BLOOD RUNS TRUE

Askula Academy 1

Kyle Johnson

kidsfitnessbg llc

As always, to Keri, for countless hours of putting up with me.

PROLOGUE

"Agheeral!"

The cry echoed across the Field of Praja, carried on a hundred thousand throats. Blood flowed across barren soil so thickly that even the parched earth couldn't hold it all. Screams of pain, terror, and rage swirled about so intensely she could almost see them rippling through the smoke-filled air. The screeches of the spirits shattered the rocks themselves with their power. The wind roared about her as her powers, unmatched on this world or any other, carried her above the battlefield, but still, above it all, one sound filled her ears as she sped across the battlefield, her powers carrying her above her armies on invisible wings of air.

"Agheeral!"

A roar to her left caught her attention, and she veered sharply as a charge of a thousand enkatiks, massive spirit beasts tens of times larger than a human, slammed into a wavering shield wall and ripped through it. She crossed a distance that would have been an hour's walk for another mortal in mere seconds. She didn't bother to unsheathe her crystalline blade; instead, she reached deep into herself, to the place where her core of power burned like another sun, and channeled the tiniest trickle of power into one hand. With a thought, she could call forth fire or lightning, bring tornadoes down from the sky, or open the earth beneath the attackers' feet to swallow them whole. Any of those would have been a mercy for the enkatiks, though – and after decades of warfare against the spirit armies, Agheeral no longer had a shred of mercy left in her soul.

The dark power of the void ripped from her hand, tearing a hole in the fabric of reality. Webs of darkness blacker than any night lashed down on the hapless enkatiks and plunged into their gray, glowing flesh. The spirits' hides were impervious to mortal weapons, immune to the human concerns of age, disease, or poison, but they yielded like water to her powers. She felt it in her core when the lines of power connected to the pulsing nodes at the spirits' cores, and she pulled, drawing that energy into herself to replace a little of what she'd used in this battle already.

The enkatiks didn't die. Their bodies didn't drop to the unyielding earth. Not a drop of their eldritch blood spilled to the soil. Instead, they simply ceased in that single instant. A thousand spirits vanished, their power and vital essences both stolen to fuel Agheeral's power. The ravening, insectoid burlats that rushed behind the mammoth spirits stumbled as they found themselves facing not a ragged, broken line of defenders but a solid wall of sahr-enhanced shields. Someone barked out an order, and those shields opened to let a line of burning spears through, stabbing into the uncertain bodies of the burlats. The spears, boosted by the power of mages, tore into the burlats and killed them quickly. The entire front line of the enemy simply collapsed as the enchanted weaponry robbed them of the vital power they needed to maintain their solid forms.

Agheeral didn't stop to watch any of that. She had no place in that battle, a fight her soldiers would win without her assistance. She fought the battles others couldn't, faced the foes that would have devastated them. With her superhuman senses, she could see the entire battlefield at once, hear individual heartbeats an hour's run away, and smell the unique scents of each race of mortals banded together to face their great enemy. No spirit escaped her gaze, but she withheld her power to deal with those worthy of her notice.

She felt the rumbling in the earth seconds before the huge peylonitog exploded from the ground in the middle of her army. Bodies flew in all directions as the serpentine monster soared upward, rising twenty times a man's height toward the ash-choked sky. Men and women screamed as tendrils shot out from the monster's side, ripping and tearing them to shreds. It opened its long, snakelike jaws wide, preparing to breathe a cloud of death that would kill a thousand of her soldiers at once, but Agheeral never gave it the chance.

Her finally unsheathed blade, long as a man stood tall, blazed with power as she struck at the peylonitog. The creature's scales were harder than the best metal, impervious to even magical weapons, but her power flowed in her blade. No force in the world could withstand it. With her sword, she could cleave mountains, carve diamonds, and destroy cities. The snake's armor gave it no more protection than if it had been draped in sheer silk. Her blade cut into its body, unleashing a spray of glowing blue essence, then flashed back as the spirit snapped at her. The monster screamed in pain and fury as its jaws flew free of its body, then dropped to the earth as her next strike cleaved it in twain.

Her soldiers cheered as she drained the power of the dead spirit, but she ignored them as she raced from battle to battle. She struck with bolts of lightning as thick as trees and waves of fire larger than the greatest houses. Mountains of ice entombed fiery spirits, and spears of glittering granite pierced towering monsters, holding them above the battle like a forest of writhing death. She rarely unsheathed her blade; her powers were sufficient to deal with all but the greatest spirits, but she felt a fierce joy when she faced those that gave her a reason to unsheathe her weapon.

She was born to battle, quite literally, and it was the only place she felt truly alive.

"Agheeral!" The cry followed her wherever she went, bolstering her forces, encouraging them to fight harder and longer, knowing that their general and savior fought among them. She darted back and forth across the battlefield, but as she did, she knew that the time had come for her to withdraw, at least for a time. She'd broken the spirits' offensive; her armies could do the rest. Almost regretfully, she raced back across the battle toward a distant hilltop, one that glowed with the power of the sahr-shield encasing it. Her banner, golden with an azure sword decorated with the heraldry of every mortal race, fluttered and gleamed atop that hill beside a tent that housed her commanding officers.

She slipped effortlessly through the shield – no working of sahr, no matter how powerful, could hold her out – and landed on the firm soil of the hill with a twinge of regret. She yearned to rejoin the battle, to slaughter the spirits as only she could, but she pushed those desires aside as she lifted the side of the leather tent and stepped within its confines. She was more than just a warrior; she was a general and the supreme commander of this allied army, and she had responsibilities beyond battle.

"My Lady," a voice greeted her as she entered. She focused on the speaker immediately; her eyes needed no time to adjust to the dim sahr-light in the tent. The man was taller than she by at least two hands, with pointed ears and narrow eyes that marked him as one of the race called shayeni. He wore their typical light chain armor, glowing blue with the power of the sahr enchanting it, and he had a slim blade only a finger's width across belted at his hip. Despite its delicate appearance, Agheeral knew that blade had taken the lives of a hundred thousand spirits in this war.

"Lord Aelritar," she inclined her head to him, removing her golden helmet to reveal hair the color of the sun, eyes as green as emeralds, and an olive face that could only be described as perfect. Of course, it was designed to be, so that was no surprise.

"We monitored your progress, my Lady," the man spoke, pointing to the glowing orb in the center of the tent that revealed the battlefield outside. "It seems that your efforts have broken the spirits' advance."

"As we all knew they would," a woman half Agheeral's height spoke gruffly. Like all thelnis, Hegglenath was short, sturdy, and far stronger than she looked. Her heavy armor gleamed silver in the dim light, forged with the techniques that only the half-heighted knew, and the spear on her back glittered dangerously.

"This battle is done," the thelni added. "The spirits just don't know it yet."

"They know," the slim fernar Willinel spoke softly, as he always spoke. His delicate fingers traced the fine, almost invisible fur on his hands, fur that Agheeral knew covered his entire body. His long, copper tail swished agitatedly behind him, and his feline ears twitched atop his head. "They almost have to. Even the rank-and-file soldiers can tell which way the wind is shifting."

"The question is, what will they do about it?" Agheeral asked, her voice smooth and melodious, deep and rich without being throaty. She walked past the orb and pointed to the large map pinned to the tent's wall.

"We've driven the spirits from every battlefield," she said touching the map that showed the entirety of the continent of Umpratan, stretching halfway around the globe. The Fields of Praja lay at the far west of that continent, a peninsula bounded by the ocean on three sides, along which Agheeral's ships patrolled ceaselessly. There would be no escape that way; there was no way off this battlefield for the spirits, and everyone knew it.

"It's taken three decades, but we've done it. Praja is their last refuge. When we take it, we drive them out of our world."

"They'll be desperate," Aelritar suggested.

"Desperate people do foolish things," Willinel added.

"Or desperate ones," Hegglenath said quietly.

"Or both," Agheeral agreed. She turned back to the others. "When we first beat them at Fahrinad, they slaughtered their captives to unleash the peynolitogs. When we turned their counteroffensive at Braymor, they opened a volcano beneath the front lines and killed a quarter of their own army. Now that they're about to lose the war entirely..." She fell silent, letting the others pick up her thoughts, which they swiftly did.

"How far will they go?" Aelritar said in a near whisper.

"We need to get to their leaders," the thelni spoke up after a few moments of silence. "We need to stop them before they can do whatever they'll have planned."

"Easy to say. Hard to do." Willinel shook his head slowly, turning back to the battlefield and pointing toward a dome of utter blackness at the rear of the enemy lines. "The ashurae still hide behind their barrier, and even Lady Agheeral hasn't been able to penetrate it."

"Yet," Agheeral corrected with a smile. She reached down and touched her blade. "I think the time has come to truly show the spirits what I can do."

"You mean, you've been holding back all this time?" Hegglenath asked in disbelief.

"Yes. I have." Agheeral let a trace of her power flow out of her, and the others drew back from her slightly as her body began to glow. "I've held power in reserve in each battle, never letting myself drop too low." She saw Aelritar's face crease in a frown and added, "Yes, that means that people have died, but how many more would have died if the spirits counter-attacked and I was out of power?" The shayen grimaced but nodded in acquiescence.

"Now, though, the time for holding back is at an end," she declared. "We have a chance to end this war, to free our people from the threat of the spirits forevermore." She looked them each in the eye, letting her power flow through her gaze into them, linking them to her and filling them with hope and excitement. She could manipulate their wills with ease, dominate them with a thought and a moment's concentration, but stealing the will was the spirits' way, not hers. She led through example and inspiration, and those who followed her did so because she was the world's best chance for survival, and because she had led them through ten thousand battles together.

"Together, we can destroy the ashurae and save our world. Are you with me?"

"To the ends of this world and back," Hegglenath said stoutly, banging her fist against her chest.

"We've always been with you, my Lady," Willinel practically purred.

"What must we do?" Aelritar asked simply.

"Fight at my side, Lord Aelritar, and you'll have done everything I could ask." She extended her power, and the three gasped slightly as they rose into the air, carried on the wings of her ability. "Now, let's go show the ashurae the meaning of fear – and teach them to shun our world!"

Reaching the ashurae's shield was child's play. No force on the battlefield could stop Agheeral alone, much when less accompanied by her three companions. Aelritar's bow hummed as he fired arrows of pure sahr into the battlefield, each shaft killing a dozen spirits or more. Hegglenath's spear flashed and danced whenever a spirit got near, the silvery metal rending their immortal flesh with ease. Willinel's fingers twisted and writhed, hurling ropes and lashes of sahr down on enemies, flaying them with fire and lightning in equal measure. They left a swath of destruction through the center of the spirit army a hundred paces wide, further shattering the invaders' will to fight.

Agheeral simply absorbed the power of those dying spirits, pushing the energy into her core until it pulsed and rumbled dangerously, barely within her control. As they raced toward the half-sphere of glossy, gray-black energy, she drew her blade and began to pour power into it. The crystal sword thrummed and hummed as it amplified the energy she pushed into it, and the air around the blade grew hazy and wavy as the dense power twisted even the light nearby. Still, she poured more power into it, until she felt the blade starting to unravel from the sheer energy it held. She leaped forward, quickly outdistancing the others, lifted her blade overhead, and slammed it down on the perfect, flawless globe enclosing the leaders of the spirit army.

The explosion of power roared with the fury of a million enkatiks. Wind blasted past her, hurling every creature nearby but her back. Every spirit within a hundred paces of the globe simply died, their mortal vessels extinguished by the force of the blast. The earth shattered and groaned; rocks shivered into dust and gravel that soared outward to pelt the spirit army harmlessly. The dome split, unraveling as the power of the void shattered its perfection and unbound its energies, and that freed power arced and crawled across every living thing it found.

Agheeral ignored the blast and the maelstrom of released energy; neither could harm her, and while the power of the shield wasn't suitable for replenishing her stores, the liberated energy of the ten thousand dead spirits nearby was certainly welcome. She hung in the air, waiting for the tempestuous fury to ease, until at last, the air cleared enough for her advanced vision to penetrate the haze of dust and ash beneath her.

The seven ashurae masters of the spirit army cowered below her, staring up at her revealed form. She felt the mingled awe, fear, and hatred wafting up from them, a stench that overpowered the ever-present miasma of blood, death, and worse coating the battlefield like a thick syrup. The creatures were tall, perhaps twice her height, slender, with long arms that had one too many joints and hands that sported six fingers. Their alabaster skin shone with its own light, illuminating the metallic sheen of their hair. They looked noble, regal, beings worthy of respect and admiration, but Agheeral knew this to be a lie. These were the masters of the spirits, the slave lords of all mortal races, and only their deaths would free her world.

"Foul creatures!" she declared in a ringing voice, still holding her blade despite the flaws and cracks that now ran through its crystal structure. "You who have held this world in bondage these centuries, flee our world now or die!"

"Ignore the mortal!" one of the creatures hissed, its voice nearly as pure and melodious as hers. "Focus on the construct..."

Agheeral was certain the creature had more to say, but none would ever know what words it intended. A blazing shaft of pure green light streaked past her and pierced the monster's open mouth, plunging through its throat and jutting out the back of its head. Its eyes widened in pain and shock, and it grasped at the arrow to pull it free – only to have the shaft erupt in green flames that coated its face and hand, burning and searing.

A roar far too loud to come from such a small throat ripped the air as Hegglenath leaped over the shattered earth. Her spear, glowing with sahr and the force of her own rage, stabbed into an ashurae, tearing into its flesh and spilling its essence into the air. The thelni ripped the weapon free and spun it, slamming the haft into a second spirit before burying the spearhead in that one, as well.

Agheeral charged her blade and struck, flashing down into the group of spirits. Two turned to face her, one holding a long lance that pulsed with darkness while the other swung a chain flail as long as she was tall. She struck at the first with a blast of lightning that knocked it backward, then caught the crackling metal ball of the flail as it soared toward her in one hand, crushing it with a flex of her fist. Her blade darted out, tearing a hole in the stunned ashurae, then slid upward to slice it in two.

The ashurae's moment of shock seemed to pass, and they struck back at her with their own prodigious powers. Waves of flame and shards of ice the size of a person soared toward her. Chains of blazing darkness streaked at her, and crimson lightning arced from the sky to hammer at her skin. Agheeral laughed as the attacks struck; finally, she'd found an enemy worth fighting! The ashurae were potent and powerful. Their attacks burned her skin, drove her back, and forced her to use her power to shield herself from them. She exulted even as she tore apart their strikes and struck back with her powers. This was the reason she'd been born; this was the purpose of her creation!

At the same time, though, part of her seethed in fear and frustration. This was it. This was the reason she'd been born, and when it ended, so would the reason for her existence. Her armies would disband. The gathered nations would disperse to their homelands. The cries of "Agheeral!" would fall silent as the mortal races slowly turned away from her. She was bred for battle, crafted to be an instrument of war. When that war ended, what would be left for her? What would be left of her?

"Agheeral!" Willinel's cry pulled her from her contemplations. The fernar's sahr rippled about, tearing into the ashurae, but when she glanced his way, his face looked alarmed, even frightened. "Look down!"

She blocked a slash from a blade as large as her own, the force of the blow shivering up her arms and sending a few crystal shards flying from her sword. Her power lashed out as a line of lightning crackled into the ashurae's face, sending it hurtling away from her and giving her the chance to look at the ground below the battle. She froze for an instant, a near-fatal one as a mass of ice crashed into her, knocking her backwards and threatening to engulf her in its depths. She shattered the ice with a blow, then looked once more at the pulsating glyphs written across the stones.

"It's a crafting!" Willinel shouted. "A powerful one!" His words told her very little. Agheeral was no master of the sahr – she had no need to be – but even she could tell that the glowing runes spread across thirty paces of floor, etched with the essence of a million slaughtered spirits, was a potent working. She could feel the power held within it, energies that rivaled the intensity and density of her own but dwarfed hers in sheer scope and breadth.

She flitted back to the fernar mage's side, leaving behind a shield to keep the ashurae off her for a few seconds. "What is it?" she asked in a flat voice.

"I – I don't know," the fernar admitted. Agheeral stared at him in shock; Willinel was a true master of the sahr, probably the single most powerful worker of it among all the mortal races. She'd never seen a working that he didn't recognize, no matter how powerful or complex.

"The glyphs – they're ones of destruction," he continued in a bleak voice. "Of unmaking and unbinding. They way they're put together, though – it's a form I've never seen, and I don't recognize any of the linkages. It's like they're mingling sahr and something else, maybe something from their world, I don't know."

"Whatever it is, it can't be good. We have to finish this before they can activate it." She lifted her blade and charged into the fray once more. All doubt and hesitation vanished. She couldn't let the ashurae finish what they started, even if that meant the end for her. She was born to be mortality's savior; she would do her duty, no matter the cost.

Power exploded from her as she released her final restraints. Lashes of energy tore into the ashurae, shredding their immortal bodies. Webs of void darkness drained their power, and she pushed that power back into them as blades of fire and ice, turning their strength into hers. Her blade burned with sapphire light so bright that even she had trouble looking at it, and crystal shards fell away from it with every strike as her power consumed the single greatest artifact ever crafted in the world.

She felt Aelritar fall as one of the ashurae plunged a black, poisonous blade into his back. Hegglenath dropped to a knee beneath a mighty hammer blow, then collapsed as a golden spear tore through her silver armor. Agheeral didn't care; she couldn't care. She'd lost far more than those few in this war; death and loss were her constant companions. All she could do was make all those deaths meaningful, and she gladly did so.

The ashurae died swiftly in the face of her fully unleashed power. Her blade cut one in half; a spear of the void sapped the power and existence from another. Molten lava exploded beneath a third, encasing them in liquid rock while a web of lightning burned a fourth from existence. Her power was unstoppable, overwhelming, the single greatest force in this world, and even the masters of the spirits had no choice but to fall before it. At last, only one remained, and that one faced her bearing a sword larger than her own. Its blade shook and trembled in its fist as it stared at her, and although its lean face held no expression, she felt the rage and terror emanating from it.

"Curse you, child of the hated sahr!" the thing snarled at her. "Curse you and all your descendants, through all of time!"

"Curse me as you will, foul spirit. I'll bear it willingly if it drives you and your kind from my world."

The spirit's face grew sly at her words. "No, foolish child. My kind will never leave your world. You've gained nothing here today."

"With your death, the threat of your kind ends." She hefted her blade. "The last of the spirits will be banished to the void today, ashurae, and Umpratan will finally belong to the mortal races as Ak-lahat intended."

"None may know the mind of the Creator of All, mortal! And though you may kill me today, I will still claim victory!" The spirit suddenly dropped its blade and sped earthward, flashing toward the pulsing crafting of sahr and other energies that lay below. The ashurae was swift, moving faster than an arrow's flight – but Agheeral was quicker than thought, and even as the creature reached toward the working, her blade plunged through its chest. The ashurae screeched as her power ripped into its deepest essence, tearing it apart and drawing that energy into herself. It felt death and something worse than death approaching; the end of existence swept toward it, an immortal lifetime cut short as the power of void obliterated all that it was and would ever be. Even as her power consumed it, though, the spirit reached out with one trembling finger – and gently touched the crafting beneath it.

Power swept outward, energies so vast that even Agheeral quailed at seeing them. This was more power than she'd ever seen, forces that dwarfed the armies behind her and made the ever-present sahr a vaporous shade. Energy plunged into the earth and clawed at the heavens. It lashed out farther than even she could see, embracing the distant horizons and shrouding them in its clutches.

The battle beyond fell silent as every spirit on the Field of Praja vanished, their essences sucked into the spreading mass of power. The groaning wounded gasped their last as that same energy sucked the life from them, drawing it into its working and feeding that power into it. The air hummed and seethed, warping visibly from the sheer density of energy crackling through it.

The earth beneath her trembled and shook. Waves of earth and stone higher than her head rippled across the battlefield, flinging everyone off their feet and killing thousands. The sky darkened, and fingers of lightning crawled across the ground. The wind rose to a gale and continued to strengthen, keening and battering her now terrified and demoralized army with its force. Reality itself seemed to lurch as power flooded the atmosphere.

Agheeral lifted her blade once more. She didn't' know what was happening, but she knew that she had to stop it. She was no master of the sahr, no mage to subtly unbind the ritual. Willinel, the only mage she knew who might have a chance, lay prone and unmoving behind her, although the sound of his heart beating assured her that he at least lived. She was a warrior, and she knew how to do one thing.

Her blade chimed as it slammed into the working below. Any other weapon would have passed through the ritual without touching it, but nothing could ignore the power of the void filling her weapon. The blade cut into the earth and lodged there as it sucked the crafting's power into itself, drawing energy out of the ritual and hurling it into the endless void. The chiming rose in pitch and volume, swelling into a clear ringing sound that echoed over the clamors of despair and fear coating the battlefield. The single note climbed through the registers to the edge of hearing and expanded to blot out all other sound, even all thought.

Agheeral staggered as the sound assaulted her ears, and she grabbed her blade, intending to pull it free, but the sword remained locked in place, held not by the feeble grip of rock but the bloating connection between the void and the terrible power of the working. She strained, pouring her power into her muscles, but the blade refused to yield. Strength that could lift house-sized boulders, crush glaciers, and flatten hills found itself stymied by this single sword. She refused to submit, though, reaching deeper into herself to push more of her swiftly dwindling power into the blade. The earth groaned as her strength met the power of the void, battling that primal energy for supremacy. For a moment, the entire world seemed to pause as those two forces balanced on a razor's edge – until with a sharp snap, a crack shot down the length of her blade, introducing a single impurity into the delicate balance of terrifying energies.

Agheeral screamed as the ritual beneath her exploded. Its energies battered her, burning her flesh and giving her true pain for perhaps the first time in her life. Her golden hair shriveled and vanished; her perfect skin seared and scorched; her crystal armor shattered and plunged into her otherwise flawless flesh. Agony ripped through her as power surged into the world, tearing not just at her but at all reality.

How long she existed that way, held in the grip of torment, she couldn't say. When at last the power faded, she found herself kneeling on the earth, panting and sobbing, her nude body covered with burns. She reached inside herself for power to heal her injuries, but the core of her essence hung dark and empty, bereft of power. She reached outward, seeking the energies of death she knew had to surround her but felt nothing. No swirling energies of spirit and life filled the air. No ephemeral mists of sahr enshrouded her, waiting to be tapped. The world felt – empty.

She stretched farther, reaching beyond the horizons, extending her senses in a way she'd never known she could – and there, to the west, hanging beyond the ocean bounding the Fields of Praja, she felt a source of power at last. Her thoughts recoiled from that energy, though. It felt like an ending, as if reality itself stopped at a wall of nothingness. She touched it, drawing the tiniest bit of power from it, and as she did, she recognized its flavor.

The spirits. The Field of Praja ended at a wall of spirit energy, a wall that seemed boundless in depth. The world of spirits existed beyond that boundary, a place no mortal could enter. Somehow, the ritual had brought the spirit world into Umpratan – or hurled Umpratan into the world of spirits, she didn't know which.

Even as she healed herself with that stolen energy, Agheeral smiled. A hundred thousand had died, her companions were lost, and the world had changed, possibly unalterably. She had no idea what it all meant, but she knew one thing.

Her people would still have need of her. Her time wasn't done yet.

The Empire of Umpratan

CHAPTER 1

One of the least pleasant ways to awaken was to a bucket of ice-cold water directly to the naked genitals. At least, so Marl discovered as the frigid water splashed over his now-flaccid member. He screeched unmanfully, which felt only fair to him since it felt like he'd just been unmanned. His stones ached and throbbed from the cold, and his stem tried to shrivel its way into his body in a vain attempt to escape the icy numbness spreading through it.

He bolted upright, blinking as the morning sun wafting through the cracks in the roof of the barn pierced his eyes. His long, silver hair, unkempt as always, swept across his face, and he spat and spluttered as it floated into his open mouth. He rubbed his clear blue eyes to free them of the dust and gunk that accumulated from a night of sleeping in a hayloft, then blinked in astonishment at the two rusty, dirt-coated tines hovering just past his arm's reach and pointed at his bare chest. His eyes tracked up along the pitchfork's shaft to the pair of grubby, gnarled hands gripping it, then to the grizzled owner of those arms.

"Filthy half-breed," Kelwat the farmer growled. The man stood a bit over a reach in height, the length of a man's outstretched arms from fingertip to fingertip, but a back bowed from decades of labor made him a span shorter, the length of Marl's thumb to pinky with his hand outstretched. He wore coarse overalls of poorly dyed blue denim, the tough fabric preferred by most laborers for its durability and resistance to staining. Scuffed leather boots, unlaced in his obvious hurry to put them on, enveloped feet that Marl suspected were horny and gnarled – and probably covered with the same graying hair that slowly receded from the old man's scalp.

"Da!" Marl winced at the soft, feminine voice beside him. He'd have preferred that Elmra remained asleep. She wore no more than he did, and as she sat up, her generous and noticeably female assets swayed and bounced on her chest. He tried not to look, but his eyes seemed to drag themselves to the paler olive of her breasts and the dark circles of her nipples. His libido, he'd long suspected, had something of a death wish, a fact doubly proven as his icy member began to warm at the thoughts of those breasts and the things he'd done with them during the night of passion he'd shared with the young woman…

"Don't 'Da' me, Elmra!" Kelwat's snarl quickly drew Marl's attention back to where it belonged. "I warned you about this – this ishtai! I told you to stay away from him…"

"Look, I can see that the two of you have a lot to discuss," Marl spoke in as reasonable a voice as he could. He'd long ago stopped taking offense at being referred to by his caste, even if it were the lowest one a person could possess without being a branded criminal. "I should go and let you talk…"

Even as he spoke, though, his traitorous eyes once more darted down to glance at Elmra's curved body and the dark patch of hair nestled between her thighs. His treacherous member continued to respond, and he subtly shifted his hands to cover it before the farmer could notice. Sadly, he'd moved too slowly for that.

"You're not going anywhere!" Kelwat barked. The old man leaned forward, poking Marl in the chest with the tines of his pitchfork. "You think I don't know about you, Marl Tem? That I don't know the stories about your philandering ways?"

Marl barely kept from rolling his eyes. "Wait, you know me, Kelwat?" he asked incredulously. "What a shock! I'm the only hizeen in a village of maybe five hundred of you naluni; what are the odds you'd recognize me?"

"Quiet your acid tongue, boy!" the old man snapped, poking Marl in the chest once more.

"Da, it isn't what it looks like," Elmra spoke up, and Marl couldn't help but snort at that. The old man had walked in on the pair of them naked, in his barn's hayloft, wrapped around one another. About the only way things could be more obvious would be if Kelwat came in during the actual act. The farmer would have to be an idiot not to realize instantly what they'd been doing. Kelwat was many things – narrow-minded, short-sighted, stubborn, and maybe a bit lax about his body odor – but he wasn't an idiot.

"I'm not a fool, Elmra," Kelwat agreed unwittingly with Marl's assessment, which the young hizeen took as confirmation that everything else he'd thought was equally true. "I know what you two were doing." He looked back at Marl. "And now, you're going to pay for it, boy!"

"Pay?" Marl swallowed nervously, fidgeting his feet as he did. "What do you mean, pay?"

"I mean, you owe me a maidenprice," the farmer growled. "You took something from me, and..." The farmer broke off irritably. "Don't laugh at me, half-breed!"

"S-sorry," Marl gasped between breathless chortles. "But – maidenprice? Are you serious? Ow!" He winced as Elmra punched his shoulder. The girl was young, only two years older than his fourteen, but she'd spent her childhood laboring in her father's fields and handling his animals. She was strong, and she knew how to hit. He rubbed his shoulder; he'd have a bruise there, he just knew it.

"Elmra?" Kelwat said a bit uncertainly. "Is – what's he saying?"

"Ignore him, Da," she assured the older man. "He's just trying to get himself out of trouble."

"Now, it's REALLY obvious that you two have some things to talk about," Marl snorted, shifting his weight so he wasn't resting on his hands. "Like Proll the carpenter's apprentice, or Drack the merchant's son, or – ow!" He winced again, rubbing his shoulder. "Seriously, stop that! It hurts!"

"Shut *up*," she hissed at him in reply. "Or the next one will be somewhere that hurts a lot more!"

"Elmra, what's going on here?" Kelwat demanded. "Tell me the truth..." The old man turned his gaze away from Marl, gazing a bit forlornly at his daughter, and in that moment, Marl struck. Kelwat howled as the stick Marl had found scrabbling around in the straw swept up and caught him directly between the legs. Marl wasn't large – he stood a span and a couple fingerwidths shorter than Kelwat would standing fully erect, and his iron-gray body was lean and lanky compared to the average nalu – but his half-spirit heritage made him strong and quick, and the blow landed with surprising force. The farmer dropped the pitchfork and fell to his knees, his hands clutching his stones as he swore and moaned, curling around his wounded genitals.

"Marl!" Elmra gasped in astonishment, her face horrified, but the hizeen didn't bother to stay and explain to her. He sprang to his feet, scooped up his clothes, and rushed to the edge of the hayloft. He slid nimbly down the ladder, landing easily at the bottom, then raced out of the open door into the morning sunlight.

Churl, Kelwat's hired hand and apprentice farmer, stood ten paces before Marl, his hand holding the lead to one of Kelwat's draft horses. The dun-haired man, tall and thick bodied with a faint greenish tinge to his skin that marked the presence of half-giant blood somewhere in his ancestry, stared at Marl's nude form in astonishment. Marl hoped that the part-vadnik was simply amazed and not admiring; he was fairly ecumenical in his passions, but coupling with an imbecile like Churl was stretching even his limits.

He ran up to the stunned young man and slipped the horse's reins from his hands. "Thanks, Churl," Marl said as he mounted the tall beast somewhat awkwardly.

"Wait – what?" Churl stammered, still gawking. "What are you – that's Kelwatirika's!" The man's eyes tracked down below Marl's waist, and the hizeen rolled his eyes, although he wasn't sure if it was at the vadnik's use of Kelwat's full name – no one used full names of adults, they were simply too long – or at his obvious interest in Marl's member.

"It won't be the first thing of Kelwat's I've used today," Marl said gleefully as he turned the horse away from the farm and toward the village. "Tell him I'll send the horse back when I'm done – but the other thing I took is mine to keep!"

Churl sputtered a protest as Marl rode awkwardly away, but he didn't offer chase. There wasn't much point; Churl was very strong but slow and awkward, and even though the horse was a draft animal meant for power instead of speed, it would have left the farmhand behind in the dust.

The trip to the village only took fifteen minutes or so, although part of that was when Marl stopped to put his clothes back on. Tem wasn't a town or city, walled and with guards at the entrances, but it was filled with curious people. If he'd entered the village naked, the story would be all over the place within minutes. He had enough tall tales spreading about him; he didn't need any more. As an orphan and a half-spirit, he was barely tolerated as it was. He couldn't be sure what straw might crack the hayloft floor at last.

Which was why instead of riding into the village, he dismounted out of sight and smacked the horse on its flank. It obediently turned and began trotting back to Kelwat's farm. The animal knew where its food was, and it was probably eager to return there. He walked the remaining five minutes, gazing up at the peaks of the Silverband Mountains to the west with a palpable longing. His mother had come to Tem from those mountains, appearing one morning in the mining village with enough money to pay for a small house at the edge of town and no questions asked. She'd died when he was but a babe, leaving nothing behind for him, not even her name. One day, he knew he'd leave Tem – or be kicked out, he admitted candidly – and when he did, he'd follow the mining road up into the peaks to see what lay beyond and maybe learn where he'd come from.

He shook off his musings as he entered the village proper. Like most villages, Tem was built along a single road, the mining road that led up into the mountains to the west and wound past farmsteads to the east. He knew that eventually the road, little more than a dirt wagon track really, joined the central highway that started at Lepild far to the north nestled beneath the Northwall Mountains and wound through the provinces of Lepild, Aggath, and Nemmbar to the city of Nemmbar on the Gulf of Danaru far to the south. He'd never seen that road, of course – Marl had never been more than five walks from the village in his life, each walk being about two hours' travel by foot – but he'd heard stories about it from the wagoners and traders who came to Tem to buy and carry the tin the miners dug from the nearby mines. He didn't know how accurate those stories were, but he intended to find out one day.

"Tem's getting too small for me," he thought ruefully as he walked along one of the paths winding into the village from the south. *"Or I'm getting too old for it. That's probably it. Tomorrow is Naming Day, and I'll be fifteen then, an official adult and free to leave this place without being sent back. Maybe that's the time to leave at last."*

He idly entertained himself for the next few minutes by imagining his departure from the village. He didn't own much, but he could steal what he needed. Tem's locks had yielded their secrets to him long ago. He'd march out triumphantly – no, *ride* out on a horse he stole from Kelwat. One of the merchant Brezam's traveling ponies would be better, of course, but Brezam would chase Marl over a horse, while Kelwat wouldn't. The farmer would be too happy to see the hizeen leaving.

All the women of the village would mourn his departure, of course. Well, probably not all the women. A handful of the village's matrons had yielded to his charms, but most of them saw him as a pest at best and a threat to their daughters' virginity at worst. Not that they had anything to worry about with that. Marl had never slept with a virgin; he wasn't remotely willing to risk their family finding out and demanding maidenprice that he couldn't pay. That would land him in indenture for five years, and he wanted to be long gone from Tem well before that.

Personally, he thought the whole concept of maidenprice was stupid. Intellectually, he knew that innocent women typically had a larger group of older, more successful men clamoring to marry them, but he had no idea why. He knew from experience that older women had far more skill, and even better, they knew exactly what they wanted and weren't shy about going after it. Wooing younger women was work; older women did half the work for him. Still, it was the custom in Umpratan that a man who lay with a virgin outside of wedlock pay her mother for the loss of potential husband options, and Marl had very little money to speak of.

He made his way to the baths, where he paid a single ak, the smallest coin in the Empire, for the privilege of getting clean in warm water with soap rather than heading to the stream and scrubbing with snowmelt and gravel. Normally, he didn't mind, but the memory of the bucket of water on his crotch was too fresh, and he luxuriated in the wooden tub of lukewarm water and bit of coarse soap. When he finished, he dressed and headed for the main street, stopping before a white-painted house with elaborate flowerbeds in front. Like most homes in Tem, the building was built from stone taken from the nearby mountains; unlike the others, though, the smell of baking bread and sweet pastries wafted from the open windows.

Marl opened the door and took a deep breath before stepping inside to the jingle of a bell. He loved the smell of Helowa's bakery. It was one of his favorite places in Tem, and it was one of the reasons he hadn't left the village long ago. The main room of the house was warm and homey, with dark walls and wood everywhere. Wooden shelves behind glass dominated one wall, all stacked with fresh breads and pastries. A door in the back wall led deeper into the house, to Helowa's kitchen, living room, and sleeping chambers.

That door opened, and a woman of about forty years with dark hair streaked with blonde stepped into the room. She wore a simple dress of white cotton, the light fabric cooler in the heat of the bakery and less likely to show flour and sugar spilled on it. The dress couldn't hide her lush figure, ample curves, or round bottom, though – either that, or Helowa was deliberately trying to emphasize those traits. Plenty of male workers and laborers came to Helowa's for breakfast each day, and while they certainly appreciated her baking, Marl was certain they stopped by to admire more than just the smells. He wouldn't blame the baker for encouraging that sort of behavior. It made her money after all, and while she hadn't chosen to remarry after her first husband died in a mining accident, if she ever wanted to, half the single men in the village would come by to woo her.

"Good morning, Marl," she said warmly as she recognized him, a genuine smile lighting up her olive-skinned face. "You made it after all. I thought you might have forgotten that you'd agreed to come help me this morning."

He gave her a grin that was deliberately sly. "Forget you, Mistress Helowa?" he asked with a grand bow. "No man in his right mind could ever forget you, I assure you."

"Ah, your silver tongue strikes again," she laughed, her brown eyes sparkling as she looked at him. "You forget, though; you aren't officially a man yet, are you?"

"I'm as much a man as I need to be," he replied archly. "And besides, tomorrow is Naming Day. I'll officially be a man then – not that it makes any difference."

"No, not really," she agreed, walking out to stand before him. "You won't be any different tomorrow than you are today, after all." She laid a hand affectionately on his shoulder, tracing her fingers down his arm. "And I'm not complaining about what you are today, either."

"I hope never to give you reason to complain," he assured her.

"I'm sure you won't." She gave him a smile, then stepped back. "However, work first. I've got breads to make for the Naming Day feast, and that means I need someone to clean and watch the shop. I'll pay you two aks, plus your choice of pastries for breakfast and lunch. As for dinner..." She smiled at him seductively. "That, we'll just have to see, won't we?"

The day passed much as every day in Tem did for Marl. Without parents to get him into a trade or pay for an apprenticeship, he was doomed to the life of a common laborer. That meant he either had to work in the mines or take whatever odd jobs made themselves available. His typical pay was an ak a day; the small bronze coin could buy him a simple meal, a bath, or a hayloft or attic to sleep in when the weather turned. Helowa always paid him extra, but he suspected that was because he helped the widowed woman deal with her loneliness in addition to his other, more mundane duties.

After the shop closed – and he and Helowa had seen to his other, far more pleasant duties for her – Marl walked outside into the cool air. He resisted taking a wistful glance backward at the building. Helowa was a skilled lover, and her bed was warmer and softer than whatever he'd find to sleep in that night. However, it was one thing for her to sport with the young hizeen; it was another to invite him to stay the night with her. No one begrudged the woman her pleasure, and Marl knew he was about as harmless a diversion as possible. He had no family to worry about; as an orphan and member of the ishtai, the lowest caste above criminals, he had no standing to be concerned with; as a hizeen, a half-breed product of a nalu and a spirit made flesh, he was unable to produce children, so she didn't even have to take precautions against pregnancy.

However, if he spent the night, tongues would wag. Rumors would spread about her falling for him, a mostly useless orphan of the lowest caste. Like practically everyone in Tem, Helowa was of the akorai caste. That caste was only a step above his own, but it was a large step. Consisting of simple laborers, farmers, miners, soldiers, and crafters like Helowa who didn't have to go through a full apprenticeship, akorai was reportedly the largest caste in the Empire, and the first one who could own property, and the first 'respectable' caste. Doing more than dallying with an ishtai, one without status but also without the outcast status of the criminal annatai caste, would hurt her standing and make any man who she might have considered taking as her husband think twice about accepting. Having a lover for pleasure was one thing; falling in love with them was totally different.

When he was younger, he'd railed against the caste system every chance he got. It was a patently unfair system; just as a person inherited their mother's name, they were also born into her caste, and nothing could change that. No one in the village knew anything about his mother – she'd spoken to no one about her past, not even revealing her name or family name for the Head Bureaucrat to record in Tem's annals – so he had no status in the Empire, and nothing he did would change that. Becoming a successful merchant wouldn't let him join other merchants, peddlers, and magic-wielding haros in the tagarai caste; mastering a trade or becoming a priest or artist wouldn't grant him the umanai caste; joining the Bureaucracy or becoming an officer in the army wouldn't even land him in the shalai caste. Theoretically, he supposed, if the Shashana, the ruler of the entire Empire, granted him a noble title, he'd join the rest of the nobility in the zahai caste, but that was obviously never going to happen. Even if he one day discovered that his mother came from that caste herself, as a half-spirit hizeen, he couldn't claim it.

He'd given up on the entire concept of fairness long ago. The Empire of Umpratan wasn't fair, and that was all there was to it. It was a hard place, and according to the stories he'd been told for as long as he could remember, it had to be. Once, eons ago, the Empire had been part of a larger world, a world where spirits roamed freely in the flesh rather than subtly invading and taking the bodies of others to wreak their harm and havoc. Back then, according to the stories, all the mortal races lived as slaves under the yoke of the spirits, cattle and servants to the more powerful creatures. That lasted until the rise of the ithtaru, the legendary defenders of the Empire, who waged war against the spirits and drove them from the world. In return, the spirits unleashed the Sundering, shattering that world into fragments that drifted separate from one another, each surrounded by the world of the spirits. Although they'd been banished, those spirits still slipped into Umpratan through the boundary between their world and the Empire, and someone like him who'd been touched by their hands was seen as unlucky, untrustworthy, and possibly dangerous.

His mother had been the one who let herself be seduced by a spirit-possessed – or gave herself willingly to one – but he was the one to suffer for that. He'd been called 'half-breed' and 'dirty blood' his whole life. Ak-lahat, the god above all others, decreed that all must care for the lowest in equal measure, and no one wanted to risk the high god's curse, so the villagers took just good enough care of him to keep him dying. That didn't mean they welcomed him. He'd never been allowed to play with the other children his age when he was younger; he'd never be given the chance to learn a trade or apprentice with one of the childless crafters; no woman would ever select him for marriage from her crowd of suitors. He couldn't even run away; as a member of the ishtai, he was considered the property of Tem until he reached his fifteenth year, and if he fled, the first settlement he reached would ship him back to the village. It was utterly unfair, but then, nothing about life was fair. He'd decided that accepting that was easier than trying to fight it.

Of course, the Empire's inequalities didn't just affect him. Everyone in Tem suffered from them in some small part. The province of Aggath, in which Tem stood, was a minor province of no real standing or importance, valuable only for its iron and silver mines. Anyone from here was automatically less important than someone from, say, the fabulously wealthy province of Dairon far to the south, or the politically important province of Menith just across the Silverbands. A crafter in Tem would never be accorded real status anywhere else in the Empire; the traders who came to Tem did so because they weren't important enough to make a living in places like the city of Aggath or a large town like Mala. From what Marl had picked up by listening to those traders in the brewer's beer garden, Tem was ridiculously backward compared to the rest of the Empire, and the village and its people were barely considered worthy of being called Imperial citizens.

He stepped outside into the encroaching evening and walked to the well just past the village, along the eastern wagon trail. The villagers mostly ignored him as he strolled past. In another village, his ancestry might make him an object of curiosity, but the people of Tem had watched him grow up. He'd stayed in many of their homes when he was younger, before he turned ten and was deemed fit to work for his living. The few glances he got were either appraising ones that he returned with a sly smile or flat ones that he blatantly ignored. Not every woman who'd taken him into her bed was a widow, after all, and every young woman he'd slept with had a mother and father. He wasn't worried about the looks, though. None of the husbands were willing to risk their wives' displeasure, and if the parents were going to do anything, they would have long ago.

He stopped before the well and stripped off his shirt. He pulled a lever beside the device, and with a grumbling squeal, pumps deep below activated, bringing water from the depths and pouring it out a black iron spout jutting half a reach above the ground. The well and pumps were some of the few bits of technology the village could afford, and most of those went into the mines to keep them well ventilated and drained of water. He hefted the bucket, intending to rinse off the accumulated flour, sugar, dust, and sweat from his body, but he froze as a rumbling noise to the east drew his attention.

Marl turned and stared at the horizon as a dark shape appeared in the distance. It was wide as a wagon but higher, looking almost like an enormous carriage. A plume of gray smoke drifted behind it as it rapidly approached the village, moving faster than a galloping horse. It grew larger as it neared, resolving into a wide, ornate wooden carriage carried on six steel wheels, with an unwieldy engine of steel and iron roaring behind it.

Marl stepped back as the steamwagon neared, marveling at the contraption. From what he knew, the steamwagons were twice as fast as horses, far more secure than wagons or carriages – and notorious for refusing to yield to those in their way. Wagoners told tales of crushed horses, pulped nalu bodies, and broken wagons driven off the road by the machines. Of course, Marl realized, those wagoners probably had no love for the vehicles that hauled several times the load at much faster speeds than they could manage, so he took those stories with a large helping of salt.

He'd heard that such wagons roamed freely on the highways, but Tem hardly rated a regular visit from such a rare and costly machine. He'd seen one twice before when important merchants came to the village, but that happened very, very rarely. Someone once said that booking passage on one cost actual akats, the larger bronze coins each worth seventy-two of the handful of aks in his pocket. He'd never even seen an akat, much less possessed one, and he doubted there were more than a few dozen of them in total in the entire village.

The wagon screamed as steam blasted from its rear, jetting into the sky, and sparks flew from the wheels as vehicle slowed noticeably. Marl winced and forced himself not to cover his ears at the piercing, fairly awful sound and decided at once that he much preferred nice, quiet horses and wagons to the metal monstrosity. The steamwagon rolled to a stop before him, and the glass window in the rear of the carriage swung open, revealing a face hidden in shadow in the twilight.

"Boy," a woman's voice spoke imperiously from the depths of the carriage. "Where can we find the Head Bureaucrat of this village?"

"I – he..." Marl stared at the woman, his glib tongue suddenly silenced for perhaps the first time in his life. He couldn't see her in the darkness of the carriage, but something about her drew his eyes to her. He felt an almost palpable aura surrounding her, an energy that he'd never felt before and that threatened to overwhelm him with its intensity.

"Great," a male voice muttered from the darkness. "The first person we meet in this hole is an idiot."

"Quiet, Herel," the woman spoke softly and coldly, and the voice in the dark fell silent. His words, though, were enough to shatter whatever paralysis gripped Marl, and his thoughts flowed once more.

"Forgive me," he said with a smile to the unseen woman, one that he'd found particularly effective against older women in the past. "I was simply overwhelmed by your presence, my Lady, and needed a moment to recover myself."

The woman snorted. "Keep it in your pants, hizeen," she said shortly. "The Head Bureaucrat?"

"He lives in the largest house in the village, of course." Marl's smile grew wider. "If you'd like, I could climb up with you and guide you."

"Directions will be fine," she replied in an even voice. "I've got enough problems in here as it is, thanks."

"As you wish, my Lady," he bowed slightly to her. "The house is along this street, on the southern side of the main square in the village center. It's painted blue, and as I said, it's the largest one on the street."

"My thanks," she said. Her hand appeared, and a moment later, a glittering disc spun through the air toward him. He snatched it deftly without looking at it and slipped it into his pocket. He opened his mouth to thank her, but her window slammed shut, and a moment later, the engine behind the steamwagon rumbled as it rolled into the village.

As the carriage pulled away, Marl slid the coin from his pocket and examined it. An aka, as he'd suspected; smaller than an akat, the bronze coin was worth six aks, three days of work at the bakery or six of most jobs, and he'd gotten it for giving the woman the simplest information. It was a ridiculous amount of money for answering a question, and part of him wondered if he could make himself more useful to her during her visit.

He stared at the woman, bemused and somewhat mesmerized. He never heard the dark shape that crept up behind him until something harder than flesh cracked into the back of his skull. A bright light flashed across his vision as he hurtled forward, catching himself on his hands and knees as pain blossomed in his head. A foot slammed into his stomach, knocking him onto his back, and his vision began to tunnel as the large, curly-haired figure of Churl appeared above him, holding a heavy stick.

"This is from Elmra," the farmhand said gruffly. "For what you told her father. Learn to keep your mouth shut, half-breed."

"Oh, that's rich coming from your half-giant ass," Marl thought briefly before the stick slammed into his stomach, doubling him up around it. Another blow fell across his back, and mercifully, darkness reached out to welcome him in its embrace.

CHAPTER 2

"Pah!" Marl spluttered as for the second time in two days, he woke up to cold water pouring over his body. This time, at least, the water splashed over his face, not his genitals. Still, he woke up gasping and sat up quickly, then winced as his head throbbed painfully. He reached up gingerly and touched his head, feeling a hard lump on the back of it coated with a sticky, crusty substance. His vision swam as the world lurched, and he swallowed hard to keep the sudden surge of bile down in his throat. He closed his eyes and waited for the spinning sensation to stop, then opened them slowly.

Sunlight greeted him, forcing him to squint against its brightness. He closed his eyes again, giving them a moment to rest, then opened them slowly once more. The light still stabbed at him, but he kept his eyes squinted nearly shut, giving them a few seconds to rest. The world slowly stabilized around him, and while his stomach still felt queasy, he didn't think he was in any danger of vomiting. At least, not as long as he didn't move too quickly.

"Normally, I'd warn someone against sleeping out in the open like this," a familiar voice spoke from above him, one that he struggled to place. "However, it appears that it wasn't by choice."

He opened his eyes as much as possible and saw a pair of dusty, black leather boots standing in front of him. The boots looked like they'd once been glossy, but time and wear eroded their shine until they appeared dull and muted. Even so, he could tell that they were of high quality, with tight stitching that was probably waterproof and thick soles that barely looked worn. They rose to just below their owner's knee, where black cotton pants tucked into them, the garment simple but obviously well dyed and finely stitched.

His eyes traced up those legs, his mind absently appreciating how they flared into finely curved hips at the waist, but his gaze fastened on the woman's belt – specifically, on the slim sword, heavy dagger, and pair of flintlock pistols all strapped to it. All the weapons looked well made –

not that he really had any idea how to tell the difference between a finely crafted blade and one likely to shatter, of course. Lines of silver and copper wound around each weapon, though, inlaid into the hilts of the blades and handles of the pistols, and he didn't think someone would go to the trouble of decorating a piece of junk.

He tried to look further upward, but the sun's gaze burned into his eyes, forcing him to look away. He blinked rapidly and finally squeezed his eyes shut as the brilliance made his already throbbing head pound. Tiny blacksmiths roamed the inside of his skull, hammering out a tune that only they seemed to enjoy, and until he could shut them up, the sun wasn't his friend.

"Light sensitivity?" the woman asked with a grunt. "Happens sometimes with a bad head injury. It means you've got more damage than you think, hizeen." She seemed to hesitate, then spoke again. "Here. Drink this. It'll help."

He felt something cool pressed into his hand, and he pried his eyes open to look at the object she'd given him. A long, copper tube rested in his fist, sealed at the top with a lid with strange indentations in it. He tried to pull off the lid, but it refused to budge, no matter how he yanked.

"Damn villagers," she sighed with obvious exasperation. "Try twisting it. No, the other – yes, like that."

He turned the lid, and it slowly spun off as he watched in amazement. The cap dropped into his hands after several full revolutions, and he peered into the tube to see a dark liquid mostly filling it. He took a sniff and winced at the harsh smell.

"Wine?" he asked hopefully.

"Hardly," she snorted. "It's a revitalizing elixir, charged with sahr and…" Perhaps seeing his stupefied face, she sighed again. "Just drink it, child. It'll make your head stop hurting."

He stared into the tube dubiously. He knew about herbal remedies – the healer Lathania brewed some for sale in the village – but most of them worked only slightly better than leaving well enough alone. At least Lathania's tonics smelled good; this stuff had a pungent odor, almost like someone took a piss in it and left it for a few days to ferment. It was more likely to poison him than help him. Of course, he reasoned, if the woman wanted him dead, she could have simply stabbed him in his sleep. Plus, as shitty as he felt, a little poisoning probably wouldn't make things much worse.

Shrugging, he pinched his nose shut and chugged the tube's contents. The liquid burned his throat and tongue, not with the searing bite of acid but with a fiery taste he didn't recognize. His mouth and throat tingled and throbbed, and that tingling moved down into his stomach. A warmth filled his abdomen and spread outward, flowing up his body. The warmth seemed to pool in his lower stomach, upper back, and head; in his skull, in particular, the sensation strengthened until it nearly burned, and he winced and clutched his skull, letting the tube fall from his fingers. A moment later, though, the burning passed, leaving his head feeling remarkably clear. It still ached a bit, but the chorus of smiths in his brain fell silent at last, and when he opened his eyes, the light no longer stabbed into them.

"That – that's much better," he said after a moment, then remembered his manners. "And thanks."

"It's the least I could do since I was probably the reason you were mugged," the woman replied, bending to pick up the fallen tube. As she did, he caught a glimpse of her face, and in that instant, he recognized her, and with that recognition, memories came flooding back. He hadn't seen the woman's face in the steamwagon last night, but he felt the same aura of power rolling off her in waves. Her eyes seemed to almost glow with energy, and he had to fight not to curl up into a ball and whimper at the sheer strength that emanated from her gaze.

She stared at him, her lips curling down into a frown. "Are you okay?" she asked. "The elixir should have cured most of your injuries."

"I..." He swallowed hard, his mouth suddenly dry, then cursed himself for being an idiot. Twice he'd met this woman, and both times he'd acted like a stammering fool. He rose slowly to his feet, marveling at how quickly his body had recovered. "I'm fine, my Lady." He swept into a low bow. "Once again, I'm simply mesmerized by the sight of you."

She gave him a contemptuous look as she tucked the empty vial into a pocket in the back of her belt, and secretly, he understood why. Her body was practically flawless. She had the type of figure that came from hard, constant exercise, lean and trim. Her torso was covered by a steel breastplate etched with the same whorls of silver and copper as her weapons, and the armor ballooned out in front of her chest, concealing her womanly features beneath. Black leather covered with enameled steel plates covered her arms and throat, conspiring to create the image of a woman who was lethally dangerous and designed for violence – and her face reflected that violence. White scars crossed the olive skin of her left cheek, and pock marks of some kind speckled her right. Her crooked nose had obviously been broken at least once and reset poorly, and an angry, red scar creased her mouth, pulling it into a perpetual grimace. Her hair was short, cut to about a finger's width in length, and gray speckled it liberally. Hers was a face that inspired caution and respect, not lust.

She apparently agreed with his silent assessment. "That blow to the head must have damaged your vision, boy. And if you're just trying to get into my pants, save us both the trouble and stop."

He opened his mouth to give a witty retort, but something in the set of her eyes warned him off. He simply nodded. "As you wish, my Lady," he bowed his head.

"Good. You've got a brain after all."

"I do," he agreed with a wry grin as he remembered Churl's attack on him the night before. "Although sometimes, I suppose I don't use it very well. I can't believe I let that vadnik idiot get the drop on me!"

"Vadnik?" she repeated, her hand drifting down toward the sword on her hip as she frowned. "There's a half-giant in this village?"

"Not a full one, no. Churl's got some blood in his ancestry, though. It makes him tall, strong, and stupid."

"Vadniy aren't stupid, boy," she shook her head, visibly relaxing. "People think they are because they're so big, but that's being foolish. Never assume that someone who's big is dumb; it's likely to be the last assumption you make."

Marl nodded slowly as he processed what she said. "Churl must just be uniquely idiotic on his own, then," he mused, tapping his chin.

She barked a short laugh. "Well, at least you know who robbed you. You can report him to the bureaucracy and get your coins back."

A spike of alarm went through Marl's chest, and he quickly patted the purse hidden beneath his shirt. He relaxed as he felt the weight of the coins still hanging there and shook his head. "Nope, he didn't rob me. He just knocked me out." He chuckled. "Probably didn't even occur to him to check me for money, the moron."

"Something personal, then?" she grunted. He opened his mouth to speak, but she waved a hand. "Not my concern, and honestly, I don't care." She sighed. "And I wasted an elixir on nothing."

"Wasted? I wouldn't say it was wasted."

"I would," she replied bluntly. "I thought that maybe someone had seen me toss that aka to you last night, and they mugged you for it. That would have made it my fault if you died, and I didn't want that on my conscience."

"Died?" he asked, startled.

"You were bleeding in your head, boy. That's why everything was too bright. It might not have killed you – just left you blind or crippled – but it might have." She shrugged. "Oh well. What's done is done. Try not to let it happen again; next time, you're on your own."

She paused and looked him up and down. "How old are you?"

He considered lying to make her think he was older than he was. Half-spirits like him never got very tall, after all, and they developed slowly, so it was feasible that he could be eighteen or even twenty and look as he did. Again, though, something in the set of her eyes advised him that honesty was by far the best policy.

"Fourteen."

"I thought so." She turned away from him. "I'll see you at the Naming Day ceremony, then."

"Probably not," he shook his head.

She turned and looked at him, her face perplexed. "You aren't interested in being named an adult of the Empire?"

"It's not that. It's just that I'm an orphan…"

"Ah," she cut him off, her expression giving way to understanding. "No one to give you your fifth letter, then. Surely, though, you'll go to see your friends get theirs."

"There are only four others in the village being named adults this year, and I wouldn't call any of them 'friends'," he shrugged. "Everyone else can get named just fine without me. I'm more interested in the feast afterward, to be honest. I've seen the ceremony a few times, and it's pretty boring."

She nodded, then hesitated. "You'll still want to come watch, boy. This year will be different, trust me."

He frowned, and before he could reply, she turned and walked away from him, heading away from the village toward the fields. He watched her for a moment, part of him wondering what she was talking about while another part couldn't help but admire how she swayed as she walked. He blinked, then gasped at the empty road; the woman had vanished, disappearing as if she'd never been there, leaving nothing behind but a settling cloud of dust where she'd stood an instant ago. He spun around, looking for her, but he couldn't see her no matter how hard he looked. Either she was hiding – and was very, very good at it – or she'd somehow disappeared into thin air.

He swallowed hard, then turned back to the well, pulling up more water and jamming his head underneath the flow. The water ran pink for a moment, and he gingerly reached up to wash the blood from his hair, but to his surprise, the lump on his skull was gone, as was whatever cut Churl's blow gave him. It still took him two minutes to scrub the blood from his shoulder-length hair, though, and when he finished, he glanced around, making sure the strange woman hadn't reappeared, then stripped down and used a bucket of water to scrub himself. He wasn't remotely modest, but something about the woman made him more cautious than usual.

He hadn't planned on going to the Naming Day ceremony, really. As he'd told the woman, he had no one to give him a letter for his name. His mother died when he was still a toddler, and Axanor the Head Bureaucrat had to change his name from Ar to Mar on his fifth Naming Day in celebration of his surviving the dangerous first years of life. He'd turned that to Marl on his tenth Naming Day himself, the day he'd become a productive member of the village. He'd been sorely disappointed that day. The others received their letters from whichever parent shared their gender, and each time, the assembled villagers had cheered and applauded, congratulating the family on gaining another set of useful hands and a possible apprentice. He'd walked up to the Head Bureaucrat alone, surrounded by utter silence, and when he announced his letter, there'd been a scattering of polite applause, nothing more. He'd walked away from the stage shamefaced and angry, and since that day, he'd realized that while he lived in Tem, he wasn't part of it, and they didn't really want him there. He wasn't going to give them the satisfaction of making him so uncomfortable and ashamed again. He'd go around to the Head Bureaucrat's office later to register his new name; that was all that was really necessary. Everything else was just an excuse for people to celebrate.

He looked back in the direction the woman had been when she disappeared and pursed his lips. He still wouldn't give them that satisfaction, of course, but maybe – just maybe – he could watch from some quiet spot and see what she was talking about. Nothing ever happened in Tem; he wasn't going to miss it when something finally did.

CHAPTER 3

Tem's central square was crowded to capacity for the Naming Day ceremony. The mines were shut down for the day; the fields were empty; the crafters shuttered their shops. Everyone came to Naming Day without exception. It was the most important holiday of the year, a remembrance of when the great Ak-lahat, One Above All, created the world and all the living things within it. It was the last day of the last week of the year, the final moon of the spring growing season. Tomorrow, a new year would start with the warm season of summer – and with the turning of the year, Amarl would be well away from Tem. At least, he hoped so; if he were still in the village, there'd be the spirits' hells to pay after the morning he'd had.

Akio, the last day of each week, was the day set aside for Ak-lahat, and as such, it was supposed to be a day of rest and contemplation. Amarl – he'd already mentally added the fifth letter to his name even though he couldn't officially claim it yet – had spent the morning quite differently. While the villagers gathered in the square, congratulating the parents whose children would be gaining a letter and those adults who'd be adding to their already lengthy names, he'd slipped from house to house, picking locks and helping himself to the supplies and coins he'd need to leave the village once and for all. Two large packs on his back bulged with his ill-gotten gains, and his hidden purse strained at the seams. The villagers thought themselves clever, hiding their aks and akas beneath floorboards and false bottoms of drawers, but he'd found most of them. Brezam the merchant kept his coins securely stored in a heavy steel safe beyond Amarl's ability to open or carry, much to the boy's discontent, but every other place he'd visited had yielded at least something useful.

He climbed up the trellis on the rear of Heldir the vintner's house – sampling a few of the grapes that dangled from the vines shrouding that trellis on the way up – and scrambled onto the low-pitched roof. Heldir's vintages were one of Tem's few luxury exports, so the winemaker could afford a large house overlooking the central square, directly across from the Head Bureaucrat's house. Amarl crawled up until his head and arms were above the peak, then lay flat on the roof. He'd chosen his vantage point well; he could see the main stage in front of Axanor's house over the heads of the crowd, so he wouldn't miss anything of note that might happen.

His eyes scanned the crowd. He spotted Helowa quickly enough, standing chatting with a pair of men who eyed her admiringly. He also found Kelwat standing toward the edge of the crowd. He held Elmra's upper arm in his hand, and the girl's face looked downcast. Churl, standing on the other side of her, looked triumphant, and Amarl felt a surge of anger as he looked at the green-skinned young man. He owed Churl for knocking him out and leaving him for dead, and he always paid back his debts. Besides, if he let the man attack him without retaliation, he'd be asking for every bully in the village to hunt him down. Amarl had no parents, no friends, no protections. Only fear of reprisal kept him safe.

He shook off thoughts of revenge and refocused on the stage. It was nothing but a series of sanded wooden planks laid atop a platform of matching wooden crates and lashed in place with rope. Two more planks made ramps allowing people to mount and dismount the stage at each end. A lectern in the middle had the Imperial Seal on it, a circle broken into a diamond-shaped grid, the symbol of Ak-lahat, with a hook-pointed spear overlaying it vertically up the center crossed at a right angle by a long stalk of wheat, the main staple crop of the Empire. A bronze, eight-pointed star covered the center of the seal, gleaming in the midday sun.

Seats had been set up behind the lectern, along the back of the stage. To the right to Amarl's point of view sat Vernir the priest of Ak-lahat, the highest religious official in the village – which wasn't saying much since there were only the priest and his two acolytes to perform the village's religious duties. Heldir, the man whose house Amarl adorned, sat beside the old, gray-haired priest, chatting amiably. Axanor sat to the left of the lectern, talking animatedly at the short-haired woman who'd apparently saved Amarl's life earlier. She, on the other hand, seemed to be saying little or nothing in return. Her eyes swept the crowd constantly, seeming to see everything at once. In fact, the moment Amarl popped his head up over the roof, her eyes pierced him, and her hand shifted toward one of her pistols. She seemed to recognize him quickly, though, and her body relaxed at once.

He settled in as Axanor rose from his seat and took the stage. The large, round-faced man wore his finest bureaucrat's robe, a long affair of golden silk, the costly material that Amarl had heard was made by worms of some sort and shimmered with a telltale sheen. The robe was decorated with an Imperial Seal and had four crimson slashes at the collar that the hizeen assumed denoted the bald man's rank as a bureaucrat, not that it meant anything to him. Amarl could read and write and knew the basic history of the Empire, but he hadn't continued in the bureaucrat's school after his fifth year the way most other children had.

"People of Tem," Axanor spoke in a voice that carried loudly over the crowd, silencing them instantly. "We gather together today in the name of Ak-lahat, the One Above All, to bid farewell to another year of the great Empire of Umpratan. On this, the final Akio of the final week of the third moon of Spring in the year 1619, we look back on the joys of the past year and celebrate the new…"

Amarl tuned out the man's speech. While Axanor had a good voice and used it pretty well, his speech each year was basically the same. He thanked Ak-lahat for the blessings the village received, and Vernir came up at that point to lead the crowd in a prayer to the One Above All that Amarl didn't repeat with the others. He didn't exactly get to share in whatever blessings the great god bestowed on Tem beyond not having it burn to the ground or be destroyed in an avalanche, so there was no real need to thank the god, as far as he was concerned. Besides, Amarl figured that if Ak-lahat really did create the entire universe, he had a lot more important things to concern himself with than a tiny village in a mostly unimportant province in the Umpratan Empire. Amarl barely noticed the place; surely the god of everything was watching something more interesting.

Instead, the hizeen kept his gaze on the woman he'd spoken to that morning. She didn't repeat the ritual phrases either, he noticed. Her gaze swept the crowd continuously, stopping here and there to examine one person or another. It took him a few minutes to realize that she was picking out the people around his age, giving each of them a brief examination before moving to the next.

Axanor droned on as he began the official process of naming. He began by bringing up the new babies in the audience and recording the two-letter names their mothers gave them. Next came those who were about to start their fifth year, gaining a third letter to celebrate not dying in infancy, followed by those going into their tenth year who could officially begin working for their families.

"Next, let us greet those who are leaving their apprenticeships and becoming true citizens of the Empire," the bureaucrat intoned. Amarl perked up instantly; the fat man should have gone on to introduce those like him entering adulthood next, but he'd skipped it. That was a serious breach of tradition, and Amarl had never seen the bureaucrat breach tradition before. The crowd seemed equally amazed; people muttered to one another and stared at the lectern in confusion. Lania, apprentice to the weaver Burnig, hesitated at the base of the ramp leading up to the stage as her name was called, but she eventually made her halting way to the top, her face worried as she announced the two-letter addition that made her new name Laniria to sparsely scattered applause.

After the apprentices, the couples who married in the past year mounted the stage, again seeming unsure and hesitant if they were doing the right thing as their names were called. Each husband renounced his maternal surname in favor of his wife's, and both spouses added two more letters to their names. They wouldn't use them, of course – full adult names were long and cumbersome, saved for formal occasions – but it would be the last time they got multiple letters until they reached their forty-fifth Naming Day, so most of them took care choosing those letters. Applause grew stronger with each name announced, but there was no cheering, and many people cast doubtful glances at the shocked faces of the fourteen-year-olds who, it seemed, might not be named adults this year after all – and the enraged faces of their families.

A handful of women mounted the stage to gain a letter for producing their first child, followed by the few people who got another letter for reaching the end of their forty-fourth year. Only one person, an old woman named Zherista, came up to receive the three letters she gained by completing her seventy-ninth year. Typically, that would have ended the Naming Day ceremony and began the feast to cheering and exultation, but an expectant hush fell over the crowd instead. Every eye fastened on the sweating Axanor, who gave them an apologetic smile in turn.

"You may have noticed a small change in our typical custom," the bureaucrat said deprecatingly. A few laughs broke out among the crowd, but if Axanor expected to lessen the tension, he'd obviously failed, in Amarl's opinion.

"We are honored – no, more than honored, we are *blessed*," he went on hurriedly, "to have with us a guest of the highest honor and standing in the Empire. It is her presence that mandated such a change in our honored traditions, and her request that such a breach remain unexplained." Amarl snorted at that; Axanor was making very sure that no one blamed him for the lapse in protocol and lack of warning about it.

"She has come to us from the far distant realm of Askula," the man declared, and the crowd's silence dissolved into confused and uncertain muttering. "And she is here for a special reason, a very special reason indeed. Please, offer the greatest respect to Danmila, Malim of the Academy of Askula and a venerated Ithtara, one of the great defenders of our Empire!"

As the woman rose holding a large wooden box in her hands, no applause or cheering greeted her. The crowd stared at her in frozen silence, stunned into incredulity at what they'd heard. Amarl found himself paralyzed with shock. He didn't know much about the ithtaru, the superhuman guardians of the Empire, beyond that they were gifted with abilities beyond anything mortals could match, and they lived in another world entirely, a place called Askula. They kept the Empire safe from the spirits who would eradicate all life and secured the Mistways leading from Umpratan to other worlds. They were something of a law unto themselves, not answerable to the bureaucracy that ran every other aspect of life in the Empire, and everyone spoke of them in hushed tones if at all, fearful of summoning one by speaking of them too loudly. As the saying went, "Where the ithtaru tread, death follows."

"And I was flirting with her!" he reminded himself. *"Stupid ass! I'm lucky to be alive!"*

Danmila walked in utter and total silence to the lectern that the bureaucrat hastily vacated. If she were surprised or upset by the crowd's reaction, it didn't show on her face. Her expression was calm and neutral as she surveyed the crowd. Nothing about her suggested threat or anger, but the villagers drew back from her, nonetheless.

"People of Tem," she spoke in her slightly raspy voice, "I've come to your village from Askula for a specific purpose. First, let me assure you that your village is in no danger. There've been no incursions nearby, and I'm not here to pass judgment."

A relieved sigh swept over the crowd. Amarl had never seen an ithtara before, of course, but he'd heard stories of them. They were sent to deal with incursions, times when spirits entered the mortal world, and their presence usually heralded a time of violence and bloodshed. Tales abounded of ithtaru who burned entire villages to the ground to make sure that any spirit-touched within were destroyed, or ithtaru who hunted down entire family lines to make sure no one of them could spread a spirit's taint. The ithtara's presence could spell Tem's destruction, and if the tales about ithtaru were even half-correct, if that was what Danmila wanted, there was nothing anyone could do to stop her.

"I've come to offer a gift to those who become adults today," she continued. "A gift from Askula to celebrate their coming of age. Let those ending their fourteenth year and their parents come forth and join me on the stage."

Her last line had been a command, not a request, and one thing that everyone knew was that an ithtara's commands were always obeyed without argument or delay. Amarl watched as the four families whose children were about to enter adulthood slowly and with obvious reluctance mounted the stage, standing as far away from the woman as they possibly could. Danmila placed her box on the lectern and opened it. The lid lifted away and the front unfolded outward. As she raised the lid, the sides spread apart until the interior was fully revealed.

The inside of the box was dark green fabric of a kind that Amarl didn't recognize. The lid, sides, and back of the box had what looked like small shelves built into them, a finger's width wide and running the length of the box. Amarl gasped as the midday light shone into the box, revealing glittering, polished gemstones placed haphazardly on the shelves. Hexagonal and octagonal stones of every color and size dotted what he now recognized as a traveling merchant's display box, from sapphire to ruby to emerald. The stones burned with a deep fire, and the entire crowd gasped in amazement as they saw the gems. That one box likely represented more wealth than the entire village of Tem possessed – and the ithtara was apparently planning to give some of it away!

Amarl, however, didn't care about that. His gaze fastened almost against his will on the least opulent crystal on display, a pale lavender shard of misshapen quartz. Spikes grew randomly out of the cloudy hexagonal prism, and it neither sparkled nor gleamed in the sunlight. Still, Amarl stared at it, fascinated. Something about the crystal spoke to him, calling his name and beckoning him to come take it. It took all his willpower not to immediately slide down the roof and rush forward to snatch up the stone, claiming it as his own, but he managed to restrain himself. Danmila knew he was there and hadn't summoned him to join the others; that meant that, like the rest of the village, she didn't want him there.

"You," Danmila pointed to Fora, one of the children gathered on the stage. The girl gulped audibly and stepped back, her eyes wide, but the ithtara beckoned her forward, and her mother behind her pushed her toward the ithtara. Fora's eyes were wild as she neared the woman, and her entire body shook with fear.

"Relax, girl," Danmila said reassuringly. "I simply want you to take one of these stones as your own."

"Wh-which one?" Fora asked in a trembling, small voice that Amarl only heard because of the encompassing silence.

"Whichever one appeals to you the most, girl. There's no wrong choice except to not choose. Take one."

Fora hesitated, her hand twitching toward the display before falling at her side. "I – I couldn't," she protested. "I'm not worthy of…"

"Damn it, girl, pick one!" Danmila snapped. Fora flinched, but she hurriedly reached out and grabbed a gleaming ruby the size of her pinky, pulling it off the display.

Danmila grunted. "Good. Now, go back to your parents, girl." She pointed to a boy named Wirn. "You. You're next."

Wirn came forward and just as hesitantly took a small green emerald for himself. Danmila grunted once more and pointed to a girl named Pasa, who didn't hesitate for a second before stepping up and grabbing a glittering sapphire. A boy named Char went last and hesitated longer than the others before taking a gleaming blue topaz.

Amarl watched it all happen in amazement. Why were they taking those worthless gemstones? They should have picked the lavender crystal; it was obviously the best one! Char even seemed to drag his finger across it without choosing it. There was obviously something wrong with him; with all of them, in fact!

Apparently, Danmila agreed. She looked over the children with hard eyes. "Are you sure of your choices?" she asked each of them. "Last chance. Does any other stone call out to you?" None of them moved, and the woman turned to glare at Axanor. "Are you sure there are no other children reaching adulthood today?"

"Well, there is one other, my Lady," the bureaucrat stammered. "A hizeen boy, Marl…"

She shook her head, cutting him off. "We've met. It's not him; it can only be a pure-blooded nalu. And it's none of the ones you've shown me. I warn you, Bureaucrat, if you're hiding something from me…"

"I would never, my Lady!" the man protested. "Those are all of the children reaching adulthood in Tem, I swear it upon Ak-lahat!"

She grunted, then closed the case, snapping it shut. "I know they're here, Bureaucrat. I'll be here for another day, in case you suddenly remember someone you haven't shown me." She leaned forward. "I suggest that you do. Otherwise, I'll have to look myself, and that might be somewhat –

damaging to this village."

Axanor swallowed nervously, his face white, and Amarl didn't blame him. The man told the truth; there weren't any other children coming of age in the village. Amarl didn't know what the woman was looking for, but whatever it was, it obviously wasn't in Tem – and she just as obviously thought it was. If she didn't find it, things might go badly for Axanor and Tem in general.

Amarl's eyes followed the woman as she walked off the stage carrying her box – the box with the lavender crystal inside it. His mind yearned for that irregular gem. He longed to feel its cold facets in his hand, to stare at it once more. The wealth of a city lay in that box, but his memory recalled only the pale purple stone. Everything else faded into the background of his thoughts. He knew he had to have it; the question was, how could he get it?

He slid back down the roof and scrambled down the trellis. He listened absently as the ceremony concluded in the square. Each family announced their child's new adult name, but no one cheered or applauded, and Amarl realized that the ithtara had been right. This year's ceremony was entirely different. No one would be rushing forward to congratulate the newly minted adults. No one would be offering them an apprenticeship or words of advice. The ithtara's presence robbed the proceedings of joy.

"I guess I could have participated after all," he mused with a dark chuckle. *"Everyone's getting treated the same way I did last time."*

He stowed his packs and slipped into the edge of the crowd as Vernir spoke once again, the old priest blessing the new names in the name of Ak-lahat, sealing them in the registries of the Empire. The old man's words were terse and formulaic, lacking the fervor and faith with which he normally spoke, and the crowd's response of, "Bi'k-lahat", an ancient phrase that supposedly invoked the great god's favor, seemed decidedly flat and dispirited.

Amarl was halfway to the food tables by the time Axanor dismissed the crowd and officially declared the beginning of the feast. He was glad of his head start as the villagers left the square and moved down the street in a nearly silent but determined mass. He grabbed a glazed ceramic plate and loaded it with dripping meat, steaming vegetables, and smoking bread as quickly as possible, then moved into an alley between two mine owners' homes as the villagers reached the banquet. To his complete lack of surprise, many of them bypassed the food entirely and went straight for the casks of beer and wine. Axanor was one of these; the round bureaucrat poured himself a clay mug of wine and drained it in a single pull, then refilled it and repeated the process. The man had the look of someone who wanted to get drunk as quickly as possible, and he wasn't alone.

Amarl eyed their foaming tankards a bit enviously; now that he was officially an adult, he could openly drink regular alcohol instead of the half-fermented versions meant for children. He'd drank both beer and wine before, of course – he preferred beer, but he wasn't picky – but he'd always had to do it secretly, stealing mugs that adults set down or tapping a cask himself when no one was watching. Drinking openly was supposed to be one of the great privileges of a fifteenth Naming Day, and typically, the new adults drank their first official alcohol to shouts of encouragement. They also typically got very drunk and spent the first day of the new year extremely hungover, but that was to be expected.

That last part was why Amarl reluctantly sipped a mug of water. He wanted to be gone just after first light, and he'd already woken up this morning with a blinding headache. He didn't need to go through that again. Plus, if he overslept, he'd likely find himself waking up in the basement of Axanor's house, the closest thing the village had to a jail, and the bureaucrat would likely sentence him to servitude to pay off what he'd stolen from the village. That was unacceptable, and he kept the idea of being trapped in the village for another five years firmly in mind as he swallowed the tasteless water.

Besides, it wasn't like the others were really getting to enjoy their first night as adults, anyway. He watched as Wirn – now Wirin – drank several swallows of a mug of beer, then looked around expectantly for some sort of praise or encouragement. The young man's face fell as he realized that no one was watching, not even his parents, and he settled in with the beer with a sullen air. Fora, who'd changed her name to Flora, sipped her wine dispiritedly, making an occasional face as she stood utterly ignored. Pasa and Char – now Pasat and Ochar – talked quietly together, each holding a mug and wearing dissatisfied expressions as the praise, apprenticeship offers, and general revelry they'd been expecting refused to materialize. Amarl almost felt bad for the group. He knew they'd looked forward to this night for the past couple of years, at least. Pasa was convinced that she was going to get an apprenticeship with Heldir the moment the ceremony concluded, and Wirn was looking forward to entering the mines as a full adult, receiving an adult wage instead of a child's half-pay. Fora was going to follow her mother's trade as a potter, of course, but Char was hoping to join Brezam's guards and get out of the village. This night was supposed to be the start of their new lives, the one time that they'd be the absolute center of attention, but the ithtara took that away from them.

At the same time, he couldn't quite bring himself to pity them. It was just one night, after all, out of the rest of their lives. They'd still get their apprenticeships and accolades, just not exactly when they expected it. They'd live out the lives they wanted, and years from now, today would just be an odd memory and maybe a story they shared every time they got too deep into their cups. It wouldn't matter in a year, which meant it really didn't matter.

He finished his food and passed through the crowd, not speaking but simply listening. There was only one topic on everyone's tongue, of course. Speculation ran rampant about what Danmila wanted – and what she'd do to get it. Would she execute Axanor? Punish the newly raised adults or their families? Would she raze the entire village to the ground? No one knew, but everyone had an opinion, and they all seemed to have a story to back it up, a tale of an ithtar doing exactly what they predicted in some other village. Of course, all these stories came from a friend of a distant relative on the husband's side of the family or some such – meaning they were utterly fabricated – but the people who listened nodded their heads sagely as if hearing utter truth.

As the feast continued, the mood grew darker and more frantic. The sun sank slowly in the west, and the shadow of the Silverbands spread across the village, the jagged peaks spreading cold fingers of darkness across the proceedings. With the approach of nightfall, musicians gathered and began to play, their cheerful airs almost gruesomely laid over the heavy atmosphere. A space was cleared in the center of the street, and couples took to dancing, their bodies skipping and cavorting in a frenzy as if they could push back the pall of trouble with the exertion of their muscles.

He worked his way around the dance floor, toward a pair of familiar-looking figures half-hidden in the darkness at the edge of the lamplight ringing the feast. The corpulent Axanor and the slim, almost emaciated form of Vernir huddled together at the edge of an alley, well out of view of most of the revelers and definitely out of earshot. Amarl slipped through the crowd without drawing much attention – no one bothered to congratulate him on reaching adulthood, and he wasn't expecting them to – heading toward the pair. Before he reached them, though, a familiar voice pulled him up short.

"Marl," a deep, flat voice spoke, and the young man turned to see the hulking figure of Churl standing behind him. The big farmhand stood with his arms crossed, glaring at the smaller hizeen, and Elmra stood at his side, her eyes flat and angry.

"Churl," Amarl said curtly. "It's Amarl now, by the way."

"Not until you register it with the Head Bureaucrat," Elmra replied with a smile. "Until then, you're still just a child, *Marl*." Her eyes flattened. "A child who got me in a lot of trouble, I might add."

He barked a short laugh. "I think you got yourself in that trouble, Elmra," he pointed out. "If you'd just kept your skirt down and your knees together, you'd have been fine."

Churl took a threatening step forward, but Elmra tightened her grip on his arm, and the farmhand paused.

"This isn't the end of this, Marl," she said flatly.

"I'm not sure why you're blaming me," he shrugged. "Half the village knows what you get up to. It was only a matter of time before your father found out. In fact, I'm surprised it took him this long." He looked at Churl. "Is that why you're helping her, Churl? Did she promise you her favors in return? You could probably get them just by asking, you know. Everyone else has."

"Shut up, half-breed," the big farmhand growled.

"Yes, because that green skin of yours is pure naluni blood, no question," Amarl rolled his eyes. He looked back at Elmra. "Look, we had some fun together. It was nice, and I'd happily do it again if you want to ditch the idiot, here. But blaming me because you can't keep your knickers on isn't exactly..."

He caught the movement in the corner of his vision as Churl lunged for him. The big farmhand was strong but clumsy, and Amarl ducked under his blow. He kicked out as the man's rush carried him past Amarl, landing his foot directly on the seat of the farmhand's ass and making Churl stumble into a group of adults. They turned irritably, then saw the trio of young people, shared a look, and slowly stepped back.

Amarl almost snorted in disgust. Granted, he hadn't really expected anyone to help him, but there was a strong tradition that all grievances were settled on Naming Day. It was an important custom; as people got deeper into their drinks, old slights and past insults tended to bubble to the surface, and in a tiny place like Tem, there were a lot of old slights lurking. Fighting was prohibited, and anyone starting a row was sent home in disgrace. At least, that was the usual standard. This time, the villagers spread out, opening a space for the pair to battle it out. He didn't know if that was because they didn't care what happened to an orphan or because of the stress of the day's events, but it didn't matter. He'd tried to goad Churl into attacking him to get the man kicked out of the feast, but that plan backfired, and now he had to deal with the lout.

His first thought was to run. After all, no one in the village really thought much of him anyway, so losing their respect wasn't much of a concern, and he could visit retribution on the bigger boy later. A glance around at the dark mood of the villagers, though, suggested that might not be an option. An undercurrent of anger ran through the crowd. They wanted to see blood, and as the least-liked and lowest-caste member of the village, Amarl's was the blood that could spill with the least consequence.

"I'm going to make you pay for what you did to Elmra, half-breed," the farmhand growled, clenching his fists and raising them to his face. He lunged forward once more, and Amarl again slipped out of the way of the clumsy attack. Churl spun quickly, swinging a wild punch. Amarl ducked and kicked upward, his foot slamming into Churl's crotch. The bigger man groaned and staggered, but he seemed to push through the pain and charged forward. Amarl, shocked by how easily the farmhand ignored a kick to the stones, moved too slowly to dodge, and Churl's arms wrapped around him as the bigger man's weight bore them both to the ground.

Amarl fought viciously, punching, kneeing, and even biting as his back crashed to the dirt road. His fingernails tore long lines in Churl's cheek, and one of his fists clipped the man's jaw, knocking his head backward. His knuckles screamed in pain at the contact, but he ignored it as he bucked and thrashed, trying to get out from under the bigger man. His knee came up, catching Churl in the stones again, and the farmhand swore loudly before sweeping a backhanded punch that crashed against the side of Amarl's head. Stars flared in the hizeen's vision, and he fell limp for a moment, allowing the farmhand to jam a forearm into his throat, pinning him down. Amarl's eyes widened as a long knife suddenly appeared in the man's other hand, raised high above his head.

"I'll show you!" Churl shouted. "This is for...urk!"

Amarl blinked as Churl literally disappeared from atop him, his weight vanishing at the same instant. The hizeen rolled sideways and scrambled to his feet, his hands raised defensively as his eyes darted around, looking for something that might be a weapon. He dropped his hands and straightened as he saw Churl two reaches away and realized that the young man wasn't much of a threat to anyone anymore. Churl moaned in pain, his face pressed into the dirt of the road and his arm twisted painfully up and to the side. A black leather boot rested on the back of his neck, pushing his head down, while a hand wearing a gauntlet of the same material gripped his extended arm. Danmila gazed around at the suddenly silent crowd as her free hand toyed with the knife she'd obviously taken from Churl's hand, her glare openly disapproving.

"In every city, town, and village in the Empire I've ever visited," she said, her raspy voice carrying clearly across the villagers, "there's a tradition that anyone fighting on Naming Day is expelled from the feast and sent home in disgrace." She glanced over her shoulder, and Amarl looked that direction to see the cringing form of Axanor standing at the edge of the crowd. The damn bureaucrat had been watching as well! While the villagers didn't really have a duty to intervene in a Naming Day brawl, Axanor certainly did, and he'd been standing there, watching!

"Is that custom part of Tem, as well, Head Bureaucrat?"

"O-of course, it is, Ithtara," Axanor stammered.

"Ah," she nodded. "Then perhaps you don't apply it to those of mixed blood?" She looked at the crowd. "That would be a shame, since I can tell that at least half of you have a trace of non-naluni blood in you."

"I – we certainly don't have different rules for half..." Axanor swallowed as the woman's gaze snapped to him, her eyes flat. "I mean, those of mixed blood, my Lady."

"Good to hear," she grunted. "And I suppose it was just a mistake that no one moved to stop this, then?"

"Of course! A simple mistake, my Lady. It's been a long day for us all, and..."

"What about this, then?" she cut him off, holding up the knife. She looked around at the crowd. "A brawl is one thing, but what about when someone draws steel? No one thought to intervene, even when this boy's life was at stake?"

Amarl's gaze swept the crowd, but no one met his eyes. He read shame and sullen anger on every face, and he matched that anger with his own. He was fine with them standing back to let him get a beating, but no one had moved when Churl drew his knife? Not one villager, the people he'd grown up with, had thought to do something to save his life. He sucked on his swelling bottom lip and tasted blood that he spat on the ground, willing a curse on the village as he did. He'd planned to leave; now, he only wished he'd taken more from them when he had the chance.

"Head Bureaucrat, what's the penalty in the Imperial Code for drawing steel in a brawl?" the ithtara asked, her tone suggesting she already knew the answer.

"It…" Axanor swallowed hard again. "Ten days confinement for a first infraction, my Lady."

She stepped back and hauled Churl to his feet, releasing his arm and shoving him none-too-gently at the bureaucrat. "I judge this man guilty of breaking the peace and violating the Imperial Code. Begin his sentence at once."

Axanor stared at the woman, then bowed his head. "Y-your will, my Lady." He pointed to a pair of large miners standing nearby. "You and you, take this criminal into custody, and…"

"Fuck you!" Churl shouted, spinning suddenly and flinging himself at Amarl. "I'll…"

Churl's cry cut off as Danmila suddenly appeared in front of him. Amarl blinked; the woman hadn't seemed to move. One second, she stood a couple reaches away, twice the height of a tall nalu; the next, she was in front of Churl. The farmhand choked and gasped, his hands grasping weakly at the slim blade protruding from the front of his chest, the blade that jutted from his back and gleamed scarlet in the lamplight. Blood gushed from his open mouth as panic filled his face. He shuddered, then went limp, falling to the hard packed dirt of the road as his final breath rattled in his throat.

CHAPTER 4

Silence reigned over the village as Danmila took out a cloth and wiped her blade before slipping it easily and silently back into its sheath. She turned and faced the pale-faced, stunned Axanor.

"I judge this man guilty of ignoring the commands of an ithtara," she said simply. "As there's only one punishment, I saw to it myself. Do you wish to issue a formal complaint, Head Bureaucrat?"

"I – no!" the fat man stammered. "No, my Lady. You acted justly, and it will be so recorded in the Imperial ledger." He cleared his throat. "Let it be known that Churl um'Nerwina Tem has been deemed a criminal deserving execution. His name shall be stricken from the Imperial rolls, and he will receive neither reward nor acclaim for his life's accomplishments. May Aklahat have mercy on his soul."

"Bi'k-lahat," Vernir murmured. A few villagers echoed his phrase, but most stood in stunned silence, their eyes darting between Churl's body, the impassive ithtara, and Amarl. The young hizeen caught more than a few angry looks tossed his way, not the least of which came from Kelwat, who'd moved to stand beside his daughter. Elmra's face was blank and pale as she stared at Churl, her lower lip trembling and tears shining in her eyes.

Danmila looked at the old farmer and shook her head. "Take your daughter in hand, Farmer," she said bluntly. "Her manipulations led to this moment. By the Code, she could be punished alongside her puppet." She stared at the ashen-faced girl and shook her head. "But I think this night has seen enough death."

"I – my thanks, Lady," Kelwat stammered before once more glaring daggers as Amarl.

"Come, hizeen," the ithtara said dryly, walking over to Amarl and grabbing the shoulder of his shirt. "You were also involved in that disturbance, and that needs to be seen to." She looked around. "Besides, I think the day's celebration is over, and it appears that more than a few people are still tempted to break the peace. Best to remove that temptation from their sight." She looked hard at Axanor. "See to it that nothing like this happens again during my stay, Head Bureaucrat, or I might begin to question if you belong at your position."

"O-of course, my Lady," the rotund man bowed deeply.

"And see to that matter we discussed. The one I seek is in this village somewhere. Perhaps someone has deceived you about their age, or perhaps there's an error in the ledger. Find them."

"I'll do my best, my Lady."

"Do that, and we'll hope it's good enough." She looked back at Churl's cooling body. "Although I have my doubts about that."

As she dragged Amarl away, he opened his mouth to protest, but she spoke before he could utter a word. "Don't say anything, boy," she instructed. "Let them think I'm going to punish you. It might keep you safe for a day or two."

He clamped his lips shut as she dragged him down the street to the house beside Axanor's. She pulled open the door and shoved him through, and he staggered into the common front room of the building, catching his balance before he fell. He straightened and wiped his hands down his clothes, adjusting and fixing them. He grimaced as he realized the tussle had left his brown shirt coated with dust and ripped his sleeve at the shoulder. He'd have to fix that later. Blood spotted the front of the shirt, whether from his cut lip or the furrows he'd dug in Churl's cheek he didn't know, and the knee of his trousers sported a hole.

"Who the hells are you?" a voice spoke up, its tone clear and precise as if the speaker chose every word with exact care. He looked up and took in the room surrounding him.

The building was designated as a guest house for the few important visitors to Tem, which meant it stood empty most of the year. It was kept locked up, but Tem had broken into it so often that picking the lock was almost second nature to him, and one of the rear windows had a permanent groove in the sill from him sliding the bolt so many times. The empty but well-kept house was simply too good of a place to sleep for him to ignore it, especially during the long, cold moons of winter, when snow came down from the Silverbands and piled half a reach deep in the village. He wasn't alone in his use of the house, either; the younger, unmarried folk of the village had been using it for their amorous activities for more years than Amarl lived.

Because of that, he recognized his surroundings at once. The room inside the door was a common area, sparsely decorated and furnished with several chairs and a table for eating in the center. An elaborate lamp hung above the table, its curving branches holding multiple wicks that all drew from a central pan and gave the room far more light than it truly needed. A fire crackled in the stone fireplace to his right, and a door to his left led to a short hall. That hall ended at the large main guest room in the back of the house, and three smaller rooms led off it, two to the left and one to the right.

He cataloged all that without really seeing it. His gaze fastened instead on the young man he'd seen earlier sitting behind the ithtara on the stage. The boy sat at the table in the center of the room, wiping down what looked to be a finely made if appallingly slim blade. He wore a fine white shirt of smooth, glossy silk and had dark blue pants of the same material. A matching vest covered his chest, and a wide leather belt with a gleaming silver buckle wrapped about his waist. His glossy black boots glowed in the light of the room and looked like someone had spent hours polishing them. His face was long, narrow, and handsome, with pointed features and oiled black hair pulled back into a tail behind his head. A sneer lay across his face as he looked at Amarl, a sneer that slowly gave way to recognition.

"Wait, I remember you," the boy said contemptuously. "You're the idiot by the well, yes?" He laughed, his voice dry and sardonic. "What, are we taking in strays, now?"

"That's unkind, Herel," a second voice spoke, and Amarl glanced over to see the young woman he'd seen on the stage as well sitting in a chair against the wall. Her round face looked disapprovingly at the obviously wealthy boy, and her hands smoothed the folds of her cotton dress against her thighs.

"It's accurate, Betha," Herel said dismissively. "This one obviously isn't who the ithtara is looking for in this…" He glanced around at the room contemptuously. "This pathetic hole of a village."

"Our village might be a hole," Amarl said easily, giving the young man a sly smile. "But at least we know how to be courteous, here – and the customs of how a guest is supposed to behave. Maybe where you come from, people aren't taught that sort of thing, though."

The boy's eyes flashed, and he half-rose from his seat. "You dare take that tone with me?" he demanded, gripping his sword. "Why, I ought to…"

"You ought to shut your mouth and sit back down, Herel," Danmila growled as she entered the room and slammed the door behind her. "And keep your hand off that sword unless you want me to feed it to you."

The young man's face flushed red in the lamplight, but he bowed his head deeply to the woman. "Of course, Ithtara," he said glibly. "Forgive me for..."

"I said shut up," she cut him off before whirling to face Amarl. "And you! Do you cause this sort of trouble everywhere you go?"

Amarl shrugged and grinned at her. "Mostly, my Lady. I have a bit of difficulty controlling my tongue sometimes, and I find myself funnier than others do."

She stared at him for a moment, then barked a short laugh. "Ha! At least you know it, hizeen. That's more than most naluni twice your age." She walked over to the table and set down two plates of food. "Here. The dinner I promised the both of you. Come eat."

"Thank you, my Lady," Betha said politely, walking over to the table and sitting down while Herel simply took the plate without a word and began eating.

Amarl looked at the two plates with confusion. The woman hadn't been carrying them when she dragged him into the building, and she hadn't had time to go fetch them from the feast down the road. Had she sent someone to go grab them earlier, then noticed the fight while she waited? That made the most sense, but it didn't feel right to Amarl. How had she gotten to the fight so quickly if that were the case?

"Sit down, hizeen," she instructed, pointing to a chair against the wall. "And try not to antagonize anyone. You've given me enough problems today."

"I don't think I was the one who caused those problems, my Lady," he protested as he took a seat. "Churl attacked me first, after all."

"Only after you goaded him into it," she shook her head. "I saw what you were trying to do. You wanted him to attack you, so that he'd be sent out of the festival."

"There was a fight?" Betha asked, her eyes wide as she looked at Amarl. "And you were in it?"

He looked down at his clothes. "No, of course not," he said dryly. "We villagers rub dirt and blood on our clothes regularly just for fun. It's the latest style here, you know." She blushed and looked down, and he forced himself not to roll his eyes. "Sorry. As I said, my tongue is sometimes faster than my wit."

"I get the feeling that 'sometimes' means all the time," Herel muttered, then fell silent as Danmila shot him a warning glance.

"That," she said, looking back at Amarl. "That sarcastic tongue of yours. That's what got you into trouble – that, and the fact that you didn't take the villagers' fear into account. The whole thing was clever but poorly done."

"What do you mean?"

"I mean that the entire village is on edge, boy. They're all worried that I'm going to raze it to the ground or slaughter everyone within it. A fight is a natural release for that sort of tension; I'm honestly surprised it took that long for it to happen. You should have considered that."

He nodded, then looked at her gravely. "Will you?" he asked quietly. "Raze Tem to the ground, I mean?"

She remained silent for longer than he'd expected before shrugging. "I'll do what I have to," she finally said. "Why? Do you care? Honestly?"

He thought about it for a moment, then returned her shrug. "Yes and no," he admitted. "There are some good people in the village, and I wouldn't want to see anything bad happen to any of them." He shook his head. "Not that it matters. You don't strike me as the kind of person who'd kill everyone in a village to get what you want. I think you're trying to scare the Head Bureaucrat into giving you whatever it is – whoever it is that you're looking for."

She gave him a flat stare. "You don't know anything about me, boy," she growled. "You have no idea of the things I've done – the things I'll do to see my duty clear. Yes, I hope to scare the fat old man into giving me what I want, but if he fails…" She fell silent, and Amarl swallowed hard as he felt a surge of some dark power well up within her. He didn't understand it, but she suddenly seemed colder than the deepest snows of the moons of Winter – and far deadlier. He felt far less certain that she wouldn't slaughter every man, woman, and child in this place if she had to – and that she hadn't done exactly that before.

"However, you might be able to help me avoid that," she said, pulling a chair opposite him and sitting down, the sense of threat and danger fading as she did. "If you help me find what I want, then I won't have to do anything that either of us would regret."

His eyes narrowed as he stared at her. "Is that the real reason you brought me here?" he asked quietly.

"Yes," she admitted without a hint of remorse. "What, do you think I care if you live or die, boy? I don't. I don't care if the people of this village tear you apart or stone you to death. I don't care that the farm boy pulled a knife on you, or that the villagers would have let him kill you."

She leaned forward, and he shivered at the ice in her eyes. "This morning, I saw a young man beaten almost to death and left on the side of the road. I watched dozens of people pass him by without stopping to offer him help. Then, I saw them clear a space so that a partially blooded vadnik could beat him again. What do you think that told me, boy?"

"That I wasn't exactly popular here," he replied softly.

"Exactly. And an unpopular orphan…" She shrugged. "Well, this isn't the first village I've visited, boy. Let's just say that I guessed you might not have much loyalty to this place. Have I guessed correctly?"

He sat in silence, thinking over her words and how best to respond. It was true, he didn't really feel a kinship with the village of his birth – but neither did he want to see it and everyone in it destroyed. The people of Tem hadn't always been kind to him, but they hadn't been openly hostile, either. He wasn't willing to simply betray them. At least, not without gaining something in return.

"Take me out of here," he finally spoke.

"What?" she asked, leaning forward.

"You want information from me. Fine. I want something in return. I was planning to leave Tem anyway, but if you take me with you, it'll be faster and easier. Agree, and I'll answer any questions you might have about the village."

She leaned back, her face cold. "I could simply order you to tell me. If you refuse…" She touched her sword hilt. "Well, you saw what happens when you refuse a command from an ithtara."

He swallowed hard, remembering her dripping blade emerging from Churl's back, but he steeled his courage and forced a smile. "I wouldn't refuse, though. I'd answer any question you asked – just not as completely as I might otherwise. I might forget some information, or not offer something that I know you would like even though you didn't ask for it." He shrugged. "All it costs you is giving me a ride in that steamwagon of yours."

She glared at him for long moments, and he felt nervous sweat dripping down the back of his neck. He was bluffing, of course, and they both knew it. If she wanted to, she could drag the information she wanted from him, and he'd give it up to spare himself what she could do. No one would even say a word against her. Some of the villagers might thank her for it. However, she could have done that at any time, and she hadn't. He was gambling that meant she'd prefer not to, and he was asking for very little in return, a ride on a wagon she'd already hired.

"I could carry you as far as Thind, the town across the border in Lepild," she finally spoke. "From there, you'd be on your own, but the highway runs from there to the provincial capital of Lepild, so it would be easy to find a ride to the city from there."

He grinned as a sense of relief swept over him. "That's more than good enough for me," he agreed.

"And that's all you want?" she asked skeptically. "Just to ride along in the steamwagon? No money to help you when you get there?"

He shook his head. "I've got money," he assured her. He hesitated. "However, there is one thing. In that case you brought..."

"Don't bother," she interrupted with a laugh. "Those gems aren't real, boy. They're colored glass, nothing more. You couldn't buy a decent meal with one."

His face fell at her words, and he sighed. "Even the lavender one?" he asked heavily. "Damn. I thought..."

A sudden pounding on the door caught his attention, and he turned toward it as it burst open. If he hadn't, he would have seen the look of shocked surprise on all three of the faces in the room. Instead, he jumped to his feet as Axanor strode into the room, his face an angry storm cloud as he clutched the two packs that Amarl had hidden away earlier – and apparently hadn't hidden well enough.

"My Lady Ithtara," Axanor bellowed, his voice outraged as he stared at Amarl. The fat man's face was red with anger or exertion, Amarl couldn't tell which, and his chest heaved as he stepped fully into the room.

"Forgive my intrusion, my Lady," the bureaucrat puffed. "I would never have entered your residence unbidden, except that you harbor a dangerous criminal!"

"I – a what?" Danmila replied. Amarl looked at her sharply as he heard confusion and uncertainty in her voice, two things he'd never heard before.

"A criminal!" Axanor repeated. "This boy, Marl Tem, has broken the Imperial Code!" He hefted the two packs in his hands. "You thought you could rob this village, boy? That you could steal from us – from *me?*"

"I don't know what you're talking about, Head Bureaucrat," Amarl replied as calmly as possible, but the fat man tossed a pack at him, knocking him backward into the wall.

"You think to lie?" he roared. "Vernir is on his way, and when he arrives, he'll craft the Chant of Fidelity. You'll tell the truth then, boy; you'll have no choice!" He turned to the two miners standing behind him. "Grab him!" he commanded. "Take him to my basement to be held – until his execution!"

"Execution?" Amarl demanded, taking a step backward and looking toward the door behind him. The two men moved before he could, though, each of them seizing one of his arms and twisting them behind his back painfully. "Let me go!" he demanded, kicking at the men futilely. "Thievery isn't punishable by execution! Servitude…"

"You think I want you in our village for years more, you filthy, rot-blooded half-breed?" Axanor sneered. "I couldn't kick your disgusting whore of a mother out of Tem, but I can rid us of her tainted offspring! Take him…"

"Enough!" Danmila suddenly shouted, rising to her feet. Axanor fell silent, swallowing hard, but he straightened, his face confident as he spoke.

"My Lady, I have proof that this criminal violated the Imperial Code," he said firmly. "And I intend to wring a confession from him under a Chant of Fidelity, under which no person can lie."

"Chants of Fidelity aren't quite as foolproof as you think, Head Bureaucrat," she said coldly. "However, this is all beside the point." She looked over at Herel, who stared at Amarl with stunned eyes. "Herel, fetch my case."

"My Lady Ithtara," the boy stammered. "He – he's a hizeen…!"

"Do you think I'm both blind and stupid, boy?" she demanded. "I know what he is! Now, fetch my case, or by all the gods in the firmament, you'll be running from here to Thind while I drag you along by a leash!"

He flinched and stood up so quickly his chair flew back, then rushed from the room. Danmila turned back to face the now-pale Axanor, whose face looked uncertain.

"M-My Lady," the round man stammered, "this – this isn't possible! A hizeen!"

"Blood holds true, Bureaucrat," she growled in reply. "If his human bloodline is pure enough, it's possible."

"But – to be that pure, his mother…" The man's face drained of what little color it held.

"Would have to be a direct descendant, yes," the ithtara nodded. "One of the most important and venerated people in the entire Empire – and I believed you called her a 'filthy whore'."

"I – I never said filthy," he protested lamely.

"It doesn't matter. If this turns out to be true, then it means you ignored your duty to check her blood. By doing that, you condemned her to die here, alone in this village, unheralded and unattended…" She shrugged. "If that's so, I suggest you run as if the spirits themselves were chasing you before the Grand Bureaucracy finds out – or before I report this to Askula. I guarantee the Order will want to have a chat with you about it."

"H-here, my Lady," Herel spoke as he entered the room, handing her the wooden box. She set it on the table and quickly opened it, revealing the gems within. The lavender gem pulsed in the lower right corner of the box, instantly drawing Amarl's eyes to it. He felt it calling him, heard it begging to take it up and claim it.

"Release him," she ordered, and the two men holding Amarl's arms let go and stepped back. "Amarl Tem, choose…"

Amarl didn't wait for her instructions. The moment his hands came free, he stepped forward and reached for the glowing purple crystal. He grasped it carelessly, ignoring the bite of its spikes in his palm. He stared at it in growing wonder; he'd expected it to be cold and lifeless, but the crystal burned warmly in his grip. He felt the energy inside it, a strange form of life, and that power sang in his blood. Unthinkingly, he reached out for the energy in his fist, not with his hands or his mind but with some deeper part of him, and as he touched it, the power surged into him.

He laughed aloud as a flood of euphoria filled his body, and his blood burned with a fire that warmed his soul. This, this was right! This was how it was supposed to be! A part of him he'd never known was missing now felt whole. A place inside him he'd never known was empty felt warmth for the first time. He drew that power greedily into himself, the energy little more than a trickle, but that trickle eased an ache he'd never known he had. At the same time, the crystal flared with a violet glow, then faded, becoming misty and transparent, as if it barely clung to reality.

"What – what happened?" Herel's voice was shocked as he spoke. "Why can't I feel the crystal anymore?"

"He quickened it," Danmila said grimly. "With no training, no instruction – he quickened it. His blood is strong." Amarl glanced at her and saw a mingling of curious expressions on her face. Surprise dominated, but he saw confusion and a little awe there as well as she stared at him. She seemed to shake herself and looked over at Axanor, whose mouth hung open and whose pale face looked almost gray.

"That clinches it, Bureaucrat," she said flatly. "I claim this one in the name of Askula, under the decree of the Blood Compact. All his grievances are forgiven, and all his debts are erased. His family name is no more, and blood price will be paid to his parents…" She grimaced. "Or would, if he had any." She glared at the fat bureaucrat. "Do you dispute this, Head Bureaucrat?"

"N-no, my Lady," the man shook his head, bowing low. "Marl Tem is of Tem no more, and I deliver him into the care of Askula."

"Good." She grabbed the two packs and tossed them to the bureaucrat. "Take these and return what was stolen to the rightful owners. Do as you wish with the rest. Askula will provide for him from now on."

"Y-yes, my Lady." The fat man bowed toward Amarl, his gaze uncertain. "May Ak-lahat bless you and keep you in his hand."

Amarl barely noticed this, enraptured as he was by the crystal in his grip. Now that he'd touched it, it no longer called to him; instead, it sang quietly, its song a barely heard hum in the back of his mind. That song soothed and comforted him, easing his cares and banishing his troubles. He roused himself as the woman's hand fell on his shoulder, gentler than he'd felt it before, and he looked up into her face.

"Put it away, Marl," she instructed softly.

"But…"

"You'll still be able to feel it, no matter where it is. Until you've drained it, nothing will be able to separate you from it." Reluctantly, he slipped the stone into his pocket. To his relief, the trickle of energy continued to flow unabated, and its song in his mind still purred warmly.

She took a deep breath. "I'll summon the steamwagon," she said shortly. "Everyone, get some sleep. We leave at first light tomorrow." She glanced at Amarl. "It's a long way to Askula, and I think we're going to find a strange reception when we arrive."

CHAPTER 5

marl's grand departure from Tem was not happening the way he'd imagined it. He'd envisioned riding out on horseback, sitting proudly in the saddle. The people of the town would line up to each side to watch him leave, the men grinning at his departure while the women bid tearful farewells. Helowa would rush up to him, begging him to stay, and he'd give her one final kiss – and perhaps a friendly squeeze or two – before trotting off grandly.

Not a soul stood in the street as the group moved through it. The sun peeked above the horizon to the east, meaning Tem should be waking up and beginning a new week, but not a single soul was visible except as faces peeking out behind curtained windows. The group walked down the street toward the waiting steamwagon in utter and complete silence.

"Not exactly a thrilling send-off, is it?" Herel muttered dryly, looking around at the locked doors and covered windows. "You'd think at least one person would say goodbye to you, hizeen – although, after what we saw last night, I'm not sure I blame them."

"Did you grow up as a half-spirit orphan in a provincial naluni town, Herel?" Danmila asked.

"No, of course..."

"Then shut the fuck up."

"I – I don't understand," Betha said quietly, her face both confused and a little pained. "Why is everyone hiding? Shouldn't the priest and the bureaucrat be here, at the very least?"

"I'll be surprised if that bureaucrat ever shows his face in this province again," Danmila said bleakly. "If he has a vestige of honor, the villagers will find his body in his house sometime today or tomorrow. If not, he'll spend the rest of his life running." The woman didn't explain further, and Amarl couldn't be bothered to ask.

He wasn't a fool. He'd always known that his image of his departure was a ridiculous, even childish dream born of pure fantasy. Despite how the village treated him, he wanted to believe that secretly, deep down, they actually cared for him as one of their own, and his daydream reflected that. He knew that, in reality, most of the people of Tem considered him a nuisance, something they had to tolerate, not a real part of the village.

Even so, he thought that he had made a few friends over the years. Surely, someone would show to wish him farewell. At the very least, Axanor and Vernir should have overseen his leaving, the former to formally record his departure from the village and the latter to wish him Ak-lahat's blessings in his life. That no one bothered – that not a single person from the village he'd grown up in had the damn courtesy to give him a simple farewell – stabbed deep into his heart. He kept his head forward and his face stoic as he walked, but his heart dropped more with every step.

He'd woken up on the floor of the main room of the guest house, huddled before the long-dead fire with his arm for a pillow while the others slept in the bedrooms. He knew that was fair – they were all certainly higher caste than he was as an orphan – but they also hadn't taken a decent beating the night before. He'd expected to awaken stiff and sore, his body and face throbbing, his eye blackened or even swollen shut, but to his surprise, when he woke up, he felt – good. His back and sides weren't stiff, his shoulder didn't ache from sleeping on the hard floor, and his head didn't pound and throb. His lip still ached faintly, but when he probed it with his tongue, it barely twinged, and his jaw worked fine without popping or cracking. He went to the water closet and examined his face in the silvered mirror; his lip had scabbed over and looked like it had been healing for days, while the side of his face had a faint yellowing to it, like a fading bruise.

He mentioned this to Danmila as she gave them breakfast, just some crusty bread and a few pieces of fruit, and she simply nodded.

"Why do you think I let you sleep out here?" she asked.

"Because I'm one of the ishtai, I assumed." He shrugged nonchalantly. "I'm one of the lowest of the low; only branded criminals are lower."

"Not anymore, you aren't." She gave him a serious look. "You gave up everything when you took that crystal, and that includes your caste. You're outside the castes, now." She looked at the others. "All of you are."

"We – we're above the noble zahai?" Betha asked tentatively.

"No, not above. Outside. Caste has no meaning for you anymore." She looked at Herel as she spoke, and the young, obviously wealthy and probably noble young man fidgeted uncomfortably. "Whatever you were is gone, now. It's best to realize that early and let it go."

Amarl had thought that would be easy for him. After all, while he didn't hate Tem, he knew he didn't belong there. There were things he assumed he'd miss, but not very badly. Putting a village that barely tolerated him behind him – one that had been ready to execute him for petty theft the night before – should be a simple enough matter.

Yet, as he walked through the silent town, he realized that Tem meant more to him than he thought. It was his home, the only one he'd ever known. Everyone he knew, everything that was important to him was in that little village, and he'd be leaving it behind, possibly forever. He walked into an unknown future, one that he'd neither sought nor understood. Part of him wanted to run and hide in one of the nearby farms until the ithtara and her entourage left, and he had to fight to keep his face from reflecting that bubbling fear and anxiety.

Two things kept him from seriously considering trying to run, though. The first was the certainty that Danmila wouldn't let him. He'd realized the night before that he was what she'd been looking for in the village, and he recalled her implied threat to tear the village apart looking for him. Running wouldn't help him, and neither would hiding. So far, she'd treated him decently, but he was certain that would end the moment he attempted flight, and he really didn't want to see her angry.

The second was the vast silence surrounding them. He was leaving Tem forever; surely, that had to matter to someone. At least one person had to be saddened by his departure, didn't they? Apparently not, and that fact hurt far more than he would have imagined. The pain of leaving, magnified by the sting of betrayal, dug into his chest like Churl's knife, twisting in his heart.

The closer he came to the edge of the village, though, the more the villagers' apparent refusal to see him off annoyed rather than hurt him. From what Danmila said, they'd walked past him the night after Churl attacked him and just left him there for dead. Then, they'd watched in silence as Churl drew a knife with the intent to kill him. Now, they stood in utter apathy as he walked away from them forever, and for all he knew, they were glad to be rid of him. His pain flared into anger, rage blooming in his chest as he realized that all these years, he'd just been a burden to these people, one they were certainly glad to be rid of.

"Fuck them," he muttered, slowing to a stop and turning to look back at the silent village. He raised his voice as he spoke and let his anger flow into his words. "Fuck all of you! You think you can get rid of me? Fuck that! One day, I'll come back here, and I'll remember every shitty thing you ever did to me! You hear? I promise you that!" His final shout rang throughout the empty streets, lingering far longer than it should have, seeming to ride an invisible breeze across the entirety of the village.

He turned back to find the others had stopped and watched him. Herel's face showed nothing but scorn, while Betha's held a look of mingled shock and pity that somehow annoyed him even more. Danmila, though, watched him intently, her gaze narrow as she stared at him in silence that finally grew uncomfortable. His anger faded as he realized he was being childish and foolish, and he hung his head in embarrassment. To his surprise, though, instead of chiding or mocking him, she nodded once.

"What's done is done," she said simply. "If they weren't terrified already, they certainly are now." He blinked in surprise, not at her words, but at the surprising lack of sarcasm in them. "Come on. It's well past time we were gone from this place."

The steamwagon rumbled in the road at the edge of the village. A man dressed in a gray leather overcoat with lightly tinted goggles pushed up onto his forehead stood beside it, bowing low as the group approached.

"My Lady Ithtara," the man said obsequiously. "Thank you for giving me the honor of once again serving you and Askula."

"Ha!" the woman laughed shortly, reaching into her pouch and flipping the man a coin. "Who needs honor when you have coins, right Pergint?"

"There's no reason a wise nalu can't have both, is there, Ithtara?" The man straightened from his bow and looked the group over. "One more, then? Where is his luggage?"

"He doesn't have any. We'll have to detour to Haveld and get him some clothing, at least."

"Of course, my Lady." The man opened the steamwagon door and bowed low once more, holding the door open as Danmila climbed inside. Herel followed her, and Amarl gestured for Betha to go next; despite what the ithtara had said, he still considered himself to be the lowest caste of the group, and that meant giving precedence to the others whenever possible. At last, he climbed inside and got his first ever look at the inside of a steamwagon.

The interior of the wagon was dark, with black lacquered walls and matching leather benches. Dark curtains were tied back away from the windows but could obviously be dropped to provide privacy or shade as needed. A single lamp glowed overhead, shielded by frosted glass so it illuminated the wagon without being overly bright. The space was fairly large, long enough for him to stretch his legs inside and wide enough that he guessed three people could sit side-by-side easily enough.

Herel sat beside the ithtara, of course, so Amarl took the seat beside Betha, facing Danmila and looking toward the front of the wagon. He settled onto the black leather seats, enjoying the padding beneath him and behind his back. It was as soft as the nicest chairs in Tem, the ones he only enjoyed when no one else knew about it – and he wondered if someone could sleep in the wagon, or if the noise would keep him awake.

As the contraption started up, he decided he wouldn't be sleeping in it, after all. The noise wasn't bad – it was a little loud, but not intolerably so – but the wall behind him vibrated so fiercely that he doubted he'd ever be able to fall asleep, even if he wanted. The wagon rolled forward, slowly at first but rapidly gaining speed, and he decided that a lack of sleep didn't matter. He stared out the window, fascinated as the farms surrounding Tem sped by at a ridiculous speed, at least twice as fast as his best sprint, if not faster.

"What are you gawking at, hizeen?" Herel asked, his voice both bored and scornful at the same time.

"We're moving so fast," Amarl breathed, still staring out the window and doing his best to ignore the haughty boy's tone. "I've never seen anything like it."

Herel laughed contemptuously. "This? Fast? This is nothing compared to one of the sahrwagons."

"Sahrwagons?" Amarl turned toward the other boy, his face mirroring the curious tone in his voice. "I've never heard of those."

"Of course not. Why would one ever come to a place like…?" He waved his hand absently toward the swiftly retreating village behind them. "They only travel between true cities."

"I saw one, once," Betha offered timidly.

"Really?" Amarl asked. "What was it like?"

"It was larger than this – and very fancy. I remember thinking that just the gold filigree on it was worth what mother made in an entire year. It was much quieter, too, and it didn't make any smoke."

"Amazing," Amarl said, shaking his head. "I'd like to ride in one, one day."

"Ha!" Herel snorted. "Not likely. The cost of passage on one is likely more than your entire village sees in a year, hizeen."

"Actually, it's very likely that you'll all ride in one at some point," Danmila cut into the conversation. "At least, assuming you survive."

"Survive?" Amarl asked suspiciously, his heart suddenly pounding, all his wonder at the speed at which they traveled and the thought of one day riding in a sahrwagon vanishing. "What's that supposed to mean?"

"Just what it sounds like." She reached past Amarl and yanked the tie holding the curtain closed, allowing the drapes to drop across the window and cutting off his view. He made a small sound of protest that he quickly cut off when he saw the serious look on her face.

"Tell me, Marl," she said once she realized he wasn't going to object to her actions, "what do you think is happening, here?"

His initial response was to make some flippant remark about her taking him on a scenic tour of the Empire, but he quickly swallowed that down after another glance at her face. Instead, he considered her question seriously, frowning as he mulled it over.

"It's obvious that you're taking us to Askula," he said slowly. "I'm guessing that you did the same presentation with your box in other places, and both Betha and Herel picked the lavender crystal – although I still don't know why no one else did."

"That doesn't matter," she shook her head. "You'll find out about all that if and when it becomes necessary." She leaned back in her seat. "What do you think it means that I'm taking you to Askula?"

"My first thought is that you're going to make us all ithtaru somehow – and it's got something to do with the lavender crystal." He frowned. "Wait, you said that I did something so that it can't be taken from me. Did I make a mistake? Does it mean the others can't become ithtaru, now?" He felt a brief surge of guilt and malicious glee at the same time, guilt at the thought of Betha missing out and glee at the idea that he might have taken something from Herel.

"No." Danmila shook her head and leaned toward him. "All three of you have been both blessed and cursed with the natural ability to become an ithtar. Just because you can doesn't mean you will, and if you fail..." She shrugged, and Amarl swallowed hard as he realized her implication, and what she meant by not surviving.

"Don't we get a say in this?" he asked plaintively.

"No. By law, every child with the ability is found between their fourteenth and fifteenth Naming Day and brought to Askula. They leave behind whatever they had before and become the property of Askula."

"And what if they don't want to? What if they run away, or hide?"

"Then they're hunted down and executed." Her face didn't remotely change expression, and her voice was remorseless as she spoke. She gave him a grim smile. "Fortunately, I don't think that will be a concern for any of us, will it?" He shook his head vehemently.

"Good. Oh, and while I'm thinking of it: give me your coin purse."

"Why?" he asked, taken by surprise by the request.

"You won't need it. I told you: you're now the property of Askula. We'll see to all your needs." She held her hand out, and slowly, reluctantly, he pulled the purse off his belt and handed it to her. She hefted it, frowned, and dropped it on the seat beside her. Her hand extended once more, snapping her fingers.

"And your other one."

"My other one?" he asked as innocently as possible, his heart pounding rapidly in his chest.

"Yes. You said you had enough money to get by in Thind, and there's not enough for that in your purse, here. Give, Marl. Don't make me search you; neither of us would like that."

He suppressed an urge to joke that he certainly would enjoy it, then reached beneath his shirt with a sigh and pulled out a large, flat leather pouch, handing it over to her. She took it, bounced it in her hand a few times, and pulled it open, glancing inside, then pulled out a handful of large, bronze akatos, each a standard skilled craftsman's weekly wage.

"This is a thief's pouch," she observed.

"A thief's pouch?" Betha asked, her eyes wide. "What's that? Are all those stolen?"

"It's just a pouch designed to hide coins and keep them from being found. It's padded, and there are layers of lining on the inside to keep the coins from clinking together or moving around." Danmila looked coolly at the young hizeen. "As far as them being stolen, I'd guess the answer to that is, 'yes'. Am I right, Marl?"

"Yes," he said heavily.

"We already know the hizeen is a common thief," Herel said

scornfully. Amarl's anger flared, but before he could say a word, Danmila replied in a voice like ice.

"He could have stolen everything in that village and still be less of a thief than some of your family, Herel, so be still." Herel's face went pale, then flushed beet red, and he looked down at his chest, his lips moving but no sound emerging.

Danmila looked at all three. "People come to Askula from every caste and every background, from royal malakai to the branded annatai, and they all enter it as equals. Everything you were, is gone, as of this moment. The person who chose that crystal died the second they touched it. Any privilege they had is lost, and their family won't acknowledge or recognize their existence. Any crimes they committed are forgiven. Askula strips all that from you, and what's left behind?" She shrugged. "Whatever you bring with you – and whatever you earn."

She leaned back again and closed her eyes, folding her arms over her chest.

"Now, everyone shut up and enjoy the ride as best you can. It's a long way to Haveld and then to Mount Askula, and if I have to listen to bickering and arguing the whole way, I'm likely to start cutting out tongues."

Amarl said nothing and lifted the curtain beside him, gazing back out the window at the land racing by. They were well beyond Tem's farms now, into areas he'd never seen before, but his eyes barely took in anything that they saw. He'd understood Danmila's words, both what she said and what she didn't say. There was a message for each of them hidden in there, and he heard what she was saying to him clearly. The others brought something to Askula, but he was entering empty-handed. If he wanted to be more than an ishtai, he'd have to earn it.

And he was determined to do so.

CHAPTER 6

Amarl stepped out of the steamwagon and stretched, breathing in the cool, crisp air that wafted down from the Northwall Mountains. He smoothed the new shirt and pants he'd gotten in Devald two days' prior, trying to flatten out the wrinkles the simple cotton fabric had picked up from sitting for so long. The material, woven from the off-white fibers of plants grown far to the south, was cheap and durable, making it the fabric of choice for most of the people he'd known in Tem, but it wrinkled and stained easily, and in the past few days, he'd become far more interested in looking presentable than he once was. He finally abandoned his efforts as fruitless and looked around at the small village they'd stopped in for their break.

The village only reminded him slightly of Tem. Its buildings were mostly gray stone, and they spread out along the southern shore of a gleaming lake that stretched to the north. Beyond the still water, the distant peaks rose, jagged, black teeth coated with a thick white frosting of snow. The range was still distant, several marches at least, meaning at least five or six days' hard walking in a straight line, but the huge peaks loomed tall and brooding despite the distance, meaning they likely dwarfed the Silverbands under whose shadow he'd once lived. He froze as his eyes looked past the mountains and saw only a wall of swirling gray, like a distant storm that stretched across the northern horizon, dwarfing the mighty peaks.

"Another pathetic village," Herel complained as he exited the steamwagon. The young man also stopped and stretched, swinging his arms and bending down to touch his toes, and Amarl noticed that his glossy, silk outfit remained perfectly smooth and wrinkle-free. The hizeen suppressed a sigh at the realization that Herel's clothes – his "traveling clothes", as he put it – were probably worth more than Amarl had ever seen in his entire life, and the boy had no idea how valuable they really were.

"I like it," Betha said as she emerged, also brushing the wrinkles from her dress and giving Amarl a soft smile. "It's better than Devald, to be sure. I'm not a fan of large cities. They're too loud, and everyone is so unfriendly."

"They're not unfriendly; they're busy," Herel corrected pompously. "And Devald barely qualifies as a city. In one of the southern provinces, it would be called a large town."

Amarl rolled his eyes at the arrogant boy. "Yeah, yeah, Herel. We know. Everything's bigger and better down south." He paused, then grinned at the former noble. "Too bad the same thing can't be said about you. I've heard that down south there is really, really small."

Herel's face reddened as Betha stifled a giggle, and the other boy took a half-step toward Amarl, placing a hand on the sword at his side.

"Don't start with this already," Danmila growled as she stepped out of the steamwagon. "I've listened to enough of your bickering the entire way here, and if I have to listen to more, I'm going to break both of your jaws to shut you up."

"Forgive me, my Lady," Amarl said grandly with a sweeping bow, grinning as he spoke.

"Not likely. One of these days, I'm going to let Herel stab you a little just to teach you a lesson."

"I'm happy to offer instruction," the noble said flatly, his eyes narrow and angry.

"Shut up, Herel. Or I'll have Betha, here, kick you in the stones again. You're lucky that's all she did the first time."

Herel turned red once more, this time from embarrassment, his flush matching Betha's. The noble boy had gotten it into his head to seduce the young woman at some point in the trip – probably, Amarl thought, in an attempt to make the hizeen jealous. While Betha was initially receptive to his efforts, the noble had apparently assumed that she'd be honored to spread her legs for him and pressed the issue a little too far. She'd given him a sharp kick to convince him otherwise, and after that, she avoided him as much as possible.

Amarl could have told the noble his efforts were pointless. Betha was shy, inexperienced, and even a little prudish. Amarl had her pegged as someone who considered sex to be more than just a physical act, and she wouldn't just give herself randomly to a man because of his looks, money, or attention. She would want romance, even love, and she'd probably fall for whoever she lay with immediately. Under other circumstances, Amarl would have been happy to give her all that. While Betha wasn't terribly beautiful, she had an appealing sweetness and softness to her, and while he preferred experienced women, it was a preference, not a requirement. Besides, the only experienced woman around scared the shit out of him on a daily basis.

Danmila threatened bodily harm to both of the young men pretty much every day. He'd originally thought she was just prone to making idle if graphic threats – at least, so he'd believed until he'd ignored her promise to stab him if he didn't shut up, and she'd done just that. He'd screamed as the steel of her blade plunged into his thigh; he could feel the blade sliding through his leg, the edge scraping against his bone. He passed out when she twisted the weapon in the wound, then woke up later to find the injury mostly healed and Danmila smiling viciously at him.

"Still feel like testing me, hizeen?" she almost purred. "Next time, I won't heal it, and we'll see how long it takes you to bleed out."

After that, he took her threats very seriously, and she'd threatened to castrate Herel if he tried to push himself on Betha – or any woman – ever again. Amarl didn't know if that threat applied to him, as well, or how Danmila would feel about him attempting to seduce the young woman, but he had zero interest in finding out. He'd treated Betha very carefully indeed, trying to cultivate some sort of acquaintance without seeming like he wanted more from her, something he really wasn't used to. Fortunately, the two of them had a common dislike of Herel to bring them together, so he didn't have to work that hard.

Amarl bit back a sarcastic reply and instead pointed to the north. "What's that?" he asked curiously, looking at the featureless gray curtain sweeping across the northern horizon.

"Those are mountains, idiot," Herel said, barking a laugh. "Didn't you grow up right next to some? How did you not notice them?"

"I was too busy bedding your mother," Amarl replied pleasantly. "She was a decent ride, but nothing to brag about, I'm afraid."

Herel roared in fury and took a step forward, then collapsed as Danmila's fist swept across his face. He dropped to the ground, clutching his chin and moaning in pain, rolling around on the paved stones of the road.

"I warned you," the ithtara said calmly, not even looking at the fallen boy. She looked at where Amarl pointed and grunted. "That's the Edge."

"The Edge?" Betha asked.

"Of the Empire. The realm. This world. The place where the Realm of Spirits begins." She gestured to the north. "Beyond the Northwalls, the land simply stops. If you go that way, you'll enter the world of the spirits, and anyone who does that never returns." She paused for a moment. "Oh, and before I forget…"

Pain flared in Amarl's stomach as she suddenly appeared beside him, her knee buried in his gut. He dropped to his knees, gagging and fighting to breathe as every breath of air left his lungs. His lunch sprayed out his mouth and burned its way up his nose to splatter on the rocks, and he choked and coughed as he finally managed to suck in a breath and breathed in some of his own vomit.

"What…for?" he gasped, fighting not to lose the rest of his stomach contents. "Herel…started!"

"Because you could have just kept your mouth shut and let me handle it, and you chose not to. You didn't start it, so your jaw stays intact, but I'm losing my patience, so you lose your lunch. Understand?"

The woman turned toward Betha and handed the girl a slim metal tube. "This is as far as the steamwagon can go. I'm going to arrange for horses; if Herel's moaning gets annoying while I'm gone, feel free to give him this to shut him up." She looked down at Amarl, who shuddered and sucked in heaving breaths, then gave the girl a second tube. "And if he keeps vomiting and the smell bothers you, give him this." Betha nodded, and the woman turned and stalked away.

Betha knelt carefully by Amarl, cautiously avoiding the puddle at his feet, and unscrewed the lid from the second tube. "Here, Amarl. Drink this."

The boy gave her a grateful smile and downed the liquid in one gulp, ignoring its burn. Instantly, his cramping stomach eased, and he rose unsteadily to his feet. He took in a deep breath, then winced as the smell of the vomit splattering his shirt and pants wafted into his nose. He instantly began pulling his sodden shirt up over his head.

"W-what are you doing?" Betha asked, her face going slightly pink.

"I can't ride like this. I'll scare the horses." He glanced down at himself, shrugged, and began stripping off his pants. Betha quickly turned around, her cheeks bright pink as she put her back to him.

"Me?" Herel managed to mutter through his broken jaw.

"If I give you this, will you promise to behave yourself?" Betha demanded, putting her hands on her hips and sounding for all the world like someone's mother to Amarl. "Your word of honor?" Herel hesitated before nodding, and she tossed him the vial.

"So, that's the Edge," Amarl said as he went to the luggage compartment and rifled through the bag Danmila had bought him, pulling out another pair of trousers and a clean shirt. He yanked on his pants first. "I'm decent, now."

"I guess so," Betha nodded, turning back to face him as he slipped a new shirt on. "Do you think all the stories about it are true?"

"My mother says that most aren't," Herel said, also rising to his feet, working his jaw back and forth and wincing. Amarl knew that Danmila's elixirs never fully healed an injury, so the boy's jaw had to be sore and aching, just as his stomach still felt bruised and queasy.

"She says that most of the stories are just that: stories. Spirits don't come out of the Edge and steal babies or inhabit naluni. They would, but they can't. The towers stop them."

"Which towers?" Amarl asked.

The noble's face twisted in contempt, but Betha cleared her throat meaningfully, and the young man took a deep breath before speaking.

"The sahr towers. They regulate the sahr field so we can tap it without danger, but they also hold the spirits back beyond the Edge. So long as the towers stand, the spirits can only enter through incursions, and those are rare."

"How do you know all this?" Amarl asked. "I've barely even heard of the sahr towers, and those only through stories."

"I went to school," the boy said shortly, not looking at Amarl. "All children of the upper castes do. History is a mandatory class." He looked like he'd make another comment, but he bit it off and remained silent. Amarl thought about mocking him – after all, he hadn't promised to behave – but he thought better of it. If Herel was willing to play nice, so could he.

"There was a school in Fento, where I grew up," Betha said wistfully. "Everyone attended from their fifth Naming Day until their tenth." She looked at Amarl. "Does Tem have anything like that?"

"No." He laughed ruefully. "Even if it did, though, I probably wouldn't have been able to attend. No parents to pay my way, and all."

"In Fento, the town pays for orphans to attend. That way, everyone has at least basic literacy and math skills." She glanced quickly at Amarl. "Um, not that I'm saying you don't, of course!"

"Yes, I can read," Amarl said with a sigh. "And do sums and

everything. The Head Bureaucrat made sure that everyone was given at least a nominal education." He looked at Herel. "Although it sounds like yours was a bit grander."

"I should hope so," the noble said with a snort. "Our schooling lasts until the fifteenth Naming Day..." He made a face. "Which means that technically, I didn't graduate. Not that it matters, of course, but still..."

Amarl blinked in surprise as realization struck him. "That's right. Danmila would have had to found you both before Naming Day..." He frowned. "Assuming it's the same day everywhere, that is. Is it?"

"Yes, of course it is, hizeen. Having it be the same day everywhere in the Empire allows the bureaucracy to standardize ages and name lengths. The bureaucracy is very big on standardization." Herel shook his head.

"Then – how did you get your fifth letters? Both of you?"

"The ithtara took care of it, of course. How else?"

"She arranged for the bureaucracy to let me choose my letter early," Betha added. "Just like she arranged for the bureaucrat in Thind to register your name, Amarl. I assume she did something similar for Herel."

"I did." Amarl jumped as Danmila seemed to appear from nowhere. Betha let out a small yelp, and Herel scrambled back in alarm, his hand reaching for his sword before he recognized the woman. She ignored their reactions and gestured toward the steamwagon.

"I've made arrangements for mounts. Everyone, grab your bags. It's two days' riding to Mount Askula from here."

Amarl grabbed his single bag and slipped the strap over his shoulder, then followed the woman as she led them down the street. Betha followed behind, carrying a somewhat larger pack slung high on her back, while Herel trailed behind, lugging two large leather bags and one stiff leather case. The noble struggled to juggle all this, and while Amarl could certainly have given him a hand – he had a spare one, after all – he didn't offer. Herel was the one who'd chosen to bring so much, after all. He could deal with the results of that choice.

The stable stood at the edge of town and stank of manure and horse piss. The stable master, a lean woman with a prominent scar across her left arm, led out five horses, her movements fawning and almost servile as she did. Danmila directed the young people to load their baggage onto one of the horses, then told them each to pick the one they wanted. Herel moved immediately to a light gray stallion, as Amarl suspected he would, while Betha chose a smaller, chestnut mare. Amarl was left with a dappled gelding, and he quickly inspected the animal's hooves, lifting each in turn, then checked its saddle cinch and bridle to make sure they were secure.

"What are you doing?" Herel asked him contemptuously from atop his mount, gazing down at the hizeen.

"If we're riding these for two days, I want to be sure they're sound." Amarl shrugged as he patted the side of the horse's neck.

"The horse master has checked them already," Danmila said reassuringly.

"I'm sure, but I don't know that horse master or how thorough she is. If I do it myself, then I know it was done right."

"Trust me, she was thorough, Amarl. This town is the closest approach to Mount Askula. Every ithtar comes through here at some point, and we all deal with this stable master. If she ever gave one a faulty horse…" She shrugged. "Well, there would be a different stable master here, have no doubt."

Amarl nodded and clambered into the saddle, not sitting as easily as Herel but feeling far more confident than Betha looked. The girl rode awkwardly, her legs clamped onto the horse, pushing her ass out of her saddle. Danmila sighed and rode back beside the girl.

"Betha, have you ridden a horse before?"

"No, ithtara." Betha looked down as she spoke, seeming ashamed by her confession. "I've – I've never had a reason to."

"No, I suppose you wouldn't. Try to relax your legs a bit, or you're going to have trouble sitting down for a week."

A simple dirt road wound west from the town, weaving between the rolling hills of western Lepild. Short, dark green grass covered the hillsides around them, dotted with gray-mantled goats and black-coated sheep. Small herding communities nestled to the sides of the road, but none lay within easy shouting distance of it, and none of the herders came near to watch the passage of the small party. The wind blew down from the north with a cold, icy scent, and that night, the party huddled around a campfire, bundled beneath blankets against the rising chill.

As they rode west, a distant peak rose on the horizon. It stood apart from the Northwalls, standing gray and solitary in the distance. A dark cloud wreathed its apex, shrouding it from Amarl's view, a cloud that swirled and twisted about the summit but never drifted away from it. Flashes of lightning lit the dark cloud and bathed the peak below, but no thunder drifted across the hills and valleys, no matter how close they came. The herding communities thinned out and vanished entirely the farther west they traveled, until at last, they rode in solitude, their only companions some wild goats that must have escaped their herds and taken up residence in the area.

At the base of the mountain, the road turned into a steep, winding path leading up the slope, ending at last at a cluster of stone buildings built against a sheer cliff face. There, Danmila had the group dismount, and she handed the horses over to an armored man with a light beard, unusual in the Empire, and graying hair.

"Everyone, gather your things," she spoke crisply. "We walk from here."

"Walk?" Herel protested, staring at the bleak, gray cliff face towering above them. "Walk where?"

"You'll see, boy," the bearded man said in a deep, growling voice that instantly silenced the young noble. The man looked over the trio, his eyes curious. "A hizeen? What are you playing at, Danmila?"

"I never play, Dermalo," she said grimly. "And this hizeen not only passed the choosing, he quickened the ithtu crystal by instinct."

The man stared at Amarl and whistled. "Show me, boy," he demanded, taking a step toward the half-spirit. Amarl drew back nervously, and the man stopped, taking a deep breath and plastering an obviously forced smile on his face. "The crystal, boy. I'd like to see the crystal you quickened."

Amarl glanced at Danmila, who nodded tersely, then reached into his pocket and slowly drew out the lavender crystal. It still shone with a pale violet glow, but it seemed even more translucent than it had when he'd first attached himself to it. The man stared at it, then shook his head, his face amazed.

"By the spirits of damnation," he breathed softly before turning to Danmila. "You know what this means, right? His parent – which one?"

"His mother. She died when he was young, unrecognized in a village that mistreated him his whole life." She shook her head, her face scornful.

"What? No one ever performed a Ritual of Blood on her? Or the boy?" The man seemed incensed for some reason, and Amarl took another step backward.

"Apparently not. Don't worry about it. The boy made a vow to return and make them pay for it. A vow that his ithtu witnessed." Danmila's face twisted ruefully as she spoke, and the man stared at her, then barked a quick bellow of laughter.

"Ha! That'll teach them." He looked at Amarl. "Now, he just has to live to see it through."

Amarl wanted to back away and run; something about the man cowed him even more than Danmila did. Before he could take another step, though, a tiny spark seemed to ignite within him. All his life, people had treated him like he wasn't there and didn't matter. He was tired of it, tired of being ignored and spoken down to. He knew that this man could probably kill him as easily as he would step on a bug, but suddenly, he simply didn't care.

"Oh, I will," he spoke up, startling both of the adults. "I don't know what we're facing, but whatever it is, I'll live through it. That, I can promise."

Once again, his words seemed to ripple through the air, echoing off the stone wall and bouncing around them, repeating his last phrase over and over until, several seconds later, the final, "...I promise..." drifted to silence in the still air.

"Boy, you need to stop making promises," the man shook his head. "Still, that was interesting to watch. Only time will tell if it helps or hurts you." Curiosity nibbled at Amarl, but he bit down his questions. He had a feeling that the man had said all he was about to say on the subject, and further investigation would be more than unwelcome.

"I'll be back with your crystals, then," the man said, turning away from the group. He walked away, disappearing into a nearby building. As he did, Amarl turned to Danmila, opening his mouth to speak, but she quickly shook her head.

"Not now, Amarl. Get through the next few days, and you'll get all the answers you could ever want – some to questions you never knew could be asked." She glanced back at the building into which the man disappeared. "Until then, the best thing you can do is stay silent and keep your eyes and ears open." She looked at the others. "That goes for all of you. The less you speak and the more you listen, the better off you'll be."

The man returned a moment later carrying a cloth sack that bulged oddly, clinking slightly as it swung in his fist. "Here. Four crystals. The Mistway's open to you. Luck."

"Thanks," she muttered before gesturing to the others and walking toward the cliff face. "This way."

Amarl followed the woman toward a sheer section of dark black stone. She stopped before it, reached into the bag, and pulled out a small, glowing pale green crystal the size of Amarl's thumbnail. The crystal pulsed with an inner light, one that drew Amarl toward it. Only the comforting song of his own crystal in his ears kept him from reaching for this new one – that and Danmila's hard face glaring at them.

"I'm giving each of you one of these. Hold it in your hand and squeeze it hard enough to draw blood; it's the only way forward." She placed the crystal in Betha's hand, and the girl hesitantly closed her fist around it, grimacing as she tightened her grip. She gave Herel one, and the young noble stoically gripped it, a flash of pain in his eyes the only sign that he'd followed her orders. She lifted a third one and held it up toward Amarl, then stopped.

"This shouldn't be an issue, but just in case, don't quicken it," she instructed. "No matter what it wants you to do."

"Wants?" Betha asked curiously.

"You'll see. You understand, Amarl?"

He nodded, and she placed the stone in his hand. He wrapped his fist around it, feeling its spikes pressing against his skin. Even more, though, he could feel the life within it, the power inside it calling out to him, begging him to embrace it. The song of his own crystal, though, swelled in a cacophony that drowned out the new one's pleas, and he felt the emerald gem's voice slowly fade to a whisper. He clenched down, grimacing as the spikes bit into the palm of his hand.

"Good. Now, follow me." The woman turned and walked toward the cliff face, reaching it – and vanishing, seeming to slide into the solid stone.

"What?" Betha gasped. "How?"

"A Mistway," Herel said, fumbling with his luggage as he staggered toward the wall. "It's fine. Just follow her." The boy stepped into the stone and disappeared, as well. Betha looked back at Amarl, who gestured toward the rock face.

"Lady first," he said, bowing. She gave him a weak smile, then slid past the wall, vanishing into the stone. Amarl took a deep breath, closed his eyes, and stepped forward. The stone seemed to liquefy as he touched at, parting around his skin and wrapping about him in a cool embrace. His eyes snapped open, expecting to see darkness, but he found himself standing in the middle of a burst of deep blue light. The radiance spilled about him, simultaneously cold and hot on his skin. Clouds of pale blue mist shrouded him, blocking sight past a reach or so in every direction, including above. Shapes seemed to move in that mist, figures he felt he could almost recognize, and their voices whispered just below his hearing, demanding his attention. The voices sounded warm and inviting, but he felt the coldness hovering beneath them, and he shivered at the thought of walking into that mist and meeting one of its inhabitants face-to-face.

He looked away and realized he stood on a narrow stone bridge that led forward into the mist. More fog hung below the bridge, obscuring the depths beneath it. Curiously, he pulled out a coin and dropped it off the edge, but the bronze ak simply hovered in midair, refusing to fall. He snatched it back up and took a single cautious step forward, into the mists, followed by another. His feet fell in utter silence, even when he stomped on the stones beneath him. He tried to whistle, then to call out, but no sound came from his throat. Swallowing hard in sudden fear, he hurried forward, careful to keep his feet on the path. Shadows floated past him, half-seen images of things he thought he should know and recognize but didn't. Shapes passed overhead, casting no shadows on the ground but leaving a trail of darkness within the mists. His walk turned into a trot, and then a run as he sprinted through the mists, desperate to be away from the mocking shapes and their cruel calls...

He struck a yielding barrier that halted his rush, enfolding him in its embrace. Darkness slid around his vision, and a moment later, he blinked as light – real light, not some azure mimicry of the concept – stabbed into his eyes. He stepped forward and took a shuddering breath, noting that the air seemed dry and oddly tasteless, as if all scent had been stripped from it. He blinked again and looked around.

He stood in the center of a long valley. Sheer cliff faces of pale gray stone rose about him to either side, stretching ten reaches or more above his head, with a rosy, pink sky floating overhead. Gravel crunched beneath his boots, and he glanced down to see that he stood on a well-worn path leading between the rock walls. The others stood in front of him, Betha looking slightly confused while Herel just looked around impassively. Danmila stood beyond them, near where the path disappeared around a bend in the canyon walls.

"What in the spirit's hells was that?" Amarl asked softly, looking back over his shoulder to see a rune-covered arch embedded in the otherwise featureless rock wall behind him.

"A Mistway, of course," Herel said contemptuously. "What did you think it was?"

"What were those shapes in it?" Amarl chose to ignore the boy's contempt; he was still too shaken from the Mistway to come up with a clever quip anyway.

"Shapes?" Betha asked curiously, her brow furrowing. "I didn't see any shapes. It was just a path and lots of black mist."

"It was dark blue to me, and there were figures in it." He shuddered. "They called out to me, and I could almost hear them."

"I didn't see or hear anything," Herel shook his head. "It must have been your imagination."

"Yes, I imagined that the entire world was another color," Amarl said, rolling his eyes. "You must have a hell of an imagination yourself, Herel, if you imagine someone could do that."

"Stop fighting and follow me," Danmila called out, cutting short whatever reply the noble had been about to make. "I told you all: talk less, listen more."

She led them around the bend to a gate five reaches high and three across. The gate was formed of some metal Amarl didn't recognize with silver tracings throughout it in strange, arcane patterns. It stood closed before them, but as they approached, the doors swung ponderously outward toward them, groaning as they rotated around huge stone pillars that seemed to be cut directly out of the living rock. The path led upward through them and leveled off, widening into a large terrace bounded by a stone wall. Danmila led them to the terrace and gestured outward, toward the panoply spreading out below.

"This…is Askula."

The Realm of Askula

CHAPTER 7

Amarl gawked openly at the scene spreading out before him. The terrace jutted out from the peak of one of the highest mountains, allowing him to see for walks in every direction, revealing a landscape that looked almost like a shallow bowl, bounded in mountains to every side. A forest of dark trees spread out before the peaks to his far left, while to his right, snow covered a wide stretch of low hills

– beyond which, a small sea of sand shimmered and glistened with waves of heat that didn't seem to touch the nearby snow. A tall tower stretched up from the peaks directly opposite him, glittering oddly in the light, while directly below him, what looked like a normal village stretched out, ending in a series of fields and pastures that ringed the area.

His eyes barely registered any of that though. A single building dominated the view, a monstrous fortification that filled the center of the land, standing upon a gentle rise in the landscape. The building gleamed with the white of marble and the pink of quartz, stretching over a walk across, an hour or more walking at a reasonable pace. Towers and parapets topped the huge building, and hundreds of narrow, arched windows dotted it. A single banner flew atop its highest, central tower, fluttering in a breeze that Amarl didn't feel, a golden field with a bright blue blade running along its length. The castle took his breath away; alone, it was larger than the entire village of Tem. Thousands could live inside it; tens of thousands, most likely. And it didn't stand alone; a half-dozen smaller buildings encircled it, each capable of holding perhaps a hundred people within.

And those people moved throughout the area, as well. Figures made small by distance walked through the fields, tended the pastures, and moved along paved roads that spread from the center like the webs of a spider. They traveled along the streets of the village below and rode on horseback toward the massive central keep. Amarl couldn't make out what most were doing, but thousands of them seemed to inhabit this small land, and he guessed there were as many more doing things he couldn't see.

"By all the gods in the firmament," he breathed, astounded by the sight.

"It's – amazing," Betha said in a similarly astonished tone.

"Impressive," Herel said evenly. Amarl glanced at the noble and found the boy's gaze matched his indifferent tone.

"Impressive? That's all you've got to say, Herel?"

The noble shrugged. "If you haven't seen the Crystal Palace, it's probably overwhelming. I have, though, so..." He let his sentence fall away, and Amarl made a silent promise that one day, he'd see that palace and determine if the noble was right or not.

"This is Tenestra's Leap," Danmila said in a quiet voice. "Before you ask, no one knows who Tenestra was, if she actually leaped from here, or why she might have done so. It's been named that way since the founding of Askula, and whatever story might be attached is lost to time."

She pointed to the huge central building. "That's the Citadel, the true home of the ithtaru. It's where most of the Order live when they aren't on assignment, and where novices attend most classes. The smaller buildings surrounding it are the novice dormitories, where students live and sleep."

She dropped her hand to point directly below them. "This is Askula Village. The people there are descendants of ithtaru who lack the ability to join the Order themselves. They provide everyone in Askula with food and vital services that the members of the Order don't have time to perform."

She turned and headed to the right, leading them down a rocky path that switched back and forth toward the village below.

"You'll spend the day in the village," she told them over her shoulder. "Tonight, you'll get the chance to join the Order as novices."

"The chance?" Amarl asked. "I thought that we were already novices."

"No. You're potentials. You each have the ability to sense and see ithtu, which means you have a chance to become a novice. Whether or not you do is up to you." She shrugged. "And perhaps the gods."

"What do we have to do?" Betha asked nervously.

"You'll see." The ithtara glanced at the girl. "Trust me. The more I tell you, the worse it will be." She looked over at Amarl. "People are going to take notice of you and may comment on your parentage. I suggest you get used to it; you're the only non-naluni in Askula. Ever, as far as I know. It's going to create a stir."

He nodded, then remained silent as she led them into the village. The villagers stopped and watched them as they passed, and Amarl noticed that most of the gazes sent their way were admiring, although a few faces held expressions of pity or sorrow. While all three of them got their share of glances, people stared openly at him and commented frequently on his silver hair, his gray skin, and his non-naluni features. He thought he'd gotten used to being singled out for his heritage, but the villagers seemed to take it to an extreme. They talked excitedly about him and whispered constantly as he passed. People literally pushed others aside to get a look at him, and he was tempted to ask them if they wanted him to stand for a portrait so they could remember him better.

Danmila took them to a small stone building and led them inside into a large, low room filled with tables. Several of these were occupied by other people about the same age as the trio who sat around, talking quietly and seriously. Danmila stopped and turned to face the three.

"This is where we part," she said, her voice tired. "Feel free to eat or drink as much as you want. The Order will pay for it."

"Why?" Amarl asked with a tinge of suspicion.

"Because if you become a novice, that small expense won't matter. And if you don't..." She shrugged. "It still won't matter." She hesitated and looked them each in the eye as she spoke.

"Remember this. Who you were isn't who you are, and you bring more than your past to the Order." She nodded at each of them, then walked toward the door leading out of the room.

"Wait," Betha said, her voice plaintive. "What are we supposed to do?"

"Someone will come get you all at sundown. Then..." The woman sighed. "You'll see." She walked out the door, shutting it firmly behind her.

"Are you the new arrivals?" a girl with raven-black hair and olive skin called out from one of the tables. "Come, join us." She turned toward a long counter running across the far side of the room. "Sasofit! New arrivals!"

A door in the back wall opened, and a small man with slightly greasy black hair emerged from it, stepping out to see the trio of newcomers.

"Come in, come in!" the man gushed, lifting up a section of the long counter and walking over to the group. "Please, you can leave your belongings wherever. I guarantee no one will touch them."

Herel let his luggage drop to the floor with a sigh. "I don't know about you two, but I could use a drink. Barkeep, a glass of your finest red vintage, please."

"Of course, of course," the man nodded. "And for the rest of you?"

"I – I'd love a glass of wine," Betha said almost timidly. "Anything will do, really."

"Ale or beer, thanks," Amarl smiled at the man, who looked him up and down hesitantly before shrugging and hurrying back toward the back once more.

"Come on, sit down," the black-haired girl said, pushing out a chair. "Sasofit or his children will bring your drinks out to you."

"My thanks," Herel said, walking over and taking a seat. Betha looked at Amarl who shrugged, and gestured toward the table. She hesitantly moved to sit down beside Herel, leaving the spot beside her for Amarl.

The noble looked around at the dark-beamed, low-ceilinged room.

"Adequate, I suppose," he sighed. "I'd have expected more in Askula, though."

"The Ithtar Order is a league of warriors, not merchants," another boy with short-cut, dark brown hair said, his tones clipped and precise as he spoke. The boy loomed larger than the others at the table, his muscles pronounced beneath his shirt.

"Let me guess: son of a soldier?" Herel asked unconcernedly. "Yes, a common soldier might not care about the niceties of life."

"My mother is *First Staff* Alowenatera um'Proteran Tennshin, an officer of the Shalai, not a mere soldier," the young man said firmly, his voice almost growling.

"Is that good?" Amarl asked with a grin. "I don't know what it all means, but her name certainly sounds impressive. With all those letters, she's either had an amazing life – or you were born frighteningly late in that life!"

The boy glowered at him for a moment, then barked a laugh. "Ha! Yes, exactly. Her name is longer than most twice her age, and she's earned every letter!" He smacked his hand on the table. "I think I like you."

"I'm very glad to hear it," Amarl grinned. "I wouldn't want someone with such a fearsome mother to dislike me, to be sure!"

"You're a hizeen," a small girl with copper hair cut just below her ears and wide eyes observed suddenly in a voice that was surprisingly resonant for someone so petite.

Amarl refrained from rolling his eyes. "I am? What an amazing thing! Thanks for telling me; I might never have known otherwise."

"What I mean is, you shouldn't be here. How are you here?"

"The same as you all, I imagine. I picked the wrong crystal." He grinned at them. "Anyone else wish they'd picked the glass, instead?"

"Does it matter?" the raven-haired girl asked quietly. "Here we are, and what's done is done." She took a sip from the cup before her, but Amarl noticed that she didn't swallow afterward.

"True," the large boy nodded. "As my mother says, 'There's little point to railing against fate, as fate doesn't care.'"

"A wise woman, your mother," Amarl nodded.

"Yes, she is. She'd like you, too."

The girl smiled at the others, her eyes piercing as she examined them. "You came from the Silverband Basin, yes?"

"Indeed," Herel said pompously. "Allow me to introduce myself. Herel um'Shemerla Menith, at your service." He bowed his head to the girl, who smiled at him.

"A pleasure to meet you. I'm Meder um'Goranda Dairon."

"Dairon? A fine city, one of the wonders of the Empire. I've visited it on occasion, as my family has holdings northeast of the city."

"Many do." She turned to face Betha. "And you are?"

"B-Betha um'Forilna Fento, my Lady," the girl said awkwardly.

Meder laughed. "There are no 'ladies' here, Betha. Haven't you heard? We all enter Askula as equals."

"A fine conceit," Herel sniffed. "Of course, some do bring more training and education with them when they enter."

"And some just bring a fancy attitude and nothing more," the large boy growled. Herel bristled, but the boy glared at him fiercely. "Go ahead and draw that pigsticker at your side. I'll break it over your head." Herel glared back, but Amarl noticed his hand drifted away from his blade. The larger boy grunted and looked at the others.

"I'm Burik, Burik um'Alowenatera Tennshin, although you should have been able to guess that last part." He gestured to the small girl beside him. "This is Riyah. She never introduces herself. I don't know why."

"Why should I, when you keep doing it for me?" the smaller girl said without a hint of humor or sarcasm.

"Because it's polite, and people expect it, Riyah," Meder said smoothly.

"Oh. Well, in that case, then I'm Riyah um'Winholdir Onla. I guess it's nice to meet you all."

"Onla?" Herel asked. "Along the Imperial River in Shujish?"

"Yes, I suppose it is. I don't really go to the river much, though. Too many fish."

"Fish?" Amarl laughed. "What's wrong with fish?"

"Nothing's wrong with them, I just don't like them, and I don't think they like me, either." She looked steadily at Amarl. "Who are you, and why are you here?"

"My name is Amarl, great lady," he bowed his head to her. "Amarl

Tem, although I'm seriously considering dropping that last part."

"You claim no matronym?" Meder asked.

He shrugged. "I have no maternal name to claim, I'm afraid. My mother died when I was young, and no one in the village knew her name. So...I'm simply Amarl Tem." He grinned at her. "Although I could certainly make one up for you if it makes you feel better."

"Perhaps another time," she smiled back. "I'm honestly more interested in hearing the answer to Riyah's question. I didn't think it possible for a non-naluni to be chosen for Askula."

"I wish I had an answer for you, but unfortunately, only the ithtaru seem to know the truth of it, and they aren't telling." He laughed. "To be honest, until Danmila arrived in Tem, I didn't even know how the Order chose novices – or that they did, for that matter. I never gave any thought to it."

"It has something to do with your mother," Betha noted. "And the ithtara was very, very angry that your village allowed her to die."

"Well, they did, and she left nothing for me to tell me who she was or why she might be important, so..." He spread his hands wide. "I'm afraid I have no great secrets to share with you all. I just know that I'm apparently the same as the rest of you."

"Not all of us," Herel muttered.

"Still, a fascinating story," Meder observed, ignoring the noble. "An orphan with a mysterious mother, chosen by fate to join the Order. Quite exciting, if you think about it."

Amarl laughed again. "Probably nowhere near as exciting as your story. Tell me, how did you all end up here?"

They passed the next few hours sharing stories of their homes and families. Amarl steered the conversation carefully, keeping it away from his mother and origins. He'd thought that he'd long ago gotten over the pain of her death, but the thought that she might have been someone notable or important – as opposed to a prostitute who accidentally lay with a spirit-possessed, as he'd always been led to believe – stirred longings in him that he believed long-dead. Part of him wanted to know her, to see if any of her lived on in him, and to feel that, perhaps, she might have loved him before she died. He would never know any of that, though, and hoping was pointless and fruitless. He'd tossed that dream away long ago, but now, the hints that the ithtaru knew something about her – or her lineage, at least – fanned that dormant ember into a glowing coal that burned inside him.

They all drank more than was probably good for them, and privately, he knew why. The others had arrived days before the trio – Riyah and four others from the western provinces; Meder, Burik, and two more from the east – and Amarl's group was the last to arrive. Whatever test awaited them to enter Askula would be held that night, and as the moment drew closer, their nerves steadily frayed. For a while, Amarl merely sipped at his beer, noting that Meder did the same, but as the tension mounted, he took larger swallows. Silences grew longer as they each retreated into their cups and their thoughts, and he noticed the same occurring at the other tables.

At last, the door opened, and a quartet of armed and armored men and women entered the tavern. "It's time," one of the men announced. "Everyone, follow me."

"W-what about our things?" Herel asked, lurching slightly as he stood. Despite his apparent distaste for the local vintage, he'd partaken heavily of it, and it showed in his speech.

"Leave them. If you enter the Order, they'll be brought to you. If you don't, they won't matter. Now, come."

Amarl followed the ithtar out the door into the cool darkness of evening, absently noting that the other ithtaru spread out to surround them, as if worried they would try to run. That wasn't a real concern for most of them. Betha and Riyah both moved with noticeable drunkenness, and Herel stumbled as he walked. Amarl felt only slightly tipsy, and both Meder and Burik moved like their drinks hadn't affected them in the least, but most of the other youngsters would have had trouble walking away from the ithtaru, much less running.

They passed through the village, and Amarl felt surprised at seeing people lining both sides of the street, watching the group as they passed. Again, while most of the faces he saw held a look of admiration, several displayed pity or sorrow, and he swallowed hard at the thought of what might await them. He glanced up at the Citadel ahead and noticed lights blazing from its towers and windows, illuminating the darkness.

The effects of the alcohol had mostly worn off by the time the group reached the Citadel. They passed through a huge gate, along a stone courtyard, and into another gate that led deeper into the building. Sentries watched them pass in silence from atop the walls, while ithtaru stood aside and gazed at them as the group strode down a long hallway decorated with banners, portraits, and old weapons that Amarl couldn't even bring himself to inspect.

His stomach churned, and he trembled with every step as they marched in utter silence. Sweat broke out on his body as fear pooled in his chest, making his heart race and his head swim. He bit his lip, focusing on the pain to distract him, and he tasted blood as his clenched jaw pierced his lip. He jammed his hand in his pocket and felt his crystal there; as he touched it, its song seemed to swell in his ears, and his hammering heart eased its frantic rhythm. He focused on its gentle trilling, clung to it desperately.

At last, the leader stopped before a large door and turned to face the group. "I'll bring you each one at a time," he said. "When your name is called, come quickly." He pulled a piece of paper from his pocket. "Burik um'Alowenatera Tennshin! You're first."

The big young man nodded and stepped forward, his chin high and his face grave. He looked at the others and gave them a wink. "Wish me luck."

"You won't need it." Amarl forced the smile on his lips the same way he forced the words from his mouth. "This is the first step to earning enough letters to make even your mother jealous."

"Right. Exactly. I knew I liked you." The boy drew a deep breath and walked out the door, which boomed shut behind him.

The next hour lasted for at least several lifetimes. One by one, the others were called and made their way out the door. Some went confidently; others seemed barely able to make their legs move. When Betha's name was called, she took two quick steps, stopped, and walked back over to Amarl.

"Just in case," she said, blinking tears from her eyes as she grabbed his face and gave him a long, deep kiss. She turned quickly and practically ran out the door, and one of the ithtaru grinned at the speechless hizeen.

"Don't see that every year," the woman laughed.

Amarl gave her a weak smile before walking over to a nearby wall and sliding down it into a crouch. He closed his eyes and tried to let his thoughts drift to visions of finding Betha after the testing and pursuing the logical next steps to that single kiss, but his brain kept showing him images of the girl standing, her face stunned and pained as Danmila rammed a sword through her chest, just as she had Churl's. He flung the thoughts aside and listened to the soothing song of his crystal, trying desperately to push the fear from his mind. He barely noticed when Herel's name was called;

he honestly didn't care how the noble did one way or the other. He knew the number of potentials was slowly dwindling, and he wondered if it was possible to die of fear.

"Maybe that's what Danmila meant by surviving," he joked weakly, his jest falling flat even in his own ears.

"Amarl Tem." The name rang out, and Amarl felt a surge of panic that he brutally suppressed. He took a deep breath and opened his eyes, discovering that he was the last of the potentials remaining. He supposed that could have been a coincidence, but he doubted it. He was the only hizeen in the entire realm of Askula, which meant he was probably the only one who'd ever gone through this test. His going last was no coincidence; it was obviously meant to be the finale of whatever this testing was.

He rose to his feet and followed the ithtar out the door, surprised as he stepped out of the large room into the coolness of the night. A path led down from the door behind him to a lake that gleamed and glittered in the darkness. A dock extended into that lake, and he noted absently that something bobbed on the water beside that dock, something that looked like a small barge carrying a long, bulky load.

He walked down the path toward the lake, toward a bier of white stone about waist high and more than a reach long. A man with long, gray hair pulled back in a tail behind his head and a wrinkled, wizened face stood behind the bier, his face grave and solemn in the light of the pair of torches burning to each side of the stone.

"Amarl of Tem, approach," the man intoned, and the ithtar beside Amarl grabbed his arm and led him none-too-gently toward the bier. Amarl glanced at the top, and his stomach lurched as he saw the dark stains glistening on the pale stone. His heart hammered in his chest, and part of him wanted to flee, but before he could take a step, another ithtar grabbed his free arm in a grip like iron.

"Amarl of Tem, this night, you seek to join the Order of Ithtaru," the man pronounced. "First, however, you must be tested to see if your heart has the strength needed." He looked at the two men flanking Amarl. "Lay him upon the altar."

Altar? Amarl thought in sudden terror. "No!" He managed one shout before a strong hand clamped over his mouth, silencing him. He began to kick and thrash, fighting to break free, but the men holding him had grips of steel, and they lifted him off the ground, carrying him easily to the bier and laying him roughly upon it. He continued to fight, but two more ithtaru came and pinned his legs, binding him securely in place. His eyes widened to see Danmila holding his left leg, the woman's face grim as she stared at him.

The older man lifted a small, flat crystal etched with runes and wrapped in gold filigree, holding it up to the sky above. Amarl absently noted that the black sky was strangely empty of stars, but a large, silver moon hung over his head, shining its light upon his apparent sacrifice. He quieted a bit; a crystal wasn't nearly as terrifying as a knife, and he wondered if he'd jumped to a conclusion.

"Beneath the eye of Ak-lahat, may your soul's journey be brief and fruitful," the man stated, and Amarl's eyes widened once again. The crystal flared with power, and the man slammed it down on Amarl's chest. Pain exploded in him as something tore through his skin and plunged into his heart, and the world swam away into darkness.

CHAPTER 8

Amarl gasped as he sat up, looking around in confusion. He sat in the middle of what looked like a garden filled with flowers of all shapes, sizes, and colors. A fountain depicting a man and woman entwined in a lewd and almost obscene embrace sprayed water into the air, and that water flowed through the garden, feeding its thirsty soil. Amarl blinked as he glanced at the fountain again and realized it now depicted two men in an act of love. Another blink, and two women stood wrapped about one another.

He shook his head in confusion, wondering where he was – then sucked in a deep breath as memory rushed into the void of his mind. Fear roared through him as he remembered his sacrifice, and he quickly touched his chest, relieved to feel whole, unbroken skin rather than the gaping wound he'd feared. He took a deep breath, pressing his hand to his chest, then froze.

Nothing pulsed and beat beneath his hand. His heart was still and unmoving.

"Am I – dead?" he asked aloud, his voice echoing oddly.

"Yes, Amarl of Tem," a musical voice boomed, echoing across the entire world, and Amarl reeled as the words struck him. The sound slammed into him with the force of a hammer to his skull, and if his heart had been beating, he was fairly sure the noise would have stopped it.

"Forgive me," the voice spoke again, this time in a much more normal tone, although the sound of it burrowed into Amarl and writhed beneath his skin. It wormed its way into his blood and sank into his silent heart, plunging down lower into his nether regions. He shuddered at the sound's caress and fought to keep from crying out in sudden ecstasy.

"I haven't spoken to a mortal in...wait. What year is it?" A woman suddenly appeared before Amarl, beautiful beyond his ability to describe, with golden hair and alabaster skin. Her sheer lace gown clung to her lushly curved figure, revealing as much as it concealed, and if his heart weren't stilled, he had no doubt it would hammer its way out of his chest at the sight of her. He opened his mouth to speak, but words refused to emerge; the woman's beauty left him spellbound and awestruck, his mind unable to function.

"Oh, I see," she said in a rich timbre that made every nerve in his body throb. "Is this better?"

He blinked once more, and instead of a woman, a man stood before him, a man as handsome as the woman had been beautiful. His muscles looked etched in granite; his inky black hair swept perfectly off his head; his silk pants revealed a member that put Amarl's to shame. The hizeen swallowed hard and closed his eyes, forcing his rising lust down.

"N-not much," he stammered.

"Hmm. Perhaps a bit of both, then?" His eyes snapped open to see the woman's face atop the man's muscular torso. That frame narrowed precipitously to a slim waist, then ballooned outward to a pair of lush hips and curved thighs – between which, an obviously male member hung. He blinked in surprise; while every bit of the man – woman – whatever they were was individually appealing, the whole presented a macabre image that dampened his desire instantly.

"Y-yeah. Much better. Thank you."

"Of course," the person said, moving to sit beside him. "I came here to talk to you, after all, and that wouldn't work well if you were unable to speak." Their scent wafted to him, filling his nostrils with an intoxicating aroma, and he quickly began breathing through his mouth as he felt that scent plunging down into his crotch.

"C-can you do something about – about how you smell?" he asked.

"Not really, sorry. You're not really smelling anything, you see. You're simply sensing my essential nature and interpreting it in a way that makes sense to you."

"I – I'm pretty sure I'm smelling that."

"But you aren't – any more than you're actually seeing all this. You can't. Remember? You're dead."

He blinked and pressed his hand to his chest once more, feeling the stillness within him. "So – that's it? I'm dead?" He looked around. "Is this the afterlife? It seems – small."

"No, it's not," they chuckled, and a thrill of pleasure raced through

Amarl at the sound. "It's…let's call it the place where your soul and the world beyond meet. Your soul is still joined to your body, so it can't travel into whatever waits you when you finally die."

"I thought I already did that." He stared at the person in bewilderment. "I don't understand. What's happening here?"

"The Joining. For a mortal to become an ithtar, you first have to bond with your Joining Crystal." They made a face. "Actually, that's only required for you to join the Order. It isn't necessary to become an ithtar, although the Order will tell you that it is."

"My what?"

"You'll understand once you revive – assuming you do, of course. Not all potentials live through the Joining."

He looked around at the beautiful garden. "So, this place is my soul?"

"Yes, but most of what you're seeing is my presence here. Your actual soul isn't very developed yet." They smiled, and the warmth of it sank into his silent chest. "How could it be? You're barely an adult, after all. A soul grows through experience, and you've barely had any."

He closed his eyes and rubbed his face with his hands. "I'm totally confused," he muttered. "What's going on here? Who are you?"

"Ah, now there's a good question. I go by many names, but in Umpratan, I'm called Khima by most."

He jumped and scrambled back from them, his eyes wide with sudden fear. "K-Khima? The god of love? You…" He swallowed hard. "You're a god?"

"Part of one, yes," they nodded. "A tiny part, to be sure – but then, the entirety of Khima would destroy your mind, I'm afraid."

He stared at them, his mind reeling as he tried to understand what he was looking at. "What – why are you here? Are you speaking to the others, too? Don't the gods have better things to do?"

They laughed, and another thrill of pleasure rippled through him, but this time, his terror quickly silenced it. "So many questions! No, none of the other potentials met me. They might have met another god – we do pay attention to the Joining when it happens – but it's not very likely." They made a dissatisfied face that made his chest ache with longing and disappointment.

"Usually, during the Joining, the potential has to confront their past, accept responsibility for their mistakes, let go of old ties, blah, blah, blah."

They made a dismissive gesture with one long-fingered and slightly hairy hand. "It's really quite boring, to be honest. Those who are too tied to their past lives don't survive it, though, which is probably for the best."

"Why is someone dying for the best?" he asked in astonishment.

"Because it's far better that they die now than have their souls destroyed by ithtu – which can happen to those without the will and desire to control their abilities. That's the true reason for the Joining: to separate the weak in spirit." They shrugged. "However, I don't think that's going to be an issue for you, considering that you've already quickened an ithtu crystal, and it doesn't seem to be damaging this place. You'll likely survive the Joining."

He blinked, and suddenly they were next to him again, their scent thick in his nostrils, their presence a physical pressure on his senses.

"And as for why I'm here – well, that's mostly because of your heritage, Amarl."

"M-my what?" His mind reeled, struggling to function under the weight of the god's presence. They gave him a knowing look before withdrawing, and he took in a deep, shuddering breath as his thoughts began to flow freely once more.

"My heritage? You mean, my mother? You know who she was?"

"Of course, I do," they laughed easily, making his silent heart sing in his chest. "Remember who I am, Amarl." He opened his mouth, but they held up a single finger, and he found himself unable to speak, his tongue utterly frozen. "No, I won't tell you of her. Survive the Joining, excel in the Order, and you can learn all you need to on your own.

"Besides, she's not the reason I'm here. Your father is."

"M-my father?" He shook his head in confusion. "I don't know anything about my father. I know he was a spirit-possessed..."

"Oh, no. Nothing like that. Your mother would never have lain with a spirit-possessed, Amarl. She knew her blood. Your father was one of mine. A true spirit, one of the ruhlubi to be precise."

"That – that's not possible, is it? Spirits can't enter our world. At least, that's what they say."

"That's not completely true, but it's close enough. Your mother didn't meet your father in your world, though. They met in the Mistways." The goddess smiled fondly, and Amarl's entire body thrilled with delight. "Their love shone briefly but brightly, the way love always does with the ruhlubi, and I thrilled to watch it happen. He was a true follower of mine, and I celebrated their joining exuberantly."

Amarl's mood sank at their words. "Was?" he echoed dully. "So – he's dead?"

"Oh, yes, I'm afraid so. That's how you were born, you see. Your mother took his essence into herself and joined with it – and that made you." They smiled sadly, and the ache of melancholy swept through his body, bringing tears to his eyes.

"Oh, don't cry, dear. There's good news, as well. You see, they say that the parent lives on in the child, and in your case, that's quite literally true. You have your mother's blood and your father's essence, and you've been a shining example of both! You have her strength, her courage, her sense of vengeance; you have his whimsy, his humor, and his skills in seduction." They laughed again, and the melancholy fled as joy filled his being.

"In fact, you've served me almost as well as he did, Amarl, and because of that service, you've earned a boon."

"A – a boon?" he asked in a trembling voice. "What does that mean?"

"It means that I'm granting you a small gift." He blinked, and once more, they appeared beside him, their presence smothering him with its intensity. "Would you like to accept my gift, Amarl?" Their voice purred in his ear, and he had to fight to form a coherent thought.

"What – what's – the gift?" he managed to stammer out.

"Oh, something minor, just a nudge, really. Your blood is powerful, but it slumbers. I can stir it, set it to awakening. It won't grant you earth-shattering power or anything – at least, not in and of itself – but it will certainly benefit you in the long run." They leaned close to him, their lips next to his ear, their hot breath seeming to pour through his body and slink along his nerves as they spoke. "Would you like my gift, Amarl?"

"Y-yes," he forced out, his mind blank and empty. He wanted whatever this being was offering; he wouldn't refuse any of their desires!

"Then let it be so." Their lips moved to touch his, and as their soft skin brushed against him, fire seemed to leap from them and pour down his throat. The heat of it burned its way down into his core and flooded his body, spreading out through his veins and warming every part of him.

And deep within him, he felt something awaken. A slumbering power stirred, a power that had slept for eons. It drowsed still, but the fire in his blood prodded it gently, and he knew it wouldn't sleep forever.

<DO YOU KNOW WHAT YOU HAVE DONE?>

The voice crashed in his soul, roaring thunderously and shattering the spell the god of love and desire held over him. The goddess flew backward, seemingly hurled from him to tumble awkwardly through the garden. They sprang to their feet, their face outraged as they turned it up to the sky.

"I have done what is my right!" they screamed, their voice also booming powerfully, forcing Amarl to cower on the ground, covering his ears. "He is one of mine, descended from mine, and I have done nothing to harm him!"

<YOU KNOW NOTHING OF WHAT YOU SPEAK, FOOL.>

"I know that what I have done is with precedent! It is within the bounds the One Above All has set! It is a kindness to him, nothing more!"

<SO IT MAY HAVE BEEN INTENDED. AND YET, YOU HAVE INFLICTED A GREATER CRUELTY THAN YOU CAN POSSIBLY IMAGINE. BEGONE FROM THIS PLACE.>

The goddess opened their mouth to speak, but before they could utter a sound, they whipped backwards as if snatched by some terrifying force. Their face had a moment to register shocked surprise before they vanished from his soul, hurled from it in a terrible instant.

Amarl saw none of this, curled up as he was in a weeping ball at the center of the garden as the titanic powers boomed and clashed around him. When silence at last settled, he slowly raised his head and looked around. All about him, flowers wilted and faded, their stalks yellowing and crisping to brown in an instant. Crimson liquid bubbled from the fountain, which now looked like a skeletal pair of figures, each burying a knife in the other's back, locked together forever in an embrace of death.

In the center of this horror, a single shoot rose from the ground. It stretched as high as the boy's face, unfurling dark purple leaves that dripped red blood. A bud burst from its tip, a single blossom that bloomed into a rose blacker than night, darker than anything he could ever imagine.

<Attend me, child.>

The voice that rolled from the flower no longer boomed majestically across his soul, beating him into submission. It sounded gentle, almost comforting, and he felt a strange peace fall over him as it spoke. He rose to his knees and stared at the single bloom – and the crimson eye that opened in its center, gazing unblinkingly at him.

<The divine mortal's gift to you is no blessing,> the voice spoke soothingly. <It will grant you great power – but at a terrible cost.>

"Cost?" he echoed. "What cost?"

<It will bring fire and terror to your world. It will shatter barriers meant to be sealed forever. It will unleash a plague of death upon the land. This, I can foresee.>

He stared at the flower in terrified astonishment. "You – you can see the future? Who are you?"

<I am an aspect of the One Above All, the great Ak-lahat. I am the silent mistress of eternity, the bringer of peace and sorrow, the one who embraces all mortals at the last. I am...> Amarl's mind reeled at the god's next words, as it spoke a language his very existence refused to comprehend. <Forgive me. Your mortal mind cannot comprehend my true name. In your world, I am called Ispuqua, the Dark Harbinger.>

"The god of death," Amarl moaned, dropping his face into his hands. "Then – I'm truly dead, aren't I?"

<No, child. You live yet, hanging on the cusp of life and death. However, I offer you a choice.> A single tendril grew from the flower, extending toward him. <Reach out to me, and I will end your life.>

"What?" Amarl demanded. "You want to kill me? Why would I do that?"

<All mortals die, child. That is the nature of the universe, the will of the One Above All. That fate may be delayed, but it can never be unmade. However, if you take what I offer you, you will enter the world beyond having lived a life of peace, and you will be rewarded for that peace.>

"And if I say no?" he asked, swallowing hard. "What will you do then?"

<I will do nothing. It is not in my nature to take life before its time, only to harvest the crop as it ripens naturally.> The crimson eye began to glow, and Amarl swallowed another fearful gulp. <However, should you refuse me, I foresee a life of sorrow and pain, of misery and death. You will reap a bountiful harvest in my name, and you will be both adored and reviled for all time.>

"How – how do you know this? How can you tell the future? I – I haven't even lived through the Joining yet! How do you know what I'll do?"

<The currents of fate flow ever forward, child, beyond the perceptions of mortals and divine mortals alike. Only we aspects of the One Above All can see them, and then only in part. I can see the death lurking behind you, and that death gives me great insight into how events will surely flow, and the inevitable results of the fool's gift.

<More, I cannot say, for it is forbidden for an aspect to interfere with mortal will, and to tell you more would rob you of the greatest gift mortals receive: choice. You must decide. A peaceful ending now, or a life of pain and power mingled as one. Choose.>

Amarl stared at the flower. It was no choice at all, not really. "I – I don't want to die," he said slowly. "I'm sorry. I'm just…I'm afraid. I want to live."

The eye's glow faded, and the extended tendril withered and crumbled. <The choice is made, and the world will have to live with its consequences. That is the balance to Ak-lahat's great gift to mortals, child. Every choice comes with consequences, and you must endure them. So be it.>

The flower began to fade and wither, and as it did, the dying garden around Amarl faded, as well.

<We will meet again, child,> the god's voice whispered in his mind. <Return to your world, recall nothing of this, and reap the fruits of your choice.>

The garden swirled away, and Amarl opened his eyes to a different sort of darkness.

CHAPTER 9

Amarl's chest heaved, sucking in a deep breath that burned all the way down his dry nose and throat. He blinked rapidly, his eyes tearing up as he stared at the blessed darkness blanketing the world and the glowing light of the silver moon overhead. He sucked in another breath, reveling in the sound of his heart pounding in his ears. A single sob escaped him as he realized that he lived; he'd survived whatever the ithtar had done to him. Relief flooded his body, mingled with a burning fire of resentment.

They had killed him! Whatever their reasoning, the ithtaru had killed him, taken everything from him in an instant. Granted, he'd survived, but they couldn't have known that he would. In fact, thinking back to Danmila's veiled hints about survival and the pitying looks the potentials had gotten from some of the villagers in Askula, they obviously knew there was a good chance he wouldn't, and they'd done it anyway. He could have accepted it if they'd asked him, given him a chance to agree, but they hadn't. They'd held him down, violated his body somehow, and ended his life. He promised himself that he wouldn't forget that, no matter what happened – not that they'd killed him, but that they'd stolen his choice from him.

"After all, choice is Ak-lahat's greatest gift to mortals."

He frowned; the voice in his mind sounded familiar, as if he should recognize it. A vague hint of memory nagged at his thoughts, a touch of some compelling scent he couldn't quite recall, the sound of a laugh that thrilled him utterly. He struggled to grasp the memory, but even as he reached for it, it raced away from him, fading swiftly. In a moment, it was gone, leaving nothing but the sure knowledge that something had happened – something important – that was lost to his memories. He gave a mental shrug and let it go; whatever it was, he'd remember it eventually – probably at the most inconvenient possible time.

Strong hands still pressed against him, and he opened his mouth to tell them in the most sarcastic manner possible that in case they hadn't noticed, he was alive, thanks very much, and he didn't need them crushing his limbs anymore. Before he could speak, though, a strange image flashed before his eyes, freezing his tongue. The image was a rounded, sea-green rectangle, translucent enough to see through but solid enough to obscure the glowing moon behind. The edges of the rectangle faded into transparency, made it look like it floated in the middle of his vision, while the center appeared more solid and stable. As he watched, letters swam up from the depths of the rectangle, gleaming silver against the background.

INITIALIZING...
PERFORMING BODY SCAN...

Amarl opened his mouth to ask what was happening when he swore that he'd just been struck by lightning. A jolt of power exploded into his body, and every muscle seized at once. His back arched in pain, and if someone weren't holding him down, he was pretty sure his skull would have slammed into the stone beneath him. His heart practically buzzed in his chest it beat so hard, and he choked as he found himself unable to take a breath and thus to scream in agony.

Darkness flooded his vision, blacking out everything around him, while a low hum filled his ears. The sudden absence of sensation lasted for less than a second before flashes of brilliant color flared before his eyes, sparkling and shimmering in odd, kaleidoscopic patterns. A cacophony rang in his ears, sounds beyond describing mingling into something he couldn't even understand, much less describe. Ants crawled across his entire body, and thoughts and images flashed randomly in his mind, blurring through his consciousness in an endless whirl.

And then, as suddenly as it began, the assault on his senses ended. His muscles relaxed as the pain vanished from them. Darkness returned to his vision and bled away, revealing the night sky above. No sounds but that of his desperate breathing and pounding heart rang in the silence of his ears. The pressure vanished from his body as those holding him stepped away, but he lay there, too exhausted to move. As he stared into the sky, the sea-green shape bubbled up into his vision again, new letters shimmering into view upon its face.

"Wh-what the actual fuck?" he gasped, staring at the rectangle uncomprehendingly. "What the fuck is this?" Panic started to rise within him; he was hallucinating. He had to be. He'd seen it before, in people with severe head injuries, or who'd spent too much of their lives in drink. It started with seeing and hearing things no one else could, and it ended in madness and death. He'd survived their stupid ritual just to die from brain damage.

"Relax, Amarl," a calm voice spoke, and he saw the older man who'd killed him – killed him! – smiling down at him in an almost fatherly way. "Just will it away, and it'll vanish."

He looked at the rectangle and mentally commanded it to begone from his sight, and the image shimmered and faded, disappearing at once. "What the hell?" he muttered, blinking in amazement. "I've never heard of a hallucination you could order to go away."

"It's not a hallucination, boy. It's part of being in the Order." The old man grabbed Amarl's arm and hauled him to a sitting position with surprising strength. "You'll learn more when you start classes tomorrow. In the meantime, go change, then join your new classmates."

Amarl rose unsteadily to his feet and looked where the old man pointed to see a cluster of figures standing well off to the side, out of his earlier sight. He stopped and looked around, realizing that he was surrounded by grim-faced ithtaru who lined the path leading from the Citadel down to the bier. He wondered if they'd come while he was dead, or if he just hadn't noticed them when he first came out. Considering his state of mind at the time, it really could have been either.

He froze as the man's words sank into him – along with a familiar if unpleasant smell rising all around him. He looked down at himself and saw that at some point, he'd soiled his clothing, front and back, and he'd done it in front of everyone watching. He felt his face warm as a blush spread up his cheeks, and he looked around frantically, trying vainly to cover the wetness staining the front of his clothing.

"This way, boy," a man said, gesturing down toward the lake, where a few sheets or blankets hung to provide some semblance of privacy. "You'll want to wash, too."

Amarl hurriedly stripped off his clothing and waded into the cold water, rinsing the foul odor from his body. A splotch of blood stained his chest, and another crusted his cheek from nose to chin, and he cleaned those off, as well. He stepped out, shivering and pale, and found his pack waiting for him. He pulled out a new set of clothing and yanked it on, raking his fingers through his damp hair. Hefting his pack, he walked back out to find the group waiting for him – and somewhat smaller than it had been.

"You made it!" Burik said expansively, lifting his arm in greeting. "Congratulations!"

"I had a feeling you might," Meder added with a smile.

He glanced around and saw Herel standing with two other richly dressed boys, talking animatedly, but as his gaze swept the group, two figures were clearly missing.

"Riyah?" he asked, his voice thick. "Betha?"

"They didn't make it," Burik shook his head, his expression turning grim in an instant. "Betha never woke up. Riyah did, but she didn't survive the body scan." He took a deep breath. "Of the twelve of us, only we six survived, I'm afraid."

"No wonder Danmila kept saying, 'if we survive'," Amarl shook his head. "If half of all potentials die each year…"

"It's not always that bad, apparently," Meder volunteered. She pulled a sour face immediately. "Although, they say, sometimes, it's worse."

"New novices!" The voice carrying over the crowd cut off Amarl's sarcastic reply, which was probably for the best. He was badly shaken, stung by Betha's loss, and more than a little angry at the Order. It was probably wiser for him to keep his mouth shut and his ears open – just as Danmila had advised.

The two trios turned to see the crowd parting, allowing a much older man in flowing silk robes that shimmered with a multihued sheen to pass through. The man looked ancient to Amarl, his hair white with age and his face as deeply lined as a prune, but something in his eyes took the boy's breath away. There was power there; power that radiated from him and stole any hint of insolence that might have bubbled up on the boy's tongue. The others fell silent as well, and he wondered if they could feel the man's strength, too.

"Welcome to the Order of Ithtaru," the man said in a grand, ringing voice. "You are the newest members of the ancient sect devoted to defending the Empire – and all life in general – from the threat of the spirits and incursions from other worlds. You will be given a terrible responsibility, and with it will come terrible power. You will be feared and shunned, hated and adored, reviled and worshipped in equal measure across the Empire and into the realms beyond. It is a heavy burden we bear, but none other can carry it, so we do as we must.

"You are each the newest entrants to Sabila, the novice school. Look to those above you in your school for guidance and wisdom, and as you grow, pass that knowledge on to those who come after. Give your all in your classes, and absorb the teachings of your instructors as deeply as possible, and one day, you'll advance from novice to student, and then to a full ithtar!" The man paused as if for dramatic effect, then beamed a smile at the groups.

"But all that is for tomorrow. Tonight, you will receive what we were forced to deny you: the celebration of your Naming Day! Drink, eat, and receive the acclaim that should have been yours. Mourn those you left behind, or those who proved unable to follow you. Drink in their memories, and celebrate your triumphs!"

Applause rang out as the man finished, and the crowd parted once more as humbly dressed villagers drove wagons loaded with ale and carts laden with food into the midst of the throng. Amarl watched in amazement as tables were quickly set up, food was spread before them, and a foaming tankard of beer was shoved into his hand.

"Well, you made it." He turned as Danmila sidled up to him, her eyes bright. "You and Herel both – not that I'm surprised, really."

"Betha didn't," he said soberly, glancing past the burgeoning celebration to the dark barge moored to the dock in the lake and understanding its significance at last.

"No, she didn't. I was afraid she wouldn't; she cared too deeply for those she left behind. She couldn't let go of the past and embrace a new life." She shook her head, then lifted her own ceramic tankard. "Let the first drink of the night, then, be to her, and to her memory." She lifted the mug, and after a moment, Amarl did the same, taking a deep swig of the heady brew. He had the feeling that the celebration wasn't just about their missing their Naming Day; they'd all died, and drink and merriment would ease that painful memory a bit. After a long drink, Danmila lowered her mug, wiped her lip with the back of her hand, and grinned at the boy.

"Okay, you'll be asked this a hundred times tonight, so I'll be the first. What's your status?"

"My what?" he asked.

"Your status. That thing you saw when you first revived. I'm curious about your stats, and especially your ability – I'm sure everyone is."

"My stats? Oh, you must mean those numbers. I don't remember them, I'm afraid."

"Just concentrate on seeing them, and they'll come back. Go ahead. I want to know."

He nodded and thought about that green rectangle, willing it to appear once again. Instantly, the image flowed up from the bottom of his vision, once more filling his view without blinding him.

STATS
FORCE: 5.2 (122%)   SKILL: 5.3 (135%)
SPEED: 5.6 (183%)   TOUGHNESS: 4.5 (61%)
MIND: 5.3 (135%)   WILL: 3.8 (30%)
PRESENCE: 6.2 (332%) SOUL: 9.4 (8,145%)

QUICKENED ABILITY: MEZ
TIER: F
PERCENT QUICKENED: 0%

CURRENT ITHTU: 11.7
TO LEVEL: 0
TO STATS: 0
TO SKILLS: 0
TO TAK: 5 (INACTIVE, TAK FULL)

CURRENT TAK: 5/5

He dutifully read the numbers off for her. She nodded at the first few, seemingly unsurprised, and grinned as he told her his Will score. When he mentioned his Presence, she frowned, but when he told her his Soul score, she gasped in astonishment.

"Did you say – 9.4?" she asked, her eyes wide. She shook her head. "No wonder you quickened that crystal so easily. Wait, what tier is your ability?"

"Um, F. What does that mean?"

Her eyes went wide, then quickly narrowed. "Tell no one that, Amarl. No one except the awals – and the Rashiv, of course. Not even the other ithtaru."

"Awals? Rashiv?"

"The awals wear black. The Rashiv is the one who spoke to you earlier in the rainbow outfit. They run the school." She shook her head. "I have to report this at once, but if anyone asks, just say you've got a Tier D ability. That's believable." She sighed. "Blood truly does run true."

"What do you mean?" he asked curiously.

"You'll learn all this in classes, but..." She hesitated. "Every stat is important, Amarl. They all matter to an ithtar, and a wise one doesn't neglect any of them. However, Soul is by far the most important one. It controls the flow of ithtu, the amount of power you can hold, how quickly you can drain crystals..." She shook her head. "It's the cornerstone of everything we do, really. And yours is high, very high, many times a standard nalu's, as you can see by the number beside your stat." She took a deep breath. "Which, all things considered, shouldn't be much of a surprise. You'll go far in Askula, Amarl. Very far, indeed."

She left him gaping after her and vanished before he could follow and ask her more questions. He willed the rectangle away, then took another deep swallow of his beer. He had a feeling it was going to be a long night.

Sadly, he was right. He tried to grab some food and hide at an edge of the crowd, but the ithtaru wouldn't let him. They hunted him down relentlessly and demanded to hear his status; after the first hour, he could repeat the numbers by heart. Each of them got that same frown on their faces when they heard his Presence score and the same look of astonishment when he told them his Soul stat. He didn't understand either of their reactions, but he learned quickly not to bother asking about them. Their response was universal: "You'll learn about it in classes." He wondered if they were under orders to respond that way, or if they were just all too lazy and indifferent to take the time to explain.

He ran into Burik later in the evening, and the bigger boy insisted they drink a tankard together in memory of Riyah and Betha. It was Amarl's fourth already, and he was feeling the effects of it, no question.

"So, I hear you've got a really high stat!" Burik said after they finished, slurring his words as he spoke. "Me too!"

"Oh yeah?" Amarl asked. "Which one?"

"Tougness, at f…" He hiccupped slightly. "Five-nine. Almost 250% normal, whatever that means. What about you?"

"My Presence is six-two." Amarl decided not to mention his Soul stat; he'd seen enough people goggle over it to last a lifetime. In Tem, he'd hungered for attention from those around him; now, he longed for the days when everyone ignored him utterly.

"That – that's high."

"So they keep telling me."

"Who's been telling you what?" The two boys turned to see Meder walking unsteadily toward them, a tankard of wine in her hand and a foolish smile plastered to her lips. As Amarl watched, though, he noticed that her movements were just a little too precise, a bit too deliberate. Just as she'd pretended to drink in the alehouse earlier, he guessed that she was feigning intoxication for some reason.

"Amarl's got a – a high stat," Burik hiccupped again. "Presence at six-two."

"Aww." She made a dissatisfied face. "That beats mine. Mind at six." She grinned slyly and giggled as she spoke. "It beats Herel, too, you know. I hear his highest is five-five, in Skill."

"How did you hear that?" Amarl asked.

"I – I asked him." She wobbled slightly as she stood, but again, Amarl felt that the wobble was deliberate, as was her uncertain speech. "Of course, first I told him that my highest stat was five-two. If I'd told him the truth, he might have…might have lied."

"You're pretty clever," Burik noted.

"I am. And you're really big, did you know that?"

"I did, yeah. Everyone in my family is. It's kind of a tra-tradition." He looked at Amarl. "You're small, but you're kind of funny. I still like you."

"I like you, too," Amarl laughed. "You're honest. Not many people are, you know." He looked at Meder as he spoke, and her eyes twinkled. For a moment, she seemed a little less unsteady than she had been, and he grinned as he realized that his guess was correct. She was faking her drunkenness so people wouldn't push more alcohol on her. He had absolutely no intention of letting her get away with it.

"You know, Burik," he said slyly, "Meder, here, hasn't drank a tankard to Riyah, yet. I think she should, don't you?"

"Yes!" the bigger boy roared. "That's right, Meder. You need to drink a tankard to Riyah's memory!" The boy plucked the half-empty cup from the girl's hand, ignoring the stunned look on her face as he grabbed a full one from a nearby table and pressed it on her. "Go ahead, now. Drink to Riyah!"

Meder flashed Amarl a quick scowl that promised vengeance before lifting the cup to her lips. The hizeen watched with glee as she slowly downed the entire cup of wine, then he reached over and replaced it with another.

"And now, one for Betha!"

"Yes! One for Betha!" Burik agreed. Meder sighed but quickly drained the second cup. She staggered slightly halfway through, but she managed to put it all down. She glared at Amarl, but he gave her a sly wink and grabbed two more cups.

"And now, a drink to beating that ass Herel!" he proclaimed.

"Oh, I will definitely drink to that," Burik laughed.

"D-damn you, Amarl," Meder said, shaking her head. "I – I'll get you for this."

"I look forward to it with endless anticipation, my Lady," he bowed toward her. "Now, drink up! I've got a few other things that need celebrating, and I can't imagine two people I'd rather celebrate them with!"

CHAPTER 10

"**W**ake up!" The call was accompanied by a pounding sound that matched the pounding inside Amarl's skull. "Everyone up! First class begins in thirty minutes!"

"Whoever that is needs to go on a long trip," Amarl groaned, burying his head beneath his pillow. "Preferably to the bottom of that lake."

"And you should join him, you ass." He lifted the pillow to see Meder huddled beneath the blankets of a second bed across the room, squinting and shielding her eyes against the dim light filtering past the heavy curtains over the window. "I think I'm going to die."

"You won't die, trust me. You'll just wish you were dead." Burik rose from the third bed, rubbing his eyes blearily.

"Wait, why should I join him?" Amarl protested. "What did I do?"

"You were the one who made me drink so much, ass. If it weren't for you, I'd be feeling fine right now."

"I don't think I made you do anything. You were the one who actually drank."

"You made me drink to Danmila's backside." Meder's voice was waspish as she spoke. "To an ithtara's backside!"

"You seemed happy enough to do it," Burik pointed out. "And Danmila seemed amused by it."

Meder's face rose from her pillow, her dark hair half-obscuring but not quite hiding her horrified expression. "Wait – she was watching that?"

"Of course. What would have been the point in drinking to her if she wasn't there to appreciate it?" The big man shrugged and rose to his feet, wincing as he did. "Now come on, get up. We can't be late to our first class."

"Of course, we can," Amarl sighed as he threw back his blanket. "I'll bet that Herel and his new friends are late, as well. That was the whole point of last night: to make sure we're all hungover this morning."

Burik frowned. "Do you really think so?"

"It makes sense," Meder said wearily, also rising to a sitting position and wincing, putting a hand to her temple. "At least, I think it does. I mean, I think I think it does. It's hard to tell what I think right now."

"We all died yesterday, Burik," Amarl said, sitting up and groaning as a spike of pain throbbed in his skull. "And while we came back, some people we knew didn't. Then, the ithtaru offered us free, unlimited alcohol right after. They knew that we'd all want to drink to forget. So, why would they make our first class the first thing the morning after, unless it was to make us suffer?"

"Which was why I was trying not to drink so much last night," Meder said crossly. "Ass."

Amarl grinned at her. "And it's why I made sure you did. I wanted us all to suffer together, to bring us closer."

"I'd say it worked," Burik laughed. "We're roommates now, aren't we?"

"Yes, we are," Meder sighed. "Drunk me is apparently an idiot, agreeing to room with the two of you."

"Yes, she was," Amarl agreed, pulling off his shirt. "I can't wait to see her again."

"Well, you'll be waiting a good, long while. Now, both of you get dressed and get out of here so I can change."

"That's not fair," Amarl protested. "You get to watch us change, but we don't get to watch you?"

"Absolutely. Now, go ahead, my pretty boys. Take them off."

Amarl laughed as he turned his back on her and stripped down. He wasn't remotely shy about his body, and he knew that while he wasn't large, he was in good shape, with lean muscles that stood out plainly beneath his gray skin. At least, so he thought until he saw Burik strip down. The bigger boy's muscles shone tautly beneath his skin and rippled as he moved; he'd obviously earned them through hard work and exercise, two things Amarl had done his best to avoid.

"Oh, my," Meder murmured appreciatively. "Maybe drunk me was brighter than I thought after all."

Amarl opened the trunk by his feet and pulled out a simple cotton shirt in bright green. He unfolded it and gazed at it with a frown. The shirt was well-made, short-sleeved with a golden circle crossed by a blue sword on the left breast and the number one emblazoned below it. It also wasn't his; he'd never seen it before in his life. He rifled through the trunk, finding similar shirts with longer sleeves and pants in the same emerald-green, several pairs of underclothes, and a dozen pairs of high, green socks but nothing he recognized as his own.

"Wait, where are my clothes?" he asked. He held up one of the shirts and a pair of pants. "And what are these?"

"Your uniforms," Meder answered, giving him a curious look. "Don't you remember? One of the ithtaru told us all last night that we'd be given school uniforms and that we had to wear them."

"I must have missed that," he shook his head.

"It was probably when you were singing," Burik suggested. "Or trying to, at least." He grabbed a larger shirt from his own trunk and pulled it over his head. "Come on, just put it on. We don't want to be late."

The young men dressed and stepped out into the hall, heading to the end to use the privy, then waiting for a few minutes for the girl to emerge, wearing trousers and a shirt identical to theirs and tying back her black hair with a cloth thong. She took advantage of the facilities herself, then returned a moment later, gazing expectantly at the pair.

"So, any idea where we go?" she asked.

Burik pointed down the hall, where other students, all older than the trio but all wearing identical green uniforms, headed toward a staircase, talking quietly and glancing back at the new novices with occasional grins.

"That way. It's breakfast time, so if we follow the crowd, it should lead us to food."

"Ugh. Don't mention food." Meder pressed a hand to her stomach. "I couldn't eat anything this morning."

The three followed the others down the staircase to the first floor, then along a series of corridors. Amarl looked around curiously, seeing details he hadn't noticed the night before in his inebriated state. The halls were polished stone, with flat ceilings hung with glowing lamps. Doors stood open at regular intervals, and he glanced inside to see various empty rooms with things like laundry basins, mops, brooms, and cleaning supplies resting inside. He grimaced as it occurred to him who would likely do all the cleaning in the school; as the lowest ranked members of the school, they'd probably get the dirtiest jobs.

They stepped into a large room filled with other students. The smells of freshly baked bread, sizzling meat, spicy pastries, and sweet fruit juice all hung in the air, and Amarl inhaled deeply of the scent. His stomach rebelled at the thought of anything solid in it, but he ignored it and followed Burik as the larger boy led them to the back of a line of students. He glanced at them over his shoulder.

"Either of you eaten at a meal line before?" Amarl shook his head, and Meder did the same. Burik nodded. "Didn't think so. Just copy what I do, and you'll be fine. Don't take any meat, milk, or kaffee; your stomach won't be able to handle them. Stick to bread, juice or water, especially water. You're going to want a lot of that."

"Why?" Amarl asked.

"It'll make your head feel better faster. Most of what you're feeling is because you don't have enough water in your body right now. You just need to put it back, and you'll be fine."

Amarl mimicked the boy as he took a wooden tray, a cloth napkin, and a fired clay plate, then carried them along a long counter. Burik stopped before a tray piled high with pastries and picked up a pair of metal tongs, using them to grab several pieces of plain bread. Amarl took up another set of tongs and reached for a sticky sweet bun, but Burik reached out and stopped his hand.

"Stick with plain bread, trust me. That thing will come right back up on you in no time." With a disappointed sigh, Amarl also took a couple slices of bread and put them on his plate. Copying Burik, he ignored the sizzling strips of bacon and sausage and the steaming piles of fluffy eggs; his nose begged him to sample them, but the thought of it made his stomach rebel. He followed the boy to the end of the line and grabbed a tankard of plain water, ignoring the tantalizing scents of kaffee and breakfast wine emanating from metal carafes.

"Now, we find a place to sit," Burik said. "Anywhere open should do." As the boy spoke, Amarl caught a few amused glances shot their way, and he grabbed the larger boy's arm and pulled him to a halt, then turned to look at one of the students who didn't seem amused by what Burik said and looked closer to their age.

"Pardon me. We're new novices. Is there a place we're supposed to sit?"

The girl nodded slowly and pointed. "Yes, back over there, next to the kitchen. Worst tables in the mess hall."

"Of course, they are," Amarl sighed. "Thank you."

The trio wound their way around the food line and settled in at a battered, wobbly table with a stained, cracked surface. Meder looked at it and grimaced, then shrugged and set her plate down and pulled out a chair. She looked over at Burik as the large boy also took a seat, lowering himself somewhat more cautiously into the rickety chair.

"How did you know all of that?" she asked, waving a hand back toward the food. "How to get food, what we'd want to eat, what to avoid?"

"It's similar to life in a barracks," he shrugged. "Food is served in meal lines, and half the soldiers wake up hungover every day. They know how to fix it." He looked at Amarl as the hizeen settled into a chair, feeling it wobble precariously beneath him. "How did you know we had a special place to sit?"

"I didn't," Amarl admitted, taking a sip of his water. "But it occurred to me that since we're the lowest of the low, here, it might be a possibility." He smiled wanly. "And if we sat in the wrong place, there probably would have been a consequence for it. I have a feeling the older students were waiting to see it happen."

"Do you really think they would?" Meder asked dubiously. "They were new novices themselves once, weren't they?"

He nodded. "And they probably got the same treatment. Now, they get to inflict it on others." He took a small bite of bread, chewing slowly and washing it down with a sip of water.

"I never would have considered that. I mean, it makes sense, but it never would have occurred to me that they might act that way." She shook her head, then winced again and took a sip of water.

"I'm one of the ishtai, remember? I'm used to being the lowest of the low. It's sort of second nature to me."

"You were," Burik corrected. "Now, you're not anything. None of us are."

"Oh, I think caste probably still matters – at least to some people." Amarl pointed at the door, where Herel and his two new friends had entered together. The three of them ignored the line and walked over to an empty table, taking a seat and looking around in anticipation. Amarl grinned. "And now, we get to see what happens when new novices make a mistake."

"What the hells do you think you're doing?" The girl that marched up to stand over Herel's table had a number two emblazoned on her shirt with a golden line beneath it. Apparently, that line mattered, considering the way she bellowed at the three young men, who stared at her in shock and confusion. "On your feet! Now!"

"Excuse me, but there's no need to shout…" Herel's pained protest cut off when the girl lashed out with a foot and kicked his chair, knocking him sprawling. One of the other new novices jumped to his feet, while the third made a move like he was going to grab the girl. Before he could, she reached out and snatched his shirt, hauling him toward her, and slammed her forehead into his face. He fell back, clutching his nose and moaning.

"I said, on your feet!" she roared, and Herel quickly clambered to his feet while the already-standing boy reached down and pulled the last boy clumsily to stand. "Better." She stood before Herel, her face directly in his, and pointed at the table. "What do you see here, new meat?"

"Uh – a table," Herel stammered, his face shocked and confused.

"This isn't just a table, you idiot!" she bellowed, drawing a wince from the obviously hungover boy. "This is a second-year table! A sacred place where your betters can eat in peace! And you just dirtied it with your new meat asses!" She ran a finger across the table and held it up before her, making a disgusted face.

"You three are going to clean this table – and every second-year table in this mess hall – until they shine, you understand me? I want to be able to see my face in one!"

"But – we have classes," the boy who'd stood first said weakly. The girl spun toward him, putting her face directly in his.

"Then you damn well shouldn't have dirtied my table, should you? You'd better get to cleaning, quick. The malims get pissed if you're late – and you really, really, don't want to piss them off!"

She turned and stormed away, and Herel looked down at the table helplessly, then around at the nearby people. "How do I clean it? I don't have anything to use!"

Amarl rolled his eyes and half-rose to his feet, stopping when Burik grabbed his shoulder and pressed him down.

"Don't get in the middle of it," the larger boy advised. "Or you'll be cleaning tables with them."

"I was just going to tell them where I saw some cleaning supplies when we were on our way here, Burik. I wasn't going to stick up for them or anything."

"And that girl will tell you that since you're so familiar with cleaning supplies, you should use them on the hallway outside, or the walls, or something." He shook his head. "I've seen it before. She's like a First Spear; they all think that humiliating work creates discipline."

"First Spear?" Amarl asked.

"Yeah. A low-ranking infantry soldier, just senior enough to give orders but not senior enough to have any real authority. That girl's probably the same way, judging from that extra mark she's got on her uniform."

"It sounds like our smartest course, then, is to keep our heads down and our eyes and ears open," Meder suggested, looking at Amarl as she spoke. "And our mouths shut – assuming you're capable of that, Amarl."

"I can keep my mouth shut. I just rarely choose to do it." He grinned, then looked over at the three boys trying to wipe a table clean with napkins and mugs of water, and the grin fell from his face. "Although I think this might be one of those times."

They wolfed down their bread and water as quickly as their stomachs would allow, then asked around until they found that they were supposed to meet in the common hall. A few more questions revealed the location of that hall in the center of the building, near the exit to the Citadel, and they hurried down to it to make sure that they didn't miss their first class. The common hall was a large, open room with chairs and divans around the edge, as well as a large fireplace that could probably warm the entire room when the months got colder. Assuming they did, of course; Amarl had no idea what the climate in Askula would be like. It looked like a place where students would gather, but that morning, every student walked quickly through it without even slowing, no doubt on their way to their first classes.

"I – I guess we sit and wait?" Meder said tentatively, but Burik shook his head.

"I'd stand, just in case. Sitting might look lazy. If this was basic training in the army, and a sword walked in to find a bunch of footmen sitting around talking, they'd have them standing for hours to teach them a lesson."

"I don't know what you just said, but my head hurts too much to care," Amarl laughed. "We'll do it your way."

"A sword is a senior infantryman, usually in charge of a knife of soldiers or two. A footman's a recruit."

"I'm not going to remember that, but okay," Amarl laughed. "Tell me again when I'm feeling better, and we'll see."

Meder opened her mouth to speak, but before she could, a middle-aged woman walked into the room radiating power and authority. She was short, a span shorter than Meder, who stood a couple fingerwidths taller than Amarl, with a round face and graying hair, and she wore a black silk dress with emerald slashes along the sleeves and down the chest. Thin threads of copper, silver, and gold gleamed among the silk, and tiny gemstones speckled it, twinkling like multicolored stars in the light streaming through the hall's windows. Amarl guessed her to be in her sixties, although she moved easily and well, without any signs of stiffness or age.

A young, muscular man in white cotton pants and a sleeveless shirt of the same color followed behind her, his chiseled face narrow, and his black hair cropped close to his skull. An ornate, black tattoo decorated his left cheek and swirled down around his neck before disappearing beneath his shirt. He looked to be about ten years older than the students, and he moved with a casual grace that Amarl envied.

"New novices, stand at attention!" the man called out, and Burik quickly stood straight, his right hand at his side while his left crossed his chest and pressed against his heart. His feet snapped together, and his chin lifted. Amarl quickly copied him as best he could and noticed Meder doing the same beside him.

The older woman stopped and gazed at the trio, her eyes flat and her gaze unreadable. "Novices Amarl, Burik, and Meder," she said impassively. "Where are your fellow novices?" Amarl blinked in surprise; he'd expected the woman's voice to be dry, harsh, or scratchy for some reason, but it was deep, smooth, and mellow. It had a strangely alluring quality to it that drew him; he found himself hanging on her every word, and he felt eager to answer her question. A flash of irritation passed through him as Burik beat him to it.

"Cleaning tables, ma'am!"

The woman glanced at the tall boy. "Ah, yes. You come from a military family, and your mother had you trained to army standards. That will serve you well here, Novice, but know that the standards set for our Empire's soldiers are far, far below the standards required of an ithtar."

"Yes, ma'am!"

"We will wait for your wayward fellows to arrive; if they haven't joined us within five minutes, I will send you, Novice Amarl, to fetch them."

Amarl forced himself not to frown at that; the other three novices certainly wouldn't appreciate Amarl telling them what to do, and he had a feeling the woman knew that.

Fortunately, the others joined them in a couple minutes, looking harried, wet, and somewhat stained but arriving before Amarl had to fetch them. The old woman grunted and looked at the three latecomers.

"Novices Hadur, Herel, and Norag, I take it that you learned a valuable lesson today?"

The three looked confused, and eventually, Norag spoke. "Um – don't argue with the second-year students, ma'am?" he asked tentatively.

"Sound advice, but not what I meant." She gave them a serious look. "Things here in Askula are seldom as simple as they seem. Question everything and make no assumptions."

She straightened and looked at the gathered students with a critical eye. "My name is Awal Tekasoka. You will address me as 'Awal' or 'ma'am' at all times. I am in charge of Sabila School, the school for all first and second-year novices, which means that after today, it is highly unlikely we will meet again until the end of the year. If we do, then you've likely caused some sort of difficulty for me, and I don't like difficulties. Pray that you have no reason to discover how much I dislike them."

Amarl swallowed hard and stood up straighter as a chill passed down his back. The woman thoroughly intimidated him in a way that even Danmila never had, and he decided at that moment that he would go out of his way not to gain her attention. That would be hard for him, but after recalling how Danmila never made idle threats, he was determined to put in the effort.

"As of this morning, you are students of Sabila School," she continued. "As such, you represent this school in everything that you do. You are my charges, and I have certain expectations of you. You will do everything you can to meet those expectations."

"First, Sabila – and Askula in general – is an orderly place. You will not disrupt that order. You will be given a schedule, and you will follow it. There are clocks everywhere, and the Citadel will chime the bells every hour, so there is no excuse for tardiness. Hour one begins promptly at dawn, as you should now be well aware.

"Mornings in Askula are set aside for physical training and conditioning. Academic classes are after the midday meal, and additional classes take place in the late afternoon. As first-year novices, you have a reduced schedule that ends at hour eight; from hours nine to twelve, you will be assigned cleaning duties in Sabila or the Citadel."

Amarl nodded; as he'd thought, the newest students would be given the nastiest jobs. Even as he thought that, though, he reconsidered. He wasn't sure if cleaning was the nastiest job they could give. He'd worked plenty of jobs in Tem, and many of them – such as working the waste wagon that carried shit from the village to the fields to be used as fertilizer – were far worse than scrubbing tables. He suppressed a shudder at the thought of shoveling the shit from every student in Askula.

"You have been given six school uniforms and six sets of training clothes intended for your physical training. You are responsible for maintaining these. You will not attend any class looking slovenly and unkempt. There are laundry facilities in the dormitory; you will use them to keep your clothing clean and presentable. If your clothing is damaged through the normal course of training, it will be replaced. If it's damaged due to your own foolishness or incompetence, you will pay for the cost of that replacement out of pocket."

That didn't bother Amarl. He'd been cleaning his own clothing since he was ten, and no one had ever given him new clothing when he'd torn or damaged his. He'd had to patch it up as best he could or save up for a replacement if it was beyond his ability to fix. He stifled a grin, though, as he imagined Herel cleaning his own underwear for the first time and discovering that it was hard work.

"You will attend classes six days a week, Shimio through Nashio. Akio is a day off for all students, and you may spend it as you will. During that time, however, you still represent this school, and you will behave as if I were standing over your shoulder, watching you, because in a very real sense, I will be. The awals, the masters of this school, are not blind or deaf; there is practically nothing that happens here that we don't know about. Keep that in mind at all times."

She stared at them, her eyes intent. "Understand this. Whoever you were before, whatever you were before, you are now part of Askula. This is your home, and the other students are the closest you will have to family. Each of you died last night, and that death was recorded in the Imperial rolls. That person no longer exists, as far as the Empire is concerned. Your former families are mourning you even now, and with your death, all your former ties are severed. You are no longer of the zahai, tagarai, or ishtai.

"You are of Sabila, the school of novices. You'll remain here until your third year. At that point, assuming you've quickened your ability, you'll be placed in one of the higher schools based on the tier of your ability. You'll remain in that school until the end of your fifth year, at which point you'll become a journeyman for two years before finally becoming a full ithtar. You have a very long way to go, and the more powerful and experienced you are, the higher you rank in this school, and in the Order in general. That means that you, as new novices, are the lowest of all those in Askula, no matter what you were a moon ago.

"Know this, though. While you are the lowest caste in Askula, you still represent me and your fellow students in everything you do. Your successes are the school's successes. A failure for you is a failure for the entire school. As you can imagine, the other students don't appreciate such failures – and neither do I. I expect you to do your utmost to succeed in everything set before you. I don't care if it's difficult. I don't care if you think it impossible. You will do your best, and then you'll do better than that. You will not give up, no matter how hard something is, no matter how much it hurts, and no matter how much you want to quit. You will push until you're ready to collapse, and then you'll push harder. I will accept nothing less."

Amarl stood straighter as her words sank into him; something in them stirred him and made him eager to please her. He couldn't wait to get started, despite his pounding head and queasy stomach. He glanced around and saw the same fire in the others' eyes. He refocused on the woman as she spoke.

"Good. Consider this your welcome to this school, and to Askula in general." She held out a hand toward the man in white. "This is Nadar Periteth, who will be your instructor for this morning. Listen to him and to all your teachers as if they were me, because if you don't, I will know about it – and I will not be pleased. Understood?"

"Yes, ma'am!" Burik said smartly, and Meder and Amarl echoed him a second later, followed far more reluctantly by the others.

"Good. Periteth, I leave them in your capable hands. Make them useful."

"I will, Awal," the man bowed his head as Tekasoka swept out of the room, not even glancing at the thoroughly cowed novices. The man waited for her to leave, then looked back at the students. "Attention!"

Burik still stood straight, but Amarl realized that he and the others had taken on more relaxed postures, and he snapped himself erect once more.

"As the awal said, my name's Nadar Periteth. Nadars are junior instructors, ithtaru cycled in to teach for a year at a time. Assuming you survive your training, one day, you'll be here as well. You can tell nadars by our white uniforms; malims, the full instructors, wear gray, and awals wear black. Whatever we're wearing, though, you address every instructor you meet by their title or the terms 'sir' or 'ma'am'. Is that understood?"

"Yes, sir!" Once again, Burik spoke almost a full second ahead of the others.

"Good. Now, it's my job to whip you into decent enough shape that you can actually perform the other physical training such as unarmed combat and weapons."

He stopped and stared directly at Meder, his eyes intense. "I ask for one thing, and one thing only. You give me everything you have, all the time, and never quit. Do that, and we'll be good." He walked over to Amarl and looked him in the eye, his expression hardening. "If you give me a half-assed effort, or whine about how hard and unfair it is, though…" He leaned closer to the hizeen. "We'll have problems. And you don't want us to have problems. Understand me?"

"Y-yes sir," Amarl nodded, copying Burik's response from before.

"Great." The man stepped back and walked to the end of the line, to the boy who'd gotten headbutted earlier, who the awal had called Hadur. He paused and peered at the young man. "What the hells happened to you?"

"Some bitch headbutted me," the boy muttered, then cried out as Periteth grabbed his shoulder and pinched, hard. He tried to pull away or twist free, but Periteth's grip held him like a vice.

"Sir," the ithtar said calmly. "You will always address me – and every instructor in Askula – as 'sir' or 'ma'am'. Got it?"

"Y-yes, sir," the boy stammered.

"Good." He let go of the novice. "You say someone headbutted you? Who?"

"I – I don't know her name, sir."

"Did you do anything to cause her to attack you?"

"N-no, sir. She kicked Herel, here, over, and I tried to push her away from him, but she hit me in the face."

"That would count as cause," the ithtar sighed, pinching the bridge of his nose, then looking at the others. "Free advice since it's your first day, and listen hard because I won't repeat it. No senior student is allowed to put their hands on you – *unless* they can claim they're defending themselves. Then, they can beat you as hard as they want, as long as they leave you able to attend classes."

He clasped his hands again and started walking back down the line. "There will be senior students who make it their mission to get you to attack them. They'll antagonize you, insult you, even threaten you, just to get you to take a swing at them. Before you do, though, remember this: these students have gone through two years of the hardest, most intensive combat training in the entire Empire. Whatever skills you believe you have, they can and will hand your ass to you. So, keep your hands to yourselves, and they'll have to do the same."

He nodded, seemingly satisfied with his lecture. "Now, before we begin, let's see what we're working with." He stopped in front of Burik. "Novice, give me your name – first name only, no matronym or birthplace – and your Force and Toughness stats."

"My name is Burik, my Force is five-seven, and my Toughness is five-nine, sir," Burik replied immediately.

"Good." He moved to stand by Amarl. "The same, novice."

"My name is Amarl, my Force is five-two, and my Toughness is four-five, sir."

Periteth made a face. "Let me guess: you're strong, but your endurance is shit, am I right?" Without letting Amarl answer, he moved to Meder. "Novice?"

"My name is Meder, my Force is four-four, and my Toughness is four-nine, sir."

"Lived a pampered life in the zahai caste, no doubt," he nodded. "Common for women in the nobility. We'll fix that, no worries."

He went down the line, and Amarl discovered that Herel had a flat five for Force and a four-eight for Toughness. Norag, the noble's friend who'd been smart enough to stand up first in the mess hall, had a five-one in Force and five-two in Toughness, while Hadur, the boy with the bruised face, had a four-six in Force and a four-two in Toughness.

"Pathetic," Periteth sighed. "Utterly pathetic, the lot of you – with the exception of Burik." He straightened. "And it's my job to make you less pathetic. We'll start that with a tour of Askula – a running tour. Follow me, and try to keep up. If you fall back, keep running. If you vomit, keep running. If you pass out..." He shrugged. "Then you can take a break."

The next two hours were the spirits' hell for Amarl. He knew he was stronger and faster than most nalu, a legacy of his mixed heritage, but that was over short distances. He'd never really had occasion to run for walks at a time, so he'd never realized that what the nadar said was true. He had very little endurance. He stayed with Burik and Periteth for the first thirty minutes, but he quickly found he had to drop back. His heart hammered in his chest, his lungs labored for air, and his breakfast threatened to make a second appearance. Norag quickly passed him, followed by Meder, whom he'd left behind earlier when her legs simply couldn't keep up the pace with the others. After an hour and a half, Herel passed him as well, and while Amarl dug in deeper, trying to catch up to the arrogant noble, his body simply refused to cooperate. At last, he caught up to the others around a well and collapsed to his knees, sucking in huge breaths and trying to ignore the stars flashing in his vision. Ten minutes later, Hadur straggled in, his face beet red, barely moving faster than a walk. The boy collapsed in a heap before he reached the others, and Periteth walked over, rolling him over and lifting the lid of one closed eye.

"Passed out," he shrugged. "The rest of you, catch him up later." He walked over to stand before the others, framed from behind by the towering peaks surrounding Askula with the pinkish sun floating high overhead.

"Your first lesson is about your stats," the ithtar told them. "What they are, what they mean, and most importantly, what they aren't." He looked over at Burik. "Burik! Tell me what you think the Force stat is!"

Burik leaped to his feet, standing erect. "How strong you are, sir!" he said confidently.

"Incorrect." Periteth shook his head. "Your Force stat says that you're around twice as strong as the average nalu your age. Do you think that's accurate?"

Burik frowned. "No, sir, I don't. I think I'm stronger than that."

"You are." He looked at Meder. "What's your highest stat, Meder?"

She quickly stood up as well. "Mind, sir, at six."

"Then you should be smart enough to answer this. What does the Mind stat mean?"

She frowned. "Is it – is it your ability to process information, sir? How quickly you learn?"

"Close, but not quite." He turned to Herel. "Tell me, Herel, what's your highest stat?"

"Skill at five-five, sir," the noble muttered, not looking at the other two.

"And you're probably thinking right now how unfair it is that they've both got higher stats than you, right? That they're somehow better than you because of it?" The ithtar shook his head.

"Novices always misunderstand their stats. They think that your stats are a measure of your strength, or your intellect, or your charm. They think that their stats define them and set a hard limit on them. And they're wrong. For the most part, your stats don't mean shit."

Amarl blinked in surprise at the man's words. He remembered how people had murmured about his Soul stat, how they'd told him it was ridiculously high and that he'd go far in the Order with it. That didn't track with Periteth's assertion that stats were meaningless, which meant that either the ithtar was lying – and Amarl couldn't see anything the man could gain from that – or Amarl was misunderstanding.

"Stats are a measure of your raw ability. They tell you what you're naturally talented at, and what you have an affinity for. Each stat tells you how easy or hard it is for you to improve one aspect of your existence, and that's it. For Force, that's your ability to gain and retain muscle mass; Skill is about fine muscle control; Speed covers your reflexes and how quickly your muscles can work; Toughness is your stamina and ability to recover from exertion and wounds."

His gaze passed over the silent group. "Those are your physical stats. You have mental ones, as well: Mind is your natural talent for learning and processing information; Will is your willpower and intuition; Presence is how easily you relate to others. You won't be training those here, but you will be training them." Meder looked like she would speak, but before she could, he added, "Soul is its own animal, and we won't be discussing it here.

"The point is, your stats aren't hard limits placed on you." He looked at Amarl. "Your Toughness is well below average. Does that mean that you're fragile? Delicate? That you'll never be able to run a mile without gasping for breath? No, of course not. What it means is that you'll have to work harder than most to run that mile. Endurance training won't be as effective for you as, say, Burik, but it will still be effective – if you're willing to put in the time and effort!"

He pointed to Meder. "This young lady has a natural talent for academics. She may find learning easier than you, but more importantly, she'll gain more than the rest of you with the same amount of study. Which means that if you want to be as educated as her, you have to put in more work, more effort, more time! It doesn't mean she'll always be smarter than you."

He turned to face Burik. "Burik, here, has a natural aptitude for physical training, but more importantly, he's undergone significant training already. He's ahead of you because he's already put in the work, not because of his stats. You can all catch up to him if you simply work harder, train harder, and push harder than he does."

He swept his gaze across the group. "Take this one thing away from your lesson today, and I'll be happy. Your stats do not define you! Your stats are a framework around which you'll build yourself, nothing more. It's up to you to decide what you'll create of yourself, but with enough hard work – and ithtu – that can be anything you want."

He held up a hand as Meder opened her mouth again. "Within reason, of course! The simple fact is, Burik is going to get more from physical training than the rest of you. You can catch him, but only if he slows down. If he focuses on that training, pushes himself to his limits, he'll always be stronger and faster than the rest of you. If Meder applies herself fully to her academics, she'll always do better in them than the rest of you. Some people are simply better at some things than others, and focusing on what you're good at can bring huge benefits.

"What's important is that you understand that just because a stat is low doesn't mean you'll always struggle with it! You can improve that aspect of yourself with training and effort, but only if you choose to do so. If you don't…" He shrugged. "That will become a weakness, and ithtaru with weaknesses seldom live long lives."

He clapped his hands. "Enough rest! Someone wake Hadur; it's time for calisthenics, then we run back to the Citadel!" Amarl couldn't quite conceal a groan, and he was gratified to hear that everyone but Burik echoed it. Periteth simply grinned at them. "How in the hells else did you think you were getting back? Did you expect a sahrwagon to show up and daintily carry you?" He laughed.

"Now, everyone on your stomachs, and I'll teach you how to do a pushup – even if it takes a couple hundred repetitions!"

Amarl dropped to his stomach with a weary sigh. Pushups, whatever they were, had to be better than running, at least. He really wasn't looking forward to the run back. So far, his first day at Askula was kind of shit.

CHAPTER 11

"Okay, I'll say it," Meder grumbled as she speared a small slice of dark brown meat dripping with gravy. "Physical training is the spirits' hell."

"It's not that bad," Burik protested, mumbling around a mouthful of bread as he spoke.

"Yes, it is, and don't talk with your mouth full." She turned to Amarl. "Back me up, here. It's awful right?"

"Moderately awful, yes." He took a swig of cool cider and sighed. "However, I have a feeling that in a few moons, we'll look back at today and remember it fondly."

"What do you mean?" she asked, also taking a sip from her mug. Although light ale and wine were both available with the midday meal, none of the three had even considered touching either after the previous night. Amarl and Burik had chosen cider, while Meder stuck with water.

"I mean that I'll bet Burik thinks this was pretty light exercise. Am I right, Burik?"

"I wouldn't say light, no. It wasn't too tough, though."

"Exactly. This was an easy day just to see where we all are. Now that Periteth knows what we can handle – and what we can't – he'll start pushing us all the way to those limits. And as we get stronger, he'll keep pushing harder." He shoved a carrot in his mouth and crunched down. "Mark my words, one day, we'll be screaming at our today selves for thinking that was hard."

"Well, that's just depressing," the girl sighed.

"Probably right, though," Burik said. "At least, that's how it is in the military. The training starts easy and gets harder as you go along."

"Enough! I don't want to think about it." She turned her attention back to her food, and Amarl let his eyes wander about the mess hall, watching the other students.

His gaze rested on the nearby table where Herel, Norag, and Hadur sat, all three of them eating in silence, their faces pale and wan looking. Herel seemed to be deliberately ignoring him, and Hadur looked like he was barely keeping himself upright – the boy had passed out twice more during the exercises – but Norag caught Amarl's eye and gave him a quick, appreciative nod. Amarl simply nodded back; Norag seemed okay, so he'd mentioned to the boy that the new novices were supposed to sit at the worst tables. He didn't expect Herel to be grateful, of course, but he was glad to see that Norag appreciated his small kindness.

"Any idea where we're supposed to go next?" Burik asked the others.

"Nope," Amarl said with a shrug. "I suppose we could ask, though."

"You ask," Meder suggested. "I'm too tired."

"Not to mention a bit ripe," Amarl grinned at her, then leaned back to dodge the quick slap she sent toward his arm.

"We're all a little ripe," Burik noted. "You included, Amarl. When you ask where we're going, find out if we have time to bathe first."

"Your wish is my command." He bowed dramatically to the others, then scanned the crowd around them for someone who looked less than a year older than them. He settled on a young woman with short, dark hair and a deeply tanned complexion, mostly because she was heading toward the tray cleaning area. He rose to his feet, carrying his own tray, and stepped up beside her.

"Hi there," he said, giving the girl his best smile and ducking his head low. She glanced over at him, looked furtively around, and inclined her head quickly.

"Hello," she said softly.

"I'm Amarl. I'm one of the new novices." She nodded but remained silent, and he plowed on. "I was just wondering: how do we find out where we're supposed to be during the day? Will the instructors come find us, or is there a schedule somewhere?"

She glanced around again as if making sure no one was watching, then leaned closer to him. "Try heading back to your room," she half-whispered. He opened his mouth to speak, but she shook her head slightly. "Just do it. Trust me." She walked away, and with a shrug, he walked back to join the others, reporting what he'd learned.

"They must have delivered a schedule while we were at morning training," Meder mused. "I wonder if they thought we'd clean up afterward and would see it."

"I'd say it's more likely they put it there without telling us on purpose," Amarl shook his head. "I have a feeling people like to watch the new people struggle and suffer."

"Or they're encouraging us to find solutions to our problems," she countered. "We are supposed to be learning here, after all."

"Does it matter?" Burik said. "Let's head back to the room and see if there's something there, and if we have time to clean up."

The schedule in question was tacked to the back of their door, and Meder examined it carefully. "Looks like our next class is in the Citadel in an hour. 'Introduction to Ithtu' in training room twelve, wherever that is."

"We can figure that out when we get there," Burik said. "Let's get cleaned up and dressed first. I doubt our instructor will appreciate us showing up reeking of last night's celebration and this morning's training."

The washroom at the end of the hall had a communal shower, and when they entered, Amarl noted that men and women seemed to be bathing beside one another without any concern or modesty. He let his eyes roam quickly over a few rounded backsides, not letting his gaze linger long enough to be caught and called out, then began to strip down. Beside him, Burik did the same thing, but Meder looked far more hesitant.

"Maybe I can wait until everyone's done," she suggested.

"That's up to you," Amarl said with a grin. "But if everyone had physical training this morning before the meal, I'm betting they'll be coming in for the next hour or so. You might miss classes."

"It's no big deal, Meder," Burik assured her. "Men and women shower beside one another in soldiers' barracks all the time."

"Yes, but I'm not a soldier, Burik."

"I'm pretty sure that we all are," Amarl said with a laugh. "Or at least, we're all in training to become one."

"For a soldier, there's no such thing as modesty and privacy, Meder," Burik said seriously. "We're going to be sleeping together, eating together, training together, and probably traveling together in the field. You might as well get used to the idea."

She made a dissatisfied face, then sighed and lifted the hem of her shirt. "Fine. But if I catch either of you staring, I swear, I'll remove your reason for wanting to look, got it?"

"Don't worry, Meder," Amarl said with a grin. "I promise you won't catch me."

The girl glared at him, then turned her back and slipped out of her clothing. Amarl managed to sneak a few glimpses, but he was careful not to look too long or let his mind wander inappropriately. Meder was very attractive, there was no doubt, but they were probably going to be working closely together for the foreseeable future. He didn't need any complications to make things awkward. Besides, there were plenty of girls around; while they probably wouldn't look twice at him now, he felt certain that would eventually change.

He quickly cleaned himself off and dressed, using the silvered mirror on the wall to arrange his silvery hair in some semblance of order, straightening some tangles with his fingers and slipping it back behind his ears. Meder was somewhat more meticulous, drawing a comb through her still wet hair and wincing as it dragged through tangles, then once more tying it back out of her way.

The trio returned their dirty clothes to their room, then headed downstairs. Meder stopped back in the mess hall to let Herel and the others know when and where the next class was, then the three went out the door and up toward the towering Citadel. Meder stopped and asked for directions from one of the sentries at the front gate, and twenty minutes later, they stood before a door marked with a gleaming brass "12". Amarl lifted his hand to knock, but Meder simply opened the door and led the way inside.

The room beyond was small and dark, lit only by a single guttering lamp. Wooden desks ringed the room with chairs placed behind them against the wall so the desks faced toward the middle of the room. A wooden podium stood there, with the lamp directly above it, shining down on the lectern. Slabs of slate were fastened to several of the walls, and someone had written numbers all over them with some soft, white stone Amarl didn't recognize.

"Is this the right room?" he asked, looking around at the empty space.

"I think so. We're just early." Meder walked confidently into the room. "Let's go ahead and take seats."

"Can we sit anywhere?" Burik asked.

"Probably. I doubt any higher students will be here, so there's no need to worry about taking their seats."

"Are you sure?" Amarl asked dubiously.

"Well, no, but this is an introductory class, so there really isn't any reason for them to be here, I would think. Typically, introductory classes are for first-year students only." She looked at the others curiously. "Did either of you ever attend formal classes?"

"Only until my tenth Naming Day," Burik said. "Then I switched into barracks training."

"I, of course, attended the finest academy in the village of Tem," Amarl said sarcastically. "That being the church of Ak-lahat, where the priest taught us our letters and numbers."

She nodded. "That makes sense. Well, I think this is more like formal academics. We can probably sit anywhere we want, although the instructor might move us around." She pointed to a row of seats against the far wall. "We should probably sit there. The lectern's facing that direction, so we'll be able to hear the instructor better – and it'll look better, as well."

"Look better?" Burik asked. "Why?"

"Well, typically the students who are most interested in a lecture sit toward the front of the lectern, while students who are more inclined to ignore the lecture sit toward the back, where the instructor can't see them." She shrugged. "At least, that's how it was in the academy in Dairon."

"Sounds good to me," Amarl laughed. "Considering the fact that I have no clue what you're talking about."

The other students entered a few minutes later. Herel's hair still hung lankly about his face, and while his clothes were dry, a faint reek of stale perspiration followed him as he entered the room. That stench grew stronger as the other two followed behind, and Amarl made a face as they move to sit in the same row of desks as the trio.

"Umm...how about you sitting a bit farther over?" he asked, waving his hand at them in a shooing gesture. "You three stink."

"Excuse me?" the noble said, his voice outraged. His hand dropped to his hip, as if reaching for a sword that wasn't there. "How dare you?"

"I dare because it's true. You reek. You should have showered before you came here." He waved his hand in front of his face.

"Amarl, you're being unkind," Meder said chidingly. She looked at the young noble. "However, he's not inaccurate. Would you mind moving to the end of the row? You'll still be able to see, and we'll all be more comfortable."

Herel huffed but slid several seats down, plunking heavily into a seat.

Hadur settled in beside him, while Norag hesitated, looking at the three seated students.

"How did you know when and where the class was?" he asked quietly. "And that you had time to get clean first?"

"There's a schedule in your room," Amarl said with a shrug. "We found it when we went upstairs to get clean."

He nodded. "Thanks for letting us know. I hear that the instructors aren't gentle with novices who miss their classes."

"Of course," Meder smiled at him warmly. "We're all going to be studying together for quite a while, aren't we? It makes sense for us to look out for one another."

"Yes. Ak-lahat teaches that we all have a duty to care for our fellows." He glanced over at Herel, who gave him a subtle glare, then sighed. "It's a shame we don't all feel the same way. Don't worry, though. I'll do what I can." He walked over and sat down with the other two.

"What's that all about?" Burik asked curiously.

"Herel doesn't much like me," Amarl said deprecatingly.

"Yes, we guessed that," Meder replied in a dry voice. "So?"

"Well, I'm guessing he's talked about me to the others. I think that was Norag saying that so long as we look out for him, he'll try to keep Herel from trying to sabotage me."

"Sabotage?" Meder asked dubiously. "You don't really think he'd do anything like that, do you?"

"I don't know. I don't really know him all that well, to be honest, but I suspect he'd feel more comfortable if I weren't here." Amarl shrugged. "Or I could just be paranoid, I suppose."

They fell silent as the door opened, and a woman perhaps twice Amarl's age wearing simple white clothing walked into the room. Her light brown hair fell beside her oval face in short, tight braids that swung as she turned her head to look over the students. As she walked to the lectern, she glared at Herel, Norag, and Hadur, and her nose wrinkled in distaste.

"From now on, you will shower before attending my class, or I will eject you from the class, and you'll spend your Akio making up your missed work. Is that clear?"

"Yes," Herel muttered.

The woman lifted her hand, and a loud crack sounded throughout the room. Herel cried out and clutched his face, where a rosy handprint appeared on his cheek. He blinked rapidly, the rest of his face reddening to match the handprint, and opened his mouth, but Hadur kicked him in the ankle, and he clamped his lips shut.

"You will address any instructor as 'Ma'am', 'Sir', or by their title," the woman said coldly. "And you will do the same for any full ithtara or ithtar you meet. Consider this your only warning. The consequences for disrespect will be severe." She gave them all a frosty glare. "Am I clear?"

"Yes, ma'am," Amarl said, echoing Meder and Burik.

"Good." She glanced at Amarl and the others approvingly. "At least someone found time to make themselves presentable. Well done."

Herel glowered at the trio, but Amarl ignored it. He was sure the young man blamed him somehow for not having a chance to bathe before class, but Amarl couldn't see how that was his fault. The noble could have gotten the same information simply by asking around as he had. He'd chosen not to – or it simply hadn't occurred to him – and so, he suffered the consequence. It was a little unfair since the school certainly could have just given them their schedules instead of expecting them to figure everything out on their own, but Amarl knew well that very little in life was fair. Herel hadn't learned that lesson, it seemed, which made sense, since the hizeen guessed that most of life's unfairness to that point had probably been in the noble's favor, and he wouldn't have seen it as unfair.

"My name is Nadar Lilenpur," she said. "If you haven't worked it out already, 'Nadar' is my title and means junior instructor. For your first year, all of your instructors will be nadars, as the malims – the full instructors – are busy working with students who are actually meeting their potential." Her lips twisted in a grimace, and Amarl got a strong sense that Lilenpur really didn't want to be teaching the new group. He didn't much care, so long as she taught him whatever it was that he was supposed to learn.

"This class will introduce you to ithtu. You will learn what it is, how it is harvested, the different types of it, and most importantly, how to quicken it." She gave them a hard look. "This class is not about ithtar powers, and I will not entertain questions about them. You will learn about powers in another class."

The group remained silent, which she seemed to take for assent, as she went on.

"Ithtu. What is it? Do any of you know?"

Meder slowly raised her hand, and both Herel's and Hadur's shot up quickly. Lilenpur pointed to Herel. "Yes, you. What is ithtu?"

"Ithtu are crystals that the ithtaru use to empower their abilities," the boy replied instantly, speaking in a sing-song voice that made Amarl think he was quoting from memory. "It's believed that…"

"Wrong," she cut him off, then pointed at Meder. "You."

"I – I don't know, ma'am," the girl said, lowering her hand. "I was taught the same thing."

"Nobles," the instructor said in a disgusted tone. "That description was created by some scholar who'd obviously never spoken to an ithtar in their life, and now it's taught in every academy across the Empire. I'm sure you were going to go on with theories about its origins and potential interactions with sahr, but it's all crap. It's technically correct, but it's a description of what ithtu can do, not what it is." Her eyes fastened on Amarl. "You. I hear you quickened a crystal already. Is that correct?"

Amarl nodded, and everyone but Herel looked at him in amazement.

"Fine. You tell me what it is."

"It's – it's alive, ma'am," he said slowly. "It sings to me, and I can feel its life inside me."

"Good. That's a better description than that scholar ever gave, and all it took was asking someone with actual experience." She stepped down from her podium and walked over to stand before the group.

"Ithtu isn't just alive; it's life. It's the energy and essence of life, condensed into a crystallized form. Later, we'll get into matrices and lattice diagrams, but for now, all you need to know is that ithtu is pure, distilled life, the most powerful source of energy ever discovered."

She pointed to Norag. "You. If ithtu is life, then how do you gain it?"

"By…" He hesitated. "By taking it from something alive, ma'am?"

"No. If that were the case, then you'd see ithtu crystals sticking out from every plant and animal you meet." She looked at Burik. "You. What do you think?"

"By killing, ma'am?" he asked quietly.

"Exactly." She looked at them. "Ithtu is the condensed remains of a living creature slain by an ithtar. There are other ways to get it, but for now, keep that fact squarely in mind. Every ithtu crystal you've ever seen or ever will was very likely taken off the corpse of a living, breathing being."

Amarl touched the crystal in his pocket, is eyes widening as he did. Something – or someone – had died to create that crystal, and he was slowly drawing in that being's vital essence. The thought made him feel vaguely dirty, but also powerful. It was no wonder the ithtaru were so strong. They literally gained from their enemies' deaths.

"Ithtu crystals come in various shapes, sizes, and colors," the woman went on. "Typically, you can judge a crystal's overall power by its size, the type of creature it came from by its shape, and its rank by its color. You'll learn to identify these properties of a crystal at a glance, and being able to do so is a vital skill. An ithtar can only quicken so many crystals at a time, and once you've begun to quicken one, you're bound to it until the process is complete. If you quicken an inferior crystal because you didn't recognize it for what it was, you're wasting your time and a crystal that another ithtar might have been able to put to better use. If you try to quicken a crystal that's too much for you, you'll either harm yourself or waste it."

She reached into a pocket and pulled out a small bag. "To enter Askula, you each received a crystal. Is there any hope that any of you thought to bring it with you?" Meder quickly pulled hers out of her pocket, as did Amarl – he valued the crystal and hadn't wanted to leave it where someone else could take it – but the others simply shook their heads. "Well, two of you have at least some sense. That's better than most new classes."

She reached into the bag and pulled out a handful of small, pale green crystals, holding them up.

"As you should know, these are ithtu crystals. I presume you can all see them? Good. Don't take that for granted. Anyone who isn't an ithtar would see me holding up an empty hand right now. The ability to perceive and interact with ithtu is the defining characteristic of ithtaru."

She moved before the students, placing a gem on the desks of the students who didn't bring a crystal with them, making a face as she passed before the three unwashed novices. "Go ahead and pick it up," she instructed. "Again, the fact that you can do so isn't something you should take for granted. Non-ithtaru not only can't perceive ithtu crystals, they can't hear, touch, or feel them. Their hands would pass right through that crystal that you're holding so easily.

"You receive one, and only one free crystal upon entering Askula. And one is all you'll need for the time being. This means that those of you who forgot their crystals will bring the ones you were given before and return them when you next see me. If you fail to do this, it will be considered stealing, and you'll be assigned to disciplinary duties. Trust me, you don't want those."

She slipped the rest of the crystals back into the bag and returned the bag to her pocket. "Now, look at the crystal. I mean, really look at it and concentrate on it. Think about understanding it, about knowing what it is."

Amarl frowned but looked at the crystal, focusing his gaze on it. He could still hear its song, but the sound was muted and distant. He thought about understanding it, about knowing what it really was, and as he did, another screen floated into his vision.

"What you've just done is activated your Analyze ability. This is an ability that every ithtar has, one granted by the crystal implanted in your chest. It analyzes the amount of life and sahr energies flowing through a person or object and gives you basic information about it.

"As you should be seeing by now, these are feeble level 1 crystals, the weakest you will ever find. You can tell they're feeble by the color; feeble ranked crystals are always a shade of green. The size tells you they're level 1, and the smooth hexagonal shape tells you that it came from something unthinking, like a plant. In fact, these were generated by felling trees in the forest."

She looked around at the students. "You're probably wondering: why do you need to know that when Analyze can tell you the same information? Well, it's because Analyze has a limited range. Right now, you can only Analyze something within a reach of you that you're directly observing. As you practice and your Joining Crystal deepens its bond with you, that range will increase, but even awals can usually only Analyze things within five or six reaches of them.

"That's why relying on Analyze is a dangerous and foolish crutch. You'll learn how to tell the rank, power, and origin of a crystal at a glance – just as next year, you'll start learning to identify dangerous creatures at a glance instead of needing to Analyze them."

Curious, Amarl turned to Meder sitting beside him and concentrated on understanding her. After a second or so, another screen appeared, this one much less detailed than the last.

ANALYSIS REPORT
CREATURE: ITHTARA
ABILITY: UNKNOWN
POWER DENSITY: 0
THREAT LEVEL: MINOR

"By this point," Lilenpur went on, "at least some of you will have tried to Analyze your classmates. If you haven't, do so. I'll be walking by; as I pass you, use the ability on me, as well, to compare the differences."

Amarl waited until the woman strolled past, then focused on knowing all about her, as well.

ANALYSIS REPORT
CREATURE: ITHTARA
ABILITY: UNKNOWN
POWER DENSITY: 6
THREAT LEVEL: FATAL

"As you can see, you don't get very much information when Analyzing a person," Lilenpur said. "That's because your crystal simply doesn't have the information to give you. As you gain in knowledge, your crystal will, as well. You'll learn the energy signatures of different abilities and creatures, the power matrices of sahr workings, and more, and with that information, your Joining Crystal will be able to tell you more about a person or creature. What sort of skills might they possess? How easily can they use sahr? How much ithtu will you gain from killing them? Eventually, Analyze can become one of your most powerful tools. Knowledge of an enemy can be a deadly weapon to use against them."

She waited for a moment, then nodded when no one spoke. "Good. Now, when you Analyzed one another, you saw a power density of zero…" She glanced at Amarl. "Or perhaps one. That tells you how much ithtu the individual has within them. For most of you, that's none because you haven't quickened a crystal – and we're going to start fixing that right away.

"Take the crystal in your hand. It doesn't matter which one. There's no need to squeeze it, simple contact will do." She waited for the novices to comply, then continued. "Today – and probably for the next several weeks – we'll be learning how to quicken that crystal. It doesn't matter how much you know about ithtu – or think you know – until you can quicken it, that knowledge is useless."

She looked at them each in turn as she spoke. "Each of you has the ability to quicken ithtu within you, and ithtu wants to be quickened. It's eager for it. All you have to do is let it happen. Hold the crystal in your palm and close your eyes."

Amarl obediently shut his eyes, feeling the crystal in his hand. Its life pulsed within its depths, and he felt it reach tentatively toward him, extending a tendril toward his thoughts. Before he could respond, his crystal's song swelled in his ears almost protectively, drowning out the hesitant chorus of the crystal in his hand. The green crystal's melody faded into a distant hum that Amarl could barely perceive, and he sighed as he realized that he wouldn't be able to quicken it. He opened his eyes, but before he could speak, Lilenpur raised a silencing hand.

"Yes, hizeen, I know. You can't quicken this one with the one you've already got. We'll talk about that, but for now, sit there in silence and let me teach." He nodded and leaned back in his chair, watching and listening as she spoke.

"Try your best to feel the crystal, not with your skin or mind, but with your heart. You heard the hizeen say that it sang to him; that's how he feels it. It will probably be different for you. It might be a strange flavor or scent, a pattern of colors, or even an odd sensation in your spine. It could be a whisper only you can hear, or a warmth only you can feel. There's no way to know, and until you can feel it, you can't quicken it.

"Relax your thoughts. Don't try. Just let it happen."

She spent the next ten minutes offering advice and suggestions, and Amarl sat quietly, watching looks of confusion and frustration ripple across the others' faces. He didn't understand; how were they struggling to do this? It was the simplest thing in the world. Like Lilenpur said, the ithtu wanted to be quickened, they just had to allow it to happen.

"Keep working on it. Remember, the harder you try, the farther from succeeding you'll be." She pointed to Amarl. "You, come with me, out in the hall where we won't disturb the others. It's time we had a private talk."

CHAPTER 12

A snarky comment about what they might be doing that needed such privacy leapt to his lips, but he swallowed it down and rose from his desk, following the woman out into the hall. Once he stepped outside, she shut the door behind him and gave him a serious look.

"Pull up your ithtu screen," she directed.

He blinked in confusion. "I'm sorry, my what?" Her face hardened, and he quickly corrected himself. "I mean, I don't know what that is, ma'am."

"Better," she grunted. "You know that image you saw yesterday? The one with all your stats on it?"

"Yes," he nodded. "The green rectangle."

"It looks different to everyone, so instead of trying to figure out what shape and color everyone's is, we just call it your 'status' or 'screen'. Bring it up, but instead of the screen you saw before, think about examining your ithtu."

He did so, and a slightly different image swirled into view before his eyes.

ITHTU REPORT
MAX ITHTU: 1
QUICKENING RATE: 5.4%
MAX ITHTU RANK: MINOR

CURRENT CRYSTALSQUICKENING: 1
1 — RANK: MINOR   DENSITY: 3   POWER: 11.7   QUICKENED: 47%

POWER QUICKENED TO:
SKILLS — NONE
STATS — NONE
LEVEL — NONE
ABILITY — 6.7 (0%)
TAK — 5 (INACTIVE, TAK FULL)

"Got it?" she asked. He nodded. "Good. What's the power level of your crystal?"

"Uh – eleven-seven, I think, ma'am."

She made a disgusted noise. "Ridiculous. I can't believe a new novice quickened a spirits-damned minor crystal. We use those because that's supposed to be impossible. What's your Soul stat, anyway?"

"Nine-four."

"That's utterly absurd. Good for you." Her gaze sharpened. "Do the others know?"

"Other novices? No, ma'am. I didn't tell them."

"Probably smart. They'll find out eventually – I'm sure you told a dozen ithtaru last night, and the only safe secret is one you alone know – but for now, best that they aren't aware. It could cause problems."

She took a deep breath. "Okay. So, this is something I'm going to discuss with the others eventually, but you need it now. Once you've begun quickening ithtu, you have to decide what to do with it. By default, ithtu will flow into your tak, but I'm guessing yours has stopped doing that, right?"

"The picture says that it's full, ma'am."

"Of course, it is. It's probably, what, six or eight?"

He frowned, trying to recall the image of his stats, and as he did, the vision before him shifted to display those numbers.

"Five, ma'am."

"Five? You must have a shit Will stat, then." She took another deep breath, as if to calm herself down. "Whatever. The point is, think of your tak as a well where ithtu can be stored and retrieved. Once that well is full, you'll stop quickening, because the power has nowhere to go."

He nodded in understanding. "So, how do I get it to go somewhere, ma'am?"

"First, you have to find your tak, and that's not always easy. Like the feeling of ithtu or the appearance of your status, it's different in everyone, but the one commonality is that it feels like a wellspring of power deep within yourself."

He frowned again and closed his eyes. He'd never felt anything like that inside himself, but the moment he began looking, he could see it in his mind's eye. It floated just beneath his heart, a gently rotating ball of energy that glowed the same silver as his hair. It felt like he could reach down and touch it if he wanted to, cup it in his hands and feel its warmth and power. Instead, he simply opened his eyes and refocused on the woman.

"So, while they're trying to quicken – and probably failing – you can work on finding your tak," she said. "It might take some time, so don't worry if you can't sense it for a few days. I needed weeks to find mine."

He debated what to say; he had a feeling that she wouldn't like hearing that he located it, but at the same time, he didn't want to spend the next hour pretending to be looking for something.

"I – uh…" He cleared his throat. "I already found it, ma'am."

She stopped, her hand on the door, and glared at him. "You what?"

"I found it. It's a ball of silver energy that's spinning around slowly." He touched his heart. "Right about here."

She stared at him in silence, then rubbed her eyes with her hand. "You found it. Of course, you did. And it's on your spirits-damned heart channel." She shook her head. "Blood runs true, they say." He opened his mouth to ask what she meant, but before he could say a word, she continued.

"Fine. Then you can learn how to channel it into a stat." She let go of the door and straightened. "Close your eyes." He did so, and she continued. "Picture your tak in your mind. Feel it floating inside you."

That was simple enough. Now that he knew what he was looking for, he found the orb in an instant. It hovered before him, its warmth gentle and comforting, filling an empty space within him he'd never known was there but that now he couldn't imagine being dark once again.

"Got it? Good. Now think about touching it. Not grabbing it, not cupping it, not embracing it. Just touching it as lightly as possible."

He pictured a single finger stretching out toward the orb, making the gentlest contact possible. A spark seemed to jump into his mind as he connected to it, and he felt the power behind it, eagerly straining for release. The energy wanted to be used, to be freed of its fetters, and he had to fight not to let it surge into him.

"Okay. I'm touching it." The strain of holding it sounded plainly in his voice, even to his own ears, and he guessed that she heard it as well since she ignored his lack of the proper respectful term.

"Now, you need to decide which stat to feed," she said. "There are channels throughout your body, and each one will empower a different stat. The channel for Force is in your stomach, Speed is in your groin, Toughness in your lungs, Skill is below your throat, Mind is in the front of your head, Will in the back, and Presence behind your eyes."

"What about Soul?" he gritted, struggling to hold the power in check.

"You can't feed Soul like this – at least, not safely. Hurry and pick one. I'd recommend Mind, but that's just me."

"Why Mind?'

"Because it will help you quicken additional ithtu. In the long run, it'll make you more powerful." She shrugged. "In the short term, it won't matter, though. Pick any of your weaker stats, and then pull that contact from the ball to the area I told you."

He was tempted – sorely tempted – to boost his Toughness to help with his physical training, but he remembered Periteth's admonition that weak stats just meant he had to work harder to improve them. Besides, if Mind really let him quicken more ithtu, eventually, he'd be able to drain enough crystals to fix all his weak stats. He focused on the contact with his tak, then imagined his fingertip touch sliding away from it, moving up his chest and into his throat. Nothing seemed to happen as he drew the phantom finger up into his skull and toward his forehead, finally imagining it resting against the inside of his forehead.

"Okay. Now what?"

"Now, let go of your hold."

He hesitated; it seemed like he'd screwed up somehow. He'd expected to see something, a line of energy, a glowing ribbon, something rise up from within him, but nothing seemed to be happening. With a mental shrug, though, he banished his imaginary finger, ready to try again when he failed.

To his shock, a whiplash of energy surged up through him and swept into his forehead. The energy spread out, washing over his brain, seeming to be carried along down invisible currents and sinking into the depths of his mind. The surge of power quickly faded to a slow, gentle flow that snaked up into his head, coursed gently around the inside of his skull, then sank beyond his perception.

"I – I think it worked, ma'am," he said slowly, shaking his head from side to side in an attempt to dislodge the odd current. It didn't hurt – in fact, he couldn't even feel it – but it was still a strange sensation, seeing a phantom ribbon of nearly invisible power attached to his brain.

"I'd tell you that you're probably mistaken since it never works for anyone the first time," she sighed, "but I'm starting to realize what that Soul stat of yours really means. Fortunately, there's an easy way to check. Pull up your ithtu screen again." He did so and immediately saw the difference.

ITHTU REPORT
MAX ITHTU: 1
QUICKENING RATE: 5%
MAX ITHTU RANK: MINOR

CURRENT CRYSTALSQUICKENING: 1
1 – RANK: MINOR   DENSITY: 3   POWER: 11.7   QUICKENED: 47%

POWER QUICKENED TO:
SKILLS – NONE
STATS– 1 (MIND, 0.01%)
LEVEL – NONE
ABILITY – 5.7 (0%)
TAK– 5 (99.99%)

"It says that I've got one power quickened to stats, ma'am," he reported. "What does that mean?"

"Each ithtu is finite; you can only drain so much energy from it before it disappears," she said. "The number you see for a crystal's power is the number of units of energy you can get from it. Before you ask, a unit is defined as the amount of energy you can drain from a feeble, level one crystal. You can assign units of energy to quicken other things, like stats, skills, or your personal level.

"How much each unit of energy actually improves those depends on how high they are. The higher a skill or stat, the more units you need to raise it. Typically, a stat between four and six goes up about a tenth of a point for each unit to quicken to it, though."

"My crystal has 11.7 units of power, ma'am. Does that mean I can assign a unit of power to each of my stats and my tak at the same time?"

"No. Each crystal can only quicken one stat or skill at a time, and if you assign it to your personal level, then it can't be used for anything else. It would be a terrible idea, though, even if you could. Extra power that you aren't using goes to quickening your inherent ability. It'll take moons to mature even so, but if you don't put any power into it, it'll never develop, and an ithtar without an ability is just a common soldier. A well-trained one, to be sure, but just a soldier."

She shook her head and put her hand back on the door. "When we go back in, don't tell the others about this. They'll learn it when it's time. If you tell them, they'll either be jealous or eager to try it themselves, and either of those will make it harder for them to quicken their first ithtu."

"I don't understand why they haven't done it already, ma'am," he admitted. "It wasn't hard. I heard it calling for me, and I reached for it. It didn't take any effort at all."

"Don't tell them that, either. They're likely to give you a beating for it, and I'd be inclined to look the other way." She gave him a piercing stare. "For most ithtaru, the first quickening takes weeks of practice and training. The other students are going to have to practice mind calming exercises, guided meditation, and hone their visualization skills before they finally manage it. That you did it instinctively, without any effort..." She took a deep breath.

"It's beyond unusual to the point that I've never heard of it happening before. That doesn't mean it hasn't, just not in the last few generations." She glared at him.

"In other words, don't try to compare their efforts to yours. What you just did to quicken a stat? That usually happens about four to six moons into your first year. I expected you to spend the next few weeks using those exercises I was talking about to find your tak, then at least another moon trying and failing to connect it to a channel. If you tell people that you worked it out in a few minutes, you're likely to piss off every student in Nabila. Understand?"

He nodded, then followed her back into the classroom. While the others worked on trying to feel the crystal in their hand, he closed his eyes and simply watched his tak and the ephemeral ribbon of energy flowing from it. The whirling ball of energy fascinated him, and some deep part of him felt there was more he could do with it, more ways to manipulate it than he'd been told. He was sure that it could be larger than it was, that he could draw on it for other things, but he left it alone and just basked in its radiance. When Lilenpur finally ended the class, he jumped in surprise. He opened his eyes, banishing the image of the core of his new power, and quickly smothered a smile after seeing the frustrated looks on the others' faces.

The ithtara had probably been right. If they knew how easily things seemed to come to him, they'd probably take turns beating the shit out of him. That was one secret that he decided he would hold onto.

CHAPTER 13

"So, what did you talk about in the hallway?" Meder asked as they left the classroom and headed back to their room to check their schedule. Herel, Norag, and Hadur had rushed out the moment they were dismissed; Amarl hoped it was to see if they had time to shower, or at least change before the next class.

"She wanted me," he shrugged nonchalantly. "Right there in the hallway. Said she couldn't stand it anymore and needed it right away." He grinned at her. "I think it's safe to say that I'm going to do well in this class."

"Ha." She rolled her eyes. "Ha, ha. You're hilarious. Seriously, what did she want?"

"I can't tell you," he said with a sigh.

She stared at him, her face slightly hurt. "What do you mean, you can't tell me?"

"According to Lilenpur, if I tell you, it might make it harder for you to quicken your first crystal. I don't want to mess with that, so…" He shrugged again.

"Keep it to yourself, then," Burik said firmly. "I had no idea what she was telling me to do. The crystal felt like a damn rock as far as I could tell." He glanced at Amarl. "You never told us that you'd already quickened a crystal."

"You never asked, did you?" He grinned at the bigger boy, who barked a quick laugh.

"You never offered, either," Meder pointed out.

"Honestly, it never occurred to me. I wasn't trying to hide anything; I just didn't think about it. Herel knows – he was there when I did it – and most of the ithtaru know, so it wasn't like I was keeping it secret."

She walked in silence for a few seconds, obviously considering his words, then nodded as if in acceptance. "Okay, so answer me this, if you're allowed. Was it easy or hard for you?"

He fidgeted uncomfortably. He didn't really want to tell her, but he also didn't want to lie. He'd learned long ago that secrets always came out eventually, and if the two found out he'd been lying to them, their burgeoning friendship would probably shatter. He glanced around, making sure no one else was in earshot.

"It – it was really easy," he admitted. "I didn't even try. It just sort of – happened."

He expected recriminations from the pair, but Burik just looked impressed, while Meder nodded as if it confirmed something she suspected.

"Do you know why it was so easy?" she pressed.

"Maybe it's because he's a hizeen," Burik guessed.

"No," Amarl shook his head. "I mean, no, that's not why, and yes, I know. The ithtaru told me a bunch of times last night. It's because of my Soul Stat. It's – it's really high."

"Really high?" she echoed. "How high? Mine's five-four, and nothing about today was easy for me."

"Five-four?" Burik asked in an impressed voice. "Mine's only four-eight."

"From what I heard, most people have Soul stats below five. It's the stat with the lowest average score. Most stats average out around five for the students, but Soul is closer to four-six or four-seven." Meder nodded at Burik before looking back at Amarl. "So, what's yours? At least six, right?"

"It's..." He hesitated again, then shrugged. As Lilenpur said, it wasn't really a secret. Too many ithtaru knew about it already. "It's nine-four."

The girl stopped walking, frozen, and Amarl paused as well. "Did – did you say...?" She looked around furtively, then stepped close to him, lowering her voice to a whisper. *"Nine-four?!"*

"Damn, that's high," Burik shook his head. "What's the percentage for that?"

"Eight thousand or so," Amarl mumbled.

"How do you have a Soul stat that high?" Meder hissed.

"I have no idea. It's just – that's what it is." As he'd feared, Meder was angry with him. He wished he could take it all back and go back to hiding his true nature, but part of him was glad that he'd told her. He'd thought they were becoming friends, but if she got that angry just because of who he was – well, Amarl had tons of experience with that. Most of the people in Tem hated him because of who and what he was. He'd learned to deal with that long ago. He'd hoped for better from these two, but…

"Meder, ease up," Burik stepped in, gently moving the girl away from Amarl. "Why are you angry? It's not like he did anything wrong, and I think you're hurting his feelings."

"Wrong?" she repeated, looking at the bigger boy. "What are you talking about? I never said…" She blinked in surprise as she looked at Amarl, and her face softened. "Oh. Oh, Amarl, I'm sorry, I didn't mean to sound like I was angry. I'm just – surprised, is all." She shook her head and laughed weakly. "And maybe a little jealous. Okay, a lot jealous. It's so unfair that you have that stat, and how easy it's going to make things for you, but that's not your fault. I'm sorry if I acted like it was."

"My mother always says that the only people who think the world is fair are the ones who already have everything," Burik said. "Everyone else knows it's unfair."

"She's right," Amarl nodded. "The world isn't fair, and there's no point in worrying about it. All you can do is the best with whatever's given you."

"Now, that sounds like something else my mother would say," Burik chuckled, clapping Amarl on the shoulder a little painfully.

"Well, maybe you can help us do the best with what we've got since you've already gone through it," Meder said cheerfully, smiling at the boy. "You can start by telling us what it felt like to quicken your crystal."

Amarl knew the girl's smile was forced. He had a feeling that Meder was used to being the best at things in school, and it was likely that she wouldn't be as good at using ithtu as Amarl was, just as she wasn't as good as Burik at physical training. That probably hurt or even annoyed her, but he hoped she was willing to let it go and keep building their friendship. He decided that if she could try, so could he, so he forced his own smile back at her.

"Hmm. It felt like…" He paused and thought how to explain the experience. "I could hear the crystal calling me, even from halfway across the village." He looked at the two of them. "I wasn't invited to be part of the testing, obviously, but I watched it from a distance, and I could feel it beckoning me the moment I saw it."

"You know, I never thought of that. As a hizeen, you wouldn't have been invited to the testing, would you? So, how did Danmila discover that you could see the crystal?"

"It's not all that great of a story." He quickly told them how Danmila had stopped Churl from stabbing him, how he'd tried to bargain with her to get out of Tem, and how he'd mentioned the ithtu crystal in passing, cluing her in that he was a potential. He left out his attempted thefts and how the Head Bureaucrat threatened to execute him – he couldn't see any reason for them to know that – and described how he'd picked up the crystal and quickened it.

"The moment I touched it, I felt the life inside it," he recalled with a wistful smile. "It sang to me, begged to be taken into me, and I was happy to do it. I just reached out for it, and it flowed into my body." He sighed. "And that's it. I can't take credit for doing anything special because I have no idea how I did it; I didn't even know what I was doing. It was total instinct, and nothing more."

"Well, I certainly didn't feel anything like that today," Burik laughed.

"I really do wonder if all this has something to do with your heritage," Meder mused. "Maybe there have been other hizeen ithtaru in the past who had stats like yours."

"Maybe, I don't know. Like I said, I have no idea what I did or how I did it. If I had some special secret to it, some trick I used, I promise, I'd tell you both in a heartbeat."

"Just hearing how it felt for you might help, actually. It seems that it's more of a feeling and less of a mental exercise." She made a face. "I'd prefer if it were something I could puzzle out, but it doesn't seem like it is."

"It will happen when it happens," Burik predicted. "No point to worrying about what you can't control."

"It's the fact that I can't control it that worries me," she sighed.

"Lilenpur says she's going to be teaching you all sorts of exercises that will make things easier," Amarl supplied. "That might help."

"It might, at that. I don't mind not being able to do this, but I hate not knowing how to get better at it."

They headed back to their room, and Burik checked the schedule, then looked at the others with a sigh. "Skills Training is next," he said. "In the Geralz Training Center, whatever that is."

"When?" Meder asked.

"An hour."

The girl frowned. "That seems like a long break, doesn't it? I can understand the break between physical training and classes so we can clean up, but why an hour after an ithtu lecture?"

Amarl sighed and stood up from where he'd been laying on his bed. "I'm sure there's a reason, and I'm equally sure that if we wait to find out, we'll regret it. Come on, lets go see where the – what was it, Burik?"

"Geralz Training Center."

"Yes, where that is."

As it turned out, there was an excellent reason for the hour break. The center wasn't part of the Citadel; instead, it was a thirty-minute walk to the southeast, along one of the paved roads. The trio didn't get to walk on that road, though; horses and wagons rolled back and forth often enough that, after the fourth time they had to scramble out of the way, they just walked along the soft, grassy ground to the side of the road instead. The afternoon sun beat down on them, and by the time they arrived, they were all somewhat sweaty and disheveled.

The training center lay in a valley tucked in among the mountains ringing Askula. As they approached, the short grass gave way to bare stone and gravel, but the ground sloped upward only gently, rather than rising into foothills and slowly swelling into mountains the way it did near Tem. The peaks simply rose from the plains abruptly, stretching toward the pink sky overhead to both sides and shading the road from the sun at last. The road turned around a bend, then spread out into the wide valley, revealing the Geralz Center at last.

The Center wasn't a single building. Instead, a series of buildings spread out before them, all built of the same gray stone as the mountains. Most were a single story, with pointed slate roofs, while a few stood two or three stories tall. Many had narrow windows, some of which were barred or blocked with iron shutters, but others had wide windows of gleaming glass or simply stood open to the elements. Smoke rose from many of the buildings' chimneys despite the heat, and Amarl wondered what they needed fires for.

"So, what do you think skill training is?" he asked curiously.

"Probably just what it sounds like," Burik shrugged. "I assume we're going to be learning new skills and training them."

"Yes, I guessed that much," Amarl rolled his eyes. "I'm wondering, specifically, what sort of skills they might be teaching us."

"Who knows?" Meder replied. "It could be anything, from weaving and sewing to blacksmithing and carpentry." She pulled an expression of distaste. "I hope it's not the last two, though. I'm dirty and sweaty enough as it is."

"Or combat skills," Burik suggested, his eyes lighting up.

"No, probably not," Meder shook her head. "Weapons training and unarmed combat are their own classes. I saw it on the schedule."

"Oh." His face fell, then immediately brightened. "Well, at least I have those to look forward to."

"I kind of hope its shoemaking," Amarl said, shaking one of his feet. "If we're going to be walking this much, I could use some better boots."

Meder glanced up at the sun and grimaced. "We'd better hurry a bit. We're cutting it close as it is." She looked around behind them at the mostly empty road. "Herel and the others are going to be late. I hope they don't get in trouble."

"Yeah? I kind of hope they do," Amarl laughed. "It might teach them a little humility."

They picked up the pace and half-jogged to the largest building in the group. When they stepped inside, they froze at the sight of Herel, Norag, and Hadur waiting for them, looking perfectly fresh and not at all tired.

"How did you get here ahead of us?" Meder asked curiously.

Herel smirked at the girl. "I arranged for one of the villagers to give us a ride in their wagon. That way, we had time to clean up, and we didn't have to arrive all sweaty and disgusting." He made a face at the three, waving a hand before his face. "And all it cost was a pair of aks, one for the trip there, the other for the trip back." He plastered a smile on his face as he leaned toward Meder. "You know, there's plenty of room on the wagon if you'd prefer to ride back. Those of our caste shouldn't have to walk anywhere, don't you think?"

"Actually, I found the walk rather pleasant," she smiled back at him. "The sun was warm, the breeze was nice, and the scenery was lovely. Perhaps you'd rather join us on the way back?"

"No, thank you," he said with a slight sneer. "I got enough exercise this morning, and those of our caste aren't meant to sweat." He turned away from her, and Amarl leaned close to Meder.

"Weren't you complaining the entire way that the sun was too hot and there wasn't enough breeze?" he whispered in her ear.

"Shut up," she whispered back. "I'd rather take a walk through the spirits' hells than ride anywhere with him." She looked at the two of them. "Besides, he didn't offer a ride to all of us, did he?"

"I don't think he's interested in riding all of us," Amarl said dryly. The girl's face blushed, but she lifted her chin slightly.

"He can wish for that all he wants. He's got a better chance with Burik, here."

Burik looked at the noble boy, his lips pursed and his eyes appraising, then shook his head. "Nope, not for me. Too soft and weak. I'd break him in half."

Meder let out a tinkling laugh, and even Amarl had to chuckle at that thought. Herel turned and glared back at the three, but Amarl chose to ignore it. He was glad that he did as a door leading back into the building opened, and a white-clad man that looked to be in his mid-thirties with onyx black hair, well-muscled arms, and a scar along his left jaw walked out. He took in the two groups at a glance and nodded his head.

"Good. You're all on time. That's rare on the first day. Come with me." He turned and strode back into the building, and the novices followed gamely along behind him into a long hallway that seemed to lead through the center of the building. Doors opened on each side of the hallway. Most stood closed, but Amarl peeked into a few empty ones and saw that they had long tables with stone tops, stools instead of chairs, and wooden shelves lining the walls, packed with boxes whose contents he couldn't make out.

The man turned at the end of the hall and led them into a smaller version of the rooms Amarl had seen. He walked to the front and gestured toward the tables.

"Sit anywhere. It doesn't matter where, at least not today." Meder made for the one of the tables closest to the front, and Burik and Amarl joined her, while the other three sat opposite them. Once the novices were seated, the man walked to the front of the room and cleared his throat.

"I'm Nadar Sengeloh," he said simply. "I'll be your instructor for skill training this year."

He folded his arms across his chest. "I'm sure you're all wondering, 'What is skill training?' What will you be learning? What skills will we teach you?

"First, skill training is not combat. You'll learn about weapons and unarmed tactics elsewhere." Meder beamed triumphantly as he said that, then looked relieved as he added, "It also isn't crafting. Crafting – things like leatherworking, blacksmithing, and carpentry – is taught north of here, at Tarmis Hall, and you won't start that until second year.

"Besides those exceptions, skill training can encompass almost anything you can imagine. If it requires training and skill to do it, there's a good chance there's a trainer here for you. Want to learn how to paint or sing? You can. How to jump higher than a nalu's head? That's possible. How to imitate another's voice well enough to be mistaken for them? You can learn that here."

He uncrossed his arms and folded his hands behind his back. "There are skills that all ithtaru learn, such as how to track, how to conceal yourself, how to question others, and how to behave in various social situations. However, much of what you learn will depend on you. You'll learn skills that complement your stats and personality as well as ones you find most interesting. As you can imagine, you'll find it easier to achieve competency and even mastery in a skill that you have both the talent for and desire to learn."

He pointed to Norag. "You. What's a skill you'd find interesting to learn?"

"I…" The boy looked around and swallowed hard. "I've always thought that learning how to sail would be interesting, sir."

"Small boats, or full ships?"

"Um, ships, sir."

The man nodded. "Seafaring, then. That's a skill we teach." He pointed to Meder. "What about you?"

"I'd like to learn more about alchemy and chemistry, sir," she responded instantly.

"Chemistry, yes. Alchemy, no. That's a crafting skill; however, it's complementary with chemistry, biology, and herbology, all of which are skills you can learn here." His gaze shifted to Herel. "What about you?"

"I don't know, sir," the boy shook his head. "If I've ever wanted to learn something, I was given tutors to learn it."

"Zahai caste. That's actually a common answer among your peers, and it's fine. We can help you discover things you might enjoy, or we can focus on skills you already possess and make them better."

He swept his gaze over all of them. "Which leads to the main point of today's lesson: unlocking your skill sheet. Each of you have come here with skills of your own, things you're already somewhat good at." He looked at Burik. "What's a skill you think you have?"

"Probably something with weapons, sir," the boy replied.

"Military family?" Burik nodded. "I thought so. Yes, you probably have a number of weapons skills – but also things like endurance training, running, discipline, possibly even combat tactics or strategy."

He looked at Amarl. "What about you? What sort of skills do you think you might have?"

"It's hard to say, sir," the boy shrugged. "In my village, I did a little bit of everything – whatever needed doing, really."

"Then you probably have a wide array of low-leveled skills. There's nothing wrong with that; being somewhat good at a lot of things can make you more flexible than someone who's very good at a few." He looked at Hadur. "You?"

"Probably things like mathematics, bargaining, appraising items, and maybe diplomacy, sir."

"A merchant's son," Sengeloh said. He glanced at Herel and Norag. "A very wealthy and successful merchant's son, I'd judge by the company you keep. Those are useful and valuable skills, especially combined with a crafting skill – and you will all learn at least one crafting skill. Every ithtar does."

The ithtar looked at them approvingly. "You have an idea of what you might be good at, but thanks to your status, you don't have to guess. The crystal implanted in each of you during the Joining can not only read your bodily stats, it can judge how skilled you are at specific tasks. However, first, we have to unlock that part of your status."

He reached into a pocket and pulled out a glowing, hexagonal crystal, and all six of the novices drew back in sudden alarm.

"Relax. This isn't a Joining Crystal. Your skill status starts locked to minimize the stress of having your brain and nervous system analyzed immediately after the initial body scan. This will simply trigger that analysis." He looked at Burik. "You. Come stand here in front of me."

Burik looked nervous, but the big boy rose to his feet and slowly walked over to stand before the ithtar. Sengeloh touched the crystal to the boy's forehead, and Burik faltered slightly, looking like he'd lost his balance for a moment. He recovered quickly, though, and stood up straight once more.

"There. Was that so bad?"

"No sir," Burik shook his head.

"Good. Each of you, line up in front of me. I'll unlock your skill status, then we can talk about what you see and what it means."

Amarl hesitantly lined up behind Meder. His heart pounded furiously; despite having seen Burik's mild reaction, his brain kept recalling the searing pain of the Joining, the agony of the body scan immediately afterward, and the fact that a crystal like that had killed him once. He noticed Meder shaking slightly in front of him and knew that she felt the same fear; he reached out and put a comforting hand on her shoulder, and she looked back at him gratefully with shining eyes.

The process wasn't nearly as bad as he'd imagined. The crystal touched his forehead, and he felt a pulse rush through his brain. His thoughts seemed to freeze as tiny fingers crawled across his mind and raced down his spinal cord. Ants scurried along the nerves running down his arms and legs, and everything seemed to pause for a moment. As quickly as it had come, the feeling vanished, and he stepped away, stumbling slightly as he regained his balance.

"Good," Segeloh said when they were all seated once more. "Now, think about what skills you possess, and your status will display them for you."

Amarl concentrated on a list of what he was skilled at, and the now-familiar green rectangle immediately flowed up into his vision.

SKILLS REPORT	
CURRENT SKILL LIST	
ANIMAL CARE	2
BAKING	2
CARPENTRY	1
CLIMBING	3
DECEPTION	6
DRIVING	2
EMPATHY	3
ESCAPE	3
FARMING	2
HIDING	4
INVESTIGATION	3
LOCKPICKING	5
RIDING	2
PERSUASION	7
SEDUCTION	8
SLEIGHT OF HAND	4

He stared at the list. He assumed the numbers to the right of each skill were an indication of how good he was at that skill. Considering that he was much better at picking locks than building bookshelves, he also guessed that higher numbers were better. That was especially true as he realized what his highest ranked skill was, and he smothered a grin that he was afraid might turn creepy. He was happy with what he saw; like Segeloh had said, he was a little good at a lot of things, but the thing he was best at was the thing he enjoyed the most. He wondered if the training center would be able to help him with that skill, then began to fantasize exactly how they might do that.

"You should see a list of skills, followed by a number," the ithtar explained. "This is your skill's level or rank. Skill levels are based on the idea that a person with a rank ten skill can be considered an expert in it. Each level means you're around twenty percent better than you were at the previous level, although there's some variation in this. This increase scales up exponentially, meaning it grows faster the higher you level, and that means it's harder to reach the highest levels. A person with a rank five skill is about one-and-a-half times better at that skill than someone without training; by rank ten, you're typically between four and six times better. This isn't always easy to quantify, but the important thing is that the difference between levels five and six isn't the same as between six and seven, and certainly not nineteen and twenty.

"This means that it's easier to gain levels at first, and leveling slows down a great deal. Once you've quickened your ithtu, you'll find it easy to gain level one of a skill, but it will always be harder to improve the higher-level ones.

"As you've probably guessed, a higher rank typically means you've had more training in that skill, but it can also mean that you're naturally gifted in or suited for that skill. Occasional training in a skill you've got talent in will yield better results than constant training in a skill you've no aptitude for."

He looked around at them. "Because of that, your initial training will focus on your three highest ranked skills, other than combat or crafting ones. They're likely to be the ones you've got the most talent for, and you'll gain levels in them faster, especially once you quicken your first ithtu."

"Why then, sir?" Meder asked curiously.

"Because your ithtu will help your skills develop faster. Ithtu is a dynamic energy; it wants to be used and called upon, and when you're training or working hard on something, it will aid you unless you explicitly restrict it." He looked at her curiously. "Tell me, what's your highest skill, and what level is it?"

"Analysis, sir, at level six."

"A useful skill, and a high level for a starting novice. It will help you break down and resolve various problems and challenges far more easily. You've probably been using it regularly since you were a child, so perhaps eight to ten years, and you got it to level six." He looked around the room. "I'm not exaggerating when I say that once you've quickened your ithtu, you could gain a new skill and bring it to the same level in four to five years, easily. Over the next two years, you'll bring a half-dozen skills to level three, something that would have taken you five or six years before."

The novices muttered in amazement and disbelief, and Segeloh nodded in approval. "Yes. The ithtaru aren't just powerful warriors. Our members are some of the most skilled artisans, trainers, crafters, and scientists in the Empire – if not the most skilled. That's what you're going to learn here: how to master a skill in a decade that would take others a lifetime." He smiled at them.

"We're going to go around the room and find out your three highest skills now. I expect them to be between levels three and five; that's typical for new novices. Outside of Askula, it can take a decade to get to level five in a skill, and half a lifetime to get to level ten." He looked at Burik. "Go ahead.

Your three highest non-combat skills and their level."

"Endurance at level five, combat tactics at level four and..." He hesitated. "Intimidation at level three, sir."

Segeloh nodded. "Don't be ashamed of intimidation. It's a valuable and useful skill. Think about it this way: isn't it better to scare someone into doing what you want than to have to kill them?"

"Yes, sir. I suppose it is, sir."

"Exactly." He looked at Herel. "You?"

"Etiquette at five, diplomacy at three, and politicking at three, sir."

"Good skills for a young noble, especially one from a less-important family trying to rise in the Empire. They can also be valuable for an ithtar; while we can run roughshod over the zahai, it's better to convince them to let us do what we want willingly." Herel looked around a bit smugly, but Segeloh had already moved on to Meder.

"And you?"

"As I said, analysis at six, then investigation at four, and diplomacy at three, sir."

"That's a potentially useful combination, especially for discovering and resolving incursions among the cities. You can find the spirit-possessed, discover the source, and then soothe ruffled feathers once you've closed it." He nodded, then looked at Amarl. "And you?"

"I..." He hesitated and glanced at Meder. "I'd rather tell you in private, sir."

Herel grinned triumphantly, while Burik and Meder looked at Amarl in confusion. Segeloh, though, was having none of it.

"Now, boy. Tell me your three highest-ranking skills. I'm not asking."

Amarl sighed. "I've got deception at six, persuasion at seven – and seduction at eight."

"Fucking liar," Hadur muttered, while Burik burst out with a bark of laughter. Meder looked at him interestedly, then blushed slightly as she realized everyone saw her expression.

"Those are remarkably high levels," Segeloh frowned. "However, he's telling the truth. I have the Lie Detection skill at level ten, and he at least believes what he said was correct."

"Seduction is a skill?" Norag asked curiously.

"Of course, it is. I told you: anything that requires talent and training to do well can be a skill. To get that skill to rank eight in such a short time, he must have considerable talent for it – and plenty of practice." The ithtar nodded. "And don't discount those skills, boy. Diplomacy and intimidation can get people to agree with you, but seduction can make them eager to help you. Most nalu are easily manipulated through sex, and if you're good at it, you can turn them into your puppets." He frowned again. "Tell me, what's your Presence?"

"Six-two, sir."

"That explains a lot. Presence is the stat most associated with things like diplomacy, seduction, and sex. You've got a serious talent for that sort of thing; we'll definitely be training those."

"Wait, you can train people in sexual intercourse?" Meder asked in disbelief. "Um, sir?"

"Of course. You can learn about human anatomy, techniques in seduction, herbs and compounds that act as aphrodisiacs, and the psychology of seduction. It's an art, but it's also a skill, and there are methods to hone those skills without resorting to something as crude as prostitutes." He shrugged. "There are no useless skills, and each one you train is another strength you've given yourself."

He moved on to the others, but Amarl let his mind drift with thoughts of how we was going to improve Seduction. He decided that he was going to really like skill training.

CHAPTER 14

They'd spent the rest of their skills session being assigned to various rooms and junior instructors. Skills sessions, it turned out, weren't broken up by year but by skill level. Thus, even though he, Meder, Herel, and Norag would all be training what Segeloh called "Presence skills", Amarl's higher levels in those skills put him with a group of mostly third and-fourth-year students, while the others trained with second-years. Amarl's instructor was a woman named Povanac, a full instructor rather than a junior one, probably three times his age but still strikingly beautiful, with copper hair and light olive skin that barely showed her age. She promised to help him train his skills, and he couldn't wait to take her up on her offer, even though he doubted she meant it the way he hoped.

After their skill classes, the trio trudged back to their dormitory for dinner, then trudged back to the Citadel with buckets, rags, and mops, and spent three hours scrubbing floors, wiping down bannisters, and cleaning staircases. They fell into bed at last a couple hours after sunset, exhausted.

Ammio, the second day of the week, began with the same pounding on the door as Shimio, the day before, but without their hangovers, they had no problems getting up, dressed, and out to physical training in plenty of time. Once again, their training started with a run, then moved into simple calisthenics and exercises before finishing with another run back to the dormitory.

"That was still the spirits' hell," Meder complained as they trudged down to lunch after cleaning up a bit.

"It'll get easier," Burik predicted. "Right now, your bodies just aren't used to the exercise. Give it a few weeks, and you'll be fine."

"A few weeks? By all the gods, I can't even think of doing this for another few days!"

"It's not that bad," Amarl laughed, stretching his tired and sore arms. "I could do without the running, but the exercises aren't horrible."

"Considering your highest ranked skill, I'd think you'd want a lot of endurance," Burik said slyly.

"I've got plenty for that. It's the running that gets me."

"Can we not talk about this?" Meder pleaded. "Seriously, it's weird enough thinking that Amarl's got something like a decade of experience at seduction when he just reached his fifteenth Naming Day." She shuddered. "That's just so creepy."

"I wasn't seducing people in my fifth year, Meder." He rolled his eyes, then paused. "I waited until my sixth. That's much more reasonable."

"Gosh, Amarl. You're hilarious." She glared at him, opening her mouth for another retort.

"You heard what Segeloh said, Meder," Burik cut in. "It's not just about how long you've been doing it. It's about how talented you are at it. Amarl, what's the percentage for that Presence of yours?"

"Over three hundred."

"There you go, then. Periteth said that means you've got about three times the natural talent in Presence as most of us, so it makes sense that you'd advance those skills a lot faster." He looked at Meder. "And with you having about the same in Mind, you'll probably blow the rest of us away in academics and those sorts of skills, while I'll probably excel at anything physical."

"That's true," she nodded. "Okay, that's a lot more palatable than imagining Amarl in his sixth year hitting on adult women." She shuddered again. "Just – it's just wrong."

"But it felt so right," Amarl grinned at her, then ducked with a laugh as she swiped her hand at his head.

"Enough! I'm not letting you spoil the rest of this day for me. I can't believe we're finally getting to go to sahr class. It's so exciting!" Meder's eyes sparkled as she spoke, but it seemed no one else shared her enthusiasm.

"Maybe for you," Burik rumbled, shaking his head. "I'm not looking forward to it."

"Neither am I," Amarl admitted.

"What?" She looked at them, obviously flabbergasted. "Why not? It's sahr-working! How can you not be excited about sahr-working? If we learn to use sahr, we could use it for so many things!"

"I doubt we'll be learning any workings, Meder," Amarl pointed out.

"It'll probably be like ithtu training yesterday. We'll have to learn all kinds of theories, and we'll spend weeks just learning how to feel sahr, much less use it. It's not like we can just pick up a wand, mutter a magic word or two, and become haros. That would be ridiculous."

"A wand?" Burik laughed. "Why a wand?"

Amarl shrugged. "We had a charlatan hara come to Tem once. You know, one who uses sleight-of-hand instead of actual magic. She had a wooden stick she waved around while she muttered strange words, and she used a lot of flash powder and smoke to make what she did seem magical. It was entertaining, at least the tricks I couldn't figure out were."

"I saw one of those," Burik agreed. "He called himself 'Veldmert' and dressed in a strange black robe that looked like it would be hard to move around in. He said he could kill someone with a few words from three reaches away." The boy laughed. "My mother said she could do the same thing from twice as far with a pistol, and that she could do it faster and more times in a row."

"Well, I've seen an actual haro," Meder said dreamily, her eyes going vacant. "It was amazing. He made a whole flock of butterflies appear just by waving his arms, then he had them dance around while he created music from nothing."

"They probably won't be teaching us to make butterflies," Burik pointed out. "More like fire or ice, I would think."

"Well, I want to make butterflies," Meder said, then grinned at the others. "Or ants. I could send a swarm of them into your beds while you sleep if you annoy me. That might be fun."

"Worms would be worse," Burik said. "Or centipedes. They bite and sting, and they've got all those legs. Having a bunch of them crawling across your face would be scary."

"Gee, thanks for that image, Burik," Amarl sighed. "I hope you're okay singing me to sleep tonight."

"Sure, but you'd rather have the centipedes, trust me. My mother always said she wished she could turn my singing into a weapon. She'd win every battle when her enemies gave up and ran away."

After lunch, the three walked through the Citadel and along a stone path bordering the lake. Marjan Tower lay on the opposite side of the lake, nestled in another hidden valley in the encircling mountains. As the group passed the lake after cleaning up and grabbing a quick meal, they saw rows of well-built but small houses ringing the far shore and spreading out up the hills leading to the mountains behind. The homes were narrow and tall, each house sharing walls with the ones beside it, with sharply angled slate roofs. They looked quiet and comfortable nestled far from the bustle of activity surrounding the Citadel and dormitories, and no path led around the lake to reach them.

"Who lives there?" Burik asked, pointing at the distant homes.

"The malims and awals," Meder said absently, staring ahead into the distance. "The awals live on the shoreline, and the malims have homes farther back."

"How do they get to them, though?" He looked around. "There's no way around the lake to get over there."

"I honestly don't know," she shrugged. "I'm assuming that if they can't fly, jump, freeze the lake, walk on water, or use some other ability to get there, though, they take one of the boats." She pointed to the dock near the Citadel, where a dozen large boats floated at anchor.

"Why would they make it so hard to get to where they live, though?"

"Probably to make it hard for the students to get there, too," Amarl laughed. "If you spent all day tormenting students, would you really want them to be able to find you where you sleep?"

"They aren't going to torment us, Amarl," Meder rolled her eyes.

"That's not what you said this morning after physical training," he grinned at her.

"That wasn't torment. It was just putting us through the spirits' hell." She continued to stare straight ahead, and he glanced in the direction she peered.

"What are you looking at?"

"That," she pointed toward one of the closer peaks rearing far in the distance. Amarl had to stare for a few seconds before he saw a thin, needle-shaped spire stretching into the sky behind the mountain, seeming to touch the thin, rosy clouds overhead. The spire glittered in the sunlight, reflecting every color of the rainbow.

"What's that?" he asked curiously.

"Askula's tower," she breathed.

"That's where we're going to practice?" He stared at the thin structure, confused. "I don't think we'll fit!"

"No, it's the realm's sahr tower," she shook her head. "It regulates the sahr field here and keeps spirits from entering Askula."

"I didn't think spirits could use the Mistways," Burik rumbled.

"They can't, but Askula has an Edge, just like Umpratan," she explained, waving a hand. "It's somewhere out there, beyond the mountains. If we went high enough on one of those peaks, we'd see it. Without the tower, spirits could leave the Edge and invade here." She shivered, then looked back at the spire. "I've never seen one before. The one in Dairon is in the middle of the Honeyed Forest, and no one's allowed near it."

"How do you know all this?" Amarl asked her in amazement.

"I ask," she shrugged. "When I want to know something, I find someone willing to tell me, and I always want to know things." She made a face. "I would look things up in one of the libraries, but we don't get access to those until we're second-years. Until then, I just try to make friends with people and ask them what I'm curious about."

"I should try that," Amarl nodded. "Although I've never really been good at making friends."

"Maybe if 'making friends' to you didn't mean practicing that seduction skill of yours, you'd have better luck," she said archly.

"Maybe, but I prefer to get lucky in my own way," he grinned at her, and she rolled her eyes, smacking his arm with the back of her hand.

As they walked closer, they rounded the mountains, and the valley of Marjan spread out before them. Towers rose from the earth, ringing the valley and stretching from four to ten stories in height. Each was made of stone, solid and functional, with glassed-in windows dotting their walls and conical roofs to shed rain and snow. Even the tallest of these, however, looked tiny in comparison to the massive structure dominating the center of the valley. A huge tower, easily fifteen or sixteen reaches in diameter, rose from the solid stone. Built of white, glossy stone that shimmered prismatically, the structure rose at least thirty or forty stories overhead, if not more, narrowing as it stretched to a tapered point. No doors or windows pierced the structure, but streaks of gold, silver, and copper decorated it in swirling bands that seemed to be buried in the opaque stone.

"That's amazing," Meder breathed, holding up a hand palm-first toward the tower. "Can you feel that?"

Amarl frowned and lifted a hand, shaking his head. "I don't feel anything."

"The energy radiating out from it," she said, looking at him curiously. "You can't feel that?"

"No." He glanced at Burik. "You?"

"The hair on the back of my neck is standing up," he shrugged. "That's about it."

She looked at them in obvious confusion. "Really? Neither of you can feel the power coming from that thing?" She breathed deeply, as if trying to take that energy into herself. "It's intoxicating."

"Maybe we'll get to see you drunk again, then," Amarl grinned. "That's always entertaining."

She lowered her hand and glared at him. "Not that sort of intoxicating, idiot." She stopped and looked past him, her glare fading into a frown. "I wonder what's going on there?"

Amarl turned and looked behind him, toward the valley spread out before them. Herel, Hadur, and Norag had beaten the trio to Marjan, of course, probably hitching another ride with a villager. Herel and Hadur stood before a tall boy, even taller than Burik, who was obviously at least a third year. The boy had short-cut black hair, was heavily muscled, and had an elaborate, black tattoo pattern spiraling down the side of his face and disappearing beneath his purple shirt that oddly reminded Amarl of Periteth's.

"Who's that?" Amarl asked curiously.

"I don't know," the girl shook her head. "He's at least third year, and that purple shirt says he's in the Baquena School, meaning he has a Tier B ability. And that tattoo says he's Nicelian like Periteth; they're all tattooed."

"What do those tiers mean, anyway?" Burik asked.

The girl shrugged. "No clue. No one wants to explain about them. But I know that when you get to third year, if you've got a Tier A ability, you're put in Risha School, Baquena for Tier B, and Libba for Tiers C and D. Risha's student wear yellow, Baquena's purple, and Libba's blue."

"So, Herel and the others are talking to a third-year," Burik shrugged. "What's the big deal?"

"The big deal is that most third-years won't even speak to novices, but that one looks friendly to them." She frowned. "I wonder what they're up to."

"They're probably trying to arrange for protection from the second-years," Amarl shrugged. "Herel paid for his wagon rides each day; he might be paying older students to keep the second-years off his back."

"Maybe. I wonder if he's trying to get some extra instruction." She glanced at Amarl. "Does he know about your Soul stat?"

"I never told him, but I told a lot of ithtaru that first night of our Joining. He might have overheard, or one of them might have told him."

"If he knows, he might be trying to get extra help to keep up with you. I hope he's not trying to get private sahr lessons, though. That wouldn't go over well."

"Why not?" Burik asked. "Seems like a sensible thing to do, if you ask me. I have a feeling I'm going to need all the help I can get with this."

"Because while the tower regulates the sahr field, it also limits how much of it is available to be used. That's why haros are so tightly restricted in the Empire; if they use sahr carelessly, it could drain the local field and cause all sorts of problems." She shook her head. "If they're caught practicing without permission, they could be in trouble."

"That's their problem, not ours." Burik shrugged. "We just have to worry about making it to class in time. Any idea which tower we're supposed to be in?"

Asking around revealed the correct tower, and the trio hurried up the stairs to their classroom. Amarl followed the others in, curious what a sahr classroom might look like. To his disappointment, it wasn't filled with arcane devices, colored lights, exotic creatures, or anything else that he might have considered "magical". Instead, it looked exactly like the ithtu classroom, save that it was shaped like a piece of pie rather than a square, with the lectern near the door and seats spread like a fan before it. Blackboards covered with complex equations and graphs covered the walls, and a pair of large, arched windows in the outer wall let light into the room.

"Well, this is disappointing," he said with a sigh as they sat down.

"A little, yes," Meder nodded, pointing to the nearest board. "Although that looks interesting."

"We have vastly different ideas of what that word means, Meder," Burik chuckled. "My head hurts just looking at those. I think this class is going to be painful."

"You're probably right, Novice." All three students jumped at the sudden voice that seemed to come from nowhere and looked frantically around the room. Amarl blinked as a shadow seemed to pass over one of the windows, a shadow that swiftly darkened into a humanoid shape and finally resolved itself as a short, slim man with long, graying hair pulled back in a series of braids. The man wore the white uniform of a nadar and stood staring out the window, not even glancing back at the trio as they twisted in their seats to gawk at him.

"Wow," Meder whispered, her eyes wide. "Did you do that with sahr, sir?"

"Yes," he replied, turning to give the girl an amused look. "A simple bending of light to make me appear invisible. Not as effective as an ithtu ability, of course."

"Why not, sir?" she asked. "We couldn't see you at all. That seems effective to me."

"You weren't looking hard. If you were, you'd have noticed distortions in the air in front of the window. Also, it only works when you're utterly still; any movement causes you to be temporarily visible until the sahr field acclimates to your new position and posture. Finally..."

The man faded into insubstantiality once more, but this time, Amarl looked closely and saw what he was talking about. Ripples and shimmers that looked like heat rising from rocks warped the light before the window, and as the nadar breathed, Amarl caught flickers of the edges of his shoulders moving. Worst of all, two black dots hung in the air, a span-and-a-half below a reach in height. The dots vanished and reappeared, and Amarl realized they were the man's pupils.

"What are you all staring at?" Amarl looked back at the door and saw Herel, Hadur, and Norag enter the classroom. Herel looked at the others with a sneer. "Thinking about getting out of here already? Did the math on the board frighten you?"

"It should." The nadar spoke again, and Herel and his friends jumped in surprise as the man slowly faded back into view. "And they were looking at me. Or rather, looking for me." The man glanced at the seated trio. "Did you see the fatal flaw?"

"Your eyes," Meder nodded. "I could see them." She frowned. "Is that because you have to let light hit them, or you're blind?"

"Very good. Yes, that's exactly the problem. If you redirect all light around yourself, you also stop light from reaching your eyes, and that leaves you blind. Part of learning to master sahr is foreseeing these problems and working out solutions to them." He looked at Herel and the others, still staring at him in surprise. "Take your seats, please. We have a great deal to cover."

The three boys hurriedly sat down, while the man strode down the center aisle between the seats and moved to stand behind the lectern. He turned to face the class, his squarish face impassive and his eyes calm and deep.

"I'm Nadar Furemas," he said in the same calm, even tone he'd used before. "I'll be your instructor on the basics of sahr."

He swept his eyes over the group, fastening on the eager-faced Meder. "Before we begin, let me tell you that yes, you will have the opportunity to both handle and use sahr in this class – eventually." He emphasized the last word, and Meder's face fell slightly. He looked at her with a soft smile.

"What is sahr?" he asked. Meder, Herel, and Hadur's hands shot up, but he ignored them as he walked out from behind the lectern, his hands clasped behind his back. "There are several definitions I could give you. For example, I could say that sahr is an energy field capable of being manipulated to do work and create effects that defy the normal laws of science." He looked at the students slowly lowering their hands. "Let me guess. That's what you were going to say, yes?" All three nodded, and he shrugged.

"That's not a bad definition, but then, it's not a good one, either. It doesn't tell us what sahr is, just what it does – which is a flaw in many of the classes the nobility and wealthy merchants take in academy, to be honest. They focus more on the utility of something, not its essential nature."

He turned to face the class. "I could tell you that sahr is a universal energy field present in every realm of which we know. I could say that it's magic, or that it's a fifth element, or that it's the omnipresent aether. All of these would be correct, but they would all be incomplete – as they must be."

He shifted to walk back to the podium. "They must be because the simple fact is, no one truly knows what sahr is or where it comes from. It simply exists, and it seems to exist everywhere. It can be harnessed by any living creature with the will to do so, and many animals and beasts in other realms use sahr instinctively or even as a fundamental part of their biology. This implies that it has existed long enough for evolution in those realms to include it in its presence, but it also suggests that it must not always have existed in those realms. Can anyone make a guess as to why?"

Meder slowly raised her hand, and he gestured to her. "Yes, you.

Stand, introduce yourself, and tell me what you think."

The girl slowly rose from her seat. "My name is Meder, sir. Is it because if those realms always had sahr, then everything would have adapted to use it, not just certain creatures?"

"Good. You may sit down." He waited while she took her seat again, then continued. "Yes, that's correct. The point of all this is that sahr is something universal, with an unknown origin, but that it hasn't always existed and came into being at some point. The priests say that sahr was a gift from Ak-lahat to the Mortal Realm, but no one truly knows, and the One Above All hasn't yet deigned to come to our world and tell us." The man smiled thinly as he spoke those last words, but Norag's hand shot up immediately.

"Sir," the boy protested, "the Book of the One is the high god's word in this world, and it states..."

"...That sahr was gifted to the world to allow the mortal races to throw off their shackles," the nadar cut Norag off. "Yes, Novice, I know the story. Sadly, a religious text that's been altered repeatedly over the past three millennia isn't a reliable source."

The man's eyes narrowed as he spoke. "Understand, Novice, that while I believe in the existence of the gods – only a fool wouldn't when there are so many records of their presence in this world – I don't hold that sahr is the divine hand of Ak-lahat and part of his powers of creation. It's far more likely that sahr is a naturally occurring phenomenon whose nature we simply don't understand than that the Creator of All took pity on us and gifted us with his powers."

Norag's face was angry by that point, but the nadar ignored the boy's distress and pressed on.

"However, that's simply my belief. You are welcome to your own, and if you continue into the advanced classes, you'll find that we delve more deeply into sahr's origin there. For now, though, we'll be discounting the religious explanation since we simply lack evidence either way."

The instructor turned back to the rest of the class.

"That tells you what sahr is: an energy field of unknown origin that permeates all of the Mortal Realm, one that affects all living things and that any living creature can touch and even tap. However, the fact is, sahr is vastly inferior to ithtu in practically every way. While sahr can generally replicate the effects of a Tier A or B ability – such as the invisibility I just showed you – its effects are never as powerful and are often drastically limited. Becoming invisible takes every drop of sahr I can channel, and it has serious flaws. I could boost my strength with sahr, but someone with that ithtu ability would easily overpower me.

"So, you might be wondering, why bother to learn to use it when ithtu is better?"

He placed his hands atop the lectern, and his face took on a grave expression. "Simply put, sahr is a tool. It's a method you can use to accomplish your tasks, not a replacement for ithtu. In that way, it's no different than your sword or spear, although it's infinitely more versatile. I like to equate it to a hammer: it can repair or shatter, craft or destroy, create beauty or ugliness, often all in the same hands." He stared at them intently for a long moment as if to let that sink in, then visibly relaxed.

"At its core, using sahr is easy. Every intelligent species can do it. Without the towers, you could draw sahr in right now and project it however you wished with very little effort, and in other realms, it's often that easy. However, uncontrolled sahr is also unpredictable. Haros wielding uncontrolled sahr are as much a danger to themselves and those around them as to their enemies, and they often consume that which they would create. This is why we have the towers. The towers keep the sahr field smooth and calm, operating within predictable parameters that allow its effects to be known and understood. You walked past a tower on your way here, obviously. Did anyone sense the sahr coming from it?" Both Meder and Norag raised their hands, and the man nodded.

"You're both sensitives and probably have a decent Will stat. That will make using sahr far easier for you, as the higher your Will stat, the more in tune you are with Sahr."

He looked around. "So, what is sahr manipulation? Sahr manipulation is nothing more than gathering sahr, focusing it into a matrix, and releasing it to perform your will. It sounds simple, and as I said, at its core, it is. Your brain can perform the calculations necessary to manipulate sahr at a deep level below consciousness, in the same way it can calculate how to walk or run, or how to throw a ball.

"However, to truly master sahr, you'll need to be able to understand and guide its flows consciously, not intuitively. Who here has seen a haro in action?" Everyone but Amarl and Burik raised their hands, and the nadar nodded. "If you paid attention, you probably noticed that the haro used multiple methods of crafting the same working. They waved their hands around, spoke quietly, might have shifted their body as if dancing, and perhaps drew an inscription on the ground or a piece of paper. What you saw them doing was creating a multi-dimensional matrix, using each of those techniques to build a different dimension of the matrix, then collapsing it down into the effect they wanted.

"If that sounds complex, it is." He waved his hand at the nearest board. "These are field equations that describe the local sahr field. To truly master sahr, you'll have to learn how to turn these equations into a part of the matrix needed, then break that matrix up into performing elements that will help your mind craft the working. Will is important, but you'll also need strong Mind and Skill stats to truly excel." He shrugged. "Which means that most of you won't. It doesn't matter. This isn't about making you into a sahr master; it's about gaining proficiency in sahr, nothing more. Those of you with true potential will be allowed to continue the study of sahr into your third year and beyond, but the rest will become competent this year and the next, and that's it. Anything beyond will be up to you."

"However, we'll begin by going back to our discussion about the nature of sahr, and of energy in general..."

Amarl leaned back, concealing a frown as he listened to the nadar speak. Using ithtu came naturally to him; he seemed to be able to do it as naturally as breathing. He had a feeling sahr wasn't going to be so simple.

CHAPTER 15

Sahr class had dragged by for Amarl. As he predicted, they didn't learn any workings or even use sahr in the class. Instead, they'd spent the entire class learning math, a subject he was woefully ignorant in. He and Burik both struggled through the class, barely keeping up with the teacher, while the rest breezed through the calculations effortlessly. His hands clenched into fists every time Furemas called on him to answer a question and he got it wrong – which was most of the time – and he caught Herel and Hadur both smirking as he fumbled for answers. He left the class with his head aching, his jaw clenched, and a decidedly miserable outlook on the possibility of using sahr.

"You were wrong earlier, Meder," he said grimly, shaking his head. "That was the spirits' hell."

"What?" the girl asked, looking at him in confusion. "It was a little dry, sure, but it wasn't that bad."

"Wasn't that bad?" Amarl asked incredulously. "That's the worst class we've taken!"

She looked at him and then back at Burik, who nodded affirmatively.

"That was awful," the large boy rumbled. "My head is pounding, and I feel like it's stuffed with cotton. That math was way too much for my brain."

"Really? I thought it was fairly simple," she frowned.

"Maybe for you. For me, it all sounded like another language, one I couldn't understand."

"But it's mostly review of maths seven and eight of the academy," she protested. "Which...oh. Which neither of you ever took."

"Nope," Amarl said cheerfully. "I learned addition, subtraction, multiplication, and division, and I've been fine with that so far."

"I hadn't thought of that." She frowned. "You would think that Askula would have, though. Surely, they'll give the two of you extra instruction to catch you up!"

"Maybe they will," Amarl shrugged. "They haven't yet, though, and almost none of that made sense to me."

She looked at them a bit speculatively. "Maybe I could help you," she suggested. "I know all of this pretty well, and we could spend some time studying it in the evening before lights-out."

"That might work," Amarl agreed.

"Not today, though," Burik groaned. "My head hurts too much for today."

"Fine. We'll start tomorrow. Now, we'd better get moving if we're going to make it to weapons training in time."

The Sitjak Complex lay southwest of the Citadel. Like Geralz, it was accessible by a paved road, but unlike the road to Geralz, the stone pathway heading toward Sitjak was occupied only by naluni walking or riding to or from it and wasn't particularly crowded. That, combined with the light overcast overhead, made their trip to the compound a lot more pleasant than the walk to the skills center had been yesterday. It was also much longer, though, and they had to hurry their steps to make it in time.

Like Geralz, Sitjak occupied a small valley within the mountains ringing Askula. The complex was a series of low, single-story buildings, set in a ring around two long, rectangular structures in the center. Most were built of wood rather than stone, with thatched roofs instead of slate. There was no obvious place for them to go, but fortunately, they spotted Herel, Norag, and Hadur standing with a white-shirted man about ten years older than the novices with muscled arms covered with thin, white scars.

"You the rest of the novices?" the man called as the group approached, his voice higher-pitched and lighter than Amarl might have suspected from his appearance.

"Yes, sir," Burik called back.

"Good. Hustle over here. If everyone's here early, we can start early."

The three jogged over to join the group, and the man nodded to everyone.

"Excellent. I'm Nadar Yamacol, your weapons training instructor." He swept his gaze over the group. "I'm not going to give you a speech or tell you why you're getting the sort of training you'll receive today. If you can't figure it out, then you're likely to have a short career in Askula."

He began leading them toward one of the rectangular buildings.

"Here in Sitjak, we train weapons skills, nothing else. Over the next two years, you'll become competent with every major class of weapon plus unarmed combat. If you show skill in a specific weapon, you'll receive advanced training in that weapon. Who here has a weapons skill already?"

To Amarl's complete lack of surprise, Burik and Herel both raised their hands. The instructor pointed at Herel. "You. What skills do you have, how long have you been practicing, and what level is it?"

"Fencing at level four, sir, and Knife Fighting at three. I've been practicing since my eighth Naming Day." The noble looked at the others a bit smugly as he spoke.

"Seven years to get to levels three and four? Not sure you're suited for those weapons, then." The instructor either didn't see or chose to ignore Herel's indignant expression and pointed at Burik. "And you?"

"Firearms at five, halberd at five, longsword at four, shield at four, military boxing at four, and spear at three, sir. Been training since my tenth Naming Day."

Yamacol paused and looked at the boy, his face clearly impressed. "Not bad. That's a wide range of skills, even for a military brat, and most of them are decently leveled for only five years. You clearly have talent, boy."

"Thank you, sir."

"Of course, talent means shit without hard work." The man opened a door and led them inside, into a room that reminded Amarl of Helowa's bakery, with a long counter and a door behind it leading into the back. Instead of steaming breads or fluffy pastries lining the walls, though, racks of weapons gleamed along the wall behind the counter, with a few displayed elsewhere around the room. Swords of various lengths and shapes rested on vertical stands from floor to ceiling; sledgehammers with narrow heads and spiked backs hung upside down on hooks; spears and things that looked like spears with fancier heads stood stacked tightly together. Amarl didn't even know the names for most of what he saw, much less how to use them.

"This is the armory," Yamacol announced. "Don't touch any of the weapons here; they're for display only." He directed this at Herel, whose hand froze as it reached toward one of the swords.

The back door opened, and a young woman walked out wearing bright blue clothing with the number three beneath the Askula emblem, denoting her rank as a third-year. "New novices, sir?" she asked in a light, respectful voice, brushing her light brown hair back out of her face.

"Yes, Andra." He looked back at the students. "Line up at the counter. Andra will ask about your stats and existing skills; answer her honestly. Her job is to help you discover what weapons will suit you best for your initial training. Do not argue with her decisions. You'll start with weapons that are likely to match your talents, then expand from there once you have a solid base to start from."

The group lined up, with Burik in front as usual, looking far more eager than Amarl had seen him in any other class. Andra looked him up and down appraisingly.

"Force, Skill, and Speed stats?" she asked.

"Five-seven, five-two, and five-one, ma'am."

"You don't have to call me ma'am. I'm just a student here, too." She tapped her chin thoughtfully. "Do you have any axe or bladed polearm skills?"

"Halberd at five. I've also got firearms at five…"

She waved a hand at him, and he fell silent. "Firearms are easy to level at first, but you need a high Skill stat to really master them. All your physical stats are good, but with Force that high, you need a crushing or chopping weapon." She turned away from him and walked over to the wall. She grabbed what looked like an axe with a sharply angled blade and a spearpoint atop a tall pole nearly a reach and a half long, as well as a shorter axe with a narrower blade and a long-handled sledge. She stacked each weapon on the counter, paused, then went back and grabbed a small shield a little more than two handspans in width.

"There. Take these, go over to the side, and test them out a bit. If one doesn't feel right, line back up, and we'll look at replacing it."

Burik looked a bit discontented but obediently walked over to a clear space and hefted his weapons. He went through all sorts of exercises and tests that Amarl couldn't really see the point of, but as he worked, the unhappiness slowly fell away from his face.

He watched as Meder was handed an iron-banded staff and a pair of long daggers, while Norag received a heavy hammer and an axe on a long wooden shaft. He couldn't keep from grinning as Herel was given a spear and a sword that was longer and wider than the one Amarl had seen him with, not the slim blade he'd obviously been hoping for.

"You don't have the Speed stat to be a good fencer," she said when he mentioned his Speed of four-six. "The rapier is a weapon of speed as much as skill. If you're too slow, you won't be able to riposte effectively, and you'll have difficulty recovering from your lunges. The spear doesn't need as much speed but is just as precise, and this longsword will take advantage of your Force and Skill without needing too much quickness."

The noble almost opened his mouth to complain, but he took a single look at Yamacol watching closely and snapped his lips shut. Amarl almost laughed aloud, though, at the boy's face when Hadur received the rapier that he hadn't, along with a shorter sword and a long, wooden stick with bronze knobs studding it.

When Amarl reached the counter, the girl gave him the same critical gaze as the others. "Force, Skill, and Speed?" she asked.

"Five-two, five-three, and five-six," he replied promptly, having looked it up while he waited. "I don't have any weapons skills already."

She nodded. "Good stats. Typically, for someone with those stats, I'd recommend a polearm, maybe a halberd or glaive, but you don't have the height and mass for that. With your Speed and Skill, I might recommend a light sword like a rapier, but that wouldn't take advantage of your Force stat. You need fast slashing weapons, maybe a light pick, or..." She grinned at him. "Oh, I've got the perfect weapon for you – at least, if you can master it."

She walked away, then came back and began laying weapons on the counter. The first was a lightly curved sword with a blade that widened a bit toward the tip, narrowing sharply into a wicked point and edged along the outward-curving side. The second was a metal rod a third of a reach long with a small, spiked metal ball at the end. After that came a small shield maybe a span and a half across. She smiled as she lifted the last weapon and placed it on the counter. It was a simple wooden shaft a couple spans more than a reach in length. One end had a crescent-shaped blade two spans wide that curved away from the shaft like a bull's horns. The other end had a pair of narrower, axe-shaped blades that faced away from one another, topped by a conical spear point.

"What's this?" he asked curiously, picking it up and examining it.

"A moon axe," Andra told him, her voice a little excited. "It's a pretty rare weapon because you need to be strong, fast, and skilled to use it well. The outward crescent can pierce, slash, and trap an enemy's weapon or limb, and the rear axe blades can cut through bone if need be. It's fast, it has some reach, and if you're strong enough, you can shear through armor with it." She pointed off to the side, where the others were all handling their weapons. "Go ahead, give it a try!"

"Thanks," he smiled at her before lugging the three weapons and the shield to an empty corner of the room.

He laid them all on the floor, then picked up the sword first, holding it in one hand. It wasn't as heavy as he'd expected, weighing maybe three or four tankards, each being the weight of a mug of water. The curved blade was probably excellent for cutting, and he supposed that he could stab something with the sharp point, as well. The way the blade widened toward the end made it feel almost axe-like, which he guessed would be good against someone wearing armor, but a round metal orb on the bottom of the handle kept it from being unbalanced. He moved it from side to side and lifted it up and down, then shrugged and put it down. He had no clue how to use it, but it didn't feel like it would be particularly hard.

The rod with the spiked ball, on the other hand, just felt strange. It weighed more than the sword, despite being a couple handspans shorter, and the steel ball at the end dragged the weight far forward. He suspected using it would tire him out faster, but he also guessed that getting smacked in the head with it wouldn't just be painful, it would probably crush a skull, and it likely didn't take a lot of training to crack someone in the head with it.

At last, he hefted the moon axe. The weapon was longer than he was tall, and it was heavy, heavier than the sword and rod both. It felt balanced in his hands, though, the moon blade on one end offset by the axes on the other. He gripped it tightly and swung it gently from side to side, getting a feel for it. It was ungainly and awkward, to be sure, but then, all the weapons were in his unskilled hands. Andra said the weapon was fast, but it didn't feel that way to him as he moved it around. That probably meant there was some knack or trick to it that he simply didn't get but hopefully would.

"You don't look all that happy about what you got," Meder said quietly from his side.

"I don't know enough to be happy or unhappy," he laughed. "I've never used a weapon other than a knife, and that only for cutting things, not people."

"Neither have I," she agreed, hefting her staff. "This feels okay, though. I could smack someone in the head with it pretty easily."

"Or cave in their chest or crush their throat," Burik added, walking up to the pair and gesturing at the staff. "That's a more versatile weapon than you probably think, Meder. You can use it for defense and offense, and it doesn't take a ton of training to become competent with it." He looked askance at the weapon in Amarl's hands. "That, on the other hand, looks like it will be really hard to be even competent with, Amarl."

"Looks like it?" Amarl asked, holding up the moon axe. "You mean, you don't know this weapon?"

"Nope. It looks too exotic for the military, though. Too short for formation fighting, too long for in-close work. It's obviously meant for someone to use in single combat." He pointed to the other two weapons. "Me, I'd stick with the scimitar and mace, but that's just me."

"Good." Yamaloc's voice broke in before Amarl could ask which of his new weapons was a scimitar and which a mace. "Now that you each know what weapons you'll be training on, go ahead and give them back to Andra. Those weapons belong to Askula, not you. You'll come here before each class and check the weapon you'll be working with that day out from here, then return them when your lesson is done."

Amarl shrugged and walked back to the counter, laying his weapons atop them, with his companions close behind. Herel seemed almost eager to get rid of his weapons, pushing them across the counter at the older girl, while Norag and Meder both looked a little crestfallen to hand theirs over. Burik seemed to have been expecting it, and Amarl assumed that taking out weapons just for training was common practice, something the larger boy had seen several times.

"Now, come with me," Yamacol said, leading the group out of the armory and into one of the nearby circular buildings. When they entered, Amarl was surprised to see that the building was a single, open space lacking interior walls. The floor was soft sand rather than stone, and raised wooden rings dotted the floor, each about three reaches across. Students older than the novices stood around those rings, watching as other students moved around inside, their movements concealed by the wall of bodies. People cheered or jeered, called out criticisms and advice, and the whole place rang with the sounds of those voices.

"This is the short blades training circle," Yamacol said loudly, his voice carrying over the din. "Knives, daggers, hatchets, fang blades, punch daggers, wrist razors – these are all small blades, and we train all of them here."

He gestured toward a nearby circle, and Amarl peered through a gap in the crowd to see a pair of students maybe two years older than him crouched low, moving about smoothly and swiftly in the circle. One held a pair of large knives or daggers – Amarl didn't really know the difference – while the other had a set of what looked like forward-curving claws strapped to her wrists, each set with two long blades that extended more than a span past the woman's closed fists. They whirled and darted around one another, attacking not just with their weapons but also lightning-fast kicks, as well as accurate elbow and knee strikes. He watched for a moment in fascination, noting the others doing the same; the pair was obviously at a level well beyond anything Amarl had ever seen. If Churl had attacked either of them, they would have handed him his ass in a heartbeat.

"You'll begin your training by learning knifework," Yamacol informed them. "Knives are the smallest of small blades, but in skilled hands, they're as lethal as any other weapon. Learning their use will teach you the value of footwork and coordination, skills that are vital for any weapon, not just small ones." He led them to a wooden barrel near one wall and reached inside, pulling out a wooden weapon about two spans long that was nothing more than a dull blade and a cloth-wrapped handle.

"Training blades. Everyone grab one, then join me in this empty ring." Amarl obediently followed the others to the barrel and took out a dull, too-light wooden knife, then walked over to an empty ring and stood before Yamacol.

"All right. First, we'll work on how to grip your weapon…"

Amarl watched the man and did his best to imitate him. He wasn't really looking forward to weapons training, but he supposed he didn't have much of a choice. Ithtaru were warriors, and he guessed that a warrior who didn't know how to fight was probably close to useless. He didn't know what happened to novices that Askula decided were useless, and he seriously hoped he never found out.

CHAPTER 16

"**A**cademics," Amarl said distastefully as the freshly showered trio walked through the Citadel's halls, doing their best to avoid the older students. Meder had accidentally bumped into one the day before, and the older girl responded with a knee to the younger girl's gut that dropped her to the floor, groaning. Both Burik and Amarl moved to defend her without thought, and Amarl never even saw the fist that crashed into his face and knocked him back against the wall. Stars flashed in his eyes, and he barely managed to hold his feet. He forced his eyes to focus in time to see Burik block an older girl's elbow and shove her backwards before taking a foot to his ribs that knocked him backward as well and left him gasping for breath.

"Keep your bodies to yourselves, Meat," the girl who'd struck Meder snarled at them. "The halls belong to the real students."

Meder had been shocked by the treatment – and the fact that students passing by either said nothing or laughed at the altercation – but Amarl more or less expected it. Periteth told them on the first day that older students would do their best to harass and antagonize the novices, and he'd suspected that included looking for any excuse to hit them. Afterward, the three walked carefully, keeping their eyes open and staying well away from older students who might "accidentally" lurch into them.

"I don't even know what that is, and I already don't like it," he added.

"Academics means general studies," Meder explained. "In the academy, it covered things like literature, history, sociology, economics, and political theory."

"I know you think you're explaining, Meder, but you're not," Amarl laughed. "Did you make up half those words?"

"She just means that it's useless stuff," Burik rumbled. "Poetry and dead people and whose ass you have to kiss to get ahead."

She giggled at that but shook her head. "I don't think any of that would be useless for an ithtara," she said, then paused. "Well, maybe literature. I'm not sure being able to correctly compose a Marrikethian sonnet will come in all that handy. But understanding history, how society works, and the subtleties of politics are all probably very important. You two shouldn't dismiss them."

"Hey, I didn't dismiss anything," Amarl protested. "I just said I didn't know what any of that was. No one taught anything like that in Tem – or even really worried about it. I know a little history, but that's mostly just famous battles and the like because the older people liked to talk about them when they drank."

"Fine. Burik, they aren't useless."

He grunted. "We'll see."

They walked into a classroom that was essentially identical to the one for their sahr classes, except that one wall was covered with a series of detailed maps. Meder immediately moved to those, gazing up at them with an awed expression.

"I've never seen a map this exacting," she said admiringly. "Look, it's got even the smallest villages and hamlets on it, as well as streams and even ponds! Have either of you seen anything like it?"

"Most of the maps I've seen were strategic ones," Burik grunted. "They didn't have all this extra noise on them."

"I don't think I've ever seen a map of the Empire," Amarl said cheerfully. "I didn't know it was this big." He scanned the map, looking for his village. Tem was in the province of Aggath, he knew, which ran along the northeastern face of the Silverband Mountains. The village sat close to the border with Lepild, to the north, and lay in the mountains' shadows, but even with that knowledge, it took him a minute to locate the tiny dot buried in the north-central part of the map.

"Hey, there's Tem!" he said, pointing to the dot. He looked at Burik. "You're from Tennshin, right?"

"Yep. Right here." The boy pointed to a large dot on the end of a peninsula jutting out of the northeastern-most part of the continent. "Tennshin, capital of Tannshin province."

Amarl pointed to a black, irregular line in the ocean just northeast of the city. "What's that?"

"The Edge. It's a day's sail from Tennshin; less by steamboat or sahrship. It's the whole reason Tennshin was built."

"What do you mean?"

"Well, back before the Empire, when Tannshin was its own nation, we used to get incursions from the Edge fairly frequently, so the rulers of Tannshin – twin sisters named Tann and Tenn – decided to build some fortifications to stop them. Tann started building the Seawall, a stone wall running for marches along the coast, while Tenn constructed a fortified harbor and began building ships. They argued about whose idea was more effective, right up until the next incursion. Tenn's fleets sailed out and destroyed the invading spirits before they ever got near the Seawall, which was good since it wasn't even a quarter of the way finished. Tann never forgave her sister for being right and abandoned the northern coast, working to settle the rest of the province, while Tenn built up her port and expanded her fleet. The province ended up taking Tann's name, but the largest city – which eventually became its capital – took Tenn's."

He shrugged. "At least, that's the story. That's why the provincial capital has a different name from the province, unlike every other province in the Empire. I don't know if it's true or not, though."

"It is, Novice," a voice spoke, and the three students turned to see a tall man with light skin, slightly reddish hair, and a long chin step into the room and walk toward them. Unlike most of the novices' teachers, the man wore dark gray clothing that marked him as a malim, a full instructor.

"At least, at its face, it's basically true," the man added in a high, reedy voice. "The story leaves out a great deal, though – primarily because the main version handed down through generations came from Tenn's descendants, not Tann's. However, the truth is, the rivalry between the sisters began long before the building of Tennshin and the Seawall, and things weren't quite as simple as the story tells."

He gave them a smile as he spoke. "You see, the story leaves out the fact that Tann was the idealistic sister, while Tenn was ruthless and grasping. Tell me, Novice. Are there a great many stone quarries in Tannshin?"

Burik frowned. "No, sir, not really. Tannshin's a marshy sort of place, and the only mines there are the gold mines along the Goldspur Mountains and the salt mines on the northern coast."

"Precisely. The Goldspurs, while rich in ores, actually provide terrible building stone. It weathers poorly, and it fractures too easily. The province has to import all its stone from outside. So, if stone is scarce and expensive, how were the sisters able to build both a Seawall and a stone fortress at the same time?"

"I – I don't know, sir," Burik admitted.

"They couldn't, that's how. Tann controlled the southern part of the province, so she brought the stone into Tannshin for her wall – and Tenn stole it from her. She sent soldiers disguised as bandits to slaughter Tann's caravans and take the stone for herself. When her sister accused her, Tenn proclaimed her innocence and said that the bandits were dumping the stone in the marshes to firm them up and create farmland – which is a workable idea and how much of Tannshin's farmland was created – but Tann noticed that as her wall's construction ground to a halt, Tenn's fort mysteriously never ran out of stone.

"Plus, what the stories leave out is that when that first incursion happened, Tenn's fleet lost half its ships – and immediately after the incursion ended, a dozen ships with no markings raided the coast where the Seawall was being built, killing a hundred workers and stealing lumber and supplies. At that point, Tann had enough and declared her sister an outlaw in the province. So long as Tenn stayed in her city, though, Tann couldn't do much about it, and the sisters never spoke again until Tann's death – which happened quite mysteriously, as she went to sleep one night and simply never woke up."

"Tenn killed her own sister?" Meder gasped.

The man shrugged. "Most of those in power believed Tenn had her sister assassinated, yes, but they said nothing since they had no proof, and with Tann gone, Tenn quickly moved to take the reins of power. She named the province Tannshin in memory of her sister, but she moved the capital from the city of Torkas – now the town of Tork – up to Tennshin. She closed Torkas' port to foreign merchants, forcing them to travel all the way to Tennshin to trade, and she stripped the lands and titles from anyone who refused to acknowledge the new center of power."

"That's horrible," Meder said, shaking her head.

"Moderately, but it was effective. Under Tann's rule, Tannshin was a fairly backwater province. It had only one active gold mine, and otherwise its main export was peat harvested from the marshes, which makes excellent fertilizer. Tann knew about the additional veins of gold and the salt deposits in the north, but she also knew that the stone around the other veins was unstable, and working in a salt mine is a torment. She cared for her people, so she refused to take advantage of those resources. Tenn, on the other hand, happily dug two new shafts in the Goldspurs and opened the first salt mine, sending those who opposed her into that mine as her first workers. Hundreds died in the process, but in the end, those extra resources turned Tennshin from a fortress at the edge of the world into the fourth-largest port in the entire Empire."

"I never heard any of that, sir," Burik said dubiously.

"Of course not. As I said, Tenn took power quickly, and she made sure that the official accounts of the founding of Tennshin reflected what she wanted them to say. If Tann's private journals hadn't been spirited out of the province by her daughter – who fled with her family when she realized that Tenn would solidify her power quickly – we might never have known the truth of any of this."

He looked at the students. "A good lesson for you all. Some say that history is written by the victors, but that's not true. Official records are dictated by the survivors, it's true. History is written by scholars, though, and scholars never stop seeking the truth."

Meder frowned. "But sir, you said that all that came from Tann's journals. What if she was lying to make herself look good?"

"A good point, Novice, and one that has to be considered. The fact is, we'll never truly know what happened. Had Tann's family released those journals on their own, they would be highly suspect. However, Tann's journals were her private ones, discovered two centuries after her death almost by accident, and the family had forgotten that they existed. Of course, it's possible that the family held them for ten generations in the hope that they'd have a chance to 'accidentally' find them, but that stretches incredulity a bit, so most take them at face value." He smiled. "At least, until we have reason not to. Now, please, find your seats, so we can begin."

He stepped back, and Amarl noticed that while they spoke, Herel, Hadur, and Norag had come into the room and taken seats. He followed Meder and Burik to seats next to the other novices, and the malim moved to the central lectern with a smile.

"Good afternoon, students. My name is Malim Warahid, and I'm your history academics instructor. Unlike other subjects such as sahr and ithtu, you'll have multiple instructors in this class, covering myriad subjects."

He looked around the room. "Who in here attended the academy past their tenth year?" Meder, Herel, and Hadur all raised their hands. To Amarl's surprise, Norag didn't. "Then each of you took courses called 'history'. However, what you actually learned wasn't history; it was the Imperial record. Often, that bears as much resemblance to true history as the old myths of Ak-lahat and the early gods, most of which are nothing but legends passed orally through generations, corrupted with each retelling until they have little in common with the events that spawned them. The Imperial record has been altered, destroyed, embellished, and even made up out of whole cloth hundreds of times over the millennia of empire, sometimes maliciously, sometimes accidentally, sometimes even with benevolent purpose. However, what we're left with is often arbitrary, confusing, or even self-conflicting."

He smiled at them. "What you'll learn is also arbitrary and confusing, but at least it has the distinction of being as correct as possible, with what we know – and of admitting when we don't know what is and isn't true."

He walked around the lectern. "What you learned in the academy as 'history' was simply storytelling. You were told the Empire's official version of the past, and you were required to memorize and repeat it. However, that's not the point of this class. Here, we focus less on the stories and more on their meanings. There's something to be learned from every mistake and triumph of history, and if you learn it, you're less likely to repeat those mistakes and more likely to replicate those triumphs."

He stopped in front of Burik. "What did the story of Tann and Tenn teach you, Novice?"

Burik frowned. "I guess that just because everyone believes something doesn't make it so, sir."

Warahid nodded. "A valuable lesson. Never take someone's tale at face value. Always question everything." He turned to Meder. "And you, Novice?"

"What occurred to me is that history always has two sides, sir," she said slowly.

"Yes, that's true. There is no coin with only one side, and nothing in history happened in isolation. Remember that when you think of the Imperial record: you are hearing the Bureaucracy's side of the story, and nothing more." He glanced toward Amarl. "What do you think, Novice?"

Amarl grinned at the man. "Me, sir? I think that the point is that in real life, you can never tell who the bad guy really is."

Warahid chuckled openly at that. "An excellent lesson, Novice, and one that's hard for many students and even scholars to accept. It's true, though. Some of our greatest heroes were in fact great fools or failures, and some of our darkest villains were responsible for saving the Empire, although the records will never show that. As I said, the records reflect what the Empire wants them to reflect, nothing more."

He turned back to the rest of the class. "A case in point. What was the single most catastrophic and thus important event in the history of Umpratan? Raise hands." As Amarl expected, Herel, Meder, and Hadur all raised their hands at once, but to his surprise, so did Burik. The malim pointed at Hadur. "You."

"The Sundering, sir," the boy said promptly.

"Yes, the Sundering, when one world became many. And what caused the Sundering?"

"The spirits invading our world, sir. When they knew that victory was beyond them, they broke our world rather than leaving it to mortals."

"According to the Imperial record, you're correct. Officially, the spirits were driven from our world by the first ithtaru, but they gathered their power in a single, final blow and shattered the world, hurling the pieces out into the realm of the spirits and separating them with the Edge. The ithtaru joined their powers together and stopped the Sundering from breaking up Umpratan, driving the spirits from the world in the process. Is that more or less how you learned it?"

When all the novices nodded, even Amarl, Warahid gave them a thin smile.

"Unfortunately, that record is false, and the story you were told was mostly fiction. Three facts dispute this record. One: the record claims that spirits invaded our world and were driven out, but also that all mortals of that time were born into slavery to them. If the spirits invaded our world, how would mortals have been born into slavery? The war against the spirits wasn't a defense of our world, it was a rebellion of slaves, which means that either they weren't invaders, or they invaded long before the war and had conquered our world by then.

"Two: we have it on good authority that the Sundering was an accident, a mistake caused not by the spirits but by the leaders of the mortal armies."

Some of the others grumbled at this, but the malim seemed to ignore them.

"Three, and most important: there were no ithtaru before the Sundering. Of this, we have no doubt."

The man smiled at them again, and Amarl looked around to see the doubt the man spoke of plainly written across Herel, Hadur, and Meder's faces. Norag raised a hand, but the malim ignored it and pushed forward with his story.

"You might wonder how we could possibly know this. After all, the Sundering took place over three millennia ago, and much of the world's knowledge and science was lost in it. Fortunately, the Order has always kept its own records, ones separate from the Imperial record, and that record clearly states that the first appearance of ithtu happened *because* of the Sundering, not before it. Thus, it's clearly impossible for the Order to have driven out the spirits."

"But sir," Norag spoke up at last, apparently tired of waiting to be called on, "the Book of the One clearly states that Ak-lahat gave the naluni race the ability to use ithtu so they could free the world from the spirits' tyranny!" The boy's voice took on a sing-song quality that Amarl took to mean he was reciting something from memory. "'For so did Ak-lahat love those of his world that he gave them the powers of creation and destruction which were once his alone, so that they might cast off the chains of tyranny and live free once more. And he granted this power to the naluni, most beloved of his people, and they took the strength of their foes and turned it against them.' That's ithtu, isn't it?"

"Ah, a true believer, are you?" The malim smiled, and Norag bristled, opening his mouth as if to speak again, but the instructor held up a restraining hand. "I'm not mocking your beliefs, Novice. I respect the teachings of the One Church; most of them focus on love, fellowship, and acceptance, which puts them far ahead of the dogmas of most other religions.

"And you are correct that the Book of the One says that – at least, it does now. The original version did not. In the original texts, sahr was the gift Ak-lahat gave all the mortal races to combat the spirits, a power that mortals could use, and spirits could not. Those texts were altered later into their current form."

"But sir, the Book of the One is Ak-lahat's word on this world!"

"Perhaps, but over time, that word has been changed and corrupted by mortal hands." The instructor shook his head. "This isn't a lesson on comparative theology, Novice. I'll be happy to discuss it with you some other time and show you the oldest versions of the texts compiled into the Book of the One, so you can see how much they've changed over the millennia. For today, though, I'm going to ask that whether you believe what I say or not, you withhold your arguments so we can move on." Norag bit his lip but remained silent.

"But, sir, why would people change the record like that?" Meder asked dubiously. "Why not just tell what actually happened?"

"Because the truth isn't as pleasant as fiction, Novice," Warahid sighed. "The texts were changed once the Mistways were discovered, and contact with the other races was reestablished. The intent was to keep the citizens of the Empire from trying to leave it by suggesting that they were special, and that the Empire itself is something blessed by Ak-lahat."

"The truth, though – at least, as much of the truth as we can know – is that the naluni who would one day become the first ithtaru were bred, not gifted by the gods. Their bloodlines were selected for their natural strength with sahr, and each generation was magically purified to be a more perfect vessel for that power until at last, they created a group of haros of unbelievable power. They rose to become champions and generals of the armies of the mortal races, and with their power, they drove back the spirit hordes.

"And the truth – again, as close to it as we know – is that the spirits, believing their war lost, attempted to shatter the barriers between their realm and ours and bring the world of the spirits into ours. We don't know what that would have done to the sahr field, but since the spirit realm is the only place sahr doesn't exist as far as we know, it probably would have weakened it at least, while empowering the spirits.

"The progenitors of the ithtaru attempted to stop this ritual with brute force, and that attempt is what caused the Sundering. It also drastically weakened the sahr field and created the first ithtu, two things that most scholars believe are related, even if no one can prove it."

Amarl looked over at the others once more. Burik and Herel appeared to be curious about what the malim had to say, and Meder looked uncertain but thoughtful. Hadur, though, appeared dissatisfied with what he'd heard, and Norag's face was red with apparent anger.

"It's obvious why the Empire would blame the spirits for the Sundering and venerate the forebears of the Order, and honestly, it's probably for the best that the general populace believes that story," the instructor continued. "The Order often has to make hard decisions to protect the Empire, but the idea that it's existed since before the Sundering, defending this world, makes it easier for people to accept that what we do is in the service of the Empire. You, though, are all here to learn to serve the Empire, as that is the point of the Order. To truly do that, you have to know the Empire – including the parts it wishes you didn't. Only when you understand its deepest flaws and know its secrets can you truly know how best to preserve it.

"I'm sure some of you won't like hearing this, but the simple fact is that much of what you think you know is whitewashed, skewed, or blatantly false. Some of those falsehoods might seem harmless – like the fiction that the naluni are chosen by the high god – but lies are never harmless. That story has caused more harm over the millennia than plague and famine combined. Millions have lost their lives in wars over which families were the most favored, and non-naluni were almost completely purged from the Empire during Lasheshia's reign primarily because of this belief. That nearly invited a mass invasion through the Mistways from all the other races combined and only Lasheshia's dethronement and execution stopped millions more from dying in that invasion.

"That's why my job is to open your eyes to the truth. That awakening will be uncomfortable, even painful for some of you. You may even choose to disbelieve me, and that's fine – in fact, I encourage you to doubt me, and once you have access to the Citadel's libraries, to research these matters yourself. All I require is that you listen and think about my words. Remember, in this class, we care less about what happened and more about what we can learn from it, and how we can apply it to the Empire of today."

Amarl leaned back and refocused on the malim, suppressing a grin. A class that dealt with the evils of the Empire was a class he just might be interested in.

CHAPTER 17

The morning sun of Akio dawned in blessed silence. At least, it was nearly silent. A steady rumbling sound echoed from the bed across the room as Burik snored steadily, but after five days of sleeping in the same room as the boy, Amarl barely noticed that. What mattered was that no one came pounding on their door to announce classes. They didn't have to rush to dress or race through breakfast to meet Periteth for physical training. They didn't have to dread another day of mental exercises trying vainly to quicken their ithtu or painful equations to master sahr. It was Akio, the day dedicated to Ak-lahat, when everyone in the Empire was granted rest, and the new novices could sleep as long as they liked.

Amarl gloried in it. While he wasn't usually a late sleeper – he'd spent far too many nights in places he shouldn't have been, and he typically had to wake early to make sure he wasn't caught – that didn't mean he couldn't lie in bed and bask in the quiet and total lack of responsibilities. He lay there, beneath the thin blanket, his eyes closed, just enjoying the stillness while his mind wandered.

He didn't think he was lazy by nature – at least, no more so than the next person – but the past few days in Askula had been a whirlwind of activity. Amarl was used to waking up with the dawn and working through the day, but getting up to run and sweat for hours, sit cross-legged on a pillow imagining a burning candle until the image was seared into his mind, muddle through incomprehensible formulas, and stab people with wooden knives was a lot different than baking bread for Helowa – along with the other services he provided her.

Not that he hadn't benefitted from the training, of course. To his surprise, when he'd pulled up his skill screen after skill training the day before, he'd found it somewhat longer than it had been.

```
                    SKILLS REPORT
                   CURRENT SKILL LIST
ANATOMY                         1
ANIMAL CARE                     2
BAKING                          2
CARPENTRY                       1
CLIMBING                        3
DECEPTION                       6
DRIVING                         2
EMPATHY                         3
ENDURANCE                       1
ESCAPE                          3
FARMING                         2
HIDING                          4
INVESTIGATION                   3
KNIFE FIGHTING                  1
LOCKPICKING                     5
MEDITATION                      1
PERSUASION                      7
RIDING                          2
RUNNING                         1
SEDUCTION                       8
SLEIGHT OF HAND                 6
```

He'd gained a few new skills over the past six days: Anatomy, Endurance, Knife Fighting, Meditation, and Running. All were at level one, but the simple fact was, he'd gotten them in a matter of days – and the others hadn't. He'd asked his roommates about it indirectly, wondering aloud how long it would take them to get a skill in Knife Fighting after a particularly grueling training session, and neither of them had gotten the skill yet. He hadn't checked with the others, of course, but he was pretty sure if Burik, who seemed to excel at anything physical, and Meder, who Andra said had an affinity for knives, didn't get the skill, it wasn't happening for the others.

He could only guess that he was improving his skills faster because he'd already quickened his ithtu crystal, and once the others did the same, they'd catch up to him quickly enough. Because of that, he'd waited until the three of them were alone to mention his new skills; he assumed that Lilenpur's advice about not telling the other novices he was improving his Mind stat with ithtu also applied to keeping secret about his skill gains. He wasn't going to keep it from his friends, but he already had to deal with dislike from Herel and Hadur. He didn't need to add jealousy to that as well.

He pushed thoughts of ithtu and ithtaru from his mind. He didn't want to worry about those things, at least for one day. Akio was his day, and he would spend it how he liked. Well, probably not exactly how he liked. After all, Meder was the only girl he really knew in Askula, and he wasn't quite stupid enough to try seducing her. Not because he didn't think he could – although he wasn't sure about that, as the young woman was extremely smart and perceptive – but because he didn't want to deal with the fallout when things went wrong, as they inevitably would. Burik and Meder were the closest people he'd ever had to actual friends, and he didn't want to lose them for a tumble or two, no matter how attractive she was.

The other students were out of his reach, as well, at least for the time being. As a new novice, he was again the lowest of the low, and most of the first and second-years wouldn't give him the time of day. Literally, most of them wouldn't even tell him the time when he asked, so his attempts at flirtations hadn't gone well. In a few moons, once they'd gotten used to having him around – and the novelty of trying to bait and torment the newbies wore off – that might change, but for the time being, he had no realistic chance with any of them.

However, there was an entire village of regular, non-ithtaru within an easy walk of his dormitory. There had to be impressionable girls about his age or a bit older, or perhaps a lonely widow or two who might enjoy some company. He'd have to convince the others to check out the village that day, so he could scout out potential amorous adventures to be had. He settled back in the bed, his thoughts drifting to fantasies about the possibilities...

A pounding at the door jarred him from his daydreams. He felt a momentary disorientation, as if he'd suddenly gone back in time to the wrong day, or he'd only dreamed it was Akio.

"Novice Amarl! Get up! You've been summoned!"

Burik shot up in bed, his snoring cut off instantly, and Meder roused sleepily, her eyes blinking blearily.

"Wazzat?" she mumbled, still half-asleep. "It's Akio."

"Amarl?" Burik rumbled, rubbing his eyes. "Answer the door, so we can go back to sleep."

"Who the hell's waking us up on fucking Akio?" he asked waspishly, getting out of bed and stamping to the door. He threw it open and found one of the older first-year students, one who'd started a few moons before his group, standing outside, his fist raised to pound again.

"What in the spirits' hells is going on?" Amarl demanded.

"You Amarl?" the boy asked, seemingly unfazed by Amarl's irritation.

"Yeah, that's me. Why are you waking us up on Akio?"

"You've been summoned to the Citadel. Get dressed and be there in thirty minutes."

"Summoned by who? For what?"

"How the fuck should I know?" The boy glared at him, and Amarl finally noticed the irritation on his face as well. "I was told to pass the message, and I'm doing it. You don't like it, take it up with the malims. I'm sure they'd love to hear you bitch and whine."

Amarl stepped back inside and slammed the door, and the others jumped once more, staring at Amarl with a mixture of irritation and consternation.

"Sorry," he muttered, stomping back over to bed.

"What did you do?" Meder asked, rubbing her eyes blearily.

"Nothing!" He paused, thinking furiously, but his mind came up blank. "Nope, nothing. I can't think of a damn thing."

"Whatever it is, you'd better get going if you want to eat anything this morning," Burik rumbled, laying back down in bed and flinging an arm over his eyes.

"Don't forget to shower first," Meder advised, also laying back down. "You don't want to meet whoever it is smelling like you probably do right now."

He stared at them both as they closed their eyes and snuggled back into bed. "That's it? You're both just going back to sleep?"

"We weren't summoned," Burik pointed out.

"It's not like we can go with you," Meder added.

"You could get up with me for moral support."

"We could, but we won't." Burik opened one eye and peered at him. "If it makes you feel better, I'll be cheering for you the whole time I'm still awake – which should last about two minutes after you walk out that door."

"Amarl, there's no need for us to get up, get dressed, and go downstairs, then sit around and wait for you," Meder said reasonably. "I'm sure this has something to do with your having bonded a crystal already. Go meet them, get it over with, and come back here to tell us about it."

He grabbed some clothing, grumbling as he stalked out of the room and down the hall to the shower. He cleaned himself hastily, then grinned wickedly as he turned the water to cold and doused his dirty clothing in it. He walked back down the hall, carefully carrying the dripping bundle away from his body, and opened the door to their room.

"Catch!" he yelled, tossing half of the bundle at each of the prone forms huddled beneath their blankets. Meder screeched as a cold, wet shirt slapped across her face, and Burik swore as Amarl's pants splattered across his arm and chest.

"What the fuck, Amarl?" Meder demanded, flinging the shirt onto the floor, her face angry.

"Oops. Sorry about that." He grinned at them. "They really should teach us a throwing skill, don't you think?"

He slammed the door and heard the pants Burik had flung at him splat against the wood, then walked down the hall, whistling cheerfully. It sucked that he had to be up so early, but at least he got to spread his misery around a little. After all, what were friends for?

He wolfed down a breakfast in the mostly empty mess hall, then headed up to the Citadel. With it being Akio, most of the students still slept, and the road leading from the dormitory was oddly quiet and peaceful. He knew he should be walking swiftly to whatever meeting awaited him, but the silence and serenity soothed his irritation and beckoned him to take his time. Because of that, he arrived at the Citadel dangerously close to the thirty-minute time limit he'd been given.

He walked through the main gate and approached one of the students standing guard outside, noting that they hadn't gotten Akio off, either.

"Excuse me, I was told to report to the Citadel. Do you have any idea where I'm supposed to go?"

"You Amarl?" the woman, a fourth-year in yellow, asked gruffly.

"Yep, that's me."

"Wait here." She turned and walked into the Citadel. Several minutes later, she returned with a second-year boy with an irritated expression.

"Follow me," the newcomer said bluntly, gesturing peremptorily at the hizeen and turning his back to walk into the Citadel. Amarl hurriedly caught up to him, having to walk swiftly to match the boy's pace.

"Do you know what this is all about?" he asked curiously.

"No," the boy replied. "Just that I'm to escort you to the Rashiv's office."

"The Rashiv? Who's that?" Amarl thought he'd heard the name before, but he couldn't quite recall when or from who.

"The head of Askula." The boy made a face. "Well, technically that's the Zajinik, but she spends her time in the Crystal Palace, so the Rashiv is the one who's really in charge."

"Do most students visit the Rashiv?"

The boy gave him a look like Amarl had just farted. "What do you think?"

Amarl decided that probably meant no, and his heart started beating faster. Despite Meder's assurances that everything was fine, he felt fairly certain that everything was pretty damn far from fine. He doubted that the head of the entire school brought people to see them because things were "fine". His palms began to sweat as he imagined all the possible reasons he might have been summoned. Maybe his ridiculously high Soul stat wasn't an advantage, it was a problem. Maybe they took issue with the fact that he'd quickened a much more powerful and valuable crystal than he was supposed to. Perhaps the Rashiv just didn't want a hizeen in their school, or a member of the ishtai. Maybe they'd learned something about his parentage, and there was a reason his mother had fled to a tiny village like Tem to die. In his imaginings, each of these resulted in his messy and public execution, and Akio – the day when no one had classes and could therefore gather to witness it – would be the perfect day for something like that. Fear soured his stomach, and he felt his breakfast trying to rise back up on him.

His feet dragged as he followed the rest of the way in silence. His jaw clamped tightly shut, and his heart hammered in his chest as the boy led him through hallways, up a couple flights of stairs, and finally up a winding set of stairs that Amarl guessed meant they were in one of the towers. They reached a door at the top, one made entirely of steel instead of the usual banded wood and lacking any sort of handle or lock. Amarl fought the urge to scream and flee back down the stairs, to run to the Mistway leading into Askula and try to vanish into the Empire. Only the sure certainty that he'd never make it out of the Citadel kept his feet in place as the boy leading Amarl took a small mallet out of his pocket and banged on the door several times in a slow pattern.

"Yes?" The voice that spoke seemed to come from the air directly above the pair, and Amarl jumped at how loud and close it sounded. He looked wildly about, trying to find some sort of speaking tube that might be carrying the sound, but the walls were smooth, polished stone while the floor and ceiling were nearly seamless wooden planks.

"Novice Fando escorting Novice Amarl as ordered, sir."

"Excellent. Send him in." The door in front of them clicked, and the boy – apparently named Fando – pushed it open, looking back at Amarl.

"Don't just stand there. Go on in."

Amarl bit back a sarcastic reply fueled by his rising fear and stepped through the door, which shut behind him with a soft clang and a loud click. He jumped as he realized that he was trapped here; any thoughts of flight were effectively quashed. He swallowed hard and looked around, examining the place that he was sure was going to be the scene of his death – or at least, where he'd be sentenced to death.

The room he entered was open and hemispherical. A large window pierced one wall, and a glance outside revealed a view of Askula Village and the southern mountains beyond. A thick crimson carpet covered the floor, decorated with the same golden circle and blue sword symbol he'd seen on the banner flying above the castle. Bookshelves lined the walls, filled with books of all sizes and colors, and a stand in one corner held a suit of silver armor decorated with golden filigree, a long-handled axe, and a gleaming golden shield.

"Novice Amarl?"

Amarl tore his gaze away from his examination of the room and saw a middle-aged man dressed in black seated behind an ornate wooden desk. The man's face was lightly lined, and strands of gray shone at the temples of his dark hair. He radiated an aura of power that awed the hizeen, and he could only stare at the man, nodding dumbly as his brain scrambled to process the energy emanating from him.

"Good. You're on time. Take a seat over there until the Rashiv is ready for you." The man gestured behind Amarl, and he turned to see a row of plush seats in the middle of the room, chairs he'd overlooked in his earlier examination. He walked over to one and sat down heavily, his mind still struggling to process the man's overwhelming aura. The man looked down at his desk and lifted a metallic pen that began scratching at whatever paper rested beneath it.

Amarl forced himself to look away and glanced at the nearest bookshelf. His eyes swept past random books, not really noting their covers or titles but just taking in their shapes and colors. He examined the armor and weapons, noting the elaborate lines of filigree and small, sparkling gemstones decorating each of them. He didn't know much about the value of jewelry, but he did know that clarity, color, and sparkle were more valuable than size; judging from the sheer number of gems dotting those armaments, they were probably worth more than the entire village of Tem combined.

His fear grew as he sat, idly waiting for the decree that would end his life. He tasted bile in his throat, and sweat broke out on his forehead. His hands felt cold and clammy, and he fought to keep from panting as his heart raced in his chest.

"An unsettled mind is a powerless mind." Lilenpur had taught them that during her training, trying to help the others touch their crystals, and her words echoed in his chaotic thoughts. He bit back a laugh; if that were true, then he was even more powerless in this situation than he imagined. He took a deep, shuddering breath. That, at least, was something that he could try to control.

He forced his eyes closed and took another deep breath, counting slowly to three as he inhaled and releasing it slowly to the same count. He repeated the effort, focusing on his breathing, trying to calm his racing heart and still the screaming in his mind. He felt his body relax as he breathed. Clenched fists uncurled; his feet stopped tapping on the carpet; his jaw loosened. With his body more relaxed, he turned his focus inward to calm his whirling, chaotic thoughts.

He pictured a single candle with a flame dancing atop it. It took him several tries to envision the image correctly – his brain kept trying to scream at him to find a way out of his mess – but he stubbornly kept at it until the image was clear in his mental eye. As always, his flame burned the same silver as his tak; he didn't know why it felt more natural to him, but it did, and it didn't seem to hamper his efforts. He imagined the flame while focusing on his breathing, watching it dance and whirl in his mind. He could hear the hissing as it burned its wick, felt its soft warmth on his face, and smelled the odor of melting wax as the flame devoured the candle beneath it.

He focused his thoughts on that flame, pushing out everything else. Nothing mattered but the fire. He let its light fill his mind, its radiance burning away the dark thoughts swirling in his head. His fear still crouched at the edge of his mind, ugly and black, waiting to plunge its claws into him once more and sap what little strength he had from his body, but for the moment, his thoughts were calm and clear. He didn't do anything, just stared at the fire as it danced merrily. His body relaxed even further as the fear released its hold on him, and he gave himself to his meditation, ignoring the world outside.

"Novice Amarl!" The voice shattered his stillness, and the candle flame flickered and vanished as he jumped in his chair. He snapped his eyes open and saw the powerful man staring at him, his face unreadable. The man pointed to the flat wall of the room, to a door that Amarl swore hadn't been there when he first entered. "The Rashiv is ready for you."

Fear bubbled back up in Amarl as the reality of his situation crashed in on him once more, but he carefully controlled his breathing. He might die that day, but if he did, he wouldn't meet his end as a blubbering, spineless mess. He'd face it with as much courage as he could muster, which to be fair probably wasn't a lot. He rose to his feet and nodded at the man, then walked to the door and pushed it open.

The room beyond the wall was very similar to the one he'd just left. It was hemispherical in shape, with bookshelves lining most of the walls. A large window allowed light to pour into the room and displayed a majestic vista of the lake and northern mountains. The carpet beneath his feet matched the one from the previous room, as well. Arcane devices lay scattered around the room, their purposes utterly eluding him. The entire space had a slightly haphazard, disorganized feel to it. The books on the bookshelves lay in piles or leaned against one another rather than being stacked neatly upright. A faint haze of dust gleamed in the light streaming through the window, and dust covered many of the devices thickly.

"Come in, Novice." Amarl ceased his examination of the room and focused on a large desk spread out in front of him, its back to the window so it faced the door he'd just entered. A man sat at that desk, a man he recognized as the one who'd welcomed the new novices to Askula that first night. He was the oldest person Amarl had seen in Askula – not that he'd seen that many people, of course – with wisps of pure white hair on his head, a deeply wrinkled face, and a snow-white beard on his chin. He wore a long coat of richly decorated, multicolored silk covered with whorls of gold and silver thread and studded with twinkling gems.

Most of that barely registered in Amarl's senses. His mind reeled at the sheer sense of power radiating out from the man, an aura of majesty that terrified and humbled the boy. He felt like a chick faced with a deadly viper, stunned into helplessness and awed into paralysis. Whatever calm he'd gained from meditation fled instantly, leaving him gripped in sheer terror. He couldn't move, couldn't speak, could barely force himself to breathe in the face of the man's might.

The man glanced up at him, taking in his terrified face and stiff body, and sighed. "Yes, of course. You're a sensitive. I should have thought of that." A moment later, the sense of power pouring off the man eased, and Amarl took in a deep, shuddering breath as feeling returned to his body. His frozen thoughts kicked into motion once more, and he realized that this man could probably have killed him with just the sheer force of his presence. Part of him wanted to escape immediately, hurling himself out the window to his death if need be, but he realized that the man could freeze him back up in an instant if he wanted. Amarl was utterly powerless and helpless, and that knowledge sapped the strength from his legs. He grabbed a nearby chair to keep from collapsing and bit his lip to keep from sobbing in fear.

"You're afraid," the man observed calmly, his eyes narrowed shrewdly. "No, beyond afraid. Petrified." The man shook his head. "I suppose that's reasonable. An orphaned hizeen in a backward naluni village probably hasn't had the best experiences with authority, and your last moments with that Head Bureaucrat weren't exactly amicable, were they?"

The man looked away from Amarl and glanced at a strange device set up on his desk. The object looked like three flat boards stacked in a cube shape. The top board gleamed like cloudy, translucent glass or crystal; the middle one glittered an opaque golden color; the bottom one shone with the black of onyx. A metal pole pierced the center of each board, holding them a span above the one below. Every board had a grid of boxes etched into it, and small, flat stones decorated many of those boxes.

"Have you ever seen labah before?" the old man asked, not waiting for the boy to answer. "No, probably not. The people in your village were certainly far too busy with things like survival and family to bother with an esoteric game." The old man examined the boards for several long seconds, then looked back at Amarl.

"Labah is called the game of life. There's an old saying: 'Life is the game, and the game is life'." He gestured to the boards. "At its most basic, labah seems deceptively simple. The goal is to advance across the middle board, taking your opponent's pieces as you can to penetrate their sanctuary, the two rows closest to them. To do this, you must claim influence across the board, build up forces to support your attack, and strike swiftly and decisively when possible."

He shrugged. "And of course, it's far more complex than that." He touched each of the three boards in turn. "The middle board is Alar, the earthly layer. Above that is Saima, the spirit world above, the realm of the gods and their servants. Below is Jahin, the spirit world below, the realm of those beings we call spirits. Controlling Alar requires acquiring power and influence over both Saima and Jahin, as well. Each turn, you must choose to place a piece, take an opponent's piece, or evade an opponent's assault. Each has costs, risks, and consequences."

He turned away and looked at the boy. "Do you know why labah is called the game of life, Novice? Some people see it as a metaphor for politics, others warfare, but the fact is, labah can represent any aspect of life that you wish it to because it's a game of endless choices. There's no one way to win, and no two games are identical. Just as in life, each choice has a consequence, some good, some terrible, most meaningless in the grand scheme. Each of us can be seen as a stone placed on the board of life, and just as in life, our efforts are often aided or hindered by forces beyond our control, even beyond our understanding."

He chuckled and turned away from the game. "You're confused now, wondering why the most powerful person in Askula summoned you here to tell you about a game. Fear not; that's not the reason I called you on your day off. I was a student myself once, and I know how important Akio is. Step closer to me, Novice."

Amarl swallowed hard but took a step toward the man's desk, then another as the man beckoned him closer.

"Give me your hand."

Amarl hesitated before slowly reaching his hand out toward the Rashiv, his arm trembling in fear as he did. The Rashiv took Amarl's hand in a firm grip and closed his eyes. The boy felt a sudden warmth roll over him, sweeping through his body before sinking into the center of his chest. It wasn't painful or even uncomfortable, and a moment later, the energy left his chest and raced down his arm, returning to the Rashiv and leaving him feeling oddly empty.

"So, it's true," the old man sighed, releasing Amarl's hand. He leaned back in his chair. "And it was beneath our noses all this time." Amarl wanted to question the man, but he recalled the terrifying power the Rashiv displayed before and kept his mouth tightly shut.

"Sit, Novice." The old man waved a hand at a chair, and Amarl sank gratefully into it. "I called you here for the obvious reason: you have a natural gift with ithtu. I assume you've realized that by now, yes?" Amarl nodded.

"Good." The Rashiv twisted his chair, which spun easily, and looked out the window behind him. "What do you think the purpose of Askula is,

Novice?"

Amarl frowned. There was an obvious answer, which meant it had to be wrong, but it was the only one he could think of. "To train ithtaru, sir."

"Yes, but also no. We aren't simply training students here. We're forging weapons. Every ithtar is a powerful weapon to defend the Empire, each worth hundreds of soldiers, and that means that we have to craft each of them with both care and precision. A flaw in a weapon can cause it to shatter, after all, and a poor weapon can be more dangerous to its wielder than its foes."

He turned back to face the hizeen. "Every student here goes through the same training their first year. We hone their physical bodies with exercise, teach them to quicken their ithtu and use it correctly, and make sure they have a basic set of skills that will allow them to continue more advanced training. However, that training won't work for you, for obvious reasons. Can you see what they are?"

Amarl repressed a shrug and nodded. "I think so, sir. If I've already quickened ithtu, I don't need a lot of the ithtu training they have."

"It's not just that. Your ithtu will aid you in all your training, Novice. Your skills will grow faster; you'll gain strength and endurance more quickly; you'll learn things faster than you would have before. Lilenpur tells me that you've learned how to access your tak and assign it to improve your stats?"

"Yes, sir," he nodded.

"That's going to put you far ahead of your classmates in no time. What's your quickening rate?"

"Sir?"

"Look at your ithtu status and tell me what your quickening rate is."

Amarl pulled up the screen and glanced at it. "Five-four percent, sir."

The old man laughed wryly. "That number is the percent of a single unit of ithtu your body can process each day toward something like your tak, a stat, a skill, or an ability. It's typically around one percent for novices, and since it takes around six moons for most students to work out how to bind a stat to their tak to improve it, they usually only get one or two tenths of a point to a stat in the first year. You, on the other hand, can increase a stat by a tenth of a point every twenty days or so – at least until you get them to six. It slows down after that."

He leaned back once more. "You might wonder where the rest of your quickened crystal's energy goes. Well, it goes to awakening your ability. You've seen your ability in your status?" Amarl nodded. "We'll discuss it in a moment. For now, you need to know that while your Joining Crystal assesses your ability, it's sleeping within you. It takes an infusion of ithtu to awaken it, quickening it, and your body automatically routes any unused ithtu into doing just that. As you stand here, listening to me, your body is trickling energy into your ability in an attempt to rouse it.

"This is why first-year novices only receive the weakest of crystals, Novice. Can you see why?" The boy shook his head, and the old man smiled. "We teach them to quicken a crystal, then immediately have them focus that crystal's single unit of power into boosting their stats. That leaves very little energy to awaken their abilities. We don't want first-year students with active abilities; we don't know them yet, and they're typically too stressed and overwhelmed by the sudden changes in their life to use an ability wisely."

He leaned back in his chair, gazing up at the ceiling. "Now, to the crux of the matter. For nearly every student, I can tell with a simple Analyze what their ability is, and how close they are to quickening it. I know what abilities the other novices in your group possess, how they function, and even how they can improve and upgrade them if they wish. I can do that thanks to my experience at seeing abilities and using Analyze, and with time, you can gain that proficiency, as well. I've seen thousands of students quicken their abilities, and I haven't had difficulty determining those abilities for well over thirty years.

"So, you can imagine my surprise – no, my shock and excitement when I Analyzed you after your Joining and found a word I almost never see anymore: unknown." The old man chuckled. "My crystal couldn't process your ability, which means more than you might think. So, tell me, Novice: what is your ability called?"

Amarl blinked and had to pull up his screen to answer the man's question. He'd seen his ability's name before, of course, but he had no idea what it meant, and in the chaos of the past week, he'd been too busy to stop and consider it.

"It's – mez, sir," he said after a moment. "M-E-Z."

"Z?" the old man asked, his eyes widening. "Ah, that explains it." He leaned forward, his eyes twinkling. "And what tier is it?"

"F, sir."

"A base Tier F ability with the letter 'Z'," the Rashiv shook his head. "Astounding." He tapped his fingers on the desk thoughtfully. "Although with a Soul stat like yours, I would expect no less."

He leaned back once again. "We have certain expectations of students in their first year, Novice. We expect them to quicken at least one crystal, find their tak, and improve at least one stat one time. They should gain basic proficiency with sahr, meet certain physical standards, and have a weapons skill at level three. I understand that you already reached level one in some weapons' skills this week, is that correct?"

The boy blinked in surprised and slowly nodded. "Y-yes, sir." He couldn't understand how the man knew that; he hadn't told anyone but Meder and Burik, and neither of them had any reason to tell anyone else.

"That typically takes at least a moon, which means you're advancing around four times the normal speed. At that rate, your weapons skills will be at least level three within the year, if not four. A second-year with talent in a skill might reach level four by the end of their second year, meaning within six moons, you'll likely have skills on par with those students. Yet I can't put you in with the second-year students, either. Do you understand why?"

Amarl didn't really have to think about that. "I don't think I know enough to be with the second-years, sir."

"Good. You understand your limitations. Yes, you lack the basic knowledge that most second-years have about ithtu, the experience they have in combat, and the required physical fitness. As well, the rigorous training and discipline second-years have already undergone grants them a certain maturity that most first-years lack, although your friend Meder seems fairly close. The first-year training program won't challenge you; the second-year program will be too much. That leaves me with only one option.

"Starting tomorrow, instead of ithtu classes, you'll report to classroom 314 for private lessons with Awal Ranakar. You'll receive a crash course in the use of ithtu, as well as advanced weapons and combat training, and additional physical training. You'll continue your regular physical, weapons, and skill training as well, of course. Oh, and you'll receive additional math education, as Nadar Furmeras assures me that you are grievously lacking in this area."

Amarl swallowed in shock and dismay. "Sir? I'm doing normal physical training – plus even more? I can barely handle what I'm doing now!"

"According to Periteth, that won't be the case for long. He says he's already seen improvement in your physical abilities. Have you gained the

Endurance skill?"

Amarl hesitated, then nodded. "Yes, sir. Along with Anatomy, Knife Fighting, Meditation, and Running. All at level one."

The man shook his head. "And that's why you need this, Novice. Within a moon, you're going to find the morning physical training barely challenging, and within six, you won't even break a sweat doing it. Your ithtu is helping your body adapt at a remarkable rate, and the only way to challenge you without breaking the rest of your class is to do it personally."

The man leaned back in his chair and spun toward the window once more. "There will be no discussion of this matter, Novice. This is what you will be doing. Consider yourself fortunate: the awal is one of the most senior and respected instructors in Askula, and he specifically requested to assist with your training. With his assistance, we'll forge you into a very dangerous weapon indeed."

A sarcastic reply sprang to Amarl's lips, but he wisely swallowed it down. "Yes, sir."

"Good. You are dismissed; return to your barracks and enjoy the rest of your Akio. Many new novices find the village interesting. I highly suggest you avoid the Halit Sparring Grounds until you've reached at least level three in Unarmed Combat and Knife Fighting." He glanced at the boy with pursed lips. "Actually, in your case, it might be better to wait for level four. I have a feeling people will be lining up to test themselves against you." He waved his hand. "Go. I have much to do, and I've spent enough time with you already."

Amarl rose quickly to his feet and left the room, wanting to put as much distance between him and the Rashiv as possible. The door leading to the stairs clicked open for him, and he practically slammed it open, finding the boy who'd led him up waiting for him.

"That was fast," the boy said. "Where are you supposed to go?"

"B-back to my barracks," Amarl said, stammering slightly as his heart began to pound again, not with fear but with relief. The boy grunted and turned down the stairs, and Amarl followed silently along. As he walked, he couldn't help but consider the reply he'd almost made to the Rashiv.

He'd seen things forged in a smithy before – and the process always looked like a bad time for the thing being forged. He wasn't looking forward to feeling that old man's hammer blows fall on him.

CHAPTER 18

"Ooh, special training," Meder said admiringly as they walked down the paved road away from the Sabila dormitory. "I thought they might do something like that."

"You could have mentioned it to me," Amarl groused. "I nearly shit myself thinking that they were going to execute me for being a hizeen or something."

She stared at him, her eyes puzzled. "Why would they do that? If they wanted you dead, they could have just killed you during the Joining – or Danmila could have anytime she wanted. No one would have said a word about it, would they?"

"That's true." He grimaced. "I guess I wasn't thinking very clearly. I don't exactly have a great history with authority figures, as you can imagine."

"Considering your three best skills, I can see why." She laughed lightly and held her hand to her forehead. "Wait, I think my ability's quickening! I'm seeing visions of the past! Dozens of angry fathers and husbands, and Amarl lying his ass off to get away from them!"

He tried to stay grouchy, but he couldn't help but laugh at her dramatic statement. "There was some of that," he admitted. "Mostly, though, I tried to make sure no one who would get angry found out. It's easier to avoid trouble in the first place than to get away from it once it happens."

"My mother says something similar," Burik agreed. "It's better to dodge a strike than to block it."

"She sounds like a wise woman. At least, she must be if she agrees with me." Amarl grinned at him, and the bigger boy laughed openly.

"She'd say the same, except it would be you agreeing with her. I can hear her now, in fact. 'Burik, making friends with someone who agrees with me is the smartest thing you've ever done.'"

Amarl had returned without issue and found his friends up and waiting for him in their room. He'd entered carefully, wary of them taking revenge for his prank earlier, but it seemed that they'd had a chance to cool down while he was gone.

"Welcome back," Burik had said. "Good to see you're in one piece."

"We thought we'd head down to the village this morning," Meder added. "We heard in the mess hall that their shops are usually open on Akio to sell to the students."

"I'll walk with you, but I don't have any money," Amarl shrugged.

"You do now." Burik tossed a small leather bag at the boy, who caught it easily in the air. He opened it up and peered inside to see a jumble of coins.

"What's this?" he asked curiously.

"Those are called coins, Amarl," Meder answered. "You use them to purchase goods and services you want. Did your little village not have them?"

"I meant, where did they come from?" he asked, rolling his eyes. He hesitated, looking at the girl. "Wait, this isn't from you, is it? I don't really want charity, Meder."

"No, not from me or Burik. All our coins were taken from us by our escorts here."

"It's our stipend, Amarl," Burik said. "Apparently, all students get one each week."

"Nice," Amarl said, closing the bag. "Have you counted yours yet?"

"Two akats," Meder shrugged. "Or, more specifically, one akat, six akas, and thirty-six aks."

Amarl whistled. "That's quite a stipend."

"It's probably adequate." She shrugged. "Either way, we were thinking it might be fun to go spend some of it down in the village."

"Of course, before we can do that," Burik added, "there's something else we need to take care of."

Amarl didn't have time to so much as shout as Burik bounded off the bed and tackled him. He fought back, striking out with his new unarmed combat techniques, but the far more skilled Burik easily pinned him down and held him on the bed.

"This is for this morning," he said solemnly. "Meder, please do the honors."

"I hereby proclaim you to be Amarl, lord of the dirty laundry," the girl announced, scooping up a large, dripping pile of clothing and stepping over to him. "Receive your bounty from my hands!"

Amarl squawked as she dumped the entire load on his upturned face and pushed her hands down on it, grinding it against him. He tossed his head from side to side, trying to escape, but Burik held him firmly in place despite his best efforts.

"And what did we learn from all this, Amarl?" Meder asked sweetly, stepping back away from him as Burik let him up.

He sat up quickly, wiping his face and eyes, then grinned at the girl. "Well, I just learned the easiest way to get your wet panties in my mouth, Meder. Thanks for the lesson."

Burik burst out in laughter and fell back onto his bed, clutching his stomach. Meder turned beet red, but a moment later, she erupted with laughter as well, putting her hand on his head and shoving him backwards.

"You're utterly incorrigible. It's a good thing we're friends, or I'd have to hurt you."

As they'd left the dormitory a while later – after he'd changed into dry clothing – he couldn't help but smile as he thought of that moment. She'd called him her friend, and her words somehow made it true. They were his friends, the first he'd ever had, and he was far prouder of that than he was of his ridiculous special training – or anything he could remember doing in his life, really.

"Well, as it turned out, you weren't punished." Meder returned to their original line of thought and pulled his focus back to the present. "You were rewarded. That's good, right?"

"I don't know that I'd call it a reward. I'm getting extra physical training, and more math. How is that a good thing?"

"They must think you'll be able to handle it with your ithtu quickened," Burik shrugged. "Segeloh said that ithtu helps us learn skills faster; it must also help our bodies get into shape faster."

"In that case, I can't wait until I quicken my crystal," Meder groaned. "I wake up every morning feeling like I've been beaten by a stick."

"Me, too," Burik admitted. He looked at Amarl. "What about you?"

"No, not really," he frowned. "I mean, I feel like shit after physical training, but by the time we get to the next class, I'm usually fine."

"That must be the ithtu," Burik nodded solemnly. "It probably helps restore your body so you can recuperate faster. That's why they want to give you more training. Your body can handle it, and ours can't."

"If that's the case, I wonder if it works for other things, as well," Meder mused. "Do you think ithtu would help someone, say, learn another language? Or memorize mathematical equations?"

"I don't know, Meder. Those aren't physical things like exercising or gaining skills. It might only improve your body."

"Maybe, Burik, but we don't just have physical stats. We have mental ones, too, and it seems that if ithtu can improve your muscles, it can improve your brain, as well." She looked at Amarl. "What do you think?"

"I think you're probably right, Meder," he said after a moment's thought. "If you think about it, to improve our skills, ithtu can't just affect our bodies. Wouldn't it have to affect our minds, too, to help us remember and retain what we've learned?" He didn't mention that he knew that ithtu could improve their minds, and that his was busily working to bolster his Mind stat as they spoke. That, he decided, wasn't a lie. It was part of the stuff he couldn't tell them because it might interfere with quickening their ithtu.

"That's a good point," Burik nodded. "I hadn't thought of that, but being good with weapons isn't just about being able to swing them around more efficiently. It's also about knowing how to use that weapon and recognizing when to attack and when to defend. If our skills are going to improve rapidly, our brains have to be getting better at understanding combat, not just at how to stab with a knife."

"Oh, it'll be so exciting when we finally quicken our crystals," Meder sighed. Her face perked up. "I've always wanted to learn Shayeni, but I've never really been able to pick it up. I wonder if I'll be able to then?"

"Probably," Amarl shrugged. "And if not, it sounds like a skill that Segeloh could help you with."

"I'll have to ask him next skill class. You're still doing that with us, right?"

"Yep. I'm only missing ithtu and sahr class. I'm doing weapons, unarmed combat, and skill training with you."

"Enough about training," Burik cut in. "This is supposed to be our day off. Besides, we're almost there." He gestured, and Amarl looked up to see them passing the last of the outlying farms ringing Askula village. A wooden arch stretched over the road up ahead, looking like it had once been part of a gate or wall that no longer existed, and beyond it, the buildings of the village spread out before them.

"Amarl, you grew up in a village," Meder said. "Where should we go first?"

"I grew up in a different village, Meder," he chuckled. "They aren't all the same." He paused. "However, I'd like to check out their bakery. I like bakeries. And maybe we could visit that taproom. I barely remember what we drank that first day."

"I barely remember anything from that first night, thanks to you," she said, smacking his arm. "So, no trying to get me drunk again."

"Deal. Burik will have to do it."

"Oh no, not me," Burik laughed. "I'd like to see if they have a smithy, though."

"Oh?" Meder asked curiously. "Why?"

"We're all supposed to get a crafting skill at some point, right? I'm thinking blacksmithing might be a good one for me. I could forge my own weapons and armor that way."

"I totally forgot that we're supposed to get a crafting skill," Amarl sighed, rubbing his head. "One more thing to worry about."

"Do you think there might be an alchemist in the village?" Meder asked hopefully.

"There wasn't one in Tem. We had an herbalist, though. I'm not sure what the difference is."

"Alchemy infuses compounds with sahr to give them properties beyond what they would normally hold." Meder spoke almost formulaically, as if recalling something she'd memorized. "It uses exotic components, elaborate preparations, and precise recipes to channel sahr into a solid or liquid state."

"Meaning what?" Burik asked.

"A doctor – or an herbalist, Amarl, who is like a doctor that doesn't operate on you – can use natural remedies to help the body fight off diseases or infections or heal more efficiently, but your body's still doing all the work, and their cures can take days or weeks. An alchemist can create a compound that would have the same effect in hours or minutes by healing your body with sahr."

"I think Danmila gave me something like that," Amarl said thoughtfully.

"Really? Why?"

"Someone attacked me the night before Naming Day and left me for dead. She gave me a drink she said was sahr-infused, and it cleared my head right up."

"Why would someone attack you?" she asked, obviously taken aback before she frowned suspiciously. "Wait, was this one of those jealous husbands or angry fathers I was talking about earlier?"

"No, not exactly. He was an idiot who was manipulated into attacking me by a girl who blamed me for her father finding out she wasn't a virgin. The same idiot Danmila ended up killing, in fact."

"And why did she blame you for that?"

"Because he walked in on the two of us in his hayloft." Amarl shrugged. "She couldn't really hide the fact that she'd been around after that."

Burik laughed and shook his head. "No, I'll bet she couldn't. Why was she angry with you, though?"

"Who else could she be angry at? Herself?" He sighed. "I never thought she'd get Churl to attack me like that, though."

"Well, you must have been pretty badly hurt if Danmila used a healing elixir on you," Meder said with a small hint of disapproval in her voice. "They're very expensive."

"She said I might have died without it, so I guess I was." He stopped and looked around the village, quickly spotting a sign that read, "Bakery" above a door. "Over there. I'd like to stop there first if we could."

The bakery wasn't as good as Helowa's, in Amarl's opinion. That might have been because the baker was a middle-aged man with a noticeable paunch, of course, but the building didn't smell as good, and it didn't give him the feeling of nostalgia and comfort he'd been hoping for. Standing inside, smelling the ever-so-slightly different spices the baker used, instead of nostalgia, he simply felt more disconnected. It drove home that he was in a different place, far from his home. He hadn't really loved Tem or anyone within it, but he knew it, everyone knew him, and he was at least comfortable there.

He wondered if Helowa missed him or even thought of him. Did she mourn his leaving, or was she, like the rest of the village, simply glad that he was gone and no longer a burden for them? He hoped for the former, but the plain truth was probably that no one either in Umpratan or Askula would mourn him much if something happened to him. It was a depressing thought, and he walked along with his companions in silence as he nibbled at a flaky pastry he didn't really want anymore.

They wandered through the village, stopping in a few stores, but the sound of music and crowds drew them deeper into it. As they walked toward the middle of the village, the street widened into a ring that surrounded a tall fountain depicting a woman in armor with long hair. One of her hands gripped the hilt of a sword almost as tall as she was, while she held the other overhead, palm skyward with her fingers splayed. Water sprayed out of her palm into the air, and more shot up in several jets around her body, all of it splashing into a lower pool at the base of the fountain. Rows of flowers and small decorative bushes ringed the edge of the stone road, and beyond that, a grassy field lined with hedges held a dozen or so tables displaying various wares. Students roamed from table to table, while musicians performed off to the side as students occasionally tossed small coins into bowls set before them.

"What this?" Amarl asked, looking around in awe.

"A fair," Meder replied. "We have them all the time in Dairon. It's like a temporary market so crafters can show off their wares."

"At vastly inflated prices," Burik added.

"I've never seen anything like it," Amarl said. "This is as busy as a Naming Day celebration in Tem."

"Let's go take a look, then," Meder suggested.

Amarl goggled as they passed through the fair, overwhelmed by the sights, smells, and most of all, the clamor of noise.

"Cloth for your tailoring and sewing skills," one man called to the trio as they passed. "The best cloth gives you the best skill advancement!"

"Tired of training weapons? Get real ones here!"

"Herbs and alchemy components! Guaranteed fresh and potent!"

Burik's eyes lit up at the second vendor's call, while Meder's widened at the third. Amarl just tagged along behind the pair as they moved from stall to stall, examining the goods displayed before them. Neither of them bought anything, no matter how much they looked, and this seemed to be the norm for most students. The merchants took it in stride, never displaying anger or frustration when someone perused their goods without a purchase. Amarl took that to mean that Burik was right: the sellers had vastly inflated their prices for the day, so a few missed sales didn't matter as much to them. That usually happened in Tem whenever a prominent merchant came to town; goods that he would have paid an ak or two at most for suddenly cost akas, and beer and wine became too expensive for the villagers to afford. Of course, the merchants knew this, but they were willing to pay the premium if it kept the locals away from the brewery and vintner's and gave them some privacy.

As they walked, Amarl noticed the various looks sent his way. Most of the villagers eyed him with curiosity, and he guessed that they'd never seen a non-naluni before. The students ignored the group for the most part, but he saw a few appraising or even unfriendly glances. He wondered if the latter were because of his heritage, or because he'd already quickened a crystal. He could honestly see it going either way, and it really didn't matter.

They wandered around the fair for an hour or so, looking a lot but buying nothing. Meder looked longingly at some of the clothing, but there wasn't much point to buying any since all they could wear were their uniforms six days a week. Amarl noticed that most of the students weren't in uniform in the village, which meant on Akio, they could probably wear whatever they wanted, but he didn't see the use in wasting coins for clothing when what he had was perfectly serviceable. Burik also lingered near several of the weapons displays but again didn't buy anything; they wouldn't be allowed to use anything but training weapons, after all.

The blacksmith's shop was like the smithy in Tem: hot, loud, and filled with the smells of soot, burning coal, hot metal, and heated oil. A young man out in front, likely one of the smith's children who wasn't old enough to be an apprentice, tried to sell them custom weapons but politely refused to let Burik past the front room of the shop to watch the smith work, no matter how he asked or how much money he offered. At last, Burik gave up, and the three trudged over to the alehouse.

The tavern was close to full, not only with students but also with people Amarl guessed to be instructors at the academy, although none of them wore their uniforms. The three found a table in the back, pressed up into a corner and barely giving them room to sit, and they squeezed onto the high stools. A few minutes later, a harried-looking man hurried up to their table.

"Welcome to Sasofit's Alehouse," he said, speaking rapidly. "What can I get you?"

"Beer for me," Burik said.

"Wine, please," Meder smiled at the man.

"Make that two beers," Amarl added. The man nodded and scampered off, and the hizeen looked around at the room. "Busy."

"Everyone wants to drink on their day off," Burik shrugged. "Soldiers always do, at least."

"There are more instructors here than I would have expected," Meder noted. "Look, there's Periteth over there – and Segeloh. I would have thought they'd stay at the school."

"Really? I'd think that after a week of teaching us, they'd need the drinks even more than we do," Amarl grinned. Burik barked a laugh, and Meder smiled wanly.

"You might be right in that." Her eyes continued to scan the room, and she pointed across the tavern. "Look, there's Herel, Hadur, and Norag. Looks like they beat us here."

Amarl looked where she pointed and saw the three students seated at a table not far from the center of the room. As crowded as the place was, he guessed that meant that either they'd gotten really lucky, or they'd been in the alehouse for some time. He watched Herel hand a couple coins to a frazzled-looking woman carrying a tray of drinks, and he frowned as something occurred to him.

"Hey, how do you think Herel arranged for those rides to the training centers?" he asked quietly.

"He paid for them," Burik shrugged. "He told us, remember?"

"With what, though? Danmila took all my coins that first day – and didn't you say that your escorts did the same to you?"

Meder frowned. "That's a good point. We didn't get our stipend until today, so where did he get the money to pay the farmer?"

"Maybe he sold that rapier of his," Burik suggested.

"I don't think so. He's awfully proud of it." Herel shook his head. "Maybe he managed to conceal some money from Danmila, but that seems even less likely. They were traveling together for weeks; I can't believe she wouldn't have caught him."

"Does it matter?"

Amarl shrugged. "Maybe. If there's a way to make extra coins, it might be useful."

"You've barely touched the coins you have," Meder laughed. "Why do you want more?"

"You can never have too much money, Meder. If I'd had what they gave us as a stipend when I was back in Tem..." He shook his head. "Let's just say that a lot of things would have been a lot easier."

"Was your life there really that bad?" she asked curiously.

"Bad? No, not really. I mean, I usually earned enough to eat each day, and I could generally find a place to sleep. It's more that the village didn't really want me there, so I was always kind of a burden to them." He stopped speaking as their drinks arrived and fished a small coin from his pocket, handing it to the server.

"Why didn't they want you there? Weren't you born there?"

He shrugged and took a sip of his beer. "Sure, but my mother wasn't from there, and as an orphan, I was a member of the ishtai, so my being there brought down the status of the entire village."

"Plus, you were seducing their daughters," Burik added with a grin. "Don't forget that part."

"Also true."

Meder shook her head. "But that wasn't your fault – the being an orphan part, I mean."

"Why would that matter?"

"Well – it isn't exactly fair, is it?"

Amarl couldn't help but chuckle. "That's the second time you've talked about things being unfair. I don't know why you'd expect them to be anything else. I've never seen anything in life that was fair." He looked at her seriously. "You were born into the zahai caste. Because of that, you got all sorts of opportunities that Burik and I never did. Is that fair?"

"Well, no, but..."

He shifted his gaze to Burik. "Your mother was part of the shalai caste, the high officers and bureaucrats, right?" The larger boy nodded. "That gave you access to all sorts of military training that others who became soldiers never got. Is that fair?"

"Nope," he shook his head. "And my mother never let me forget it. 'Never discard a gifted weapon', she always said."

"The woman has a saying for everything." Amarl grinned. "Hells, I can't even complain about unfairness. I'm here with you both in Askula. I've already quickened an ithtu, and now I'm getting special lessons, all because of my heritage, not because I earned any of it. How is that fair?"

"Point taken," she sighed, sipping her wine. "You're right. Things are very rarely fair, Amarl." She shook her head. "You know, you haven't said anything about what sort of crafting you might pursue."

He shrugged, glad for the subject change. "That's because unlike the two of you, I haven't given it any thought."

"Nothing interests you?"

"I didn't say that. I said I haven't thought about it, mostly because I don't really have any idea what the choices are."

"You had to have had crafters in your village," Burik pointed out. "Did any of their crafts interest you?"

"Not really. For a while, I thought I'd try carpentry, but the splinters weren't for me. Ever got one of those under a fingernail?" He shuddered.

"What about baking?" Meder asked. "You seem to like that."

"I've seen it done enough to know it's not what I want to do for the next decade or so," he laughed, taking another swallow of beer. "I like the results, but not the process."

"You should really start thinking about it. They said we'll start our crafting skills in the second year, and while that seems like a long way away, it seems like we're going to be very busy this entire year. You don't want to lose time deciding what to do."

"I don't know. I have a feeling that we're all going to be learning more than one crafting skill – that we'll be learning a lot of different skills, in fact, not just ones we'd like. I think we're going to get a chance to try all sorts of things."

"Why do you think that?" Burik asked.

"Because of what Segeloh said about ithtu helping our skills grow." He shrugged. "Think about it. How high a level do you really have to be in a skill to be competent at it? Two? Three? Burik, how would you compare to most soldiers with your weapons?"

"I'm much better than the average soldier with a firearm or halberd. Not as good as elite ones, though."

"So, they're probably the equivalent of level one or two, and Segeloh said you can easily reach that in six moons with the help of ithtu. If that's the case, then we could become at least competent at a dozen skills while we're here and focus on a few that we like once we're on our own."

"That's probably reasonable," Meder agreed. "Give us a broad base to build on to start, then let us narrow our focus later."

"Enough talk about the school," Burik declared. "Meder, tell us what it was like growing up as a zahai."

She laughed. "I don't know what to tell you, Burik. I don't really have anything else to compare it to."

"Tell us about Dairon, then," Amarl said. "I've never been to one of the big cities."

"Oh. Yes, I can do that. Well, Dairon's on the Horkez Strait, the closest port to the Nicelian Protectorate, so all sorts of people pass through it..."

They spent the next couple hours chatting companionably, sharing stories about their childhoods. At last, they rose from their seats, slightly unsteady from the alcohol but far from drunk. None of them wanted to start another week of classes hungover, after all. They wove through the tables and stepped outside, into the afternoon sunlight. They made it all of three steps before a pair of students appeared from the alley beside the tavern and stood in front of the trio, blocking their path.

"Excuse us," Meder said politely, trying to step around the pair, but one, a tall boy with short-cut hair and hard eyes, held a hand out, blocking her passage.

"Look at this, Ronia," the boy growled. "New meat."

Ronia, a muscled girl with attractive features but a bleak expression, stared at the group with her arms folded across her chest. "Who said you could drink in our alehouse, new meat?" she demanded in a voice that jarred Amarl, being both melodic and cold at the same time.

Meder sighed. "We don't want any trouble," she said tiredly. "We're just heading back to our dormitory..."

"Not before you pay what you owe us," the boy shook his head.

"Owe you?"

"Yes. You drank beer that was meant for us and took up space your betters could have used." Ronia leaned toward the group. "Hells, I see you breathing my air right now. You're going to have to pay for that."

"We aren't paying anything," Burik rumbled, his voice flat and his body tense. "Step out of our way, now."

"Or what, meat?" the other boy demanded, taking a step closer to Burik, putting his face practically in the taller but younger boy's. "What are you going to do?"

"Let it go, Burik," Amarl said, grabbing the larger boy's arm and pulling him to the side. "They're not worth it."

"What did you say, meat?" Ronia snapped, her voice rising in volume.

"I said, you're not worth it." Amarl spoke with exaggerated volume, mouthing each word dramatically. "I'm sorry, do you have trouble hearing?"

"Who the fuck do you think you are, talking to us like that?" the older boy roared, stepping up into Amarl's face.

"Gah," Amarl said, waving a hand before his nose. "Seriously, have you ever brushed your teeth? It smells like you sucked off a dead horse." The boy's eyes bulged, but Amarl just grinned at him. "What? Are you going to yell at me some more? That's all you can do, yell and threaten, isn't it? You're not allowed to actually touch us unless we do something first – and none of us are stupid enough to do that."

He looked back at the others, who stared at him in shock. "Come on, let's leave these two to finish doing whatever they were to that horse. I'm sure Ronia needs it since there's no way his little cock will keep her happy…"

Pain flared in Amarl's skull as something slammed into the side of his head. The world spun crazily, and he felt himself crash into something solid and unyielding. His head cracked against whatever it was, and stars exploded before his eyes. His legs wobbled beneath him, and he nearly fell on his ass as everything suddenly grew quiet and distant. The older boy's face blurred in his vision, and something crashed into his stomach. His stomach lurched as he vomited, spraying beer and pastry out of his mouth. Something else cracked against his head, and he found himself unable to breathe as bands wrapped around his throat, choking off his air. Dimly, he heard screaming and saw someone yanking at the older boy, but his blood pounded in his ears too loudly for him to understand what was happening. The boy's beet-red face glared at him, its expression one of pure fury and loathing, and Amarl struggled to suck in a breath. Coldness seeped into his fingers and toes, and a dark circle appeared around his vision, slowly shrinking as the light faded from his eyes. He tried to struggle, to kick and punch, to tear the boy off him, but his body moved feebly, barely able to respond. Fear exploded in his mind as he realized that the boy was going to choke him to death, and there was nothing he could do about it.

And deep in the center of his chest, just above his spinning tak, something stirred to life.

Power flared from his tak, roaring into his body, and Amarl kicked out once more. The energy exploded down his leg and slammed into the boy with a boom that hurt Amarl's ears, and the beet-red face vanished from his vision. He greedily sucked in a breath as the pressure blocking his throat disappeared, then fell to his knees as pain flared in his leg. The older boy seemed to be floating gently through the air, his face shocked and blood streaming from his open mouth as he drifted slowly backwards. A figure with light-brown hair appeared before Amarl, shouting something he couldn't make out, and he struggled to focus. As he did, though, the power within him winked out, and his strength fled in an instant, along with what was left of his awareness.

CHAPTER 19

Amarl's eyes snapped open, and he winced as light stabbed into them. He shut them tightly, pressing the heels of his hands against them as light flashed in his vision. He groaned as awareness returned to him, bringing pain with it. His head pounded, his body ached, one foot throbbed, and his throat burned with thirst. He groaned and kept his hands pressed over his eyes to keep the stabbing pain out of them.

"He's awake," a familiar voice spoke, and he slowly lifted his hands away and slid his lids open to a squint. The light stabbed again, and for a moment he wondered if he'd damaged his brain a second time, but his eyes quickly adjusted to the glare, and he opened them fully as the pain and sensitivity fled. He looked up to see Burik standing over him, a look of obvious relief on his face.

"Step aside, Novice." Burik vanished, and a middle-aged man in gray clothing that nearly matched Amarl's skin suddenly appeared in his place. The man leaned over Amarl, peering into the boy's eyes, then straightened.

"What's your name, boy?" the man asked.

"W-water, please," Amarl croaked, gesturing to his throat.

"Answer my questions, first. I don't need you puking all over me if you're not fully healed. Your name?"

"A-Amarl."

"Good. Where are you?"

"As..." He took a breath, swallowing to try and moisten his throat. "Askula."

"Do you remember what happened to you?"

"A-asshole. Attacked me."

The man smiled thinly. "Close enough." He produced a mug and held it toward Amarl, then pulled it back as the boy reached greedily for it. "Drink slowly at first. You've had a major healing, and you're badly dehydrated. If you drink it too fast, it'll come right back up."

Amarl nodded, wincing as the motion made his head pound, and the man handed the mug to him. Amarl forced himself to take several small sips of the water, sighing as the liquid coated his throat.

"Thank you," he said after several seconds, handing the mug back. "That feels better."

"Keep drinking," the man shook his head. "You'll need all that and more. You lost a lot of blood, and we had to drain your tissues to replace it."

Amarl took the mug back and kept sipping it, sitting up and finding himself on a simple bed with no sheets or blankets. Burik stood off to one side, his face worried and his uniform soaked in drying blood. A row of simple cots like the one on which he sat spread out to either side of him, several of them occupied by obviously injured students. One of them he recognized as the boy who'd attacked him.

"Where am I?" he croaked.

"The infirmary, of course. Your friend there carried you here – that's your blood all over him." Amarl winced at the amount of crimson staining the larger boy's shirt.

"You're honestly lucky to be alive," the man continued. "You had two concussions, fractures of the skull, shoulder, and ankle, and significant internal bleeding. If Andra hadn't been there, you might not have made it."

"Andra?"

"Yeah," Burik nodded. "She got there just as you…" He paused. "Did whatever you did to the guy who attacked you. Somehow, she slowed you and him down – and that girl, Ronia, who tried to run away." He shook his head, and his face grew awed. "She didn't get far before Andra grabbed her and slammed her into a wall without even trying."

"She has the ability to slow the passage of time for individuals around her," the man spoke nonchalantly. "Quite the power, actually, and I've used her several times to stabilize critically wounded patients to give me a chance to heal them before they die."

Amarl looked over at his attacker, who still slept on his cot several beds down. "Why is he here?"

"You kind of caved his chest in, Amarl," Burik chuckled. "Not that he didn't have it coming…"

"I don't know what's funny about a fractured sternum, six broken ribs, a bruised heart, and a punctured lung," the ithtar who was obviously some sort of healer said crisply. "Dalat might also have died on the trip here if not for Andra." The man straightened, his gaze cold as he glared at Burik. "Ithtaru aren't so common that we can afford to lose any of them, especially not over foolishness."

"Yes, sir," Burik said solemnly. "I understand."

"Good. Now..." The man broke off as a door on the far wall opened, and several figures walked into the room. Meder walked at the back, with Ronia beside her looking glum and Andra in front of both of them. The three students followed behind a familiar figure, the short and round faced Awal Tekasoka, whose eyes glittered fiercely and whose jaw was set in displeasure. Amarl swallowed hard as the woman approached; she'd warned them not to attract her attention, and he hadn't even made it a week without doing so. Whatever was about to happen, it couldn't be good.

"Awal," the healer said, bowing his head toward the black-garbed woman as she neared Amarl's bed.

"Midoral. I see that Novice Amarl is awake. Is he coherent enough to speak?"

"Yes, Awal, although Student Dalat is still resting."

"Can he be safely awakened? This is a serious matter, and it must be dealt with immediately."

"Yes, Awal Tekasoka. Give me a moment." The ithtar hurried over to the sleeping boy's bed and laid a hand on the student's forehead. A moment later, Dalat gasped, and his eyes flickered open. "Give him a minute to recover and get some water in him, and he'll be able to speak."

Amarl ignored the boy, watching the woman. Her entire body radiated power, and he could practically feel her anger. He swallowed hard; he really didn't want to face the woman, but he didn't seem to have any other choice. His instinct urged him to jump out of bed and flee, but he knew that was stupid, and he'd been stupid enough for one day already. There was nowhere he could run, no place he could hide. All he could do was be honest and accept the consequences of the choices he'd made.

Dalat coughed, and Midoral patted him on the back, then rose and looked back at the others. "He's awake and cognizant, Awal. His voice may be weak from dehydration, but he can speak."

"Good. He can finish healing later – assuming that there is a later for either of these two." Dalat's eyes widened, and Amarl's heart lurched in his chest, but before he could speak or react, she stood erect and stared at them with a cold expression.

"Student Dalat, Novice Amarl. You have both been accused of brawling in the village of Askula, an area where fighting is forbidden. You have been accused of breaking the peace and damaging property."

Amarl frowned; he wasn't sure when they damaged property unless his skull damaged a building when Dalat smashed him into it. Blaming him for that seemed patently absurd.

"Student Dalat, you are additionally accused of improper use of ithtu against an unquickened student. All of these charges have very serious consequences, up to and including expulsion from Askula. Do you understand this?"

Dalat nodded slowly, and Amarl did the same.

"Good. I've spoken to the witnesses behind me, and I'll give each of you a chance to tell me your version of events. You will speak the truth, and nothing else." Her last sentence seemed to echo in Amarl's skull, sinking into his thoughts and filling his mind. The phrase, "speak the truth…" rang in his ears for long moments. At last, it fell quiet, but he felt the power of it resting in his mind, hovering just below his consciousness.

"Student Dalat, relate what happened."

The boy's eyes went blank, and when he spoke, it was in a monotonous, emotionless voice. "Ronia and I went to Sasofit's, but they were full, and we were told to come back later. As we left, Ronia saw two groups of novices sitting at tables drinking, and she asked why they could have a table when we couldn't. I agreed it was wrong, and we decided to wait for whichever group left first."

"And why were you waiting for them?"

"We were going to demand money from them that we could use to buy our drinks for the day. If they wouldn't pay, we would antagonize them until they attacked us. Everyone knows that the tall novice, the noble boy, and the merchant boy are touchy and quick to fight, so we thought if we couldn't get their money, at least we could have some fun with them."

The woman nodded, seemingly unsurprised by the news. "Continue. What happened when they came out?"

"We stopped them like we planned, and we demanded their money. They refused, and I tried to provoke the tall novice. The hizeen stopped him from responding, then began insulting us. I threatened him, but when he suggested that Ronia had relations with a horse, I lost my temper. I used my ability without thinking and attacked him. Then, someone hit me with an ability, and I blacked out and woke up here."

"Very well." She turned away from him, and Dalat's eyes suddenly cleared. He looked stricken and panicked for a moment, then his shoulders slumped dejectedly as he realized what he'd confessed to.

"Novice. Tell me your version of what happened," Tekasoka said. Suddenly, the sound of her earlier words rose up in his mind, echoing in his thoughts. "Speak the truth!" rang in his ears, washing out everything else, hammering at his brain and demanding that he submit. He felt his will draining away until nothing existed except his need to follow the awal's command, to speak the truth exactly as he knew it. He ached to do as she asked; he burned to comply with her wishes. His lips parted, and he took a deep breath.

As he did, though, something stirred in his chest, just below his heart, and the song of his ithtu crystal rose above Tekasoka's all-encompassing voice, drowning it out. Pain bloomed in his skull as her command lashed at him, compelling him to obey, but a surge of anger flared in his thoughts. How dare she try to force him to follow her will? How dare she try to control him like a puppet? His anger burned hotter, and the song of his crystal soared, shattering the command battering at his mind. He felt it break, felt its power drain from his body. He looked up at the awal, and while her face remained impassive, her eyes showed that she knew what he'd done. He saw the confusion and concern in them, but mingled with that was fascination and even excitement.

He looked away as the song of his ithtu faded, leaving him strangely tired once more. He swallowed hard and cleared his throat, taking another drink. "Dalat and Ronia accosted us as we left the alehouse, ma'am. They told us we had to pay them for breathing or something stupid like that. It was obvious they were trying to antagonize us. We refused to pay and tried to leave, and Dalat tried to provoke my friend Burik into hitting him. I insulted him and Ronia instead, and when I said he had a tiny cock and Ronia had sex with horses, he attacked me. He slammed me into a wall hard enough that I almost passed out, and then he started choking me. I kicked him away from me, and for some reason, it sent him flying. That's when I passed out, then I woke up here."

She nodded. "Were you attempting to provoke him to attack you, Novice? Perhaps to get him in trouble?"

"No, ma'am. I thought he wouldn't attack me since he's not supposed to, and I was hoping that if I embarrassed him enough, he'd leave me alone in the future rather than trade insults again." He grimaced. "Saying that out loud, it sounds totally ridiculous since making him angry like that would probably just make him come after me more, wouldn't it? Sometimes my mouth runs away with me and says stupid things."

"Apparently," she nodded. "Novice Amarl, you were foolish to provoke a full student, and you nearly died doing so. As you said, there was nothing Student Dalat could have done but continued insulting you had you simply remained silent and walked away. Are you such a childish fool that you can't handle idiotic provocations? So immature that you have no ability to walk away from a confrontation that you can't possibly win? Or are you simply so arrogant that you think yourself immune to such consequences?"

"Probably all three, ma'am," he replied, hanging his head as he realized that he'd been all of those things.

"At least you recognize it. However, knowing your flaws isn't enough. You have to work to fix them. To help with your arrogance, you will spend the next week in the laundry room for the two hours before dawn. You will wash any clothing given to you without complaint, no matter what it is or who owns it, and you will thank the person for giving it to you – and the entire school will know this. Maybe being up to your armpits in other people's soiled underwear will teach you some humility."

Amarl winced and sighed. That was a nasty punishment, as he could imagine the vile garments the older students would be bringing him to clean. And he would have to thank them for doing it! The awal was right; he deeply regretted getting her attention.

As he contemplated his next week, she turned to Dalat. "Student Dalat, whatever the reason, you attacked an unquickened novice with an ability, and that attack almost resulted in two deaths. An ithtar holds the lives of millions in their hands, and losing control is beyond unacceptable. By all rights, I should cast you from Risha school and expel you from the academy." The boy's face went white, and he trembled violently. Amarl had a feeling if Midoral hadn't been beside him to hold him up, Dalat might have collapsed back onto the bed.

"And had you attacked the novice purely because he insulted your genitalia, that is precisely what would be happening now. However, since you acted in defense of another, I'm willing to merely punish you, instead." She looked at the healer. "Midoral, how much ithtu did you expend repairing these fools?"

"Twelve units, Awal."

"And Student Andra, how much did you expend keeping them alive?"

"Ten units, ma'am."

"Twenty-two units of ithtu, wasted." The woman made a disgusted face. "Student Dalat, you will repay both Midoral and Student Andra with the fruits of your hunts until they've regained what they lost. You will then pay them that amount again as a way of thanking them for saving your life.

"However, that doesn't address the fact that when you got angry, you lost control of yourself and used your ability. What is your current duty in the village?"

"The stables, ma'am. I'm helping to care for the horses."

"No longer. Effective immediately, you are assigned to the pig farm, where you will be given the most difficult and frustrating duties possible, and you'll do them without using your ability. Wrangling angry pigs while covered with mud might just teach you how to cool that temper." She hesitated. "And because the entire school needs to know how inexcusable your behavior was, you will receive twenty lashes at the Deep tomorrow morning before the whole school."

Dalat's face paled at that, but he ducked his head in submission. "Yes, Awal."

"Good. This matter is concluded." She looked at the other students gathered around. "You both handled yourselves as well as possible under the circumstances, especially you, Novice Meder, for remaining calm during this situation and seeking my assistance, and you, Student Andra, for intervening and keeping these two idiots alive. Continue to do so."

"Yes, ma'am," Meder nodded, and Burik echoed her response.

"Now, I will require a minute alone with Novice Amarl. Midoral, please assist Student Dalat and the others into a nearby room."

The healer looked surprised at that. "Awal, the student is still recovering from his injury..."

"I understand that, Midoral, but this is a matter of some importance. Are the student's bones fully healed?"

"Yes, Awal, but..."

"Is he bleeding still? Is there, in fact, anything wrong with him besides dehydration?"

"No, Awal, but…"

"Then he can drink in the next room as easily as here. Thank you."

Midoral bit his lip, then nodded and beckoned Burik to help him lift Dalat to a standing position. "All of you, follow me."

As the group disappeared through another door, Tekasoka sighed. "Midoral will hold that against me for some time, I'm afraid. I'll have to buy him a night of drinks at Sasofit's to make up for it." She moved over to Amarl's bed and shooed her hand at him. "Move over, boy. I'm too old to stand around staring down at you." Amarl quickly scooted aside, and she sat on the bed, sighing a second time.

"You are very dangerous, Novice," she said after a moment.

"Me, ma'am?" he asked.

"Yes, you. Very, very dangerous." She looked at him curiously. "What do you think you did today?"

"I – I honestly don't know, ma'am."

"I didn't think so. Let me explain, then. When you attacked Student Dalat…"

"I was just defending myself, ma'am," he said quickly, then gulped as she stared icily at him.

"I trust that you won't interrupt me again? Good. As I said, when you *attacked* Student Dalat, which was what that was, even if it was an attack performed in self-defense, you used the equivalent of a Tier B ability. Only something that strong would have caved his chest in like that, as evidenced by the fact that Student Dalat's Tier A strength ability merely gave you a concussion and skull fracture and didn't implode your skull like a piece of fruit. How much energy did you use doing that?"

"I don't know, ma'am."

She rolled her eyes. "You have an ithtu screen, Novice. Use it. What is your tak right now?"

"Umm…one-seven out of five, ma'am."

She nodded and gave him a direct look. "You used power to emulate a Tier B ability, then more to break my ability when I used it on you. And you did it without realizing it." She gave him a direct look. "That's why I say that you're dangerous."

"I don't mean to be, ma'am."

"That may be, but intent rarely matters when it comes to matters of power. Results are what's important." She sighed. "I'm going to give you a painful truth, Novice, one that I suspect you already know, but one that you might not fully appreciate. To many students in Askula, you are an unwelcome addition."

He nodded a little glumly. "I assumed that, ma'am. That's how it was in my village, too."

"Yes, I heard about your leave-taking from Tem, and the Head Bureaucrat's little tantrum. He was a fool, but this is more serious. The older students always attempt to antagonize the younger students. However, more of them will target you than anyone else. They'll be cruel, vicious, and ruthless, all in the attempt to get you to give up and try to leave Askula."

"I'm not giving up, ma'am," he said in a hard voice.

"I never assumed you would. I'm merely warning you that you – and by association, your roommates – will be subject to far more abuse and insults than the other novices. And that is what makes you dangerous. As we learned today, when you are backed into a corner, you fight back rather viciously, with potentially deadly results for your attackers." She shook her head. "There aren't so many students in Askula that we can afford to lose them like that."

"What if you, I don't know, told them all to leave me alone, ma'am?" he asked a little bitterly.

"I can, and I will. And once word of this gets out, some will listen. Others, though, will see it as a challenge." She shrugged. "That's the nature of those who excel as ithtaru, you know. Danger is a challenge and adventure for them, something to be respected but not avoided. It's how we train them, and it's how many will see you."

She rose to her feet. "Hopefully, your training with awal Ranakar will help with this, but I would like you to do a favor for me. Avoid these situations in the future, and for the love of all the gods, keep that mouth of yours shut. A problem avoided is as good as a problem solved – at least in this case."

She stepped away from the bed. "I hope that this is the last we see of each other until the end of year, Novice, but I have a feeling it won't be. Know that I'm keeping an extra close eye on you – and you truly, truly don't want that. Am I understood?"

He nodded. "Yes, ma'am. I really don't want that."

"Good. I will send the others back in before I have to buy Midoral two days' worth of drinks to appease him. Good day, Novice." She turned and stalked out, and Amarl laid back on his bed, closing his eyes. It had been a long day, and he had a lot to process. Had he used an ability? The awal seemed to be suggesting he had – although, as he thought about it, she never said that. She said that he did something *like* an ability, a Tier B one. His was Tier F, so whatever he did, it couldn't have been his ability. And how had he just thrown her power off like that? He thought she'd be angry about that, but she hadn't seemed to be. She'd given him good advice, though. He'd do his best to just avoid the older students when he could, and try not to deliberately antagonize them when he couldn't stay away from them.

He listened as the others returned, then opened his eyes as he heard Dalat's bed creak. He looked and saw the others gathering around. Meder looked at him curiously, but he just shook his head. He didn't want to talk about it in front of the older students. Instead, he turned to face Dalat.

"Dalat, I'm sorry. I shouldn't have spoken like that to you. I'm kind of an ass sometimes."

"He really is," Meder agreed with a sigh. "And a stupid one, at that."

"No, I'm the one at fault," Dalat shook his head. "I can't believe I attacked you like that. I could have killed you." He gave Amarl a serious look. "I'm sorry, too. I should never have put my hands on you."

"You were both fools, and you both got off lucky," Andra said, her tone disappointed. "Dalat, she almost expelled you for that, and if Ronia hadn't begged her for leniency, she might have. You know what that would mean."

The boy paled again but nodded. "Y-yeah. I do." He swallowed hard, then looked at Ronia. "Thanks for helping me out. I don't know what got into me."

"I do. You still worry too much about what other people think about me, Dalat. I don't care what they say; why should you?"

"People talk about you?" Meder asked curiously, then winced. "I'm sorry, that's none of my business."

"No, it's fine. See, I look like a woman, but I wasn't born one. I just – I feel more comfortable like this." She shrugged. "A lot of people make fun of me for it, call me names like 'pervert' or 'pussy boy'." She looked at Amarl. "Which is why Dalat got so upset with what you said."

Amarl winced. "Ouch. Yeah, I can see that. I'm sorry for that. If it makes you feel any better, I thought you were a very attractive woman when I first saw you."

"Thanks. I think so, too." She frowned. "But what you did was stupid, you know. Even if the higher students can't attack you, they can make your life here the spirits' hell."

"She's right," Andra agreed, looking at Amarl seriously. "If you piss them off too much, they can make every day here torture for you. You need to be careful."

Amarl nodded slowly. "Thanks for the warning. Oh, and for saving my life. I really appreciate that."

She grinned at him suddenly. "Well, I had to. No one else is going to be stupid enough to try and master that moon axe, are they?"

"Wait, you gave him a moon axe?" Ronia asked. "Do you hate him?"

"He's got all fives, with a five-six in Speed," Andra shrugged. "And he's too small for heavy polearms. Plus, you saw what happened today. There's something special about him." She grinned at him again. "You want to pay me back, get good at that. I really want to see it in action in Halit one day."

"I'll try," he promised.

"Don't try. Do." She looked around at the group. "And don't make me step in on something like this again. Next time, I'll beat all of your asses, understand?"

Amarl started to grin, but both Ronia and Dalat nodded somberly. The girl walked out of the room, and he looked at the older students inquisitively.

"Are you both scared of her?"

"Yes, and you should be, too," Ronia said. "She wins almost every time in sparring. That ability of hers is ridiculously powerful."

"It's a Tier C power," Dalat offered. When the novices looked unimpressed, he sighed. "I forget that you guys haven't been to ability instruction yet. You know that there are tiers to abilities. Well, each tier is more than twice as powerful as the one below, close to three times – and much rarer."

"Dalat and I are both Tier A, the lowest tier," Ronia said. "Most ithtaru are. Andra is a high-ranking Tier C, so her power is about ten times as strong as ours."

"Wow," Burik breathed, his eyes wide.

"We aren't supposed to tell you this," Dalat added. "So, don't tell anyone you know it."

"Why aren't you?" Meder asked. "Why doesn't anyone tell us anything?"

"The school wants you to learn how to work things out on your own. Most of the time, ithtaru operate independently, so you usually won't have anyone to rely on but yourselves." He shrugged. "At least, that's what they tell us."

"Ha!" Meder said, grinning at Amarl. "I knew it!"

"And of course, it's also payback for the older students doing it to us when we were new novices," Ronia added with a vicious grin.

"I'm not going to say, 'I told you so'," Amarl said slyly. "However, I did warn you."

CHAPTER 20

Amarl parted from the others and walked through the Citadel hallways alone toward his newest class. It had been a long day the day before, and an even longer night in some ways, and while his body felt perfectly awake, his mind was tired and exhausted from trying to answer his friends' questions most of the night.

"How did you do that, Amarl?"

Burik's question had leaped from the larger boy's lips the moment the trio returned to their room after Midoral released Amarl from the infirmary. Amarl repressed a sigh; he knew the question would be coming, and he didn't have good answers.

"Well, first, I was dumb enough to think that I could get away with freely insulting a higher student," he said lightly, sitting down on his bed. "Then, I just kind of opened my mouth and let words fly out."

"Amarl, this is serious," Meder interrupted him. "That looked like an ability. Did you quicken an ability?"

"Of course not." He frowned. "At least, I don't think so."

"Try checking your status to see."

"Fine." He sighed and pulled up his status.

STATS
FORCE: 5.2 (122%)   SKILL: 5.3 (135%)
SPEED: 5.6 (183%)   TOUGHNESS: 4.5 (61%)
MIND: 5.3 (135%)   WILL: 3.8 (30%)
PRESENCE: 6.2 (332%)   SOUL: 9.5 (9,001%)

QUICKENED ABILITY: MEZ
TIER: F
PERCENT QUICKENED: 0%

CURRENT ITHTU: 10.3
TO LEVEL: 0
TO STATS: 1 (31%)
TO SKILLS: 0
TO TAK: 5

CURRENT TAK: 3.7/5

He stared at the screen for a moment. His Soul stat had gone up a tenth of a point, and his crystal was weaker now. Somehow, he'd touched it and used that power against Dalat – but he hadn't quickened any abilities.

"No, my ability's still at 0% quickened," he said after a moment.

"Really?" Meder looked at him suspiciously. "How strong is that crystal you quickened?"

"It was eleven-seven. It's down to ten-three. I think I tapped it today without realizing it."

"And you've been quickening it to your ability for a week since the Joining. It should have gone up at least a percent, wouldn't you think? Otherwise, it could take you three or four years just to awaken your ability."

He shrugged. "It hasn't, sorry."

"I'll bet it's because Amarl's ability is high-tier, isn't it?" Burik guessed. "With a Soul stat like his, it's probably D, at least, and I'll bet higher tiers take longer to wake up."

He hesitated, remembering Danmila's admonition to him, but he didn't think it counted with his friends. "I'm not supposed to tell you, but – it's actually Tier F, according to my screen thingy."

Meder stared at him. "Tier F? Seriously? There's a Tier F?"

"Yeah. It's still at 0%, though, so it's not like I'm going to be using it anytime soon."

She shook her head and rubbed her temples. "I have to stop being surprised by you," she sighed.

"Why, what's yours?" Burik asked. "Mine's Tier A."

"Tier C. And I was proud of it, too, after what Dalat and Ronia said about Andra. If Tier C is ten times as powerful as Tier A, though, Tier F…"

"You shouldn't think of it like that," Amarl said firmly. "I'll bet there are ups and downs to every ability. No matter what Dalat and Ronia said, I imagine abilities are like any weapons. It's not about how dangerous the blade is. It's the person holding it. I'd rather fight Herel with a perfect sword than Yamacol with just a stick, any day."

"That's true," Burik agreed. "And I'll bet lower tiered abilities take less power and are easier to use, just like a dagger's easier than a halberd."

"Okay, fine," the girl sighed. She looked at Amarl closely. "Something changed in your status, though, didn't it?" she asked shrewdly. "I saw the surprise on your face."

"Yes," he admitted. "My Soul went up to nine-five."

"Like it wasn't high enough already," she grumbled.

"Try to use your ithtu again," Burik suggested eagerly. "Maybe you can get it to go up even more!"

"You want me to kick you, Burik?" Amarl asked dryly. "Really?"

"No, nothing like that. Try kicking…" He paused then grabbed a pillow from his bed. "This."

He'd spent the rest of the night trying to recapture the feeling he'd had when he kicked at the older boy without a hint of success. He could sense his tak, even move it around, although he couldn't connect it to any other part of his body to strengthen it, as Lilenpur warned him was the case. And he certainly couldn't pull the rush of power from it he'd use to almost kill Dalat. In fact, the more time passed, the less he could remember what it even felt like, until when he stalked down to the laundry room the next morning, surly and bleary-eyed, he could barely remember the energy coursing through his leg into the boy. It was like a dream that faded swiftly, leaving a vague sense that it happened, nothing more.

His tiredness affected his physical training, and Periteth gave him a serious tongue-lashing over a lack of effort. Part of him wanted to take a nap instead of eating the midday meal, but if his "special" training was going to be overly difficult, he didn't want hunger interfering. He had a feeling things would be hard enough as it was.

He kept his gaze straight ahead and his mouth shut as he navigated the halls. Older students dressed mostly in green and yellow passed him, but he carefully avoided doing anything that might provoke them or draw too much attention to himself. Despite his best efforts, at one point, a pair of boys in purple uniforms stepped in front of him, barring his path.

"Where are you going, new meat?" one sneered.

"To meet Awal Ranakar," Amarl sighed tiredly. "You want to give me your names, so I can tell him who it was that made me late?"

The boys glanced at one another and stepped aside, allowing him to pass without another word, and Amarl smothered a smile. Perhaps there was something positive about his new classes, after all.

Room 314 was on the third floor of one of the towers, and indeed the room took up the entirety of that tower's third floor. Amarl trudged up the stairs to the classroom and pushed the door open to walk inside. He stopped as he entered; he didn't know what he'd been expecting, but it wasn't what he saw.

The room was a complete circle utterly bereft of furniture of any kind. Firm but yielding mats of woven grass covered the floor, and a huge circle had been painted on those mats around the edge of the room. Smaller circles and lines filled the space within that huge circle, with a single circle a reach wide at the very center. Ropes stretched across the room at various heights and angles, thick as his wrist and knotted to metal rings embedded in the stone walls, making it feel like he walked into a maze as much as a classroom. Wooden poles about the same thickness as the ropes rose from floor to ceiling in spots, and chains dangled from overhead, hanging just above head height. He worked his way slowly into the center of the room and looked around in awe. He didn't know what sort of training he might be doing there, but he was suddenly a lot more excited to start it.

He spun as the door opened behind him, and a familiar, black-garbed figured entered. The man was older, probably in his sixties, with a short, gray beard and dark gray hair. His face was square, with scars on one cheek and above his eye. He wore black clothing with gold trim, with metallic threads interwoven among the fabric. Tiny gems dotted the shirt and pants, glittering and flashing in the sunlight streaming into the room.

None of that registered in Amarl's head, though. He recognized the man instantly; he would never forget him. This was the man who'd killed him, who'd plunged the Joining Crystal into his chest. His heart hammered, and sweat erupted from his forehead and palms as the sight of the man's face brought back the terror of that night, the memories of being dragged to the altar and held down.

Ranakar barely glanced at the boy as he made his way effortlessly past the various ropes and poles, gliding around them in a single, flowing movement that looked almost like dancing to Amarl. When he finally spared the boy a look, he stopped and sighed, dropping his bag to the floor with a loud, wooden clatter.

"You're thinking of your Joining, aren't you?" he asked quietly. Amarl remained silent, and the man shrugged. "It's understandable. I killed you, Amarl. It was for your own good, but I did it. I've done that to hundreds of new novices."

"Why?" The question was out of Amarl's mouth before he could stop it. He winced, but Ranakar just gave him a calm look.

"Why? Why am I the one who does that? Or why is it done that way?"

"Why do you have to kill people, sir?" Amarl asked hoarsely. "Isn't there another way?"

"No. And it's been tried." The old man sighed. "Every year, someone asks that question, Amarl. And every year, the answer's the same. Because there's no other way to connect a Joining Crystal.

"The Joining isn't just a physical thing. The crystal doesn't just link to your body and brain. It uses ithtu to bond to your soul, and it can't do that while you live. You have to die, to free your soul from your body, so it can join to the crystal. Then, if you accept the bonding, the crystal rejoins your body and soul, and..." He held out his hands. "If you can't accept the bonding, then your soul moves on. It's as simple as that."

Amarl nodded slowly. "I thought – I thought it was for the Imperial rolls."

"No. That's a useful little thing we tell students, but the fact is, the Order is the single most powerful force in the Empire, with the possible exception of the Grand Bureaucracy. We could simply order the Bureaucracy to strike you from the rolls, and they would. The fact that you technically die makes it simpler, but the Bureaucracy has no problems altering the records to suit the Empire's needs – as I believe your history class is teaching you."

"Yes, sir."

"Good. Hopefully, then, that matter's out of the way." Ranakar flowed to the side of the room and lifted a mat, revealing a trap door beneath. He lifted the wooden door and pulled out a pair of large cushions, then turned and tossed one to Amarl. "Here. Sit on this."

Amarl obediently laid the cushion on the floor and settled onto it, then waited while the awal glided back and settled before him. The man reached into a pocket and pulled out what looked like a bracelet, golden and chased with silver, with gemstones inset into it irregularly.

"Put this on."

Amarl hesitated before taking the bracelet. "Are you sure, sir?" he asked dubiously. "This thing has to be worth more than half my village."

"Probably the whole thing," Ranakar corrected. "Put it on." Amarl shrugged and slipped his hand easily through the overlarge band, then gasped as the bracelet shifted and flowed, the metal seeming to liquefy as it shrank down to fit snugly around his arm.

"How...?"

"Sahrotik," the man shrugged. Seeing Amarl's blank look, he put his hand in his lap. "Yes, I suppose Tem wouldn't have had access to sahrotik. Sahrotik – or tik, as some people call it – is a way to channel sahr without using workings." He gestured at his shirt, pointing to the gems dotting it. "Sahrotik uses gems and metallic threads to channel the local sahr field into an effect, in this case, added protection and comfort for the wearer. Essentially, the gems form the lattice of the required matrix, while the metal threads connect them in a pattern to replicate the multi-dimensional nature of a sahr matrix." He grimaced. "It's obviously far more complex than that, but the upshot is that with sahrotik, anyone can replicate the abilities of a haro, at least in a limited fashion."

"I've never seen anything like it," Amarl breathed.

"You wouldn't have, no. Tik is expensive to craft, for obvious reasons, and it requires a high degree of skill and intelligence to be able to fashion. However, it's also stabler and more reliable. That makes sahrotik engineers rarer than haros and far more valuable. Only noble families, wealthy merchants, and the bureaucracy can afford to employ them, so sahrotik is almost exclusively limited to large cities. Oh, and the military, of course. The army uses a fair bit of tik to create everything from war cannons to battle wagons to airships to blast lances. It's one of the reasons invasions through the Mistways never get very far."

Amarl examined the band around his wrist, fascinated by it. "Do – do you think I could learn how to do it?"

The awal shrugged. "As I said, it's expensive, and it takes clever fingers, intelligence, and patience. We'll have to see about that third one, but we can check your stats right now. What you're wearing is called a mentor band. It's connected to this ring. Anyone wearing the ring can see your status while you're wearing that band." The awal held up a similarly ornate ring and slid it on his finger. He frowned as he stared into space, and Amarl bit his lip to refrain from asking what was wrong.

"You've got one of the most lopsided status sheets I've ever seen," the old man finally spoke. "Obviously, that Soul stat is ridiculous. Soul is the one stat that typically can't be trained, so I've never seen anyone's close to yours." He frowned. "I thought the Rashiv said it was nine-four."

"It was, sir. It went up a tenth of a point yesterday."

"Did it?" The old man looked surprised. "That might mean that there's still more potential inside of you, waiting to be unlocked. That could be good – but it could also be a nightmare." He shook his head. "And a three-eight in Will? No wonder you couldn't keep your mouth shut yesterday. Yes, I heard about that. You were a fool, and while you got lucky, you can't count on luck to keep you safe. For now, avoiding trouble is best – at least until I teach you how to manage it. And you've got an ithtu point quickening toward Mind. Why Mind and not Will?"

"Nadar Lilenpur suggested it, sir. She said that the higher my Mind stat was, the more crystals I could quicken at once, and that in the long run, it'll make me stronger."

"She's right and wrong," the old man nodded. "Until you awaken your ability, the number of crystals you can quicken at once will be sharply limited. You aren't likely to see any improvement in the number of ithtu you can quicken at once until you've used up about half of this crystal." He shook his head. "Improving your Will, on the other hand, will increase the size of your tak, and with a high-tier ability like yours, that's going to be crucial. Plus, it's easier and faster to improve lower stats than higher ones."

"Should I switch it to Will from now on, then?"

"No. In the short term, being able to quicken a second crystal is more important since it will double your ability to improve yourself and the rate at which you restore your tak. After that, though, the benefits of additional crystals drop off somewhat since once you unlock your ability, you'll want to use most of your crystals to attune your body to it. Stick with Mind until you can quicken two crystals. Then, we'll talk." The ithtar continued staring into space, then blinked and refocused on Amarl, shaking his head. "What do you think the point of this training is, boy?"

Amarl frowned in thought, but the answer came to him quickly enough after his conversation with the Rashiv yesterday. "To make me into a better weapon, sir."

"Good. That's exactly right." Ranakar nodded approvingly. "You're a weapon that's potentially incredibly dangerous, and that means you need to be sharper, stronger, and more controlled than anyone else. I'm here to help turn you into that weapon."

He removed the ring and slipped it back into his pocket, then gave the boy a serious look. "Tell me, Amarl. How much do you know about ithtu abilities?"

"Not much, sir. I know that they're powered by ithtu, that there are tiers of them, and that each tier is stronger than the one below it, but that's about it."

"That's more than most new novices, and the important thing is that you know about tiers. Do you know how they're connected to your stats?" Amarl shook his head, and the old man nodded. "I'll explain, then, because it's a big reason why you're here.

"Each tier holds abilities somewhat more than double the power of those below it. Technically, the actual multiple is a constant called the golden number, around two-seven. So, Tier B is more than twice as powerful as Tier A, for example. That also means that abilities of a higher tier take more than double the ithtu to power, and your body and mind have to be stronger to channel them without killing yourself."

"Killing yourself?" Amarl echoed.

"Oh, yes. If you quicken an ability that's too powerful for your body, simply using it can damage or even destroy you. That's one reason we train our students so hard, and why we keep them from awakening their ability too early: we want their bodies and minds to be able to withstand the power of their abilities. Usually, you need a stat of five to handle a Tier B ability, six for Tier C, and so on. Having that stat doesn't mean you'll get an ability of that tier, just that it's at least possible, or that you might be able to advance your ability to that tier eventually."

"So, if I don't improve my Will stat before my ability awakens – I might die?" Amarl swallowed hard as he considered that possibility.

"Technically? It's possible. However, it's unlikely. Ithtaru almost always develop abilities based around their strongest stat, or perhaps their two strongest – and that's the problem."

"Problem, sir?"

"Yes." He shifted on his mat. "You see, Amarl, ithtaru typically quicken one of two types of abilities. The first is a stat-based ability, like Student Dalat's strength. His ithtu can boost his Force stat until it's much higher than a normal nalu's. The ithtara who brought you here, Danmila, has a similar type ability: she can use her ithtu to move at incredible speeds by essentially making the distance between herself and a nearby point vanish. If your ability turns out to he stat-based, then there's no real problem.

"However, there's a second type of ability: an elemental one – and Soul-based elemental abilities are incredibly dangerous."

The man waved a hand, and a seven-sided circle appeared in the air between them. Lines connected every other point of the shape to make a seven-pointed star, and a different shape glowed at each point of the circle. At the top, greenish sparkles glittered and danced; to the left of it, half of a sunburst shimmered golden. Below that lay a crackling flame, followed by shifting rocks. Swirling drops of water floated above the grinding stones, and a grayish brain slowly rotated at the final point to the right of the top. A heart pulsed in the center of the shape, and Amarl thought he saw a dark, swirling hole in the middle of that heart.

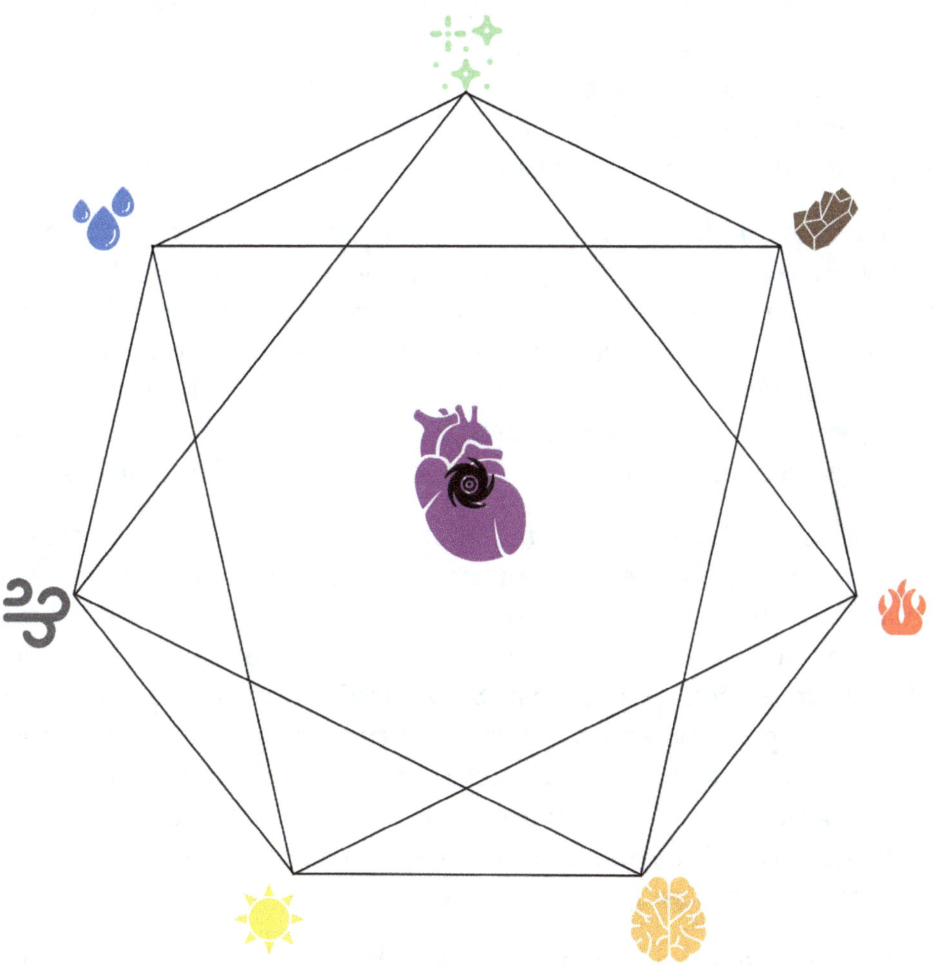

"This is Menesrav's Circle," the awal said. "Also just called 'The Circle'. It's a diagram of the different elements ithtu can manifest, and each of these forces is associated with one of your stats. Starting at the top of the circle, you have Will and aether, or sahr; Toughness and earth; Force and fire; Mind and thought; Presence and light; Speed and air; and Skill and water."

He gave Amarl a meaningful look. "And in the center, you have the Soul stat, along with two elements: life, the power of generation and creation, and the void, the power of obliteration and destruction, the antithesis of everything. If your ability is tied to one of those concepts, well…" He shook his head.

"And it gets worse. You'll notice that each element is connected directly to the two beside it and more remotely to the two beyond but has no direct connection to the two forces opposite it. That's a limiting factor, and the same connections hold for their associated stats. You'll never see an ability directly linking Presence and Will, for example, or Force and Speed. Every stat and element has two others it can't directly join with. The one exception is Soul; being in the center, it links to everything. That means that your ability could technically draw on any other concept, element, or stat."

The man made a sour face. "Soul abilities are rare, very rare, and you can see why they're exceptionally powerful, even compared to other abilities of the same Tier. I said that an ability is more than twice as strong as one of the tier below, but it's actually not that simple. Within a tier, different abilities have different powerful levels, so a weak Tier B ability like creating fire is closer to twice as powerful as a Tier A ability, while a strong one like creating a protective bubble about yourself is more like five times as strong.

"The Soul elements, life and the void, are essentially creation and destruction. They're incredibly powerful, and any ability that uses them is automatically one of the strongest in its tier. Soul-based powers can heal and restore, but they can also snuff out life, inflict plagues and curses, or simply obliterate foes. I've heard of Soul-based ithtaru being able to terrify entire armies, spread poison and disease, or even kill with a touch. There are stories of ithtaru who could animate their dead enemies to fight for them, create living flames or stone guardians to serve them, or craft weapons of pure void that would cut through anything they touched without effort, and all of those are Soul-based."

He shook his head ruefully. "Even the simplest soul-based power I know of, the ability to empower one of your stats with soul energy, is Tier D, something like thirty times as powerful as a comparable Tier A ability like superhuman strength. That means that the Soul-based ithtaru can hit with thirty times the force of someone who's already superhumanly strong, the way Dalat is. To put that into scale, Dalat can probably lift about 150 casks, the weight of three adult naluni. That Soul-based ithtaru could theoretically lift two tuns, the weight of a standard wagon of ore."

Amarl pictured a person lifting one of the heavy, creaking tin wagons coming from the mines, and he shuddered at the thought. If Dalat were that strong, he would have crushed Amarl's entire body with a punch – and might have taken out the building behind the novice. He couldn't imagine a person being that powerful, but apparently, some were.

"You, on the other hand, have a Tier F ability. That has the potential to be hundreds of times stronger than a Tier A ability. Imagine being able to lift ten or fifteen of those wagons and carry them around or run so quickly that your clothing would catch on fire. Jumping a hundred reaches into the air, or creating weapons that could cut down entire buildings with a single slash. That's the kind of power level we're talking about, here – and you can see why I said it could be a problem."marl stared at the man in stunned silence. He couldn't imagine anyone having that sort of power, and the awal was suggesting that Amarl might, one day. It wasn't possible, and his mind reeled at the thought of it, but at the same time, part of him yearned for it. With power like that, he'd never have to worry about people bullying or harassing him again. People would have to fear him instead of the other way around, and deep down, he wanted that sort of strength so badly that it ached.

"I – I don't see why that's a bad thing," he finally admitted. "Being strong – that can't be bad."

"It's not, at least not by itself. However, remember how I told you that each tier requires double the ithtu to use? You'd need to have a tremendous tak even to think about using an ability like that to its fullest extent. With a tak the size yours is right now, you could barely scratch the surface of a Tier F ability.

"Plus, being insanely powerful doesn't make you immune to the laws of nature. When you hit something, it hits you back with the same force, as you learned when you broke your ankle kicking Dalat. Throwing a Tier F punch with a body the way yours is now would destroy you as well as whatever you hit. If you run so fast your clothes catch fire, you burn, too, unless you've got enough Skill and Speed to control your body and keep you below that ignition point. You need to train your body and mind to handle the kind of strength you might one day be capable of.

"Finally, the more powerful an ability, the harder it is to awaken it. We don't allow students to put power toward awakening their abilities in their first year – with you being an obvious exception. Beginning in second year, we feed them crystals at a controlled rate that will awaken their ability by the end of the year, or early third year for Tier D.

"You, however, have a Tier F ability. I've never seen one before, but extrapolating from what we know, you would need to quicken nothing but Major or even Grand crystals to have a chance of awakening your power by the end of next year, and again, your body can't handle that kind of power. If we stick with Minor crystals, it will likely take four or five years just to awaken your ability, meaning you'll be a full two to three years behind the other students. By that time, your body and tak might be developed enough to use your power fully – and that would be a disaster since newly awakened students always lose control of their powers. Imagine someone with the kind of strength I mentioned before but no control over that strength. Not being able to take a step without bursting into flames, or hug someone without crushing them into paste. Having senses hundreds of times stronger than normal that you could never turn off. Your own ability could destroy you."

Amarl swallowed hard. "So – what should I do, sir? If I need time to train my body to handle my awakened ability without hurting myself, but doing that means I might hurt everyone around me..."

Ranakar nodded. "You see the dilemma we face. We need to awaken your ability, but not too quickly, and not too slowly. If we awaken it around the same time as your fellow novices, you should have enough strength of body and mind to use it, but only at a reduced capacity that shouldn't be too dangerous to the people around you. And we need to train your body and mind to their limits, beyond the normal training novices receive, so that when that ability awakens, you can handle it.

"So, that's why you're here. While the other students are learning to handle ithtu with Feeble crystals, you'll be getting Minor ones, the strongest you can handle. And I'm going to push you, both physically and mentally, to your breaking point and a little past it, over and over, day after day. I'm going to push you until you hate me, then push harder." His eyes were cold as he spoke. "Does that scare you?"

"Absolutely," Amarl said bluntly.

"Good. It should. Just not as much as the thought of what might happen if we fail. You're a powerful weapon, Amarl, but you're powerful enough that you could sever the hand holding you if we're not careful. I won't let that happen." He rose to his feet, and Amarl scrambled to do the same. "I hear that in the past week, you got the first level of several skills. Is that right?"

"Yes, sir."

"Then let's take advantage of that." He grabbed the bag he'd brought and pulled a pair of wooden staffs from it, tossing one to Amarl. The boy fumbled the almost reach-long shaft but managed to keep it from hitting the floor. Ranakar began twirling his, and the staff hummed and whistled as it spun through the air so swiftly Amarl could barely see it.

"We need to give you stronger crystals, but we don't just keep those lying around. If you want them, you'll have to join a hunt and claim them, and that means you'll need better weapons skills than Knife Fighting."

"A hunt?"

"Yes. It's exactly what it sounds like, except the things we hunt, hunt us back." He stopped his twirling and slammed the butt of his staff on the floor. "If you can't protect yourself, you'll die, which is why no student gets to go on a hunt without at least two weapons skills at level four. I estimate it'll take you about three moons to use up that crystal you've quickened, and if you want a new one, you'll have to be ready by then. Think you can do it?"

"I don't know, sir," he admitted honestly. Amarl had never considered himself much of a fighter, and the thought of hunting animals – or even people; he couldn't assume the students only killed creatures on a hunt – bothered and even slightly sickened him.

"Smart answer. You never know what you can do until you're facing the choice." He lifted his staff. "We'll start here, and see where your abilities take us."

Amarl lifted the staff, dread filling him as he faced the awal. He knew he was being forged into a weapon. He had a feeling Askula just got a bigger hammer to pound him with, and he wasn't looking forward to it.

CHAPTER 21

A black ball whipped past Amarl's head as he dove over one of the ropes. One hand reached out and snagged the rope as he passed, and he twisted his body to roll back under the rope rather than continuing his dive. Another ball zipped through the space he would have occupied had he not changed direction, and he rolled backward to his feet, jumping to grab a chain above his head and pulling his legs up as a ball zoomed beneath him. He let go of the rope to drop to the floor, but he'd reacted too slowly, and a ball slammed into his stomach.

The ebony cotton balls looked soft, and from what Amarl had heard, they were supposed to be. He guessed that when the balls were filled with something like dried rice or sand, they probably were, but Ranakar liked to fill his with gravel and pebbles. Getting hit with one hurt like the spirits' hell, especially since the awal threw them with terrific force. Amarl groaned as he landed in a squat, then dove sideways, expecting another ball to target his crouched form. None were forthcoming, though, and he glanced up to see Ranakar staring at him disapprovingly.

"You're dead."

Amarl straightened, ignoring his throbbing stomach and pounding heart and trying to control his labored breathing. When he first started this training, three moons ago, he was on his knees, puking and gasping for breath after ten minutes of the exercise. He'd just finished twenty, and while his body felt it, he could have kept going for another ten minutes or so had the awal not ended the exercise early. He wasn't about to mention that, though, anymore than he would say that the blow to his stomach wasn't exactly a lethal one.

Once, when he took a similar hit, he protested that he wasn't dead, just injured. Ranakar proceeded to show him why an injury like that was as good as being dead by stabbing him in the stomach and forcing him to repeat the exercise with the bleeding wound. Amarl never realized how involved his stomach muscles were in things like moving, jumping, and even standing up straight. The pain had seriously hampered him, almost crippled him, and his teacher pelted him with impunity, deliberately targeting his arms and legs to inflict more pain without "killing" him. After three minutes, Amarl was on his hands and knees, fighting not to weep with pain, and he'd learned that in combat, any serious injury was a lethal one.

"What did you do wrong?" the old man asked, as he always did. He never simply told Amarl what mistakes he'd made; he forced the boy to guess them, and if he got them wrong, the training repeated until he figured them out.

Amarl's first instinct was to say that he moved too slowly, but he'd learned that the most obvious answer was usually the wrong one. He replayed the exercise in his thoughts, going back through the moments before he'd been struck. There was only one thing he could think that he might have done differently.

"I jumped instead of dodging," he said, not bothering with the "sir". Ranakar told him that the formality just slowed things down, so when it was just the two of them, he could drop it.

"Exactly," the old man nodded approvingly. "The moment your feet leave the ground, you lose ninety percent of your ability to dodge. You're committed to one trajectory – or, in the case of hanging like that, one location – and a smart enemy will take advantage of that. Always keep your feet on the ground if at all possible."

Amarl nodded in acceptance, knowing he didn't have to say anything. Ranakar expected him to acknowledge the advice by showing he'd learned when he repeated the exercise. He went around the room, collecting the small balls, then tossed them one at a time across the room into a small basket beside the man. He made most of them, although four bounced off the lip of the basket or bounced out of it, and he sighed and dropped to the floor to perform eighty pushups as punishment for missing.

When he finished, his arms aching and sore but not burning and trembling as they once would have been, he rose to his feet and stood, his body relaxed and loose the way Ranakar liked.

"Again?" he asked.

The older man shook his head. "How much of your crystal is left?" he asked.

"One percent," Amarl said. "It's almost gone."

"That's what I thought. That means it's time for you to go on your first hunt. You need better crystals than the Feeble ones you'll get otherwise."

Amarl nodded. "How will that work? I know you've been training me in things like tracking and being stealthy. Will I just have to go out into the wilderness and find something to kill?"

"No. There's nothing in Askula worth hunting. You'll be going to another realm, Shadora, and you'll be part of a hunting team of third-years." The awal grimaced slightly. "They'll likely do must of the hunting and harvesting since they'll have the use of their abilities. You'll just be along to learn this first time."

Amarl frowned. "How will I get a new crystal if I don't kill anything?"

"Crystals are passed out to everyone in the hunt at the end of it. You might not get another Minor one – in fact, you probably won't – but you'll get at least a Weak one. Once you've seen how a hunt works, you'll understand how much you still need to learn before you can really be a useful part of one."

The old man held up a hand before Amarl could reply. "I've made the arrangements. You'll join the hunt this Ispio, and you'll return three days later, on Nashio. That'll give you Akio as the next day to recover." The old man stopped and took a pair of leather sparring gloves from his pocket. The gloves were fingerless past the first knuckle and had padding along the back. They were designed to allow someone to be hit without serious injury, but Amarl knew from past experience that "serious injury" didn't include nasty bruises, torn skin, and just the general pain of being punched in the face.

"In the meantime, unarmed sparring. We'll start with Tiger Form. Remain in contact with your tak the entire time."

Repressing a sigh, Amarl sunk into himself and found his tak floating within him. He no longer needed to close his eyes to find or touch it, although it did take some concentration, focus that he would have preferred to use to keep the awal from pummeling him. Once he had contact, he dropped into a low stance with his feet wide, his knees bent, and his weight balanced so he could move in any direction easily. He brought his hands up, keeping his fingers loose and relaxing his shoulders.

"Begin."

Amarl moved forward swiftly, his hands striking in the powerful, aggressive movements of Tiger Form. It was a strong technique, heavy on offense, incorporating combinations of punches, knife-hand jabs, and low kicks to keep an opponent constantly on the defensive. He snapped a fist at the man's face, one designed to provoke a rising block, then lashed out with a foot at the man's leading knee. He pushed forward, driving his other fist toward the man's midsection while stepping in and bringing a knee up to slam into his chest.

Ranarak ignored the feint and slid his foot out of the way of the first kick. He twisted sideways to avoid the second fist and slapped a hand against the outside of Amarl's knee, deflecting his knee strike to the side and upsetting his balance. The man grabbed Amarl's elbow and pulled, forcing the boy to step forward to avoid losing his balance entirely.

Knowing what was coming, Amarl rolled with the kick that swept out his front leg, using the momentum to twist around and sweep a low foot at the awal's knee. Ranakar slid back to avoid the sweep, giving Amarl a chance to regain his feet and unleash another flurry of strikes. Even as he did, though, he could feel himself slowly losing his balance, as blow after blow was dodged or diverted. He struggled to recover, but each tiny misstep added up until at last, one of his strikes went too fast and too hard, and Ranakar's hand lashed out to seize his wrist. With a twist and a kick, the older man knocked Amarl's feet out from under him and somersaulted him in the air, slamming the boy onto his back on the fortunately yielding mats. Amarl rolled with the landing, coming to his feet and resuming his stance, but as he stood, the awal's feet shifted, widening as he, too dropped into Tiger Form.

Amarl straightened slightly, bringing his feet closer and pulling his elbows toward his side as he shifted into Water Form. Ranakar attacked, driving a foot toward Amarl's chest and following it up with two quick punches. Amarl shifted sideways without moving his feet, allowing the kick to sail past, then slapping both punches aside, redirecting them just enough to keep them from striking his body.

Water was a soft form, primarily defensive and focused on speed, grace, and flowing movements that led from one to the other. It sought to absorb and redirect blows rather than opposing them, flowing past attacks without striking back. Like waves on the shore, the form built up slowly, constantly attacking the opponent's balance until it swept their feet out from them or struck with a single, powerful blow that held all the force the wielder had redirected to that point. At least, that was how it was supposed to work – and how it always seemed to for Ranakar. Amarl could never quite seem to get it to come together.

As Ranakar pushed forward, Amarl felt his stance and form giving way a fraction of a span at a time, the awal's strikes just a little too precise and powerful for him to fully redirect them. His gathering waves began to swirl against one another, interrupting their slow build to power. His feet stumbled slightly, and his hands pushed a little too hard, driving his balance even further off. Finally, his form crumbled, and a punch blew past his defenses, crashing into his chest as a foot swept his knee, hurling him to the floor once more. He rolled with the fall and came to his feet, his momentum lost and his chest throbbing painfully.

Ranakar dropped his hands and crouched low, and Amarl quickly widened his stance and spread his hands as he moved into Bear Form. His right hand grabbed the awal's shoulder as the man moved in on him, while his left seized the opposite elbow. Ranakar did the same, grasping the boy, and shoved, trying to force him backward. Amarl slid with the push, his feet gliding across the mat, his weight centered across his hips and shoulders. The man pulled, trying to force Amarl forward, then twisted, dragging him to the side.

Through it all, the lighter boy slid his feet, allowing himself to be moved but never letting his balance waver. Bear was a close form, designed to grapple and tumble opponents rather than striking them. That didn't mean there were no strikes in the form, but they were there to finish a fallen opponent, not to bring one down. Like Water Form, Bear Form was all about redirecting a foe, but instead of tiny nudges, it used constant pressure in varying directions to confound an opponent's balance and topple them.

Amarl pushed and pulled, trying to disrupt the man's form. He was lighter and weaker than Ranakar, but that didn't matter much in Bear Form. He wasn't trying to overpower the man; he wanted the man to try and overpower him. The technique goaded his opponent into pushing or pulling harder than they should, losing their balance and allowing him to hurl them to the ground. Ranakar, though, refused to yield; his body was like an oak tree, planted deep in the ground and impossible to uproot. Amarl, on the other hand, felt his own balance wavering as he fought to keep from being moved too far, and at last he pulled back too hard, shifting his balance away from the man, then leaned forward to try and recover it. Ranakar spun as he dragged the boy toward him, his arm snaking over Amarl's shoulders while his hips slammed into the hizeen's stomach. Amarl relaxed as he felt himself fly over the man's back and crash into the floor with the awal atop him, the man's arm pinning him in place.

Ranakar released him and rolled to his feet, and Amarl sprang up quickly. The awal just stood, though, and the boy sighed and released his tak. Once again, he'd failed. If that had been a real fight, he'd have been dead. Ranakar could have shattered his arm when he first threw him, or crushed his chest with his punch, or choked the life from him when they fell together. The boy stood, rubbing the sore spot on his chest where he knew a bruise was forming, his shoulders slumped.

"You lost," the man spoke, his voice even. "Why?"

"You're too fast," Amarl shook his head. "Too strong. I keep making little mistakes, and they add up until…" He tapped his chest and shrugged.

"That's an excuse, not a reason." Ranakar's face was disapproving. "There's always going to be someone faster than you, someone better. Are you accepting the fact that you're going to die if you face someone like that?"

Amarl almost responded by telling the man that yes, that was exactly what he was saying, but he stopped. The awal was right. Someone was always going to be better than him. What would he do if he faced a real opponent that just had more skill? Give up and die?

"No," he shook his head with a sigh. "But I don't know what to do about it."

"I suggest you think on it, then. You might want to ask yourself who you're really fighting." He lifted his hands. "Again."

Amarl trudged tiredly toward the Citadel entrance, his body aching and sore as it always was after his classes with Ranakar. The man pushed him hard, to his body's limits and a little beyond every day, and Amarl walked with trembling legs and shaking hands. He'd started weight training this moon, and they always finished class by having the boy lift heavy objects while touching his tak. The awal added to the difficulty of the exercise by giving him instruction while he worked, occasionally asking questions about what he should have learned. Incorrect answers were punished by a staff blow to a shoulder or thigh, making his weights even harder to hold, so Amarl made sure to focus on the old man's words. This left him utterly exhausted, and Ranakar was right: part of him hated the man. Another part, though, rejoiced at the progress he'd made, and he pulled up his skill screen, filtering it to only show what had changed since he'd started his training.

SKILLS REPORT	
CHANGED SKILLS	
Acrobatics	3 (+3)
Anatomy	2 (+1)
Bear Form	3 (+3)
Climbing	4 (+1)
Endurance	4 (+3)
Investigation	4 (+1)
Knife Fighting	3 (+2)
Meditation	3 (+2)
Memorization	2 (+2)
Perception	2 (+2)
Riding	3 (+1)
Running	3 (+2)
Scimitar Fighting	2 (+2)
Silent Movement	2 (+2)
Staff Fighting	2 (+2)
Survival	2 (+2)
Throwing	2 (+2)
Tiger Form	3 (+3)
Tracking	2 (+2)
Water Form	3 (+3)

He'd grown a great deal in the past moons. Acrobatics helped him with his tumbling and jumping exercises, which had also given him a point in Climbing. Having to constantly touch his tak while he worked boosted his Meditation, and his three unarmed forms were at level three, a level that would be considered competent in most places outside Askula. His weapons skills weren't quite as advanced, but Ranakar didn't train him as hard in those, either.

The incredible growth actually bothered Amarl a bit, mostly because his friends hadn't grown at the same pace, even though they'd quickened their crystals weeks ago. He knew that while he'd trained with Ranakar, they'd both gotten the first level of Knife Fighting, but that had come only recently. Meder hadn't gotten Staff Fighting yet, despite her training, and none of the other novices had gotten a new weapons skill beyond knives, either. According to Ranakar, Amarl had gained as much in the past three moons as most novices would achieve in more than a year. Amarl credited that to his ithtu helping him and the intensity of his daily training – which was up to twice a day now instead of just once, replacing normal physical training in the morning – but Ranakar seemed to think otherwise. Apparently, he was learning quickly even for an ithtar, and Amarl couldn't help but wonder why that was the case.

He closed his screen as he spotted Meder and Burik waiting for him at the entrance, and he smiled at the pair as he approached.

"How did it go?" Meder asked, smiling back at him. The girl had cut her hair above her shoulders last moon, claiming that the longer ponytail got in her way during training, and her black hair framed her face to just below her chin. The moons of training showed; her body was lithely muscled where it looked soft before, and she moved more fluidly and gracefully than she had.

"Same as usual," he shrugged, rubbing his chest once more. "I've got a sea of bruises, and I didn't successfully complete a single training exercise. Ranakar didn't stab me this time though, at least, so that's something."

Meder shivered. "I still can't believe he does that sometimes. It seems so – abusive."

Amarl shrugged again. "I can't exactly tell him that, can I?"

"Besides, look at the results," Burik rumbled. The bigger boy didn't look much changed in the past moons, although Amarl thought his muscles looked a bit more defined than they had, and he could feel a tiny spark of power emanating from the boy's eyes that he'd learned was quickened ithtu.

"Amarl's advanced his skills way faster than we have. Hells, I might see if I can volunteer for that training if it gets me the same kind of growth."

"You'd let someone stab and beat you just to improve your skills?" Meder asked dubiously.

"Absolutely. As my mother always says, 'Nothing worthy is gained without pain.'"

"You say that until you get a knife stuck in you," Amarl laughed. "It's a lot less academic when your blood is pouring out of you, trust me." He shook his head. "Enough of that. How was your class?"

"Herel finally found his tak," Burik replied with a grin. "I was starting to think he was broken, to be honest."

"He isn't broken, Burik. He just needed more time than the rest of us, that's all." Meder shook her head. "We all got here, and that's what's important."

"Says the girl who quickened her stat already," Burik snorted. "Pretty soon, they're going to put you in special classes like Amarl if you aren't careful."

"No, thank you," she shuddered again.

"You got it?" Amarl asked. "Congratulations! What did you pick?"

"Skill." She looked at Amarl curiously. "You've been boosting your stats for a while, right?"

"Yes. Only Mind, though. I think just a unit or two more, and I'll be able to quicken a second crystal."

"That's great, but how long did it take you to figure out how to do it?"

"Do you really want to know?"

She grimaced, then sighed. "No, not really. I'll just assume it was fast and let it go at that."

"Smart," Burik laughed. "You always get pissed off when you hear how these things come so easily to him."

"Not anymore, I don't," she protested. Both boys gave her a dubious look, and she sighed. "Fine. Not as much as I used to, though."

"So, why'd you pick Skill?" Amarl asked.

"Well, it'll help with my staff and knife training, but mostly because I think it's what's holding me back the most in working with sahr. I can't do anything with it, not really, and I think that's why."

"Can't do anything?" Burik said incredulously. "Just yesterday, you built a matrix that sucked all light out of the room! The rest of us could barely make shadows! And last week, you were the only one who could start a fire! Well, you and Norag, but still!"

She made a face. "Yes, but those are all really basic things. I want to try some advanced stuff, and I think my Skill is holding me back. At least, that's what Furemas says."

Amarl shuddered. "Sahr's still my worst subject," he noted. "See, Meder, you're way better than me at that."

"She's better than everyone at that," Burik laughed.

"Norag's about as good," Meder pointed out. "He struggles more with the matrices, but his flows are amazing. I think Will is his highest stat, and it shows."

"He can do stuff, but you're the one who figures out the best way to do it," Burik said dismissively. "I still say you're better than him."

"So, now that everyone's found their tak, do you think anything about your class will change?" Amarl asked.

"Probably not," Meder shook her head. "We'll still spend half the time learning about ithtu and the other half trying to connect it to our stats." She frowned. "I wonder if I could get permission to do extra sahr classes on the days where everyone's working on that?"

"Lilenpur will just have you doing more meditation and visualization practice," Burik shook his head. "At least you get to miss that, Amarl."

"Are you kidding? Ranakar still makes me do it, but I have to do it while I'm training and sparring." Amarl laughed a bit bleakly. "It's a lot harder that way, trust me."

"He's probably preparing you for when your ability quickens," Meder said sagely. "We'll probably all have to learn that, I imagine. I don't think we'll be able to stop and meditate to use our tak in the middle of battle, do you?"

"You certainly could, but it might not go well for you. And you're probably right; I'll bet everyone has to learn to do that. I'm just lucky to get to learn it early, is all."

"Stop complaining," Burik shook his head. "Would you really rather be sitting in ithtu class, bored to tears because you can already do what everyone else is learning?"

"Hmm. Being bored or being stabbed. Such a tough decision." Amarl chuckled, then ducked away as Burik swiped at his head. "Fine, I'll stop complaining." He looked at Meder curiously. "You know, I never asked you guys where you found your tak."

"Just behind my nose," she replied.

He nodded. "Deep channel, then, most likely. That's a good spot." He frowned. "Although with your Mind stat, it might also be the anterior channel, which isn't quite as good."

"Deep channel?" Burik rumbled. "Anterior? What's that?"

"You haven't learned that?" Amarl asked, surprised. The two shook their heads, and he shrugged.

"Well, I don't think it'll hurt for you to know. There are eight channels in your body, and your tak will always lie off one of them. Meder's is near the deep channel that goes into the lower part of her brain, through her eyes, and loops along the inside of her spine. However, it might also be near the anterior channel that goes from her forehead though the front half of her brain and ears."

"Why is that a good spot?" Meder asked.

"Because the deep channel is a major channel, along with the ventral one in your chest and stomach. Those channels can carry more power than the five minor channels, so having your tak near one of them means you'll probably quicken your ability faster. That's good, since yours is a higher tier that takes longer to quicken normally."

"What are the minor channels, then?"

"Anterior, posterior, upper, lower, and dorsal. Anterior is in the front of your skull and includes your eyes, posterior is in the back of your skull and touches your ears, upper goes through your throat and arms, lower your crotch and legs, and dorsal your lungs and back."

"That's seven," Burik noted. "You said there are eight channels."

Amarl nodded. "The heart channel is in your heart, obviously, and it's where all the other channels connect. It's a strong channel, not minor or major, bigger than either of them and linked to all the others."

"You said that with my Mind stat, my tak might be linked to my anterior channel," Meder noted. "Does that mean that each channel has a linked attribute?"

"Yep. Anterior is Mind, posterior is Will, and deep is Presence. Upper is Skill, lower is Speed, ventral is Force, and dorsal is Toughness."

"Meaning the heart channel must be linked to Soul," she guessed. He nodded, and she narrowed her eyes shrewdly. "That's where your tak is, isn't it, Amarl?"

He sighed. "Yeah. It's next to my heart," he admitted. "It's on the strong channel."

She nodded. "I had a feeling. I'll bet that's part of why things come easily to you, and why your Soul stat is so high."

"Maybe," he shrugged.

"This all seems like something they should have told us," Burik grumped. "My tak is just above my navel, which puts it on that ventral thing, which is linked to Force, my strongest stat, right? Why was I wasting time looking all over when they knew it would be there?"

"Because it's not always next to the channel for your highest stat. I guess it's more likely to be closer to the channels for your three highest stats, but for you, that's dorsal, ventral, and upper. That covers everything from your bellybutton to your chin, more or less."

"And if it's not always there, then they probably don't want us focusing on just those places when it might be somewhere else," Meder nodded.

"Fine," Burik sighed, kicking a rock. "You never gain anything on the first try, right?"

"One of your mother's sayings?" Meder asked with a smile.

"No, I just came up with it." The boy grinned. "I'll have to remember it. Maybe one day, I'll get a chance to tell her."

They walked to Sitjak but stopped outside the armory as they saw a crowd of third-years lined up, waiting to enter it.

"I wonder what that's all about?" Meder asked curiously.

"Probably the hunt this Ispio," Amarl shrugged. "It's supposed to be a bunch of third-years."

"How do you know about it?" Meder asked.

"Oh, I forgot to tell you. I'm supposed to be going on it to get a new crystal."

"What?" Burik demanded, putting his hands on his hips. "How could you forget that? You're so lucky!"

"At least I'm not the only jealous one," Meder laughed. "Seriously, Amarl, you're going on a hunt? I hear that they can be dangerous!"

"I'm not really supposed to do much hunting," he said deprecatingly. "I think I'm mostly along for the ride, and to see what a hunt is like." He scanned the crowd of third-years. "Hey, Andra's in that group. Think that means she'll be going, too?"

"Maybe." Meder's eyes narrowed, and she lifted her chin toward a tall boy in purple clothing. "It looks like Nihos is, too."

"Are Herel and the others still getting private training from him?" Amarl asked.

"Yeah, and they seem to be paying him. I'm not sure where they're getting the money, though."

"They're probably pooling their stipends," Burik suggested.

"No, that's not it. They're still spending money on Akio. Plus, I hear that the third-year stipend is pretty high; Nihos probably wouldn't care about a little extra money. They're getting extra coins from somewhere, and I have no idea where."

"Well, it's not our problem," Burik shrugged. "Besides, even with their training, Herel's the only one who can take you in sparring, Meder, and none of them can beat Amarl or me. Obviously, it's not working out for them."

"It could be a problem for Amarl," she said quietly. "If Nihos is on a hunt with him, and there are no malims around..." She let her voice trail off, but Amarl felt a chill settle into his chest as he looked at the tall, muscular third-year.

Suddenly, he really didn't want to go on this hunt.

CHAPTER 22

"I can't believe you get to go on a hunt without me," Burik complained as Amarl finished stuffing the dark gray knapsack with extra clothing. "We have to wait until our second year for that!"

"I think I'd rather wait," Amarl laughed as he closed up the knapsack. "It's going to be me and a bunch of third-years. I'm pretty sure it's going to be a bad time."

"There are ithtaru going along," Meder shook her head. "They won't let anything bad happen to you."

"According Ranakar, they won't let you die or be seriously injured. That isn't the same as not letting anything bad happen to you."

"It's in the Kurlag Forest, though, right?" she asked. "There can't be anything too dangerous in the forest. They wouldn't let really dangerous creatures live in Askula in case one broke out and attacked the village."

"No, we're taking the forest's Mistway," he corrected. "Some realm called Shadora. I don't know anything about it, but it's obviously not too safe of a place."

"Why won't they tell you more about it?" Burik asked. "It seems like the more you know, the safer you'll be."

"'Ithtaru must prepare for the unexpected'," Amarl said sonorously, trying and failing to imitate Ranakar, standing straight and crossing his arms before his chest with a scowl. After a moment, he relaxed and shrugged. "That's what Ranakar said, at least. I'll bet the third-years know more than I do, though. Remember, I'm just supposed to be along for the ride."

Meder frowned. "I still say that Nihos being there could be dangerous. You've improved your skills a lot, Amarl, but do you really think you're in the same class as a bunch of third-years?"

"No, I'm not. Not only do they have better skills, they've all quickened their abilities. I don't really have a choice, though. My crystal's almost used up, and despite getting my Mind stat up to almost six, I can still only quicken one crystal at a time. Ranakar doesn't want me using the Feeble crystals they feed us novices, and if I want to get a Weak or Minor one, I'll have to go gather it myself. So…" He held out his hands.

Burik sighed again. "It sounds exciting. Three days in another realm, fighting monsters and harvesting ithtu beats constructing sahr matrices and learning how to manipulate them."

"I personally think those are fascinating," Meder smiled. "And the equations are important to know. The towers keep the sahr field from being chaotic, but…"

"Yeah, yeah, I know," the boy sighed. "But a single untrained haro can disrupt it and cause ripples across the local field if they don't know the power calculations. I get why we're doing it, but I don't have to like it. You're lucky you don't have to take that stuff, Amarl."

"Oh, I do," the boy laughed ruefully. "You think Ranakar is letting me off without learning how to use sahr? I'm doing the same math you're doing. It makes my head hurt, but at least you can solve a matrix function. I guess when we get to advanced field equations, you can't solve them, you can only come up with a best estimate." He shook his head. "I'm not looking forward to that." He grimaced. "Or this trip, either."

"You'll be fine," Meder assured him. "Andra will be there, right?"

"Yeah." He shrugged. "That doesn't make me any less worried. She and I aren't really friends or anything."

"My mother always says, 'No use worrying about what you can't change'," Burik told him, clapping a hand on his shoulder and grinning. "Besides, think of it this way. You're going to be around a bunch of older girls with limited supervision. It could be fun, right?"

"Well, when you put it that way…" Amarl grinned back.

"Ugh. You two." Meder got up and gave Amarl a hug. "Keep your mind where it belongs, and your pants buttoned, and you'll be fine, Amarl."

"I thought what we were just talking about was where my mind belongs," Amarl told Burik in a puzzled voice, scratching his head while he hugged Meder with one arm.

"That's what I thought, too," Burik shrugged.

Meder pushed away from Amarl and smacked his arm, but her face held a smile as she spoke. "You're both disgusting, and I don't know why I'm friends with you."

"Because your other choices are Herel and Hadur," Amarl replied with a laugh.

"Ugh. True. I need to find some better-quality people." She pushed him toward the door. "Go on. You don't want to be late."

"No, I definitely don't. I don't know what they'd do if I was." He strapped on his sword belt with his scimitar and two daggers attached, then made sure his staff was tied securely to the knapsack before slipping it on his shoulders. He reached out and clasped arms with Burik, who nodded at him.

"Good luck. Kill something big."

"I'll be happy not to become monster food, personally." Amarl looked at the two with a pang as he realized it would be the first time he'd be away from them for more than an hour or two in three moons. For the next three days, he'd be surrounded by older students who would have nothing to say to a first-year novice. He'd been used to isolation in Tem, but having friends for even a short time suddenly made the pain of loneliness a lot sharper and more intense.

Shaking off his sudden melancholy, he walked out the door and headed down the hall. Whining about things wouldn't make them better, even if he was only complaining to himself. Besides, he knew that most ithtaru worked alone; once he graduated, he'd probably be dealing with loneliness for much of the rest of his life. He might as well start getting used to it again.

Once he left the dormitory, he set out toward Kurlag Forest at a swift trot. Running to the mountains no longer fatigued him, and while the pack on his back would certainly tire him a little, he knew he'd be fine. Ranakar made him run with a pack of lead bars that had to weigh ten casks, around a quarter of his own weight, for hours at a time. The extra three or four casks of weight he carried wouldn't matter much for such a short distance. The sun hung low before him, barely visible behind the mountains – he didn't know why they were leaving so late in the day, but he assumed the school had reasons – and he held his gaze low as he ran to keep from being blinded.

The forest was nestled in a large valley slightly north of Sitjak, and as Amarl neared it, the scent of pine wafted across his nose. He inhaled deeply; the scent reminded him a bit of Tem. When the winds came gently down the mountain slopes, they bathed the village in this resinous scent, and sometimes late at night, he'd lay in someone's attic – without their knowledge, typically – and just enjoy the smell of the trees. To his surprise, though, his remembrance of Tem no longer sent a pang of loss or regret through him. That place wasn't really his home any longer, and the Amarl who'd lived there was slowly fading.

Part of him hated that thought. Amarl Tem was a scoundrel and an annoyance, to be sure, but he was also carefree, unconcerned with his future, and only lightly entangled in the worries of others. Amarl Askula – assuming he could one day claim that name – suffered from constant stress and pressure, had to consider the consequences of his actions daily, and had people to look out for. Askula promised him power, but it also bound him in chains of responsibility and obligation that he couldn't figure out how to escape. He wasn't honestly sure which of those lives was better, and which was worse.

He pushed aside his somewhat depressing thoughts as he spotted a large group of students gathered at the edge of the forest. He angled toward them and slowed down as he neared the group, trotting to a halt as he approached the crowd. He scanned the group and guessed about twenty students stood in front of him, all a couple years older than he was and all dressed in the colors of their schools. Most wore the deep yellow of Risha, the Tier A school, but around a third of them sported the rich purple colors of Baquena, the Tier B school. Only two students wore the royal blue of Libba, the school for higher tiers, and he recognized Andra as one of them. He tried to catch the girl's eye, but she just glanced at him, gave him a curt nod, and looked away. He suppressed a sigh as he realized that the weekend was probably going to go exactly the way he'd thought.

"What in the hells do you think you're doing, meat?"

He turned to see a group of three students, two boys and a girl, standing beside him, glaring at him. All three wore yellow, marking them as Tier A students from Risha School, and all three had their chests puffed out belligerently.

"This hunt is for third-years only," the boy in the center stated. He stood maybe a couple finger-widths taller than Amarl but was significantly wider and probably heavier, and from the heavy axe hanging from his belt, Amarl guessed he had a high Force stat but not much of a Skill or Speed stat. "Get the fuck out of here now, and we won't have to beat you for trying to sneak in."

Amarl shrugged. "Awal Ranakar assigned me to this hunt," he said simply. "I guess you can go tell him that he's wrong, and I don't belong here.

I wouldn't, but you feel free."

The boy's eyes narrowed, and he took a step closer to the hizeen. "Lying about the awals will get you a flogging, boy. Now turn around and get out of here..."

"Student!" a voice snapped, and all four of them turned quickly to see a short, muscular woman with inky black hair, a wide face, and light olive skin storming toward them. She wore the dark gray uniform of a malim, a full instructor, with a black metal chainmail vest laid atop it.

"What in the hells do you think you're doing?"

The boy snapped to attention, facing the woman. "This novice was trying to sneak into the hunt, Malim," he said. "He lied about Awal Ranakar giving him permission..."

"He does have permission, you idiot," the woman cut him off. She walked up to stand before the boy. He stood a little taller than her, but the student still looked properly intimidated as she spoke. "Do you think I'm stupid, Student?"

"N-no, Malim!" the boy said hastily.

"Blind, then, perhaps? Unable to see the color green?"

"No, ma'am!"

"Then how the fuck did you think I wouldn't see this novice? Do you perhaps think that I'm too weak-willed to kick his ass out if he doesn't belong here?"

"No, ma'am!" the boy practically shouted.

"Then get the fuck away from him and find someone else to pester." The trio of students quickly walked away, and the malim turned to face Amarl.

"I've heard about your sharp tongue, boy. Keep it in check during my hunt, you understand? You'll be working with a team, and if you piss them off, they might conveniently be too busy to help you when something's trying to eat your face. Got it?"

"Yes, ma'am," the boy nodded, his heart quickening slightly as she reminded him that he was going to be in real danger on this hunt, no matter what anyone thought.

"Good." The woman looked around. "For those of you who don't know him, this is Novice Amarl. He's coming on the hunt because he needs Weak and Minor crystals, like most of you. Don't complain about how you had to wait for three years to go to Shadora, or how unfair it is. If you haven't realized by now that your life is going to be ridiculously unfair, then you're probably going to die young, and it won't matter anyway."

She turned back to him, and her voice lowered until only he could hear it. "I'm going to be blunt with you, Novice. I don't like that you're here. No matter what anyone says, you don't belong on a third-year hunt. All I ask is that you don't fuck up too badly and screw things up for your team. Got it?"

She spun and walked away from him, leaving him staring after her with an empty feeling in his chest. Even the malim in charge of the hunt didn't want him around. There was no way this was going to go well for him. Part of him wanted to turn and walk away right then, but he knew that wasn't an option. He'd have to see this through and hope for the best – or at least, that the worst didn't happen. That was probably a more realistic thing to wish for.

He refocused as the woman's voice lifted over the group of students.

"Listen up! For those of you who don't know, my name is Malim Nirecina. You will address me as Malim or ma'am. I'm one of the main trainers for hunting, tracking, and creature lore. I've gained that position because I'm fucking good at it, and I've been doing it since before your father squirted you into your mother's womb. That means that if I tell you something, you listen! Don't argue with me, and don't question! If I say hide, you hide; if I say run, you run. Do you understand?"

"Yes, ma'am!" Amarl's response was half a heartbeat behind the almost perfectly synchronized shout of the older students.

"Good! We will be hunting in Shadora. Shadora is a realm of twilight and mists, with limited visibility, which is why we're leaving so late, to let your eyes adjust on the way. Sahr is unstable there, so be careful with workings, and be sure your power equations are accurate. The creatures there are dangerous, but most lack magical abilities, so you shouldn't have too many problems if you work as a team.

"The Mistway will deposit us in the middle of a forest similar to Kurlag, but there are differences. I want you to take note of them; spot as many discrepancies as you can. Tiny details can and will save your life, so pay attention to them!

"During this hunt, you will be split into teams of four. You will stay with your team the entire hunt and will not go off on your own for any reason. If one of you has to take a piss, all four of you go together. If two of you are a couple, either deal with having an audience for whatever you do or keep it in your pants for the hunt. If you go off alone for any reason, I will find you, and I will make you regret it. Is that understood?"

"Yes, ma'am!" That time, Amarl managed to shout in synch with the others.

"Outstanding. First, I'll sort you into your teams. These have been preselected based on your individual abilities, so don't bitch about it." She pulled out a piece of paper and began shouting out names. As she called a name, the student came forward and joined their group, then each team moved off to the side together.

"Team four!" she called out. "Andra! Veter! Amarl! Tukos!"

Amarl gave an internal sigh of relief; Nihos still waited to be placed in a group, and Amarl foresaw disaster if they'd been placed together. He walked silently forward, ignoring the whispers and dark glances that accompanied his passage. Andra gave him another curt nod as he approached. Veter, a boy slightly taller than Amarl and almost as lean, ignored him, while Tukos, a boy standing over a reach in height with broad shoulders and heavy muscles, openly sneered at him. The four walked off to the side in silence, and Andra turned to the group.

"I'm Andra. Tier C Ihuye. Most swords and polearms, level six and higher."

"Veter," the purple-clad shorter boy said next. "Tier B Apo. Bows, crossbows, and Throwing, level five each, Healing at four."

"I'm Tukos. Tier A Es. Spears at five, Endurance at six."

The three looked at Amarl, who shrugged. "I'm Amarl. I assume you were telling each other about your abilities, but obviously, mine hasn't quickened yet, so it doesn't matter. I've got a lot of skills; which ones do you want to know about?"

The boys both scoffed at his ignorance, but Andra just sighed. "Any skill that could be useful in a hunt, Amarl."

"Oh. Well, Ranakar's been preparing me for this, so I've got a few. For weapons, I've got three unarmed forms and Knife Fighting at level three; Scimitar and Staff Fighting both at two; Hiding and Climbing at four; Endurance, Silent Movement, Throwing, Tracking, and Perception at two."

"Not one skill at level five?" Tukos sneered.

"I didn't say that. It's just that my higher skills probably won't be very useful on a hunt. They mostly deal with people." Amarl shrugged. "If you want my whole skill list, we'll be here a while."

Tukos' eyes narrowed, but Andra touched his arm, and he stilled instantly. She looked at the hizeen curiously. "Amarl, I remember your first day at Sitjak. You said you had no weapons skills. Was that a lie?"

He shook his head. "I didn't. I got those mostly from training with Ranakar."

"Wait," Veter said, holding up a hand. "Did you say that you got three unarmed and three weapons skills, all at level two or higher – in the past three moons?"

"Yeah," Amarl nodded. He shrugged. "I think the fact that I came here with a quickened crystal helped a lot."

"Not that much," the boy shook his head and sighed. "Well, that answers the question of what the hells you're doing here."

"And what role he can take," Andra nodded.

"Role?" Amarl asked.

"Yes. There are different roles to a hunting team, and each of us will fill one. Tukos' Es ability makes him our shield. Veter's Apo ability makes him ranged, and my Ihuye ability makes me the damage dealer."

"I know what your ability does," Amarl said. "And I'm guessing that each ability has its own name, but I never learned them."

"Not exactly," Veter shook his head. He glanced at the others, who looked expressionless, then shrugged. "You'd normally learn this next year, but what the hells, right? Might as well know it now. There's a standardized system for naming abilities. Each letter of the alphabet is assigned to one effect or action, and when they're joined together, they describe the ability."

"I have no idea what that means," Amarl laughed.

"Take my ability, Apo. A stands for 'create' or 'fashion'. P is 'water' or 'ice', and O is 'project'. So, I can create ice and use my crafting skills to fashion it into specific shapes, from walls to weapons. I usually make blades I can throw or bolts I can fire from my crossbow since my ranged skills are my highest."

Amarl nodded. "Wait, so are longer names higher tiered, then? I noticed that Tukos' ability is Tier A and has the shortest name, while Andra's has the longest."

"Not always," Andra shook her head. "Longer names are almost always higher tiered, but the tier depends on the base principle. Tukos' base is S, which is Toughness, a Tier A principle. My base principle is Y, which means 'drain' or 'reduce' and is Tier B, but all the modifiers bump it up to Tier C."

"You'll learn all the letters next year," Veter added. "But there are three rules. Vowels tell what the ability does; consonants tell what it uses to do it or affects; and the more common a letter is in the alphabet, the lower its principle's tier and the more common it is in abilities, while the less common a letter is, the higher the tier, and the less likely you are to see it."

"So, what are the highest tier letters?" Amarl asked as sudden realization dawned in his mind.

"Q and Z. Nobody knows what they do, though. No one's ever recorded an ability with either."

Amarl nodded, but he suddenly understood why the Rashiv hadn't been able to Analyze his ability. If no one knew what concept 'Z' stood for, then the Joining Crystal couldn't map out how it worked. He decided then and there never to share his ability's name with anyone unless he had to.

"Enough of the fucking lesson," Tukos growled. "The point, meat, is that with your skills – pathetic as they are – you're going to be our scout. You'll go out ahead of the group and try to find things for us to kill as well as watch to make sure we aren't ambushed."

Amarl frowned. "I thought we weren't supposed to go off alone?" He looked at the tall boy suspiciously; was his group setting him up to fail already? His cynical mind screamed yes, but he didn't really want to believe it.

"You won't be that far ahead," Andra assured him. "We'll be close enough to step in if something happens, and with my ability, we'll have plenty of time to reach you if it does."

"Okay, listen up!" the malim snapped, and everyone fell silent. "By now, you should know one another's abilities and skills as well as have roles chosen. If you haven't done all that, you belong back in second year and not on this hunt!" She glared at the groups, and Amarl looked around as well, but no one looked uncomfortable or frightened. It seemed the higher students knew what to do; he'd just have to watch and follow them.

"Good. Let's get moving."

She turned and led the way into the forest. The teams followed in order, and as his group entered the woods, Amarl looked around curiously.

The edges of the forest showed signs of activity – stumps of felled trees, broken branches, and tons of footprints, too many for him to make out much beyond the fact that a lot of people had been there – but once they passed into the forest, those signs vanished instantly. A worn path wound through the trees, which crowded closely enough overhead that they blocked out the last rays of sunlight completely. Stepping inside felt like stepping into twilight, and he blinked several times as his eyes slowly adjusted to the dim light.

They walked for a little over twenty minutes before Nirecina halted them before a massive tree. The tree's branches spread out in all directions, shading a huge part of the forest, many of the limbs as thick as Amarl's waist close to the trunk. The malim looked them over, her eyes sharp and glittering even in the dim light of the forest.

"We will be going through the Mistway in order of teams. Once we reach the other side, we'll reconnoiter the area, then set up base camp. Team one will head straight, team two left and ahead, team three left and behind, and so on. Clear the immediate area, then return in fifteen minutes. Everyone, get out your crystal."

Amarl reached into his pocket and pulled out the Feeble crystal he'd received to first enter Askula. He looked at the others in his group and saw that they each had Feeble or Weak crystals, but that theirs had multiple points jutting from them, meaning they came from creatures, not plants. Tukos glanced down at the smooth, green stone in the hizeen's hand and snorted contemptuously once more, shaking his head. Amarl ignored the larger boy; hopefully, after this hunt, he'd have more crystals than this simple one.

"Follow me, three second delay," the malim ordered before clenching her fist and walking into the face of the tree's trunk, vanishing into the dark brown bark of its surface. Three seconds later, the first team did the same, and one by one, each team vanished into the tree before Amarl.

As he approached, his heart hammered in his chest. He still remembered his first passage through the Mistway into Askula, and he wasn't excited to experience it again. He found himself hanging at the back of his group, and he had to force himself to clench his fist enough for the crystal to pierce his skin. He closed his eyes and stepped forward, entering the Mistway.

CHAPTER 23

The blue radiance of the Mistway surrounded Amarl, wrapping him in its chill embrace. The light seemed faintly brighter than it had last time, painting his skin in flickering azure patterns. Those patterns seemed random, but something about them screamed of a deeper order and meaning, something beyond his understanding. The mist swirled around him, obscuring but not hiding the dark shapes that moved through it. Whispers echoed in his mind, purring seductively, urging him to come closer, to delve into the mist to investigate, and he took a half step toward them.

His foot scrabbling at the edge of the bridge broke the hypnotic spell the whispers held over his thoughts, and he slid his foot back, his heart pounding suddenly. He glanced down; once more, he stood on a bridge above a mist-filled rift whose bottom he couldn't perceive. The narrow crossing gleamed cerulean in the pervasive light that seemed to come from nowhere and everywhere at once, the stones smooth and polished, stretching forward into the mist beyond his sight. The whispers called to him again, the shapes flickered at the edge of his vision, but he ignored the sounds and walked hastily forward, keeping his eyes glued on the bridge ahead.

Darker shapes rose around him, small at first but swiftly rising to tower over his head. He couldn't help but glance at them; to his relief, the monolithic forms remained still, and no whispers rose from them. The shapes were tall and slender, too obscured for him to see clearly. As he walked, though, the shapes loomed closer and closer to the path, until they crowded him to either side closely enough to tell that they were bare, leafless trees. One of the dark shapes swirled out of the mist in front of him, its surface blocking the path completely. Glowing symbols covered its dark blue, wrinkled surface, and when he reached out to touch it, his hand slid through it. He heaved a sigh of relief; it was the exit. He'd made it through the Mistway.

He stepped through the surface, feeling it glide along his skin, and emerged into a gloomy, fog-filled forest. Trees stretched around him, fading slowly into a grayish mist until they disappeared after ten reaches or so. The trunks looked black in the grayish light bathing them. The trees were almost unnaturally straight, with no branches until two or three reaches above Amarl's head. Underbrush crowded the space between the trees, standing taller than Amarl and growing thickly enough in places that he knew anything could be hiding inside.

Part of him reeled in awe. He stood in another realm, a whole different world than Umpratan, carried there by powers beyond his comprehension. He had no idea what to expect in this world, and he realized that there was no real way for him to know. He could encounter beings and creatures totally unlike what he knew, things he couldn't even imagine! He shivered as the reality of it struck him, rooting him in place for a moment.

"Okay, our area is straight back behind the Mistway door. Amarl, you're on point." Andra's voice broke the spell the new world held over the boy, and he gave himself a mental shake to refocus himself.

"Point?" he asked.

"Yes, out in front, like the point of a spear. Head out first, stay hidden as best you can, and use your skills to see if anything is lurking nearby. If it is, mark it and come back to tell us."

He nodded and walked around the massive tree through which they'd just exited, glancing once over his shoulder to make sure they were actually following him. He thought about unsheathing his scimitar, but the gleaming blade might catch the eye of anything or anyone waiting in ambush. The same went for his knives, so he slipped his staff off his back and held it out before him. He crouched slightly as he entered the underbrush, skirting the large bushes that would rustle and shift as he passed through them. He walked slowly, lowering his heel carefully, then placing the outer edge of his foot down and listening and feeling for anything that crackled or popped beneath his feet. The movement was slow and somewhat tiring for long periods, but it also let him move almost noiselessly across the forest floor.

The fog swirled around him as he slipped through the leaves, his eyes scanning the ground before him. He looked for tiny imperfections in the turf: leaves pressed into the soft ground, claw marks in the soil, or broken sticks and branches that would indicate the passage of an animal or person. To his surprise, the forest was full of tracks, so many that he couldn't always tell one from another. The mist kept the soil damp, making it great for impressions, but also kept all the prints looking fresh and new, rendering them basically useless for tracking purposes.

He kept moving, listening as much as watching now that he knew that his admittedly fledgling tracking skills weren't going to help him much. Unfortunately, the group of students walking a few reaches behind him complicated matters. None of whom apparently had any ability to walk silently, and their feet crackling through leaves and snapping twigs drowned out any sounds he might have heard in the first place. He gritted his teeth in frustration; he could try to move faster, but that would make him louder, and his skills were far too new and untested for him to trust them moving at any speed. Plus, the students could easily keep up with him. He was setting the pace for all of them, not the other way around.

A flicker of movement in his vision and his reflexes, trained by moons of being battered by Ranakar, saved his life. He spun as a dark shape descended toward him, his staff spinning instinctively. The end cracked against the head of a huge snake, easily big enough to swallow him whole, knocking its skull sideways. The force of the blow slid his feet in the wet leaves, but he held his balance and whipped his staff upward, taking the creature under the chin. Its head swiftly retreated, and it drew back, its neck arching as it opened its jaws wide. Its eyes seemed to bore into him, its body swaying hypnotically, and he found himself fascinated by it, staring at it in awe and letting his staff drop slightly.

The serpent struck at its bemused prey, and once more, only Ranakar's training saved Amarl. His staff moved almost of its own accord, slamming again into the monster's skull and knocking it sideways. As its head slid past him from the power of its strike, Amarl thrust with his staff, plunging the butt end into the serpent's black, unblinking eye. The eye collapsed with a pop beneath the steel-shod shaft, and the serpent recoiled swiftly with a loud hiss. It reared back once more, but before it could strike, a shimmering dart streaked past Amarl and plunged into its other eye. The blinded serpent thrashed madly and struck toward Amarl again, but someone shoved him to the side, and he fell hard, rolling in the leaves and coming quickly to his feet, his staff held before him.

Tukos stood where Amarl had been, the snake's mouth wrapped around his chest, dimpling his skin but unable to penetrate. He wrapped his arms around the serpent, pinning it in place, and a moment later, Andra swept past Amarl, the long blade in her hand flashing as she cut. The sword sank into the snake's neck, and she jerked the blade free and slashed once more. Her blade struck the same spot, cutting through the serpent's spine with a muffled thunk, and the snaked ceased thrashing instantly as it dropped to the ground. Tukos pried its jaws off his body and stepped back, allowing Andra to stab down into one of its ruined eyes and the brain behind. The paralyzed creature didn't twitch or move as it died, its heart falling still there in the mists.

Andra yanked her blade free and began to clean it, then walked over to the dead serpent and laid a hand on it. Amarl looked at the girl as she knelt silently, totally confused.

"What's she doing?" he asked quietly, not wanting to disturb her. Tukos sneered down at him and walked away, but Veter gave the younger boy a shrug.

"She's harvesting it for ithtu," he explained. "And no, I'm not going to tell you how to do that. We don't want you to. You won't be able to, anyway, even if I did."

"Why not?"

"Because you can only harvest a creature you kill." A crackling sound filled the air, and Veter gestured toward the snake. "There, look. Here comes the crystal."

Amarl watched in amazement as a yellow crystal the size of his thumb with three points sticking out of it rose out of the monster's ruined eye, seeming to almost grow out of the wound. When it ceased growing, she grabbed it and pulled it effortlessly off the snake, examining it critically.

"Weak crystal, level six," she said diffidently.

"That's not terrible," Veter pointed out. "Not for the first kill of a hunt."

"Not great, either," Tukos grunted as Andra slipped the crystal into a pouch at her waist. The tall boy looked at Amarl. "Think his being here affected it?"

"He didn't kill it or harvest it, so no," Veter replied. "Which reminds me: Amarl, try not to kill anything. Let Andra do it if possible."

"Why?" Amarl asked curiously.

"Because the stronger the ithtar killing and harvesting something is, the stronger the crystal they'll get. From something powerful, Andra might get a Strong ranked crystal when you'd get eight or ten Feeble ones, and trust me, one Strong one is way better for everyone."

"It won't matter," Tukos snorted. "Meat's not going to kill anything, and we all know it."

"I don't know, Tukos," Andra shook her head. "His reflexes are good, and at least he attacked the snake when it went after him. Most novices freeze up on their first hunt. If he'd had a better weapon, he might have killed it himself."

"Whatever." The tall boy looked at Amarl again. "Next time, meat, try looking up every once in a while."

"Yeah, I figured that out," Amarl chuckled, refusing to let the older boy's taunts bother him. "Thanks for the advice, though." He paused. "Although if you guys could stop deliberately making all that noise behind me, it would help."

Andra looked a little shamefaced, but Veter just grinned at him. "Figured it out, did you?"

Amarl nodded, matching the boy's grin. "Yeah, there's just no way that with everything else the school teaches you, they never bothered to show you how to walk quietly. I'm guessing this is another way to screw with the new guy, right?"

"More or less, yeah. You knowing takes the fun out of it, though." He sighed. "I thought we'd get a couple days of driving you crazy, at least."

"Sorry to disappoint – but not very sorry." Without waiting for the boy to reply, Amarl turned and slipped back into the underbrush, grinning as the others set off behind him making much less noise this time.

He spotted the next ambush before it struck; tracks led into a clump of reach-high bushes ahead of him, bushes that shifted and moved slightly despite the lack of wind. He dropped back and informed the others, and Veter shot a crossbow bolt into the bush to flush out whatever lurked within. Something screamed, and a mottled, light gray shape exploded out of the bushes, racing toward the group. After three bounds, it suddenly slowed, seeming to float through the air at a normal walking speed as Andra's ability struck it. Tukos stepped in front of it, jabbing his spear into the slowed creature's chest, while Andra rushed up and slashed it across the throat. Her first cut barely made it through the beast's fur, but her second released a spray of blood that Tukos just managed to avoid. Once again, Andra harvested the creature, pulling another yellow Weak crystal from its hide.

They flushed out two more creatures in their trek away from the Mistway, a black-feathered bird that swooped on them from above and a reach-long beast that looked like someone had taken a squirrel and a fox and mashed them together. Amarl spotted the fox-squirrel clinging to a tree, its dark fur blending into the bark but its slowly moving tail giving it away, but the bird had come hurtling out of the mists above without warning. In both cases, though, he'd stood back and watched while the three older students killed the creatures with ease. After both kills, Andra harvested a pale-yellow crystal that matched the ones they'd found already.

"Okay, that's abut as far as we should go if we're going to make it back on time," the girl finally said, halting Amarl in his tracks. "Time to head back and start setting up camp."

"Fine by me," Tukos grunted. "I can't wait until we begin the actual hunt."

"Wait, this isn't the hunt?" Amarl asked in confusion.

"No," Veter shook his head. "Right now, we're just clearing the nearby area of threats so we can set up a reasonably secure camp. The actual hunt will start tomorrow."

"It can't come soon enough for me," Tukos sighed. "We're going to have to face something dangerous if we want anything better than Weak crystals."

"These things seem pretty dangerous to me," Amarl noted.

"That's because you're pathetic, meat. Any of us could kill these kinds of things all day long without even breaking a sweat."

Amarl glanced at the others to see if the tall boy was exaggerating, but neither of them reacted to his claim. Amarl suddenly realized how weak he really was compared to the older students; if he'd faced any of these creatures alone, he might have killed it, but he would have had to work for it, and he'd probably have been wounded in the process. None of them seemed remotely concerned by the beasts they'd faced so far.

"What we've seen so far, Amarl, are simple animals," Andra explained. "Like wolves in Umpratan. They're dangerous to someone unprepared and untrained, but not to anyone with a quickened ability, or even someone with well-trained weapons skills."

Amarl winced at the implication but couldn't really argue. Compared to the older students, his weapons skills were pretty paltry. In a year, that probably wouldn't be the case, at least not at the rate that he seemed to grow, but at the moment, he was definitely the weakest link in the group's chain. He didn't like it, but he couldn't really argue it, either.

"Stay on point and stay sharp on the way back, Amarl," Andra instructed. "Creatures might have moved in behind us to feed on the remains we left, and we'll need to take care of those, as well."

As it turned out, she was right. Amarl heard the sounds of something eating long before he spotted the scavengers feasting on the bodies they'd left behind, and the group collected three more Weak crystals on the way back. They reached the group to find about half the others back already and busily setting up a camp. They found the malim in the center of the group, watching everyone, and Andra began pulling crystals out of her pouch.

"Group Four reporting, ma'am," she said. "Seven weak crystals, levels three to eight."

"Good work," Nirecina nodded, taking the crystals and placing them in a larger bag that already bulged slightly with irregular shapes. She glanced at Amarl, then back to the girl. "Any problems?"

"No, ma'am," the girl shook her head, and the malim looked surprised for a moment.

"Well..." She seemed to hesitate for a moment, then shrugged. "Good. Clear and set up facing the direction you scouted. You have fourth watch, hours four to five. Fifth group has next watch."

"Yes, ma'am." Andra gestured to the others. "Come on. Let's go get set up so we can eat."

"Setting up", it turned out, meant clearing the underbrush from the area behind the Mistway and raising a large, mottled-gray tent for the four of them. Amarl had never erected a tent before, so he was given a wide-bladed hatchet and told to hack down bushes as close to the ground as possible. Veter followed along behind him, cutting stumps to the forest floor with a glittering, transparent blade of ice instead of a regular sword. Amarl thought at first that the ice blade would shatter the moment it struck a trunk thicker than his pinky, but the blade swept through even the thickest of bushes in a single blow, and he realized that Veter could have cleared everything by himself just as quickly. The others had given Amarl busy work to get him out of the way.

Once an area about three reaches across was cleared of undergrowth and stumps, Andra and Tukos swiftly erected the large tent. Amarl watched closely so he could help the next time; the process seemed simple enough. Four light metal poles with spikes at either end held up the four corners of the tent, with thin ropes looped around the top spikes and staked to the ground to keep them from falling inward. A fourth pole, this one flat on the bottom, went inside the tent to hold up the center. Amarl copied the older students as they unfolded bedrolls and blankets and laid them out inside the tent. As he made to set his up, though, Tukos stopped him and pointed toward the door.

"Yours goes there, meat," he sneered. "That way, if something makes it in here while we're sleeping, it won't get anyone important."

"Really?" Amarl asked doubtfully. "It seems like the person who's the toughest should sleep there, so they have the best chance to survive while the rest of us wake up. I'm pretty sure it would reflect badly on the whole group if someone got badly hurt because we set up the wrong way. We might all end up having to end the hunt early and go back to Askula without any crystals."

"He's right, Tukos," Veter spoke up. "Although even smarter would be for no one to sleep by the entrance. You and Andra should sleep closer to the center, so if something attacks us, you can engage it first, while I hit it from over here."

"That's probably the smartest setup," Andra agreed.

Amarl looked at the others, a little unsure suddenly. "Wait – is there really a chance something might attack the tent in the middle of the night? I thought people were going to be on watch?"

"An ithtar always assumes that no one has their back," Veter said a little pompously, his finger held high, then chuckled, lightening his statement. "At least, that's what the malims tell us."

"It's smarter to prepare for things to go wrong, Amarl," Andra said, her voice oddly intent as she spoke. "Always assume the worst is going to happen, because it probably will."

"Plus, it's entirely possible the malim will send in one of the groups as a mock attack to see if we're prepared," Veter added, looking at Tukos as he spoke. "Imagine what she'd say if they burst in here and found our weakest member in front of the entrance."

"Fine," Tukos grunted and grudgingly set up his bedroll near the center pole, with Andra on the other side of it. Amarl unrolled his padded cloth rectangle between Andra's and the tent wall, while Veter took the opposite side of the tent.

He followed his team members out of the tent and found most of the others gathered around a large fire, eating some sort of stew or soup. He mimicked the others as they grabbed a fired clay bowl from a stack, then scooped up a bowlful of the thick liquid filled with chunks of meat and floating vegetables from a pot sitting atop the fire.

His mind, though, barely focused on his actions or the food. Andra's words rang in his ears. Her tone and the look she gave him as she spoke suggested there was more to her words than she said. Was she telling him that the group was planning something for him? That the others had more little tricks like they'd played on him earlier, walking loudly to attract creatures and distract him? Or something more sinister? He didn't know, but he decided to follow her advice and assume the worst. He wasn't sure what he could do about it, but a little preparation couldn't hurt.

After the other groups finished setting up and joined them around the fire, Nirecina stood up, holding her hands up to silence the students.

"Enjoy the fire, the meal, and the company," she said in a quiet voice. "It's the last time you'll get all three for the next three days. Tomorrow at first hour, we break camp and head out."

She looked over the groups. "You'll each be assigned an area in which to hunt. You will remain in your group's area; poaching in another team's area is strictly prohibited. If you allow your quarry to escape into another team's area, too bad for you. If you're caught in another team's area, you'll forfeit your share of any crystals found on this hunt. Is that clear?"

"Yes, ma'am!" The reply from the group of students was somewhat muted, and Amarl barely stopped himself from shouting the reply.

"Outstanding." She began to walk around the fire, looking at each group in turn. "You're hunting creatures that can produce Minor or better crystals, meaning something that has at least limited sahr usage. I expect each team to bring back a minimum of two Minor or one Strong crystal, but the more you bring in, the more likely you are to get something other than a Weak crystal at the end of the hunt."

She stopped and looked over them again, her eyes hard. "This camp is the last place in this realm where you'll be close to safe. None of you – and I mean not one of you – have the skills and mastery of your ability to survive in this realm alone. Shadora is not a low-tier realm; what you've seen so far is this world's equivalent of vermin. There are things here that even a full ithtar would think twice about before attacking, but they avoid the Mistway because we kill them if they get too close to it.

"Once you leave the cleared area, you are not safe. Assume that you're being hunted by something that can and will kill you if you give it the chance. Don't give it that chance. Remain vigilant, sleep in shifts, maintain your watches, and most of all, watch one another's backs. Your safety and success will depend entirely on how well you work as a team."

Her eyes hardened, and she looked directly at Amarl's group as she spoke. "You are not invulnerable. You cannot handle what this world can throw at you on your own. Every member of your team is valuable, and you'll need to rely on each of them." She let her words sink in for several seconds, letting the silence grow.

Amarl's heart beat faster as a trickle of fear welled up in his heart. He hadn't really expected there to be real danger on this hunt, in all honesty. He'd assumed that it was possible to get hurt, of course, but he figured that there would be an ithtar nearby at all times in case they got into real trouble. It didn't sound like that would be the case, though. Once they left the main camp, it seemed like they'd be on their own, and Amarl's mind began to conjure up all sorts of terrible things that could happen. Thanks to Andra's words earlier, he wasn't just worried about what could befall the group; he was more concerned about what could happen to him in particular. Would they stand back and let him die? Would anyone say anything to them if they did, or would they call it an accident? He didn't know, but he suspected Askula would just decide that he was too weak to make a good weapon and let it go at that.

"Now, hit your tents, and try to get a good night's sleep," the malim finally spoke to break the silence. "It's likely to be the last one you have for two nights." Amarl followed the others back to their tent, but he knew that he, for one, would be sleeping very lightly indeed – and with one of his daggers tucked beneath a pillow, just in case.

CHAPTER 24

Amarl crept through the mist-filled forest, crouched low as he moved slowly and silently toward the sound of running water. He slipped through the underbrush carefully and cautiously, his mottled gray and dark green clothing blending into the foliage as he slid past branches without breaking them, trying to minimize the sounds of his movement as much as possible as he eased toward the water, his eyes searching the trees above him and his ears alert for any sound out of place. He knew from the myriad tracks on the ground that whatever water source lay ahead was used frequently by the forest's inhabitants, and he assumed at least some of them would be present at any given moment. He also assumed they'd be hungry and happy to make a meal out of a clumsy or impatient hizeen. After all, that seemed to have been the case for every creature they'd met so far.

As he predicted, he hadn't slept well the night before. Keeping a dagger under his pillow gave him a sense of security, but it turned out a thin, down-stuffed pillow wasn't enough padding to let him rest comfortably on a solid chunk of metal. He woke constantly throughout the night and started the next day irritable, tired, and suffering from a headache and a nasty crick in his neck that took most of the morning to work out. He avoided speaking to the others as much as possible and was honestly grateful when they set out and he could move out in front of them. He didn't know that they planned anything painful or humiliating for him, but all his experiences with upperclassmen suggested that it was likely they had something like that in mind for this hunt, and he found himself pissed off at all three over the thought of what they might be planning, even though they hadn't done anything so far.

Nirecina had given them their hunting area, which to Amarl's surprise was a massive square two walks across, about a four hour walk if it had been an open field or road. Each group got a similarly sized square, and the malim assured them that they'd know when they reached the boundary of their hunting grounds. Sure enough, an hour later, the team encountered an obviously artificial line of scorched earth burned into the soil, a reach across and running to either side as far as Amarl could see in the mists.

"I take it this is the edge of our hunting ground?" Amarl guessed when the others caught up to him.

"Of course, meat," Tukos snorted. "What in the hells else do you think it could be?"

"The track left behind by some fire-using monster I've never heard of, maybe," Amarl shrugged. "Or the aftermath of some weird lightning storm. I don't know how this world works, so I've got no clue."

"It's the boundary," Andra said with a sigh, cutting off whatever scathing reply Tukos might have made. "This is the edge of the area that Askula patrols, so once we're past that line, we could encounter anything. Stay alert."

Amarl nodded, trying to ignore the sudden hammering of his heart, and set off again, this time moving even more quietly and cautiously. Perhaps because of that, when the first creature ambushed the party, it struck at the three older students, not at Amarl. He didn't see the attack, just heard the shouts of alarm as the creature struck, and he hurried back to see the group fighting a larger version of the big cat they'd faced the day before.

As usual, Tukos had moved to intercept the creature, but he underestimated the two-perl-long beast's mass and the ferocity of its charge. Amarl leaped out of the underbrush to find the cat atop the larger boy, biting and clawing at him fiercely, shredding the camouflage garb Nirecina gave each of them to wear on the hunt. Andra stood over it, slashing with her sword, and a pair of glittering ice blades jutted out of its hide from Veter's attacks.

Amarl dropped his staff and yanked out his scimitar, charging forward and cutting at the beast's back leg. His blade, unlike Andra's, was designed for slashing more than thrusting, and it bit deep, nicking the heavy tendon in the back of the creature's leg. It yowled in pain and whipped its paw back at him, and while he tried to twist out of the way, the heavy leg clipped his side, knocking him back a step and almost making him fall. He regained his balance and struck at the other leg, effectively crippling the beast. It struck at him again, but he anticipated its reaction and slipped out of the way of the blow. A moment later, Andra managed to thrust her sword into the creature's side, sliding the blade between the ribs with the weight of her entire body. The cat stilled at last and collapsed atop Tukos, who laboriously rolled the thing off his body and scrambled to his feet.

"What the hell, meat?" he demanded, looking at his tattered clothing.

"You're supposed to spot things like that! What were you doing, taking a fucking nap?"

"It wasn't there when I passed," Amarl shrugged. He pointed to the beast's hide, where several bramble-covered twigs clung to its dappled fur. "Look, these are freshly broken. It probably picked them up charging at you from out of sight in the mist."

"How could it have seen us if it was out of sight?" the older boy snarled contemptuously.

"Maybe it heard or smelled us."

Tukos took a step toward the smaller boy. "Are you saying I stink?"

"No more than the rest of us," Amarl laughed easily. "None of us bathed this morning, and I'll bet that thing's nose is way better than any of ours. It probably smelled us coming, crept close enough to listen, and heard the three of you – or saw the light flashing on Andra's sword or your spear. Light probably carries farther in this mist than regular vision does."

"He's right, Tukos," Andra sighed as she harvested the creature, getting three glowing, yellow, Weak crystals. "None of us are exactly silent. We're going to have to watch for things like this. Amarl can only see and hear so much without some kind of sensory ability."

Tukos grimaced, then began stripping off his clothing. "Fine. But if I catch the meat dozing when he's supposed to be paying attention…"

"I'm always paying attention, Tukos," Amarl said quietly. "I kind of have to. If something like that cat had gone after me first, I'd probably be dead right now." He looked at Andra as he spoke, his voice and expression both deadly serious. "I have to pay a lot more attention than any of you, and I'm always looking out for danger. From anything and anyone."

The girl paled slightly, and Amarl mentally confirmed that the team planned something painful and probably humiliating for him during their hunt. He'd do his best to be wary, but he knew he couldn't keep his guard up all the time. Everyone needed to sleep sometime, after all. Part of him wondered if it wouldn't just be smarter to circle around the group and head back to the camp, but he couldn't imagine Nirecina would react well to that. What could he say? Just that he suspected that his teammates were planning some sort of novice torture for him, and so far, none of the instructors seemed keen to step in on that sort of thing so long as it didn't go too far. She'd probably be angrier at him for going off on his own. She already didn't want him along; that might be all the excuse she needed to send him back in failure.

So, he set back off into the mists, a growing feeling of isolation welling in his chest. Veter's words yesterday rang in his mind. *"An ithtar always assumes that no one has his back."* Well, he wasn't an ithtar yet – and he might never become one – but the lesson struck home for him. He could only think of two people he could trust to watch out for him, and he'd left them both back in Askula. Out there in Shadora, he was alone, and he couldn't trust anyone but himself. The others could count on one another to some extent, rely on each other in a fight, but he had to assume that they plotted something each moment. The stress and tension built inside him, and his minor headache slowly mushroomed into a pulsing, stabbing pain in his skull.

When he heard the trickling water, he headed directly for it. There would be creatures there, to be sure, and a water source was a good place to look for something stronger than the simple animals they'd fought so far. Even if nothing was there at the moment, he could probably find tracks of something larger and thus probably more dangerous, and they might be able to track it back to wherever it slept. Besides, they'd need water themselves at some point, and while any water source would likely provide a terrible place to camp thanks to the increased beast traffic, staying near it would be smart and probably fruitful.

He peered through the bushes and saw that the ground ahead sloped downward toward a narrow, burbling stream. Tracks led up and down the muddy banks toward the water, and he settled in to observe and see if anything frequented the water source. After five minutes, the only thing he spotted was one of the reach-long, black-furred squirrels plastered against a tree overhanging the brook, only its twitching tail giving away its presence. He began to go back for the others, then stopped.

He'd been relying on them so far, counting on the older students to keep him safe. They'd done so, but what happened if they stopped? No, he corrected mentally, when they stopped, as he was now certain they would at some point. Would he be defenseless? Would they let some creature savage him? He doubted they'd let him die, but they could let him get badly wounded and claim it was his fault for not seeing the attack. They might even think they'd do better without him; he certainly hadn't given them any reason to appreciate having him on their team – or to be concerned about his skills.

Maybe it was time to change that.

He slowly replaced the staff on his back and drew his scimitar. He crept forward, moving as slowly as possible. The squirrel was up out of his reach, so he couldn't just creep up on it and kill it – assuming he was even capable of being that silent, which he doubted – but the farther away it spotted him, the more time it would have to prepare its attack.

He approached to within three reaches when the animal's tail suddenly stilled, and he knew it had seen him. Its body tensed, and he rushed forward, freeing himself from the restraining underbrush as it leaped from the tree directly at him. He twisted to the side, dodging its spring, and slashed with his blade. He felt the edge of it drag along the squirrel's fur, parting its hide but only opening a shallow wound. The creature landed and spun quickly, snapping its bushy tail behind it as it turned to face him and lunged, its long teeth snatching at him.

He stepped back, dodging the attack, and slashed again, this time cutting the creature across its muzzle but missing its eyes and nose. It charged at him, bounding forward, but his hasty blow knocked it aside and cut into the side of its skull.

As he struck at the creature, Amarl felt something stirring within him. The weak song of his ithtu suddenly soared in his mind, and as the squirrel twisted once again to face him, a hot, fiery taste filled his mouth. Everything around him seemed to fade away until only he and the beast existed, and his doubts and fears stilled in his mind, silenced by the triumphant song of his crystal. All of his stress, anger, and frustration seemed to crystallize into the black-furred animal before him, and rather than waiting for it to strike at him, he moved forward, eager to vent his pain and fear on the beast.

The squirrel seemed taken aback by his sudden aggressiveness, and its hesitancy cost it. He stabbed and slashed with his blade, driving the creature back, opening a dozen small but deep cuts on its head, shoulders, and forelegs. He danced past its lunges and responded with thrusts to its throat and face. It squealed in pain as he put out one eye and scrambled toward him, biting madly, but he slipped to the side and cut rather than slashed, putting all his anger and frustration into that single blow. The scimitar sank into the back of the animal's neck and plunged through its vertebrae, cutting through bone and cartilage with ease. The squirrel tumbled to the ground, blood exploding from its half-severed neck, and it fell still at once.

Amarl felt a pulling from the creature, as if something in it spoke to him, calling out for him, and he stepped toward it in a near-daze. Life still pulsed in the animal's body, not the animation provided by blood and brain, but something deeper, more fundamental, and that life sang to him the same way his crystal did. As he reached out toward it, he heard a shout behind him, but beneath the call of the life pulsing in the body, the sound was a mere whisper, barely registering in his ears. He stretched out a hand and touched the squirrel, willing that pulse of life to come to him, to join with him, and he felt it eagerly respond. He gathered the energy to him, drawing it from every span of the creature's body, bringing it to him and begging it to show itself.

Something slammed into his shoulder, breaking his connection with the creature as he felt himself hurled sideways. He crashed to the soft mud and rolled with the landing, coming to his feet with his scimitar in his hand. Something else challenged him, and he was ready; his blood pounded in his skull, his heart pumped eagerly, and his whole body thrilled at the idea of another battle, of more life to be taken and gathered to himself. Power surged within him, rising up and filling his blade, and it danced and flickered with silver light that dappled the ground around him.

"What the fuck are you doing, meat?" Tukos' roar echoed over the song in Amarl's head, shaking his focus, and the hizeen blinked to see the taller boy standing before him. Tukos' fists were clenched, and his face purpled with rage as he took a step toward the boy.

"Are you trying to fuck up this hunt?" Tukos screamed, but Amarl simply remained silent, his blood still roaring in his ears. "Answer me!" The older boy took another step forward, his fist raised, but Amarl simply watched, his blade up and ready. Was this it? Was this the moment they would turn on him? If it was, he was as ready as he'd ever be. It probably wouldn't be enough, but he no longer cared. If they attacked him, he'd fight, and even if he lost today, one day, he'd find a way to make them regret turning on him...

"Tukos, stop!" Andra's voice rang out, but the tall boy ignored her. His fist rose, and Amarl readied his blade. The taste of blood filled his mouth and nose, and he stood ready, almost eager to face the older boy. Tukos lunged, but his punch crawled toward Amarl, moving so slowly the hizeen could watch each muscle in the boy's arm twitch individually.

Amarl twisted to the side, but as he moved, something grabbed at his body. Invisible strings wrapped around his limbs, keeping them from moving, while more plunged into his body, slowing his heart and numbing his muscles. The song of his ithtu rose furiously in his mind, filling his thoughts, and unthinkingly, he lashed out with his mind at the strings. The strands shredded and tore as his thoughts swept through them, freeing him from their grip, and suddenly released from restraint, he twisted to the side and dodged Tukos' crawling punch. He lifted his scimitar, preparing to strike, aiming a slash at the taller boy's thigh that would cripple him and make him easy prey.

Lights flashed in his skull as something hard slammed into his head. Pain flared, and he stumbled sideways, falling hard to the ground. He rolled and scrambled drunkenly to his feet, feeling something dripping from the side of his skull. He touched it and pulled his fingers away, expecting to see blood, but nothing more than slush coated his hand. He glanced down and saw a ball of slush-coated ice swiftly dissipating, and he realized that Veter had attacked him, as well. He lifted his sword, preparing to defend himself, but Andra stepped in front of him, knocking his blade aside and grabbing his shoulders as she stared into his eyes.

"Enough, Amarl!" she shouted, shaking him roughly. "Snap out of it!" He gazed into her eyes and saw a mingling of anger, concern – and fear. That last shattered his focus, and the sound of his ithtu quieted once more to a muted hum in the back of his mind that slowly waned to silence. The roaring in his ears faded, and his vision seemed to expand to take in the world around him once more. A mild wave of weakness washed over his body, making his arms and legs tremble, but he fought it off and stepped back, tearing himself free from Andra's grip. She looked at him, her gaze grave and worried, but she dropped her arms and stepped away from him, eyeing his scimitar carefully.

"Put that away, Amarl," she said softly. "You don't need it anymore."

Amarl's heart still pounded in his chest, and his anger started to rise as he pointed at Tukos, who stood to the side, his chest heaving and his eyes still flat with anger. "He attacked me! Tell me why I don't need this, Andra!"

"You ruined that kill, meat!" Tukos roared. "I saw you trying to harvest it, even after we told you not to! You stupid son of a bitch, I ought to…"

"You ought to shut the fuck up, Tukos," Veter said, stepping in front of the larger boy, his hands raised. "And maybe take a look at that shadow squirrel for a second."

Tukos stared at the smaller boy, his fists still clenched, then looked to the side. Amarl followed his gaze curiously and saw the squirrel's corpse lying still in a pool of its blood. More blood ran down the bank into the stream, mingling with the crystal water in swirls of crimson that quickly vanished in the flow. The creature's head lay twisted to the side, half-severed from its body and held in place only by the neck's muscles and tendons. A single crystal glowed and pulsed atop the squirrel's fur where Amarl had touched it, a crystal half the size of his fist. The crystal glittered and danced in the twilight, matching the gleaming water of the brook.

And the crystal shone bright blue, not the green or yellow he'd expected.

"What the fuck?" Tukos gasped, lowering his hands and walking over to the creature. "That – that's a Strong crystal!"

"Yeah," Veter nodded, glancing back at Amarl with a puzzled expression. "You were about to beat him unconscious, and he just made our minimum for this trip all by himself, Tukos. Don't you feel like an ass, now?"

"I...how? That's not possible! There's not enough ithtu in one of these to make a Strong crystal!"

"So we've been told," Veter shrugged. "Obviously, either the malims lied to us, or Amarl did something he shouldn't have been able to." The boy laughed. "Still want to hit him, Tukos?"

"Don't be stupid," Tukos shook his head, then turned to face Amarl. "How did you do that, meat?" he demanded. Amarl stared at the boy for a moment, then slowly sheathed his sword. His anger faded slightly, but the image of Tukos' fist headed for his head refused to vanish. In that moment, he felt certain he'd seen the group's true nature, and he had no intention of trusting them.

"My name's Amarl, not 'Meat'," he said quietly. "And I'm going to check the banks for signs of something bigger and stronger to hunt."

"Amarl, wait," Andra said, stepping forward. He took a quick step back, his hand going to the hilt of his sword, but she held her hands up and shook her head. "Shit, I'm not going to attack you, Amarl. I just want to know what's going on. Why did you fight that thing by yourself?"

He just stared at her, then let go of the sword and took another step away from them.

"It's like Veter said," he said quietly. "An ithtar has to assume that no one has his back."

He turned and headed toward the stream, his eyes scanning the ground, ignoring the sudden silence behind him. He hoped that letting them know he knew they were planning something would be enough to stop it, but he doubted it. Something was going to happen; he could feel the tension of it simmering in his blood. And when it did, he didn't think he'd be able to do much about it anymore.

When he lost his focus on the battle, he'd lost more than that. The song of his ithtu had faded to silence, and that silence reigned in the quiet of his thoughts. No gentle hum echoed in the back of his head. No soft singing comforted his thoughts. Where he'd felt warmth before, now he felt only emptiness. He quickly pulled up his screen to confirm what he suspected.

ITHTU REPORT
MAX ITHTU: 1
QUICKENING RATE: 6%
MAX ITHTU RANK: MINOR

CURRENT CRYSTALSQUICKENING: 0

POWER QUICKENED TO:
SKILLS — NONE
STATS — NONE
LEVEL — NONE
ABILITY — NONE
TAK — NONE

As he thought, his crystal was gone, and with it went any chance he might have had of handling whatever his supposed team had planned for him.

CHAPTER 25

The most obvious trail Amarl found came down to the water on the opposite side of the stream, near a wide, muddy spot. Tracks crowded the mud near the stream, far too many for Amarl to possibly sort out, but one set stood out from the others. Rather than hoof or paw prints, it looked like someone stabbed two lines of sharp spikes into the ground, serrated spikes that tore up the earth when they were pulled out. Even more telling, the tracks in between these spikes were blurred and muddled, as if someone had tried to cover them up, which Amarl guessed meant whatever made the spike-prints dragged something relatively heavy away from the water into the brush.

He stayed well ahead of the others as he followed the prints. None of them tried to approach or speak to him, but whenever he stopped, he heard their whispers behind him. He wasn't sure if the whispers meant they were planning something, or they were arguing about dropping those plans, but he had to assume it was the former. A coldness settled into his chest, an icy chunk of anger at his certainty that they had planned to humiliate him somehow, and he embraced it, letting its chill settle his turbulent thoughts and freeze any fear he might have still clung to.

Twice, something attacked him, and both times, he dealt with it alone. The first time, a rat nearly a reach long exploded from a nearby bush and lunged at him; the second, a bird ghosted down on silent wings, its beak wide and its claws grasping for him. Both times, he reacted with instant violence, dropping his staff and yanking out his scimitar. As he fought, the chill in his chest spread out into his blood, cooling the fear he knew he should have felt and keeping his mind calm and lucid. The rat was no real problem for him – the creature couldn't bite much higher than his thigh, and he was able to dispatch it easily with a handful of slashes to its face and throat – but the bird was a struggle. The creature refused to stand still and fight him, instead soaring into the trees and wheeling to sweep down on him again, barely giving him a chance to slash at it with each strike. Eventually, he was forced to reclaim his staff, and with the weapon's longer reach, he was able to bat the bird from the sky by smacking its wing, then finish it with a thrust into its throat.

Each time, he stopped and harvested the creatures as the lingering remains of their life essence called out to him, practically shouting for him to draw them into himself. Both times, a glittering, blue crystal rose from the beast as he drew forth every drop of energy left in the monster, and both times, he tried and failed to quicken the crystal. The song of the blue Strong crystals roared in his mind, hammering at his thoughts too powerfully for him to draw them into himself, and he had no choice but to leave the crystals for the others to gather.

He knew they hung back, watching him silently without interfering, and honestly, he preferred it that way. Any of them could have killed either of those creatures without even trying hard, but for some reason, their deaths felt mildly cathartic to him, as if ending their lives and drawing forth their lingering essence sated some deep need in himself that he couldn't explain or understand.

As he passed through the underbrush, something drifted across his face and clung to his lips. He reached up and wiped his face irritably, but the thin strand of whatever it was stuck tenaciously to his skin. At last, he pulled it free and held it out, revealing a long strand of webbing, like that spun by a spider. He paused and looked around, scanning the trees and bushes far more cautiously. It took him nearly a minute to spot the sparkle of another line of webbing stretching from one tree to the next, but once he saw it, his eyes followed the strands until he saw that webbing covered practically every bush and tree before him, all centered on a huge thicket of shrubs and small trees two reaches high and double that across, five reaches from his position. He glanced at the ground and saw that the spike trail led directly into that thicket; he'd found his quarry.

Part of him wanted to go out and deal with what he assumed was a large spider by himself. He'd done well enough on his own so far, after all. He'd watched spiders hunting their prey before, and he knew they were ambush predators, not fighters. If he could get it out of its lair, then take out its legs with his scimitar...

He glanced at the spike trail in the soft earth, shook his head, and slipped back into the bushes. The two lines of spikes were more than two reaches across, closer to three. If the thing in the bushes was a spider, it was probably big enough – and fast enough – to leap out and catch a hizeen boy in one strike. Assuming that its bite was poisonous, that one attack would probably be all it took to end Amarl's life. He was still angry, to be sure, but he wasn't stupid. At least, he refused to be *that* stupid.

He found the others more than six reaches back, moving quietly and slowly to keep from catching up with him. Part of him wanted to hide in the underbrush and startle them, but what little common sense he had told him that not only was that petty, it was stupid to startle someone who could kill you with an ability in a matter of seconds and was obviously already on edge. Plus, his Hiding skill wasn't so great that he was sure they wouldn't spot him, anyway.

He stepped out of the foliage and held up a hand, and the others stopped as they saw him. He walked over and looked at Andra, who he guessed was the leader of their little team – or whatever it was.

"Found it," he said with some satisfaction. "It's a spider, I think – a big one, too. Almost three reaches across."

"Are you sure it's a spider?" the girl asked a bit dubiously.

He shrugged. "No, but it walks on eight legs with barbed, pointed feet, and it's surrounded itself with webbing. That sounds like a spider to me."

"There are spiders, and there are things that sort of look like spiders," Veter shook his head. "Did you find its lair, or nest, or whatever?"

"I think so. It's in a really big thicket about twelve reaches that way." He jerked his thumb over his shoulder.

"How big?" Andra asked. "Is it on the ground, or up in the trees?"

"I couldn't see the spider, so it's probably hiding in the thicket on the ground. And the thicket's maybe four reaches across and two high."

"Death spinner, then, most likely," Veter nodded sagely. "Its lair is probably underground beneath that thicket."

"Death spinner doesn't sound promising," Amarl noted sourly.

"It's actually probably the best thing we could be facing," Andra shook her head with a thin smile. "If it had been a shade strider or night stalker, we'd be getting the fuck out of here and heading to the other side of our territory."

"Death spinners are one of the weakest forms of sahr-using spiders in Shadora," Veter explained. "They're fast, and their poison is dangerous, but they can't shoot webs or venom at you. They primarily use sahr to strengthen their webs and detect prey by sensing it through the ground and their webs, so one also isn't likely to get through Tukos' ability."

"They're still very dangerous, though," Andra warned. She looked at Amarl gravely. "Go ahead and show us where it's hiding, and we'll make a plan to deal with it."

He shrugged and led the three back through the forest to the edge of the undergrowth, where he pointed out the thicket in which the death spinner or whatever the thing was hid. Andra examined it, then looked at Amarl thoughtfully.

"Did you disturb its webbing at all?" she asked in a quiet but not hushed tone.

He nodded. "A strand of it caught on my face, but that's all."

"That's enough," Veter grimaced. "Death spinners can't hear, and their eyesight's not great, but they can feel anything that touches their webs. It knows that you were here."

"It knows we're all here," Andra countered. "We're fifty reaches from its lair. It can feel us standing on the ground here." She tapped her chin thoughtfully. "We need to get it to come out of its thicket, and that means we need to cut some of its webbing. Veter, can you make a blade wide enough for that?"

"No problem," he nodded.

"Good. If you cut the webs between us and that thicket, it might think we're rushing it and come out to play." She looked at Tukos. "When it does, you hold its attention with your spear. Stamp a lot and make plenty of noise." The taller boy nodded curtly but remained silent, and she turned to Veter.

"Try to take out as many of its eyes as possible first. When you've gotten a few, I'll try to sneak up on its flank and take out its legs."

"Can do," the boy smiled.

"What should I do?" Amarl asked, expecting her to tell him to stay out of the way. To his surprise, she didn't.

"When I go after one side, if it doesn't react, you go for the other. Walk lightly and make as little noise as possible, and when you're close, strike at its legs. I'll be doing the same thing on the other side. Death spinners have delicate legs, and if we can cripple it, it'll be easy to kill." She looked at the others. "And we're all agreed, right? Amarl makes the kill and harvests it."

"Oh, hells yeah," Veter chuckled. "I want to see what he'll get from something that uses sahr."

"Me, too. Tukos?" Andra watched the bigger boy for a second, who grimaced but nodded again silently.

"Good." She took a deep breath. "If we get this thing, and Amarl harvests something like a Major crystal, we'll all get Strong crystals from this hunt, no doubt. So, let's work together like an actual team. We don't have to like each other; we just have to work together."

Amarl nodded; he couldn't argue with her, there. Tukos did as well, and she sighed. "Good enough. Veter, let's get this started."

The ice wielder moved to the edge of the bushes, deliberately reaching out and tearing through several strands of webbing. He lifted his hand, and a glittering disc two handspans across that spun like a saw blade suddenly appeared before his palm. He drew his arm back and flung, and the blade shot forward, skimming and rolling across the ground, severing webs as it raced toward the thicket. It crashed into the brush, and a moment later, the bushes shook violently as something large and terrifying burst from them, leaping out into the open beneath the silvery twilight.

Amarl stared at the beast in awe and rising fear. The spider was as big as he'd feared, close to three reaches across, and its body hovered at just about Amarl's eye level. Its head and thorax were dark gray with thin black stripes running down its body that expanded at its abdomen and made the rear part of the spider glossy black with gray streaks. It stood with its forelegs raised in the air, eight black eyes gleaming above two sets of wickedly sharp mandibles that moved in and out as if testing the air.

Tukos burst from the thicket and rushed the spider, which quickly oriented to face him. He shouted and stamped his foot, stabbing with his spear at the creature's face. The spider scuttled forward him, but he thrust his spear at it, holding it at bay.

"Shit!" Andra swore. "That's a night stalker! Tukos, watch out!"

As she called out, the spider jumped back from the warrior and spread its mandibles wide. A spray of clear fluid shot out, and while Tukos dove to the side, some of the fluid spattered on his legs and back. The boy rose to his feet, moving a little unsteadily but still gamely thrusting and stabbing with his spear.

"Veter, its eyes!" Andra shouted, drawing her sword. "Amarl, move, now! Watch out if it turns toward you, either front or back; it can spray its webbing, too!" The girl rushed forward as Veter lifted his crossbow, conjuring a glittering bolt of ice to lay on the groove atop the weapon. The hizeen hesitated for only a moment, then yanked loose his scimitar and rushed forward, moving the opposite direction as Andra toward the thing's side.

The stalker turned to face Andra as she ran, and its jaws gaped wide again. The spray of liquid that shot from its mouth rolled forward with almost agonizing slowness, though, and the girl easily outpaced it, dodging the venom blast. Veter's crossbow thrummed, and a transparent bolt streaked forth to slam into the beast's head. Amarl couldn't see if it hit the target, but the spider began to turn ponderously back toward the archer hiding in the thicket.

As it moved, Amarl raced toward it, lifting his scimitar and hacking at the creature's leg. The weapon struck the black limb with a thunk, and only a chip of exoskeleton flew away from the leg. Despite what Andra said, the spider's legs obviously weren't delicate. He reared back and struck again, trying to hit the same spot, but the creature lifted its leg, and his blade cracked into an undamaged portion of the limb instead. He tried once more, but as he struck, Andra's binding seemed to shatter, and the leg suddenly whipped out at him at full speed, slamming into his chest and knocking him flying. His training kicked in, and he rolled instinctively as he landed, coming to his feet in a crouch two reaches away. His chest ached and throbbed but hurt no more than the blows Ranakar often gave him, and he pushed the pain aside and rushed back in.

As he charged, though, the spider spun in place, its backside suddenly facing toward him. Recalling Andra's words, Amarl quickly shifted directions and cut to his left. The creature's glossy abdomen lifted, and a spray of thin filaments shot from its posterior, blasting back behind it like a net. If Amarl hadn't changed direction, the web blast would definitely have caught him, and while the strands looked thin and flimsy, he doubted they truly were.

He glanced to the side and saw Tukos stabbing somewhat drunkenly at the spider, shouting incoherently at the beast. It began to turn toward the tall boy, but once again, Andra's ability wrapped around it, slowing it drastically. As it turned, Amarl glanced at the creature's iron-hard legs, then down at his scimitar. He simply wasn't strong enough to cut through the thing's armor, at least not its leg armor. He might be able to break a leg if he hammered at it for a few minutes, but he didn't know if Tukos had a few minutes. Taking a deep breath, he ignored Andra's instructions and raced forward, ducking low as he slipped beneath the spider. He ignored its bulbous abdomen and shuffled around in a crouched position as it slowly moved, getting under its thorax. He took another breath, grabbed his scimitar's hilt in both hands, then jammed the blade upward, driving the point not with his arms but with the power of his legs.

The point struck the creature's exoskeleton and skidded slightly, making Amarl's heart leap in his chest. Instead of sliding off, though, it lodged in the seam between two plates of the thing's armor. He drove his body upward, and the blade flexed slightly before punching through the skeleton and sinking into the spider's thorax with a scraping sound.

The arachnid responded instantly, dropping its body and crushing Amarl against the forest floor. He cried out as the creature's weight slammed his back into the soft soil, driving the hilt of his blade into his shoulder painfully. The motion served to plunge the sword even deeper into the spider, though, and it recoiled, jerking its body away from the metal thorn in its flesh. Clear fluid spattered from the hole in its skeleton as the spider jerked the blade free, drenching Amarl, and he panicked as he recalled the toxin it sprayed all over Tukos. The liquid bathing his skin didn't feel dangerous, though, and his head and body felt fine. Whatever coated him, it either wasn't poisonous, or it couldn't affect his non-naluni body.

He scrambled to his feet, his whole body aching, and struck again, driving the point of the blade into a second seam in the creature's armor. This time, he dropped the moment the blade pierced it, and when the spider collapsed on him again, while it squashed him a bit, it didn't knock the wind from him or jam his own sword hilt into him. He yanked the blade free as the creature rose, rolling to the side to keep the rush of clear fluid that splashed out from drenching him further.

"Amarl, get out of there!" Andra shouted, but the boy ignored her and slammed the blade up into the creature one last time, this time a little farther forward. Once more, his scimitar pierced the seam between two armor plates without too much difficulty, but this time, the creature didn't plunge down onto him in response. Instead, it seemed to sink slowly toward him as Andra's power enshrouded it, and he jammed the blade as deep as he could before yanking it out and duck walking as fast as he could back the way he'd come, hacking up into the monster's abdomen a few times for good measure. He emerged behind it and quickly cut to his right, not wanting to get a blast of webbing in the back for his efforts.

He spun to face the creature, ready to strike again, but it seemed it wasn't needed. The spider sank to the ground, its legs curling up underneath it and twitching madly, as if trying to move but unable to. He looked past it and saw Veter half-dragging Tukos away from the beast, while Andra stood before it, her sword ready but not striking. The spider struggled to stand, but its legs seemed unable to support it, and it shivered a few times before finally stilling, its legs curled up under its body.

"Amarl, harvest it," Andra shouted. "I'm going to check on Tukos!"

The boy didn't need any instruction. He felt it when the spider died. Its life force screamed at him, begged him to hurry forth and collect it, and he moved almost trancelike toward the still creature. He could feel its energy surging through it, much more power than any of the animals they'd killed before had. It sang in his mind, urged him to gather it to himself, and in a half-daze, he stretched out his hand and touched its abdomen, willing the energy to him.

Power surged toward him in a torrent, and he almost recoiled and broke contact with it as the flood poured from the creature. He managed to maintain his connection, though, and pulled, drawing the rush of power toward himself. Even as he did, he knew it was too much energy; this creature held as much life as four or five of the lesser beasts he'd killed, and his mind blanched at the thought of that much power. Unthinkingly, he split the flow as it neared him, diverting it into several lesser, more manageable ones, each just barely at the edge of what he could handle. The energy rushed forth, and he watched in awe as a half-dozen glowing, deep blue crystals bigger than his fist rose from the spider's hide, crackling with power as they formed next to his palm. The crystals spread out in a spiny shape like a cluster of midnight blue hedgehogs, growing more and more spines as they expanded.

At last, the power cut off, and he stared at the crystals, willing himself to understand them.

ANALYSIS REPORT
ITEM: ITHTU CRYSTAL
RANK: STRONG
POWER DENSITY: 10
SOURCE: NIGHT STALKER

Ten, he knew, was the maximum power density for a crystal. He'd forged six crystals at the peak of the Strong rank. He reached out hesitantly to touch the closest one. The moment he did, its song soared in his mind, the power of the melody erasing his thoughts, and he jerked his hand back, shaking his head as pain pulsed in his temples. The crystals, he knew, were beyond his ability to safely handle, much less quicken. He took out a rag he used for cleaning his sword and wrapped it around the first crystal, touching it gently through the thick cloth. The crystal's song still sang in his mind, but its powerful notes sounded faint and muted now, and he ignored them as he stuffed the crystals one at a time into his pouch.

He walked around the creature and found Tukos laying on his back, clutching a metal tube in one hand. Veter crouched over him, looking concerned, while Andra watched the tall boy carefully, her eyes assessing.

"Better," Tukos said after a moment, his voice still somewhat slurred. "Need – ithtu, though. Tak's empty."

"You're out?" Andra asked, and the boy nodded. She hesitated, then pulled a yellow crystal from her pouch. "I can only give you a Weak one, Tukos. The Strong ones have to go to Nirecina."

The boy grimaced, then nodded and held out a hand. Andra laid the crystal in his palm, and he closed a fist around it, shutting his eyes. A moment later, he sighed, and his body relaxed.

"Is he okay?" Amarl asked.

"Yeah, he will be," Andra sighed, sitting back on her heels. "The elixir healed the worst of the damage, and his ithtu will handle the rest."

"His ithtu?"

Andra looked at him in surprise. "You didn't know? If you're hurt, sick, or poisoned, your ithtu will heal you. It's not instant, the way a sahr elixir is, but unlike an elixir, it'll heal you from anything short of death itself."

"Haven't you noticed how you're never sore after physical training?" Veter chuckled. "Or how your injuries from sparring are gone in a day or two? That's your ithtu at work, serving you."

Amarl nodded; he and the others had guessed that ithtu helped them recover faster, but he hadn't realized just how much it helped him.

"With night stalker venom, though, Tukos is going to need at least a day to recover," Andra said, shaking her head. "It's sahr-enhanced, so it got through his ability, and his ithtu will need time to destroy it and heal the damage it's causing." She looked around at the clearing, then shrugged. "Might as well set up camp here, I suppose. It's as good a place as any."

"After we get rid of the giant spider corpse," Veter said distastefully. "It'll draw scavengers if we don't." He looked at Amarl. "Speaking of which, what did you get from it?"

"Six more Strong crystals," the hizeen shrugged, using his cloth to reach into his bag and pull one of the large crystals out.

Veter whistled appreciatively and took the crystal from the boy, examining it. "Look at the color," he said in amazement. "It's so deep – this thing is level ten, peak Strong!" He looked at the boy. "And you said you got six of them?"

Amarl nodded and patted his bag.

"Well, I was hoping for a Major crystal, to be honest, but I guess that's just getting greedy," the older boy laughed, handing the crystal back to Amarl, who slipped it back into his pouch.

"Sorry. I tried to keep the power together as one flow, but it was too much for me. I had to split it up."

"No need to apologize. Even Andra would have been lucky to get a single Strong crystal from this thing. She'd probably have ended up with a few Minor ones instead."

"I would have." Andra nodded and rose to her feet. "Amarl, help me pull this thing out into the forest a ways so we can set up camp."

"Are you sure this is a good place?" he asked, looking around at the web-strewn clearing.

"Yeah. There aren't many things that will intrude on a night stalker's lair, and hopefully, nothing that would is anywhere near us." She gestured to him, and he followed her into the clearing. The two each grabbed a curled leg of the dead creature and began hauling it into the woods, guiding it around trees and avoiding thick underbrush. The spider was actually lighter than Amarl thought it would be from when it crushed him, and while the pair had to work to move it, it wasn't unmanageable.

"Damn, you drained this thing dry," Andra shook her head. "I can't feel a hint of energy left in it."

"Isn't that what usually happens when a creature gets harvested?" he asked.

"No, not really. At least, not when students do it. Some energy always gets missed – a lot of it, actually – and once someone's tried to harvest it, whatever's left is lost. That's why higher-tiered ithtaru usually do the harvesting; we leave less power behind, so we get stronger crystals on average." She stopped and looked around. "I think this is far enough. Anything that comes to eat it here won't bother us in our camp."

"If you say so," he shrugged. "It feels creepy as shit to me."

"Oh, it is, but if it keeps Tukos safe, it's worth it."

Amarl and Andra helped Veter set up the tent, and the trio moved Tukos inside, where he could rest. They built up a fire and used it to warm some water and rations, then sat down to eat and recover from the battle. They sat in silence; Amarl felt no need to talk to the older students, and apparently, they had nothing to say to him, either. Eventually, Veter went into the tent, making excuses about being tired, leaving Andra and Amarl alone.

"I can take first watch," the girl suggested. "You should get some sleep."

Amarl shook his head. "I'm not tired. Not really. I'll stay up for a bit."

She nodded and made to stand, then froze as the bushes nearby crackled and shifted. Amarl jumped to his feet, grabbing his scimitar, but he froze when a familiar figure emerged from the trees and strode out into the clearing. The figure was tall and muscular, dressed in mottled gray that matched the misty surroundings well, and as he stepped out of the forest, he nodded toward the silent Andra.

"Thanks for your help, Andra. I can take it from here." Nihos cracked his knuckles and grinned evilly as he looked at Amarl. "Hello, Meat."

CHAPTER 26

"Nihos, wait," Andra said, stepping forward and holding up a hand.

"You're not getting cold feet, are you, Andra?" the older boy asked in an evil voice. His dark hair was short, almost invisible against his round skull, and the black tattoo that started at his left ear and swept beneath his chin, around his neck, and down into his shirt seemed to gleam in the dim light. "You were paid well to carry that tracker and stand back. Are you planning to give all that money back?"

"You know I can't. It's just..." She glanced back at Amarl. "I don't think this is a good idea, Nihos."

"I do." The taller boy walked forward, still staring at Amarl with dark, unblinking eyes. "Do you, Meat?"

Amarl simply stood in silence, his jaw clenched and his hand gripping his scimitar tightly. He recalled how Meder had said that he should be grateful that Andra was coming along, as if the older girl would somehow keep him safe. She hadn't, though; she'd been plotting against him the whole time. All her subtle hints coalesced in his mind; she hadn't been warning him about herself. She'd been warning him about Nihos.

"Nihos, he just killed a night stalker," she said quietly. "He harvested six Strong crystals from it."

"Is that so, Meat?" The older boy laughed. "Maybe when this is done, you can harvest me some Strong crystals, too." He grinned viciously. "Assuming that you're still around, that is."

"We agreed," Andra said quickly. "No abilities, and he has to be able to be healed by sahr. I don't want to explain anything to the malims!"

"What's to explain? The meat went off alone and got jumped by something. Happens in hunts." He shrugged. "No one's going to miss him. No one even wants him here."

"No, Nihos. You know I can take you if I want to. No abilities, and he walks away from it." She stepped toward him, her hand on her sword. "I agreed to help him get a beating. I never agreed to murder."

The tall boy grimaced, then spat on the ground. "Fine. No abilities, and he lives through it."

Andra looked at Amarl, her face stricken. "Fine," she sighed, stepping back. "Just – just get it over with."

Nihos looked at Amarl with a sneer. "What, you thinking of drawing that sword, Meat?" he asked contemptuously. "Go ahead, draw it. It won't matter."

Amarl yanked out the scimitar and stood back, waiting. He didn't want to attack first; he didn't know if that was what the boy was waiting for, and part of him hoped that if he didn't strike first, the older boy wouldn't, either. Even as he thought that, he knew it wasn't true. Nirecina had forbidden them to go into another group's territory, and Nihos had done that. If he was willing to break that rule, Amarl doubted he cared about the self-defense one. Despite what Nihos promised Andra, Amarl didn't think the older boy intended to leave him alive. He couldn't; if he did, Amarl might report what happened, and despite what Nihos thought, Amarl knew there were trackers in Askula who could tell what happened here. The only way they wouldn't be called in was if they had no reason to look, and that meant Amarl couldn't be around to tell the story.

His heart pounded, and sweat slicked his brow and his grip on the scimitar. Fear wormed up and down his spine, and his brain screamed at him to run, to dive into the trees and try to get away. He doubted he could, though. Nihos was taller and stronger than him, and he'd been training at Askula for three years. The boy doubtless had a much better Running skill than Amarl, and his long legs would eat up the ground.

"What's wrong, Meat?" the boy laughed. "Too scared to fight? Here, let me make it easy on you." Nihos bounded forward, and Amarl slashed at him, backing off as he did. The boy leaned back, letting the sword slip past him, then lashed out with a foot. The lightning-fast kick slammed into Amarl's hand, and his sword tumbled from his already slick grip. The boy's foot flashed out again, crashing into Amarl's stomach, and the hizeen curled up and fell back as every inch of his breath whooshed out of his body.

He managed to scramble to his feet, though, sucking in a deep, gasping breath and trying to ignore his throbbing stomach. He raised his hands and spread his feet as he shifted into Water Form, but the older boy just laughed.

"Oh, the Meat wants to spar!" he said mockingly. "Okay, Meat. Let's spar." Nihos lifted his hands and dropped into a stance that looked more like Burik's Military Boxing than any of Amarl's unarmed forms. His loose hands covered his face, while his elbows protected his ribs. He stood lightly on feet a little more than shoulder-width apart, bouncing his weight up and down.

Nihos' fist flashed toward Amarl, and the smaller boy slipped to the side to block it. He quickly realized the strike had been a feint as the boy's back foot snapped up and crashed into his lower back, knocking him forward. Amarl managed to tuck and roll, rising to his feet, but Nihos was there. The boy snapped a fist at Amarl's head, tagging him high on the skull, and as Amarl staggered from the blow, the boy grabbed his shoulders and slammed his knee into the hizeen's stomach. Amarl dropped again, gagging and coughing, trying to catch his breath. Before he could, though, a fist crashed into the side of his skull, and pain exploded in his head, knocking him sprawling to the ground. He groaned and coughed, clutching his head and rolling on the damp earth as the world went distant and hazy for a moment.

"Come on, Meat," Nihos laughed. "You can take more than that." The boy grabbed Amarl by the hair and yanked him up, and as he did, Amarl uncoiled. His fist lashed up, powered not just by his arm but by his whole body, and sank into the softness between Nihos' thighs. He felt the boy's balls crumple beneath his knuckles, and Nihos cried out with a loud scream as he lifted up onto his toes. Amarl grinned triumphantly, then pain blossomed in his face as another fist crashed into him.

"Fucker!" Nihos screamed. "You little fuck!" Amarl fell to the ground, barely aware, but the foot crashing into his side jerked him back to the moment. Agony flooded his side as he heard ribs pop, and he screamed as another foot crashed into his stomach, grinding the bones against one another.

"Nihos, stop!" Andra's voice sounded distant and faint as a foot swept across Amarl's face, cracking his jaw and circling his vision with blackness. "You'll kill him!"

"Fuck that!" Nihos roared, sweeping a hand toward the girl. "You see what he did? The little fucker's going to pay!"

Amarl screamed again as Nihos grabbed his hair and yanked him up to his knees. He felt the boy's arm circle around his throat, cutting off his wind, while Nihos' lips pressed against his ear.

"They paid me just to fuck you up, Meat," the boy whispered. "That's all I was gonna do. But now, I'm gonna break your fucking neck, and even Andra can't stop me. Goodbye, Meat!"

A hand grabbed the top of Amarl's head, and panic exploded within him. He thrashed and fought, striking with his elbows, but Nihos absorbed the blows harmlessly. Everything started to go dark, and Amarl heard soft, sad music ringing in his ears. Desperately, he reached for that sound, but it remained distant, untouchable. As he fought vainly, he stretched out to the sound, hearing it swell as his thoughts grew closer to it. The noise of it rose to a thunderous volume that pounded in his ears and rattled his brain, and part of him hesitated. What he did was dangerous, possibly deadly. The power could consume him, that he knew. As the pressure on his neck increased to the point of pain, though, he cast his hesitation aside. One path led to sure death; down the other, there was a choice between death and power.

That choice was his, and he made it. He embraced the power, felt it surge into his body, screaming through his veins. The song exploded into a triumphant symphony that washed out all thought, banished his pain, and battered against his very self. He fought against it, struggling to control that flood of power, but as he did, he knew that he would fail. It was too much for him, too much energy for him to hold, and he would be washed away by it. He couldn't fight it; just like Nihos, it was a power that he couldn't match.

"You might want to consider who you're really fighting."

Ranakar's words rang in his mind, piercing the cacophony in his skull. The awal had somehow predicted this moment, seen that Amarl would face a foe that he couldn't simply defeat with power and skill. He'd asked what Amarl would do; would the boy give up and die?

"No. No, I won't. I'll die fighting, but I won't give up."

That thought echoed in his skull, and with it, something in his chest rose up. Fire surged in his blood, but it didn't burn, it purified. He knew who he'd been fighting; he fought himself, not Nihos, not Ranakar, not Askula. He fought his own nature. He rejected his power. He'd denied it, downplayed it, refused to accept it, but no more. The power flooding through his body belonged to him; he couldn't have called it if his soul couldn't handle it. It would serve him. The ithtu always wanted to serve.

He lashed out with an elbow, and Nihos cried out as the power filling Amarl's arm surged into the boy, cracking his leg. Amarl felt the pressure around his throat ease, and he twisted, slipping into Bear Form as he grabbed

Nihos's legs and yanked, driving his shoulder into the boy's midsection. The tall boy swore as his feet flew out from under him, and he crashed hard to the ground, but he held out a hand, and Amarl felt himself flung backward as a visible wave of force slammed into his chest. He expected to feel pain, but the impact was barely noticeable, and he rolled swiftly to his feet.

His body felt alive in a way it never had before. Every muscle and nerve trembled with power. His senses shivered as they took in every detail, watching almost impassively as Nihos rose to his feet and thrust his hand out again. Amarl slipped into Water Form easily, leaning aside and letting the flattened globule of force slip past him.

"No abilities!" Andra's voice was a roar in his sensitive ears, a roar that the triumphant song in his head quickly drowned out. Nihos snarled and lunged forward, lashing out with a foot and following it with a pair of punches, one high to draw off Amarl's guard and one low to crash into his solar plexus. Amarl slid past the kick, ignored the feint, and blocked the body blow, redirecting the force around and past him.

Nihos stumbled slightly but recovered quickly, lashing out with a rapid barrage of punches and knee strikes. Amarl flowed around each one, finally moving like the water the form was named after. He marveled at how easy it was once he stopped fighting his own body, stopped thinking about what to do and simply did it. Water didn't think or plan; it simply existed, moving from one place to the next because it had no choice but to flow. Amarl allowed his thoughts to drift and floated with the tide of the battle, rolling around the older boy's strikes. Each dodge, each shift, every movement undercut Nihos' balance, eroding at his base like the endless tide. At last, Nihos stumbled, and the wave Amarl had gathered stood ready to crash against the shore.

He shifted his feet and yanked the older boy forward, pulling him off-balance. Nihos' arms windmilled as he struggled not to fall, and Amarl's hands flowed outward almost gently as they crashed into Nihos's chest. The power building in the boy exploded outward, and Nihos screamed as he was hurled backward, tumbling to the earth. The tall boy struggled to rise, his eyes wide and his face pale, clutching his ribs with one hand. He coughed, and blood streamed from his mouth as he held the other hand up pleadingly. He shook his head, his lips moving, but Amarl didn't care to hear what he said.

The boy had come to take Amarl's life. That was his choice, and now he reaped the consequence.

Amarl rushed forward as he slipped into Tiger Form, readying himself to strike at the older boy. As he did, strands of energy suddenly whipped around him, grabbing at his limbs and plunging into his body, trying to stop him. Power flared in him as the song in his mind soared even higher, and the strands blackened and curled away from his body, unable to touch him. A flare of power surged behind him, and he spun, swiping the solid ball of ice from the air with a swat of his hand. He charged forward, ducking beneath a sloppy blow from Nihos. His hand lashed out, palm-first, fingers curled like a tiger's claws. Nihos tried to dodge, but the blow slammed into the center of the boy's chest, and Amarl felt the surge of power roll out through it. Nihos flew back once more, crashing limply to the earth, blood flowing freely from his mouth and his body still and unmoving.

"Shit!" Andra rushed forward, placing her hand on Nihos' chest and throat. She looked at Veter, who stood unmoving near the tent, his eyes wide and his face pale. "Get an elixir! Hurry!"

The boy blinked and vanished into the tent, emerging a second later with a metal tube. He froze as Amarl stepped toward him, holding up a hand.

"Amarl, if he doesn't drink this, he'll die!" Veter said. "Hurry, get out of my way!" He took a step forward, but Amarl swept his foot and shoved gently against his chest, and he tumbled backward, landing in a roll, his face panicked. "What the hells, Amarl?"

"He came here to kill me," Amarl said quietly. "He was trying to kill me; to snap my neck. He made his choice. Choice is Ak-lahat's gift to the world." He didn't know where the words came from, but they felt right, and as he spoke them, he felt a cold touch ripple across his spine. He looked at Andra. "And you helped him. That was your choice, too."

The girl rose to her feet, tears blinking from her eyes. "Fine. Yes, it was my choice, Amarl. And it was the wrong choice. It was selfish and stupid. But now you have a choice, too. You can choose to let him live or let him die." She stood straighter. "Which choice do you think Nihos would make? And which one would your friends?"

Amarl took a step back as her words impacted him, and the song in his head quieted to a murmur. She was right. Burik and Meder might understand if Amarl killed Nihos, but they'd never look at Amarl the same way again. This death would change him, make him someone else, and he didn't know if they'd still like the person he'd become. He took a deep, shuddering breath and stepped back, nodding to Veter once. The boy raced across the clearing and knelt beside Nihos, unscrewing the lid from the elixir and gently pouring it into the unconscious boy's mouth. Andra just watched, but Amarl stared at her, his anger seething within him.

"Why, Andra?" he asked softly. "Why? What did I ever do to you?"

"I'd kind of like to know that, too," Veter muttered as he slowly administered the liquid. "I mean, teasing him is one thing, but this is fucked up."

"Nothing, Amarl," she shook her head, blinking tears from her eyes. "You didn't do anything."

"Then WHY?" he suddenly shouted as rage surged over him. "You brought him here to kill me!"

"No!' she protested. "No! I wouldn't! He – he gave me a lot of money, Amarl. Money I need. Crafting components are expensive, and…"

"Alchemy?" Veter demanded in disbelief. "You did this to help your fucking Alchemy?"

"I didn't think it would be like this!" she half screamed. "Nihos told me he was just going to rough Amarl up and scare him, that's all! It's what we all do to novices, Veter, even you! I made him promise not to use any abilities and to make sure we could heal him right up."

"And that makes it better?" Veter shouted back. "You know Nihos! He's a fucking psychopath! Why would you trust him?"

"I – I thought it wouldn't matter. I thought that I could stop him if he got out of hand. I'm stronger than him, and I've always beaten him at Halit…" She blinked again and wiped her eyes. "I thought I had it under control!"

"Yeah, great fucking job," Veter shook his head. "Nihos will be lucky to live the night, and you're lucky Amarl didn't do the same thing to you! I saw how he broke your ability." He glanced at the silent hizeen. "And I really fucking want to know how you did that."

Amarl ignored the boy's tacit request and stared at Andra. "So, you betrayed me for money," he said quietly.

"Betrayed you?" She laughed weakly and wiped her eyes again. "Amarl, I didn't betray anyone. Sure, I let things get out of hand, but this kind of shit? This is what the fucking malims *want* us to do. This is what they *tell* us to do to novices."

"What?" His voice reflected his confusion. "What are you talking about?"

"Malim Nirecina told us to haze you until you quit," Veter said woodenly. "Said that you don't belong on a hunt, and she would prove it. That was why we were walking so loudly earlier, and why we didn't jump in when you fought that shadow squirrel. You were supposed to panic and run, and then we could say that you were a danger to the team."

Amarl's anger still burned within him, but now it glowed like banked coals rather than roaring flames, and as the flame of his rage cooled, the song in his head grew quiet. Weakness suddenly washed over him as the power filling him retreated, and he had to force himself to stand upright as his legs trembled beneath him.

"She did?"

"Yes," Andra said. "And before you get all bent out of shape, that's the kind of shit that happens to us all when we first come out here. Older students harass the younger ones, try to get them to break, or cry, or scream for help, or something." She grimaced. "My first hunt, in my second year, the third-years pinned my arms while one held a rot wolf a foot from my face, letting it snap and lunge at me." She shuddered. "I pissed myself, and they thought it was hilarious."

"That's fucked up," he said coldly. "And you were all planning to do something like that to me?"

"Yeah," Veter admitted. "I thought that the snake would do it, honestly. Most second-years would have broken and run from that if it attacked them on their first hunt. Then the shadow squirrel – I was sure we'd have to save you from that, and that you'd realize that a first-year had no business being out here." He shook his head. "I was wrong, though. You're scarier than that fucking night stalker." He turned and glared at Andra. "And I thought we all *agreed* that we weren't doing anything like that to him anymore! That he'd proven that he deserved to be here!"

"I'd already taken the money!" she shouted. "Where do you think all these elixirs we've been using came from? I pulled them out of my ass? Each one of these things costs two or three akatos to make, Veter! I figured that as long as I was using what I made from the money for the team, not just for me..."

"Yeah, you're a fucking spirit of kindness," Veter shook his head. He stopped and took a deep breath. "Okay, Amarl, here's the simple truth. Every older student is told to harass the younger ones. We're told it's to make you independent and strong, able to handle the hard life of an ithtar, but I think that's bullshit. There's some other reason.

"Be that as it may, though, what Andra and Nihos did – that went way beyond what we're supposed to do. Nihos broke the rules coming here, broke them again attacking you first, and then tossed them out the fucking window by trying to kill you. And Andra helped him with all that, so as far as the school's concerned, she's just as guilty.

"Now, the question is, what are you going to do about it?"

Amarl looked at Andra, who stood with her shoulders slumped, looking defeated. "What choices do I have?" he asked quietly.

"Choice number one, we go get the malim and bring her here to sort all this out," Veter sighed. "If you do, Nihos will probably be expelled – and expulsion means execution. Anyone who flunks out of Askula doesn't live to talk about it. There can't be any rogue ithtaru. Andra will probably be flogged, barred from any further hunts, and put on disciplinary duty for a year or so, but it depends on the awals. She might join Nihos.

"The problem with that is that Tukos can't be moved, and that means you either have to leave her here with Nihos and trust that she'll watch him, or you have to take her with you and trust that she won't just try to silence you to make all this go away."

"I wouldn't do that," Andra protested quietly.

"Yeah, like he's going to fucking trust your word, Andra. Would you right now?"

Amarl nodded. "Choice two?"

"Choice two is that we let him heal up here for a day, then send him on his way. We don't say anything to anyone about all this. If his teammates raise a stink about his being gone, that's up to them and not our concern. Of course, if you do that, there's a chance that Nihos will come after you again seeking revenge." Veter snorted. "He'd be a fucking idiot after the way you beat his ass, but he might do it – or go after your friends.

"Is there a choice three?"

"Choice three..." Veter hesitated. "We drag Nihos out into the woods and leave him for something to find. It's brutal, but it keeps Andra out of trouble, and honestly, it's no worse than what he probably deserves."

"Why not just let me kill him, then?" Amarl asked. "Why waste an elixir on him?"

"Because if we heal him and leave him for dead, you didn't kill him." The boy shook his head. "You don't get it, Amarl. If you kill him, then you can harvest him, and your Joining Crystal will show that. Any awal who wants to can access those records, and they'll be able to tell that you killed him just by Analyzing you. Then, you'll be the one expelled. Understand?"

"That's why Nihos said he wanted to make it look like a creature got you," Andra said sadly. "He wanted to do what Veter's talking about."

Amarl thought for several seconds. "The fair thing to do is to get the malim and let them both face their consequences. That would stop Nihos from hurting anyone, and Andra would pay for what she did."

"Yeah, probably," Veter agreed.

"But that might hurt Tukos, and we'd have to trust Andra – which I don't." The girl winced but didn't protest. "Letting Nihos heal up, though, seems stupid. He seems like the kind of person who'd do whatever he could to hurt me, even if it meant hurting my friends. Am I right?"

"Yes," Andra said sadly. "I could see Nihos doing that. And like I told you once, an upperclassman can make a novice's life the spirits' hell if they really want to without getting in any trouble."

Amarl nodded. "If it was just me, I'd probably say, heal him up. It's not, though. I've got friends, and I have to look out for them, too." He took a deep breath. "Drag him out to the woods and leave him for the beasts."

Veter nodded. "Yeah. That's probably what I'd do, too. Nihos isn't someone I'd want as an enemy." He rose to his feet and grabbed the boy beneath the shoulders, but as he did, Andra shook her head.

"No. I'll do it. I caused all this. I should be the one to do this."

Veter's eyes narrowed. "How about we both go? We can drop him by the night stalker's corpse; that will attract scavengers, and it'll look like he was trying to poach our kills." He shook his head. "And honestly, Andra, I don't much trust you right now. I don't think either of us do."

"Okay," she said quietly. "We'll go together." She grabbed the boy's feet, and the two of them vanished into the trees, leaving Amarl alone.

The power that sustained him had fled his body, but he could still feel its song soaring in the back of his mind. He reached into his pouch and pulled out the source of that song, the Strong crystal he'd quickened without touching it in his terror and desperation. Its surface no longer singed him, and its song no longer drowned out his thoughts. He'd claimed it, trusting his soul and whatever heritage gave him his abilities with ithtu to carry him through, no longer fighting against his nature. He quickly pulled up his status and ithtu screens and read the results of his efforts.

STATS
FORCE: 5.2 (122%)　　SKILL: 5.3 (135%)
SPEED: 5.6 (183%)　　TOUGHNESS: 4.5 (61%)
MIND: 5.7 (201%)　　WILL: 3.8 (30%)
PRESENCE: 6.2 (332%)　　SOUL: 9.6 (9,948%)

QUICKENED ABILITY: MEZ
TIER: F
PERCENT QUICKENED: 32.1%

CURRENT ITHTU: 47.4
TO LEVEL: 0
TO STATS: 0
TO SKILLS: 0
TO TAK: 13

CURRENT TAK: 1.1 / 13

ITHTU REPORT
MAX ITHTU: 2
QUICKENING RATE: 6.6%
MAX ITHTU RANK: STRONG

CURRENT CRYSTALS QUICKENING: 1
1 – RANK: STRONG　　DENSITY: 10　　POWER: 47.4
QUICKENED: 0%

POWER QUICKENED TO:
SKILLS – NONE
STATS – NONE
LEVEL – NONE
ABILITY – 34.4 (32.1%)
TAK – 13 (0.01%)

Whatever he'd done bumped his Soul stat up another tenth of a point, which increased his tak to thirteen. That tak was practically empty thanks to his fight against Nihos, but it would fill back up quickly enough. That would be easier since completing his last crystal raised Amarl's Mind stat to five-seven, which apparently was the threshold for being able to quicken two crystals. He was glad about that; it meant that at the end of the hunt, when crystals were doled out as rewards, he'd be able to take and quicken a second one – not that he was sure he really needed it. The new crystal was incredibly powerful, and Amarl could draw on it for a long time. It was also stronger than he should have been able to handle, but he'd never really been a fan of worrying about what he should do.

He dismissed the screens and stared into the slowly darkening forest. His heart ached inside his chest, and it felt like he'd lost something, or it had been taken from him. He wondered what Meder and Burik would say if they knew what he'd just done. Burik, he guessed, would probably agree with his decision. Meder, though, wouldn't, and he didn't know how it would change her feelings toward him. For a moment, he considered hiding his deed from them, but he dismissed that thought immediately. He would never tell another soul – but he'd tell them. They deserved to know, to decide if they wanted to stay his friends. He wasn't sure they would, and the fear of their reaction hovered in the back of his thoughts.

He pushed it aside. That, he could deal with later. First, he had to survive to get back to them. He hoped that the night's events had firmly driven any thoughts of hazing him from the other students' minds. Hopefully, they were too afraid of him and what he might do to try something. Even so, he knew he wouldn't be sleeping that night.

It was going to be a very long hunt.

CHAPTER 27

Night in Shadora, at least in the mist-filled forest in which they hunted, wasn't much different from day as far as Amarl could tell. He had no idea what provided the silver light that filtered through the dark trees, or if that light was silver because of the mists or if the mists were silver because of the light. What he did know was that the light source apparently moved around overhead, and at some point, it must have dropped low in the sky. The shadows of the trees darkened and mingled, spreading out to create a rough semblance of darkness, and the silver hue bled away from the fog, leaving roiling white clouds in its wake. Visibility, already limited, dropped to a handful of reaches, blocking sight beyond a dozen paces or so. The biggest difference, in fact, seemed to be the fact that the forest came alive once the shadows deepened.

Andra was wrong in her prediction about other creatures avoiding the night stalker's nest. Either that, or she was right, and if they'd camped somewhere else, things would have been much worse. Creatures entered the clearing at least once or twice an hour, and each time, the three able students had to kill them quickly, then drag their bodies away to keep their blood from drawing more predators. Amarl spent the night grabbing sleep in ten and fifteen-minute bursts, dozing off only to awaken seemingly seconds later to the sounds of battle. By morning, he was exhausted, and he wasn't the only one. Dark circles ringed Andra's eyes, and Veter's shoulders slumped wearily. They all moved slowly as they ate a cold meal of prepared rations in silence, and the fourteen Minor and Strong crystals they'd collected from their efforts hardly seemed worth the interminable night.

"There's no point to trying to hunt today," Andra said in a subdued voice, obviously still worried about the night before. "Tukos can't go, and someone has to stay with him. Two of us can't handle something like another night stalker if we run into one."

"Agreed," Veter nodded wearily. "We should rest while we can, especially if tonight's going to be like last night."

They spent the day sleeping in two-hour shifts, two of them resting with Tukos while the third stayed awake and kept watch for an hour. It didn't really leave Amarl feeling rested, but at least exhaustion no longer tugged at his body and mind. Tukos seemed to recover late in the day, and Andra had them break down the camp once he was up and moving. He seemed confused by the silent tension filling the air, but he didn't ask about it, and no one volunteered. None of them, Amarl guessed, wanted to admit what they'd done.

"If tonight's going to be like last night, sitting still and staying put is probably a bad idea," she said. "Every animal we kill will draw others, and pretty soon we're going to be overrun. We need to stay mobile and deal with things as we find them. Amarl..."

"Yeah, I know," he said tiredly. "I'm on point."

"Yes, please. But please, no fighting things alone tonight. There's a chance that the night stalker's nest actually did ward things away, and if that's true, there are going to be a lot more animals wandering around than normal. If noise from a fight attracts something else to the battle, you could be in trouble. Okay?"

"Fine." Part of him wanted to keep hunting on his own when he could, but he saw the logic in her statement. He didn't trust her – or any of them, really – but he didn't really feel like becoming something's dinner, either. Plus, he was too tired to argue.

The night passed in a bloody haze. The forest really had come alive with the deepening of the shadows. Creatures like the squirrels and rats that were probably food for many others scurried out to forage beneath the blanket of the night's concealment, and that lured the greater predators out to hunt them down. Most of these were simple enough for the group to deal with, but twice, they were ambushed by powerful beasts wielding sahr.

The first was a bird with wings more than a reach across, huge eyes, and a long, curved beak, looking like a giant owl with darker feathers. The creature swept down on them in total silence, its wings unmoving as it rode the air currents, and they only discovered it as it let out a loud, hooting cry. That cry smashed into the group like a hammer, knocking Amarl and Veter sprawling and staggering Andra. Only Tukos remained unharmed, which was probably what saved the group since the tall boy's spear held the creature at bay. Amarl's head spun, and his thoughts swam lazily in his skull, refusing to form together into coherent thought for several seconds. During that time, both he and Veter were basically helpless, and if Tukos hadn't been there, the bird might have badly wounded or even killed one of them. Fortunately, the tall boy fended it off until Veter recovered and used his ranged attacks to ground it, making it easy prey for the group.

The second time, a creature that looked like a three-reach-long weasel with glossy, black fur and claws as long as Amarl's hand exploded out of the forest floor, emerging from a hole in the ground that had been covered with the illusion of solid ground. The creature's body blurred and shifted as it attacked, making it hard to focus on, and it struck with fierce savagery, clawing and biting at all four of the students almost madly. Working together, they managed to kill the creature, but not without taking some injuries themselves. Andra ended up with a slash to the stomach, Veter got a long cut on his cheek, and Amarl's arm pulsed painfully where the weasel bit him. Only Tukos ended up unharmed, although he once again had to replace his tattered and shredded clothing.

Andra handed out more small metal vials of healing elixir after the battle. "Drink up," she said wearily. "We can't afford to hunt injured like this. The blood will draw predators from walks away."

At last, the tired, battered group trudged back toward the base camp. Even Tukos' endurance was flagging by that point, and the group did their best to avoid any more encounters rather than triggering them. Hours later, the massive Mistway tree emerged from the fog, and they hurried toward it almost eagerly. As they rounded the tree, they found Nirecina waiting for them, sitting by the fire, a look of mild disapproval on her face. The malim looked pointedly around the otherwise empty campsite and then back at the group, shaking her head.

"Gave up already?" she asked gruffly. "You still had hours to hunt, you know."

"Yes, ma'am," Andra nodded. "But we thought we'd gathered enough crystals already, so we decided to come back in early."

The woman rolled her eyes. "Let me guess. You got your two Minor crystals and figured that was enough, right?" She sighed, looking at Amarl. "I knew letting you join was a bad idea. Novices have no place on a full hunt..."

"Actually, ma'am..." the girl interrupted the woman. Andra froze as Nirecina's expression turned into a flat, cold glare, but she took a breath and pushed on. "I'm willing to bet that we've got the best haul in the hunt."

She gestured to the others, then opened her pouch and began pouring out crystals onto the soft ground. Veter and Tukos did the same, and when they finished, Amarl used his cleaning cloth to pull out a total of eleven large, deep blue crystals he'd gotten from the three sahr-using creatures they'd fought. They stepped back, and Nirecina stared at the pile of almost three dozen crystals, a few of them pale yellow or deep violet but most various shades of blue. The woman's mouth hung open, her anger vanished in an instant, and she stood, speechless, as the students shared knowing glances and concealed grins.

"This…" the woman stammered, her expression shocked and confused. "How – you harvested all these from your hunt? In just two days?"

"This isn't our entire haul, ma'am," Andra admitted. "Tukos got poisoned by a night stalker and ran out of ithtu, so I gave him a Weak crystal to help him heal." They'd all agreed not to mention Amarl quickening the Strong crystal; they didn't want to have to explain why it had been necessary, for obvious reasons.

"You killed the night stalker?" the woman echoed. "You shouldn't have been able to kill that…"

"We did, ma'am."

The malim shook her head, seeming to recover herself, and her gaze turned into an angry frown. "Student, I don't know what you're playing at, here, but I don't have the patience for games! Where did you get these crystals?"

"We – we harvested them, ma'am," Andra replied, her eyes wide.

"Bullshit." The woman picked up one of the deep blue crystals and hefted it. "This is a peak Strong crystal, almost a Major one. There's no way a Tier C student harvested it, even from something like a night stalker. It's not possible. So, where did you really get them?"

"I didn't harvest them, ma'am," Andra said quietly, glancing over at Amarl. "Amarl did."

The malim turned quickly to face Amarl, her eyes radiating disbelief. "No. He hasn't even quickened an ability, let alone learned how to harvest. Even if he got lucky and figured it out, he'd get nothing but Feeble crystals."

"It's true, malim," Veter spoke up earnestly. "Amarl harvested everything except the Weak crystals. Andra got those." The girl gave him a sharp look, but he shrugged. "What? It's true."

"Student Tukos," Nirecina said sharply, glaring at the tall boy. "Remembering that a single infraction will have you banned from hunting for a year and chopping trees for Feeble crystals, tell me the truth. Where did these crystals come from?"

The boy shrugged, his face disgruntled. "It's true, ma'am. The meat..." He stopped and glanced at Amarl, then grimaced. "Sorry. Amarl harvested them all. I don't know how, but he did it. We all watched it happen at least twenty times."

She glared at the students, her eyes piercing as she scanned their faces, Amarl guessed in search of any sign they were lying to her. At last, she turned to face Amarl. "Fine," she said flatly. "Show me."

"Show you, ma'am?" the boy echoed, glancing around the campsite. "How? There's nothing here to harvest."

"You three, stay here and don't budge from this spot," she snapped, pointing to the older students. She reached out and grabbed Amarl's shirt, hauling him close. "The novice and I are going to go find something he can demonstrate on." She hesitated. "Last chance. If you're making me waste ithtu on this, I swear to all the gods above and below that I'll have all your asses flogged every day for a week, understand?" She waited, but none of the students spoke. At last, she shrugged.

"Have it your way." She looked at Amarl. "Close your eyes. I don't want you puking all over me."

He looked at her, startled not only by her words but by the sheer strength of her grip. She glared at him, and he quickly slammed his eyes shut. The moment he did, the world lurched around him. Wind roared in his ears and tore at his clothes, whipping his hair across his face in a furious frenzy. The world spun dizzily as the direction "down" vanished and vertigo overwhelmed him. The feeling lasted for long seconds before he felt a slight shudder run through the malim, and the world skidded to a halt. He tumbled to the ground, dizzy and reeling, afraid to open his eyes.

"Stand up!" the malim snapped. Amarl pried his eyes open, but the forest lurched around him, and he quickly snapped them shut. "Oh, for fuck's sake." He felt himself hauled to his feet, and a cool hand pressed against his forehead. Energy flowed from that hand into him, and the spinning in his head faded slowly. The hand withdrew, and the malim released him. He staggered slightly as his legs adjusted to his weight, but when he slowly peeked his eyes open, the world no longer swam and spun around him.

"Kill that and harvest it," Nirecina said harshly, pointing her finger to her left. Amarl glanced over and saw one of the large squirrels lying on its side on the ground, its chest heaving and its forelegs scrabbling at the ground while its hindlegs lay still and limp. Its spine twisted at a weird angle, explaining why it couldn't move, and Amarl stared at it in shock. From what he could tell, Nirecina had shattered the creature's back just by running into it at an incredible rate of speed. As he stared, something hard struck the back of his head.

"Now!" she said harshly, withdrawing her hand from where she'd smacked him. "Show me this amazing harvesting ability of yours, or I will beat you until you're an inch from death for wasting my time. Go!"

Amarl swallowed hard and drew his scimitar, approaching the squirrel warily. The animal chittered and hissed at him as he approached, but with its rear legs useless, it couldn't do more than snap helplessly at him. He lifted the blade and aimed carefully, then slashed, cutting into the beast's throat. He jumped sideways as blood sprayed from the wound, jetting down into the ground, and he watched silently as the animal's struggles slowly weakened and stilled. At last, it collapsed on the ground, its heartbeat ceasing as the last of its blood oozed into the dark soil.

Its life sang to him, not the triumphant song he usually heard but a mournful dirge, and he understood. Killing it wasn't a joyous battle but a simple slaughter, and he hadn't earned the life force he was about to take. The squirrel's essence wept at the knowledge that it was going to be stolen, not gathered in victory, and Amarl's already wounded heart lurched at the melancholy of its song.

Pushing his sorrow aside as much as he could, the boy stepped over to the creature and laid a hand upon it, gathering and guiding its energy. The power swirled up within it, rising unwillingly at his command, but rising, nonetheless. He drew every drop of it he could and called it forth, and with a tinkling sound, a pale blue crystal the size of his middle finger grew like a tree from the creature's fur. When the last trickle of power flowed out of the animal, Amarl removed his hand and plucked the crystal. The shard sang in his mind, its song gloomy and distraught, and he quickly handed it to the malim, blinking as a wave of sorrow swept through him.

She took the crystal with a trembling hand, staring at it, then looked up at Amarl with an awed expression. "This – how?" she stammered. She walked past him to the squirrel and touched it, then pulled her hand back, shaking her head. "You sucked it completely dry, boy! How did you do that? And how did you keep the power flows coherent?"

Amarl shrugged. "I don't know what that means, ma'am. I just did it."

"You – you just…" She stopped and took a deep breath, clenching the crystal in her fist. "And you did this for all of those crystals back at camp?"

"Yes, ma'am. Well, the Minor and Strong ones. Like Veter said, Andra harvested the Weak ones."

"Do you know what you did, boy?" she asked in the same quiet voice. "Do you know what this means?"

"No, ma'am," he shook his head. "I mean, I don't know what it means."

She brayed a sudden burst of laughter. "Ha! Neither do I!" She clenched her fist around the crystal with a determined expression. "I'll tell you this, though. I'm hauling your ass along on every hunt they'll let me. If you can do this to something really powerful, you could get Major or even Grand crystals!" Her eyes shone, but he shook his head regretfully.

"I don't think so, ma'am. When I harvested the night stalker – or the other sahr animals we killed – I found I couldn't handle enough power to make anything more than a Strong crystal."

"Not yet, but we'll fix that." Her eyes shone, and the doubt was gone from her face. "I'll talk to Ranakar; I'm sure we can work something out." She stopped and looked at him, then shook her head. "Sorry. We should get back to the others. I'm sure they're starting to worry."

Amarl grimaced, but Nirecina chuckled. "Don't worry, boy. I'm not pissed anymore, so the trip back will be better than the trip here." She grabbed his shirt and yanked him close once more. "You might still want to close your eyes, though."

He snapped his eyes shut, and the wind began to pick up, but it rose around him much more gradually this time. The sensation of motion and weightlessness rose about him slowly, and while it still felt mildly dizzying, his head didn't swim or spin. The sensation lasted longer, a full minute or more, before it slowly faded. As the world stabilized around him, Nirecina set him back on his feet, and he opened his eyes to see the others staring at them expectantly.

"Well, it seems an apology is in order," the malim spoke, her voice even and calm. "I doubted you all, and I was wrong. You did well – outstanding, in fact – and I think it's safe to say you'll be getting first pick of the crystals when everyone returns." She looked at the group, taking in their exhausted and bedraggled state. "In the meantime, sit down, grab something to eat, and tell me about it."

Amarl wasn't hungry – he just didn't have the emotional energy left to feel hunger, really – but he took a slice of bread to chew on just so he wouldn't have to speak. The others got bowls of the same stew they'd eaten the first day of the hunt and settled in around the fire. Andra began to relate the story of their hunt, fortunately giving the woman a heavily edited version of events. She told how Amarl killed and harvested his first squirrel but left out Tukos' attack on him and how he somehow broke her ability. She talked about the night stalker battle but didn't mention Nihos' presence. When she finished, the malim leaned back, her eyes thoughtful.

"No wonder you all look like shit," she said wonderingly. "A night stalker, a mist screecher, and a blur weasel? That's more than most groups see in a dozen hunts. And you faced at least double the animals you should have."

"Double, ma'am?" Veter asked.

The woman nodded. "You think we just send you students out here?" she asked. "Fuck no. Too many of you would die or be seriously injured. The day before this hunt, we had a team sweep the hunting areas and drive out most of the creatures. We left a couple stronger ones in each area, so you could get your Minor crystals – including the night stalker, although I thought you'd be smart enough to avoid that – but we chased out most of the others."

She leaned back on her log seat and folded her arms. "It sounds like you had a pretty normal first day, but those nights..." She shook her head. "Even I've never heard of a night like those here in Shadora. In Necronia or Malefican, sure, but not Shadora. It's like you faced a week's worth of creatures over two days."

She rose to her feet and grabbed an obviously empty pack, tossing it on the ground beside the pile of crystals. "Go ahead and load those into the pack. After everyone gets back, we'll announce an official winner and let you pick your crystals." She snorted. "Not that there's any doubt, but if everyone faced the same numbers of creatures your group did, this hunt's going to be very profitable." She hesitated, then bent down and gathered up the large, deep blue crystals.

"These, though, are going to the school. I doubt any of you would be able to quicken them, and if you did, it would take you years to empty one. They can be put to better use."

Amarl saw minor disappointment in both Veter and Andra's faces, but it didn't bother him. He'd already quickened one, and while he thought he could do it again, he wasn't eager to try. It had nearly broken his mind, and he decided he'd stick with Minor crystals for a while.

"Once you're done, try to grab some rest before the others return. You really do look like shit." The malim rose and walked away, and the students put down their food and began wearily dumping crystals into the bag. Once they finished, Amarl followed them back to the spot where they'd first camped.

"I'm not setting up the tent," Veter said emphatically. "We're just going to have to take it down again when everyone starts coming back."

"That's fine," Andra sighed. "I don't really want to bother, either. Someone's going to have to keep watch, though. If the others get back and find us sleeping, there's no telling what they might do. I don't want to wake up with something inappropriate drawn on my face, do you?"

"I'll watch for a bit," Amarl volunteered. "I'm tired, but not really sleepy."

"Same here," Tukos nodded. "I'll stay up with him."

Andra looked at the tall boy, her face concerned, and exchanged a look with Veter. The other student just shrugged, and she sighed. "Fine. But please don't start fighting, okay? I want to get at least a couple hours of sleep."

Andra and Veter unrolled their bedrolls and lay down on them, falling asleep within minutes. Amarl walked back to the fire and sat down, staring into the flickering flames. He felt numb and empty inside, as if all his emotions had been wrung out, and he didn't have the energy to focus on anything. Most of all, he didn't want to think – to think of what happened, of what Nihos had done, and of what he'd done in response.

A moment later, he felt as much as saw Tukos settle in beside him, and he flinched without thinking. He didn't want to talk, but he knew the boy wouldn't have sat down just to be near him.

"I, um…" Tukos took a deep breath, obviously uncomfortable. "I just wanted to say thanks."

"For what?" Amarl asked in a puzzled voice.

"For not mentioning what happened after you harvested that first shadow squirrel." The tall boy shifted uncomfortably on the log. "You could have, and I'd have gotten in trouble for it. So, thanks for not saying anything."

Amarl shrugged. Tukos had slept through Nihos' visit, and they hadn't told him about what happened so that the boy didn't have to keep their secret. Amarl wasn't worried about the others saying anything – Veter and Andra had been the ones to actually leave the student in the forest, so they obviously wouldn't talk about it – but Tukos had no real reason to keep silent. So, the boy probably thought that everyone was upset over him, when honestly, Amarl had almost forgotten about the incident.

"You've probably noticed that I've got a bit of a temper," Tukos added.

"What, you?" Amarl asked dryly, shaking his head. "You're the soul of gentleness and patience, Tukos. Ask anyone." He bit his tongue; he hadn't meant to say that, but he was too wrung out to catch himself.

The boy's eyes flattened, but he took another breath and let out an obviously forced laugh. "Yeah, that's me. Glad you noticed." He shifted again on the log. "See, my temper's already gotten me in trouble on a couple of these hunts. People screw up or make mistakes, and I don't handle it well. The last hunt I went on, we came back with no crystals because we were too busy fighting to harvest."

He grimaced. "No, because I was too busy arguing. I fucked up the whole hunt, and the malims told me that if I did it again, I'd be banned from hunting. You know what that means?" Amarl shook his head. "Well, it means that the only way for me to get crystals is to work in the fields or the forest, harvesting crops and cutting down trees for Feeble ones. It's the worst possible way to get crystals, and it seriously limits your growth and advancement."

He sighed. "I think that's why they paired me with Andra, you know. Her ability's really good at keeping people under control, and it's hard to counter if you don't have a speed ability of your own. Even then, I've seen her catch both Ehe's and Ehee's with it in sparring." Seeing Amarl's puzzled face, he added, "Those are two of the basic speed-boosting abilities, one Tier A and the other Tier B. If someone who can move at double or triple normal speed can't beat her ability, what chance do the rest of us have?"

Amarl didn't bother to mention that he'd somehow evaded her power. He didn't need more questions and speculations.

"The point is, that's why I was so pissed off when you were put in my group. I thought the malims were setting me up to fail, pairing me with a novice with no ability and barely any skills. I was afraid that if we had a bad hunt, I'd lose my chance to get any more crystals like this." He chuckled. "Instead, having you in the group basically secured my chance to go on future hunts, no question. Nobody can argue that we weren't successful this time. So, I was wrong, and I'm sorry."

Amarl sat in silence for a few moments, considering the boy's words. The simple fact was, Tukos' apology didn't mean shit. He wasn't sorry that he'd attacked or mistreated Amarl, just that he'd thought Amarl was worthless when he wasn't. The boy had lost it over the potential for a single Weak crystal, not a Minor or Strong one that would have mattered for the hunt. Everything he'd said was nothing but excuses, and pretty shitty ones at that.

He tried to imagine what would have happened if Tukos had come to Tem instead of Danmila. When none of the first candidates turned out to be a potential ithtar, would Tukos have kept his cool? Or would he have attacked people, venting his frustration on the helpless? Amarl guessed the second option was far more likely, but he also guessed that Askula wouldn't let someone like Tukos out into the world. The boy would be as much a danger to those around him as to the Empire's enemies. He now knew what the Order did to students who turned out to be unsuitable to become ithtaru. He had a feeling Tukos didn't have much of a future at Askula – or at all.

However, that wasn't Amarl's problem, not really. Tukos made his own choices, and he'd have to deal with the consequences. Choice was Aklahat's gift to the world, after all, and he doubted the older boy would listen to any advice he might bother to give.

"Thanks," he said at last.

"Yeah." Tukos sighed again and rose to his feet. "I'm gonna go watch near our camp, just to make sure no one creeps up on us that way."

"Sounds good," Amarl nodded.

He stared at the fire as the older boy walked away. It occurred to him that ithtu crystals might not be the only harvest a student could reap while at Askula, and not every bounty would be a welcome one. He sighed and poked at the fire with a stick. He was ready for the hunt to be done and to head back to Askula. At least, with Burik and Meder, he knew who had his back.

And now, thanks to Andra, he knew for a fact that no one else did.

CHAPTER 28

"Holy shit," Burik said, his eyes wide as Amarl finished telling the story of his hunt. "I mean – you – holy shit!"

"Yeah. That about sums it up," Amarl agreed with a heavy sigh.

"I can't believe that Nihos actually attacked you – and tried to kill you!" Burik's face turned red and angry. "Herel, that son of a bitch! I'll bet he was behind it! The next time I spar against him…"

"Amarl, why did you do that?" Meder asked quietly, interrupting Burik. "You could have gone to the malim. They would have punished Nihos."

He nodded. "Yeah, but I would have had to either leave Tukos behind with only Andra to protect him – and that would have given her a chance to try and drag Nihos away and hide what happened – or to take Andra with me, and I wasn't about to do that."

He took a deep, ragged breath. He couldn't look her in the eyes, afraid of what he'd see there. "And I couldn't let him recover. Nihos – he was crazy, out of control. Even if he was too scared to come after me again, he might have gone after you two. And I didn't want anything to happen to you…so, I…"

He took another breath, blinking as tears welled in his eyes. The enormity of what he'd done suddenly struck him. He'd taken a nalu life. Oh, he hadn't slit Nihos' throat, but he'd killed the boy, just the same. There was no doubt about that.

When Team Six returned one person short, the camp went up in flames. Nirecina screamed at them, demanded to know where Nihos was and why they hadn't stayed together. The other members of the team tried to explain that they didn't know; he'd volunteered to stand watch, then disappeared without a trace. They'd searched to no avail. Nirecina grabbed one of the girls from the team the same way she'd hauled Amarl around and commanded the girl to show her where they'd been camped. They vanished from the camp and returned thirty minutes later, carrying torn and half-eaten remains.

"Everyone come take a look at this!" Nirecina bellowed, tossing Nihos's corpse onto the ground. "Look at it! This is why you don't go off alone on a hunt, no matter how fucking strong you think you are!" She looked around at the others. "This student left his territory, on his own, and went hunting in someone else's, and this is what he got for it!"

Amarl felt some relief that the malim believed that Nihos had gone off and been overcome by creatures. He suspected that might not have been the case had the other groups not all come back with a common complaint.

"There were hardly any creatures to hunt, ma'am," a muscular girl who apparently headed up Team Five had reported as she held out four Weak crystals and one Minor one. "Especially once night fell. It was like the forest emptied as it got dark."

Team One managed a decent haul of three Minor and eight Weak crystals, but the other teams had similar luck to Team Five's. As each reported, Nirecina glanced at Amarl, and it didn't take him long to make the connection. As far as he could tell, the other teams faced fewer creatures because they'd all headed to Amarl's team's area for some reason. That made it seem reasonable that Nihos had followed the animals into Amarl's territory and been overcome by the sheer number of them.

Nirecina hadn't suspected anything amiss, but guilt still gnawed at Amarl's gut. Once he'd returned to Sabila, he'd asked Meder and Burik to join him in their room, and once the door closed, he poured out everything. It hurt to admit it, but it also felt cleansing. Still, the thought of how they might react – what they might think of him – terrified him.

"I – I'm sorry," Amarl said hoarsely. "I know it was an awful thing to do, but it was my only real choice. I don't blame you if you don't want me around anymore..."

He stopped as Meder's arms wrapped around him, pulling him close to her, and suddenly, all the stress of the hunt seemed to explode from his chest. He clutched her tightly, pressing his face into her shoulder as sobs wracked his body. She simply held him, letting him get it all out. He clung to her fiercely; no one had ever comforted him like that before, and part of him never wanted it to end.

At last, though, his sobs quieted, and he relaxed his hold on her. He didn't feel good, but he felt – cleaner, as if he'd purged something foul from inside him. As he regained himself, she leaned back and took his face in her hands, looking down into his eyes.

"Amarl, you are an idiot," she said, shaking her head.

"W-what?" he asked, caught by surprise.

"You are. Did you really think you were going to tell us that, and we'd hate you for it?" She sighed. "I'm so sorry that you had to make that choice. It sounds awful, but I understand why you did it."

"My mother always says, when every choice is evil, it's impossible to be good," Burik said quietly. "Those were some evil choices you had, Amarl. Personally, I think you made the right one."

"Honestly? So do I," Meder sighed.

Amarl looked up at her, surprised. "You do?"

She nodded. "I've been asking around about Nihos for a while, but I really started digging once you went off on a hunt with him. Apparently, he's a borderline psychopath."

"That's what Veter called him, too. I don't know what it means, though."

"In Nihos' case, it meant that he liked hurting people. He enjoyed giving people pain." She shook her head. "He's been on disciplinary duty and been publicly flogged multiple times, but everyone is still afraid of him. No one wants to spar with him because he likes to make it as painful as possible." She made a face. "Well, he liked it, I guess."

She gave Amarl a very serious look as she continued. "If you'd gone hunting for Nihos, that would be one thing. But he came for you. He tried to kill you. And I think you're right that he would have tried to hurt us to punish you for beating him. What you did isn't what I would have done, but – it was probably the best solution."

"I have a feeling that we're all going to have to make a lot of those sorts of decisions as ithtaru," Burik said solemnly. "I know my mother's had to in the service of the Empire. I don't know why it would be any different for us."

"Your mother's had to do things like that?" Meder asked.

"Well, not exactly the same, but yeah. That's part of being an officer. Sometimes, you have to sacrifice one life to save two – or a thousand to save ten thousand."

"Well, I hope you're wrong, and I don't have to do that again," Amarl said heavily. "Thanks, though – for listening, and for understanding."

"Of course! You're stuck with us, my friend. We're not going anywhere."

"No, we aren't," Meder smiled at him before sitting back down on the bed. She frowned. "It concerns me that the older students are told to harass us, though."

"That's what Andra said," Amarl shrugged. "And I don't think she was lying. I'm pretty sure if I hadn't been able to harvest better crystals, they'd have made that hunt even worse for me than it was."

"It wasn't all bad," Burik pointed out. "You learned something about yourself, and you got a new crystal, right?"

"True. And it was one of the peak Strong crystals, the ones that Nirecina didn't share. Not that it matters. We brought back enough that everyone got at least a Minor crystal – well, everyone except Team Six, that is. They lost a person, so they forfeited their crystals. Usually, though, most people have to settle for Weak crystals, from what Veter said."

"I want to know more about how you ignored Andra's ability," Meder said. "What did you do?"

"I have no idea," he admitted. "I just didn't want something holding me, so I didn't let it. I didn't do anything on purpose."

"That's amazing," the girl sighed. "From what everyone says, she has one of the strongest Tier C abilities. How could you just stop it from affecting you?"

"No clue," he shrugged. "I can barely remember how it felt anymore, to be honest."

"Really?"

"Yeah. That's how it always is when this happens. It's like a dream, and the memory of how it felt or what I did starts to fade the moment that I wake up. I still remember what happened, but how I did it?" He shrugged. "No clue."

"I'm sure Ranakar will ask him all about it," Burik pointed out. "He might even have an explanation."

"He might not know, actually. It's not like it was in our report to Nirecina."

"Are you going to tell him?" Meder asked.

"The part where Tukos attacked me? Probably," Amarl sighed. "It doesn't make any sense to keep it from him, does it?"

"Not really, no."

He grimaced. "Nirecina's going to try to make me go on more hunts now."

"I'd call that lucky," Burik offered.

"After what he went through?" Meder scoffed. "I would be a lot more than hesitant, Burik. I'd be terrified to do it again."

"By almost any standards, they were wildly successful, though. No one was seriously wounded, they didn't lose any members of their team, and they came back with a shitload of crystals. Plus, Amarl scared three upperclassmen into leaving him alone. Most people would call that a win."

"And each time he goes out, he'll have to do that again with a new group. Or he'll have to endure whatever they've got planned for him."

"Exactly," Amarl nodded glumly. "I don't want to have to try to intimidate every third-year in Askula – especially when I have no clue how I did it in the first place. What if it doesn't work next time, or if trying makes them angry enough to really hurt me?"

"You should tell Ranakar that," Meder suggested.

Amarl snorted. "I don't think he'll care. No one listens to the blade's complaints when it's being forged, after all. If he thinks more hunts will make me stronger, he'll send me on them, whether I want to go or not."

"But he won't want anything bad to happen to you, will he?"

"Probably nothing permanent, but getting terrorized by some older students?" He shrugged. "I think any of the malims would call that instructional."

"Harsh, but probably true," Burik agreed.

"You know that means we're going to have to deal with the same thing eventually, Burik," Meder pointed out.

"Probably, yes."

"That doesn't concern you?"

"There's nothing I can do about it, at least not now. I'll worry when I have to."

"So, what did I miss while I was gone?" Amarl asked, wanting to change the subject. He knew Burik was right – there wasn't anything any of them could do about the situation – but part of him rankled at that helplessness. The more he thought about it, the angrier it made him, but he had no real outlet for that anger, so he decided the best thing was to try not to think about it.

"They've started bringing in a new group of potentials," Burik replied nonchalantly. "I think they're planning to test them this Akio."

"A new group already?" Amarl asked in surprise. "I thought they'd let us get further along, first."

"Apparently, the malims like to bring students into the school in small groups," Burik shrugged. "A new group comes in every three moons or so."

"Why would they do it like that?"

"It's actually very reasonable if you think about it," Meder said. "It seems to take about one to two moons to quicken a crystal, then another moon or so to find your tak. At this point, we're all working on improving our stats, which doesn't take as much focus and guidance, so they can start teaching a new group of novices how to quicken a crystal while we work on other things."

"The same goes for physical training," Burik added. "Even Hadur doesn't struggle with running anymore, and we've all moved into advanced training with weights instead. Periteth can start whipping a new group into shape."

"Wait, does that mean they're changing your schedules around?" Amarl asked.

"Yeah. Starting next week, we'll only do an hour of physical training in the morning, then we'll be doing daily weapons training for the second hour, and skills training goes to six days a week as well."

"I can't wait," Meder laughed. "I'll take more skill training and less physical training any day. It's still the spirits' hells."

Amarl's mental exhaustion caused him to oversleep the next morning, and he practically ran to Ranakar's tower without eating, not wanting to be late for class. That had happened once, and the old man hadn't been pleased. Amarl had spent that morning running up and down the tower stairs, six flights of them, carrying two barrels of water on his shoulders to teach him how to hurry up stairs. He'd ended up separating one shoulder and vomiting all over the stairs; Ranakar healed his shoulder and made the boy clean up his puke with his own shirt. Amarl had never been late to class again.

He burst through the door in time, but as he entered, something moved in the corner of his vision. He reacted instinctively, diving forward beneath the closest rope and grabbing a pole to help him spin to his feet facing the threat. He found the awal standing next to the door, a short staff in his hand, nodding appreciatively.

"Good awareness." The man set the staff against the wall and moved in his normal flowing gait into the center of the room. "Sit." Amarl quickly moved to obey and settled himself before the man, who joined him on the floor.

"I read the records about your hunt," the awal began without preamble. "Before we discuss them, I'd like you to tell me your impressions of it."

"I'm not sure what you mean," the boy replied cautiously. "My impressions?"

"Yes. I'm not interested in what happened – we'll discuss that as well as what happened that didn't make the report. I want to know what you thought of it. Give me your honest opinion."

"My opinion?" Amarl hesitated. He knew that most of the time, when people asked for an honest opinion, what they really wanted was for him to tell them what they wanted to hear. Ranakar, though, wasn't the kind of person he wanted to lie to. The old man had an uncanny ability to find things out, and he was free with his punishments.

"Honestly, I hated it," he said at last, expecting to see a look of disapproval or disappointment on the man's face. To his surprise, though, the instructor just nodded.

"Why did you hate it?"

"Why wouldn't I? We spent two days with barely any sleep. We fought more than double the number of creatures of any of the other groups, and one of our team members got seriously hurt. We came back exhausted and hungry, and my ithtu crystal ran out halfway through." He finished, and Ranakar stared at him.

"And?" the awal asked.

"And what?" Amarl wouldn't lie to the awal, but he hoped the man might miss a lie of omission. Andra hadn't mentioned the internal friction in the group, and he hoped that meant no one knew about it.

Ranakar shook his head. "Students never give the malims enough credit, Amarl. They think we don't know what's going on beneath our very noses." He gave the boy a sharp look. "You got to experience Nirecina's ability, yes?"

"Yes, sir. She could move really fast."

"Not exactly. Increased speed is a Tier A or B ability and is relatively common. Nirecina has a Tier C ability to lower the effective mass of herself and anyone she touches. That lets her move incredibly quickly without needing an actual Speed ability. However, she has the same passive ability as most ithtaru with a Speed-based power."

"Passive ability?" Amarl asked, confused.

"Yes. Every ability has two components: an active part that drains your tak to use, and a passive part that your ithtu maintains without losing any power. Almost anyone with the ability to move at high speed also has improved senses and reflexes, allowing them to react to obstacles in their path without crashing into them and killing themselves or someone else." He gazed at the boy calmly. "For Nirecina, that includes hearing."

Amarl felt his face go cold as he realized what the awal was saying. "So, then – she heard…"

"Yes. She overheard your conversation with Tukos. She also heard part of your conversation with Andra and Veter on one of her check-ins on your group, so she knew that you'd been attacked. It didn't take much to figure out that Tukos got angry at you and tried to harm you."

"Check-ins?"

Ranakar laughed. "You don't think she just sent you out and left you all to your own devices, do you? Students are valuable, Amarl, and we don't waste them. One reason Nirecina is frequently chosen to supervise these hunts – beside her skills and experience at hunting – is that she can move fast enough to get within sensory range of a group, check in on them, and move to the next without being noticed. She watched each of your groups constantly."

Amarl frowned. "Then – why didn't she know that I could harvest more powerful crystals?"

"She missed that," he shrugged. "Just as she missed Nihos going missing because the others were busy looking for him, and she assumed they were hunting creatures, not a lost student. Most of the time, a malim checks in by getting close enough to hear that everything's going fine, then moving on. She didn't hear the others talking about what you'd done, or she'd have known – and she probably would have stayed with your group to hunt something more powerful down to see what sort of crystals you'd harvest."

He gazed at Amarl. "So, tell me the rest."

The boy sighed, then explained what happened with Tukos. He should have known it was pointless to conceal anything, but he hoped that the awal didn't know about his decision with Nihos.

"I suspected from the start that I couldn't trust my team," he said wearily. "I was almost certain they planned to do something to me once we were out of sight. I felt totally alone, and having to watch out for animals and my own team was frustrating and exhausting. It sucked knowing that they wouldn't have my back." He looked up at the man. "They said that they have to, though. That the malim told them to. Is that right?"

Ranakar nodded, his face grave. "And how does it make you feel?"

"Angry," Amarl said flatly. "It makes me think that I can't trust the school or the malims, either."

"And that's why Andra and Veter shouldn't have said anything to you," Ranakar sighed. "Normally, I wouldn't tell you this, but the simple fact is that you need to trust your instructors. Andra told you that she and the other third-years are ordered to harass second-years on their first hunts. Did she tell you why?"

Amarl nodded. "To get us used to the life of an ithtar," he said in a monotone.

"That's part of it, but not the main reason," the awal shook his head. "The main reason is to help students develop their ability faster."

"Their ability?" Amarl asked in a puzzled voice. "How?"

"You know that in some ways, your ithtu is like a living thing," the man explained. "It serves you; it wants to serve you, in fact. It wants to help you, protect you, keep you safe. It heals you when you're wounded, makes you stronger, faster, smarter. It answers your needs, whatever those are." He shrugged. "So, we give you needs for it to serve."

Amarl's eyes widened. "So, if we're afraid of being harassed or hurt by the older students..."

"Your ithtu is more likely to come to your aid," the man nodded. "For most students, that means it bonds with you, becoming part of your body and quickening into an ability. Not all at once, to be sure, but stressing a student like that speeds up the process."

"I think..." Amarl hesitated. "I think it might have worked. Tukos tried to attack me for harvesting that squirrel thing, and Andra used her ability on us to keep us from hurting one another. I kind of – shook it off, I guess."

The man's eyes widened. "Nirecina missed that. What happened?"

"I don't know," Amarl shook his head. "I can barely remember it. It's like a dream that starts fading once I wake up. I just remember something trying to hold me, and I didn't want to be held. So, I didn't let it happen. That's all I remember – that and my ithtu singing, then going silent. That was when it finally vanished."

"You drew on it to do whatever it was you did," the old man nodded sagely. "And shrugging off a Tier C power like that takes a lot of energy."

"So – does that mean my ability is going to be ignoring other people's?" Amarl asked, curious.

Ranakar laughed. "You're getting ridiculously far ahead of yourself, Amarl. What you did wasn't an ability. It was just your ithtu coming to your service, nothing more. It did the same thing to protect you from Danat, you may recall." He grimaced. "Which is a real concern."

"Why?"

The old man eyed Amarl gravely. "Your ithtu is acting without your will or control, Amarl. It responds to your needs, nothing more. That's normal for a student or novice, but typically, those responses are weak and barely noticeable until their ability quickens. Before that, their bodies just can't channel enough ithtu for it to be dangerous.

"That's not the case with you. Your ithtu's responses are powerful enough that your uncontrolled ithtu unraveled a Tier C ability and nearly killed someone who attacked you." He shook his head. "And it's barely developed. As it grows stronger and bonds more completely with you, those responses could be dangerous even to a full-fledged ithtar."

Amarl swallowed hard. He hadn't set out to hurt anyone; he just didn't want to be hurt himself. "So, what can I do?" he asked quietly.

"First, I think that's your last hunt for a while," the awal chuckled. "No matter what Nirecina begs. The students will keep trying to harass you, and I worry what might happen if someone pushes you too far. Here in Askula is one thing, but out there, away from the prying eyes of the malims, things can get out of hand." He gazed at Amarl calmly. "And we already lost one student on a hunt this year. We don't want to lose any others, do we?"

Amarl swallowed hard and shook his head. "No, sir, we don't."

"I'm glad we agree. Now, second, did you quicken a stat with your new crystal already?"

The boy shook his head. "No. Finishing my last crystal brought my Mind stat to five-seven, and that lets me quicken a second crystal, now. You told me to stop boosting Mind when that happened."

"You can quicken a second crystal already?" The old man looked surprised, then shook his head. "Fine. I'll get you a second Minor crystal."

"I already have two. I quickened one of the ones I'd harvested after mine ran out, and then I picked one as a reward for the hunt. I wanted to be able to protect myself, just in case."

"That's fine," Ranakar nodded. "Normally, taking a higher tier crystal like that would be a problem, but all things considered, I think we can overlook it. Go ahead and attune them both to your Will stat. You know how to do that?"

"Lilenpur told me how. I haven't done it yet, though."

"Go ahead and try it and be sure you remember."

Amarl closed his eyes and pictured his tak glowing beneath his heart. The ball of energy pulsed dimly compared to its usual radiance, which he guessed meant it was low – he hadn't checked his regular status since leaving Shadora and didn't know. He reached out a mental finger and touched it, drawing a line up along his spine, following his posterior channel until he reached the back of his skull. He released the strand, and a surge of energy rolled up the back of his neck, making him shiver as it settled into the rear portion of his brain and spread out, following the channel that flowed there. He repeated the process, and another tendril of power flowed up his spine into the back of his skull.

"I think it's done," he announced.

"Don't think. Check. You have a screen for a reason, Amarl. Use it."

The boy nodded and pulled up his ithtu screen. "It's there. Two units, assigned to Will at zero percent."

"Good. Improving your Will stat should make it easier for you to control your ithtu and rein it in as necessary. Right now, it's basically doing whatever it wants because your Will is abysmally low." He shook his head. "That's all we can do for right now." He rose to his feet. "Did the others tell you about the class schedule change?"

"Yes. They're starting weapons training in the mornings now."

"You'll join them twice a week for weapons training to help you practice against opponents of a similar skill level. Which brings me to this morning's training. You need a better weapon than that staff, and one that takes advantage of your stats better than the scimitar." The man walked over to a wooden case lying against one wall and flipped it open. "Fortunately, Andra already had a good idea for that."

The man reached into the case and pulled out a familiar looking weapon. It stretched a couple spans longer than Amarl was tall, with a curved crescent blade on one end like a bull's horns and a thin, double-bitted axe on the other. The awal pulled out the moon axe and spun it, making it flash and whirl in the air, whipping it around his back and across his body. He slammed the spear point onto the ground with a smile.

"The moon axe is one of the hardest weapons you can master, and it only shows its worth in the hands of someone truly adept." He lifted the weapon and touched the crescent blade. "While this blade can cut and thrust, so can your scimitar." He turned it around and looked at the other end. "The axes can cut through armor and bone, but then, so can a glaive or halberd. And the point can thrust, but so can a spear.

"More importantly, each of those weapons is simpler to learn, faster – at least at first – and specifically designed to do that one thing. Which might lead you to ask: why bother with a moon axe at all?"

Amarl nodded; that was exactly what he had been wondering.

The man set the blade spinning once more. "Because in skilled hands, the moon axe can do all three just as well. It can slash as well as your scimitar but has better reach and more power." The weapon slid out through his hands, extending in a wide circle, and all around him, ropes sang and hummed as he severed them in a broad arc, not missing a step as he kept the weapon moving.

"It can chop as well as a glaive but recovers better." He stepped sideways, and the weapon slid out in the opposite direction. The nearest pole cracked as one of the axes cut right through it, and Ranakar brought the axe in close once more, turning it around his body.

"And it can thrust as well as a short spear but with more mass and thus force." He slid his foot forward, and the weapon shot out, stopping less than a span from Amarl's stunned face before darting back to its wielder.

"The moon axe is like a high-tier ability in some ways," Ranakar went on. "It's complex and takes a large investment of time and energy to make it useful. However, while simpler weapons and low-tier abilities both do one thing well, they lack flexibility. The moon axe, once you learn how to use it, can be far more powerful and versatile." He stopped the weapon abruptly and tossed it to the boy, who caught it, his mind whirling with amazement.

"Just like a high-tier ability," the awal finished. "Now, let's begin with some of your simple staff exercises to feel how the weapon is different..."

CHAPTER 29

"Look at that! It snowed!"

Amarl groaned as Meder's voice rang through the room. The girl was entirely too cheerful for it being barely after dawn. None of them slept in anymore, of course – six moons of waking before dawn to make it to classes on time made that impossible – but that didn't mean they wanted to get up.

"Meder, it's Akio," Burik groaned. "Go back to sleep!"

"How can you sleep? It's snowing right now!"

Amarl cracked one eye open and peered at the girl standing before the window in nothing but her underclothing. They'd all lost whatever modesty they had around one another long ago, and he barely noticed her state of undress. He did, however, take note of the fat, swirling flakes falling from the sky beyond the window, and the thought of being out in them made him burrow deeper under his blanket and shut his eyes tighter.

"Yes. It's snowing. I see it. We'll go out in it later when we go to the village. Now, go back to bed."

"But it might not be snowing by then!" He heard her moving around and opened both eyes. She'd left the window and stood by her foot locker, pulling out a heavy shirt, pants, and jacket that she'd bought in the village weeks ago as the weather turned.

"Are you seriously going out there?" Burik asked. "It's just snow, Meder!"

"It never snows in Dairon," she said, turning back to gaze out the window. "It's too hot. I've never even seen snow except at the tops of the Northwall Mountains when we came here."

"Well, it snows every year in Tem," Amarl groaned. "Spans at a time sometimes. I spent half my childhood trying to stay out of the snow."

"Yes, yes, your childhood sucked, Amarl. We all know. Boo hoo." The girl grinned and leaned easily to the side to dodge the pillow Amarl flung in her direction. She moved far more gracefully than she once had, and even in the dim light, her muscles rippled and shifted beneath her skin. With her warrior's body and her hair cut even shorter, down to her chin in the front and up to the base of her skull in the back, Meder barely resembled the pampered noble she'd been when she arrived in Askula.

"You can stay in bed if you'd like," she continued. "I'm going to go outside and enjoy the snow while I can."

"Fine," Burik groaned, flipping back his blanket. "I'll go with you."

"You don't have to, Burik."

"Yeah, I do. Remember the deal we made after Amarl's hunt? None of us go anywhere alone if we can help it." He sat up and rubbed at his eyes blearily, wincing as he put his feet on the floor. "Damn, that's cold. You coming, Amarl?"

"You just said the floor was cold, then asked if I'm coming?" Amarl said testily. "Hells, no. I'm staying here where it's warm and toasty. You go have fun freezing bits of yourself off."

"Aww, is the scary hizeen afwaid of a wittle, cold fwoor?" Meder laughed. "I can fix that." She raised her hands and closed her eyes, waving her fingers about and swaying her body as she mumbled under her breath. Amarl felt a brief sense of power coalesce around the girl, and suddenly, a wave of warmth rolled across the room. "There. Now, it's not cold anymore."

"Huh. That is better," Burik noted. "You've gotten a lot better with sahr, Meder. Can't you get in trouble for using it without permission, though?"

She shrugged. "I've been working on that matrix for a while, so I balanced it well enough that there isn't much drain. The showers get cold in the mornings these days, and cold doesn't go well with wet and naked, if you've noticed." She picked up the pillow Amarl had tossed and hurled it back at him. "Go on, get up. Otherwise, I might have to sneak a snowball back in here and dump it under your covers."

"You wouldn't," he groaned.

"You know she would," Burik chuckled. "Might as well get up, Amarl."

"Fine." He flung the covers back and sat up. "I'm not going to enjoy it, though."

"You don't have to, as long as I do," she grinned. "Now, get dressed so I can go play in the snow!"

A span of snow had fallen overnight, and since it was Akio, most of the students, teachers, and villagers were either still in bed or hiding inside the dormitories where it was warm. A blanket of pure, unsullied white stretched out before them, dotted only here and there by footprints. Amarl stopped and inhaled deeply, taking in the crisp, clean air. The sharp, icy scent of the snow stirred his memories, reminding him of his far-off birthplace. Those memories no longer panged him, though; Tem wasn't his home anymore, and he almost never thought of it these days.

"Oh, it's amazing!" Meder squealed, tromping into the snow. She bent down and scooped up two handfuls, lifting them to her mouth and touching her tongue to them.

"Don't do that with the yellow snow," Amarl told her with a grin. "It's flavored, but not a flavor you'd like."

She ignored him as she threw the snow up into the air, tilting her head back and laughing as it cascaded over her face. She turned back toward them with her tongue out, grinning happily, and Amarl couldn't help but laugh. Snowflakes covered her eyelashes and clung to her dark hair, and her cheeks were already pink from the cold. She looked like a giant kid, and he couldn't stay irritated seeing how happy it made her. At least, not until she scooped up a handful of snow and flung it at his face. He dodged easily, and she bent down, scooping up another handful.

"Come on!" she urged the boys. "Let's have a snowball fight!" She whipped the ball at Burik, who swatted it from the air with a gloved hand. She stamped her foot in the snow. "Come on! I've never had one before!"

Burik and Amarl shared a glance, then they both bent down and scooped up snow, flinging it at the girl. Meder squealed as a snowball struck her stomach while another exploded against her hair. She laughed excitedly and bent down to grab more snow. "Yes! Just like that!"

The trio spent the next hour in the snow, playing like they were five years younger. Meder insisted they try everything she'd ever heard about, from building snowmen to laying on their backs and making snowbirds. At last, though, the cold and damp soaked through their clothing, and they retreated inside to warm up and dry off.

"That was perfect," the girl sighed as she sipped a steaming mug of cider. "Just what I imagined it would be."

"You really never got to see snow?" Burik asked curiously as he cradled a warm mug of kaffee in his hands.

She shook her head. "Like I said, it never snows in Dairon. The coldest it gets there is like autumn was here in Askula."

"You were a noble, though," Amarl pointed out. "Your family could have just traveled north in the winter to see snow, couldn't they?"

"Not all families of the zahai caste are the same, Amarl," she shrugged. "Some live off of their inherited money and property, and those families do lots of traveling and vacationing. Others, though, actively manage their estates and businesses, and my family was one of those. My parents were too busy for us to travel much, and when we did, it was usually by sea to Menith, the Crystal Palace, or the Nicelian Protectorate. All of those places are warm, too."

"You've been to the Protectorate?" Burik asked. "Ships from there docked in Tennshin pretty regularly, but I've never heard of anyone going there."

"They don't welcome casual visitors," she shook her head. "You can only go there if you have legitimate business and are sponsored by a native. My mother owns a couple of shipping concerns there, so my family was allowed to visit."

"What's it like?" Amarl asked curiously. "I've barely even heard of the Protectorate before."

"Uncomfortable," she shrugged. "They've got two castes there: Kakan and Wahan, basically men and women. Just like in the Empire, women are higher ranked and head the family, but they're also treasured and protected, so they've got all sorts of restrictions on them. They wear silk from head to toe, and while they veil their faces, the silk doesn't do much to cover the rest of them."

"So, the women basically walk around half-naked?" Amarl grinned.

"Yes, more or less. It's really hot there – hotter than summer in Askula but all year long – so the silk they wear is pretty thin, and they don't wear much beneath it. The men aren't much better, but they leave their faces and chests uncovered to show off their tattoos."

"Tattoos?"

"Yes, it's a rite of passage over there. People get tattoos as well as letters to celebrate milestones in their lives. They get a face tattoo on their fifth Naming Day, then a neck one on their tenth and one on their chest for their fifteenth."

"Nihos was Nicelian," Amarl remarked. "You mentioned that once."

She nodded. "Yeah, but they're not all like him. Periteth is, too, remember?" She grimaced. "Actually, it kind of makes sense that they both came from there. The men are all obsessed with being strong, while the women try to be as beautiful as possible."

"Why worry about how you look if you always keep your face covered?" Burik asked puzzledly.

"Oh, they only cover their faces in public so men can't see them. They show them off around other women so they can compete to see who's prettiest. See, they consider their beauty to be too valuable and precious to allow most men to see it and only reveal themselves to a man they consider worthy. That's why the men try so hard to be strong and successful: it's the only way they'll get to see a woman except their mother or sisters."

"Did you have to dress like that?" Amarl asked.

"I had to veil my face, yeah. They wouldn't have let me out in public otherwise. A woman who walks around with her face displayed is considered a harlot and either jailed or executed."

"They'd execute a noble daughter?" Burik asked.

"Oh yes. Our castes don't mean much to them. They're officially part of the Empire, but they don't see it that way. They consider themselves independent allies, and they generally refuse to accept our traditions. The Empire's never cared enough to force the issue, so…" She shrugged again.

"That doesn't sound like much of a vacation," Amarl laughed.

"Oh, don't get me wrong. There were some beautiful things to see down there, things I'd only read about in books before. I saw trees so old and large that people build villages in their branches. I got to swim down to a coral reef that had more colors than I imagined existed. I ate exotic foods and sat on the beach at sunset, watching the sun sink below the ocean." She sighed. "That was pretty great."

Amarl suppressed a quick flash of jealousy at everything the girl had experienced. "Maybe we'll all get to go there someday," he suggested.

"Maybe. The Order is obviously always welcome in the Protectorate, mostly because the Nicelians are terrified to try and stop them, just like the rest of the Empire." Her face brightened. "If I went back as an ithtara, I wouldn't have to wear those stupid veils, either!"

"Speaking of traveling," Amarl said, finishing the last of his kaffee, "do you guys want to hit the village today?"

"Absolutely," Meder nodded. "I want to see what it looks like in the snow." She frowned. "Do you think they'll still have the fair?"

"Snow never stopped the fairs in Tennshin," Burik laughed. "My mother always says that no force in the Empire is more powerful than a merchant's greed."

"I seriously want to meet your mother one day," Amarl grinned. "I want to see if she really says all these things, or if you're making them up and just saying it's her so no one argues with you."

"Trust me, if you meet her, you'll find out right away. She's got a saying for everything."

They dressed in another set of warm clothing and trudged toward the village. Someone had planned for heavy snowfall by erecting stone markers regularly along the road's edges, and both wagon tracks and dozens of sets of footprints marred the snow between those markers. The trio entered the village, and as had become their tradition, headed to the bakery first but froze as they saw the crowd of students milling around the door, pushing to get in and stumbling back out bearing some sort of steaming pastries.

"What do you think this is?" Burik asked. "Galiber's is never this busy!"

"Must be something special," Meder said, her eyes brightening. "Maybe something to do with the snow! We should go see!"

The three of them wormed their way into the crowded bakery, and Amarl slipped around older students until he reached the main counter. Bodies packed the counter, and Galiber's three children all worked furiously, pulling out ring-shaped pastries and taking money from students almost feverishly.

"Amarl!" The boy looked over as a slightly pudgy, balding figure emerged from the back room. The baker stood a span taller than Amarl and at least three wider, the consequence of constantly sampling his own wares. He pulled off a flour-dusted apron and wiped the bits of dough clinging to his hands on a damp cloth as he stepped forward to greet the boy. The nearby students glanced at Amarl, and he saw a few ugly looks, but Galiber lifted a hand and made a stern face.

"No trouble in my shop, you understand? Anyone who starts trouble is banned for a year, and that means no cider circles! Now, let them come forward." The students grumbled but moved out of the way, allowing the trio to approach the counter.

"How are my best customers today? I wasn't sure if you'd brave the snow to come see me or not."

"Hi, Galiber," Amarl laughed. "Of course, we came. Although I think we all know that we're not even close to your best customers. I'm pretty sure that Ranomi buys more bread from you in a day than we have all year."

"Details, details," the wide-faced man laughed.

Amarl looked around. "What's going on? This is the busiest I've ever seen you!"

"First snowfall of the year! The only day that I make my cider circles. I'm glad you came early; they sell out fast!"

"Cider circles?" Meder asked. "Is that what everyone's buying?"

"Yep. Old family recipe. I got it from my mother, who got it from her mother, and so on. It's a tradition that we only make these to celebrate the year's first snowfall. They're very popular." He bent down and lifted a plate with three ring-shaped, steaming pastries on them. "Here, try them."

Amarl hesitantly took a ring-shaped pastry and hefted it. It looked like it would be dense and solid, but it felt surprisingly light. He sniffed it dubiously, then shrugged and took a small bite.

"Mmm," he moaned as the flavors of apple cider, honey, and warm bread hit his tongue all at once. At the same time, a hint of something cold, like a touch of peppermint teased his tongue. The treat held the flavors of fall with just a touch of ice that promised winter's arrival.

"Galiber, this is really good!" he moaned.

Beside him, Meder took a bite, and her eyes went wide. "Oh," she said in surprise. "Wow, this is incredible!"

"This is the best thing you've given me," Burik mumbled through a mouthful of pastry. "It's so good!"

"Burik, don't talk with your mouth full," Meder scolded. "Galiber, I can see why you're so busy today..." She hesitated. "But these are amazing! Why don't you sell them all year?"

"Because then they wouldn't be special, would they?" he laughed. "Go on, those are on the house; the three of you have spent more in here than any other group of students this year. If you want more, though, you have to stand in line like everyone else."

The three novices quickly finished their treats, then lined up to purchase a second before walking toward the fair in the center of town. The music echoing through the air told them that despite the snow, the fair still went on. Amarl guessed that Burik's mother was right. No power, not even the weather, could stop a merchant from making coins.

They emerged into the fairground and stopped, staring in surprise. While the booths and stalls still ringed the fair, the center of it had become a wonderland of ice and snow. Sculptures of glittering ice dotted the grounds, each carved to resemble a person or creature. Buildings of packed snow reared high above the students' heads, with tunnels dug through the structures allowing students to wander through them. Someone had put a large pond in the very center of the grounds, and the cold weather turned it into a sheet of ice. Students wearing strange, bladed boots glided across that ice with various degrees of grace, and Amarl grinned as he watched a second-year girl's feet slip out from under her, sending her crashing onto her ass on the frigid surface.

"Wow," Meder breathed, her face astonished. "Just – wow."

"Yeah, I have to agree," Amarl said admiringly. "I mean, I grew up with snow – but never like this!"

"I've been ice skating before," Burik said, pointing to the sheet of ice with the figures gliding across it. "Tennshin's harbor freezes every year, and most of the city's kids skate on it. I've never seen anything like these sculptures or buildings, though."

"Then you can teach Amarl and me how," Meder said brightly, grabbing both boys' hands and pulling them forward. "It looks fun!"

Ice skating, Amarl decided, wasn't as much fun as it looked. The skates that they rented for an ak each were old and worn, and they barely fit Amarl's feet. The ice was slippery, and the blades on his skates wobbled slightly, making his balance unsteady. The frozen surface was also hard, as he found out several times when his feet went out from under him and deposited him on his backside. His only consolation was that Meder went down as often as he did; only Burik was comfortable and graceful.

After ten minutes or so, though, Amarl began to figure out how to move on the skates and how to keep his balance, and within thirty, he was gliding along the ice. He wasn't exactly graceful, but at least he didn't fall down. Meder picked up the knack almost as quickly, and soon enough, the trio found themselves racing across the ice, crossing back and forth in front of one another, and trying to mimic Burik's ability to skate backwards, on one foot, or even to spin in place without falling.

"Now, you're just showing off," Meder panted as Burik built up speed and leaped into the air, spinning his body before landing on one foot and gliding along.

"Yeah, pretty much," he grinned at her. "Like I said, I did this a lot, and most of us had special skates that made tricks like that easier than they are with these." He lifted a foot and shook the skate, looking at it with minor scorn.

"That's great, but I think I'm about skated out," Amarl said with a laugh. "How about we head to Sasofit's? I'll bet they're serving something warm today."

"That sounds like a good idea," Meder nodded, reaching up and touching the sides of her head. "My ears are half-frozen."

The three returned their skates and began walking toward the taproom. The moment they left the fairground, Hadur and Herel appeared around a corner with a pair of third-years following along behind them. Amarl ignored the other novices, but Hadur made a beeline for the hizeen and walked up to him, slamming his shoulder into Amarl's chest. Surprised, Amarl fell back, rubbing his chest and staring at Hadur in mild shock.

"What the fuck?" he muttered. "What was that about?"

"How dare you touch me, half-breed?" Hadur snapped, brushing at his shoulder as if trying to sweep off dirt. "I'm going to have to burn this jacket, now!"

Herel smiled, and the third-years both laughed at Hadur's words. Amarl bit his lip, determined to say nothing, but to his surprise, Meder stepped up to Hadur, her face inches from the boy's.

"What did you say?" she asked, her voice flat and quiet.

"I called him a filthy half-breed, because that's what he is," Hadur purred. "He doesn't belong here, and now that he's contaminated you, neither do you."

"Contaminated me? What exactly do you mean, Hadur?"

"What, you think we don't know?" The boy turned and looked at the others, laughing. "Everyone in Askula knows that you spread your legs for both of them every night. You may come from the zahai, but you're just a common whore..."

Amarl and Burik both moved, but fast as they were, Meder was faster.

She grabbed Hadur's shirt and yanked him close, slamming her fist into his face. He cried out, his hands flying to his lips, then groaned as her knee crashed between his legs. He bent over, grabbing his crotch, and her elbow slammed into the back of his skull, knocking him into the snow, which quickly began to turn crimson as his bleeding mouth and nose stained it.

"If you ever say anything like that to me again," she hissed, kicking him in the stomach as she did, "I will beat you so hard your own family won't recognize you. Understand me?"

"Pthucking bitch!" he moaned, spraying more blood into the snow. "One day, I'm going to..."

She stepped forward to kick him again, but Herel stepped forward and shoved the girl back. "You've made your point," he said dryly.

"Maybe I'm not done making it yet," Meder said angrily.

"Yes, you are." Herel reached down and rested his hand on the hilt of the sword at his side, and Meder's eyes narrowed.

"Are you threatening to draw a weapon on me, Herel?" she asked in a dangerous voice. "Right out here in public, where everyone can see?"

"If necessary. Step back, and we won't have to find out." He half-turned his head, his eyes still fastened on Meder. "Pick him up, please." One of the third-years grunted and hauled Hadur to his feet. Herel eyed the girl.

"That was pretty impressive. You know, my friends and I have been taking extra training. You have talent; you could come join us. I wouldn't even charge you anything." He looked her up and down with a smirk. "At least, not in coins."

She gave him a contemptuous snort. "The only way I'll ever touch you or your friends is the way I just did to Hadur. You're welcome to some of that, if you'd like."

He laughed dryly. "Feisty. I like that."

"You need to walk away, Herel," Burik rumbled, taking a step toward the boy. As he did, though, one of the third-years moved to stand before him.

"Or what, Meat?" the older boy drawled.

Burik looked at the boy contemptuously. "Without your ability, I'd tie your ass up into a bow."

"You think so? Maybe you'd like to try."

"What the fuck is the point of all this, Herel?" Amarl said tiredly, reaching out and pulling Meder and Burik back.

"I'm not sure what you mean, hizeen," Herel said contemptuously.

"You went out of your way to get our attention. Why? To try and pick a fight between us and your little pets?" Amarl shook his head. "That's not going to happen."

"Who are you calling a pet, Meat?" the other third-year growled.

"You. You come when you're called, stay when you're told to, and attack on command." Amarl shrugged. "That makes you a pet, as far as I can tell." The older boy took a step forward, but he froze as Herel raised a hand. "See? Stay. Good boy."

He looked back at Herel. "Do you really want to stand here and trade insults? You'll lose, and then your pets will get mad and do something stupid. That'll get them expelled, and all the money in the world isn't worth risking that, is it?" He looked at the two boys, who both suddenly seemed uncertain.

"What would you know about money, hizeen? Except that, from what I heard, your mother had to earn it on her back." Herel sneered at Amarl, but the smaller boy just smiled in response.

"Oh, no, you insulted my mother," he said, rolling his eyes. "No one's ever said that about her before." He snorted. "Now, your mother on the other hand – well, from what I hear, she likes to head down to the local barracks once a moon and spend a couple nights motivating the soldiers, sometimes three or four at a time, while your father watches and wishes it was him instead of her." His eyes widened theatrically. "I wonder if one of them is your real father, Herel – since your actual father couldn't get it up if someone tied a stick to his cock." He laughed. "You still want to play?"

Herel's face went white, and he took a step forward, partially drawing his sword, but Amarl grabbed his wrist and held it in place. The hizeen stared into Herel's eyes without blinking.

"You pull that out, and you're expelled – and that means they execute you," he said flatly. "Now, I wouldn't mind that in the slightest, so go ahead and do it. Or shut up and back the fuck off. I don't know what your problem is..."

"You're my problem, hizeen," Herel snarled. "You get all this special treatment, all this extra favor, but your kind doesn't even belong here. Nihos died right next to your camp, but no one cared enough to even question you..."

"How would you know that, exactly, Herel?" Amarl asked calmly despite the anger that suddenly stirred up inside him. "Hells, even I didn't know where that happened, and I was on that hunt. Nirecina just told us that he'd gone into someone else's territory and died for his trouble. How would you know right where it happened?"

Herel's face paled slightly, and Amarl shoved the boy's sword back into its sheath, then pushed him away. "Go bother someone else, Herel," Amarl shook his head.

"You think this is over, hizeen?" Herel hissed. "I'm going to make your life miserable here – yours, and your friends'. You'll have to look over your shoulder every time you walk to the distant classes, worry about every hunt, and wonder which of the upperclassmen are looking for an excuse to beat you senseless, for the rest of your time here."

Amarl's anger flared again, and he stepped up into Herel's face. "You're threatening my friends?" he said coldly. "Maybe you're the one who needs to start looking over his shoulder then, Herel. Who knows what might happen if you happen to be alone, out of sight of the malims?"

"Why don't we find out? Right now. We'll go somewhere, and..."

"No," Meder said sharply. "Not like that. Halit."

"Halit?" Herel echoed, his face puzzled. "What are you talking about?"

"The two of you can settle this in Halit. That way, you can fight all you want, and no one gets in trouble. If Amarl wins, you leave us alone, period."

"Why would I agree to that?" Herel laughed. "What's in it for me?"

"For you? Halit has the thing you really want, Herel: an audience. If you fight there and win, everyone will see it. Everyone will talk about it." The girl looked at him archly. "Isn't that what you really want? To humble Amarl in public, so everyone's talking about you instead of him?"

Herel stared at the girl and stepped back. "Fine. Halit, two hours. If you're not there, then my friends, here, will make your existence the spirits' hell, starting tomorrow."

"I'll be there," Amarl nodded.

"Good." The noble turned and strode off, and in the sudden silence, Amarl realized that half of the fair had stopped to watch their altercation. He looked around and saw dozens of students watching him, some angrily, others in approval, but most seeming simply curious.

"Why did you do that, Meder?" Burik demanded quietly. "You should have let them go somewhere and have at it privately."

"And the moment we were out of sight, those third-years would turn on us," she shook her head. "They'd claim it was self-defense, and while I believe that the malims would uncover the truth, that wouldn't help us in the infirmary, would it? This way, everyone is watching, so everything has to be done correctly." She looked at Amarl fiercely. "Now, you just have to kick his ass, and he and his people will leave us alone."

Amarl just nodded, but secretly, he doubted she was correct. Herel had planned this encounter; he had more in mind than a scuffle, or even a simple beating from the older students. What the noble said about Nihos confirmed to Amarl at least that he'd been the one paying the older boy to attack Amarl, and that had been fairly well planned. They'd somehow known that Andra and Amarl would be in the same group, and they'd bribed the girl at least a week or more before the hunt if she had the chance to use that money to make the elixirs for the hunt. Amarl doubted Herel would leave the result of this match to chance.

He sighed as the trio turned and left the village. His earlier happiness evaporated, replaced with a cold anger. Whatever Herel plotted, Amarl was determined to convince the boy to leave them alone – no matter what it took.

CHAPTER 30

"We should head back to the dormitory, so I can get my gear," Amarl sighed as the trio headed away from the fair and the imagined warmth of Sasofit's taproom.

"You can't use real weapons in Halit, Amarl," Meder shook her head. "Someone could get killed that way. They have special sparring weapons there."

He made a face. "Ugh. I hate fighting with wooden weapons. It throws their balance off too much."

"That's not a problem when you use a staff," she said with a small grin. She looked at the hizeen. "Ranakar's never had you compete at Halit, has he?"

"No. He says I should wait for next year for that."

"Yamacol says the same thing," Burik agreed. "Although he said my halberd skill was high enough that I could try it if I wanted – as long as I didn't face anyone with a quickened ability."

"And I've only heard about it, never seen it. So, I think the first thing we should do is go there and see how everything works. There are usually matches going on all day on Akio, and we could watch a few to see how they're run."

"Smart." He sighed as he looked mournfully back at the village and the idea of the warm alehouse waiting for him. "Might as well go there now. There's no point in waiting around, and I probably shouldn't have a beer before a sparring match."

"No, probably not," Burik laughed.

The more Amarl thought about it, the more this fight seemed like a stupid idea – and the more suspicious Herel's requested two-hour delay felt. However, his only choices were to see it through or to find Herel before the match and deal with him. He doubted Herel would be without his constant third-year protection, so that second option wasn't a great one.

The Halit Sparring Grounds were southwest of the Citadel but almost directly west of the village. The trio left the roads and cut overland, walking beneath the towering peaks of the southern mountains. As they approached, they heard shouting and screams, and Amarl's heart lurched until he realized the screams were cheering, not cries of pain. They rounded a peak, and Halit's valley spread out before them.

Unlike most of the training centers, Halit was mostly open ground. A single long, low, stone building stood at the entrance to the valley, and the road from the Citadel led directly to it. Beyond lay dozens of sparring rings, each surrounded by tiers of wooden seats, most of which were empty due to the snowfall. Students of all ages crowded around the rings, some shouting and cheering, but most just watching whatever happened in the ring quietly.

Meder led the three to the large building, where they found three second-year students standing behind a counter similar to the armory's in Sitjak, bringing and retrieving weapons for older students standing before the counter. A student in a yellow uniform with the number four on the chest stood behind a sort of lectern or podium with a large, angled surface on top. The older student held a charcoal pencil and seemed to be making notes on a large piece of paper spread out before her. When Meder led the group closer to the older student, Amarl caught a glance of the paper and saw that it was actually a piece of glossy silk with a dozen or so large circles inked on it and names and numbers written inside.

"Names and year?" the girl said without looking up as the group approached, and Meder stepped back, gesturing to Amarl.

"Um, I'm Amarl. First year." His throat felt dry as he spoke, and his palms were suddenly sweaty. The girl looked up sharply at him, her eyes narrowing.

"First year? Oh, you're the hizeen." She shook her head. "Look, kid, you don't want to do this yet, trust me. Wait until you get your weapons skills to level four or five."

Amarl opened his mouth to protest that some of his skills were already close to that, but before he spoke, Meder slipped forward.

"Excuse me, but how does this all work? This is our first visit, and we're not sure what to do."

The older girl grunted. "Anyone who wants to compete puts their name on a list. Once you're signed up, you can challenge or be challenged by anyone on the list within a year of you, and if you're challenged, you fight, or you get taken off the list. Fights are to first blood. It's that simple."

She looked at Amarl again. "Like I said, kid, you don't want to be on this list. Every second-year in this place will want to challenge you, and you're not ready for that. Go watch some matches, maybe make some wagers, and enjoy your day."

"What if two people want to fight each other but don't want to be on the list?" Meder pressed.

"A duel? Yeah, you can do that, but the rings are pretty busy. Might take a while for them to open up."

"Another first-year, Herel, challenged me to a fight in two hours," Amarl said.

"Two hours?" She looked down at the silk cloth for a few seconds, then nodded. "Yeah, I can make that work. Ring seven in two hours. Check in here thirty minutes early to get your weapons, and I'll go over the rules then." She scribbled something onto the silk, then looked up at the group. "In the meantime, if you don't want to be part of the general fighting, go watch a match or something. I'm busy."

"Thank you." Meder smiled at the older girl, who grunted again in response, then led the two boys out of the building toward the rings. As they stepped into the open, Meder glanced back at Amarl over her shoulder.

"Where do you want to go?" she asked loudly to be heard over the noise, to which Amarl merely shrugged. To him, one ring was as good as another.

Burik apparently agreed. "Might as well just head to the first ring," he said, gesturing to the nearby crowd. "See if we can find somewhere we can watch from, and maybe figure out how it all works."

The crowd near the ring was fairly densely packed, but Burik spotted some students standing on the nearby bleachers watching, and they made their way there and climbed up until they could see over the heads of the crowd. The sparring ring was a fenced-in circle, just like the ones in Sitjak, but the fence here was metal rather than wood. The circle was still filled with snow, although most of that was trampled into the sand beneath, especially in the center. And the center of the circle was where Amarl stared in fascination.

Two students circled in the center of the ring, both in their fourth or fifth years. The girl stood about the same height as Meder but had far more muscle, and she gripped a solid metal maul half a reach long in one hand, moving it as easily as if it were a rapier, while her other hand held what looked like a very short spear only four spans long, solid metal with a barbed spike on the end. The boy was taller than Burik and had light gray skin that shone glossily in the wan sunlight filtering through the overcast sky and gently falling snow. He wielded a wicked-looking battle axe with a wide, flat blade that looked like it could easily take off an arm or a leg – which, Amarl supposed, was the point.

"Those are real weapons," Meder gasped. "They're not training ones! Isn't that dangerous?"

"Nah," one of the students standing nearby spoke up, shaking his head and not looking at the novices. "They're sahrotik, designed to draw blood or crack a bone but nothing more. Galea could smash her hammer into Marik's skull all day and give him nothing more than a nasty concussion, even with her strength."

Amarl opened his mouth to thank the student, but he froze as the pair burst into activity. The girl, apparently Galea, moved first, leaping toward Marik and slashing at him with her maul. The heavy hammer had to weigh three or four casks, easily, but she whipped it toward him like it was a light blade. Amarl expected the boy to dodge the blow, but Marik simply raised his arm and took the strike on his forearm. The hammer struck with a loud clang, and Marik's feet slid backward in the snow from the force of the impact, but he seemed otherwise unharmed, and he lashed out with his axe, cutting toward the girl's chest. Galea lifted her spear and blocked, then countered with another hammer smash that knocked the boy sideways but left him uninjured.

Amarl watched in awe as the two moved back and forth across the snow. Galea struck swiftly with her hammer, darting in and slamming the steel head into Marik's body over and over again, but the boy ignored her blows, letting them clang harmlessly against his seemingly impenetrable skin. He retaliated with his axe, slashing and cutting at her, driving her back time and again. Both of them moved with incredible speed and skill, their blows almost too swift for Amarl to even see, and he knew that if he'd been the one in that ring, he'd have lost in a heartbeat. He simply didn't have the skill, speed, and experience to compete with the high-ranked students – at least, not yet. He would one day, and the thought of what he might become capable of scared him a little.

The pair battled across the ring, cutting and smashing, dodging and blocking, but to Amarl, it seemed obvious who the winner was going to be. "Marik's going to win this," he observed after a couple seconds. "Galea can't hurt him, and while he hasn't hit her yet, he just has to do it once."

The student who'd spoke before turned to face him, grinning and with their eyes sparkling. "Care to make a wager on that?" the boy, probably a third-year, asked archly.

"Um – not really, no. Sorry." Amarl shook his head.

"Shame. Galea's gonna win this, easily."

Amarl looked at the boy doubtfully, but as he did, in the ring, Galea's hammer crashed into Marik's thigh with a crack instead of a muted clang. Marik staggered, and his skin suddenly darkened from gray to an odd grayish brown. Galea struck swiftly, swinging her maul at the boy's axe to knock it to the side, then stepping in and driving the spike in her left hand up under the boy's ribs, piercing his armor and sinking into his skin. Meder gasped in surprise at the apparently lethal strike, but the spearpoint stopped less than a fingerwidth into Marik's skin, and when Galea withdrew it and stepped back, only a trickle of blood oozed from the wound rather than the gout of it Amarl had been expecting.

"See? Sahrotik. Sure, you could overcome it with a full-power ability, but no one's going to do that because they'd get expelled." The older boy shrugged.

"How did you know Galea was going to win?" Meder asked curiously.

"Marik's steel skin ability is powerful, but it makes him a little arrogant, especially since Galea's only got Tier A super strength. He should have been dodging since every hit she landed weakened his ability." The boy shrugged. "It was only a matter of time until she broke it, and he's not fast enough to hit her before that happened."

Burik nodded sagely. "It's not the tier of the ability that matters, it's how well you use it."

"Well, tier matters, too. If his ability had been Tier D instead of B, she'd have worn herself out trying to get through it." The older student laughed. "And if it had been Tier A invulnerability, she'd have knocked him out in twenty seconds. But yeah, skill is more important than power, most of the time."

Amarl watched as the two students clasped wrists and left the ring, and two more entered. These were both girls, both he guessed in third year, one carrying a long, slim spear and the other with a whip coiled in her hand. He watched as an older student, probably a fifth-year, walked to the middle and spoke to both contestants. They each nodded, and the older boy stepped back. The two women exploded into movement; one rushed forward in a blur, while the other leaped into the air, and to Amarl's shock, remained hovering there. The hovering student unfurled her long, whiplike lash that glittered metallically and snapped it at the girl below, but she easily dodged the attack and stabbed with her spear, forcing the other student to dart out of the way.

The two flitted about the ring faster than Amarl's eyes could track. At first, he'd thought it would be a simple enough battle: the girl who could fly could stay out of the reach of the one who couldn't easily enough and rain whip blows down on the other girl's head. Eventually, one would land, and the match would be over. That wasn't what happened, though. The flying student didn't stay aloft perpetually; she used her superior mobility to counter her opponent's speed, leaping into the air and zipping around the spear-wielder before touching down and striking with her whip. The faster student, similarly, used her ability to close quickly and charge rapidly at the other girl, then relied on her normal speed to stay close and strike. It was a fairly balanced match, at least until the spear-wielder charged, driving the flier into the air once again, then reared back with her spear and flung it. The surprised flier didn't dodge, and the spear took her in the side, ending the match.

"That was a good trap," Burik observed.

Meder nodded. "The girl on the ground got the aerial one into a pattern, then changed it up on her. Smart."

They moved from ring to ring, watching different matches, and Amarl got a sense for how things worked as he watched. People who wanted to fight consulted the list the girl they'd first met talked about, which was posted just outside the building, written in chalk on a piece of black slate. They called out when they wanted to challenge someone, and once the word reached the other person, they both grabbed weapons from the armory and got assigned a ring. There was no bowing or pageantry involved; the fifth-year student overseeing that ring reminded the contestants of the rules, and the moment the referee was clear, the fight started. It lasted until someone was injured or was unable to continue; he didn't see anyone surrendering or bowing out gracefully. He didn't know if that meant they couldn't, or that it was just frowned upon, but he had a feeling it was prohibited. He knew that if he'd been challenged by someone with a fully awakened ability, he'd have given up immediately if he could, and he assumed the same would happen if someone got challenged by a person well out of their league.

However, he really couldn't be sure of that. To his surprise, he didn't see any one-sided matches, where one person simply dominated the other. Most of the matches were fairly close and probably could have gone either way. A student with Tier C invulnerability, basically skin as hard as gemstone, seemed unbeatable to Amarl but fell to a girl who could create weapons of shimmering, nearly invisible air that quickly cut through his invulnerability. One who hurled waves of fire around lost to a slim boy who seemed to be able to throw knives with incredible speed and accuracy, but that boy later lost as well to a girl who could blur and distort her body, making it nearly impossible for him to target her.

The one constant seemed to be that power wasn't the biggest deciding factor in most of the duels he saw. The person who had the best control of their power, the most skill with it, or could use it creatively was more likely to win. He saw multiple Tier A students defeating Tier B and Tier C students with clever ability usage or just superior tactics. It was a sobering reminder that while his Tier F ability had the potential to be incredibly powerful, power wasn't everything. If he could kill with a glance, he could still lose to someone who fought blindfolded and stabbed him in the heart.

"We should head back up," Meder said, pulling her watch out of her pocket and glancing at it. "Herel should be here soon."

"Fine," Amarl sighed. "Let's get this over with."

The trio walked back to the main building, where they found Herel, Hadur, Norag, and one of the two third-years waiting for them. Herel sneered at the hizeen as he approached and glanced at Hadur.

"I guess I owe you an ak. The hizeen had the courage to show up after all."

Amarl simply rolled his eyes. "Really? How long have you been standing here, Herel, waiting for me to arrive? You had two hours to think of something to say, and the best you could come up with was a bet that I was a coward?"

Herel's eyes narrowed, and his face flushed. "I can't wait to beat that insolence from you once and for all," he growled. "I've been waiting to do this since the moment I laid eyes on you back in that filthy pigsty you call a village."

Amarl didn't bother to respond to the boy's insults. "I arranged a ring for us. Ring seven. We just have to check out weapons, and we can get this farce over with."

He walked past the spluttering noble and into the building, where a different fifth-year stood behind the counter. "I'm Amarl. We're supposed to be in ring seven for a private fight in about thirty minutes."

"Amarl?" the older boy asked, glancing down at the silk below him. "Yeah, I've got you. Go ahead and get weapons, then head out to the ring. You know where it is?"

"Yeah. We've been here watching for a couple hours, so we found it."

"Smart. You've got two groups ahead of you there; you're after Lapek and Varnai. If you're not there when you're called, you forfeit, and you can't fight again today. Understand?"

"Got it. Thanks." Amarl walked away from the older student and joined the line heading up to the counter with his friends. When he reached the front, the second-year gave the trio a scornful look.

"Who's fighting?"

"Me," Amarl raised a hand.

The girl snorted derisively. "What weapon?"

"Can I only choose one?"

"You can choose what you'd like, Meat. You just have to be able to carry it." She smirked at him. "Not that it'll matter. You wouldn't last ten seconds in the ring carrying a damned war cannon."

"Then moon axe and scimitar, thanks." The girl looked startled at his request, but she walked into the back room and reappeared carrying the moon axe and a sheathed scimitar on a belt.

"Here. Try not to cut yourself on those, Meat. Next!"

Amarl handed the axe to Burik and slipped the belt on while waiting for Herel to get a longsword and buckler. He started walking toward ring seven, toward the center of the sparring grounds, but as he did, he spoke quietly to his friends.

"I don't trust this," he said just loud enough to be heard over the noise. "I think Herel's got something planned – and where's that other pet of his?"

"No clue," Burik shrugged. "But yeah, this all feels off to me, too."

"It's not like he can cheat," Meder protested. "Everyone will be watching."

"That just means he can't get *caught* cheating. He can still do it if no one realizes it." He shook his head. "Just keep an eye out for me, okay? I'm not worried about Herel if everything's on the level, but I don't think he's planning to fight fairly."

"We'll keep an eye," Burik assured him. "You just worry about the match, and don't get cocky. Herel's better than he lets on during sparring practice."

"So am I," Amarl smiled grimly, hefting the moon axe.

The trio reached ring seven without incident. A crowd of students surrounded the ring, cheering and shouting as two students, both apparently with strength-based abilities, fought unarmed in the ring, wearing nothing but leather training gloves. Amarl barely noticed the fighters as he scanned the surroundings, looking for anything suspicious or out of place. Nothing caught his eye, and he realized that with the crowd around the ring, he'd never be able to see anything anyway.

"Amarl and Herel!" The shout rang out, and Amarl took a deep breath and hefted his moon axe. He stopped as Meder laid a hand on his arm.

"Good luck, and be careful," she said quietly. "I think you're right; something doesn't feel right about this."

"Don't worry. We've got your back." Burik smacked him on the shoulder. "Go teach the brat a lesson."

Amarl smiled at the pair, then ducked under the metal railing surrounding the ring and moved toward the center. Herel approached from opposite him, smiling viciously, but Amarl kept his expression bland and expressionless. The pair stopped two reaches from one another, and a fifth-year boy walked up to stand between them.

"The rules are simple. You can use weapons and abilities, but no sahr or sahrotik other than the weapons given you. You fight until first blood or until I call the match. Understood?"

"Yes," Herel said with a smile.

"Got it," Amarl nodded.

"Good. When I step back, you can begin."

The boy took a step back, and Herel swiftly drew his sword and raised his shield as if expecting an attack. Amarl simply stood, unmoving, holding his axe lazily in his hand; he suspected the boy assumed he would rush to attack, and he still wasn't sure what Herel had planned. He figured his best option was to do nothing and wait for the boy to come to him. It gave Herel a minor advantage – the moon axe was at its strongest on offense – but Amarl would rather hand the boy a small advantage than screw up and give him a big one.

"What's the matter, hizeen? Afraid?" A sneer crossed Herel's face as he stood in readiness.

"No, just bored." Amarl faked a yawn, bringing laughter from several students watching. "Are you here to fight, or are you just trying to look pretty for everyone? Maybe you should have taken up dancing instead of fencing."

Herel's face reddened, but he didn't rush forward as Amarl hoped. Instead, he advanced cautiously, leading with his blade and holding his buckler up, ready to deflect a blow. Amarl doubted that the small shield could do more than slow the moon axe's strikes, but that could be enough if it let Herel land a solid thrust. He waited until the boy neared, then pulled the moon axe from the ground and held it before him like a staff.

Herel lunged, stabbing with the longsword, but the thrust was a simple feint designed to draw Amarl's guard into a high position. He ignored the thrust and twisted to the side, allowing the follow-up strike to slip past him. Herel twisted his wrist and cut to the side, but Amarl spun his axe, slapping the blade into the air and knocking it up over his head.

"Come on, Herel! Are you even trying? I know pig farmers who can fight better than that!" Amarl grinned at the noble boy, and Herel's face purpled in anger, but the noble held his temper and attacked calmly and coolly. He moved forward with a series of rapid thrusts and short slashes designed to drive Amarl back, but rather than allowing himself to be pushed, Amarl retreated in a circle, his axe blocking each quick, probing strike as he forced the noble boy to follow him.

Herel had gotten better, Amarl realized quickly. The boy held his balance excellently, never overextended himself, and attacked with simple, fast thrusts and slashes that kept Amarl on the defensive. He refused to fall for the fake openings Amarl offered and never let his shield drop, always ready to block a sudden attack. The boy wasn't an expert by any means, but Amarl could see the work and effort he'd put in, and part of him couldn't help but be impressed.

However, Amarl had improved quite a bit, as well, and he quickly realized that could win the fight easily. Herel had been practicing, but sparring with third-years a couple hours a week wasn't the same as the grueling, punishing training Ranakar had put Amarl through. He'd spent hours each day fighting, knowing that if he faltered, his teacher would happily stab him in the stomach, break one of his limbs, or knock him out, then heal him up and do it all over again. Herel was competent, but Amarl was used to fighting against perfection, not 'pretty good'.

Herel thrust against, then turned the feint into a low slash toward Amarl's feet, and the hizeen decided he'd given the boy enough chances. He spun his axe, using the crescent blade to catch and trap Herel's sword and push it into the ground, then slapped the double axes forward, striking with the flat side of the blades. Herel stumbled off-balance as the tip of his sword plunged into the frozen sand, and his shield came up too slowly to block Amarl's counter. The boy reeled as the axes smacked against his face, knocking him backward but not doing any real damage.

Herel backpedaled, bringing his sword up, but Amarl went on the offensive. His axe blurred and spun as he slashed and thrust at the noble boy. Herel parried and blocked, but the moon axe's strength was that the momentum of a failed attack led directly into the next strike. The axes whipped past the noble's chest; the crescent blade trapped his sword and knocked his buckler out of position; the spearpoint thrust at his face, barely missing his throat and eyes each time. Amarl drove him steadily back, never pressing the attack as hard as he could. Instead, he pulled each strike just before it hit, allowing it to pass by the unharmed noble.

Herel's careful defense crumbled as Amarl's relentless attack drove him across the slippery, slush covered sand. He lashed out with wider swings to drive the hizeen back, and his feet stumbled over one another as Amarl's blows forced him from side to side. The crescent blades swept behind his knee, tripping him, but a blow with the flat of the axe to the face knocked him backward and kept him upright. He slashed wildly, spitting and snarling, and Amarl decided to end it. He parried the boy's hasty swing and knocked it downward, into the sand, then allowed the axe's momentum to carry the double axe blades into Herel's side just below his armpit. The boy cried out as the axe sank a finger's width into his ribs, but even as it struck, Amarl felt something restraining it, a force pushing the blade back and keeping it from sinking deeper.

Amarl stepped back, but as he did, something seemed to grab hold of his back foot, locking his heel in place. He stumbled and crashed into something soft but unyielding behind him that knocked him forward. Herel's sword flashed up as Amarl tripped, and the tip of the blade punched into Amarl's stomach below his ribs. Instead of stopping, though, the sword tip slid up into Amarl, tearing through muscle and shredding the organs beneath. Hot pain flared in his stomach as Herel thrust, driving the blade deeper, a triumphant sneer on his face.

That sneer vanished as the wall behind Amarl shattered, and the hizeen staggered backward a step. The sword slid from his stomach, and he clutched a hand to the wound, trying to hold in the sudden flow of blood. Herel rose to his feet and readied his sword, then screamed as a flash of fire shot past Amarl's shoulder and splashed into the noble's face. The boy dropped his sword and fell back, clutching his face and falling to his knees. Amarl's legs sagged, and he fell to a knee. Blood soaked his fingers, making them slippery, and ran down his shirt, pooling in the dirty snow beneath him.

A hand fell on his shoulder, and something warm and metal was placed against his lips. "Drink, kid!" a deep voice urged. "Hurry!" The metal on his lips tilted, and liquid poured into his mouth, liquid he swallowed gratefully. The liquid burned all the way down his throat, but the fire of it quickly spread out into his body, flooding the pulsating wound in his stomach with heat. He tried to pull away as the fire seared his wound, but liquid kept flowing into his mouth, and he had no choice but to swallow or choke. Thankfully, a moment later, the pain began to ebb and dull, fading to a muted throbbing that he could easily ignore.

"Are you okay? Can you stand?" A hand went under his arm, and Amarl rose to see the fifth-year refereeing the match looking at him with mingled concern and anger.

"I – I'm okay," Amarl gasped, wincing as straightening pulled on muscle tissue that was still healing. "I've been stabbed in the stomach before. I'll be okay."

The boy looked at him, startled, but nodded. "Um, okay, I guess. Good thing we keep healing elixirs on hand in case of accidents." He turned and glared at Herel, who groveled on the ground, still clutching his face. "Not that this was any accident!" he roared at the fallen boy.

"Wh-what happened?" Amarl asked, but the older boy ignored him and gestured to one of the fourth-years standing nearby.

"Grab the cheater and get him healed up. I have to go report this. All of it." He looked around, and for the first time, Amarl did, too. Burik stood across the ring, kneeling atop an unconscious third-year, the one that Amarl had seen with Herel before but who had disappeared. Burik's lip bled, and one eye looked like it was swelling shut, but he grinned triumphantly at Amarl. Beside him, Meder stood over a kneeling Norag, her eyes fierce and her jaw set. Norag clutched his jaw and moaned incoherently, while the girl held up her right hand, which looked burned and blistered.

"What the fuck just happened?" Amarl mumbled.

"That's what we're going to find out, kid," the older boy sighed. "At least, that's what the awals are going to find out – and somebody's in serious shit for this."

CHAPTER 31

The last time Amarl had seen Awal Tekasoka, she'd looked a little angry. When Amarl walked into the large room that he thought was her office, he realized that he'd only seen her mildly annoyed. This time, she was furious. Her jaw clenched, her nostrils flared, and the only color in her face was the crimson in her cheeks. Her eyes flashed fire, and the power rolling out from her awed and cowed the boy as he walked inside the room, and he lowered his eyes although he honestly wasn't sure why he did. He hadn't done anything wrong, as far as he could tell.

The awal's office was a large room at the top of one of the Citadel's towers. Like the Rashiv's, it was semicircular, sharing the floor with an antechamber, inside which a gray-garbed malim sat and watched the procession as it made its way into the office. Its window looked down on Sabila dormitory and the farmlands beyond, letting some light into the room, but it still felt a little dark and menacing to him. Of course, that might have been the awal's presence, as well. Bookshelves lined one wall, a large map that showed Umpratan, Askula, and several other regions Amarl didn't recognize dominated another, and a huge desk occupied the center of the space. He noticed one of the tri-level game boards on her desk that matched the one he'd seen in the Rashiv's office, although it looked to be less ornately crafted.

A row of chairs lined the wall opposite the awal's desk, but the woman gave no indication she wanted the novices to sit, so they stood in a line, staring uncomfortably at anything but the angry woman. Only the fifth-year escorting them met the woman's gaze, and she looked up at him somewhat expectantly.

"I understand there was an altercation at Halit today, Student Zirso," she said in a deceptively calm voice.

"Yes, ma'am. That's one way of putting it."

"Enlighten me, Student Zirso. What, precisely, did my novices – possibly soon-to-be ex-novices – do?"

"Novice Amarl and Novice Herel scheduled a duel today, ma'am. I don't know what it was about, obviously, but they were placed in my ring for their match. They were each given sahrotik sparring weapons, I explained the rules of the match, and I let them have at it."

He shifted in his chair. "It quickly became clear to everyone watching that Novice Amarl was going to win the match. He was simply the better fighter. He scored first blood, and I was about to call the match when the sahr alarm triggered. At the same time, something hit Novice Amarl in the back and knocked him forward, into Novice Herel's sword – only it wasn't a sahrotik sword. It was an actual longsword, and it took Novice Amarl in the liver. Novice Amarl couldn't back up, and Novice Herel continued what could have been a lethal blow.

"I moved to intervene, but before I could, these two novices..." He gestured at Meder and Burik. "...ran into the ring. The girl somehow threw a bolt of sahr fire at Novice Herel, stopping his attack on Novice Amarl but burning him and her own hand in the process. She and the boy ran across the ring and attacked this novice and a student that I hadn't seen." He gestured at Norag and the battered-looking third-year. "She broke the other novice's jaw, and the tall one fought with the third-year, knocking him unconscious.

"I gave Novice Amarl a healing elixir, ordered my assistant Bekol to do the same for Novice Herel, and sent a runner to report the incident."

"Do you know why Novice Herel didn't have a sahrotik weapon?" the awal asked calmly.

"No, ma'am. I questioned Maira at the counter, and she swears she recalled giving him one. I didn't find it on him or his companions, however."

She nodded, then looked at Meder, her eyes blazing. "Novice, would you care to explain what happened from your point of view? Speak only the truth." Amarl winced as the woman's voice rang strangely in the room once more, and Meder's eyes went blank and unfocused.

"Herel, Hadur, and two third-years accosted us in Askula Village this morning," she said in an emotionless monotone. "Hadur deliberately ran into Amarl, then called him a half-breed and accused me of sleeping with him and Burik. I knocked him down, and Herel threatened to pull his weapon on me."

"He was carrying a sword in the village, then?" Tekasoka interrupted.

"Yes, ma'am. He tried to start a fight and started to pull his sword, but

Amarl stopped him. Herel wanted them to go somewhere private and fight, but I suggested they settle it at Halit."

"Why did you do that?"

"Because I knew that Amarl could beat Herel, and that Herel wouldn't stop pushing until that happened. Herel thinks that training with third-years has made him better than anyone, but Amarl's gotten better faster than any of us, even Burik. And if it happened at Halit, everyone would know about it – and Herel's third-year bodyguards couldn't get involved."

"Very well. That seems a wise and well-thought-out decision. Continue. What happened at the actual match?"

"Amarl thought that Herel was planning something, and honestly, so did Burik and I, so we were watching Hadur, Norag, and the other third-year as much as we watched Amarl. When Amarl fell onto Herel's blade, I noticed Norag mumbling under his breath, then I caught a glimpse of the eyes of someone being hidden by sahr. I told Burik, and we ran over to stop them from doing whatever they were doing. I knocked Norag down with an elbow, and Burik attacked the third-year, who became visible when Norag fell. Burik knocked him out, and whatever was holding Amarl vanished."

"And the fire you threw at Novice Herel?"

"Herel was still attacking Amarl and hurting him. I had to make him stop, so I used a fire matrix. I only meant a flash of fire in his face, but the matrix collapsed faster than I was expecting, and I had to keep rebuilding it all the way to the target. I think that gave it too much momentum, so it hit his face – and it backlashed on me, burning my hand." She blinked rapidly as her eyes went back into focus, and she frowned and looked down at the floor.

"I see. Novice Burik, do you have anything to add to that?"

Burik shook his head. "No, ma'am. Meder said it better than I could."

"Which was why I asked her." The awal's gaze swept across to Norag. "Your turn, Novice. Tell me what happened. Was this planned out in advance? Speak the truth."

Norag's face went as blank as Meder's had, and he spoke in the same flat voice. "Yes, ma'am. Herel and Hadur had been planning it for a while. Originally, they wanted to lure Amarl into a duel out where no one could see, and Yashi would use his air weaving ability to push Amarl onto Herel's blade. They would claim it was an accident, that he stumbled into the blade by mistake. I told them it was a terrible plan that went against the high god's teachings, and I wanted nothing to do with it, which is why I wasn't with them in the village this morning."

"And when Novice Meder suggested the battle take place at Halit, what happened?"

"Herel wanted to do the same thing, but Yashi said it wouldn't work, that everyone knew about his ability, and that they'd suspect him. He didn't want to risk getting expelled for some coin. Herel suggested that I could shield him with sahr, so no one would know he was there, and I agreed to do it. Yashi erected a barrier behind Amarl, then tripped him so he'd fall onto Herel's blade."

"And the sahrotik blade Herel was given?"

"Hadur returned it almost immediately, but to a different second-year so no one would ask questions."

"And why in the spirits' hells would you go along with this, Novice?" she asked in a dangerous voice.

"I thought they would fail, ma'am. I know that the rings dampen sahr within them, so I thought when Yashi got close, the veil would shatter, and they'd abandon the plan."

"And why didn't you tell someone?"

"Because Herel and Hadur are my only friends here. Being with them destroyed any chance of befriending the other novices. If I alienate them, I'm alone."

Tekasoka's face was white with fury, and Herel practically cowered in his chair as she turned to face him. "Novice Herel," she said in a whispered voice, her words cold enough that Amarl was sure he felt the air in the room cool around him. "Why in the name of all the gods, both above and below, would you even consider doing something like this? Speak the truth!"

Herel seemed to struggle silently for a moment before his eyes went blank. "Amarl is a hizeen, ma'am," he said in an emotionless voice. "The Order is and has always been only for naluni for a good reason. Lesser races lack the strength of character and morality to handle the power of ithtu, and Amarl's among the worst of them. He's a thief, liar, and seducer by his own admission, and someone like that shouldn't be allowed to have the power of ithtu. He can't be trusted with it. Getting rid of him is for the good of the Order and the Empire."

She stared at him, her face shocked. "That is the most disgusting thing I've ever heard, Novice!" she gasped. "You think that you have the right to determine who does or doesn't belong at this school? Even worse, that you can determine who at this school should live or die?"

"No, ma'am. I didn't decide that. I was told that it had to be done, that it was my duty to the Empire."

She froze, her face astonished. "Told? Who told you that?" He opened his mouth, then shook his head and clamped his lips shut. The woman's face hardened, and she leaned closer to him. "Novice, tell me this instant. Who told you this? Speak!"

Her voice rang in the room again, and once more, Herel's mouth opened as if he'd speak, but no sound came from his lips. His hands began to tremble, and his eyes widened until they bulged. His face drained of all color, and he suddenly screamed, clutching his skull and dropping to his knees. He shook his head frantically from side-to-side, still screaming, then collapsed to the floor, his eyes shut and blood streaming from his nose.

"Get him to the infirmary! Now!" Tekasoka's voice filled the room, and Zirso sent his chair flying as he scooped the boy up and charged out the door, smashing it open with his shoulder. As he rushed out, the malim from the outer office appeared, her face concerned and lightning crackling on her fingers.

"Awal? What's wrong?"

"Nadishia, go find the Rashiv at once!" Tekasoka said, rising to her feet with an ashen face. "Have him meet me at the infirmary as soon as possible!"

"Yes, Awal." The woman vanished, and Tekasoka looked at the others, her face grave.

"There's more here than is apparent, but that doesn't free the rest of you from your responsibility in this matter. Novices Hadur and Norag, you both should have done all in your power to stop Novice Herel, and if that was insufficient, you should have come to me. Allowing him to proceed with a plot that was intended to kill another novice is so immoral and irresponsible that I can't even fathom it. Right now, I'm of a mind to expel you both!" The pair flinched, and she turned to face the older Yashi.

"And you! These novices are young and foolish, but you are a third-year! You know better! Why would you even consider being part of this?"

The older student looked down. "Herel – he paid me, ma'am. Lots of coin – enough to fund my sahrotik skill and then some. And I didn't think he'd succeed, either; most of his plans are idiotic and complicated."

"Then you can be bought? How can you possibly serve the Empire when you can cast aside your morals for mere coins?" She shook her head, her voice disbelieving, then turned to Meder and Burik.

"While the two of you are less culpable in all this, you still behaved foolishly! Zirso would have intervened immediately had the two of you not distracted him. Your ridiculous heroics could have cost your friend his life rather than saving it! And Novice Meder, the sparring rings are warded to damp out sahr! The spirits know how you still managed to collapse a matrix inside one, but you're lucky it didn't collapse fully onto you and set you on fire!"

She took a deep breath. "For the two of you, the punishment is simple. You will spend two hours after classes each night for the next two weeks serving at Halit in the most menial possible capacities so you can understand that you aren't needed to save anyone there! Is that understood?"

"Yes, ma'am," the two mumbled.

"Good. You may return to your room." Amarl turned to leave with them, but she held up a hand. "Not you, Novice. You will stay right there and not move a muscle. I'm not finished with you yet."

She turned back to the rest of the students. "The three of you, return to your rooms and remain there. I'll be speaking to the Rashiv about this; he will decide if there's a place for you in Askula or not. I strongly suspect the latter, but perhaps I'm mistaken. Dismissed." She hesitated. "And don't even think of trying to run. There's nowhere you could go that you wouldn't be hunted down, and it will be far worse for you if that happens. Understand?" Hadur, Norag, and Yashi all nodded grimly, then turned and walked out of the room.

"You," Tekasoka said, pointing to Amarl. "You will come with me to the infirmary. We still need to discuss this."

"Yes, ma'am," he sighed.

She strode out the door, and he followed behind her, finding himself walking quickly to keep up with her despite her shorter stature. Students and malims took a single look at her face and cleared out of their way, and Amarl noticed a few commiserating looks – but far more smirking grins. She remained silent as they strode through the corridors, until at last she pushed open the double doors leading into the infirmary. When the doors shut, she stopped and turned to face him.

"Tell me, Novice," she said crisply. "Do you consider yourself blameless in all this?"

He frowned, thinking through the day, then shook his head. "No, not totally, ma'am. I knew something was wrong. I could have just not shown up to the duel."

"Yes, you could have. However, all things considered, I believe you showed considerable restraint and foresight. You tried to contain the situation in the village, and your participation in this ridiculous event stemmed from your desire to protect your friends."

Amarl paused in confusion. "Wait – wait, no one mentioned that, ma'am…"

She smiled grimly. "No, they didn't. Consider that before you think to conceal things from me, or assume that I don't know what's truly happening in Askula."

"In any case, while your actions weren't the wisest, they weren't abysmally stupid the way practically everyone else's were. Well done."

He stared at her in shock. "Uh – th-thank you, ma'am."

"You're welcome. Don't do anything like this again. Now, come. Let's see if there's a resolution to be had in all this."

She pushed past a heavy fabric screen hanging before her and led him into the now-familiar infirmary. A handful of beds were occupied, but the one that drew Amarl's attention was in the center of the room. Herel lay unconscious on his back, with a malim Amarl didn't recognize kneeling beside him, her hands resting on the boy's forehead and chest. Zirso stood well back, his eyes wide as he stared at the thin, wizened, rainbow-clad Rashiv standing beside the fallen boy's bed, his face calm. As Tekasoka and Amarl neared, the old man turned and looked at them, inclining his head.

"Awal, Novice," he said evenly.

"Rashiv," the woman breathed with obvious relief. "Thank you for coming so quickly."

"Nadishia impressed the urgency of the matter on me sufficiently." He glanced down at the boy. "While Tanaret heals his most immediate injuries, what can you tell me of what occurred?"

"Novice Herel created a scheme to murder Novice Amarl and make it look accidental. When I questioned him, he spouted some Lasheshian rhetoric and claimed he'd been told it was his duty. I used my ability to compel him to tell me who told him that, and something resisted me."

The Rashiv glanced at Amarl. "And your passive ability?"

"Nothing. Something held me out."

The old man frowned. "Concerning. Few powers are strong enough to hold you out." He looked down at the unconscious boy. "How is he, Tanaret?"

"Minor hemorrhaging, Rashiv. Nothing severe. I've healed the damage; should I wake him?"

"No, this will go easier if he sleeps." The old man reached down and placed a hand on Herel's forehead, and Amarl once more felt the Rashiv's power wash over him. He froze, his body unable to move, his mind blank and empty of all thought as that titanic presence battered him. How long he stayed like that, he didn't know, but when the man's aura receded, stars floated in Amarl's vision, and his lungs ached from the need to breathe. He sucked in a deep, shuddering breath and heard Zirso doing the same. He glanced over and saw the boy looking pale, white, and shaking.

"Interesting," the Rashiv said. He glanced at the healer kneeling beside Herel. "Tanaret, step back a reach, please."

"Yes, Rashiv." The woman nodded her head and rose to her feet, walking back away from the bed. The old man gestured, and a shimmering curtain swirled into being around the bed, enclosing Amarl, the awal, the Rashiv, and the sleeping Herel within it.

"The boy's family are Lasheshians," the Rashiv said simply. "The sentiments were instilled in him since birth, but he holds them in check. At least, he did until someone unearthed them and gave them power to dominate his thoughts."

"Who?" the woman asked.

"He doesn't know – at least, he doesn't remember. That knowledge was wiped from him when you commanded him to reveal it. Their first meeting was during the feast after the Joining, when the person apparently unlocked the boy's latent hatreds and supplied him with a significant amount of coinage. He has since seen this person on three separate Akios. He considers this person to be an authority figure, a person who spoke to him of Lasheshia's teachings and of Novice Amarl's flaws. He believes that someone in great authority here in Askula instructed him to find a way to remove Novice Amarl for the good of the Order and the Empire."

He sighed. "Whoever it was, their repeat visits had a purpose: to forge a soul binding. Novice Herel could have thrown it off, but only by going against his most fundamental nature. And that binding radiated power;

anyone near the novice for any length of time would have come to believe in his cause, especially if they were already so inclined." He grimaced. "The binder was someone of exceptional power and talent."

"You can't divine their identity?" she asked, her voice sounding surprised.

"No. They apparently foresaw my involvement and took steps. Each time they approached Novice Herel, they made a point to interact with everyone around them, buying drinks, telling stories, hurling insults, and so on. They made enough of an impression that their presence disturbed the lines of everyone nearby, tangling them together, but not enough to carry any of those with them, ensuring they wouldn't be remembered. It will take weeks or even moons for me to sort it out and trace it back to its source, and by then, it will probably be immaterial."

"Why?"

"Because, Tekasoka, there are only three people in Askula at the moment who could have done any part of what this person accomplished. You could have suppressed the boy's memories and wiped them. Ranakar could have crafted the soul binding. Ninalow could have charmed the entire bar. But none of you could have performed each individual piece of it together. So, either three of my awals have mysteriously banded together to kill one novice – calm down, Tekasoka, that's obviously absurd – or the person who did it entered Askula, performed their task, and left the realm. I'm certain that once I untangle their line, I'll find it leads back into Umpratan, probably into another tangle in Sik and an even larger one in Lepild."

He shook his head. "I'll continue to search, but I fear that whoever this is has covered their trail well. I'm not optimistic."

She nodded. "And Novice Herel?"

"I removed the binding. He should recover, and his need to harm Novice Amarl should be gone. However, the Lasheshian sentiments are part of his nature. They won't be so easy to remove."

"What of his consequence? And that of his companions?"

"His companions?" She quickly related the full story, and the old man's eyes hardened. "It's possible that the binding affected Novices Hadur and Norag, making it harder for them to go against Novice Herel – but Student Yashi's actions are beyond absolution. He acted for the love of money, nothing more, and an ithtar who can be swayed by coin can never be trusted in the Empire. Do what must be done."

"Yes, Rashiv. And the Novices?"

"Punishment is certainly in order. Something painful that remains in their memories and reminds them of the consequences if they ignore their common sense. Perhaps a moon spending their evenings hauling rocks in the quarry."

"As you wish, Rashiv." She bowed her head.

"Return this Novice to his dormitory if you would. Perhaps with a suggestion to keep all this to himself."

"I will, Rashiv, but…" She glanced at Amarl. "He's already thrown off one of my suggestions. He may do the same to another."

"Really?" The old man's eyes fastened on Amarl, glittering with curiosity. "Blood truly does run true, does it not? Very well, then, Novice. You may tell your friends that Novice Herel was under a binding that forced him to act as he did and altered the behavior of his companions, but nothing more. I will know if you share more than that, and I will be highly displeased." He leaned toward the boy, and a hint of his power leaked out. "Is that understood?"

Amarl swallowed hard as the man's aura sent a thrill of fear through his chest. "Y-yes, sir."

"Excellent. Then return to your room, and hopefully, this will be the end of your difficulties with Novice Herel."

Burik and Meder were waiting for him when he returned to the room, their faces worried and curious in equal measure.

"What happened?" Meder asked the moment Amarl stepped in the room. "Are you in trouble, as well? You didn't do anything wrong…"

"No, I'm not," Amarl shook his head. "The awal told me that I was basically the least foolish fool of the bunch of us, at least this one time."

"Ha!" Burik snorted. "I never thought you'd be the coolheaded one, Amarl."

"Don't worry. It won't last, I'm sure."

"So, what happened?" Meder pressed. "Do you know what happened to Herel?"

"I can't say everything," he said slowly. "The Rashiv was there, and he told me what I'm allowed to tell you both. He said he'd know if I said more –

and I believe him."

Burik nodded. "I would, too. The malims and awals seem to know everything. It has to be worse with the Rashiv."

"So, what can you tell us?" Meder asked.

"Apparently, someone used something called a binding on Herel," he said slowly. "It made him do what he did."

"What?" Meder gasped. "Who?"

"I can't talk about that, sorry. I can tell you, though, that it might have made Hadur and Norag more likely to follow along with him. Although, the Rashiv did say that Herel's family was Lasheshian. I've never heard of that place before, but why would it make a difference?"

"Being Lasheshian isn't about a place," Merel sighed, rubbing her eyes. "Lasheshia was a Shashana from a couple centuries back who believed that non-naluni should be expelled from the Empire and tried to get the High Council to make that happen. You remember: Warahid talked about them at the beginning of the year."

"If she was the Shashana, couldn't she just order it?" Burik asked in a puzzled voice.

"No, it doesn't work that way – at least, not since the time of She Who Is Forgotten, the last Shashana to hold actual power. She nearly unleashed a plague of spirits on the Empire, and after that, the High Council took all secular power from her. The Shashana is the spiritual and divine leader of the Empire, but she has no real power." Meder shrugged.

"Lasheshia believed that naluni were an inherently superior species to all others, not physically but morally and spiritually. She said that the gods only claimed the souls of naluni, and that the souls of shayeni, felni, vadniy, and everyone else were impure and unclean, so the gods hurled them into the void when they died."

"Sounds stupid," Amarl laughed.

"Not stupid, hateful. The problem is that the Shashana is supposed to be the gods' voice in Umpratan, so a lot of people listened to her. She made up this whole doctrine, filled with what she called proof that naluni were superior, and she worked to convince the High Council to approve it and make it law. It obviously didn't happen, but many noble families took her words to heart, and some still do. It sounds like Herel's is one." She made a face. "It sort of makes sense. Lasheshian families tend to be insular since no one else wants to deal with them, and they usually have great heritage but little influence. I think his family's like that from the way he's latched on to Hadur and Norag."

"He latched on to them?" Burik asked. "I thought they were kissing his ass to get favor with his family."

"Oh, their families don't need it. Hadur comes from one of the preeminent merchant families in the Empire. Like all merchants, they're low caste, but they're incredibly rich and influential, and every noble house works to cully their favor. And Norag's family are renowned artists and stonecutters whose works are prized across the Empire. Again, that only makes them umanai caste, two below the nobility, but they're all invited to every noble house in every city they visit. Herel probably counts himself lucky to have met them, and he's probably hoping to use that connection to help his family become more influential."

"I thought you were all supposed to be cut off from your families," Amarl chuckled.

"Technically, yes, but realistically, it's not that simple. If Herel went back home to his family, they couldn't publicly acknowledge him, but they could privately, and while he couldn't claim their name anymore, he could still quietly use their connections, and they could quietly use his." She laughed. "Although if it got out that he inadvertently dragged Hadur and Norag into some sort of Lasheshian scheme, those connections might go out the window."

"Wait, so if they were dragged along, like she said, does that mean they're not being punished?" Burik asked in disbelief.

"Oh, no. They are, and it's worse than what Tekasoka gave you. They've got to spend a moon in the rock quarry hauling stones every night." Amarl grinned as he spoke, but the grin faded to a grimace. "And I think they're going to expel Yashi."

"Oh," Meder gasped.

"Serves him right," Burik growled. "He prized money over what he knew was right. People like that shouldn't be ithtaru. I'm glad they're kicking him out."

"They don't just kick you out," Amarl shook his head. "Expulsion means execution, Burik."

"Execution?"

"Yeah. Veter told me on that hunt."

"That – that actually answers a few questions," Meder said quietly. "Like why no one's ever seen a rogue or independent ithtar. Or why I've never heard of someone failing out of Askula. Hundreds or thousands of ithtaru came from Dairon originally, and no one's ever heard of them returning to their families, not once." She shook her head. "It adds up. If you fail here, that's the end for you."

"Makes sense," Burik said after a moment's silence. "Anyone with an awakened ability is too dangerous to let loose in the Empire, aren't they? And you can't take that ability away from them. What other choice do they have?"

"None, really," Amarl said slowly. "Think about those matches we saw today, and how powerful those students were. What could regular people do against someone like that? And those were students, not even a fully developed and trained ithtar. How could you contain someone like that?"

"I agree," Meder nodded. "And I can see why they wouldn't want someone like Yashi sent into the Empire. The Order is supposed to be incorruptible. That's why they hold the right to summary judgment. If one ithtar started taking bribes, it could undermine the entire Order." She sighed. "I still don't have to like it."

"Neither do I, but there's nothing we can do about it." Amarl rubbed his face and lay back on his bed. "Today started out so great. Where did it all go wrong?"

"When we went to get a drink," Burik noted.

"You're right," Amarl laughed. "And that thing with Dalat happened right after we got a drink. I'm thinking we need to stay away from Sasofit's for a while."

"Screw that. If I'm going to have to spend every day cleaning the sparring rings and polishing equipment at Halit, I'm drinking next Akio. May the gods help whoever tries to stop me."

Meder laughed. "At least you got out of that, Amarl."

"Yeah, but I'll still be going down with you to help if they let me," he shrugged.

"You will?" she asked.

"Of course. You got in trouble protecting me. I can't let you take the consequences alone." He grinned at the pair. "Veter said that an ithtar has to assume that no one has his back, but that's bullshit. I think an ithtar just has to find the right people to have his back."

"Now that's something I can drink to!" Burik laughed. "To always having each other's backs!"

"We don't have anything to drink, Burik," Meder said, rolling her eyes.

"Details, woman. Don't bother me with details."

CHAPTER 32

Amarl ducked as Burik snapped a fist at his head, sliding sideways in the graceful movements of Water Form. The larger boy followed with a second punch, then thrust his foot out with a side kick at Amarl's chest. Amarl's hands flowed up and redirected the kick, while his foot darted out to strike at the back of Burik's knee. Burik slammed his front foot down and twisted with Amarl's kick, thrusting an elbow at the smaller boy's head that Amarl barely blocked, but the impact of the blow threw off his rhythm, and the building wave of force that Water Form was supposed to generate once more dispersed, ruining Amarl's balance and throwing off his form. Burik snapped another punch high at Amarl's head, and the boy ducked and turned to escape the follow-up, but the strike was only a feint. Burik's knee crashed into Amarl's stomach, doubling him up, and he felt a swift but gentle blow to the back of his neck, a blow that would have been crippling or even fatal had they truly been fighting.

The blow turned into a gentle hand that rested on Amarl's shoulder and helped him straighten, and the hizeen stood and rubbed his aching stomach, shaking his head ruefully. In the moons since his hunt, he hadn't been able to recapture the feeling of doing Water Form correctly. He still struggled with himself, moving too stiffly, thinking too much and trying to plan for the inevitable crash of the building wave – which usually ended with him crashing to the ground.

"You got me again," he sighed. "I should have dodged that elbow instead of blocking it."

Burik nodded. "Moving into it would have been even better," he said. "I've got better reach than you, so staying in close negates some of my advantages."

"It also gives me less time to react and space to move," Amarl shook his head. "You're fast, and I need that."

The larger boy grinned. "For now. You're getting better fast, though. Are you still at level three on your unarmed skills?"

"Four, but I'll probably be there a while. Ranakar says that it usually takes a couple years to go from four to five in a skill, even with ithtu, so I'm not holding my breath. Have you leveled Military Boxing yet?"

"It's at five, yeah, but it'll probably be stuck there for the next few years. Nadar Lothitar says that I should look into a second form..." He broke off at the sound of slow clapping from the edge of the circle, and they both turned to see Meder standing there with an ironic smile.

"Yes, yes, you're both much better than you were. You're amazing, and songs will be written about you." She thumped her quarterstaff on the ground at the edge of the ring. "But I believe it's my turn, yes?"

"We did promise her that would be our last round," Burik agreed. "Who do you want to spar against first today, Meder?"

"Amarl, if that's okay. That axe of his keeps throwing me off, and I need to get used to it."

"Fine by me," the smaller boy shrugged, walking over to the edge of the ring and grabbing his training moon axe. "Besides, Burik's better at teaching anyway."

"That as well," she smiled, ducking under the railing and moving to the center of the ring. They faced one another and gave each other a low bow, never taking their eyes off the other person as they did.

Meder struck the moment their bow was complete, spinning her staff up and aiming it at Amarl's chin, but the nimble boy twisted out of the way and brought his axe up to block her downward slash. The two wooden shafts struck with a loud thunk, and Meder spun, using the recoil from his block to send a thrust at his midsection.

Amarl focused on fighting defensively at first. The moon axe was a versatile weapon, but its strength was in its ability to constantly attack, striking with all four blades, one after the other, interspersed by stabbing with the crescent and spear point. It was heavier than a staff, which gave it more power, but that also meant that it moved slower and didn't reverse directions as quickly. Just like the boys, Meder had gotten much better with her staff, and he had to focus on his defense to keep from being struck. He twisted and blocked, slid her high blows and tumbled over her low ones. He cracked his weapon against hers over and over, giving up ground as she pushed him back toward the edge of the circle.

After two minutes, he turned to the side, sliding her attack, and shifted his feet. He spun, whipping the axe around him, and slashed at her with the crescent blades. She leaned back and batted the trailing edge of his axe, trying to ground it, but he used the momentum of her strike to bring the axe heads chopping down toward her shoulder. She knocked the blow out of the way, and once again, he rode the momentum of her parry to bring the crescent around to slash at her face.

She stepped back to avoid the blow, now entirely on the defensive as he struck again and again. She blocked and dodged, but each failed strike led instantly to the next. That was the true danger of the moon axe; as long as he kept it moving, it left very little chance for an opponent to attack, and while it was heavier than a staff, it was light enough that he could quickly reverse its spin or thrust with it if its momentum stalled. Meder grew increasingly frustrated as he pushed her around the circle, and she batted one of his blows away with a fraction too much power. He spun the weapon, letting the force of the block flow into it as it slid out of his hand into a thrust that poked her on the left side of her chest. She stepped back, her hand flying up to her chest and her eyes wide.

"You stabbed my boob!" she said indignantly, covering her breast with one hand, her face turning slightly pink.

"I didn't mean to," he grinned. "That's just how the momentum kind of carried it. I was just trying to hit you in the chest."

She glared at him for a moment. "If you were better with that, I'd have trouble believing you," she finally said, lightening the moment with a grin of her own. "But since you're still terrible at it, I guess I can let it slide this time."

"Terrible?" he protested. "I beat you, didn't I?"

"Only by poking me in the boob, which doesn't count," she said archly, then laughed.

"Oh, it totally counts. Now, I just have to poke the other one to even things out."

"Not on your life." She lifted her staff again. "Bring it on."

They sparred for another round, and once again, Amarl focused on defense for the first couple of minutes. Not only did he need the practice, Meder needed to work on fighting aggressively. She tended to hold back, not going for the kill, staying defensive and hoping for an opening rather than creating one herself. He knew it was good for her to practice striking over and over again, and since defending with the moon axe was one of his weak points, it was a win-win for both of them.

After a couple minutes, he once more shifted to offense, this time starting with a massive swipe of the axe as he held it by one end and lashed out with the other. Meder ducked and parried the blow, and he used his other hand to set it spinning once more. He slashed and cut, thrust and stabbed, constantly striking and never giving the girl a chance to move back into offense. Eventually, he struck high, forcing her to duck, then swept the weapon back low, catching her in the side with the crescent blade.

"Okay, give me a minute," she said, panting slightly as she rose to her feet and rubbed her side. "That axe of yours is totally unfair, you know."

"Not really," he shook his head. "It's just a really good weapon against a staff or sword. A spear or Burik's halberd would do better against it."

"You think so?" she asked dubiously.

He nodded. "A spear has reach, and it can thrust pretty quickly, so I wouldn't be able to attack the way I do against you. And Burik's got reach and can both slash and thrust, so he can force me to stay defensive."

"He's right," Burik agreed, walking into the ring. "Although if you got inside my reach, you'd have the advantage." He reached out and touched the axe. "That thing would be a nightmare against an agility-based fighter like Hadur, though. You'd cut him up long before he could close with you."

"That's the hope, at least," Amarl laughed. "And I'm working on ways I can use it against someone like you. I just haven't perfected them yet."

"Well, I need to work on that, too," Meder said. "So, I'll spar with Burik for a bit, and then you and I can go again, Amarl."

"Sounds good to me," he nodded, walking back to the edge of the ring and settling in to watch. As he did, he pulled up his status sheet to examine his recent changes.

<u>STATS</u>
FORCE: 5.2 (122%)   SKILL: 5.3 (135%)
SPEED: 5.6 (183%)   TOUGHNESS: 4.8 (82%)
MIND: 5.7 (201%)   WILL: 4.6 (67%)
PRESENCE: 6.2 (332%)   SOUL: 9.6 (9,448%)

<u>QUICKENED ABILITY:</u> MEZ
TIER: F
PERCENT QUICKENED: 48.9%

<u>CURRENT ITHTU:</u> 60.2
TO LEVEL: 0
TO STATS: 2 (2.5%)
TO SKILLS: 0
TO TAK: 13 (99%)

<u>CURRENT TAK:</u> 13/13

He still had his Strong crystal with two-thirds of its energy even eight moons later, but the level 9 Minor crystal he'd gotten from that hunt gave out just days ago. Since he was no longer allowed to hunt, he'd expected to have to make do with Feeble crystals the way the others did, but Ranakar provided him with a new level 7 Minor crystal as a replacement. Having two crystals greatly sped up his ability to advance his stats, but bringing his Will up to a reasonable number took more power than he'd thought. Apparently, his lack of affinity with the stat made it harder to improve, and he'd gotten less and less for each unit of ithtu he channeled to it.

He finally got it level with his Toughness after five moons, at which point Ranakar had him switch the crystals to Toughness; apparently, it was important for an ithtar to keep stats at least somewhat balanced. Ithtaru usually worked alone, after all, so they needed to be a little good at everything. A low stat was a weakness to be exploited. Also, according to Ranakar, raising his Will stat didn't fix the fact that he didn't have an affinity for Will-based skills, and he'd always struggle with his Will compared to his other stats. He could improve his stat, but ithtu couldn't change his essential nature.

He'd wondered if adding a second crystal would boost his skill gains, but it hadn't seemed to. He'd certainly grown in the past eight moons, but he wasn't growing twice as fast as he had before. He switched his main status for his skill screen and checked out the changes he'd gotten since taking two crystals.

SKILLS REPORT
CHANGED SKILLS

ACADEMICS	3 (+3)
ACROBATICS	4 (+1)
ANATOMY	4 (+2)
BEAR FORM	4 (+1)
CLIMBING	5 (+1)
EMPATHY	4 (+1)
ENDURANCE	5 (+1)
HIDING	5 (+1)
KNIFE FIGHTING	4 (+1)
LOCKPICKING	6 (+1)
MEDITATION	2 (+1)
MEMORIZATION	4 (+2)
MOON AXE FIGHTING	3 (+3)
PERCEPTION	4 (+2)
RUNNING	4 (+1)
SAHR MASTERY	2 (+2)
SCIMITAR FIGHTING	4 (+2)
SILENT MOVEMENT	4 (+2)
STAFF FIGHTING	4 (+2)
THROWING	4 (+2)
TIGER FORM	4 (+1)
TRACKING	4 (+2)
WATER FORM	4 (+1)

The constant weapons training had proven beneficial for all the novices' skills. He knew Meder had gotten her Staff Fighting and Knife Fighting to two, and Burik had apparently boosted his Military Boxing skill, an impressive feat considering how high it was already. Norag had two levels in hammers, his preferred weapon, and Herel had the same with his longsword. He wasn't sure where Hadur was at; the merchants' son wasn't particularly forthcoming lately. They'd all improved tremendously, but even though doubling his crystals hadn't improved his skill growth rate, none of the novices had grown close to as quickly as Amarl.

According to Ranakar, most ithtaru took around a year to a year and six moons to reach level three in a skill, depending on their affinity for it, and then a similar amount of time to go from level three to level four. Amarl had reached level four in his unarmed forms in six moons, a quarter of the normal time. His skill growth was amazing, but it slowed down once he hit level four in his skills. It usually took at least a couple years to go from level four to level five; even if he kept advancing at four times the normal pace, that would still be another three moons or so before he saw another bump to his skills, which would put him into his second year.

He watched as Burik handed Meder a few defeats before re-entering the ring with her, this time using his unarmed forms instead of his axe. That was harder since the girl was fast and accurate with her strikes, and he couldn't rely on one form or another. If he spent too much time in the Water Form, dodging and redirecting her blows, when his gradual buildup inevitably crashed, he took a staff blow or two in the process. If he stuck with the aggressive attacks of Tiger Form, he'd keep her on the defensive, but once again, he'd probably get cracked with a staff at least once. He had to shift back and forth between the two forms, slipping Bear Form in every so often when he got close enough for a throw. It challenged his skills since shifting from one form to the other wasn't just a case of performing a different movement; he had to switch mindsets, shift his focus to other parts of his opponent, alter his footing, change his body positioning, and recenter his balance. He couldn't practice like this with Burik; the bigger boy was too good, and he took merciless advantage of the tiny moments of hesitancy when Amarl switched from one form to the other.

Finally, bruised, winded, and slightly battered, he stepped back, lowering his hands. "You've gotten a lot better," he panted at Meder with an approving nod.

"So have you," she said, panting just as heavily. "You're making me work much harder than you used to." Her black hair lay plastered against her face and neck with sweat, and her shirt was soaked and glued itself to her body. Amarl thought he probably looked the same; he certainly felt disgusting.

"You're both good enough that you'd probably pass advanced military standards," Burik observed from the side of the ring. "With a little training in formation fighting, spears, and firearms, you'd both fit in as elite soldiers now."

"Really?" Meder asked with a grin. "I didn't think I was that good."

Burik nodded as he walked over to stand by them. "If you knew more about formation fighting and tactics, you're probably good enough to be Third Sword, Second for Amarl."

"You say that like it's supposed to mean something to me," Amarl said cheerfully. "For all I know, though, you're saying I'd be an excellent backup weapon, which doesn't sound all that complimentary."

Burik barked a quick laugh. "No, Swords are the elite infantry ranks in the army. Third Sword is the basic elite infantry, someone with specialized training. Second Sword is the same but with a tiny bit of authority and responsibility."

"That's Amarl, all right," Meder laughed. "Tiny Authority. We should call him T.A. for short."

"My authority is as big as it needs to be," Amarl shrugged and grinned slyly at the girl. "And so is everything else."

She no longer blushed at his innuendos but simply rolled her eyes. "You forget, Amarl, I've seen everything else. Do I look impressed?"

"Damn, Meder," Burik laughed, clapping a hand on the girl's back appreciatively. "That was brutal!" He flashed Amarl a grin. "Accurate, but brutal."

"We all do the best with what we have, Burik." He paused. "Although now I understand why you prefer such a long weapon, when you're blessed with such a small natural one. Have to balance things out, right?"

"Okay, okay," Meder laughed. "Stop before you actually start comparing them. I don't need to see that. Come on, we need to get cleaned up before the meeting tonight."

"Any idea what it's about?" Amarl asked the girl as he gathered his weapons.

"Not a clue," she shook her head.

"What?" Burik chuckled. "Meder doesn't know something? How did that happen?"

She grimaced as she wrapped her daggers around her waist. "No one's talking," she said. "I don't know what it's all about, just that we all have to be there: us, Herel, Hadur, and Norag."

"I hope it's a party," Burik said with a smile. "Maybe to celebrate our first year of being here."

"What have the malims ever done to make you think they'd throw us a party, Burik?" Amarl laughed.

"Plus, there's a group of novices just three moons ahead of us," Meder pointed out. "I don't think they got a party for moving to second year – or if they did, everyone kept it quite a secret. And we're not quite finished with that first year; we've still got a moon to go before we're second years." She shook her head. "I don't know what it is, but I don't think it's a party."

"It's probably a test of some kind," Amarl shrugged. "Everything else is, isn't it?"

Burik's shoulders sagged. "You're probably right. A test does make more sense." He brightened. "Maybe it'll be a sparring tournament!"

"Why would they bother?" Meder laughed. "You'd win, Amarl would take second, and Herel and I would fight for third. Hadur and Norag would come in last. What would be the point?"

He sighed. "Fine, it's probably not that, either." His eyes widened. "Think it's something to do with sahr? Maybe a test in that?"

Meder smiled at him. "I'd be fine with that," she laughed.

Amarl grunted. "I wouldn't. I still suck at using it. I'd come in last in that, for sure."

"Yes, you would," Meder said matter-of-factly. "And Herel would come in second-to-last."

"And you'd probably win."

"It depends on the challenge, really. If we had time to think and research and craft a working, then yes, I'd probably win. If we were given a task and had to create a working quickly, then Norag would win. He has a better intuitive feel for sahr than I do, but my calculations are better than his."

"I can agree with that," Burik nodded. "And I'd be right in the middle."

"Probably, yes, with Hadur. If it's some sort of end-of-year test, though, I doubt it's focused on any one thing. I imagine the malims would want us to show a little bit of everything we've learned."

"Well, there's no point in worrying about it," Amarl shook his head. "We'll find out soon enough." He sighed. "It's weird thinking that it's been almost a year. Sometimes it feels like it flew by, and other times it feels like it's been a lot longer."

"I know what you mean," Burik nodded. "The other day, I was thinking about your duel with Herel, and I was sure it was just a few weeks ago, not five moons."

"I haven't thought about that in a while," Amarl laughed.

"Well, you haven't had reason to. Herel's behaved himself since then." Meder sighed a little sadly. "But you're right. Sometimes, it feels like our Joining was just a few weeks ago, and other days, I can barely remember what it felt like living in Dairon. That seems like a lifetime ago."

"Technically, it was. You did die, remember?"

"Yes, I remember. I also remember watching you die, and if I'd known back then what an ass you are, I might have made sure you didn't revive!"

"Oh! I'm hurt!" Amarl clutched his chest, then let out a small belch. "No, wait, I'm fine. Just gas."

"Boys," she rolled her eyes once more, and Burik and Amarl traded grins. She turned and eyed Amarl archly. "And speaking of boys, did you know that a certain gray-skinned novice was seen slipping out of the room of Kamda, Teria, and Corin this past Akio? Care to explain that?"

Amarl shrugged. "I was helping Kamda with her studies, that's all."

"Her studies?" Meder asked, obviously unconvinced. "What studies?"

"She wanted a little extra help with one of her skills. It's really no big deal."

"Which skill?" Burik asked with a wide grin.

"Anatomy," Amarl said without a hint of a smile.

"Anatomy," Meder repeated. "Seriously, Amarl?"

"Oh, yes. And she was a dedicated and diligent student. We both learned a great deal with just an hour's study. She was extremely grateful for my help afterward."

Burik brayed with sudden laughter, but Meder just shook her head. "You're ridiculous, you know."

"I do my best," he said grandly.

"So, tell us about it," Burik asked.

"Burik!" Meder gasped. "I don't want to hear the details!"

"Not that," he rolled his eyes. "I mean, how did it happen?" Amarl looked at him with a raised eyebrow, and the larger boy waved his hands. "Not how did *it* happen, obviously. How did you seduce her with your wiles?"

"His wiles?" Meder laughed. "Yes, Amarl, tell us about your wiles."

"It was last Akio, when we were at Sasofit's and I went up to the bar to get us some drinks..." Amarl regaled them with an only somewhat embellished story as they headed back to Sabila.

When they reached their dorm, the three quickly showered and got dressed in clean clothing. The sun was lowering below the western mountains as they entered the Citadel and headed for the main hall, the large room where they'd all first waited for their Joining. The room used to unnerve Amarl, but after spending a year walking through it at least twice a day, those memories had mostly faded. He'd barely noticed the room the first time he entered, but since then, he'd seen it hundreds of times.

A huge version of the sword banner of Askula dominated the wall above the door leading to the lake, with a dozen other banners spreading out from it, hanging like pennants around the walls. Each pennant was a different shape, color, and had its own heraldry on it, but he had no clue what any of them meant, and he'd never been curious enough to try and find out. The same went for the portraits hanging along the wall; he assumed they were important people to the school, but they didn't matter to him personally, so he didn't care. Staircases ringed the hall, leading up into the castle's higher levels and towers. The doors at the top of those staircases usually stood open, but someone had shut them, making the wide space feel more confined. Amarl had cleaned the Citadel enough times in the past almost year to know that those doors were usually left open, and the feeling of being shut in seemed ominous.

Herel and his friends joined the trio a few minutes later, and as they approached, Norag glanced at Amarl's group, then walked over to stand in front of them, ignoring the glares Herel and Hadur sent his way.

"Any idea what this is about?" he asked curiously.

Meder shook her head. "No clue. I've tried to find out, but no one's willing to talk about it."

"Same. None of the third-years will talk about it – not that many of them talk to us anymore after Yashi." The boy shook his head and glanced back at his friends. "Herel's furious about it."

"That sounds like Herel's problem," Burik noted a little coolly.

"Well, it's my problem, too, since I have to live with him," Norag grinned. "At least he'll be happy knowing that no one talked to you, either. If you'd known when he doesn't, he'd be impossible."

"Impossibler," Amarl corrected. "He's already impossible."

"No, just a little difficult," Norag sighed. "At least, if you're naluni." He stepped back from the group. "Thanks anyway."

Amarl opened his mouth to speak, but before he said a word, a door at the top of the stairs opened, and two figures emerged from it. Norag walked quickly back to his friends as Ranakar stepped out onto the stairs, following behind the short figure of Tekasoka. She walked forward expressionlessly, her round face serious and her back straight, and the students immediately fell silent and stared at her.

Since the duel, Amarl had only seen Tekasoka a few times from a distance, for which he was very glad. Part of him wondered if she'd tell him whatever the Rashiv found, but he knew that she wouldn't. She'd brought him along that night in case the Rashiv wanted to speak with him, not because she thought he had any reason to know what was happening. He'd been careful to avoid problems with the other novices, and they'd been equally careful to stay away from him, and everyone seemed content with that situation. Even the older novices had started leaving the trio alone after Yashi's expulsion.

The expulsion hadn't been pleasant. The entire school gathered in front of the lake outside the Citadel. Yashi was brought out, bound and gagged, his eyes blank and unseeing in a way that Amarl hoped meant he wasn't really aware of what was happening. The trio could only watch in grim silence as the reason for the boy's expulsion was read to the gathered students. He was forced to kneel before the altar, and Ranakar beheaded him with a swift blow. Amarl thought that was the end of it, but to his shock and mild horror, the awal knelt by the boy and harvested a glowing ithtu crystal from him as well as his Joining Crystal. The body was laid on a simple log raft, doused with oil, and set alight, pushed into the lake to burn. Amarl watched it for a long time, wondering how many other students' bodies covered the lake's depths in a layer of ash.

It shook them all, reminding them that there was no opportunity for failure in Askula. They were blades, nothing more, and flawed blades were flung back into the fire to be destroyed. They'd all been a little quiet for the next couple weeks, and Amarl noticed he no longer saw older students following Herel and Nadur around. It was a harsh lesson, but one well-learned. Askula didn't tolerate mistakes.

He pulled himself back into the present as the pair of awals stepped onto the main floor. They walked over to stand before the group of novices, eyeing the students in silence. Everyone stood quietly, and Amarl's heart beat so rapidly he wondered how no one else could hear it in the hush. Whatever this was, he had a feeling it wasn't good, at least judging from Ranakar's flat expression.

"Novices," Tekasoka finally said, shattering the silence, "you have been in my care for eleven moons – eleven moons that have been far too chaotic for my tastes. Be that as it may, you have all survived to reach the end of your first year here in Askula, at least so far. Your nadars have kept me informed of your individual progress. Be assured, I know where each of you excel and where you falter, whether that be academics, skills, weapons, sahr use, or any aspect of life here at Askula. Had any of you been obviously unsuitable, you would not be standing here now.

"You have mostly impressed your instructors, and none of you have displeased me beyond the possibility of atonement." She glanced at Amarl and Herel as she spoke, and the hizeen winced, noting that Herel did the same.

"Although you are nearing the end of your first year, you have not yet reached it. Every group of novices must be evaluated to see whether or not they are fit to move into the advanced second year classes. The method of evaluation varies from group to group and is chosen to test that group's strengths and challenge their flaws. I gathered you here this evening because your specific evaluation has been chosen – and it begins now."

Meder flashed Amarl a triumphant look, and he barely managed to avoid rolling his eyes. Burik's lips twitched in a grin, and beyond him, Norag looked nervous and concerned. Herel seemed relatively unfazed by this news, while next to him, Hadur seemed eager for the evaluation to begin. Amarl wasn't so sure; while he felt confident in his abilities, he knew that Ranakar knew his strengths and weaknesses well. If the test was really meant to target Amarl's flaws, it would probably be brutal.

"In fact," the awal continued, "your evaluation was specifically suggested by the Rashiv himself." Her eye twitched as she spoke, and Amarl had a feeling that what the Rashiv 'suggested' wasn't what she wanted. "You should all feel honored that he decided to take a personal hand in your education here; that is rare, and not something to be taken lightly."

Meder glanced at Amarl, and he couldn't help but grimace. He knew what she was thinking. He was probably the reason that the Rashiv took an interest in the group, and this evaluation was probably going to be harder than it had to be because of it. Once more, he was certain he could hear the sound of a hammer ringing on steel in the distance, and it seemed he felt the blows of that hammer falling on his back and shoulders.

"The test that has been chosen for you will challenge every aspect of your education so far. Tonight, you will be sent through a Mistway into another realm, and there, you must survive for five days." The woman's face was grave as she spoke, and the novices all shifted about as they listened. Amarl glanced at the others; Burik and Herel looked eager, but the rest seemed nervous or even frightened. He understood their fear, as a spike of anxiety rose up and stabbed his heart, as well. He wasn't looking forward to another hunt after the way the last one had gone.

"Awal Ranakar will give you more details," she continued. "I will simply tell you the purpose and parameters of this exercise." She gave them all a hard look. "First, once through the Mistway, how you survive is up to you. You may choose to work together, to separate into groups, or to go it alone. If you work together, you will be judged based on your contributions to your group, so relying on stronger teammates to carry you will fail. If you choose to proceed alone, your path will be much harder, but you alone will be responsible for your success or failure. As always, the choice and its attendant consequences are yours.

"Second, you will face danger, but nothing beyond your ability to handle. Several older students and a pair of nadars will precede you through the Mistway. They are there to ensure that the threats you face are within your capabilities, and nothing more. Their presence does not guarantee your safety, and they will not intervene to protect you or assist you." She glanced at Amarl. "In fact, they are under orders to avoid interacting with you in any way."

Amarl felt a huge surge of relief. If trouble came, he could handle Herel and his partners, especially with Meder and Burik to help, but he didn't want to deal with another group of older students trying to bully and harass him and his friends. He'd had enough of that for one lifetime.

"The expectations of this test are simple. Last for five days. If you do not, you fail. There will be no excuses to justify failure. You should have the skills and knowledge you need to persist in the particular realm to which we're sending you; if you don't, then you don't qualify to move to second year. Is that understood?"

"Yes, ma'am," Burik said loudly, with the others echoing him half a heartbeat behind.

"Good. Then go with Awal Ranakar, and remember. This is within your capabilities if you use what you've learned to your advantage. I will see you in five days."

She turned and strode back up the stairs, and Ranakar stepped forward with a grim smile.

"Follow me, novices," he said in a cold voice. "I'll tell you what you need to know to survive in the realm of Isolas – and give each of you your individual requirements."

CHAPTER 33

To Amarl's surprise, Ranakar led the group around the Citadel and southeast, toward the Geralz Center, where the novices went to train their skills. He guided them past the buildings to a crack in the mountainside just wide enough for someone like Burik to fit through without having to squeeze. A group of older students stood before the crack, chatting quietly and unconcernedly, and he recognized Andra and Veter in the group, although neither spared the novices even a single glance. Stacks of what Amarl recognized from his last hunt as tents, bedrolls, and full packs stood off to the side. Beside those rested piles of weapons, including a moon axe and scimitar that Amarl guessed were his.

Ranakar stopped before the crack and walked over to the older students, speaking quietly to each before handing them a crystal from a pouch at his side. Each student nodded to the awal, then turned and made their way into the crack, vanishing once they were inside. Amarl grimaced ruefully; he'd seen this crack a dozen times or more visiting Geralz, and he'd never thought that it might be a Mistway. He wondered how many other Mistways dotted Askula; the realm seemed rife with them.

He refocused his thoughts as the last of the older students disappeared, and Ranakar walked back over to stand before the novices.

"You're about to take a Mistway into Isolas, one of the realms connected to Askula," the old man declared. "It's also the safest outside of Umpratan itself. This doesn't mean that it's safe, just that the threats inside it are within your abilities to face, assuming you're cautious, use your wits, and employ your skills and talents effectively.

"Isolas is a subterranean realm, and you'll be traveling through a maze of tunnels. Food and water can be found easily enough if you simply look. Sahr is relatively stable there, so workings will typically function as you expect, and you can use sahr as freely as you're capable once through the Mistway. You'll be operating within a designated area two marches across, and the upperclassmen and nadars inside will enforce that restriction. Understand that it's for your own safety: beyond that area, you'll face creatures stronger than you're ready to handle.

"Within Isolas, you may encounter bipedal, black-shelled insects. These are the assilians, one of the native intelligent species of that realm. If you see them, do not attempt to interact with them or harm them. They will ignore you as long as you ignore them, but they can be dangerous if provoked. Don't provoke them!" He glared at the novices, who all remained silent, then gestured to the piles of equipment.

"Each of you will take a tent, bedroll, and the pack with your name on it. The pack has extra clothing, rations, water, and a fire-starting kit. That, and your weapons, should be all you need to complete this test – and be assured, it is a test. Whether or not you continue at Askula will depend entirely on your performance. If you are too badly injured to continue, you fail. If you quit early for any reason, you fail. My advice is: don't fail."

He looked at each of the students as he spoke. "In addition to the general task to survive, each of you will be given a secondary task that is unique to you; this task is on a piece of paper within your pack. Each of you has your own strengths and talents, and that task will be based on those. Failing the secondary task does not mean failing the test, but it could have other consequences."

He nodded as if to himself and straightened. "I'll call you up one at a time. When I call your name, come grab your gear, your weapons, and a crystal to allow you entrance to the Mistway. Do not lose this crystal, or you will not be able to return to Askula! Understood? Good. Amarl!"

The hizeen walked forward and grabbed his pack, quickly strapping the rolled-up tent and bedroll to the top of it as he'd learned on his last hunting trip. He slipped the pack over his shoulders, pulling it tight against his back, then strapped his sword belt to his waist. He checked the scimitar and long knife attached to it to make sure they were clear, then grabbed his moon axe and walked over to Ranakar. The awal stoically handed him a small, green crystal, and Amarl clutched it in his fist until it pierced his skin before stepping into the crack in the mountainside. The crack ended after a few feet in a blank wall, but he took a deep breath, put his hand to it, and pushed through.

The blue light of the Mistway rose around him once more. Towering slopes reared around him to each side, and his path wove down the center between them. Voices whispered in his mind, their hushed words unintelligible but enticing, but he pushed them aside and focused on the path before him. He hurried his steps, aware that the shapes in the fog followed him, their whispers growing louder as he passed. The slopes beyond those shapes curved inward overhead, finally joining far above him, and he found himself walking through a tunnel for the last several reaches. The tunnel ended at a sheer, rune-covered wall, and he hurriedly pushed through it, breathing a sigh of relief as he stepped out of the Mistway and its unseen but always heard inhabitants.

He looked around as he walked forward; he'd emerged in a large cavern, at least eight or nine reaches across. Arched tunnels led from the cavern in every direction, some sloping up, others plunging downward. Light filled the grotto, coming from crystals overhead, but that light quickly faded to shadow inside the tunnels, leaving him unable to see more than several reaches beyond the cave. The floor was smooth and flat, which he thought probably meant someone had carved it that way. He knew from carrying food and water in the mines in Tem that natural caves and tunnels tended to be either round if they were water-carved or uneven and irregular otherwise.

The cave was brownish stone, but bands of quartzlike crystals swirled through the rock, sticking out into the cave in hexagonal shapes that glittered with golden flecks in the light coming from overhead. He walked over and touched a crystal; it was cool, hard, and utterly lifeless, unlike the ithtu he'd bonded. Still, some sort of energy moved through it, something he could only faintly sense.

Movement caught his eye, and he spun, his axe at the ready. He relaxed as Burik stepped out of a sheer stone face carrying his halberd, a heavy mace, and a small hatchet. The larger boy stepped away from the Mistway exit and looked around.

"A cave." The larger boy shuddered slightly. "Have I ever mentioned I hate caves, Amarl?" Burik's voice was loud in the enclosed space, louder than normal, and Amarl winced at the sound.

"We'll have to talk quietly in here. Why do you hate caves?"

Burik looked up at the ceiling a reach overhead. "How much stone do you think is above us right now?" he asked in a quieter voice. "I can tell you: too much. You can't fight a hundred tuns of falling rock."

"It looks safe, Burik," Amarl said reassuringly.

"No offense, but how would you know?"

"I've seen unstable tunnels before. The ceilings are filled with cracks and drop little bits of gravel. This is one solid piece; it's not going anywhere."

Burik opened his mouth to reply, then shut it quickly as Hadur emerged from the wall. The merchant's son glanced around at the cavern, then walked to the other side of the cave from them, peering down a dark tunnel. He whistled sharply, then listened as the whistle echoed back to him. He stepped back, shaking his head ruefully.

"You probably shouldn't do that," Amarl said evenly. "A sound like that will carry a really long way underground like this, and it's not the kind of noise that's common down here."

The boy sneered at Amarl, shaking his head. "Don't tell me what I should and shouldn't do, half-breed," he spat. "You don't even belong here. This school is supposed to be for naluni only. You'll be lucky not to die in the first day in this realm. In fact, you'd be doing us all a favor by feeding yourself to the first thing you meet."

Burik took a menacing step toward the boy, but Amarl laid a hand on his friend's arm, halting him. "You know, Hadur, I should remind you that there won't be any nadars or malims to keep you safe during this little test. From any creatures we might meet..." He spun his axe nonchalantly. "Or from anything else. It would be a shame if you got too badly injured to continue in the first few minutes. That would probably be a record for the fastest failure."

Hadur looked at the pair, then stepped back, muttering quietly under his breath and crossing his arms over his chest but not saying anything to Amarl. They all paused as Herel stepped out of the wall a moment later. Hadur's eyes narrowed as his friend joined the group, but Herel glanced between the students and shook his head.

"Fighting now, when we're almost at the end of this year is pointless and foolish," he said firmly. "Amarl, Burik, we all know you're better fighters, but Hadur and I are good enough that we could probably injure you. Then, we'd all fail." He looked over at Hadur. "It's not worth it."

"I agree," Amarl said easily. "I think we'll all see enough blood over the next few days without spilling each other's."

"Agreed." Herel walked over to Amarl, staying out of weapons reach but keeping his hands away from his sword. "I don't like you, Amarl," he said bluntly. "I won't ever like you. You're a thief and a liar, and I doubt that will change."

Amarl shrugged. "I'm not exactly thrilled about you either, Herel.

You're arrogant, short-sighted, and overconfident. You think you're better than anyone else, and you get angry when you're wrong. That doesn't mean I want you to fail, though. We all remember when that happened to Yashi; I don't want to see that again."

Herel paled slightly and nodded. "Neither do I, which is my point. My not liking you doesn't mean we have to fight and argue. I won't work with you, but I won't work against you either, and neither will my friends. I think that's fair enough."

"Sounds fair to me."

"Good." He looked at Hadur. "Then I think that's an end to it, right?" Hadur nodded, and Herel looked back at Amarl. The noble lifted his chin and walked back over to the opposite side of the cavern, speaking to Hadur too softly for Amarl to hear before falling quiet. The group waited in silence as Meder and then Norag emerged from the wall, each joining their friends. Meder looked around at the tense novices and shook her head.

"Boys, boys, boys. This will all go more smoothly if we just work together. There's safety in numbers, you know."

"There is," Norag agreed, then glanced at Herel and Hadur with a sigh. "But only if you're worried about trouble coming from the outside, not the inside. I think it's probably wisest if we split into two groups and head in opposite directions. Ak-lahat teaches us that avoiding conflict is preferable to resolving it, after all."

"I'm all for that," Burik said, once again speaking too loudly and sending his voice echoing around the chamber. He winced and lowered his volume. "I think Meder, Amarl, and I can handle whatever this test throws at us."

"I feel the same way about my team," Herel said blandly. "So, it's agreed. We'll go..." He turned and pointed to a random tunnel. "That way. You go that way." He waved his hand absently at the opposite side of the cavern. "We'll meet back here in five days."

"This is foolish," Meder sighed. "If we could just put our differences aside..."

"I don't trust the hizeen at my back," Hadur said bluntly. "His kind are treacherous and untrustworthy. I'd rather be down here alone."

"For me, it's more of a personal issue," Herel shrugged. "Amarl and I traveled together once. I'd rather never do it again." He waved to his friends. "Come on. There's no point to further discussion. The sooner we get started, the sooner we can be done with this." He looked at Norag. "The awal said that sahr works well enough here. Norag, a light, please."

Norag looked at Meder, then at Herel, and shrugged. He lifted his hammer and laid a hand on it, closing his eyes. His lips moved, and his hand made passes around the weapon as he used his body and voice to construct a matrix to control and guide the ambient sahr. Amarl glanced past the boy and frowned as the crystals embedded in the wall closest to him began to glow, but pushed the distraction away. A moment later, the top of the hammer radiated a bright, white light, and the three boys set off into the tunnel they'd chosen, one that sloped upward.

Meder sighed again. "Well, I guess it's just us. Here, I can make a light for us…"

"Can you make it so it only faces forward?" Amarl asked. "Or maybe one that floats over our heads?"

"No to the second, sorry. I have to have something to collapse the matrix onto; if I put it in the air, it'll stay wherever I put it." She hesitated, her eyes thoughtful. "Maybe to the first, though. Why?"

"Because that light Norag made is going to blind them to anything beyond it," Amarl shook his head. "We want the light to go outward, not into our eyes."

"Smart," Burik nodded. "You seem to know a lot about being underground."

"Tem is a mining village, you know. Mountains and all. I never did any actual mining, but I worked in the tunnels carrying water and food and hauling out garbage when I was younger. I learned how to get around comfortably underground."

"Give me a moment to work out the matrix," the girl said, tapping her chin with her eyes unfocused. She muttered quietly for several seconds, then reached out and touched her staff, closing her eyes and speaking softly. Again, Amarl noticed the crystals nearby her taking on a dim, golden radiance, which he assumed meant they were sensitive to sahr somehow. They didn't seem to be affecting Meder, though, so he ignored the effect. A second later, the staff began to glow, a soft radiance spilling out from one half of it. Meder looked at it, her mouth twisted in a dissatisfied expression, and shook her head.

"I must have messed up my calculations," she admitted. "I wanted to cover half the staff, but I accidentally made the light half as bright at the same time. The sahr here is stronger than it is in Askula, but it's harder to work with, too. It's like it's heavier somehow."

"Actually, that's just about perfect," he assured her. "Light also carries a long way in dark tunnels, and a really bright light will tell anything with eyes that we're coming long before we see it."

"Then it all worked out," she smiled. "So, what should we do first? I think we should figure out what our secondary tasks are so we can decide how best to complete them."

"I vote for looking around and seeing what sort of creatures are nearby," Burik said. "No matter what anyone says, this is a hunt, so we should start hunting."

"Personally, I think we should find a campsite," Amarl shrugged. "Somewhere near but not too near water, so we can save what the awal gave us as a backup. Once we're set up, we can check our secondary tasks and scout around. Hells, if we're near water, the creatures will probably come to us."

"I'm sold," Burik agreed.

"Since Amarl's the only one of us with survival training, so am I," Meder laughed. "Burik, you should lead, I think. I'll stay in the middle, and Amarl, you can take the back."

"Sounds good." The large boy glanced around. "Any particular tunnel anyone likes?"

"I don't hear anything coming from any of them," Amarl shrugged. "I'd say down rather than up, though. Less chance of running into the others if the tunnels loop around." Meder made a face at that but didn't say anything.

The tunnel they chose sloped gently downward into the ground, and they passed through it in near silence. Despite what Amarl first thought listening from the cave, the tunnel was actually full of sound. Their footsteps echoed softly along it, especially Burik's heavy treads. Rocks shifted and tumbled, clattering in the quiet. Air flowed through the tunnel gently, making a whooshing sound like the cave breathed, and somewhere up ahead, the sound of trickling water tantalized them.

Amarl was so busy listening to the cave's sounds that he barely noticed the rapid ticking approaching him from behind. He spun at the last second and caught a glimpse of dark, shiny carapace as something scuttled from the darkness and sprang toward him. He whipped his axe across the creature – or he attempted to. The weapon struck the wall beside him with a loud clang, nearly jarring itself from his hands, and he barely managed to bring it up across his chest like a staff as the creature's leap carried it toward his face. The creature impacted the shaft, knocking him back a step. Its legs scrabbled against his clothing, and long, black pincers snapped toward his exposed throat.

Amarl hurled the creature back with a shove and a cry of disgust as he heard a second clang ring from behind him. He ignored the sound and focused on his attacker. It looked almost like an overgrown ant, half a reach long with legs stretching almost that wide. Four antennae atop its head waved in the air toward him as it scuttled forward once more, leaping forward to bite at his legs. Amarl had learned his lesson, though, and he slammed the crescent blade of the axe down toward the creature, fearing that the spearpoint might glance off its armor. The points of the crescent clanged against the floor, and the inner blade cut into the ant's armor, trapping it in place. The creature twisted and dug its claws into the stone, and Amarl lurched as the insect's strength tore it free from beneath the blade. It lunged at him again, and this time he reversed the axe and struck with the spearpoint. The sharp tip punched easily through the ant's shell and plunged into its body, and the creature curled up into a ball and fell still.

A glint of black caught his eye, and two more of the ants scuttled his way. He crouched, waiting for the first to spring, then batted it from the air with a short, controlled sweep of his axe. The second sprang immediately after, and he thrust the spearpoint at the creature, catching it in midair. The spear cracked its shell but didn't penetrate, but it did succeed in knocking the light insect back onto the ground. It fell onto its back and began thrashing and twitching, its legs wiggling furiously and frantically as it worked to flip itself back over. The first ant recovered and sprang at his legs, but he slammed the spearpoint down into it, killing it quickly, then finished the second before it flipped back upright.

A curse from behind him caught his attention, and he glanced back to see Burik dealing with two more of the ants. A third lay dead on the floor, almost bisected by the boy's halberd, which was probably the clang Amarl heard earlier. Burik jammed the spearpoint of his halberd into a second ant, but the third leaped forward, getting inside his reach. Amarl moved to help, but Meder was already there, her staff sweeping down and slamming on top of the ant, crushing its shell and killing it. Amarl glanced back behind them and looked around, panting slightly from the exertion as he made sure there weren't more of the creatures.

"Well, that was unpleasant," Meder said softly, pulling her hair back from her face and tying it behind her head.

"At least they're easy to kill," Burik shrugged. "And there weren't too many of them."

"Yet," Amarl said quietly, moving toward the first ant he'd killed. He felt its life energy beckoning him, urging him to come claim it, and he squatted next to it, laying a hand on its shell.

"What are you doing?" Meder asked curiously.

Amarl didn't answer. His thoughts were lost in the joyous flow of life energy coursing through the insect. He gathered it to him, coaxing every drop he could from the creature's body. A sharp crackling sound split the air as a dark green, almost black crystal rose from the thing's shell, growing in a sharp spike with a pair of thorny protrusions. He quickly pulled the crystal from the ant and held it up, Analyzing it.

> ANALYSIS REPORT
> ITEM: ITHTU CRYSTAL
> RANK: FEEBLE
> POWER DENSITY: 8
> SOURCE: INSECT

He closed the screen and slipped the crystal into his belt pouch, repeating the process with the other two creatures he'd killed. Each time, he pulled a deep green Feeble crystal, each dense with energy but still relatively weak.

"Is that how you harvest those?" Burik asked curiously, staring at the last crystal in Amarl's hand.

"Yeah. I don't know if we're supposed to, but I figure since I can, I might as well, right?"

"Can you harvest these, too?" Burik asked, pointing to the ants he'd killed.

"I'm not supposed to be able to. You can usually only harvest what you kill yourself."

"You do a lot of things you're not supposed to be able to," Meder rolled her eyes. "Just try and see."

Amarl shrugged and walked over to the one she'd killed, kneeling beside the crushed insect and laying a hand on it. He could sense the thing's life energy, but it felt ugly and hostile. He beckoned it to him, but it ignored him, and he almost felt it snarling territorially at him. At last, he rose to his feet and shook his head.

"No. Veter was right; you can only harvest what you kill."

Meder frowned, her lips pursed. "Can you teach us, then?"

Amarl opened his mouth, then paused. "I – I don't know, actually. I'm not a hundred percent sure how I do it, and I'm not much of a teacher."

"Just tell us what it's like, and we can try. How does it feel? Do you have to do or think anything when you do it?"

"I can just feel the life energy inside something I kill, the same way I can feel the energy in a crystal. I reach for it, just like I reach for a crystal, and I draw it out. It's almost like I'm coaxing it toward me, like trying to befriend a strange dog by offering it food. It comes pretty quickly; I think it wants to be harvested."

Meder and Burik looked at one another for a long moment, and the boy shrugged. "Can't hurt to try it, right?" He looked at Amarl. "You say it's like quickening a crystal?"

"Sort of. It's the same sense of reaching out, but I don't take the energy into myself. I just draw it toward me, and it pools in one spot, then forms into a crystal."

"Okay. Well, here goes." The boy put his hand on the ant, his face set in concentration. Seconds passed and turned into a minute, and Amarl was about to interrupt the boy when a soft tinkling sound filled the air. A moment later, two small, pale green crystals half the size of Amarl's pinky slowly rose from the ant. Amarl smiled and Analyzed one of them.

> **ANALYSIS REPORT**
> **ITEM: ITHTU CRYSTAL**
> **RANK: FEEBLE**
> **POWER DENSITY: 2**
> **SOURCE: INSECT**

As they stopped forming, Burik let out an explosive breath and rubbed his forehead.

"Damn, that's hard," he breathed, shaking his head slowly.

"Congratulations!" Amarl grinned at the boy. "You did it!"

"Yeah, but it wasn't easy. I hope it gets simpler with practice."

"Was it like Amarl described?" Meder asked eagerly.

"Sort of. I could feel the energy, just like he said, and I reached out to it. It didn't all want to come, though, and I had to work to coax what little I could get. If it was like a dog, like Amarl said, then mine was skittish and wanted to run away." He pointed to the two crystals. "Those aren't exactly as impressive as what Amarl harvested, are they?"

"No, but it's more than the other group will get," Meder grinned, kneeling beside the ant she'd killed. "Harvest that other one, as well."

"Why?" Burik asked. "It's just a low-level Feeble crystal. I'm sure the school has tons of those."

"Yes, but these are better than the ones they usually give us; level 2 instead of 1. Since this isn't an official hunt, they might let us keep them, and I think better crystals will let us grow faster."

"They do," Amarl nodded. "A stronger crystal will awaken your ability faster, according to Ranakar. They might not let you quicken that, though. Once we hit second year, the school decides what crystals you'll get so that you awaken your ability by the end of the year. If that one's not the rank and strength they think you should have, you won't get to keep it."

She shrugged. "Even if they don't, I'm sure coming back with more crystals will make a good impression. Besides, if we can do it – and get some practice at it – we'll be ahead of things, won't we?" She closed her eyes and touched the crushed ant. It took her somewhat less than a minute before a single green crystal arose from its shell, darker than Burik's but nowhere near as dark as Amarl's.

"Level 3," she smiled. "I'm fine with that." She picked up the crystal and slipped it into her pouch with a grin. "Even if it's not a level 8."

"Are you really fine?" he laughed.

"No, but I've decided that instead of being jealous of what you can do, I'm going to catch up to you, so it doesn't matter." She smiled and rose to her feet. "This just got a lot more interesting. Let's go find some more ants to smash!"

They made their way down the tunnel, following the sound of running water and ignoring silent side tunnels. After a couple hours, Amarl decided they must be inside an ant nest, considering how often the creatures swarmed them. They came from the front and the back, sometimes only two or three, sometimes six to eight at a time. The novices quickly learned how to deal with the ants; they always attacked with a springing leap, and once the creatures were on their backs, it took them several seconds to recover. Amarl used his crescent blade to catch the creatures as they sprang, twisting the axe to flip them onto their backs where he could spear them easily. Burik and Meder worked together, the larger boy holding the creatures at bay with his halberd while Meder used her staff to crack open any that got inside his reach. The insects didn't attack constantly, but they seldom went more than fifteen or twenty minutes between battles, and Amarl had a feeling that once again, he was seeing more creatures than anyone might have expected.

At last, the tunnel widened before them, and the trio paused to take in the view. A large cavern spread out in front of them, more than a hundred reaches wide and at least five or six tall. Glowing patches of something like moss hung from the ceiling, bathing the cave in an eerie green glow that provided light about equal to that of a full moon. Their tunnel entered high above the floor of the grotto. A rough path wound down a fairly steep slope toward the bottom of the cavern, crossing back and forth before disappearing into what looked like a forest. The forest filled most of the cave with something similar to dwarfed, skeletal pine trees, pale white and conical, stretching only two to three reaches above the floor and crowding together densely enough to block the sight of anything that might be within them. Gleaming stone pillars dotted the cavern, thicker near the floor and ceiling and thin in the center, columns that Amarl knew had formed from eons of water flowing from the ceiling.

The tinkling sound of that water caught Amarl's ears, and he tracked the noise. Across the grotto, a glittering cascade poured down the rock wall, disappearing behind the skeletal forest. The sound filled the cavern, blocking out other noises, and the waterfall turned the air inside the cavern humid, creating small patches of fog that drifted through the air, green and eldritch-looking in the light from the dangling moss.

"This is amazing," Meder breathed. "Guys, stop and think about this. We're in another world, seeing something that probably doesn't exist in Umpratan; something that no naluni but the ithtaru have ever seen!"

"I hadn't really thought about it until now," Burik agreed. "We really are in a whole different world, aren't we?"

Amarl smiled gently, but his eyes kept scanning the forest below. Shadora had washed away his wonder at visiting new realms in a wave of blood, betrayal, and death. He didn't see the wonder of a forest that shouldn't exist deep belowground, hidden away from the sun. He saw a place of danger, where innumerable creatures could be lurking. He didn't say anything, though. He didn't want to take the moment away from his friends. Instead, he let his eyes wander looking around for a suitable campsite, then smiled wider at what he found.

"We should go through the forest and camp by the waterfall," Meder said excitedly. "It should be filtered by the stones so that it's drinkable water, and it'll be an easy place to get back to if we're out hunting or whatever."

"I don't think that's the best idea," Amarl shook his head. "That waterfall is probably the main water source for every creature within a walk of this place, and that forest could be hiding a hundred of those ants – or something worse. If we're camped next to the water, we could be swarmed by everything in the forest."

"Are you suggesting we camp in the forest?" Burik asked dubiously.

"No. We wouldn't be able to see far enough to really keep watch, and we could be attacked from any direction."

"Fine, Mr. Survival Expert," Meder said a little testily. "What do you think we should do, then? Camp here in the tunnel?"

"I'd really prefer we not do that," Burik said with a shiver, looking up at the low ceiling again. "The cavern would be better. It's – larger."

"No, I think we should camp up there." The ledge he pointed at looked more like a shelf of rock, a place where a slab of stone probably broke loose from the ceiling and lodged itself in a break in the wall three reaches above the floor. A crumbled, rock-strewn ledge less than half a reach wide was the only way to the ledge other than scaling the cliffs behind it. He had a feeling the ants could do just that if they wanted to, but he imagined it would be a lot slower, and they'd be easier to kill if they tried.

"That ledge isn't very big," Burik said doubtfully. "And it's kind of slanted to the side."

"Not enough for us to fall off it, and it's big enough for two tents, which is all we'll need since someone will always be on watch. The important thing is that there's only one easy way up to it. The rock face behind it covers our back, and it's not really that far from the forest or the waterfall if we want to go hunt or get water."

"And no way to easily get down if we're attacked," Meder said smugly.

"Sure, but with the way those ants were swarming us in the tunnels, I think it's less 'if' and more 'when' we're attacked, and it'll probably be from every possible direction. An escape route is just another way for them to reach us."

"He's right," Burik nodded. "Trying to fight on two fronts is asking for a disaster."

"Okay, it's not a bad idea," Meder admitted. "I'll agree to check it out first and see how it looks. I still want to go see that waterfall, though."

"Yeah, we should check it out, and we should scout the forest a little and see what we find." Amarl smiled at the girl. "We can climb up there, and if it looks relatively flat and stable, we can put our stuff down and go look around a bit without carrying all this."

"You sound like you actually know what you're doing," Burik laughed. "Did you pick all this up on your last hunting trip?"

"That, and the survival lessons Ranakar's giving me. Finding a good campsite is one of the lessons. You want water nearby but not too close, an elevation to make you harder to reach and extend your sight, and limited access for enemies. I think we'll all be taking them next year to get us ready to go on a hunt."

"Well, it looks like they might come in handy," Meder acknowledged. "Come on, let's check out that ledge and see if it's really a good place to camp."

As Burik said, the shelf slanted a bit toward the path leading up to it, and rocks and gravel covered it, but it was dry and close enough to being level that they wouldn't have to worry about rolling or sliding off it. It was high enough to provide a decent view of the forest and the waterfall, as well as the sparkling pool into which the rivulet of water splashed continually. Several clumps of glowing moss clung to the wall beside it, lighting it with a dim glow, and bands of the ever-present crystals rippled through the cliff face, shimmering golden in the light of Meder's staff. Several of those had broken free of the rock and lay tumbled on the shelf below; those, Amarl realized, gleamed dully, without the sparkle of the crystals clinging to the walls.

"It's not bad," Burik admitted, kicking some stones aside. "If we clear the rocks off, at least."

"It's good enough that someone's already used it," Meder said, pointing to a scorched patch of stone. "I'll bet that was a fire pit."

"I think you're right," Amarl agreed, scanning the ground around the ledge. "And it doesn't look like many creatures come up here." He touched the wall, where several clumps of the glowing moss had taken root in cracks. "I'd have thought they would have to eat the moss."

"Maybe it's toxic," Meder said. "Some bioluminescent plants are. If that's the case, herbivores learn not to eat anything that glows."

"Maybe," Amarl shrugged. "I wasn't planning on eating it, so it doesn't matter."

"Yeah, let's hope it doesn't come to that," Burik chuckled. "I'd rather eat those ants, to be honest."

"Come on. This place is good enough, and it's been used before. Let's drop our stuff and go check out the waterfall."

Amarl smiled at the girl's eagerness to see the subterranean waterfall and pool. He didn't share in that excitement himself. He had a feeling that whatever beauty and wonder the pool and forest might hold would be overshadowed by what lurked within them.

CHAPTER 34

The small fire crackled and popped, giving off far more smoke than Amarl expected. The fungus stalks that looked like leafless trees were damp and didn't burn well, and the odor they gave off was fairly pungent. They burned hot, though, with a low, purple flame that didn't make too much light. That heat seared the pair of four-span-long fish filets hanging above the flames, resting on a nest of the branchlike arms of the conical fungus Burik chopped down.

"That actually smells sort of good," Meder noted, sniffing the air, then wrinkling her nose. "The fish does, I mean. Not that mushroom."

"Hopefully, it tastes good, too," Burik said. "Although it's likely to taste like mushroom smoke."

Amarl shrugged. "It'll still be better than rations." He sniffed as well and winced at the slightly acrid odor of the burning fungus. "Although only barely."

The trio had skirted the edge of the forest as they made their way to the waterfall, not wanting to draw the attention of anything living farther within. They'd still been attacked by a few of the ants, but they killed and harvested those easily enough, and they had no other difficulties as they made their way to the waterfall. The falls started at the top of the cavern, pouring out of a crack in the stone wall, and splashed into a pool of crystal-clear water at their base. The impact of the water had worn a deep pool in the stone, and a half-dozen large fish swam in the pool – one less, now that Burik speared it with his halberd for their meal. Meder formulated a quick working and pronounced the water clean enough for drinking, and they all had their fill. The water had a strong mineral taste to it, but it didn't bother Amarl too much, although Meder pulled a face when she took her first sip.

Building a fire was a simple enough matter; Burik chopped down one of the fungus trees with two swings of his halberd, and Amarl used his scimitar to clean it of branches. The fungus stalk was soft and rubbery, but it split easily enough beneath Burik and Amarl's weapons. They stacked some of the split pieces up, and Meder lit them with a touch of sahr. They ignited quickly, and despite their smoke, they burned with a low flame that Amarl hoped wasn't too visible. The smoke and smell of cooking food would probably draw predators from the forest; they didn't need the light of the fire to bring even more.

"How do you think the others are doing?" Meder asked.

"They're probably fine," Burik said easily. "They're all trained fighters – more or less – and these ants aren't that hard to kill."

"That's assuming that ants are all they ran into," Amarl noted. "If the things live in this forest, they might not be in all the other tunnels."

"True," Burik nodded. "But the awal said anything we met would be within our capabilities. Whatever they found, I'm sure the three of them handled it."

"I hope so." The girl looked at Amarl. "I know you and Herel hate each other..."

"I don't hate Herel," Amarl interrupted with a frown. "Hells, I don't think I hate anyone. I don't like him very much, is all."

"He said that you didn't get along when you came to Askula," Burik noted.

"Yeah, that's a mild understatement. Danmila had to stab me and break his jaw to get us to stop annoying one another."

"Why?" Meder asked.

Amarl shrugged. "Because he was an ass to me from the moment we met. He was a high-and-mighty zahai, and I was an orphan ishtai. He was wealthy; I had to steal to eat some days. He was educated, I was ignorant."

"But all those are true about Meder, and you get along fine with her," Burik chuckled.

"Hey! I am not high-and-mighty!" Meder glared at Burik, but Amarl nodded in agreement.

"Exactly. I don't care that you and he had advantages I didn't. Hells, most people did. I just hated that he rubbed my nose in it every chance he got. And he hated that I was chosen for Askula because I think he felt it diminished him. Who's going to pay attention to another noble when there's a hizeen ithtar who quickened a crystal without trying, right?" He grinned. "Plus, you know, Betha."

"The girl that came to Askula with you," Meder nodded. "The two of you fought over her?"

"I didn't, no. Herel, though, seemed to think that because she was a lower caste, she owed him her affections. She objected by kicking him in the stones, and after that she mostly talked to me. I think it made Herel jealous."

Meder rolled her eyes. "Sadly, I could see him doing that. So, you never...?" She drew out the word, and he laughed.

"No. After what Herel did, Danmila threatened to castrate him if he tried anything like that again. I didn't really want to see if that applied to flirting, as well, so I just left well enough alone. The point, though, is that I don't really give a shit about Herel. I don't like him, but..."

"But you don't want anything bad to happen to him or the others," she finished.

"It depends on your definition of 'bad', I guess. I don't want them to fail or get hurt or anything, but I'd be fine if something, say, burned all of Hadur's hair off his head and face. Or other places."

She gave him a disapproving look, but Burik shook his head. "No, Meder, Amarl's being nice. You didn't hear what Hadur was saying before Herel came through the Mistway."

"What? What did he say?"

"He apparently has a problem with my heritage," Amarl shrugged.

"Your heritage?"

"He called him a half-breed; said he didn't belong here," Burik rumbled. "That he'd die in the first day – and that he should let it happen to 'make it easier on everyone'."

Her eyes widened. "He said that?" she gasped. "Really?"

"Oh, yes. I was about to shut his mouth for him, but Amarl stopped me." He looked at the boy. "You should have let me hit him."

"It wouldn't have changed anything, Burik. He'd still have felt that way, but he would have done it with a bunch of missing teeth and an oddly shaped nose." Amarl laughed again, but Meder shook her head sadly.

"I can't believe it. I mean, I knew that Hadur didn't like you, but I thought it was jealousy, not that he was a Lasheshian, as well – although that does explain why he and Herel get along so well." She looked at Amarl. "And I can't believe you're so cavalier about it, either."

"Hells, I stopped letting that sort of thing bother me years ago," Amarl said airily. "If I'd gotten angry every time someone insulted me over my heritage, I'd have spent my whole life angry." She looked at him doubtfully, so he explained further.

"Meder, I grew up in a tiny village of all naluni, with me as the only hizeen. I was the lowest caste, an orphan, with no family ties or name to shield me. The first time I can remember being called 'half-breed' was the night of my fifth Naming Day, by a drunken sot who thought I'd bring a pestilence to the village. That's just the first I can remember; I'm sure it was happening earlier than that."

"Well, yes, some people are ignorant, but..."

"On the day that Danmila discovered I could quicken," he interrupted quietly, "the Head Bureaucrat called my mother a whore and said that I was tainted." He looked her directly in the eye. "The Head Bureaucrat. The man who'd educated me, who certified me every Naming Day, the single most educated person in the entire village. And he just said what most of the village thought. I've been called 'tainted', 'cursed', and 'a plague' for as long as I can remember."

He took a deep, shuddering breath at the pain that suddenly ached in his chest. He thought he'd put this sort of thing behind him, learned to ignore it and let it roll off him. Remembering the Head Bureaucrat's words, though, felt like a knife in his chest. He knew that Axanor hadn't always approved of him, but he hadn't realized until that night how much the man hated him – how much most of the village hated him. With the pain came anger, but it was a useless rage, something that couldn't be vented or targeted, so he pushed it away. He'd made a vow to return to Tem; he intended to keep it.

"So, you can imagine that Hadur's stupid Lashooshian or whatever it is attitude doesn't really bother me all that much," he said into the sudden silence. "He's a pompous ass who's obviously used his family's wealth and connections to ingratiate himself to Herel, so he's a terrible judge of character. Why should I give a shit about his opinion?"

"That – that's awful, Amarl," the girl said quietly. "I had no idea. How did you stand it?"

"What choice did I have? I couldn't run away. Until my fifteenth Naming Day, as an orphan, I belonged to the village, and if I'd left and gone someplace else, their bureaucrats would have just shipped me back to Tem, and then I would have been indentured to the village for the cost of getting me back. And there were a few people, mostly older women, that I felt close to."

"Now, when you say close..." Burik said with a laugh, and Amarl smiled briefly.

"Yeah, sure, I lay with them, but that's not what I'm talking about. We also talked, and they told me things about themselves that they wouldn't tell anyone else because they knew I wouldn't judge them." He smiled a little wistfully. "I knew that I was just a safe plaything for them, but it was the closest thing I had to friendship, so I treasured it."

"You weren't really with a bunch of older women, were you?" Meder asked doubtfully.

"Oh, yeah. I love older women." He grinned at her. "They know what they want, and they're not afraid to tell you about it. Plus, they tend to know what they're doing. More practice, you understand."

She blushed slightly and shook her head. "But weren't they worried about their reputations?"

"No, not really. I don't have any family that might object or demand anything from them, and they never had to worry about getting pregnant since I'm sterile."

"You're what?" Burik asked in surprise.

"Sterile. All hizeens are." Amarl shrugged. "It's something about our heritage."

"But what about their families and husbands and such?" she pressed. "Weren't they upset with you?"

"Sometimes, but not as often as you'd think. An adult woman has the right to her entertainments, after all, and everyone in Tem knew that I wasn't ever going to look for more than a tumble with anyone. I was a harmless pastime, nothing more." He laughed. "In fact, I had more trouble with fathers thinking I owed them maidenprice for their daughters than anything."

"Did you?" Burik asked with a wide smile.

"Hells, no," Amarl shook his head. "I wasn't about to deal with that headache. Another reason I like older women: no one ever thinks that you're their first."

The big boy laughed, and even Meder let out a small chuckle at that. "Still, that sounds like a pretty terrible way to live," she said in a sad voice.

"It was all I knew – at least until I came to Askula." He smiled at the pair. "Then I made actual friends and learned the difference between friendship and just being comfortable. And now, even though I know the difference, I don't have to worry about it anymore because I've got two pretty decent friends."

"Pretty decent?" Burik scoffed. "I'd say we're a lot better than that! Amazing, at the very least."

"I'd say you're both above average," Meder corrected with a grin, then deliberately looked below their belts. "Maybe a little below in some ways."

"Wow, she went there again," Amarl laughed. "Meder, if you keep talking about our stems like that, I'm going to think they're all you hang around us for."

"If those were the only things keeping me around, I'd have been gone a long time ago, trust me," she said dryly.

Amarl opened his mouth to reply, but before he could, Meder scrambled to her feet, lifting her weapon, and he did the same, spinning to face the path leading up to their camp. Burik already stood and moved to the front, obscuring Amarl's view of the entrance to the camp. He shifted sideways, but as he did, Burik stepped back, his weapon rising as he stared uncertainly at the three creatures moving up the path toward the camp.

The three things that approached weren't like anything Amarl had seen before. They looked like insects that stood upright, with dull, matte black carapaces. Their legs looked powerful, bent backward at the knee and ending in hooked claws that gripped the stone and held them upright. They bounced as much as walked, moving in a galloping gait that was oddly silent. Their four arms gripped wooden spears tipped with the crystals found everywhere in the tunnels, but these glittered fiercely in the light of their fire rather than being dull and flat like most of the broken crystals Amarl had seen. Their "hands" were little more than three claws, one opposing the other two so that they could grip but probably lacking in dexterity. Their faces were clearly insectoid, smooth and chitinous with bulbous, faceted eyes, large pincers, and two rows of small antennae running down the middle that waved about despite the lack of a breeze. As they approached, Amarl thought about understanding them, and his Analyze screen swirled into view.

The three creatures stepped onto the ledge and walked directly toward the students for a second before splitting off to go around them and approach their fire. Amarl traded confused and concerned looks with the others. He held his axe out in front of him, ready if the creatures took any hostile action, but instead they simply stood before the fire for a few moments before two of them went over to the nearby rock face and began chipping at it with their spears near one of the crystal formations. The crystal points dug easily into the stone of the wall, releasing a shower of gravel as the two creatures methodically hammered at the rock, revealing a cluster of golden crystals that branched out from the main one.

"What are they doing?" Burik whispered hoarsely.

"I think – I think they're mining those crystals," Meder whispered back. "Maybe that's why no creatures come up to this shelf – maybe these things keep them away."

"Think they'll be mad that we're planning to sleep here?" Amarl asked nervously.

"I don't know, but they don't seem to care that we're here." She watched the creatures as one of them carefully tapped their spearpoint against the base of the crystal cluster, gently rapping on it until it broke free with a quiet snap. The other one caught the crystal in one of its hands, and the pair stepped away from the wall toward the third, who hadn't moved from the fire.

<Blood. Loud.>

Amarl blinked at the flat, monotone voice that rang in his ears, and from Meder's gasp and the way Burik lowered his halberd, they heard it as well. After a moment, he realized that he hadn't actually heard the sound; nothing disturbed the quiet of the cavern save the roar of the waterfall. Somehow, though, he'd "heard" the voice anyway.

"What – what was that?" he asked nervously.

"It's sahr," Meder said quietly. "They're speaking using sahr somehow."

Burik's eyes narrowed. "Did it say it wanted our blood?" he demanded.

<No.> The insect that stayed by the fire pointed at Burik with one hand. *<No loud.>* It shifted the hand to point at Amarl. *<Loud. Bring hunters.>*

"You're here to hunt Amarl?" Burik asked with a growl.

"I don't think so, Burik," Meder shook her head before looking at the insect. "Do you mean other hunters?"

<No hunt young. Pact. Others come.> The insect seemed to hesitate, and Amarl noticed its antennae waving furiously. *<Not safe. Return to nest.>*

"You want us to leave?" Meder asked.

<Yes. Not safe. Bring others. Blood loud.>

Meder shook her head. "We can't go back, I'm sorry."

<Then die. Warning given.> The three insects turned and walked back down the path, and the novices watched them in silence, waiting until the creatures vanished from sight into the forest below. As they did, Amarl let out a breath he hadn't even realized he'd been holding.

"Well, that wasn't remotely creepy and threatening," he sighed, shaking his head. "Even in another world, I've got people saying they're going to kill me."

"I don't think they were threatening us," Meder said slowly. "I think they were warning us that other hunters might come after Amarl."

"You mean, more of those – whatever they were?" Burik asked.

"No – and Ranakar called them assilians. I think they meant other creatures." She frowned. "It must be something about being a hizeen. Maybe your spirit ancestry draws creatures to you."

"Great," Amarl sighed. "Just one more awesome thing to look forward to on this trip. I'm fucking bug bait."

"Best be careful not to leave anything dangling, then," Burik laughed.

"And on that note, I think it's time to check our secondary objectives and see what they are," Meder said, rolling her eyes.

"Good idea," Amarl agreed. "The conversation was heading south in a hurry." Meder groaned at his joke, but she said nothing as she went back to her pack and rummaged through it while the two boys did the same.

"Okay, I'll go first," Burik said, unfolding the paper and clearing his throat. He frowned. "Huh."

"What is it?" she asked.

"It says I have to fight a creature I don't think I can defeat. I'm not sure how that's going to happen if everything is like these ants. They're easy to beat."

"That might not be the case, though. The nadars might have left the weakest creatures close to the Mistway, so we have a chance to get used to fighting before we face something truly dangerous."

"Hells, there could be something like that in the forest down there," Amarl chuckled. "We can go check it out first thing tomorrow to see."

"I guess I can hope. Worst case is that if we never meet something that I don't think I can beat, then I just can't do this. Ranakar said we don't fail if we don't do it."

"But he said there could be consequences," Meder reminded him.

"Don't worry, Burik. We'll scout the area until we find something. They wouldn't have given you a task you can't complete." Amarl looked at Merel. "So, what's yours?"

"Let me see." She unfolded the paper and lifted it up, reading it carefully. "Well, that's not quite what I expected."

"What?" Amarl asked.

"Well, I have to craft a sahr array."

"You do that all the time," Burik said dismissively. "This'll be no problem for you."

"No, I craft sahr matrices. An array – well, it's something we aren't supposed to learn about until second year." She looked uncomfortable. "I've been kind of doing some extra studying with Andra to get ahead."

"You've been working with Andra?" Amarl asked flatly, a touch of anger rising up inside him. "Seriously?"

"Amarl, she's good with sahr, and she knows alchemy – which you know I want to do – and I didn't even have to pay her. She says she feels like she owes us." She shook her head. "Besides, after Yashi, none of the other third or fourth-years would even talk to me about it."

"You do remember that she betrayed Amarl?" Burik asked in a disappointed voice.

"And she feels terrible about it. She was wrong, and she knows she was – and she's trying to make up for it." She looked at Amarl. "Did you know that after your duel, she told the other third-years that if they did anything to us, they'd answer to her?"

He shook his head. "No, I didn't, but..."

Meder nodded. "And she meant it. Some of the third-years blamed us for what happened to Yashi – blamed Burik in particular – and when she found out about it, she caught each of them alone and – well, I guess you could say she convinced them to leave us alone."

"And she told you this?" Amarl asked skeptically.

"No. Veter did. I guess they became friends after the hunt, and he said she was really upset by what she did, and after Yashi, she said she was no better than he was and deserved the same punishment." She gave Amarl a grave look, but he simply shrugged.

"Maybe she did, Meder."

The girl sighed. "Maybe, but the point is, she really regrets what she did. I don't think she'll ever do anything like it again."

"Not to me, she won't," he snorted. "I'm never giving her the chance." He took a deep breath, trying to let go of the anger he still felt over that day. "Look, it's fine, Meder. You wanted extra help, and she's helping you. I understand. Just don't expect me to forgive her anytime soon."

She looked at Amarl and looked like she was going to say more, but after looking at his face, she simply nodded. "That's fair." She took a deep breath.

"So, my task. An array is an advanced matrix held by multiple people at once. Each person acts as an anchor for a single layer of the array, and together, they create an effect far more powerful than any of them could enact alone." She looked at both of them. "So, you'll have to help me."

Amarl frowned. "I mean, I'll do what I can, Meder, but you know I'm not great at sahr."

"I know," she sighed. "That's probably the point. If I'm going to create the array, I'll have to use you, and that means I have to try and help you handle sahr a little better." She stopped, her eyes narrowing. "Wait, how do you think the awal knew that I knew how to make an array?"

Amarl laughed. "I think that they know everything that happens in Askula," he said. "Even the things we think they don't know."

"That's not creepy at all," Burik rumbled. He lifted his chin at Amarl. "So, what did you get?"

Amarl opened his paper and peered at it. "Well," he said after a moment as he processed the words on the paper. "That's – interesting."

"What is it?" Burik asked.

"It's a lot simpler than I thought. I have to harvest a Strong crystal from a creature I killed alone." He frowned. "Although now that I think about it, it's not that simple at all, is it?"

"Sure, it is. Hells, you've already done it, haven't you?" The big boy frowned. "Wait, why would they give you something that you've already done? That feels like cheating!"

"Oh," Meder said, her eyes widening as she realized the same thing Amarl already had. "Oh!"

"What?" Burik asked a bit irritably.

"Burik, Amarl harvested those Strong crystals in Shadora, not here," the girl said slowly.

"Yeah. So?"

"So, I'll bet the creatures there were much stronger than the ones we'll face here. You heard his stories; he almost died several times. That probably won't happen here, at least not with the nadars and older students keeping the area safe for us. So, how is he going to get that crystal?"

"Huh. That's a good..." Burik's eyes widened, and he looked at Amarl. "You mean..."

Amarl nodded. "Yeah. If I'm going to do this, I have to leave the protected area. I'll have to sneak out of the restricted zone."

"You can't do that, Amarl," Meder said firmly. "You don't know how dangerous it is out there!"

"I'm not sure I have any choice. How else will I do this?" He held up the paper and waved it around.

"You don't know that you don't have a choice, though. What did you tell Burik? There could be something like that hiding down in that forest!"

Amarl rolled his eyes. "Oh, come on, Meder. We both know there's not. I just told him that to make him feel better."

"Hey!" Burik protested.

"In fact," Amarl plowed over the other boy, "this might be a way for both of us to complete our missions – or even all three. I find a creature that's strong enough to give us a Strong crystal, which should be one Burik doesn't think he can beat, you show us how to create one of those array things to hurt or weaken it, and I kill it and harvest it. We all win!"

A grin replaced Burik's dissatisfied expression. "Okay, I like this plan!"

"You would," Meder muttered, then hesitated. "It's not a terrible idea.

We just don't know that it's necessary!"

"How about this, then?" Amarl asked. "Tomorrow and the next day, we scout to the edges of the restricted area and see what we find. If we find something that will work inside that territory, no problem. We use the plan on it. If we don't, though, we leave the territory and spend two more days trying to find something better."

"How do you even plan on getting out of the restricted area?" she asked a little desperately. "I'll bet every way out is guarded."

"Simple. I'll get your buddy Andra to let us through. She owes me a favor, remember?"

Meder bit her lip, but Burik burst out laughing. "I like it!" he said happily, clapping Amarl on the arm.

"I don't know," Meder hedged.

"Come on, Meder, he's compromising with you. He's giving you two days to be right. If we haven't found anything in two days in an area two walks across, we're not going to find it."

"Fine," she sighed. "That is a fair compromise. Okay, Amarl. I'm in."

"Thanks, Meder," the hizeen replied with a smile.

"Yeah, thanks, Meder," Burik agreed.

"For what?" the girl asked the larger boy quizzically.

"For going along. This trip just got a lot more interesting!"

CHAPTER 35

"**W**atch its fangs!" Amarl shouted.

"You watch its stinger!" Burik roared in reply.

"Both of you, shut up and kill it! This isn't easy!" Meder grunted.

Amarl pivoted and ducked as the huge centipede twisted its body, trying to grab him with a pair of three-span-long pincers jutting out of its hind end. A slim stinger slid out of its ass every time the pincers snapped closed, and Amarl felt pretty certain that it could inject poison into him if it grabbed hold of him. In reply, he chopped one of his axe blades into its side, cracking its chitinous shell and letting clear fluid leak out. Three more holes decorated the thing's hind end, all trickling fluid, but in the narrow confines of the tunnel, he couldn't strike any farther up its body to do real damage. He knew that on the other side of the creature, Burik was having the same problem, and that if Meder weren't using sahr to make the stone beneath the thing sticky, slowing it down, he'd be having to work a lot harder. Still, he wished he could just chop the damn thing in half; dodging it and chipping away at it was annoying.

He caught the bug's pincers on his crescent blade as it thrashed toward him once more, guiding the attack past his legs but not trying to pin the creature in place. He'd learned that while the insectoid creatures of Isolas were light and easy to move around, they were also ferociously strong. He knew from hard experience that the centipedes could fling him bodily against the side of the tunnel, and that his head smacking into stone hurt like the spirits' hells. Instead, he reversed the axe and jammed its spearpoint into the creature twice in a row, cracking its shell again and leaving two more holes in its carapace.

He jumped back as the thing whipped its pincers spasmodically to free itself from the painful spearpoint, and the centipede twisted in the tunnel, folding its body in half so it could face the source of its pain. That was what Burik had been waiting for; the boy's halberd flashed in the light of Meder's staff, cutting a long gash in the thing's side. The centipede's struggles weakened at once, and Amarl stepped on its rear end, feeling its shell crumble beneath his foot as he pinned its pincers in place. He winced at the feeling of the sticky fluid that flowed into his boot, but he ignored the sensation and jammed his spearpoint into the monster's head. It thrashed feebly, trying to dislodge him, but Burik's blow had cut the long muscles running down its side that gave it much of its power, and he held it in place until it finally curled up and fell still.

He yanked his weapon free, then stepped back, lifting his boot and watching clear fluid drip from it onto the stone floor. "That's disgusting," he said with a sigh, shaking his head.

"That's what you get for trying to stand on it," Burik chuckled, taking out a cloth and beginning to clean his halberd. "It's not exactly a stepping stool, Amarl."

"It was either that, or let the damn thing sting me in the leg. I really don't want to see what one of its stings feels like."

"I don't blame you." The larger boy gestured at the fallen creature. "Well, what are you waiting for? It's not gonna harvest itself."

"It's also not going anywhere." Amarl sat down on the stone floor and slipped off his boot, tipping it upside down and shaking it to let more of the sticky liquid drain out. He glanced past Burik at Meder, who stood slumped against the wall, leaning her head back against the hard stone. "Are you okay, Meder?"

She turned toward him and gave him a weak smile. "Fine. Just a little tired, is all. It's one thing doing that for a few ants; it's another with a two-reach-long centipede with how hard it is to move the sahr down here."

"Especially on short sleep," Burik noted.

"Yes, especially that. I'll be glad when this is over, and we can head back to Askula. I think I'll sleep for a week to recover."

Amarl laughed. "They'll give us a day then expect us back in classes, and you know it." He took out his somewhat grimy cleaning cloth and used it to wipe out the inside of his boot, then cleaned up his moon axe as best he could. The centipede's blood, they'd all learned, dried hard and crusty on weapons and was a pain to get off once it did. There was only so much the rag could do, though; he'd cleaned it as best he could using water from the pond, but he couldn't soak it in the crystalline pool for fear of contaminating their main source of drinking water and getting them all sick. The same went for their clothing, which was stained and spotted with insect goo that would need a good scrubbing to wash out.

He slipped his boot back on and leaned over to harvest the creature, pulling a low-level Weak crystal from it and dropping it into his pouch to join a dozen similar crystals. He sat back and looked at Meder, shaking his head. "It's been two days, Meder. We've killed a few dozen ants, a few spiders, and a bunch of centipedes. Nothing's given us more than a Weak crystal."

"I know," she sighed, closing her eyes.

He didn't blame her for being tired. It had been a long two days already. As he expected, the creatures of Isolas attacked the group frequently if not constantly. The ants swarmed their campsite every hour or two both nights, and only the fact that he'd been wrong about their ability to scale the cliff walls kept them safe. One of them could hold back a decent number of the creatures on the narrow path leading to their camp, but even so, none of them could sleep through the sounds of battle, so they woke tired and sandy-eyed in the morning – not that there was any way to tell day from night in the tunnels beyond Meder's watch.

They spent their "days" scouting around the area looking for dangerous creatures to hunt. At first, Amarl went ahead, using his Silent Movement and Hiding skills to try and avoid pointless fights with the insectoid creatures around them, but he'd quickly learned that whatever senses the bugs used to find him, they weren't as simple as regular sight and sound. They tracked him no matter how well he hid, and after the third time he'd had to fight off an ant swarm by himself, the group had taken to sticking together.

Amarl was especially glad of that every time they encountered another group of the assilians. The insect-people always traveled in threes, and he couldn't tell one group from another – for all he knew, it was the same group they encountered over and over – but after that first meeting, none of them tried to communicate with the novices. Meder had attempted to talk to one group, but they ignored her utterly, focusing only on digging crystals out of the walls. Amarl guessed that the first group said whatever they were going to say, and that was the end of it. Even when the novices fought a pair of reach-wide, brown spiders in sight of the assilians, the insect-people didn't so much as look in their general direction.

They decided to ignore the creatures right back as they explored to the edges of the restricted zone, marking where the older students and nadars had set up camps to keep greater creatures out and the students in. They'd found the other novices' camp but left it alone; they didn't catch sight of Herel and his friends, a fact for which Amarl was somewhat grateful. Instead, they hunted every type of beast they could find to see if any would help them complete their secondary missions. So far, none had even come close.

"These centipedes are the most dangerous things we've found, and they aren't really all that dangerous," Burik rumbled, echoing Amarl's thoughts. "A little annoying, sure, but if I had to, I could probably handle one by myself. We're not going to find anything worse down here."

"I know," she repeated, reaching up to rub her eyes. "I know what we have to do. I just don't like it, that's all." She looked over at Amarl. "Should we head back and try to get some rest first?"

He shook his head. "There's no point. We're not getting any rest. Did you sleep at all last night?"

"No, not really."

"Me either. Another night will just make us groggier and more tired, I think. If we're going to do this, it's best to do it sooner rather than later."

"He's right," Burik nodded. "Once we're done, we can rest for a day or so and try to get some actual sleep."

"You had me at sleep," Meder sighed, rising back to her feet. "Okay, let's go chat with Andra."

They'd located the girl's camp on the first day, for obvious reasons, but they hadn't approached it. She'd set up in a cavern that was little more than a widening of one of the main tunnels, and her simple camp consisted of a small tent, a ring of stones containing a small fire, and a metal tripod set over that fire that Amarl supposed would be useful for cooking and heating up water. When they approached, Andra stood in the center of the cavern, holding her longsword in two hands as she moved through a series of forms that Amarl didn't recognize. As they neared, though, Amarl felt a slight surge of power, and her eyes snapped around to face them as she whipped her sword around. Seeing the trio, she lowered the blade.

"Sahr ward," Meder whispered admiringly, looking around. "Really well done, too."

"This is the edge of your area, Novices," the older girl said in an even voice. Her eyes scanned the three students, but she flinched visibly when she met Amarl's gaze. "Turn around and head back."

"We need to leave the area, Andra," Meder said, stepping forward.

"No," the older girl said flatly, shaking her head. "Out of the question."

"We don't have a choice, Andra," Meder pleaded. "Burik and Amarl's secondary tasks can't be completed in the restricted area. We have to leave it to complete them."

The older girl's eyes narrowed. "What tasks need you to go out there?"

"Burik has to fight a creature he thinks he can't beat, and Amarl has to harvest a Strong crystal. We've spent two days looking for something that will work, but the ants and centipedes aren't strong enough."

Andra winced. "No, they aren't. We aren't letting anything in here that would fit that description." She hesitated, then shook her head. "Sorry, I can't let you pass. It's too dangerous."

"More dangerous than Shadora?" Amarl asked mildly, noting that she flinched again as he spoke.

"No, not as dangerous as Shadora," she admitted in a soft voice.

"And I did okay there," he noted. "In fact, we fought side-by-side, remember? If you can handle it, I probably can, too."

"No, Amarl, I'm sorry. If it means you don't complete your secondary tasks, well, too bad. As long as you live, you succeed, and if you go out there without an ability, then you might not live."

"I didn't need an ability to deal with Nihos," he said quietly, and her face paled visibly. "Besides, Andra, you owe me a favor, a really big one, remember? Let us pass, and I'll call it even."

She stared at him, and he saw her hands trembling visibly. "Two..." Her voice was hoarse, and she stopped and cleared her throat. "Two conditions. One, I know a place that can give you what you're looking for; instead of wandering around, you go there. Two, I go with you. I can make sure you don't run into trouble you can't handle on the way, and I can give us all time to escape if we do. Deal?"

Amarl glanced at Meder, who nodded eagerly, and Burik, who simply shrugged. "Okay, but you only step in if things are really dangerous. Remember, Burik has to think he can't beat something, and if you're helping, he won't."

"Fine," she sighed, reaching out her hand toward Amarl. Before he could take it, though, a voice made him spin around, gripping his axe fiercely.

"Three, we get to go with you." Amarl watched as Herel, Hadur, and Norag appeared out of the darkness from a bend in the passage. Herel's face looked smug, while Hadur's was sullen, and Norag's looked stricken, like he didn't want to be there.

"Not only no, but fuck no," Burik growled, stepping toward the three. "I don't trust any of you at my back. Get the hells out of here, now!"

"Do you really want us to leave after what we just heard, Burik?" Herel asked, shaking his head and making a clicking sound with his tongue. "We might have to go back and report what the hizeen said about Nihos. I wonder if anyone's checked his crystal's log about that?"

"All you're doing is making an argument for why you shouldn't be allowed to go back, Herel," Amarl said with an evil smile, lifting his axe. Burik hefted his halberd as well, and Herel swallowed hard, taking a step back as his hand fell onto his sword hilt.

"Then your crystals would show our deaths, too," he said. "And…"

"Herel, by the love of Ak-lahat, just shut up for a second," Norag sighed, stepping out in front of the pair. Herel's eyes flattened, but Norag ignored him. "Look, there are two reasons you should let us go along. One, we aren't going to be able to complete our secondary quests in here, either. And two, if you all leave, you can't exactly stop us. We can just follow along." He turned and glared at the two behind him. "Which is what I said we should have done in the first place, instead of trying to blackmail people!"

"Why can't you do your tasks, Norag?" Meder asked, putting a hand on Amarl's arm to silence him and moving to stand just out of range of the boy's long poleaxe

He sighed. "I have to use sahr to turn the tide of a battle we might otherwise lose, and Herel has to save someone from being hurt. The problem is, we aren't finding anything to fight in here, so we can't do that."

"Really?" she asked dubiously. "We've been attacked almost constantly."

"I don't blame the creatures of this place," Hadur muttered, but Norag glared at the merchant boy.

"Lasheshia's teachings were a perversion of the One Above All's words, Hadur," Norag said flatly. "For the sake of your soul, put them aside – or at least keep silent about them, so the rest of us don't have to listen!"

He turned back to face Meder. "I don't know what you've faced, but we haven't seen more than a handful of creatures, and all those were on the first day. So, we either have to go with you, or we need to work together to bring enough creatures to one place to create a battle that we might not win. I'm fine either way."

"Or you can just not complete those tasks," Amarl suggested.

"I could say the same for you, Amarl, but the point is, we want to. We're all pretty sure that there's a reward for doing it; otherwise, why would they bother giving it to us? So, you either have to give up on your tasks, or you have to let us follow behind you."

"If you follow us out of sight, you'll probably die," Andra said shortly. "I won't be able to get to you in time to save you from some of the things out there."

"But if that happened, you'd have to explain how we all got out there." Norag swallowed hard. "And yes, I know that there's another option, doing to us whatever you did to Nihos, but I don't think you'll do that. I told Herel that sending Nihos after you was a bad idea, that Nihos was sick and would take things too far, and I'm guessing he did – and one of you had to kill him for it."

"Shut up, Norag!" Hadur hissed.

"No, you shut up!" Norag turned back to face Amarl. "This way, you know there's no blackmail, no coercion. I just admitted that Herel sent Nihos after you. After what happened to Yashi, if the malims found out about that, they'd expel us for sure – and we all know what that means, now. So, we can't say anything about Nihos, or we're sealing our own fates, too. We just want the same chance to complete our tasks that you're getting, I swear by the high god."

"I believe that *you* do, Norag," Amarl agreed. "I don't think Herel and Hadur necessarily agree. I think they'll take any chance they get to make sure I fail, especially if they think it won't come back to them."

"And if they did something like that, I'd make sure no one ever saw or heard from them again," Andra said in a flat voice. "You understand me? There will be no betrayals, no hidden blades and secret plots. If I take you along, then you work as a team. If you can't do that, then none of you are going, and you'll all just have to deal with failing your secondary tasks." She glared at all of them.

"What do you think, Amarl?" Meder asked quietly.

The hizeen stared at the trio, doing his best to read their faces. At last, he walked over to stand in front of Herel, staring into the noble's eyes.

"I don't trust you, Herel," he said quietly. "Or Hadur. But my choices are to let you tag along, or kill you right now." Herel's hand tightened on his sword hilt, but Amarl ignored it. "And I can do it. You remember our duel? I've gotten better since then. Either Burik or I could kill you and Hadur without even trying too hard." Herel looked like he wanted to speak, but he kept his lips pressed tightly shut.

"But I don't want to do that," Amarl added. "I just want to finish this test and be done with it. If the only way to do that is to bring you along, so be it." His eyes hardened. "But I promise you, if any of you betray me, I'll feed you to whatever is down here, and I won't lose a bit of sleep over it. You understand me?" After a moment, Herel gave a long, slow nod, and Amarl stepped back.

"Fine. You can come." He looked at Andra. "You mind showing us this place you have in mind? I think we'd all like to just get this over with."

"You think?" She snorted and shook her head. "This is going to be the spirits' hell, Amarl, but whatever. It's not the first time we've faced that together, is it?" She turned and waved to the group. "This way. Meder, you and your light up front with me. Burik and Amarl, you secure the rear. Everyone else, stay in the middle and stay sharp. And Norag, put out that damned hammer; it's blinding you more than it's helping you." She strode forward. "Let's get this shit show over with, so we can all pretend it never happened."

CHAPTER 36

The tunnels past Andra's camp looked identical to the ones in the novices' hunting zone. They were no wider or taller, they smelled and sounded the same, and they had the same bands of golden crystals swirling along the walls. However, twenty minutes into their hunt, Amarl quickly realized that they weren't the same, at least not in the way that mattered most.

As the group passed through an area, the wall beside Amarl crumbled and shattered. Stones struck his arm and side, knocking him into Burik and making both boys stagger. That was fortunate since it meant the lunging bite of the huge, half-reach-wide creature that sprang out of the wall missed them both. The creature looked almost like a round, legless centipede or a chitin-covered worm. Its head was featureless save for a ring-shaped mouth filled with rows of teeth, and two rows of antennae ran along each of its sides, each shorter than his pinky and waving as if testing the air. The worm smacked into the opposite wall, then curled about and lunged toward Amarl once more.

Fortunately, the past two days of hunting left both Amarl's and Burik's reflexes honed, and the worm's charge merely impaled it on the larger boy's halberd. It jerked back, but Amarl followed it, plunging his crescent blade into its side and ripping open a huge gash in its tough shell. He yanked the weapon free as it whipped sideways, trying to smash him into the wall, and Burik's halberd chopped into its opposite side, crunching through its exoskeleton. The creature lunged again, and the boys fell back, staying out of its range and cutting into it as it surged toward them until eventually, Burik's halberd sank into its gaping mouth, and it fell still at last.

"Well, that was exciting," Amarl chuckled as he looked around for more creatures. "Did that count as something you didn't think you could beat, Burik?"

"Nope. I never doubted we'd win for a second." The boy knelt and laid his hand on the worm's shell, concentrating. Almost a minute passed before a green crystal crackled up from the thing, and Burik grabbed it with a sigh.

"Level 4. I was hoping it would give me something like a Weak crystal."

"You both okay back there?" Andra's voice wasn't loud in the tunnel, but Amarl heard a tinge of anxiety in it.

"Yep. We're fine. Burik just had to harvest the thing. We'll be there in a second." Squeezing past the dead worm wasn't easy, but they managed to shove its bulk to one side of the tunnel and slip around it.

"Wait, Burik, you can harvest ithtu?" Andra asked in a puzzled voice.

"Meder and I both can. Amarl showed us how."

"What?" Herel demanded. "That's not fair!"

"No, it isn't," Andra shrugged. "Get over it." She looked back at Burik, then at Meder. "That's impressive for first-years, but you should really let Amarl get the kill and harvest everything whenever possible. He might have gotten a Minor crystal from that stone borer."

"You recognized it?" Meder asked.

"Yeah. They're fairly common in these tunnels. We try to keep them out of the area around the Mistway, though, for obvious reasons. They're ambush hunters, and if you aren't ready for them, they can kill you in that first lunge." She frowned. "They usually attack the first thing that passes them, though, which is one reason I'm in front. I've never seen one wait to hit the people in back of a group before."

"We're just lucky, I guess," Amarl said dryly.

"Not the word I'd use for you, Amarl. Not the right word at all."

Amarl quickly realized that the older students really had been shielding them from the worst of what was down in the tunnels. The next attack came from a swarm of the familiar ants, but these were larger than the ones they'd faced before, with thicker carapaces to protect them. When the first launched itself at Amarl from three reaches away, and wings unfurled from its back to carry it through the air toward him, it surprised him so much he nearly forgot to bat it from the air and punch a hole in its thorax. The attacks came steadily after that; ants swarmed them, stone borers erupted from the walls beside them, and beetles as long as Burik was tall scuttled out of open tunnels to bite at them with pincers as long as Amarl's arm.

At first, Andra, Burik, and Amarl did most of the actual fighting in these attacks, but as creatures came in greater numbers, all the novices were forced to join in. Amarl realized that Herel, Hadur, and Norag had learned how to work well as a team, probably something they'd been training to do with Nihos and the other third-years. Norag used his long axe to hold back insects, hacking at them and keeping their attention, letting one or two past for the others to deal with. Herel's longsword and Hadur's rapier punched holes in the insects that got close to Norag, their thrusting weapons probably more effective than Amarl's axe in the cramped tunnels. When those fell, Norag allowed more to slip around his weapon, and his friends dispatched them quickly. It was an efficient strategy, and Amarl couldn't help but feel a little impressed. He knew that, individually, none of the three was his equal in combat, but together, they were obviously more than just the sum of their parts.

At last, two hours and many battles later, the tunnel widened in front of them, spreading out into a cavern smaller than the one Amarl's group set up camp in but still a dozen reaches across. Pillars of stone filled the cavern, reaching from the ceiling three reaches above to the floor a reach below tunnel in which they stood. Water poured the ceiling in the center of the room in a constant spout, emptying into a large, black lake whose rippling waters reflected the light of Meder's staff and hid its depths. More of the treelike fungi rose thicky along the shores of the lake to the sides and along the far bank, obscuring the walls behind them, but the nearer shore lay clear of the trees.

"Here we are," Andra said in a soft voice. "We call this cavern Black Lake, for obvious reasons, and it's one of the more dangerous spots near the Mistway."

"It doesn't look dangerous," Hadur observed.

"Not at all," Amarl chuckled. "Except that anything could live in that lake, thirty or forty ants could be hiding in those trees, and there could be a half-dozen tunnels hidden behind the trees with other things in them. Plus, this is probably the water source for everything in a march or so. Beyond that, no, this doesn't look dangerous at all."

Hadur fumed, his face turning red, but Andra spoke before the boy could reply. "There are some tunnels leading out of here, you're right, but nothing uses this lake for water. If you head toward the shore, you'll see why."

"Are you coming with us?" Herel asked nervously.

"I'll be close enough to intervene if it's necessary – which it probably will be." She shrugged. "You want to complete those secondary tasks? This is a way to do so. Go for it."

"Wait," Meder held up a hand as Burik stepped forward. "I've still got my task, too – and Norag, you've got yours."

"To use sahr to change the outcome of a battle," Norag nodded. "What are you thinking?"

"My task is to set up an array, and this could be the perfect time for it." She glanced at Andra. "Could you be an anchor point?" Andra shrugged, and the younger girl smiled. "Thank you. Having you and Norag as anchors will make this much easier than using Burik and Amarl – especially Amarl."

"Hey!" the hizeen protested.

"Amarl, you're awful with sahr. Just terrible. We all know it." She looked at Norag. "So, what I'm thinking is..."

"Hold on a second," he shook his head, holding up his hands. "I don't even know what you're talking about! Arrays? Anchors?"

"An array is..." She paused. "Think of it like taking a sahr matrix and adding another dimension, then stacking matrices like layers along that dimension. When it activates, the bottom layer descends first, dragging the next layer, and so on until the whole thing collapses down into one point."

Norag frowned, scratching his chin. "But couldn't you do the same thing just by having three of us craft the individual workings?"

"No, because they're arrayed along an extra dimension, so the power drawn from each layer is exponentially greater." She grimaced. "That also makes it exponentially harder to control, of course, and a lot more likely to fragment or fluctuate, but the final result is much more potent than the sum of the workings would be. That's why I need you and Andra as anchors, to help stabilize the higher matrices until I can collapse them."

"And have you ever built one of these arrays before?" Herel asked dubiously.

"Well – no, but I know the theory, and with Norag and Andra anchoring, there shouldn't be any danger. Well, not too much."

"No," he shook his head. "I think this is a terrible idea."

"Good thing no one asked or cares what you think, then," Amarl grinned. "Meder, what are you thinking of building, and what do you need from us?"

She smiled at him gratefully. "Well, nothing damaging obviously, or it might hurt everyone. I was thinking that..."

Building the array took Meder over an hour and involved a number of failed stops and starts as whatever she was doing slipped away from her. By the fifth attempt, Amarl could feel the power in the air like the static before a lightning storm, lifting the hairs on his neck and the back of his head and filling the cave with a barely heard buzzing sound. The crystals in the walls all around them pulsed and glowed softly with a golden light that grew steadily brighter as the power swelled around them. Amarl couldn't help but look around nervously, expecting the whole thing to collapse onto him any second, and he could see the others, except Norag and Andra, seemed to feel the same.

"Okay, I think that's got it," Meder finally sighed. "It seems to be stable and holding. Although it's a lot stronger than I planned for it to be."

"For the moment," Norag said through gritted teeth. "I've never tried to hold this much power in a matrix, Meder. I'm not sure how I'm doing it right now, to be honest."

"Well, the sympathetic links between the layers act as a stabilizer, funneling excess power out of the higher layers into the lower, more stable ones, while using the inertia of the higher, more potent layer to…"

"That's great, but can we do this before this thing crashes down on us and kills us all?" Herel interrupted. "You can explain to anyone who cares some other time."

"He's right," Norag grunted. "I can't hold this long. I don't have the control the two of you do."

"Okay, people, let's get moving," Burik called out, lifting his halberd. "I'll take point. Amarl, you and Hadur on my left; Herel, you're on my right."

"How about we keep Hadur as far away from my back as possible when he's holding a sword?" Amarl said dryly.

"Yeah, good call. Hadur, you take right, but maybe borrow Norag's axe. That rapier of yours is next to useless in a real fight." The merchant's son bristled again, but Burik ignored him. "Let's move, and see if we can get this done!"

The four novices advanced in a line toward the shore, moving slowly and cautiously. Amarl held his axe crescent-first in case anything leaped out at him; the wider blade could catch a charge like that easier than the spearpoint could, and it was sharp enough to cut into anything that he caught inside it. Burik led slightly, his long halberd extended, with Hadur to the right – carrying his rapier, not the poleaxe, Amarl noticed.

Ripples covered the surface of the water, and as they moved away from Meder's light, shadows crowded around them. Even so, Amarl spotted the two long, thin, black reeds waving in the air a reach past the shoreline, moving around despite the lack of a noticeable breeze.

"Here it comes," he said softly, his voice strangely loud in the silence of the cavern.

No sooner had the words left his mouth than the lake's surface exploded into a frenzy of white water. Something that looked like a cross between a millipede and a beetle leaped from the water, its body three reaches long and half a reach wide. Its pincers gaped open, and a blast of black liquid shot from its maw at the novices. Burik dove sideways, knocking Hadur down and carrying him out of the way of the blast, while Amarl leaped into a roll, narrowly avoiding the spray of what could have been poison or acid.

"Now!" Meder's voice rang out loudly in the cavern, and Amarl felt a terrible sense of pressure as energy descended around them, sweeping past them toward the creature. A blast of wind screamed against his back, slamming into the monster and carrying it back into the water. That wind turned cold and frigid a moment later, and Amarl shivered violently as snow fell as the moisture in the air froze – as did the nearest part of the lake with a loud crackling sound, trapping half of the creature beneath the frozen surface. The air swirled and twisted, howling as it sucked the snow from the air and battered it against the monster, covering it in a fine layer of frost. At last, the wind died, and the icy bite left the air, leaving the four novices tumbled about, staring in total awe at the monster trapped in the ice.

"Holy fuck," Burik breathed. "What the hells was that?"

"An array, apparently," Amarl grinned as he rolled to his feet. "It certainly made this fight easier." The monster twisted, and the ice beneath it cracked as it began to tear itself free. Amarl frowned. "But not that easy. Let's go!"

He and Burik ran toward the lake, skidding and sliding as they stepped onto icy stone. Burik swore as he fell onto his back, but Amarl maintained his footing and readied his axe. The creature turned to face him, its pincers spread wide, and he dove forward, hitting the ice and sliding as a torrent of black water splashed against the stone behind him. He heard Herel swear and glanced back to see the noble sliding headfirst onto the ice, having apparently dived to escape the creature's blast. Burik had regained his feet and approached the creature from the side, his steps careful and his halberd lowered. He lunged forward, and the thing's head whipped toward the larger boy as his halberd's spearpoint cracked into its carapace – and slid off, leaving its shell undamaged. Beyond him, Hadur tried to move forward, close enough to use his slim rapier, but the ice and treacherous footing slowed him down, essentially taking him out of the fight.

Amarl's blood surged as he lifted his axe and closed with the creature. The song of his ithtu soared in his mind triumphantly, and he felt its fire in his veins. He lashed out with his axe, aiming for the thing's underside, and one of the double axe blades cracked into its shell and plunged inside, leaving a ragged hole in its armor from which clear fluid spewed forth. He yanked his axe, but the weapon hung up for a moment, causing him to lose his balance on the ice. His weapon came free as his feet slid out from under him, and he lifted it defensively as the creature's head swung toward him and darted down, its pincers snapping toward his chest.

Herel's blade struck the monster with a loud clang, the two-handed blow knocking its head sideways and breaking off a chip of chitin from its pincer. Herel stood over Amarl, his blade held ready. The creature recovered and struck again, but once more, the noble slashed, knocking the blow aside.

"Get up, you ass," the boy growled through clenched teeth. "Or are you really that lazy, after all?"

Amarl shook off his surprise and rolled backwards to his feet, lifting his axe. He glanced over at Burik and Hadur, then up at the monster. "Burik, I can hurt it!" he called. "Switch in and hold its attention! Herel, stay with me and keep its fangs off me while I cut it down! Hadur..." He grimaced. "Try not to die, and learn how to use a damn spear!"

Burik slipped in front of Amarl, swinging his halberd in an overhand chop that clanged against the creature's head and left a long crack in its armor. The hizeen waited for the monster to lunge at Burik before darting in, spinning his axe. The creature twisted and struck at him, but Herel swept his longsword up and slashed it into the beast's face. The sword couldn't hurt the creature, but Herel was strong and skilled enough to knock its attacks away and keep Amarl safe. The hizeen whipped his axe around his body, letting it slide through his hand to gain power, then slammed an axe blade into the insect's underside once more. The blade plunged into it, and he yanked it loose as once again, Herel deflected its attack with a sweeping blow and Burik stabbed it with his spearpoint, driving its head up and away from the hizeen.

Amarl's axe blurred as he whipped it around, slamming it over and over into the monster, targeting the same area again and again. The monster writhed and twisted as its chitin collapsed, and clear fluid sprayed copiously from its wounds. It snapped and slashed at him, but Burik and Herel kept it from landing an attack. His ithtu sang gloriously in his mind as he plunged the crescent blade into the hole he'd made, twisting the weapon inside the creature. The giant beast shuddered, and Amarl barely yanked his axe clear and jumped back as it curled up and crashed into the swiftly melting ice below.

Silence reigned over the cavern for long seconds as Amarl stood there, his chest heaving, his weapon dripping slime and coated with gobbets of the thing's insides. Herel stood beside him, panting just as heavily as he let his sword tip lower to the ground, while Burik stood back, his halberd on his shoulder, shaking his head at the dead creature.

"Now, that was a fight!" the larger boy laughed.

"Think it counts toward your secondary task?" Amarl asked with a grin.

"Oh, hells, yeah. No way I could have taken that thing alone. I couldn't even get through its armor." Burik frowned as he spoke. "Speaking of which, how did you get through it?"

"No idea," Amarl shrugged. "I must have found a weak point on it."

"Lake spitters don't have weak points, Amarl." Andra walked over to the lake shore, shaking her head as she stared down at the still corpse. "It takes an ability or very powerful sahr to get through their armor. I'm not sure how you did it, to be honest."

"Wait," Hadur said, his tone clearly unhappy, "you expected that we wouldn't be able to hurt it?"

"Honestly? Yes. I thought I would have to come in and rescue you, and you'd all understand why you shouldn't be out here and agree to go back into the designated area." She glanced at Amarl. "So much for that plan, I guess. Between Meder's array and Amarl's – whatever he did – that thing didn't stand much of a chance."

"Yeah, that was some working, Meder!" Burik said as the girl trudged wearily over to them.

"It was impressive," Herel nodded, still panting as he spoke. "Impressive enough that I have to wonder why you didn't just kill it with sahr and save us the trouble."

"I couldn't have," the girl shook her head. "Sahr just isn't that strong, and that thing had its own sahr that would have resisted me."

"Not that strong?" Hadur scoffed. "You froze the lake, Meder! You could have frozen that thing solid!"

"No, she couldn't have," Norag shook his head. "If she could have, then the working would have frozen it instead of just frosting it a bit. Trust me, that was everything we had."

"And I didn't freeze the lake, just a finger-width or two around the creature," Meder added. "And it took three of us and all the available sahr in the area to suck that much heat out of the air – which was really all we did."

"Someone like Veter with an ice ability could have done the same thing a lot faster," Andra added. "It would have taken more ithtu than he normally uses, but he could have wrapped that thing in a layer of ice a finger-width thick. I've seen him do it before."

"In other words, Meder did the best she could – and it was better than any of the rest of us could have done," Amarl said, giving Herel a hard look. His chest still heaved as he spoke; for some reason, he was having trouble catching his breath. "Well, except maybe Andra." He looked at the girl, and she opened her mouth as if to speak, but a confused look crossed her face as no sound came out. Her eyes suddenly widened, and she yanked out her sword, looking around frantically.

Amarl glanced around as well, but as he did, a tightness spread across his chest, like someone wrapped a band around it. He lifted his axe and struggled to take a breath, but no air came into his lungs, as if someone had clapped an invisible hand over his mouth and nose. He looked around frantically and saw Herel drop to one knee, clutching his throat, while Hadur staggered, taking two steps backward as if to run before his legs seemed to collapse from beneath him. Burik shook his head furiously, his face purpling as he struggled to breathe, while Andra waved her hands in the air, perhaps trying vainly to craft a working of some sort.

The blood began to pound in Amarl's head as his lungs screamed for air, and he staggered as he turned about, looking for whatever had stolen the breath from them all. Blackness bordered the edges of his vision, and the song of his ithtu suddenly blazed in his mind, sweeping through his blood and roaring in his ears. He slashed about with his axe, trying to free himself from whatever bound him, but the weapon whipped silently past him, without even a breath of air passing his knuckles or tugging at his arms.

Herel and Hadur collapsed to the stone floor, their eyes closed and their bodies still, and a moment later, Meder joined them, her face unnaturally pale. Norag fell next, followed by Burik several seconds later.

Only Andra and Amarl still stood as black, insectoid figures detached themselves from the shadows beneath the trees and moved to surround the group. Amarl's strength flagged as he struggled to breathe, and he fell to a knee despite the power raging through his blood. Beside him, Andra staggered and dropped as well, catching herself with a hand and shaking her head as if trying to clear it.

The figures drew closer but stayed well outside weapon range, not that it mattered, as Amarl's axe was suddenly far too heavy to hold and slipped from his numb fingers. He fell to his side, struggling to push himself back up as his air-starved brain slowly shut down. One of the creatures moved to stand near him, looking down at him with its expressionless face.

<Blood calls. We come. Warning given.>

As his vision faded, the last thing he saw was the insects moving to gather the bodies of the novices and drag them away. A clawed hand grasped his hair, and something hard slammed into his skull. Darkness filled his vision, and the light fled his eyes at last.

CHAPTER 37

Amarl sat up, his head pounding, and sucked in deep lungsful of air. He blinked, shocked that he was alive, much less awake. His mouth was sour, his head felt like someone was stabbing it from the inside with a dagger, and his entire body felt bruised and battered, but he lived! When he saw the assilians reaching for them, he'd been certain...

He shivered and pushed the thought from his mind. There was no point dwelling on what might have been, only on what was. He hadn't died, but that didn't mean everything was fine. As he looked around at his surroundings, he amended that thought. He lived, but besides that, things were most definitely not fine.

He sat on a hard stone floor in a small cave about two reaches across and one high. Some of the glowing moss hung from the walls, providing enough light to see and reflecting off a pool of water maybe three spans wide in one corner. The ever-present crystals lined the walls, sticking out in elaborate clumps and clusters rather than simple hexagonal prisms the way they had in the tunnels. Dark, unmoving shapes littered the floor, the greenish light washing over olive skin, and it took him a second to realize that the shapes were the other novices – and that they were all naked, stripped of weapons and clothing. He glanced down at himself and realized that he was in the same state; the assilians had taken his gear from him.

He rose into an unsteady crouch, the world spinning slightly for a moment before stabilizing, then moved to the closest figure. He rolled them onto their back and sighed as Norag's face appeared. The boy's eyes were closed, but his even breathing showed that while he was still unconscious, he was alive, at least. Amarl moved from body to body, finding the same thing true for each of them. They all lived, but none of them were awake and aware. He frowned as he realized that Andra wasn't among them; either the assilians had taken her somewhere else, or she'd managed to escape somehow. While he certainly hoped for the second option – if she'd gotten away, she'd go gather the other students and nadars, and a rescue could be on the way – he had a feeling that the first was more likely. He'd seen her fall, and he doubted the insects would have approached if she was still up and able to fight. It was a shame, really, because they absolutely needed rescuing.

The cave was roughly hemispherical, the walls solid except for a gash in the rock about four spans wide, which must have been how they were brought into the grotto. However, bars of what looked like natural stone now grew across that crevice, each only a span or so from the next, sealing them inside. The bars weren't all that thick, maybe a finger-width, and with a hammer or even his moon axe, Amarl thought he could have busted through them and freed himself, but with his bare hands, he doubted there was much he could do.

As he looked at the sealed exit, wondering if he could kick his way through, a hint of movement behind it caught his eye. He rose to his feet, waiting as the world spun about once more, then took a step toward the door. One of the assilians stood behind it, the creature's faceted eyes gleaming in the dim light as it watched him.

"Where are we?" Amarl demanded, taking a step closer to the creature. He wasn't expecting a response, of course, so when its voice sounded in his head, it took him by surprise.

<In hive.>

He stared at the creature. "Your hive? Like your home? Why?"

<Blood calls. We come.>

"You said that before. Why do you want our blood?"

<Not want. Blood loud. Must silence.>

That took him by surprise. "You can hear our blood?"

The creature pointed past him, at the other novices' still forms. *<No hear.>* It pointed at Amarl. *<Blood calls. Loud. Bring many hunters. Too many for hive. Must silence.>*

"My blood is loud? What...?" Amarl shook his head; he didn't know what the creature was talking about, but he didn't care. "Why not just kill us?"

<Kill, blood brings hunters. Silence blood first. Then kill.>

"What about Andra? The other girl? Did she escape?"

<No. Blood is strong. Feed many.>

"Y-you ate her?" Amarl gasped.

<Soon. Silence blood. Also feed many.> The creature stepped back, and Amarl rushed to the bars, grabbing them.

"Wait! What about the pact you were talking about?"

<Pact still. Black one promise. Too many hunters.> The creature vanished into the darkness, and Amarl screamed in frustration, shaking the bars but finding them utterly unyielding.

"Well, that was a depressing conversation." Amarl spun to see Burik sitting up, shaking his head and blinking rapidly.

"Burik!" Amarl moved quickly to the other boy and squatted beside him. "Are you okay?"

"My head hurts a bit, and I feel like someone hit me with a stick, but yeah, I'm okay." He looked around at the still figures. "The others – are they...?"

"No, they're all alive," Amarl shook his head. "Just unconscious, I think."

"Well, from what that bug said, we need to wake them up, I think." Burik groaned as he rose to his feet, then winced as his head struck the low ceiling of the cave. He rubbed the top of his head, wincing. "Fucking bugs. At least they could've given us a bigger cave."

Amarl knelt by Meder. "Meder!" he said loudly, shaking her gently. He slapped her cheek a few times. "Meder!" The girl's eyes fluttered, and she groaned as they opened.

"Amarl?" He moved back as she sat up, rubbing her temples and wincing. She looked around. "Where are we?" She stopped and glanced down at herself. "And why are we all naked?"

"The assilians captured us," Amarl said shortly. "We're in their hive, wherever that is. They took all our gear."

She nodded slowly. "Why would they do that? Was it because we left the area?"

"Something about Amarl's blood," Burik rumbled from where he knelt beside Norag. He reached down and clamped a hand over the boy's mouth and nose, and Norag's eyes shot open as he clawed at the hand stopping him from breathing. "That's one more awake."

"Holy shit!" Norag said, sitting up and panting, his eyes wild. He looked around. "Where the hells are we?"

"How about we wake everyone up, then I explain that just once for all of you?" Amarl said dryly.

"Where's Andra?" Meder asked, looking around worriedly. "Did she get away?"

"No. That's something else I have to explain." Amarl grimaced. "I'll wake up Herel; Burik, you get Hadur."

It took only a minute to wake the other two novices, who both came around with the same questions Norag had asked. Hadur also quickly noticed their state of undress and leered openly at Meder – at least until the girl walked over and planted her foot directly in his groin. Hadur curled up and clutched his crotch, whimpering and cursing, and Meder stood over him, glaring.

"We're all in danger of our lives, and you're being a pervert," she snapped at him. "Stop it, or I'll remove your reason for wanting to look in the first place, understand?"

"I think he gets the message," Herel said dryly. "And while I don't approve of the delivery method, I agree with the substance. We need to focus on getting out of here."

"Can you use a working?" Amarl asked Meder.

"No," Norag answered, shaking his head. "I tried already, just to make some better light for us. The sahr field down here – it's strange. It almost feels like it's being regulated, like by a tower, but when I try to use the energy, it refuses to move. It kind of feels like trying to collapse a working into one of the sparring rings."

Burik looked over at Meder. "Hey, you did that, remember?"

"I'd forgotten about that," Norag laughed. "How did you do that, anyway?"

"Poorly," she grimaced. "I burned myself pretty badly, remember?"

"But if you did it once, you might be able to do it again," Herel pointed out. "With the kind of power you used at that lake, you could shatter those bars!"

"It wasn't that much power," Meder shook her head. "Really, the hardest part was getting the air moving to create the wind that pushed the lake spitter back so I could trap it in ice. Removing the heat wasn't difficult at all. It would take a lot more power to fracture stone."

"Does it really need to, though?" Amarl asked. "I mean, if I had a pickaxe or rock hammer, I could break through those bars pretty easily, and

I'm not all that strong."

"That's true. Power density and focus are more important than raw strength." She grimaced. "I'd still need to build an array, though. I don't have that kind of power on my own."

"I can anchor it," Norag volunteered.

"I would actually need almost everyone to anchor it, I think." She looked around. "The reason workings don't work in the sparring ring is that the field inside the ring has too much of its own inertia. It's like trying to make a wave in molasses or tar – it dies out the moment you stop pushing it. I'm guessing it's probably something like that here. I'll need several layers to build up momentum, focusing the power a bit more each layer, then carry the final matrix all the way into the wall."

"So, it's possible?" Herel asked.

"Maybe." She swallowed hard. "But when I did it in the ring, the field's inertia pushed part of the working back at me. That's why I burned my hand. If the same thing happens here, with as much power as I'm thinking we'll need, the recoil could hurt all of us – maybe even kill us."

Herel winced. "Maybe we can find another way, then. Perhaps we could trick one of the assilians into opening the door for us – if one of us pretended to be sick or injured, perhaps…"

"They're planning to eat us, Herel," Amarl said dryly. "Why would they care if we died of an injury first? And do you think just one of them would open the gate and come in here with all of us inside? Or would they do whatever they did to steal our air and knock us all out again?"

The noble grimaced. "Fair point."

"Besides, it's not like we'll be any less dead when those bugs come to 'silence' our blood, whatever that means," Burik added. "I'd rather die trying to escape than be slaughtered like cattle."

"What does it matter?" Hadur muttered, shaking his head.

"What do you mean, what does it matter?" Burik demanded. "You want to get eaten?"

"Let's say this works. Then what? We don't know where we are. We don't know how we got here. For all we know, we're a hundred marches from the Mistway!" The boy's voice tinged with panic and rose in volume the more he spoke. "And we're unarmed and naked! We'll never make it back…OW!"

He fell silent as Herel reached over and backhanded him across the face. "Calm down!" the noble hissed. "The assilians obviously understand Imperial, and if they hear you, they'll come stop us before we're ready!"

"He does raise some good points, though," Norag said dejectedly. "Even if we get out, then what?"

"I have the Tracking skill," Amarl said. "I might be able to use it to backtrack our path here and find a way out."

"And we can't be too far from the Mistway," Meder shook her head. "From what Amarl said, they dragged us, and if they'd dragged us a march over stone, we'd be a lot more cut up and hurt than we are."

"Plus, people don't typically stay unconscious for very long," Burik rumbled. "Minutes at most. We're likely not very far from that lake. If Amarl can track the way we came, we might be able to escape in a matter of minutes."

"The real issue is that building and holding this array is going to be difficult," Meder said slowly. "I mean, incredibly difficult. It's likely that we're going to be exhausted from doing it – assuming we're not all badly wounded from the recoil. We're not going to be in much condition to fight if we run into any resistance on the way out." She looked up at Amarl. "Which is why you shouldn't be part of the array, Amarl."

"What? Meder, I can help…"

She shook her head. "We're unarmed, and only you and Burik have any real unarmed skills…" She glanced at Herel. "Unless one of you three developed some?"

"I have Nicelian Boxing at level 1, as a matter of fact," Herel nodded. "I stopped training it after Nihos…" He glanced at Amarl, then fell silent.

"Amarl's level is somewhat higher," she said delicately.

"Not as high as Burik's," Amarl countered. "He still beats me in sparring, too. He should…"

"He's also much better than you at sahr," Meder cut him off. "You know he is." She hesitated. "In fact, just about everyone but Herel is – and you're a better fighter than he is. You're the only logical choice to deal with anything that comes our way."

Amarl sighed, feeling defeated. "Fine. You're right; I suck at sahr-working. I'll take point."

"Thank you." She took a deep breath. "Okay, for an array of this size, we'll need more than just anchors. You'll each have to move to the correct positions at the right moment to add an extra dimension for stability..."

Amarl stepped back and watched as his friend coached the others through what they would have to do. It amazed him how much she'd learned about sahr and manipulating it; he could barely create a light, and she was talking about six-dimensional matrices like most people would discuss the weather. Sometimes he forgot just how bright Meder was until moments like this. Periteth had been right, so long ago. Amarl had improved his Mind stat until it was fairly close to Meder's, but he would never be able to match her ability to absorb and analyze information. It was part of her in a way that it simply wasn't part of him, and no amount of ithtu boosting would ever change that.

At last, she moved into the center of the irregularly spaced group. "Okay, remember, concentrate, and move to your positions when I tell you," she instructed. "And Hadur, keep your mind on the working where it belongs, got it?"

"Fine," the merchant muttered.

"Good." She looked at Amarl. "I'm going to try and focus the working into the thinnest line I can. It could shatter the bars, but it might only crack them or break them down the center."

"I'll see if I can finish the job if that's the case," he nodded.

"Yes. Whatever happens, though, it's going to be loud, and it'll probably attract attention, so you'll need to move quickly." She took another breath and closed her eyes. "Okay, here we go."

The girl began to move, swaying her body and moving her hands through the air, muttering under her breath while her feet performed an intricate dance. After several seconds, she clapped her hands and pointed to Herel, and the noble moved smoothly half a reach to his left, his hands waving in the air and his eyes closing as he did.

Light drew Amarl's eye, and he looked away from the ritual toward the wall opposite him, behind Herel. Several crystal clusters there began to glow with dull, dark gold light that pulsed in their depths. He looked back at Meder and watched as she continued her smooth dance, then clapped once more and pointed to Hadur, who turned around and walked backward toward the girl two slow steps. The crystals past the merchant boy began to glow as well, while the ones nearest Herel grew brighter, their hue lightening a shade or two as they pulsed.

Meder continued, but Amarl could see the strain building on her face.

Her hands seemed to move through water instead of air, and sweat streamed from her body as if she'd been laboring for an hour, not a couple of minutes. With every gesture and movement, the air around her seemed to thicken and congeal, and the crystals behind Herel and Hadur grew brighter. Her face looked pained, and her hands started to tremble, and Amarl knew she wasn't going to be able to build her array – not unless he did something to help her.

He jogged around the group, taking a few quick steps to reach the wall behind Herel. He held a hand over one of the crystal clusters and felt the warmth radiating from it. Just like the other crystals he'd seen, it was reacting to the building sahr, and he had a feeling that whatever it was doing wasn't helping the girl. He recalled how Meder had first said that the sahr felt heavier, and how Norag said the sahr in the cell wouldn't move...

He tensed, hoping he wasn't making a mistake, then grabbed the crystal and yanked on it, hard. The cluster resisted for a moment, then tore free of the wall, leaving behind a string of thick, sticky fluid that connected it to the wall. The crystal still pulsed in his hand, and he hurled it to the floor as hard as he could. It struck with a loud crack and split into pieces, immediately falling dark and losing its glittery luster.

He grabbed two more crystals, one with each hand, and tore them from the wall. Like the first, they hadn't grown there naturally but were attached with some sticky substance. He shattered the pair, then moved to the next. He worked as swiftly as he could, tearing each glowing crystal free and cracking it against the floor. The shards stabbed his feet, but he ignored the almost incidental pain as he glanced at Meder. She already seemed to be moving more easily, her motions smoother and swifter, and some of the strain eased from her face. He continued to destroy crystals as swiftly as he could, covering the floor in fragments of shattered stone.

As he worked, the power behind him grew, making the air seethe and hum with its intensity. He felt it building, growing stronger by the second. He heard the groans of the novices as they struggled to hold the working in place, felt the energy of it buzzing against his skin. The hair on the back of his neck and arms stood on end, and tingles of power raced down his spine, sending shivers coursing through his body.

He winced and clapped his hands to his ears as a loud boom echoed in the small cave, followed by a series of sharp cracks. He spun and saw Meder lying on the floor, while the other novices sat or knelt around the room, looking dazed and weary. He glanced at the exit, fearful that the working had failed, and the attempt would mean their swift deaths.

Triumph replaced his fear as he saw the crack in the stone, a crack empty of the restraining bars. Chunks of stone littered the space beyond the crevice, evidence of the power of Meder's working.

Movement beyond the crevice warned Amarl, and he rushed forward as two of the assilians ran into the light, brandishing their crystal-tipped spears. The first charged at him, stabbing with its spear, while the other turned toward the nearest novice to the exit, Herel. Amarl's blood raged at the sight of the creatures, and the song of his ithtu swelled in his ears. Anger surged through him as he raced towards the first insect, slipping past its stab and grabbing its extended spear. The creature yanked back on its weapon, pulling Amarl toward it, and he let it happen, using the momentum of its pull to hasten his approach.

It released the spear with two of its hands and grabbed for him, but he slid past its reach and snatched its arm, using Bear Form to lock the limb and twisting with his hips. The chitinous arm resisted for a moment before shattering, and he tore the lower part of the limb free and slashed it across the creature's face, ripping at its eye with its own severed claw. It fell back, and he tore the spear from its lax grip, spinning it in his hands and smashing it across its skull. He stepped past it as it fell and stabbed with the spear, plunging it into the back of the second creature. He yanked the weapon free and spun it once more, bringing the butt end down on the thing's eye and collapsing the faceted orb with a soft pop. Something brushed his leg, and he danced back just as the first insect's claws snapped where his foot had been. He brought the spear around and sank it into the thing's head, then swept the feet out from the other one and stabbed the weapon through its shattered eye.

Movement caught his eye, and he spun to see another of the creatures rush through the crack into the room. The song of his crystal soared in his thoughts as he moved to meet it, batting aside its initial spear thrust and plunging his weapon into its thorax. The insect fell back, and Amarl drove it back through the crevice into the darkness beyond.

The crack in the wall widened swiftly into a tunnel two reaches across, a tunnel filled with charging assilian bodies. Part of Amarl screamed at him to fall back, to use the crack in the wall to limit the number that could attack him, but the song of his crystal and the fire in his blood drowned out that voice. Instead of retreating, he moved forward, taking the battle to his enemy. Unthinkingly, he slipped into the patterns of Water Form, gliding around spear thrusts and slipping aside blows, but even as he fought, he knew the defensive form would fail him. He needed to strike his enemies, to mow them down, to bring the battle to them.

He shifted into Tiger Form, spinning his spear and thrusting it at the nearest insect. His blade tore into its head, dropping it, but another swiftly took its place. He swept the legs from a second, cracked his spear's butt into the head of a third, but no matter how hard he fought, they pushed him back, driving him toward the crack behind him. He knew that if they managed to wedge him into it, he'd fall; the narrow walls would hamper his defense, and they were too close for him to retreat back through it anymore. Fear tickled his mind, but he pushed it away.

He wouldn't fall. His friends needed him, and he wouldn't fail them, no matter what.

As if hearing his silent vow, the song of his ithtu redoubled its fury, practically washing away his thought, and in that moment, he felt his body shift, moving into something that wasn't Water Form or Tiger Form, but held aspects of both. His movements were loose and fluid, flowing around the attacks directed toward him, but each wave of his motions swept him forward, cresting in an attack that struck down an insect. He rode the momentum of a parried thrust, spinning and stabbing his spear into the attacker's chest. He parried a staff blow aimed for his legs and used its force to plunge his weapon into a nearby eye. He was the tide, retreating from the battle only to sweep over it once more, battering inexorably at his foes.

The surge of insects paused, as if straining against the force of his wave, then broke. The creatures began to fall back, but he swept forward, crashing against them. His spear spun and flashed, parried and thrust, each defense an attack, and each attack felling a foe. He slapped aside a hasty blow, cracked his spear's haft into the attacker's knee, then stabbed it as it fell, pinning its body to the stone. As he jerked the weapon free, he looked around and found the corridor empty of living foes; only the bodies of the creatures he'd killed littered the floor.

The song of his crystal faded in his mind, but as it fled, he held onto the feeling of that joining of his forms, the melding of them that held touches of both and was deadlier than either. That was his, now; he would have to practice it, to turn those feelings and sensations into instinctive movements, but he could do that. He couldn't help but grin; the next time he and Ranakar sparred, the old man would be in for a surprise.

CHAPTER 38

"B y all the gods above and below..."

Amarl turned to see Herel standing in the crevice leading into the room, holding one of the creatures' spears in his hands. The noble boy stared at the carnage surrounding the hizeen, his eyes wide and his expression disbelieving.

"What in the hells happened here?"

Amarl looked around at the shattered husks of the assilians spread out around him, then turned back to Herel with a grin.

"Is that some sort of trick question, or do you really not know?"

Herel blinked and seemed to gather himself. "I – I came to help you. I saw you go after the creatures and thought it was foolish; you should have stayed where they could only attack you a few at a time." He shook his head. "Apparently, I was wrong." He looked at Amarl, his eyes wide and slightly fearful. "What are you?"

"The same thing we all are, I think," the smaller boy shrugged. "Or what we're all becoming, at least."

"No. You're something different."

"Maybe. Maybe we're all just a little different. I couldn't have crafted that working that Meder did; could you?"

"No," Herel shook his head. "I had the easiest part, and I could barely hold it." He sighed. "You're right. We all have our talents. It seems that combat is yours."

"Are the others okay?" Amarl asked. "How's Meder?"

"She's sleeping; the others are just resting. They were more drained than I was – like I said, I held the easiest part. They might need a few minutes to recover."

"I don't know if we have that." Amarl kicked aside a body as he walked back toward the crevice. As he touched it, he felt its trapped life force calling out to him, begging him to claim it. He ignored its call, though; he had no way to carry an extra crystal, and he didn't think that leaving them behind was a good idea. He walked past the bodies, and Herel stepped backward out of the way, allowing him to pass. The smaller boy entered the cave, peering at the other novices.

"It's clear out here, but I don't know how long that'll last. We need to get moving."

"Meder's still out," Norag said wearily.

"Is she okay?"

"She's breathing normally," Burik said.

"I think she's just exhausted," Norag added. "The effort it had to have taken to carry that final matrix into the stone with all the power it held ..." He shook his head. "I wouldn't have wanted to do it."

"None of the rest of us could have," Burik chuckled. The larger boy rose wearily to his feet. "Don't worry. I can carry her."

"Don't be foolish," Hadur snapped. "You're the best fighter of us all. How are you going to fight with her on your shoulders?"

"Still better than you do," Burik growled.

"I can carry her," Norag said tiredly. Burik gave him a sharp glance, but the boy held up his hands, shaking his head. "I'll behave, I promise. I'm worried about dying, Burik, not about my hands wandering. Besides, the high god frowns on those who take liberties with women without their knowledge. I don't think we need his curse on top of everything else, do we?"

"If you can carry her, go ahead," Amarl cut in. "First, though, we need a light. Can you make one that won't blind everybody?"

"I think so. I saw what Meder did, only lighting half her staff. I think I can do the same to one of these spears."

"Good. Do that to mine." He handed the weapon to the boy, then looked at the others. "Everyone else, grab your own spear as we leave. There are plenty in the tunnel outside, and it's better than being unarmed."

Burik nodded and took a step, wincing as a broken piece of crystal cracked beneath his foot. He looked around at the shards of stone littering the floor, then back at Amarl.

"What was that all about, by the way?"

"I think they were interfering with Meder's working somehow. They started glowing when she began crafting, and she was struggling until I started smashing them. It got easier for her once I broke a bunch of them."

Norag moved to an intact cluster and touched it curiously. His lips moved, and the crystal began to glow slightly, winking out a moment later when he stepped away from it.

"Amazing," he breathed. "I think these crystals work like the towers, stabilizing sahr!" He glanced around. "No wonder I couldn't collapse a working before. With all these crystals, the sahr field would be basically immovable."

"They're just glued to the wall," Amarl offered. "I think the insects put them in here so that no one can collapse workings in this room."

"They must have done it in a hurry," Herel observed, reaching out and touching a sticky spot on the wall, then making a disgusted face. "Otherwise, they could have protected the crystals better."

"Why are we talking about this?" Hadur demanded. "We need to get out of here!"

"He's right," Herel agreed. "We don't have the luxury of standing around talking. We need to move."

"Yeah, we do." Amarl took back the now glowing spear from Norag, watching as the boy bent down and awkwardly but cautiously slid the unconscious Meder over his shoulders. He rose slowly to his feet, grimacing slightly as he straightened.

"You're sure you've got her?" Burik asked in a tone of mild concern.

"Yeah. She's not that heavy, and I'm used to carting stone for my father. He's a sculptor, you know. I might need to stop and rest at some point, though."

"Burik or I can switch off with you if you need it," Amarl nodded.

"You'll both be needed if more of the assilians attack us," Herel shook his head. "I'll relieve Norag if necessary." Amarl eyed the noble suspiciously, but Herel gave the hizeen a steady gaze. "You have my word that I will respect her as I carry her, hizeen. As Norag said, survival is our only goal, here."

Amarl stared at him for a moment before nodding. "Okay. I'll lead. Herel, you're behind me, Norag in the middle, then Hadur, and Burik in the back. We move as silently as possible. The goal is to get out of here, back to the restricted areas, and alert the nadars."

"What about Andra?" Burik asked. "If we free her, we'll all be a lot more likely to get out of this."

Amarl hesitated, then nodded. "That's true, but I don't know if that's possible. Let's focus on getting out ourselves, first, and worry about Andra if and when we have to."

He turned and led the way out into the hall, hearing Herel move into place behind him. As Norag squeezed sideways through the crack, the boy stopped and stared in amazement at the carnage before him, walking slowly out into the mass of dead insects.

"Amarl – you did this?"

Amarl didn't answer; he barely heard the boy's comment in the first place. The tunnel seemed filled with the sound of ithtu crying out to be harvested, the sound of life begging to be gathered and collected. The noise had been a faint murmur earlier, but it seemed that the longer he left it alone, the more insistent it became. Unthinkingly, he knelt and placed a hand on the creatures to each side of him, willing their energies to come to him. Crackling filled the air as two golden crystals rose from the bodies. The crystals were flatter than usual, spreading out in a ring of spikes rather than growing up in a treelike shape, and Amarl picked one up and examined it curiously.

ANALYSIS REPORT
ITEM: ITHTU CRYSTAL
RANK: WEAK
POWER DENSITY: 6
SOURCE: ASSILIAN (SAPIENT)

Harvesting the two crystals seemed to shatter the hold the overwhelming song of the fallen had on him, and he rose to his feet, carrying a crystal in his hand. He closed his eyes and shook his head, pushing aside the insistent clamoring, doing his best to tune out the noise. He glanced back at the others and saw them staring at him in silence, watching him wordlessly. He held the crystal up with a sigh.

"Anyone need another ithtu?" he asked somewhat lamely.

"Amarl – you killed all these?" Burik rumbled from the back of the line.

"Yeah," Amarl sighed, rubbing the back of his neck but adding nothing more. He expected Burik to ask questions or comment, but the larger boy simply nodded.

"Bullshit." Hadur's mouth was set in a hard line as he shook his head. "I saw you fight Herel in that duel. You're not that good. I'll bet the working took out most of these things, and you just finished them off."

"Yeah, good thing I don't give a fuck what you think, asshole," Amarl snorted contemptuously before tossing the crystal to the ground.

"Are you just going to leave those here?" Herel asked somewhat disbelievingly. "Those are Weak crystals – and decently powerful ones, too. We should bring them with us!"

"How, Herel? You don't have any way to carry them – at least, no way that I want to think about."

"I can carry my spear with one hand…"

"And if we're attacked by something like those stone borers? Or we get ambushed by the insects?" Amarl shook his head. "Are you really willing to die just for the chance at a Weak crystal?"

Herel sighed. "No, obviously not. It just feels – wrong to leave them behind."

"Yeah, I know, but we don't have much choice." Amarl turned away from the group and led them deeper into the tunnels, his eyes flicking back and forth between watching the ground and scouting the passage ahead.

Once they cleared the battle site, he found the trail of their incoming passage easily enough. The hard stone floor didn't take impressions, obviously, but the layer of dust and fine gravel coating it did. He couldn't make out the insects' tracks – their finely clawed feet didn't disturb the floor enough to leave a trace he could see – but the clear paths where bodies had been dragged were obvious enough. He led them through the silent tunnels, following that path and hoping that it led to an exit – and a nearby one.

The first ambush came after only a couple minutes. As he passed one of the side tunnels, three dark shapes exploded from it and swarmed toward him. He reacted instantly, his body slipping into the stance of his new form, sweeping his spear to the side to deflect a pair of thrusts aimed at his chest. He rode the momentum of those strikes, using it to carry the butt of his spear into the backwards pointing knee of one insect, shattering it and bringing it down. He ducked a hasty slash from a second, spinning to jab his spear into the chest of the attacker, then whipped the weapon free and stepped over a low thrust from the third, cracking the end of his spear into its head and caving in its bulbous eye. He slipped to the side, avoiding a stab from the creature he'd first taken down, and used the movement to plunge his spear into its featureless face. A quick thrust finished off the one-eyed assilian, and he stepped back, holding his spear ready, scanning for more threats.

"By the One…"

Norag's whispered curse echoed loudly in the now-silent tunnel as the boy shook his head, his expression awed. "How the fuck did you do that?"

Amarl shrugged. "They're not really great fighters," he said deprecatingly. "They're strong, but that's about it. Burik could have done the same thing."

"I probably could have killed all three," the larger boy laughed. "It wouldn't have looked like that, though. You looked like you were dancing with them, Amarl." He looked contemptuously at Hadur. "Still think he didn't kill the ones outside our cell?"

"There's no time for this," Herel broke in. "You can fawn over Amarl later. For now, we need to keep moving."

"He's right," Amarl agreed, turning back to head down the tunnel. He really didn't want to talk about how he'd killed the insects. He wasn't completely certain himself, and he certainly couldn't explain how the song of his ithtu suddenly made his two forms click together into something more. Staying silent and scouting ahead was simpler and easier.

The next attack was somewhat more serious. As they neared an intersection of two tunnels, Amarl spotted five of the insects arrayed before them, spears leveled as they waited for the students to approach. He took a step toward them but stopped as Herel put a hand on his shoulder.

"It's too easy," the noble whispered, shaking his head. "You've killed far more than this already; why would they just stand there and wait to be slaughtered?"

Amarl nodded and looked back at Burik, catching the boy's eye. He pointed two fingers at his own eyes and then swept the fingers around at the tunnels, and his friend nodded in understanding. Amarl moved forward cautiously, his spear extended, and his body relaxed, with Herel beside him. The group made it all of a reach before the wall beside Amarl crumbled, revealing a shallow cave behind it and a pair of the insect warriors that leaped at him, their claws grasping as they attempted to bear him to the ground. Behind him, he heard Norag cry in alarm and Burik curse, and he assumed they'd been attacked, as well.

He reacted without thinking, crashing his spear into one, then dropping the weapon and slipping into Bear Form as the second closed with him. He grabbed two of its extended arms and twisted, slamming his hips into its midsection and bending at the waist. The lighter creature's claws scrabbled against his skin as it flew over him and crashed into the opposite wall. The one he'd knocked down first scrambled to its feet, but he grasped one of its nearer arms and spun, dragging it along and smashing its face into the stone wall. He bent down and scooped up his fallen spear, ending the two creatures with swift thrusts, then spun to face the five who'd lured them into the ambush, finding them still standing and waiting for him. He glanced behind him and saw Herel and Hadur dealing with two of the creatures, while Burik put down the second of the insects attacking him before moving to help the others.

Satisfied that his friends were safe, he turned and ran toward the remaining five creatures, his spear twirling as he swept toward them. He realized his mistake the moment he stepped into the cavern and found the air once again stolen from his lungs, just as it had been when they captured him. The five insects moved at last, charging toward him, trying to bring him down before he could retreat into the air-filled tunnel behind him. The song of his ithtu suddenly soared in his mind as he met their attack, spinning and twisting to strike at them, stabbing into heads and thoraxes. His chest ached and his head pounded; his spear grew heavier by the second, and darkness framed his vision, but in less than a minute, all five lay dead around him, and he quickly moved back into the tunnel, greedily sucking in a deep breath of air.

"Everyone okay?" he panted slightly as his laboring heart slowly returned to its normal rhythm.

"Minor scratches, nothing worse," Burik reported. "Like you said, they're strong, but they're light and not very agile. They aren't hard to take down."

Amarl nodded. "I couldn't breathe in that room ahead of us," he told them. "Looks like this was a trap; they probably hoped that we'd try to break through the group there and get stuck in the room, where we'd pass out again."

Herel's eyes narrowed. "That suggests a significant intelligence in the creatures," he noted.

"Well, they can talk, so they have to be at least somewhat smart," Amarl shrugged. "The point is, we have to watch out for more traps like this one." He looked at the passage. "I'm going to go see how far the effect extends, then I'll be back."

He took a deep breath, then moved back into the cavern, noting the sudden silence that descended over him as he stepped into the airless region. As he walked, his eyes scanned the walls and floor, seeing that the crystals jutting from the walls glowed faintly golden. He guessed that meant that whatever the bugs were doing to drain the air used sahr; hopefully, the crystals and the sudden silence would serve to warn him of traps like that in the future. His eyes caught an anomaly on the ground, and he stopped and knelt to examine the tracks before him. He nodded, walked to the edge of the cave and stepped into the tunnel beyond, gratified as he inhaled a lungful of air. He made another quick check on the way back, then walked quickly back to the others.

"Okay, it seems to be limited to just the cave. I could breathe in the tunnel past it, and it looks like that's the way out. I could hear water running in the other tunnel, and I'm hoping that means it leads out into that cavern by the lake."

"I'm sensing a 'but' coming," Burik laughed.

"Yeah, and it's a big 'but'," Amarl grinned before his face turned serious once more. "I saw signs of someone else being dragged deeper into the tunnels, over that way." He pointed away from the hive's exit. "I'm pretty sure it was Andra. They took her somewhere else in the hive."

"Then we should go rescue her," Burik said immediately.

"No, we should escape while we can," Hadur shook his head.

"I agree," Herel nodded.

"Of course, you would want to save your own skin," Burik said contemptuously.

"Obviously, I want to live through this," Herel replied coolly. "However, that's not the point. We don't know where Andra is, how many guards she might have, or how she's being held. If it's in a cell like ours, how will we get her out with Meder unconscious?"

"So, you just want to leave her here?" Burik asked disbelievingly. "They said they were going to eat her!"

"No, I suggest we go get the nadars. One ithtar could probably clear this entire place out in minutes and rescue her with no problem."

"Unless she's dead by the time we get back!" Burik shook his head.

"That's a good point," Norag said slowly. "It took us an hour to get to the lake, and the nadars are camped twenty minutes or more from Andra's campsite. Maybe we should at least see if we can rescue her; if we can't, and she's in a cell like ours, then we could get her a weapon so she can defend herself until we can get someone here who can help."

"And if we're ambushed again, but this time it's by double the number of creatures?" Hadur demanded. "Then we'll all be dead, and how will that help anyone?"

"Fine. You and Herel run away. The rest of us will look for Andra." Burik glared at Hadur, but the merchant boy matched the expression with a glare of his own.

"That would be stupid," Herel shook his head. "Hadur and I would be killed before we reached Andra's camp. We aren't using our preferred weapons, and neither of us can fight as well as you or Amarl can." He turned and looked at Amarl. "Two of us want to stay. Two of us want to go. That leaves you as the tiebreaker. What should we do?"

Amarl rubbed his eyes tiredly. "I want to save Andra," he said slowly, and Burik grinned triumphantly. Amarl held up a restraining hand as he continued. "But we're all tired, hurt, and using weapons that most of us aren't trained well on. I think we need to get out of here while we can."

Herel nodded, and Burik's face crumpled in disappointment. He opened his mouth to speak, but Amarl cut him off before he could. "Burik, Meder's still unconscious, and we can't guarantee that we can protect her. If we hit another of those ambushes, she could be killed. Do you want to risk her to go look for Andra?"

"No," the big boy sighed, dropping his head. "It just – it feels wrong leaving her here."

"I agree. And I don't intend to."

"Exactly," Herel nodded. "We'll head back to the hunting area as fast as possible..."

"No," Amarl interrupted. "I mean..." He stopped and took a deep breath. "I mean, while the rest of you go looking for the nadars, I'm going to try and find her."

"What?" Burik shouted, his voice echoing in the tunnel and making everyone wince. "Hells, no! You can't be here alone, Amarl!"

"I have the Hiding and Silent Movement skills, Burik. None of the rest of you do."

"Fuck that. I'll go with you. We'll find her together."

"And who will keep Meder safe on the trip back to the nadars? Do you really want to trust her life to the others?" Burik made a sour face, and Amarl continued. "I'm just going to follow the trail until I see where Andra is, and if it's possible to break her out. If she's in a cage like ours, then I'll get her a weapon or two and tell her about the crystals; maybe if she breaks them, she can escape on her own with sahr. If it's something worse, or I can't help her, then I'll get the hells out of here." He shook his head. "Either way, I'll hopefully be fifteen or twenty minutes behind you, and with you carrying Meder, I can catch up quickly enough."

"And if there's another ambush like this one?" Burik demanded.

"Then I'll deal with it." Amarl shook his head. "Burik, Andra's in this mess because she helped us. I can't just leave her here, but I can't risk Meder's life, either. This is the only chance to save them both."

Burik stared at him for a moment, then stepped forward and grabbed his shoulders, pulling the smaller boy into a sudden embrace. Amarl stood there for a moment, startled, before reaching out and patting the taller boy awkwardly on the back a couple times. Burik stepped back, still holding Amarl at arm's length, and nodded decisively.

"Be careful. Don't die."

"I'll do my best," Amarl grinned at the older boy.

"Do better than that." Burik turned and looked at the others. "Norag, light up my spear the way you did Amarl's. Everyone else, here's the deal. When we get into the lake cavern, we're taking the tunnels as fast as Norag can handle. Anything attacks us, we cut through it as quickly as possible. Norag, when you get tired, you and Herel switch, but otherwise, we stop for nothing. If you fall behind, you're dead. Got it?"

The others nodded, and Burik looked at Amarl one last time. "Good luck." He turned and strode into the cavern, with Hadur and Norag right behind him. Herel stopped at the edge of the cave and looked at Amarl.

"I was wrong about you," he said quietly. "I thought you were selfish and lazy, someone who only cared about himself. I was wrong, and I'm sorry."

Amarl nodded. "I always thought you were arrogant and spoiled, and you took yourself too seriously." He grinned at the noble boy. "I still see no reason to think otherwise, but other than that, you're not too bad."

Herel barked a short laugh. "You might be right, hizeen. It's hard not to be arrogant when you're as attractive and talented as I am, after all." He paused, then nodded and stepped into the cavern, following behind the others.

Amarl waited until they disappeared in the opposite tunnel, then took a deep breath and entered the hive.

CHAPTER 39

Amarl moved as silently as he could through the dark tunnels, which was fairly quietly. His bare feet made no sound on the stone, and he moved carefully to avoid dislodging loose gravel or stones that would rattle in the silence. He watched the ground for traces of Andra's passage but also kept an eye on the walls, ceiling, and everything else he could. He eyed the crystals in the walls carefully, hoping that their glow might reveal an assilian trap or ambush, knowing that there almost had to be one waiting for him somewhere ahead.

He'd lied to the others, of course. Well, he hadn't lied, but he'd deliberately misled them. He'd told them about his skills, implying that he could use them to slip past the insects, but he knew that wouldn't be possible. The light he carried would give him away, if nothing else, and he certainly wasn't about to try to navigate the tunnels in the dark. Plus, from what the assilians said before, he couldn't hide no matter what he did. They could hear his blood, somehow – and that was the real reason he wanted the others to go on their own.

Twice he'd gone on a hunt, and twice he'd found himself almost relentlessly attacked by the natives of those realms. Both times, other groups around him found themselves without anything to hunt, while he and his teammates faced assault after assault. If the assilians were right, and they could sense his blood somehow, then he had to assume other creatures could, as well. Without him, the others might have a much easier time making it back to the Mistway to get help. Of course, without them, his chances of getting out of the hive were a lot smaller – unless he could find Andra and free her, of course.

The first ambush came minutes after he'd separated from the group. Assilians exploded from the walls behind him, charging at him and stabbing with their crystal-tipped spears. He fell back, barely managing to sweep aside a pair of thrusts, then dropped into his new form and counterattacked. The three insects worked well together, their thrusts and slashes jabbing at him without interfering with one another, but he slipped past each blow and dealt swift death to his attackers. All three fell in less than a minute, and he left them behind, ignoring their lingering essence as it cried out to be gathered and collected.

Insects attacked him from all sides as he moved through the tunnels. They struck from side passages that he swore were empty; they emerged from pits in the walls and floor that concealed them; they swarmed at him when he entered open spaces. He slaughtered them each time, but he knew he couldn't keep it up forever. The song of his ithtu rang in his mind, banishing much of his weariness, but his muscles still ached and trembled from exhaustion. Scratches and cuts burned along his skin where spears and claws had laid open his flesh when he dodged too slowly or missed an attack from the side or behind. The creatures didn't seem to care that he killed them; they threw themselves at him every chance they got, no matter how many he cut down.

His spear shattered, and he grabbed a new one, carrying the broken end of the last one so he had a light. His feet burned from where shards of broken crystal and shattered stone had cut into his soles, and when he glanced back, he saw dark splotches on the floor where he left a trail of blood. He grimaced but pressed forward. It couldn't be helped. There was nowhere to go but ahead.

Light in front of him caught his eye, and he slowed, dropping his chunk of spear shaft and creeping forward on throbbing feet. The tunnel split ahead, and the light came from his left. He stopped and listened down each tunnel. Silence reigned to the right, but to the left, he heard soft sounds that he couldn't quite make out. Something clicked, the sound of stone on stone, and a soft rushing sound like flowing water filled his ears. His eyes glanced down at the floor; as he feared, Andra's trail led down that passage.

Taking a deep breath, he headed to the left. The tunnel continued to curve, then suddenly spread out into a vast cavern at least ten reaches wide and four high. Stone pillars and jagged cones of rock rose along the sides of the cavern, glittering in the light of hundreds of clumps of moss that clung to the ceiling overhead. The far wall of the cavern, twenty or more reaches away, sloped upward to a narrow horizontal crack in the stone, from which a sheet of water flowed down to cascade into a wide pool that stretched the width of the cavern and extended three reaches into the cavern.

The cavern sloped upward toward the center, creating an elevated section around five reaches to a side in the middle. A ring of creatures surrounded that section, looking like assilians but larger, with jagged spikes and serrated edges jutting out of their armor. The figures held spears similar to the one Amarl clutched but obviously more finely crafted, with flattened blades rather than hexagonal points and spikes jutting out from each side. The creatures stood at least two spans taller than the hizeen, and they looked far more dangerous than any of the insects he'd faced so far, dangerous enough that his first instinct was to slip back down the tunnel and retreat the way he'd come. He suppressed that instinct when he looked past the creatures to the central area beyond.

No crystals decorated the walls of the room. Instead, a single, massive clump of crystals that looked like someone had packed hundreds of the things together into a smooth, rounded boulder jutted up from the center of the flat space. A figure lay bent backward across that rock, a figure that Amarl recognized at once. Her light brown hair fell back against the boulder, her naked breasts jutted up toward the ceiling overhead, and her hands stretched out to the side, fastened to the crystal with thin bands of some sticky, fibrous substance. Similar fetters held her feet against the floor, and a gag of the same material plugged her mouth, keeping her from crying out. Her muscles rippled as she struggled vainly to free herself, screaming into her gag as the creature hovering over her reached out to touch her chest with a long, clawed hand.

That creature stood half a reach taller than Amarl, with long, segmented arms. Two of those arms ended in surprisingly flexible claw-fingers, while the other two formed bladelike appendages that looked wickedly sharp. Its outer shell glittered with golden flecks the same way the surrounding crystals did. Its head was longer and narrower than the assilians he'd seen so far, its eyes smaller and less protruding. The mandibles jutting from its skull looked powerful, though, as they moved in and out, opening and closing as the thing ran its finger along Andra's bare skin.

<You have come at last.> The words echoed in Amarl's skull, the thought clearer and more complex than the messages he'd gotten from the assilians before. *<I wondered if you would. What drew you here, I wonder? Affection for this one? Duty?>* The creature hesitated for a moment before adding, *<Or is it your blood, demanding death and conquest?>*

Andra blinked in surprise at the creature and looked around, spotting Amarl as he emerged from the tunnel into the cavern. Her eyes widened, and she began to scream into her gag, her voice muffled and her words lost to him but the panic and fear in them clear. He ignored her and kept his eyes on the tall creature bending over her.

"Why do you keep talking about my blood?" he asked. "Is it because

I'm half-spirit?" He continued to walk closer; as he did, the creatures surrounding Andra shifted, tightening their ranks to keep him out.

<Your blood calls to us. It calls to every creature nearby. Its song is one of challenge and battle, a challenge that cannot be ignored. It must be silenced before it brings greater hunters down upon the hive.>

"You want me to leave? Fine. Give me the girl, and she and I will head back to Askula, and I won't return."

<That chance was given. You were warned, and you chose not to heed that warning. For cycles, you have traversed the warrens around the hive, and the scent and sound of your blood has traveled far. If you leave, the hunters will still come, following your trail, and they will destroy the hive to pursue it. It must be silenced. Only then will the hunters abandon their hunt.>

"Silenced how?" he asked. He walked sideways, circling the central ring, putting the stone pillars to his back.

<The power that makes your blood sing must be cut free, just as we have done for this one.> The thing touched Andra again. *<When your blood is silent, then it can be spilled, and your meat given to the hive. It is the only way.>*

"I'm not going to just let you take me," Amarl said, spinning his spear. "Let Andra and me go, and I won't have to kill any of you."

<Soldiers die. That is their purpose. I will make more with the blood and meat you both give me. And you will not kill many. Your kind never last long when we steal the air.>

Amarl's eyes widened, and he sucked in a deep breath as the creature reached out and touched the crystal Andra was bound to. The crystal lit up with a bright, golden glow, and everything went silent once more as the air was sucked from around him. At the same moment, the soldiers swept forward, crashing into him in a wall of spears and hardened, bladelike shells.

Amarl cut quickly to the left, angling toward one edge of the insects' line. The song of his crystal roared in his mind, pushing away fear and doubt, and he settled into his new form without thought. The first creature swept toward him, and he quickly parried its attack, knocking the blow to the side and spinning with it. The soldier was stronger than the lesser assilians had been, but that just added power to Amarl's counter as he plunged his spear into its thorax. The insect's shell splintered and collapsed, and it fell as a gout of clear fluid spurted from its chest and splattered on the stone floor.

He ducked beneath a spear thrust and met his attacker with an upward stab that tore into its head. He shifted sideways to allow a strike to slide past him and swept his spear horizontally, shattering the creature's knee. He rose to his feet and parried a blow, slipping his spear around the attacker's and plunging it into the thing's thorax, then spun to the side, letting a blow glide by him and jamming his spear into the assailant's faceted eye.

Even as he fought, though, he knew he was in trouble. The soldiers were faster and stronger than the other insects had been, and they had more skill with their weapons. A spear slid across his arm as he dodged a bit too slowly, opening a gash below his shoulder. Another swept across his back, leaving a burning sensation behind, while a clawed arm slashed at his stomach, tearing a shallow wound that bled too freely. He was forced to fall back, away from the cavern's entrance toward the distant pool. His chest began to ache, and his head started to throb as stars flashed in his vision. The song of his crystal raged in his mind, soaring through his blood and pushing aside the pain of his wounds, but it wasn't enough. He blocked too slowly, and a spear plunged into his side, sending pain flaring through his body and making him stumble as he saw death approaching.

Beneath his heart, deep in the center of him, something stirred, trying to wake, and new strength flooded his muscles. He struck at the soldiers with renewed vigor, the ache in his chest fading and his vision clearing as he stabbed and slashed at the insects. He twisted past a blow and answered with a thrust that ripped through a skull, shattering his spear in the process. He cracked the broken end against a clawed arm, crunching the elbow, then snatched that creature's weapon free and rammed it into its former wielder's head.

He moved forward instead of back, driving the soldiers closer to the center of the room. They charged toward him, sweeping out to try and take him from the sides, but he moved faster than they could, flanking his flankers and spilling their blood onto the stone. The rocky floor was slippery with the clear fluid, but Amarl's footing never faltered as he tore through the creatures. At last, the last of them fell, pierced on his blade, its head torn open and spilling its brains onto the stone.

<*The blood sings louder.*> He looked up and saw the tall creature moving away from Andra and walking toward him. Its abdomen was larger than the others and looked swollen, but it moved without seeming discomfort or awkwardness. <*It draws us to battle and leads you to slaughter. The hunters approach. This must end.*>

Amarl would have replied, but his burning lungs and throbbing skull reminded him that speech was useless. His vision flashed and darkened, and he staggered as the creature descended the slope toward him. He raised his spear defiantly, stumbling slightly as he did.

<Why do you fight so? There is but one end to this. Submit and...>

The creature fell silent as Amarl summoned what little strength he had and rushed at it, his spear spinning in his hands. The creature set itself, its blades raised, and it slashed at Amarl, moving faster than it should have been able to, faster than should have been possible for a creature of that size. Its blow missed as Amarl dove beneath it, his blood-slicked body sliding on the stone and carrying him behind the creature. He rolled to his feet, using his momentum to sweep his spear around, pouring every ounce of power he could into the swing, willing it to destroy his target.

The spear struck with a crash of glass shattering as it tore through the massive crystal. The haft shattered, splintering into fragments, but the damage was done. Andra's unconscious form slid free as the crystal exploded beneath her, the shards spraying out from under her and coating the stone floor near the entrance tunnel. The crystal's light winked out instantly, and sound rushed back into Amarl's ears as the air returned. He sucked in a deep breath, then another, gasping as his grateful lungs drew in the air.

Something slammed into him, knocking him off the center platform, and he crashed to the ground over a reach away. He rolled with the impact, then screamed as something sharp stabbed into his shoulder, pinning him to the floor. He looked up and saw the final insect standing over him, clutching one of the fallen spears and skewering it through his arm.

<What have you done?> The creature's voice rang in his mind, no longer dry and dispassionate but filled with anger and fear. *<You have doomed the hive!>*

"I – don't – care," Amarl gasped, grasping the spear and trying vainly to pull it out of his shoulder. "You attacked me first!"

<You threaten us with your existence! Now, you destroy the mask that hides us! The hunters will come, and soon, and we will all be food!>

"Then at least I know – that I'm taking you with me," he panted.

<So be it. Your blood will spill, and the hunters will come, and we will all be meat. There is no other choice.>

The creature's blade swept up, then sped toward Amarl, flashing at him with terrible speed. He forced himself to watch as it swept toward his neck. The blade arm would cut deep into his throat, possibly decapitating him, and there was nothing he could do to stop it...

The blade suddenly slowed to a crawl in midair, and Amarl's eyes widened as a spear shaft swept above him, crashing into the thing's chest and knocking it backward. Its flight tore the blade arm from his chest, and he rolled away, scrambling to his feet as quickly as he could. He grinned as he saw Andra standing in front of him, torn fetters dangling bits of crystal hanging from her wrists and ankles as she leveled a spear at the tall creature's chest.

<How? Your blood – it was silenced!>

"I've got more than one crystal, asshole." The girl looked over her shoulder at Amarl, who winced as he saw her bleeding and reddened lips from where she'd apparently torn her gag free. "Grab a spear. Let's kill this thing and see what you can harvest from it."

The creature let out a silent scream and launched itself at Andra, but its charge slowed to a crawl as her power wrapped around it. She stepped forward, stabbing with her spear, but the crystal point skittered and slid across the thing's shell without leaving so much as a mark. She knocked aside a lazy blow, then tried again, plunging her spear into its eye to no effect.

Amarl raced to his left and snatched up a fallen spear. His blood surged, and his crystal's song rang in his ears as he charged into the battle. He hefted the spear and stabbed, driving it with all his strength into the creature's side, and he grinned as the crystalline point punched through its armor and slid into its body. The thing shrieked silently and swept toward him, but he easily ducked beneath its slash and stabbed it again, piercing its thorax and letting a jet of clear blood splatter onto the stone floor.

The creature's armor suddenly glowed with a deep, golden light, and a pulse of force ripped out from it, slamming into the pair of students. Amarl tumbled backward, barely managing to turn his fall into a roll, and came to his feet as the creature swarmed toward him, now freed of Andra's ability. He ducked beneath one slash and brought his spear up to block a second, using the momentum to stab at the beast's head. The creature slipped to the side, easily dodging his blow, and responded with a double slash, crossing its arms and opening them swiftly. Amarl ducked and brought his spear up to block, but the blade-arms glowed with a golden light and cut through the spear shaft, severing it and leaving him weaponless.

Amarl rolled back as the creature lunged toward him, ducking and dodging its blows. It was faster than him, but his smaller size made him harder to hit, and he barely managed to stay ahead of its strikes. He couldn't block, and without a weapon, there was no way to attack. Unthinkingly, he slipped fully into Water Form, gliding past its strikes and redirecting its force. The creature was strong, though, and faster than him; he couldn't avoid its attacks forever, and soon, it would spill his blood out onto the stone to mingle with the clear fluid pooling across the floor.

The song of his ithtu swelled in his mind, but he knew that its power wasn't going to be enough. Desperately, he drew on it, pulling its energy into him, trying to make himself faster to stay ahead of its attacks and give Andra a chance to use her ability on it. The power surged within him, flowing into his body, and his ithtu's refrain thundered in his thoughts. As it swept over him, he gave himself to it, letting the power utterly fill his body. Fire raced through his veins, and silver light burned beneath his skin. Still, he drew more power as the creature's body glowed golden once more, and its attacks came even faster and more furiously.

Deep in his chest, the thing that stirred before shifted restlessly. His burning blood poured around it, and he felt that energy sinking into it, plunging into its depths and rousing it even further. His chest lurched as the thing within it stirred – and finally awoke.

Power flared in him, rushing through his body in a torrent, but instead of searing him from within, the energy poured into his chest and filled the thing within him. He felt it stretching out, rippling through his body. It flowed down the center of his bones, raced along his nerves, flooded his veins. Every tiny part of his body felt charged with power, power that flowed from the space beneath his heart and surged into him in waves.

He staggered as his distraction allowed the creature to land a blow, and its blade arm slashed across his chest. A surge of energy rose from his center to where the blow landed, and while it cut a thin, deep line across his chest, the wound was only skin-deep, rather than tearing deep into the muscle as it should have. The creature froze for a moment in surprise, and in that moment, Amarl dropped back into his Water Form stance. Power flowed through his body into that stance, and he stood ready when the thing struck again.

Its blades struck with terrible swiftness, but he flowed around them easily enough. He nudged a blade, knocking it into the other and ruining a follow-up slash, then kicked out at an ankle, forcing the creature to shift its stance to hold its balance. Its body glowed golden once more, and its speed increased, but Amarl glided ahead of it, letting its attacks push him back, drawing a bit of momentum off each strike and using it to fuel his short, swift counters. That, he realized, was the point of Water Form – water could be pushed and moved easily, but it always returned, using the strength of its attacker to flow over and destroy whatever opposed it.

He shifted from Water Form into his new style, and his attacks gained in power and ferocity as he stole more of the creature's own strength and turned that against it. His hands grabbed its arms above the blades and pulled; his feet darted out, cracking into its armored shell; his knees and elbows slammed into it, never inflicting any damage but always keeping it off-balance. The creature's attacks became fiercer and wilder as it struggled to touch him, knowing that it could kill him in an instant if it could just reach him, and he felt the momentum of the battle building and shifting, as the wave of tiny attacks he'd built up reached its peak and crested.

The creature stumbled as it lost its balance, and his foot slid out and knocked its leg sideways. It tripped over its own leg, and it jammed its bladed arms down into the stone to keep from falling. Amarl flowed forward, power roiling in his hands as he slammed his open palms into the joint between the thing's thorax and abdomen. It screamed as its armor crumpled and it flew backward, soaring through the air. It crashed and rolled, clear blood pouring from the shattered hole in its shell, but as it stood, its movements slowed to a crawl.

Andra stepped up in front of the creature, ignoring the blood that streamed from a gash in the side of her head. She stabbed out with her spear, driving it into the hole Amarl had opened in the beast's stomach, and he heard another silent scream as her weapon sank down into its abdomen. She looked back over her shoulder at Amarl, her face strained, and pain written clearly in her expression.

"I can't hold it long," she gritted. "Hurry up and kill it so you can harvest it!"

He nodded and raced toward the creature, snatching up the severed head of his fallen spear and gripping it like a short sword. As he neared, the thing took a swipe at him, but he ducked under the blow and came up behind it. He grabbed one of its arms and jumped, hauling himself up and driving the spearpoint into the back of the thing's head. It shrieked once, silently, then collapsed as blood jetted from the wound in its skull.

Amarl landed heavily as the creature fell and lay on his back on the cold stone, panting, his eyes closed. His body ached and throbbed; his skin stung and burned from the cuts lining it; exhaustion threatened to sweep over him in a wave. He wanted nothing more than to fall asleep for a week or so, maybe two. As he lay there, he pulled up his skill status; he wanted to see if his new form showed up there, or if it was just a combination of Tiger and Water Forms.

Skills Report	
Changed Skills	
Bear Form	5 (+1)
Hiding	5 (+1)
Nameless Form	2 (+2)
Silent Movement	5 (+1)
Spear Fighting	1 (+1)
Tiger Form	5 (+1)
Tracking	5 (+1)
Water Form	5 (+1)

He couldn't help but grin as he read the screen. He'd gained two new skills – Spear Fighting and his new form – and his form was already at level two. He guessed that was because it melded two forms he'd already gotten to a decent level, so it started higher than it should have. The forms themselves leveled up, as well, which they shouldn't have according to Ranakar, but he wasn't about to look too closely at a gifted weapon, as Burik's mother might have said…

"Wake up, you lazy ass."

He closed his screen and forced open his eyes. Andra stood above him, grinning as she held a hand out toward him. "What, you're just going to lay around all day while I do all the hard work?"

He opened his mouth to retort, but the absurdity of the situation overwhelmed him. He chuckled, the sound quickly swelling to full-blown laughter as relief and disbelief flooded his body. Andra looked surprised for a moment, then joined in, falling onto her ass beside him and resting her head on her knees as her body shook with laughter.

The moment passed, and he pushed himself to a sitting position, then looked over at Andra. "You okay?"

"Hells no. That thing was trying to steal my ithtu from me, and then it was going to feed me to its babies while I was still alive." She shuddered and shook her head. "I'm a long, fucking way from okay, Amarl. How about you?"

"Me? I'm…" He hesitated, then shook his head. He was naked, bleeding, exhausted, in pain, and still stuck in the depths of the assilian hive. He definitely wasn't okay. "I'm about the same as you, I guess."

She nodded. "And the others? Where are they?"

"They got out of the hive. Meder broke us out with an array, and I tracked the path the assilians took to bring us here. I sent them to go get help while I looked for you. Hopefully, they're doing better than we are. Your head is bleeding, you know."

She winced and touched the gash just below her hairline. "Yeah, when that bitch knocked us both flying, my head hit one of those stalagmites."

"What?"

"The cone-shaped rocks sticking up from the ground. That's what they're called. Knocked me cold for a couple minutes." She laughed. "I came to and saw you fighting an assilian queen hand-to-hand and beating the damn thing. I suppose I should be surprised, but somehow, I'm not."

She gave him a serious look and smiled gently. "We're both pretty beat up, but if you hadn't come back for me, it would have been a lot fucking worse. You saved my life."

He shrugged. "If it weren't for me, your life wouldn't have been in danger in the first place, would it? I talked you into letting us leave the hunting area."

She laughed. "You really think so?" She shook her head. "I was told that if you came to me and asked me to leave the area, I should let you, Amarl."

"Wait, what? Who told you that?"

"Ranakar, of course. Right before I entered the Mistway, he told me that you might ask, and if you did, I should let you convince me, but I should go with you." She made a sour face. "And not to tell you that, so I suppose I fucked up, there."

"I promise, I won't say anything."

"Oh, they'll find out. They always do. It's only a matter of time until they figure out what happened to Nihos – if they haven't already. I wouldn't be surprised if they had and just decided to let it stand." She gave him another intense gaze. "Seriously, though. You were free, and you came back for me – alone. Even after what I did to you. Thank you seems like such a lame response to something like that, so...”

She reached out and grabbed the back of his neck, pulling him toward her and planting her lips on his. He froze for a moment, stunned, then wrapped his unwounded arm around her and pulled her close, kissing her deeply. She melted up against him, and he felt his body reacting to her softness – and the feeling of her naked breasts pressed against his chest. He moved closer to her, and for a moment, he felt her yielding against him before she pulled back.

“Wow.” She shook her head and wiped her mouth with one hand, wincing as she touched her torn lips. “That was pretty good.”

“Yes, it was,” he smiled at her. “And you’re absolutely welcome.”

She laughed, then smacked him on the arm. “Come on. Go harvest the queen so we can get the fuck out of here. We can continue this discussion when we’re not bleeding and in danger of being attacked and killed, sound good?”

“Works for me.” He rose tiredly to his feet and walked over to the prone form of the queen, analyzing it as he did.

ANALYSIS REPORT
CREATURE: ASSILIAN QUEEN
POWER DENSITY: 4
THREAT LEVEL: DEADLY

He knelt beside the creature and reached a hand out toward it. He felt the lingering life within it straining toward him, begging for his touch, demanding to be harvested. The moment he touched it, that power rushed at him, surging through the queen’s body. The torrent of energy was enormous, far too much for him to safely handle, and he swiftly split it into manageable streams. The crackling of crystals growing echoed in the room, and he watched as a half-dozen deep blue crystals the size of his fist rose around his hand, the crystals flattened and spiky rather than tall and treelike. As the last drops of power flowed out of him, he sat back down heavily. He pulled one of the crystals and tossed it to Andra.

“Here you go. Didn’t this thing say it severed one of your crystals from you?”

"Yeah." She hesitated. "Amarl, this is a powerful Strong crystal. We should take it back to Askula."

"But we have no way to carry it, do we? So, you might as well quicken it. It's better than leaving it here."

She nodded and gripped the crystal, closing her eyes. A moment later, it grew slightly transparent as it bonded to her. She let it go, and the crystal faded into insubstantiality, vanishing into the air.

"Hey, where did it go?" Amarl asked, concerned.

"It's still here," she laughed. "It's floating around me somewhere – or in me, or something. I'm not totally sure. Yours are with you right now, too. You didn't lose them, did you?"

Frowning, he pulled up his ithtu screen. It swirled into view before his face a moment later.

ITHTU REPORT
MAX ITHTU: 2
QUICKENING RATE: 8.5%
MAX ITHTU RANK: STRONG

CURRENT CRYSTALS QUICKENING: 1
1 – RANK: STRONG   DENSITY: 10   POWER: 33.2
QUICKENED: 88%

POWER QUICKENED TO:
SKILLS – NONE
STATS – 1 (TOUGHNESS, 71%)
LEVEL – NONE
ABILITY – 12.2(0/720)
TAK – 20 (21%)

"Huh," he said, staring at the screen. "That's strange. I am missing one."

"What?" she asked, looking at him in confusion.

"Yeah. I think I drained one of my crystals fighting that thing – and I lost a lot of energy from the other one."

She nodded. "That would explain how you could even fight it. Usually, you need a team to deal with an assilian queen. They're too dangerous for most students to handle." She rose to her feet. "Go on, quicken one yourself, and let's get out of here. I'm really not in the mood to find out what those 'greater hunters' that queen was talking about are, are you?" She gave him a wicked smile. "Besides, the sooner we get back, the sooner I can finish thanking you."

Amarl grabbed a crystal and scrambled to his feet. Suddenly, the thought of fighting his way back through the tunnels to the Mistway didn't bother him in the slightest.

CHAPTER 40

Amarl trudged up the stairs of the tower in the Citadel with Burik and Meder following behind him. None of them spoke, and Amarl didn't blame them. He suspected that anything he said would just make the fear fluttering in his stomach worse than it already was – not that he was sure it could be all that much worse. He'd rather have gone back to Isolas and faced another assilian queen than deal with what waited for them at the top of those stairs.

Their guide, a second-year student, reached the steel door and rapped on it with the hammer she took from her pocket. "Novices Meder, Burik, and Amarl to see the Rashiv, as ordered." Amarl waited for the person in the room beyond to answer, but the door just swung silently open, revealing the antechamber to the Rashiv's office. The guide gave the three a sympathetic look that Amarl hadn't been expecting. "Good luck," she whispered softly.

Amarl led the trio into the somewhat familiar office and headed for the seats, but the awal seated behind the desk shook his head. "He's waiting for you. Go on in." The door to the inner office swung open, and Amarl stepped inside, his heart hammering in his chest and seemingly trying to jump out of his throat. He walked inside, and if anything, the butterflies fluttering in his stomach grew worse. The Rashiv sat in his chair, his back to the group as he stared out his window. To Amarl's extreme dismay, Tekasoka and Ranakar stood behind and to the side of the Rashiv's desk, both looking stern as they frowned at the novices.

"Come in. Stand before my desk." The Rashiv didn't look at them as the novices entered, and Amarl filed in to stand at the far end of the desk, facing Tekasoka. Meder moved to stand beside him, with Burik on the end. They stood in silence, waiting for the others to join them, and as they did, Amarl considered just how much trouble the group was probably in.

He and Andra had fled the hive without encountering any more assilians, which Andra said was expected. Apparently, the hive's queen controlled the creatures almost absolutely through the ambient sahr field, meaning that whenever the group spoke to any assilian, they were actually speaking to the queen, albeit through the filter of the insect's limited brain. Without the queen, the remaining assilians would scatter, either seeking new hives to join or becoming food for something greater in the deep tunnels.

They traveled less than an hour before they ran into a group of two older students and a nadar. It seemed that Andra's absence had been noted, and the other novices found the nadar at Andra's campsite. The ithtara had gone immediately to rescue the two lost students, and the fact that they'd managed to free themselves and kill the assilian queen didn't do anything to lessen the tongue-lashing the nadar gave them all. The test was immediately cancelled, and the novices were sent back through the Mistway to all of their great relief.

The next morning, a messenger arrived informing the trio that they were confined to their room until further notice, pending an investigation into their actions in Isolas. Amarl's heart sank as he saw Tekasoka's signature at the bottom of the order. The awal of Sabila School honestly scared him, and he couldn't imagine that she would be happy with what they'd done.

"She can't be too mad, can she?" Meder had asked a little plaintively from her bed. "Didn't Andra say that she was under orders to let us go if we asked?" The girl lay back with an arm across her face to shield her eyes from the morning sunlight. She'd woken up soon after the novices reached Andra's camp, but she'd complained of a terrific headache, and she was too exhausted to walk without assistance.

"That won't stop her from being mad," Burik predicted. "She'll just be mad at Ranakar, I hope."

"No, she'll blame us," Amarl shook his head. "After all, Andra was only ordered to let us through if we asked. We didn't have to ask."

"Yes, we did," Burik protested. "How else would we complete our secondary tasks?"

"We could have simply failed them. That was a choice. We decided to go into danger instead." Amarl shrugged. "At least, that's how she'll see it, I'm sure."

"He's right,' Meder sighed. "Just because we could do something doesn't mean we had to – which might have been the whole point, really. Being able to differentiate between what you're capable of doing and what's both wise and practical is probably very important to an ithtar."

"Maybe, but that still seems unfair," Burik grumbled. "Giving us all tasks that we couldn't possibly complete..." He frowned. "Except for Hadur. We never found out what his task was, did we?"

"I did," Meder smiled weakly. "From Norag. Hadur was supposed to follow the orders of whoever took the lead at any given moment."

Burik burst out laughing. "Ha! That had to have been a hard pill for him to swallow! I wondered why he was so willing to go along with everything anyone said."

"So did I. I expected him to fight with us a lot more – and especially with Amarl." Meder sighed. "We're all in a lot of trouble, aren't we?"

"If we are, we are," Burik said stoutly. "There's no point in worrying about it. My mother always says, 'Don't waste time sharpening other people's knives.'"

"Okay, that one went over my head," Amarl laughed.

"The awals are going to do whatever they're going to do, Amarl. Worrying about it just makes us miserable before the punishment even happens. It's like we're making their knives sharper, so they can cut us even deeper with them."

"Oh, I like that saying," Meder laughed. "It takes some thought. I might have to use that one."

"Feel free. So, Amarl, tell us about what happened in the hive again. How the hells did you and Andra kill that queen?"

"And tell us what happened with you and Andra besides the fighting," Meder smiled. "I saw the looks she gave you. Come on, spill."

That had been two days ago, and they'd awoken this morning to a summons to the Rashiv's office. They showered and dressed in silence, all of them dreading what would soon come. Amarl had hoped that the dread of the meeting – or trial, he supposed – would be worse than the trial itself. Now that he was actually in the Rashiv's office, he decided that the reality was much, much worse.

The door behind them opened, and Herel, Hadur, and Norag entered a moment later. Herel nodded to Amarl as the final three novices moved to stand in line with the others, and Amarl nodded back. He still didn't much like Herel, but the boy had been at least courteous since they escaped the assilian hive, and Amarl was content with polite animosity. It was certainly better than outright hatred, after all.

The door swung shut with a clang that sent a chill down Amarl's spine and made him jump. It had a feeling of finality to it, and that thought unsettled Amarl's stomach to no end.

As the door sealed behind them, the Rashiv turned his chair to face the novices. The old man's face was cold, and his gaze chilled Amarl. A touch of the ithtar's power rolled forth, not enough to paralyze the hizeen but enough to cause his heart to lurch in his chest. He remembered how he'd felt the first time he'd met the Rashiv and again when the old man restored Herel's mind, and he considered how easily the Rashiv could kill them all if he chose to. Fear filled him, a fear that he hadn't even felt facing the assilian queen, and he knew that his life hung in the balance at that moment.

"This tribunal into the events in Isolas can now begin," the old man said in a calm, even voice that still held the chill of deepest winter within it. "I would ask if you all know why you're here, but I'm going to operate under the assumption that none of you are idiotic enough not to know what actions brought you to my office.

He leaned back in his chair, tenting his fingers before him. "You six novices were sent to Isolas with a simple task. Survive for five days. You were given adequate supplies and gear to accomplish this task, and you were given very specific rules to follow. Those rules stated that you were to remain in the designated area at all times. Did anyone here believe that those rules were flexible?" He eyed the silent novices. "Perhaps that they were just a suggestion that could be followed or ignored as you chose?" Again, silence greeted his question, and the man sighed.

"Yet, despite your apparent full understanding of these rules, you left the designated hunting area, knowing that doing so would put you in grave danger. Can any of you give any possible reason why you made this decision?"

Amarl took a deep breath before taking a step forward. "Sir, it was my decision, and my fault," he said, his voice quavering as he spoke. "I convinced the others to follow me."

"I don't believe I asked whose fault anything was, Novice," the Rashiv replied. "I asked what drove you to convince them in the first place."

Amarl shook his head. "It was a stupid reason, sir. It was the only way that I could see that Burik and I could complete our secondary tasks, and we didn't want to give up on them."

"So, you risked your life – and the life of the other novices – just to complete a task that wasn't vital to your success?" the man asked dryly. "Am I understanding this correctly?"

"Yes, sir. That's more or less it, sir."

"Sir, Amarl isn't responsible for me and my team," Herel said, stepping forward as well. "We made them let us go along with them. I was the one who led my team out of the designated area, and I take responsibility for that."

"And was your reasoning the same, Novice? You wished to complete your secondary tasks?"

"Yes, sir."

"And the thought of seeing the other team succeed while yours failed played no part in your decision?"

Herel swallowed hard and flushed slightly. "That – was also part of it, sir."

"I thought so." The Rashiv frowned, and Amarl's heart raced at the man's expression. His gaze was flat and unfriendly, and displeasure radiated out from him in palpable waves. Amarl had to stifle an urge to turn and run rather than facing the old man's gaze, but he held himself still. He'd made his choices; he would accept the consequences.

"The rules of Askula are not subject to interpretation, novices," the Rashiv said in a cold voice. "They are there for a reason, and breaking them – whatever your motivation – is unacceptable. Those rules keep you alive. Askula is not a place for games, petty jealousies, or ridiculous rivalries. You are here to be forged into weapons to serve and defend the Empire, not to impress others or satisfy your foolish pride!"

He leaned forward, and Amarl shivered as a hint of the man's hidden power flowed from his eyes. "And I will forge you, I promise – or I will shatter you. The choice is yours. Do you understand?"

"Yes, sir!" All six novices spoke in unison, and all of their voices cracked and quavered, even Burik's.

"Good. Now, to the matter of punishment. You will, of course, receive no reward or praise for completing your secondary tasks. You will each receive ten lashes before the school tomorrow morning. You will also be assigned disciplinary duties for the remainder of this year, as decided by Awal Tekasoka." His eyes burned into each of them in turn. "Consider yourselves very fortunate that you aren't kneeling over the Altar of the Deeps, waiting for the sword to descend. Very, very fortunate, indeed."

Amarl shivered again as he remembered Yashi's execution, and his stomach churned as he realized how close he'd come to being the next one bent over that altar.

"Now," the Rashiv leaned back, "with that unpleasantness resolved, there is the matter of the results of your testing. Tekasoka?"

The round-faced woman stepped forward, her jaw set and her eyes blazing. "Novices, you were given a task, to survive for five days in the realm of Isolas. You returned, naked and half-dead, after four days. Strictly speaking, you all failed your test."

The woman grimaced unpleasantly. "However, what you accomplished was far more significant. You worked together, despite your differences, to escape from a situation that you had no chance of escaping. You fought your way out of an assilian hive, even rescuing another student in the process. And by some miracle, you killed an assilian queen, shattering that hive, precisely the punishment we would have inflicted on them for attacking our students.

"Considering these achievements, we have judged your test to be successfully completed. You will all be allowed to proceed to the second year of Askula. Congratulations are in order – and I suggest that you each take the time to send a prayer to the gods above for your luck!" She stepped back, and the Rashiv nodded.

"Yes, congratulations, novices. As of next moon, you will advance to second year, and your new course schedule will be given to you the Akio before. Until then, consider seriously how close you all came to death – not only in Isolas, but here, as well." He turned his back to them. "You are all dismissed – except for Novice Amarl." Amarl froze as he turned toward the door. "I will require you to remain, as we have additional matters to discuss."

"Y-yes, sir," Amarl swallowed, nodding. Burik reached out and patted the hizeen's shoulder, while Meder flashed him a wan smile before they exited the room, followed by Tekasoka and Ranakar, leaving Amarl alone with the Rashiv. He stood in silence until the old man turned back around and gestured toward one of the chairs.

"Sit down, Novice," he instructed. Amarl practically fell into his chair, his legs trembling and weak all of a sudden.

"Something remarkable happened in that hive, Novice," the Rashiv said, tapping the tips of his fingers together as he spoke. "Didn't it?"

"You mean, when I fought the queen, sir?"

"That seems to have been the catalyst, yes." The Rashiv frowned. "You honestly don't know what I'm talking about?" Amarl shook his head. "Have you checked your status since you returned to Askula, Amarl?"

"N-no, sir."

"Make a habit of checking it each morning and after any significant event. An ithtar who doesn't know their status intimately is operating with their eyes closed and a hand tied behind their back." He shook his head. "Go ahead and check it now."

Frowning, Amarl pulled up his status. As it swam into sight, he read it and gasped aloud at what he saw.

STATS

FORCE: 5.5 (165%)   SKILL: 5.6 (182%)
SPEED: 5.9 (246%)   TOUGHNESS: 5.3 (135%)
MIND: 6 (272%)   WILL: 4.8 (82%)
PRESENCE: 6.5 (448%)   SOUL: 9.8 (12,151%)

QUICKENED ABILITY: MEZ
TIER: F
LEVEL: 1

CURRENT ITHTU: 77.1
TO LEVEL: 0
TO STATS: 1 (TOUGHNESS 97%)
TO SKILLS: 0
TO TAK: 20 (99.9%)

CURRENT TAK: 20/20

"I – I don't understand, sir," he stammered. "My stats – my ability – everything changed! What happened?"

"Somehow, Novice, in the depths of that hive, you awakened your ability," the old man responded. "A full year ahead of when we intended, I might add."

"I – I didn't mean to, sir!" Amarl protested. "I wasn't trying to…"

The old man chuckled. "Novice, if I believed you deliberately quickened your ability, trust me, I wouldn't be angry. I would be indebted to you for discovering something that the Order has failed to work out for millennia." He shook his head. "No, this was a miscalculation on my part, I'm afraid, not a failing on yours. I underestimated your talent."

Amarl opened his mouth to ask a question, but the Rashiv silenced him with an upraised finger. "We will address all that, Amarl. There's no longer any reason to keep these things from you – especially since you'll likely learn enough to puzzle them out within the next year. For now, though, I want you to think about your ability and focus on understanding it."

Amarl hesitated, curiosity about his talent warring with that over his ability. At last, though, he clamped his lips shut and thought about that ability, focusing on knowing it and understanding it. As he did, a new screen faded into view before him, one he'd never seen before.

ABILITY REPORT
ABILITY TITLE: MEZ
"SOUL STRENGTHENS ALL"

TIER: F   ITHTU REQUIRED: 148   LEVEL: 1 (0/720)

PASSIVE EFFECT 1: GROWTH INCREASED ACCORDING TO SOUL STAT (CURRENTLY 428% OF STANDARD)
PASSIVE EFFECT 2: SOUL STAT BOOSTS EFFECTS OF OTHER STATS (CURRENTLY 2.3)

ACTIVE EFFECTS: UNKNOWN

"Well?" the Rashiv asked when Amarl had been silent for several seconds. "Did your ability awaken enough for your Joining Crystal to analyze it?"

"I – it…" Amarl swallowed. "Yes, sir. I mean, I think so, sir. I got a new screen, at least."

"Excellent," the old man practically purred, leaning over the desk. "What does your ability mean?"

"It says – it says, 'Soul Strengthens All', sir."

"All! So that's what 'Z' means!" The Rashiv leaned back with a pleased grin. "Yes, that would be a rare concept indeed, considering that it could encompass anything and everything all at once." He shook his head. "An absurdly simple and yet terribly powerful ability, Amarl. Tell me, what are its effects?"

"It has two passive effects, sir. One increases my growth by four hundred percent, and the other boosts my stats by two points." He frowned. "My stats don't look any higher, though, sir – and I don't think I've grown any taller in the last year."

"That's because that isn't how passive effects work." The Rashiv turned away, his face thoughtful. "I believe you know that every ability has both passive and active effects, yes? Well, passive effects are ones that occur as needed, without requiring you to actively pour ithtu into them. Your growth effect, for instance: obviously, it doesn't mean growing physically larger. It's likely the reason you've advanced your skills so quickly: skill ranks are a measure of growth, after all. It's also probably why you quicken your stats as rapidly as you do, and once you learn to do the same for your skills and ability, it might aid you there, as well.

"I can't be certain, but I believe that the stat boost effect is what you've been tapping in times of need. You drain ithtu to become stronger, faster, tougher, perhaps even more intelligent and perceptive. Even increasing a stat by a point would be a significant boost. Your ability will provide you those boosts as you need them, not all the time." He turned to look back at the boy. "And the active effect?"

"It says, 'unknown', sir."

"Then your ability is only partially awakened," the Rashiv said with a nod. "Not that you'd likely be able to use the active portion anyway. What is the ithtu requirement?"

"148, sir."

The old man laughed loudly at that. "148? That's the equivalent of a low-density Grand crystal!" His eyes twinkled as he looked at Amarl. "We have a lot of work to do to before you can even touch a small fraction of your power. Fortunately, that growth effect and your own natural talent will make that far easier than it would be for anyone else."

"Sir?" Amarl hesitated, biting his lip, then spoke hurriedly. "I don't understand about what you keep calling my talent. Why am I like this? Is it because I'm a hizeen?'"

"A good question, Amarl. A good question with an answer that's at once both simple and complex. Blood holds true."

The old man turned away once more, then stood and walked over to the window. "You know the lore of the Sundering, yes? I believe Warahid discussed it with you while you were still in his class. You know that the forebears of those who would become the ithtaru were created to be immensely powerful haros and drove the spirits from our world, correct?" Amarl nodded, and the man continued.

"When the Sundering occurred, ending that war once and for all, those forebears discovered that they could harvest the life from anything they killed, and doing so granted them incredible powers, even greater than the ones they gained from sahr. Our lore tells us that each of these forebears had abilities similar in power to yours, if not greater. We can only imagine the kinds of things they could do – although perhaps, as you come into your power, we won't have to imagine anymore."

The man waved a hand before his face. "The point is, with the war ended, those first ithtaru created lives for themselves. They married and produced children, and those children inherited their abilities. Their offspring had children, and so on and so forth, carrying their bloodlines down through the ages. However, with each generation, the blood of those first ithtaru was diluted and weakened, and the abilities their offspring gained were similarly less powerful."

"Does that mean, sir, that every ithtaru today…?"

"Yes. Every ithtaru shares a small measure of the blood of one of those forebears. That blood is spread throughout the Empire, mostly too weak to awaken an ability, but rarely, it is strong enough to create an ithtaru. And the stronger the blood, the stronger the ithtaru. Even after three millennia, that blood runs true and has never disappeared."

He turned back and gazed solemnly at the boy. "Do you understand, now, why people talk of your blood, Amarl? For you to take to ithtu the way you have, to quicken a power of such a high tier, your blood must be incredibly pure. In fact, it seems to be utterly pure, without a drop of non-ithtaru blood to corrupt it."

Amarl's eyes widened as he processed the old man's words. "But – wait – then my mother…?"

"Must have had equally pure blood, yes. And somehow, she managed to bear you without letting your spirit half contaminate the bloodline. I'd give a great deal to know the secret of how that happened."

"Then she was an ithtara! Do you know who she was?" Amarl leaned eagerly forward, but the old man shook his head.

"Your mother was never part of the Order, Amarl, I'm sorry. In fact, I'm certain that she wasn't even part of the Empire." Amarl's face must have reflected his confusion, and the Rashiv came back over and sat behind his desk once more, leaning forward and folding his hands on his desk.

"You see, Amarl, it's no accident that we find new novices between their fourteenth and fifteenth Naming Days. That's when the blood within you starts to awaken, at least enough to activate the wards we have overlaying the entire Empire, woven into the sahr field. When you reached your fourteenth Naming Day, you activated those wards, and that was how we knew to come find you in Tem. If your mother had been born and raised in the Empire, we would have found her."

"But if she wasn't from the Empire...?"

"Then she must have come here through a Mistway. One that no one in the Empire knows of." The old man leaned back, his eyes sparkling and a smile spreading across his face. "Quite possibly one that no one but someone of your bloodline can open, as well. Imagine, there could be an entire family – perhaps multiple families – of pureblooded ithtaru living in a realm somewhere, concealing themselves from the Empire. Dozens or hundreds of people with abilities like yours..." The old man shivered. "It's both fascinating and terrifying to contemplate."

"Then – then there's no way to find out who she was, is there?" Amarl deflated as his rising hope crumbled. He'd always held out hope that he had a family somewhere and that he'd track them down someday, if only to find out who his mother was and why she came to Tem. Now, it seemed that he likely did have a family somewhere – and that family was probably forever beyond his reach.

"I've learned not to label anything impossible, Amarl," the Rashiv chuckled. "After all, a year ago, I would have said it was impossible for a novice to quicken a Tier F ability at all, much less in their first year. And yet, here we are. However, I can't see any way to do it – and frankly, that should tell you exactly how difficult such an endeavor would be.

"I can tell you, though, that had anyone known of your mother's bloodline, they would have honored and exalted her to no end. She would have been granted a noble title and offered the sons of the highest families to choose as a husband, perhaps even those of the Shashana herself. Her existence should have been cause for rejoicing across the Empire – and had that idiotic Head Bureaucrat of your village done his job, that's what would have happened."

"What do you mean, sir?"

"Do you remember the working I used on you in our first meeting? It's called the Ritual of Blood, and it's designed to determine if a particular individual shares the blood of royalty or nobility. It can also tell its user how pure the ithtaru blood in the target is. When I crafted it on you, it told me instantly that your blood was incredibly pure, as close to absolute purity as the working allows me to determine, and anyone who'd used it on your mother would have learned the same.

"The simple fact is, by law, that rite is used on any nameless woman when she arrives at a settlement in the Empire. It's not uncommon for daughters of the zahai who have no chance to inherit to flee their families rather than be forced into a political marriage they don't desire, and while that's their choice, the Bureaucracy isn't about to lose track of a high bloodline just because a wayward daughter wants to join the military or priesthood. For some reason, though, the Head Bureaucrat in Tem ignored his duty, and the entire Empire is lessened as a result." He shook his head. "The thought that someone like that died in obscurity when it's likely that simple sahr elixirs could have saved her infuriates me to no end, Amarl."

Amarl's eyes hardened as anger curled up within him. "He did that?" he asked in a cold, quiet voice.

"Yes, but before you go making more vows, he's beyond the reach of your vengeance, I'm afraid. He was found in the city of Aggath, less than a moon after your departure from Tem, dangling by his neck from a rafter in a room in a squalid inn in the poorest part of the city. The official report is that he took his own life in disgrace, but between you and me, it was the work of the Bureaucracy removing a blight on its good name. Of course, you still have your vow to revisit the place of your birth, and since your ithtu witnessed that vow, it will drive you back there eventually to see it through. So, you'll still have the chance to gain some measure of vengeance.

"That is something to be dealt with far, far in the future, though. For now, the important thing to know is that your blood is different than most and holds a great deal more power. Your blood is likely why your Spirit stat is so high and why you seem able to handle ithtu almost intuitively. After all, the first ithtaru had no one to instruct them and certainly had to figure out how to harvest and quicken crystals by themselves, and you share their blood in its purest form."

Amarl frowned once more. "The assilian queen kept talking about my blood, too, sir. It said my blood was too loud, and that it called hunters."

"Did she, now? That didn't make it into the reports."

"Yes, sir. That was why it captured us: to silence my blood. It said it would draw greater hunters who would destroy the hive."

The Rashiv nodded, touching his chin. "She was doubtless correct. That was the true reason you were forbidden to go on further hunts after

Shadora, after all."

"It was? But sir, I thought it was about the other students…"

"No, of course not. We could have simply ordered them to leave you alone – as Tekasoka did after the debacle with Student Yashi." He shook his head. "What a waste that was."

He looked back at Amarl. "No, after Shadora, it was clear that other realms aren't safe for you – at least, most other realms." He chuckled and shook his head. "Amarl, have you ever encountered wild creatures before? Squirrels, rabbits, anything like that?"

"Of course, sir."

"And when did any of them leap to attack you? Did a wolf ever come down from the Silverbands to stalk you? A serpent hunt you as you worked in the fields?"

"Well – no, sir."

"And yet, every creature that you met in Shadora, even those that usually live on diets of leaves and berries, attacked you viciously. None of them fled, even after being gravely wounded. Didn't that strike you as odd?"

Amarl frowned. He'd honestly never thought about it, but now that he did, he realized that he'd never seen an animal behave like that before.

"Why do they do that, sir?"

"Because of your blood, Amarl. Blood that every ithtar shares, in small part. The ithtaru caused the Sundering – accidentally, but they did – and the mark of that still clings to their descendants. Every realm you've visited was once part of the larger world, and the Sundering left each realm isolated, weak, and vulnerable to the spirits. Every living thing in those realms has suffered since then, and they can feel our ancestors' guilt in our blood – especially in yours. That's why your team in Shadora faced four times the attacks that a normal team would, and why you and your friends in Isolas drew attacks away from the other novices.

"Of course, now that your ability is at least partially awakened, we can ease that restriction. There are still realms that are beyond you, but a place like Shadora would be within your abilities. And next year, your friends can join you, as second year is when we allow students to begin hunting for their own crystals."

The old man gestured flippantly at Amarl. "But you'll learn more about that next year. The whole purpose of this talk was so that you could understand what happened to you and why. You finally know why people speak so much of your blood, and why you find things so much easier than others."

"But – why not tell me this sooner, sir?" Amarl asked. "Why was it a secret?"

"A secret? It isn't, really. Every nadar and malim knows this about you – and many of the senior students, who've learned more about the history of the Order and know about the bloodlines, have likely worked out that your blood is purer than most.

"As to why no one told you, it was because knowing that could have hurt your progress. You have a tendency toward laziness, and if you knew that you would have an innate ability to use ithtu, you might abandon all effort altogether. And would you have truly wanted to go to Isolas or Shadora knowing that every creature within range of you would seek you out and try to kill you? I certainly wouldn't have."

He shrugged. "Now that your ability is awakened, though – at least in part – and you've faced those creatures and emerged mostly unscathed, those reasons are less important than your knowledge of the truth." He frowned at Amarl. "However, that truth is for you, not everyone. I'm certain you'll share this with your friends, and that's acceptable, as they've shown that they can keep these things to themselves. However, to anyone else, even malims, you have the Tier D ability Em, an improved soul. That ability mimics part of the passive effect of your true ability, allowing you to use ithtu to boost any one stat temporarily. You will tell no one else but one of the awals of your true abilities. Is that understood?"

Amarl nodded and swallowed slightly. "Yes, sir."

"Good. Then you are dismissed. Awal Tekasoka will tell you your punishment duty. Let nothing like this happen again, do you understand?"

"Yes, sir."

"Go, then. I've a great many things to deal with right now, and I've spent far too much time on you novices as it is."

Amarl nodded and rose to his feet, walking out of the door with a mingled sense of relief and confusion. He finally knew why things came so easily to him, but with that knowledge came dozens of questions, questions he didn't even know if he could ever find the answers to, and those questions rattled in his mind as he walked down the stairs to reunite with his friends.

CHAPTER 41

"What happened? You didn't get even more punishments, did you?" Meder's concerned expression matched the tone of her voice as he entered their room. "That wouldn't be fair; we all knew what we were doing, even Herel and the others!"

"I thought we already talked about fairness," Burik snorted. "It's not exactly fair to give us tasks that can only be completed by breaking the rules, then getting mad at us for breaking the rules, is it?"

"Well, maybe they were giving us impossible tasks to teach us that we can't always achieve our goals," she suggested.

"Except that most of our tasks weren't impossible. Hadur could have done his no matter what, and so could you. Norag's and Herel's might have been hard, but if they fought five or six of those centipedes, it would have been doable. It was only mine and Amarl's that couldn't be done inside the designated area."

Meder's eyes widened in sudden realization. "What if they were planning to let something else into the designated area just so you could complete it?" she gasped. "Maybe you would have been able to do it if we hadn't gotten impatient!"

Burik grunted. "Okay, that's a possibility."

"And now that I think about it, we could have just asked Andra to bring us a creature that would have fit our needs," she sighed, rubbing her face. "There was no need to go out there. We're going to get lashes – nearly got expelled – for nothing!"

"Not exactly for nothing," Amarl shook his head as he sat down on his bed. "I got something out of it. I guess I awakened my ability – at least a little bit."

Meder gasped again, and Burik whistled in amazement. "That's incredible, Amarl," he said appreciatively.

"How?" Meder asked.

"When I fought the queen, I drew enough ithtu to totally drain one of my crystals. I guess it was enough to wake up the ability – at least, the passive part of it. The active part isn't working yet."

"That's amazing," she sighed. "And I'm incredibly jealous, of course. So, what does it do?"

"Currently, it speeds up my growth – which I think means my skill training and how quickly I increase my stats – by 300%. Plus, if I need it, it boosts my stats by a couple points."

"Just a couple points?" Burik frowned. "I'd have thought that a Tier F ability would do more than that."

"It's not *just* a couple points, Burik," Meder shook her head. "I've done the math with the percentages in my status, and adding two points to a stat makes it something like five to seven times stronger."

"I don't think it works that way," Amarl shook his head. "I've gotten my Mind Stat up almost a whole point already, and I don't think I'm twice as smart as I was when I got here."

"No, definitely not," Burik chuckled. "If anything, you might have gotten dumber, along with the rest of us, considering what just happened."

"It's probably a question of affinities," she mused. "Periteth said that stats are more about affinities than anything else; maybe if you don't have an affinity for a stat, increasing it by a point doesn't mean the same thing." She shook her head as if to banish the wayward though. "But even if it's not that much of a boost, it's still significant," Meder said. "And growing four times as quickly..." She sighed. "No wonder your skills go up so fast. That's an absolutely broken ability, Amarl."

He snorted. "In more ways than one. Apparently, once I unlock the active portion of it, using it fully will take the entirety of a Grand crystal. That's each time I use it." He laughed. "It'll be years before I can store enough ithtu to even use it once, and by then, you both will be way ahead of me."

"A Grand crystal?" Meder asked, her face awed. "But – Lilenpur said those only come from ridiculously powerful creatures! How will you even get one?"

"He'll kill ridiculously powerful creatures, of course," Burik said confidently.

"Yeah, I'll pass on that, thanks. Fighting that queen was hard enough.

I would have hated to see what else was coming that scared that thing."

"What else was coming?" Meder echoed. "What do you mean?"

Amarl took a deep breath. "The reason the Rashiv wanted me to stay behind was to examine my ability, of course, but also to tell me why I was able to awaken it, and why all this ithtu stuff is so easy for me."

"He knows? And he never told you? Why not?"

"I'll bet it's because he's a hizeen," Burik guessed. "Was that it?"

"No, sorry, Burik. It's because – well, I guess because of my mother." He went on to explain what the old man had told him about the origins of the ithtaru and the purity of his blood.

He left out the idea that he might have a family somewhere, living in another realm inaccessible to the Empire. That was personal, and he knew if he mentioned it, they'd want to start making guesses about who his family might be. Thinking about them – and the fact that he'd likely never meet them – hurt too much to share, at least for the time being. One day, he might be willing to talk about it, but it wasn't that day yet.

"Wow," Meder finally breathed. "That's – it's – wow."

"I think you broke her," Burik laughed. "I've never seen her at a loss for words like this."

"It's just – so many things make sense now," she shook her head. "Like why there are so many nobles and higher castes in the Order. Zahai especially tend to marry within their caste, which means most of us are distantly related to one another."

"Wait, you're related to Herel?" Amarl laughed.

"Probably, at least a little bit. Somewhere in the past, one of his family members likely married one of mine. It's very common, and most of us can go back and find a connection if we really want to." She made a face. "Not that I really want to in this case, but it's probably true.

"The point is, wouldn't that sort of intermarriage concentrate the ithtar blood?" Her eyes widened. "Oh, and since the villagers are descendants of ithtaru who didn't have the ability to quicken, I'll bet they produce new novices all the time! I wonder if that's the point of the village..."

"Maybe. I'm not sure who you'd ask, though." Amarl laughed. "Not that I have any doubts that you'll figure it out eventually, of course. The whole point is that ithtar blood is the reason that creatures in the other realms attack us, and since mine is so pure…” He shrugged.

“You draw more attacks than anyone else,” Burik nodded.

“I wondered about that,” Meder said softly. “I talked to Norag, and he said that they barely fought anything before they joined us. Apparently, everything came after us, instead. You said that happened in Shadora, too, so I guessed that something about you drew more creatures. I thought it was your heritage, though, not your bloodline.”

“For all I know, it’s both,” Amarl sighed. “Which means, Burik, that you might be right. I might end up fighting all sorts of super-powerful monsters. Yay me.”

“Stop whining,” Burik laughed. “It’s a good thing!”

“It won’t feel like a good thing when some monster with a million tentacles is eating me for breakfast, I’m sure.”

“It is, though.” Burik leaned back, and his eyes went distant. “You know the last thing my mother said to me before I left? She said, ‘Burik, always remember: any fool can go through life safely, but that fool has never lived. Go embrace your destiny, and live.’”

“Yes, and fighting creatures out of your nightmares is a great way to follow that advice,” Amarl snorted. “You know, except for the ‘living’ part.”

“I have to agree with Amarl,” Meder said lightly. “I’ve had nightmares about the assilian hive ever since we got back. I’m not eager to do something like that again.”

“Not the point. The point is, there’s a difference between existing and living. Think about everything that’s happened just in this one year!”

“You mean, like almost getting killed by Nihos?” Amarl said dryly. “Or being stabbed in the liver by Herel?”

“Don’t forget almost dying to a giant spider,” Meder added. “And having to scout an assilian hive alone in the nude.”

“Exactly!” Burik agreed happily. “Those moments, the ones where you’re struggling and don’t know if you’ll survive, they make you really appreciate life! They make things like seeing Meder play in the snow, or drinking together at Sasofit’s, or just watching the sun sink over the mountains all feel that much sweeter! With no risk, there’s no fun, and you’re just existing, not living.”

Amarl and Meder shared a long look. “He’s kind of got a point,” the hizeen admitted.

"Yes, he does," she sighed. "I'm not sure how much more 'fun' I can take, though."

"You're strong, Meder," Burik said with a dismissive wave. "You can handle it. Besides, it's not like either of you are going to face any of this alone."

"That's also true. At least we can deal with whatever comes next year together." She smiled at the pair. "That makes the rest of it almost bearable."

Amarl couldn't help but grin as a surge of affection rose up within him. Burik was right; he really had lived more in the last year than he had his entire life in Tem. He'd learned to fight and how to use magic. He'd gone to other worlds and faced creatures he'd never even dreamed of before. He'd discovered more about the world and life than he ever could have imagined. Best of all, he'd made two friends, people he could trust with his secrets – and his life. His childhood in the little village seemed like a swiftly fading dream, and he no longer looked back at it with regret or loss. This was his life now, and he wouldn't trade it for anything.

He still felt the blows of the hammer forging him into the weapon Askula wanted, but now, he welcomed them. Whatever they were becoming, they would become it together, and for now, at least, that was good enough.

"Come on," he told the others. "Enough moping about. We're not confined anymore, and we don't have any classes today. Let's go to Sasofit's and have a drink to celebrate making it to second year. It's on me."

"That's something I can drink to," Burik laughed. "How about you, Meder?"

"Oh, gods, yes," she said feelingly. "Anything so I don't have to think about tomorrow morning. Let's get out of here."

Amarl followed his friends out of the room, smiling as he looked at them. One year would soon be over; he couldn't wait for the next to begin.

EPILOGUE

Rashiv Venidihim turned away from the window, letting the image of the three novices fade from it as they left their room. Askula's students had long believed that their teachers, especially the awals, knew everything that happened in the school. The students generally suspected that the awals had some working or ability that spied on their wards, and the scrying windows served exactly that purpose. In the hands of an awal, the windows in their offices could find and follow any student, no matter where they were, so long as they stood inside a sahr field.

Of course, that hadn't helped once the novices went into the assilian hive. The crystals that the insect people collected acted to stabilize the sahr within their hives, keeping any but their queen from using it. It made the creatures far more dangerous within their hives, and even most full ithtaru hesitated before entering an assilian hive.

Fortunately, the Rashiv's ability didn't have the same limitations as the sahr field. Closing his eyes, he followed the strands of the novices' past back into Isolas, watching them as they argued with one another and banded together to fight their captors. He observed their battle against the lake spitter and watched as they "convinced" Andra to let them leave the restricted region.

"This group has promise," he said quietly. "Well, most of them. That tagarai boy probably won't make it. He's too stubborn and closed-minded. The rest of them, though, show a lot of potential."

"They do. It would be a shame to waste it, wouldn't it? Like by sending them to die in an assilian hive, for example."

Venidihim winced at the mild tone of accusation in Ranakar's words, and he opened his eyes to see his oldest friend watching him. Ranakar's face was calm and impassive, revealing nothing in his expression, but the two had been friends for sixty years, and Venidihim could read him like a book.

"You disapprove of my actions, then, Ranak?" he asked quietly.

"They almost died, Venidi," his friend shook his head. "You insisted on giving them those tasks knowing that they'd go out of the restricted zone and run afoul of the assilians, didn't you?"

"No, the assilians were an unexpected complication. I did plan for them to leave the restricted area, though – just as I paired the boy with Andra in Shadora, knowing the arrangement she and Nihos had made."

"Why?"

"Need, Ranak. Our ithtu responds to our need, as you know, but his does even more strongly. His ability is powerful, and it slept deeply. We couldn't wait for years for it to awaken on its own, so I gave him powerful needs to stir it to awareness. And as you can see, it worked – at least, partially."

"And if the assilian queen had killed him? How didn't you see that possibility?"

"Because there's a hidden player, here," the old man sighed. "I can see the edges of their involvement – they visited the hive the day before we sent the students to Isolas, and from what the boy recalls of the queen's words, they assured her that we wouldn't respond if she took the novices. Somehow, the queen believed them."

"The same person who bound Herel?"

"Impossible to say. You know that thread vanished in Devald. This one does the same; whoever they are, they're taking precautions against my ability, so I can't get a definite read on them. It could be the same person, or it could be two people working together, operating in the same manner. I can't tell, and honestly, not knowing is more than a little frustrating. It makes the future unpleasantly uncertain."

"It would be anyway," Ranakar shook his head. "You know better than anyone that your ability's predictions aren't always accurate, especially around someone like the boy. You're gambling, and you know it."

Venidihim nodded in grudging acceptance. "It's true. He holds too much potential, too much power. His future is a mystery to me – or, I should say, which of his futures will come to pass is a mystery. I've seen dozens of them, all equally valid. He saves the Empire from disaster; he dooms it to destruction. He stops Askula from being destroyed; he razes the Citadel with his own hands. He returns an ancient evil to our world; he locks that evil away for all time." He shook his head with a rueful laugh. "I've even seen him reverse the Sundering and ascend the Crystal Throne – and in the same vision, not another one, mind you, but that same one, he shatters the restored world beyond all hope of restoration and hurls us all into the world of the spirits." He shivered. "His power to shape the world awes me, Ranak, awes me and terrifies me in equal measure."

"His ability is only Tier F, Venidi, just one tier above yours. It's going to be powerful, but not *that* powerful."

"So far, yes, but with his talent, he's sure to evolve it. He's already shown signs of how terrible his power might be; imagine what it could be at Tier H or I, thousands of times stronger than a Tier A ability. He could obliterate entire realms, wipe out civilizations. Alone, he could be a match for the entire Order, Ranak. How terrifying would that be?"

Ranakar remained silent for a long moment, and Venidihim could practically hear his friend's thoughts. Ranakar was a man of action. He made decisions swiftly, and he rarely regretted them, even when they turned out to be wrong. He would want to be proactive, to solve the problem before it became a problem. Venidihim didn't need his ability to predict what his friend would suggest.

"If that's the case, then – maybe we should remove his threat while we still have that option," Ranakar said slowly.

"And what if trying to 'remove his threat' is the thing that makes him a threat? His ithtu rose to protect him against Dalat and Nihos. It rescued him from the assilian queen. It even strengthens his friends so they can aid him when he needs them. What would it do if faced with a threat such as you, Ranak?"

"The boy's body can't handle the kind of power he'd need to be dangerous to me," Ranakar shook his head.

"The boy's body is an almost perfect conduit for ithtu. I've tested him, little bits here and there, and ithtu flows through him utterly unimpeded."

Ranakar frowned. "How is that possible? Ithtu is a spiritual power; mortal bodies can never be perfectly acclimated to it."

"Normally, no, but my guess is that his spirit half removed that resistance." The older man gazed steadily at his friend. "How many ithtu does your ability require again?"

"Twenty-three."

"He used more than that without even trying. He channeled at least thirty units of it in the battle with the queen without even being tired afterward, at least no more tired than anyone who'd been fighting through a hive on short sleep would have been. His only limitations are the ones his own mind sets for him. Remove that from the equation by threatening him, and there's no telling what he might do." The Rashiv shook his head. "No, old friend, it's smarter to hone the boy into a blade that we can use against the Empire's enemies."

"A blade that could cut us all if it turns on us," Ranakar reminded him.

"Yes. That means we just have to make sure the blade is always pointed in the proper direction."

"Then why inflict such a deliberate cruelty on him? Why punish him and his friends for doing exactly what you wanted them to do?"

"I couldn't exactly reward them for utterly ignoring the rules, could I? The boy's nature is already chaotic and mercurial. He resents authority and rules thanks to that gods-blasted village that practically abused him his entire life. If I give him even a hint that he can bend the rules to fit the situation, he'll throw them aside utterly and drag those other two along with him. He'd have this entire place turned upside down in two years!"

Ranakar frowned thoughtfully at the man. "I thought you said your ability didn't work on him?"

"It doesn't. It works on his friends, though, and I can already see his power altering the paths their lives might have taken." He shook his head. "Left alone, the girl would have focused on research and pure academics, while the other boy would have become just another warrior. Thanks to Amarl's influence, though, she's now headed toward becoming a combat haro, while he's taking a path of leadership and strategy. The less we control Amarl, the more his power will spread and drag all those around him into its influence."

Ranakar sighed and leaned back in his chair, rubbing his face. "Fine. What do you need from me?"

"To keep doing as you are. Teach the boy. Become his mentor. Gain his trust. Starting next year, his friends will be joining him for some of those 'special lessons', so you'll have the chance to guide all three of them."

"All three? Why?"

"Because just being around the boy is going to awaken their abilities and make them grow rapidly. His blood calls out too loudly to be ignored. They'll need training beyond what the other novices will receive soon enough, believe me."

"Why me? Why not Tekasoka? She's more suited to this sort of thing than I am."

"Because you're the awal of Khana School, and unless I miss my guess, at least Amarl and the girl will be joining it in their third year."

"The girl, too?"

Venidihim nodded. "She built a six-dimensional, five-level array under pressure inside an assilian hive, Ranak. Trust me, you'll want her in Khana. Maybe the other boy, too, but I'm not completely certain of that."

"Fine." Ranakar rose to his feet. "But I'll hate it every step of the way."

"No, you won't," Venidihim smiled. "That much, I can tell for certain."

As his old friend left, Venidihim turned back to face the scrying window, although he didn't activate it. A shiver ran down his spine as he thought about what he hadn't told the other man, what he'd honestly been afraid to share. Ranakar honored and respected his friend as the Rashiv of Askula, but when he thought it was needed, he didn't hesitate to act, even if those actions went against his purported superior's orders. Venidihim could see that future's line clearly; if Ranakar knew the truth about his predictions for the boy, the awal would act, and that would force Amarl's ithtu to defend him. However Venidihim looked at that confrontation, one thing was certain. Ranakar's line ended there. It wasn't a risk the old Rashiv was willing to take.

The truth was, he'd only looked far into the young hizeen's future once. He had no plans to do it again. With that glance, he'd seen hundreds of futures, not mere dozens, enough that it staggered him and left him reeling and nearly unconscious for an hour. None of those futures had been prosaic; all had involved cataclysmic events and Empire-shaking choices. And all of them left the hizeen drenched in blood and surrounded by death. One way or another, Amarl would leave a bloody trail through the Empire as he forged his path.

The old man, feeling the weight of his almost eighty years more than he normally did, turned to his labah board and slowly, carefully set down a dark grey stone with silver flecks across the top. Life was the game, and the game was life. Looking at the piece, he couldn't see the layers above or below it, and he knew there were other players on this board moving their own pieces around. The dark-robed figure who'd bound the noble brat still eluded his sight, and he felt the interference from powers beyond his ken when he'd tried to scan the boy's futures. And something more seemed to be at play, some force that guided even the Rashiv's actions without his knowing it.

He sighed and turned away. He'd laid his pieces as best he could. He could only hope that the ocean of blood following the silver-haired boy wouldn't drown them all in its crimson tides.

To be continued...

Amarl's adventures will continue in Askula Academy 2, where he'll learn more about his special ability, his heritage, and the powers arrayed against him!

If you enjoyed this book, please take a moment to rate and review it! Reviews are vital to self-published authors, and each one is greatly appreciated. Also, maybe check out some of my other series while you're at it!

Visit me online at The Singularity or my Amazon Page to see my catalog of works, find out more about what's coming up, or sign up for my mailing list to get news, promos, and an occasional free short story (from me, of course)!

Thanks to everyone who supports me on Patreon, especially my Lord Sorcerer tier supporters!

To learn more about LitRPG, talk to authors, and just have an awesome time, please join the LitRPG Books group!

If you love Gamelit and want to read more series like this, or to hear about the newest releases and best series, check out the GameLit Society!

STATUS SHEETS

Amarl

<u>STATS</u>
FORCE: 5.5 (165%)   SKILL: 5.6 (182%)
SPEED: 5.9 (246%)   TOUGHNESS: 5.3 (135%)
MIND: 6 (272%)   WILL: 4.8 (82%)
PRESENCE: 6.5 (448%)   SOUL: 9.8 (12,151%)

<u>QUICKENED ABILITY</u>: MEZ
TIER: F
LEVEL: 1

<u>CURRENT ITHTU</u>: 77.1
TO LEVEL: 0
TO STATS: 1 (TOUGHNESS 97%)
TO SKILLS: 0
TO TAK: 20 (99.9%)

<u>CURRENT TAK</u>: 20/20

SKILLS REPORT

Skill	Rating
Academics	3
Acrobatics	4
Anatomy	4
Animal Care	2
Baking	2
Bear Form	4
Carpentry	1
Climbing	5
Deception	7
Driving	2
Empathy	4
Endurance	5
Escape	3
Farming	2
Hiding	5
Investigation	4
Knife Fighting	4
Lockpicking	6
Meditation	3
Memorization	4
Moon Axe Fighting	4
Perception	4
Persuasion	7
Riding	3
Running	4
Sahr Mastery	2
Scimitar Fighting	4
Seduction	8
Silent Movement	5
Sleight of Hand	6
Staff Fighting	4
Survival	2
Throwing	4
Tiger Form	5
Tracking	5
Water Form	5

ITHTU REPORT
MAX ITHTU: 2
QUICKENING RATE: 8.5%
MAX ITHTU RANK: STRONG

CURRENT CRYSTALS QUICKENING: 2
1 — RANK: STRONG   DENSITY: 10   POWER: 33.2
                         QUICKENED: 88%
1 — RANK: STRONG   DENSITY: 9   POWER: 43.9
                         QUICKENED: 0.05%

POWER QUICKENED TO:
SKILLS — NONE
STATS — 1 (TOUGHNESS, 71%)
LEVEL — NONE
ABILITY — 50. 1 (0/720)
TAK — 20 (99.9%)

ABILITY REPORT
ABILITY TITLE: MEZ
"SOUL STRENGTHENS ALL"

TIER: F   ITHTU REQUIRED: 148   LEVEL: 1 (0/720)

PASSIVE EFFECT 1: GROWTH INCREASED ACCORDING TO SOUL STAT
(CURRENTLY 428% OF STANDARD)
PASSIVE EFFECT 2: SOUL STAT BOOSTS EFFECTS OF OTHER STATS
(CURRENTLY 2.3)

ACTIVE EFFECTS: UNKNOWN

Meder

STATS
FORCE: 5.4 (55%)   SKILL: 4.9 (90%)
SPEED: 4.6 (67%)   TOUGHNESS: 4.9 (90%)
MIND: 6 (272%)   WILL: 5.4 (149%)
PRESENCE: 5.6 (182%)   SOUL: 5.4 (149%)

QUICKENED ABILITY: BAJ
TIER: C
PERCENT QUICKENED: 0%

CURRENT ITHTU: 1.0
TO LEVEL: 0
TO STATS: 1 (SKILL 42%)
TO SKILLS: 0
TO TAK: 0

CURRENT TAK: 0/3

Burik

<u>STATS</u>
FORCE: 5.7 (201%)   SKILL: 5.2 (122%)
SPEED: 5.1 (111%)   TOUGHNESS: 6 (272%)
MIND: 4.7 (74%)   WILL: 5.1 (111%)
PRESENCE: 4.4 (55%)   SOUL: 4.8 (82%)

<u>QUICKENED ABILITY</u>: EST
TIER: A
PERCENT QUICKENED: 0%

<u>CURRENT ITHTU</u>: 1
TO LEVEL: 0
TO STATS: 1 (SPEED 14%)
TO SKILLS: 0
TO TAK: 0

<u>CURRENT TAK</u>: 0 / 1